Michael
Crichton

D0533619

For A-M
and
T

Michael Crichton

Jurassic Park

Congo

ARROW

ISBN 0 09 188979 0
UNIVERSAL PICTURES presents
an AMBLIN ENTERTAINMENT production
SAM NEILL LAURA DERN JEFF GOLDBLUM and
RICHARD ATTENBOROUGH
"JURASIC PARK" SAMUEL JACKSON BOB PECK
MARTIN FERRERO
Music by JOHN WILLIAMS
Film edited by MICHAEL KAHN, A.C.C.
Production designer RICK CARTER
Director of Photography DEAN CUNDEY, A.S.C.
Based on the novel by MICHAEL CRICHTON
Screenplay by DAVID KOEPP
Adaptation by MICHAEL CRICHTON and
MALIA SCOTCH MARMO
Produced by KATHLEEN KENNEDY and
GERALD R. MOLEN
Directed by STEVEN SPIELBERG
A UNIVERSAL PICTURE

Typeset in Baskerville 10/11.5 by Pure Tech Corporation,
Pondicherry, India
Printed and bound in Germany by Elsnerdruck, Berlin

CONTENTS

JURASSIC PARK

"*Reptiles are abhorrent because of their cold body, pale color, cartilaginous skeleton, filthy skin, fierce aspect, calculating eye, offensive smell, harsh voice, squalid habitation, and terrible venom; wherefore their Creator has not exerted his powers to make many of them.*"

LINNAEUS, 1797

"*You cannot recall a new form of life.*"

ERWIN CHARGAFF, 1972

Introduction
"The InGen Incident"

The late twentieth century has witnessed a scientific gold rush of astonishing proportions: the headlong and furious haste to commercialize genetic engineering. This enterprise has proceeded so rapidly – with so little outside commentary – that its dimensions and implications are hardly understood at all.

Biotechnology promises the greatest revolution in human history. By the end of this decade, it will have outdistanced atomic power and computers in its effect on our everyday lives. In the words of one observer, 'Biotechnology is going to transform every aspect of human life: our medical care, our food, our health, our entertainment, our very bodies. Nothing will ever be the same again. It's literally going to change the face of the planet.'

But the biotechnology revolution differs in three important respects from past scientific transformations.

First, it is broad-based. America entered the atomic age through the work of a single research institution, at Los Alamos. It entered the computer age through the efforts of about a dozen companies. But biotechnology research is now carried out in more than two thousand laboratories in America alone. Five hundred corporations spend five billion dollars a year on this technology.

Second, much of the research is thoughtless or frivolous. Efforts to engineer paler trout for better visibility in the stream, square trees for easier lumbering, and injectable scent cells so you'll always smell of your favorite perfume may seem like a joke, but they are not. Indeed, the fact that biotechnology can be applied to the industries traditionally subject to the vagaries of fashion, such as cosmetics and leisure activities, heightens concern about the whimsical use of this powerful new technology.

Third, the work is uncontrolled. No one supervises it. No federal laws regulate it. There is no coherent government policy, in America or anywhere else in the world. And because the products of biotechnology range from drugs to farm crops to artificial snow, an intelligent policy is difficult.

But most disturbing is the fact that no watchdogs are found among scientists themselves. It is remarkable that nearly every scientist in genetics research is also engaged in the commerce of biotechnology. There are no detached observers. Everybody has a stake.

The commercialization of molecular biology is the most stunning ethical event in the history of science, and it has happened with astonishing speed. For four hundred years since Galileo, science has always proceeded as a free and open inquiry into the workings of nature. Scientists have always ignored national boundaries, holding themselves above the transitory concerns of politics and even wars. Scientists have always rebelled against secrecy in research, and have even frowned on the idea of patenting their discoveries, seeing themselves as working to the benefit of all mankind. And for many generations, the discoveries of scientists did indeed have a peculiarly selfless quality.

When, in 1953, two young researchers in England, James Watson and Francis Crick, deciphered the structure of DNA, their work was hailed as a triumph of the human spirit, of the centuries-old quest to understand the universe in a scientific way. It was confidently expected that their discovery would be selflessly extended to the greater benefit of mankind.

Yet that did not happen. Thirty years later, nearly all of Watson and Crick's scientific colleagues were engaged in another sort of enterprise entirely. Research in molecular genetics had become a vast, multibillion-dollar commercial undertaking, and its origins can be traced not to 1953 but to April 1976.

That was the date of a now famous meeting, in which Robert Swanson, a venture capitalist, approached Herbert Boyer, a biochemist at the University of California. The two men agreed to found a commercial company to exploit Boyer's gene-splicing techniques. Their new company, Genentech, quickly became the largest and most successful of the genetic engineering start-ups.

Suddenly it seemed as if everyone wanted to become rich. New companies were announced almost weekly, and scientists flocked to exploit genetic research. By 1986, at least 362 scientists, including 64 in the National Academy, sat on the advisory boards of biotech firms. The number of those who held equity positions or consultancies was several times greater.

It is necessary to emphasize how significant this shift in attitude actually was. In the past, pure scientists took a snobbish view of business.

They saw the pursuit of money as intellectually uninteresting, suited only to shop-keepers. And to do research for industry, even at the prestigious Bell or IBM labs, was only for those who couldn't get a university appointment. Thus the attitude of pure scientists was fundamentally critical toward the work of applied scientists, and to industry in general. Their long-standing antagonism kept university scientists free of contaminating industry ties, and whenever debate arose about technological matters, disinterested scientists were available to discuss the issues at the highest levels.

But that is no longer true. There are very few molecular biologists and very few research institutions without commercial affiliations. The old days are gone. Genetic research continues, at a more furious pace than ever. But it is done in secret, and in haste, and for profit.

In this commercial climate, it is probably inevitable that a company as ambitious as International Genetic Technologies, Inc., of Palo Alto, would arise. It is equally unsurprising that the genetic crisis it created should go unreported. After all, InGen's research was conducted in secret; the actual incident occurred in the most remote region of Central America; and fewer than twenty people were there to witness it. Of those, only a handful survived.

Even at the end, when International Genetic Technologies field for Chapter 11 protection in San Francisco Superior Court 'on October 5, 1989, the proceedings drew little press attention. It appeared so ordinary: InGen was the third small American bioengineering company to fail that year, and the seventh since 1986. Few court documents were made public, since the creditors were Japanese investment consortia, such as Hamaguri and Densaka, companies which traditionally shun publicity. To avoid unnecessary disclosure, Daniel Ross, of Cowan, Swain and Ross, counsel for InGen, also represented the Japanese investors. And the rather unusual petition of the vice consul of Costa Rica was heard behind closed doors. Thus it is not surprising that, within a month, the problems of InGen were quietly and amicably settled.

Parties to that settlement, including the distinguished scientific board of advisers, signed a nondisclosure agreement, and none will speak about what happened; but many of the principal figures in the "InGen incident" are not signatories, and were willing to discuss the remarkable events leading up to those final two days in August 1989 on a remote island off the west coast of Costa Rica.

Acknowledgments

In preparing this novel, I have drawn on the work of many eminent paleontologists, particularly Robert Bakker, John Horner, John Ostrom, and Gregory Paul. I have also made use of the efforts of the new generation of illustrators, including Kenneth Carpenter, Margaret Colbert, Stephen and Sylvia Czerkas, John Gurche, Mark Hallett, Douglas Henderson, and William Stout, whose reconstructions incorporate the new perception of how dinosaurs behaved.

Certain ideas presented here about Paleo-DNA, the genetic material of extinct animals, were first articulated by George O. Poinar, Jr., and Roberta Hess, who formed the Extinct DNA Study Group at Berkeley. Some discussions of chaos theory derive in part from the commentaries of Ivar Ekeland and James Gleick. The computer programs of Bob Gross inspired some of the graphics. The work of the late Heinz Pagels provoked Ian Malcolm.

However, this book is entirely fiction, and the views expressed here are my own, as are whatever factual errors exist in the text.

Prologue: The Bite of the Raptor

The tropical rain fell in drenching sheets, hammering the corrugated roof of the clinic building, roaring down the metal gutters, splashing on the ground in a torrent. Roberta Carter sighed, and stared out the window. From the clinic, she could hardly see the beach or the ocean beyond, cloaked in low fog. This wasn't what she had expected when she had come to the fishing village of Bahía Anasco, on the west coast of Costa Rica, to spend two months as a visiting physician. Bobbie Carter had expected sun and relaxation, after two grueling years of residency in emergency medicine at Michael Reese in Chicago.

She had been in Bahía Anasco now for three weeks. And it had rained every day.

Everything else was fine. She liked the isolation of Bahía Anasco, and the friendliness of its people. Costa Rica had one of the twenty best medical systems in the world, and even in this remote coastal village, the clinic was well maintained, amply supplied. Her paramedic, Manuel Aragón, was intelligent and well trained. Bobbie was able to practice a level of medicine equal to what she had practiced in Chicago.

But the rain! The constant, unending rain!

Across the examining room, Manuel cocked his head. 'Listen,' he said.

'Believe me, I hear it,' Bobbie said.

'No. *Listen.*'

And then she caught it, another sound blended with the rain, a deeper rumble that built and emerged until it was clear: the rhythmic thumping of a helicopter. She thought, *They can't be flying in weather like this.*

But the sound built steadily, and then the helicopter burst low through the ocean fog and roared overhead, circled, and came back. She saw the helicopter swing back over the water, near the fishing boats, then ease sideways to the rickety wooden dock, and back toward the beach.

It was looking for a place to land.

It was a big-bellied Sikorsky with a blue stripe on the side, with the words 'InGen Construction.' That was the name of the construction company building a new resort on one of the offshore islands. The resort was said to be spectacular, and very complicated; many of the local people were employed in the construction, which had been going on for more than two years. Bobbie could imagine it – one of those huge American resorts with swimming pools and tennis courts, where guests could play and drink their daiquiris, without having any contact with the real life of the country.

Bobbie wondered what was so urgent on that island that the helicopter would fly in this weather. Through the windshield she saw the pilot exhale in relief as the helicopter settled onto the wet sand of the beach. Uniformed men jumped out, and flung open the big side door. She heard frantic shouts in Spanish, and Manuel nudged her.

They were calling for a doctor.

Two black crewmen carried a limp body toward her, while a white man barked orders. The white man had a yellow slicker. Red hair appeared around the edges of his Mets baseball cap. 'Is there a doctor here?' he called to her, as she ran up.

'I'm Dr. Carter,' she said. The rain fell in heavy drops, pounding her head and shoulders. The red-haired man frowned at her. She was wearing cut-off jeans and a tank top. She had a stethoscope over her shoulder, the bell already rusted from the salt air.

'Ed Regis. We've got a very sick man here, doctor.'

'Then you better take him to San José,' she said. San José was the capital, just twenty minutes away by air.

'We would, but we can't get over the mountains in this weather. You have to treat him here.'

Bobbie trotted alongside the injured man as they carried him to the clinic. He was a kid, no older than eighteen. Lifting away the blood-soaked shirt, she saw a big slashing rip along his shoulder, and another on the leg.

'What happened to him?'

'Construction accident,' Ed shouted. 'He fell. One of the backhoes ran over him.'

The kid was pale, shivering, unconscious.

Manuel stood by the bright green door of the clinic, waving his arm. The men brought the body through and set it on the table in the center of the room. Manuel started an intravenous line, and Bobbie swung the light over the kid and bent to examine the wounds. Immediately she could see that it did not look good. The kid would almost certainly die.

A big tearing laceration ran from his shoulder down his torso. At the edge of the wound, the flesh was shredded. At the center, the shoulder was dislocated, pale bones exposed. A second slash cut through the heavy muscles of the thigh, deep enough to reveal the pulse of the femoral artery below. Her first impression was that his leg had been ripped open.

'Tell me again about this injury,' she said.

'I didn't see it,' Ed said. 'They say the backhoe dragged him.'

'Because it almost looks as if he was mauled,' Bobbie Carter said, probing the wound. Like most emergency room physicians, she could remember in detail patients she had seen even years before. She had seen two maulings. One was a two-year-old child who had been attacked by a Rottweiler dog. The other was a drunken circus attendant who had had an encounter with a Bengal tiger. Both injuries were similar. There was a characteristic look to an animal attack.

'Mauled?' Ed said. 'No, no. It was a backhoe, believe me.' Ed licked his lips as he spoke. He was edgy, acting as if he had done something wrong. Bobbie wondered why. If they were using inexperienced local workmen on the resort construction, they must have accidents all the time.

Manuel said, 'Do you want lavage?'

'Yes,' she said. 'After you block him.'

She bent lower, probed the wound with her fingertips. If an earth mover had rolled over him, dirt would be forced deep into the wound. But there wasn't any dirt, just a slippery, slimy foam. And the wound had a strange odor, a kind of rotten stench, a smell of death and decay. She had never smelled anything like it before.

'How long ago did this happen?'

'An hour.'

Again she noticed how tense Ed Regis was. He was one of those eager, nervous types. And he didn't look like a construction foreman. More like an executive. He was obviously out of his depth.

Bobbie Carter turned back to the injuries. Somehow she didn't think she was seeing mechanical trauma. It just didn't look right. No soil contamination of the wound site, and no crush-injury component. Mechanical trauma of any sort – an auto injury, a factory accident – almost always had some component of crushing. But here there was none. Instead, the man's skin was shredded – ripped – across his shoulder, and again across his thigh.

It really did look like a maul. On the other hand, most of the body was unmarked, which was unusual for an animal attack. She looked again at the head, the arms, the hands –

The hands.

She felt a chill when she looked at the kid's hands. There were short slashing cuts on both palms, and bruises on the wrists and forearms. She had worked in Chicago long enough to know what that meant.

'All right,' she said. 'Wait outside.'

'Why?' Ed said, alarmed. He didn't like that.

'Do you want me to help him, or not?' she said, and pushed him out the door and closed it on his face. She didn't know what was going on, but she didn't like it. Manuel hesitated. 'I continue to wash?'

'Yes,' she said. She reached for her little Olympus point-and-shoot. She took several snapshots of the injury, shifting her light for a better view. It really did look like bites, she thought. Then the kid groaned, and she put her camera aside and bent toward him. His lips moved, his tongue thick.

'*Raptor*,' he said. '*Lo sa raptor . . .*'

At those words, Manuel froze, stepped back in horror.

'What does it mean?' Bobbie said.

Manuel shook his head. 'I do not know, doctor. "*Lo sa raptor*" – *no es español.*'

'No?' It sounded to her like Spanish. 'Then please continue to wash him.'

'No, doctor.' He wrinkled his nose. 'Bad smell.' And he crossed himself.

Bobbie looked again at the slippery foam streaked across the wound. She touched it, rubbing it between her fingers. It seemed almost like saliva . . .

The injured boy's lips moved. 'Raptor,' he whispered.

In a tone of horror, Manuel said, 'It bit him.'

'What bit him?'

'Raptor.'

'What's a raptor?'

'It means *hupia*.'

Bobbie frowned. The Costa Ricans were not especially superstitious, but she had heard the *hupia* mentioned in the village before. They were said to be night ghosts, faceless vampires who kidnapped small children. According to the belief, the *hupia* had once lived in the mountains of Costa Rica, but now inhabited the islands offshore.

Manuel was backing away, murmuring and crossing himself. 'It is not normal, this smell,' he said. 'It is the *hupia*.'

Bobbie was about to order him back to work when the injured youth opened his eyes and sat straight up on the table. Manuel shrieked in terror. The injured boy moaned and twisted his head, looking left and right with wide staring eyes, and then he explosively vomited blood. He went immediately into convulsions, his body vibrating, and Bobbie grabbed for him but he shuddered off the table onto the concrete floor. He vomited again. There was blood everywhere. Ed opened the door, saying, 'What the hell's happening?' and when he saw the blood he turned away, his hand to his mouth. Bobbie was grabbing for a stick to put in the boy's clenched jaws, but even as she did it she knew it was hopeless, and with a final spastic jerk he relaxed and lay still.

She bent to perform mouth-to-mouth, but Manuel grabbed her shoulder fiercely, pulling her back. 'No,' he said. 'The *hupia* will cross over.'

'Manuel, for God's sake –'

'*No.*' He stared at her fiercely. 'No. You do not understand these things.'

Bobbie looked at the body on the ground and realized that it didn't matter; there was no possibility of resuscitating him. Manuel called for the men, who came back into the room and took the body away. Ed appeared, wiping his mouth with the back of his hand, muttering, 'I'm sure you did all you could,' and then she watched as the men took the body away, back to the helicopter, and it lifted thunderously up into the sky.

'It is better,' Manuel said.

Bobbie was thinking about the boy's hands. They had been covered with cuts and bruises, in the characteristic pattern of defense wounds. She was quite sure he had not died in a construction accident; he had been attacked, and he had held up his hands against his attacker. 'Where is this island they've come from?' she asked.

'In the ocean. Perhaps a hundred, hundred and twenty miles offshore.'

'Pretty far for a resort,' she said.

Manuel watched the helicopter. 'I hope they never come back.'

Well, she thought, at least she had pictures. But when she turned back to the table, she saw that her camera was gone.

The rain finally stopped later that night. Alone in the bedroom behind the clinic, Bobbie thumbed through her tattered paperback Spanish dictionary. The boy had said 'raptor,' and, despite Manuel's protests, she suspected it was a Spanish word. Sure enough, she found it in her dictionary. It meant 'ravisher' or 'abductor.'

That gave her pause. The sense of the word was suspiciously close to the meaning of *hupia*. Of course she did not believe in the superstition. And no ghost had cut those hands. What had the boy been trying to tell her?

From the next room, she heard groans. One of the village women was in the first stage of labor, and Elena Morales, the local midwife, was attending her. Bobbie went into the clinic room and gestured to Elena to step outside for a moment.

'Elena . . .'

'*Sí*, doctor?'

'Do you know what is a raptor?'

Elena was gray-haired and sixty, a strong woman with a practical, no-nonsense air. In the night, beneath the stars, she frowned and said, 'Raptor?'

'Yes. You know this word?'

'*Sí*.' Elena nodded. 'It means . . . a person who comes in the night and takes away a child.'

'A kidnapper?'

'Yes.'

'A *hupia*?'

Her whole manner changed. 'Do not say this word, doctor.'

'Why not?'

'Do not speak of *hupia* now,' Elena said firmly, nodding her head toward the groans of the laboring woman. 'It is not wise to say this word now.'

'But does a raptor bite and cut his victims?'

'Bite and cut?' Elena said, puzzled. 'No, doctor. Nothing like this. A raptor is a man who takes a new baby.' She seemed irritated by the conversation, impatient to end it. Elena started back toward the clinic. 'I will call to you when she is ready, doctor. I think one hour more, perhaps two.'

Bobbie looked at the stars, and listened to the peaceful lapping of the surf at the shore. In the darkness she saw the shadows of the fishing boats anchored offshore. The whole scene was quiet, so normal, she felt foolish to be talking of vampires and kidnapped babies.

Bobbie went back to her room, remembering again that Manuel had insisted it was not a Spanish word. Out of curiosity, she looked in the little English dictionary, and to her surprise she found the word there, too:

raptor\n [deriv. of L. *raptor* plunderer, fr. *raptus*]: bird of prey.

First Iteration

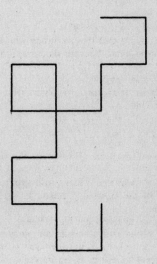

'At the earliest drawings of the fractal curve, few clues to the underlying mathematical structure will be seen.'

IAN MALCOLM

Almost Paradise

Mike Bowman whistled cheerfully as he drove the Land Rover through the Cabo Blanco Biological Reserve, on the west coast of Costa Rica. It was a beautiful morning in July, and the road before him was spectacular: hugging the edge of a cliff, overlooking the jungle and the blue Pacific. According to the guidebooks, Cabo Blanco was unspoiled wilderness, almost a paradise. Seeing it now made Bowman feel as if the vacation was back on track.

Bowman, a thirty-six-year-old real estate developer from Dallas, had come to Costa Rica with his wife and daughter for a two-week holiday. The trip had actually been his wife's idea; for weeks Ellen had filled his ear about the wonderful national parks of Costa Rica, and how good it would be for Tina to see them. Then, when they arrived, it turned out Ellen had an appointment to see a plastic surgeon in San José. That was the first Mike Bowman had heard about the excellent and inexpensive plastic surgery available in Costa Rica, and all the luxurious private clinics in San José.

Of course they'd had a huge fight. Mike felt she'd lied to him, and she had. And he put his foot down about this plastic surgery business. Anyway, it was ridiculous, Ellen was only thirty, and she was a beautiful woman. Hell, she'd been Homecoming Queen her senior year at Rice, and that was not even ten years earlier. But Ellen tended to be insecure, and worried. And it seemed as if in recent years she had mostly worried about losing her looks.

That, and everything else.

The Land Rover bounced in a pothole, splashing mud. Seated beside him, Ellen said, 'Mike, are you sure this is the right road? We haven't seen any other people for hours.'

'There was another car fifteen minutes ago,' he reminded her. 'Remember, the blue one?'

'Going the other way . . .'

'Darling, you wanted a deserted beach,' he said, 'and that's what you're going to get.'

Ellen shook her head doubtfully. 'I hope you're right.'

'Yeah, Dad, I hope you're right,' said Christina, from the back seat. She was eight years old.

'Trust me, I'm right.' He drove in silence a moment. 'It's beautiful, isn't it? Look at that view. It's beautiful.'

'It's okay,' Tina said.

Ellen got out a compact and looked at herself in the mirror, pressing under her eyes. She sighed, and put the compact away.

The road began to descend, and Mike Bowman concentrated on driving. Suddenly a small black shape flashed across the road and Tina shrieked, 'Look! *Look!*' Then it was gone, into the jungle.

'What was it?' Ellen asked. 'A monkey?'

'Maybe a squirrel monkey,' Bowman said.

'Can I count it?' Tina said, taking her pencil out. She was keeping a list of all the animals she had seen on her trip, as a project for school.

'I don't know,' Mike said doubtfully.

Tina consulted the pictures in the guidebook. 'I don't think it was a squirrel monkey,' she said. 'I think it was just another howler.' They had seen several howler monkeys already on their trip.

'Hey,' she said, more brightly. 'According to this book, "the beaches of Cabo Blanco are frequented by a variety of wildlife, including howler and white-faced monkeys, three-toed sloths, and coatimundis." You think we'll see a three-toed sloth, Dad?'

'I bet we do.'

'Really?'

'Just look in the mirror.'

'Very funny, Dad.'

The road sloped downward through the jungle, toward the ocean.

Mike Bowman felt like a hero when they finally reached the beach: a two-mile crescent of white sand, utterly deserted. He parked the Land Rover in the shade of the palm trees that fringed the beach, and got out the box lunches. Ellen changed into her bathing suit, saying, 'Honestly, I don't know *how* I'm going to get this weight off.'

'You look great, hon.' Actually, he felt that she was too thin, but he had learned not to mention that.

Tina was already running down the beach.

'Don't forget you need your sunscreen,' Ellen called.

'Later,' Tina shouted, over her shoulder. 'I'm going to see if there's a sloth.'

Ellen Bowman looked around at the beach, and the trees. 'You think she's all right?'

'Honey, there's nobody here for miles,' Mike said.

'What about snakes?'

'Oh, for God's sake,' Mike Bowman said. 'There's no snakes on a beach.'

'Well, there might be . . .'

'Honey,' he said firmly. 'Snakes are cold-blooded. They're reptiles. They can't control their body temperature. It's ninety degrees on that sand. If a snake came out, it'd be cooked. Believe me. There's no snakes on the beach.' He watched his daughter scampering down the beach, a dark spot on the white sand. 'Let her go. Let her have a good time.'

He put his arm around his wife's waist.

Tina ran until she was exhausted, and then she threw herself down on the sand and gleefully rolled to the water's edge. The ocean was warm, and there was hardly any surf at all. She sat for a while, catching her breath, and then she looked back toward her parents and the car, to see how far she had come.

Her mother waved, beckoning her to return. Tina waved back cheerfully, pretending she didn't understand. Tina didn't want to put sunscreen on. And she didn't want to go back and hear her mother talk about losing weight. She wanted to stay right here, and maybe see a sloth.

Tina had seen a sloth two days earlier at the zoo in San José. It looked like a Muppets character, and it seemed harmless. In any case, it couldn't move fast; she could easily outrun it.

Now her mother was calling to her, and Tina decided to move out of the sun, back from the water, to the shade of the palm trees. In this part of the beach, the palm trees overhung a gnarled tangle of mangrove roots, which blocked any attempt to penetrate inland. Tina sat in the sand and kicked the dried mangrove leaves. She noticed many bird tracks in the sand. Costa Rica was famous for its birds. The guidebooks said there were three times as many birds in Costa Rica as in all of America and Canada.

In the sand, some of the three-toed bird tracks were small, and so faint they could hardly be seen. Other tracks were large, and cut deeper in the sand. Tina was looking idly at the tracks when she heard a chirping, followed by a rustling in the mangrove thicket.

Did sloths make a chirping sound? Tina didn't think so, but she wasn't sure. The chirping was probably some ocean bird. She waited quietly, not moving, hearing the rustling again, and finally she saw the source of the sounds. A few yards away, a lizard emerged from the mangrove roots and peered at her.

Tina held her breath. A new animal for her list! The lizard stood up on its hind legs, balancing on its thick tail, and stared at her. Standing like that, it was almost a foot tall, dark green with brown stripes along its back. Its tiny front legs ended in little lizard fingers that wiggled in the air. The lizard cocked its head as it looked at her.

Tina thought it was cute. Sort of like a big salamander. She raised her hand and wiggled her fingers back.

The lizard wasn't frightened. It came toward her, walking upright on its hind legs. It was hardly bigger than a chicken, and like a chicken it bobbed its head as it walked. Tina thought it would make a wonderful pet.

She noticed that the lizard left three-toed tracks that looked exactly like bird tracks. The lizard came closer to Tina. She kept her body still, not wanting to frighten the little animal. She was amazed that it would come so close, but she remembered that this was a national park. All the animals in the park would know that they were protected. This lizard was probably tame. Maybe it even expected her to give it some food. Unfortunately she didn't have any. Slowly, Tina extended her hand, palm open, to show she didn't have any food.

The lizard paused, cocked his head, and chirped.

'Sorry,' Tina said. 'I just don't have anything.'

And then, without warning, the lizard jumped up onto her outstretched hand. Tina could feel its little toes pinching the skin of her palm, and she felt the surprising weight of the animal's body pressing her arm down.

And then the lizard scrambled up her arm, toward her face.

'I just wish I could see her,' Ellen Bowman said, squinting in the sunlight. 'That's all. Just see her.'

'I'm sure she's fine,' Mike said, picking through the box lunch packed by the hotel. There was unappetizing grilled chicken, and some kind of a meat-filled pastry. Not that Ellen would eat any of it.

'You don't think she'd leave the beach?' Ellen said.

'No, hon, I don't.'

'I feel so isolated here,' Ellen said.

'I thought that's what you wanted,' Mike Bowman said.

'I did.'

'Well, then, what's the problem?'

'I just wish I could see her, is all,' Ellen said.

Then, from down the beach, carried by the wind, they heard their daughter's voice. She was screaming.

Puntarenas

'I think she is quite comfortable now,' Dr. Cruz said, lowering the plastic flap of the oxygen tent around Tina as she slept. Mike Bowman sat beside the bed, close to his daughter. Mike thought Dr. Cruz was probably pretty capable; he spoke excellent English, the result of training at medical centers in London and Baltimore. Dr. Cruz radiated competence; and the Clínica Santa María, the modern hospital in Puntarenas, was spotless and efficient.

But, even so, Mike Bowman felt nervous. There was no getting around the fact that his only daughter was desperately ill, and they were far from home.

When Mike had first reached Tina, she was screaming hysterically. Her whole left arm was bloody, covered with a profusion of small bites, each the size of a thumbprint. And there were flecks of sticky foam on her arm, like a foamy saliva.

He carried her back down the beach. Almost immediately her arm began to redden and swell. Mike would not soon forget the frantic drive back to civilization, the four-wheel-drive Land Rover slipping and sliding up the muddy track into the hills, while his daughter screamed in fear and pain, and her arm grew more bloated and red. Long before they reached the park boundaries, the swelling had spread to her neck, and then Tina began to have trouble breathing . . .

'She'll be all right now?' Ellen said, staring through the plastic oxygen tent.

'I believe so,' Dr. Cruz said. 'I have given her another dose of steroids, and her breathing is much easier. And you can see the edema in her arm is greatly reduced.'

Mike Bowman said, 'About those bites . . .'

'We have no identification yet,' the doctor said. 'I myself haven't seen bites like that before. But you'll notice they are disappearing. It's already quite difficult to make them out. Fortunately I have taken photographs for reference. And I have washed her arm to collect some samples of the sticky saliva – one for analysis here, a second to send to

13

the labs in San José, and the third we will keep frozen in case it is needed. Do you have the picture she made?'

'Yes,' Mike Bowman said. He handed the doctor the sketch that Tina had drawn, in response to questions from the admitting officials.

'This is the animal that bit her?' Dr. Cruz said, looking at the picture.

'Yes,' Mike Bowman said. 'She said it was a green lizard, the size of a chicken or a crow.'

'I don't know of such a lizard,' the doctor said. 'She has drawn it standing on its hind legs . . .'

'That's right,' Mike Bowman said. 'She said it walked on its hind legs.'

Dr. Cruz frowned. He stared at the picture a while longer. 'I am not an expert. I've asked for Dr. Guitierrez to visit us here. He is a senior researcher at the Reserva Biológica de Carara, which is across the bay. Perhaps he can identify the animal for us.'

'Isn't there someone from Cabo Blanco?' Bowman asked. 'That's where she was bitten.'

'Unfortunately not,' Dr. Cruz said. 'Cabo Blanco has no permanent staff, and no researcher has worked there for some time. You were probably the first people to walk on that beach in several months. But I am sure you will find Dr. Guitierrez to be knowledgeable.'

Dr. Guitierrez turned out to be a bearded man wearing khaki shorts and shirt. The surprise was that he was American. He was introduced to the Bowmans, saying in a soft Southern accent, 'Mr. and Mrs. Bowman, how you doing, nice to meet you,' and then explaining that he was a field biologist from Yale who had worked in Costa Rica for the last five years. Marty Guitierrez examined Tina thoroughly, lifting her arm gently, peering closely at each of the bites with a penlight, then measuring them with a small pocket ruler. After a while, Guitierrez stepped away, nodding to himself as if he had understood something. He then inspected the Polaroids, and asked several questions about the saliva, which Cruz told him was still being tested in the lab.

Finally he turned to Mike Bowman and his wife, waiting tensely. 'I think Tina's going to be fine. I just want to be clear about a few details,' he said, making notes in a precise hand. 'Your daughter says she was bitten by a green lizard, approximately one foot high, which walked upright onto the beach from the mangrove swamp?'

'That's right, yes.'

'And the lizard made some kind of a vocalization?'

'Tina said it chirped, or squeaked.'

'Like a mouse, would you say?'

'Yes.'

'Well, then,' Dr. Guitierrez said, 'I know this lizard.' He explained that, of the six thousand species of lizards in the world, no more than a dozen species walked upright. Of those species, only four were found in Latin America. And judging by the coloration, the lizard could be only one of the four. 'I am sure this lizard was a *Basiliscus amoratus*, a striped basilisk lizard, found here in Costa Rica and also in Honduras. Standing on their hind legs, they are sometimes as tall as a foot.'

'Are they poisonous?'

'No, Mrs. Bowman. Not at all.' Guitierrez explained that the swelling in Tina's arm was an allergic reaction. 'According to the literature, fourteen percent of people are strongly allergic to reptiles,' he said, 'and your daughter seems to be one of them.'

'She was screaming, she said it was so painful.'

'Probably it was,' Guitierrez said. 'Reptile saliva contains serotonin, which causes tremendous pain.' He turned to Cruz. 'Her blood pressure came down with antihistamines?'

'Yes,' Cruz said. 'Promptly.'

'Serotonin,' Guitierrez said. 'No question.'

Still, Ellen Bowman remained uneasy. 'But why would a lizard bite her in the first place?'

'Lizard bites are very common,' Guitierrez said. 'Animal handlers in zoos get bitten all the time. And just the other day I heard that a lizard had bitten an infant in her crib in Amaloya, about sixty miles from where you were. So bites do occur. I'm not sure why your daughter had so many bites. What was she doing at the time?'

'Nothing. She said she was sitting pretty still, because she didn't want to frighten it away.'

'Sitting pretty still,' Guitierrez said, frowning. He shook his head. 'Well. I don't think we can say exactly what happened. Wild animals are unpredictable.'

'And what about the foamy saliva on her arm?' Ellen said. 'I keep thinking about rabies . . .'

'No, no,' Dr. Guitierrez said. 'A reptile can't carry rabies, Mrs. Bowman. Your daughter has suffered an allergic reaction to the bite of a basilisk lizard. Nothing more serious.'

Mike Bowman then showed Guitierrez the picture that Tina had drawn. Guitierrez nodded. 'I would accept this as a picture of a basilisk lizard,' he said. 'A few details are wrong, of course. The neck is much too long, and she has drawn the hind legs with only three toes instead of five. The tail is too thick, and raised too high. But otherwise this is a perfectly serviceable lizard of the kind we are talking about.'

'But Tina specifically said the neck was long,' Ellen Bowman insisted. 'And she said there were three toes on the foot.'

'Tina's pretty observant,' Mike Bowman said.

'I'm sure she is,' Guitierrez said, smiling. 'But I still think your daughter was bitten by a common basilisk amoratus, and had a severe herpetological reaction. Normal time course with medication is twelve hours. She should be just fine in the morning.'

In the modern laboratory in the basement of the Clínica Santa María, word was received that Dr. Guitierrez had identified the animal that had bitten the American child as a harmless basilisk lizard. Immediately the analysis of the saliva was halted, even though a preliminary fractionation showed several extremely high molecular weight proteins of unknown biological activity. But the night technician was busy, and he placed the saliva samples on the holding shelf of the refrigerator.

The next morning, the day clerk checked the holding shelf against the names of discharged patients. Seeing that BOWMAN, CHRISTINA L. was scheduled for discharge that morning, the clerk threw out the saliva samples. At the last moment, he noticed that one sample had the red tag which meant that it was to be forwarded to the university lab in San José. He retrieved the test tube from the wastebasket, and sent it on its way.

'Go on. Say thank you to Dr. Cruz,' Ellen Bowman said, and pushed Tina forward.

'Thank you, Dr. Cruz,' Tina said. 'I feel much better now.' She reached up and shook the doctor's hand. Then she said, 'You have a different shirt.'

For a moment Dr. Cruz looked perplexed; then he smiled. 'That's right, Tina. When I work all night at the hospital, in the morning I change my shirt.'

'But not your tie?'

'No. Just my shirt.'

Ellen Bowman said, 'Mike told you she's observant.'

'She certainly is.' Dr. Cruz smiled and shook the little girl's hand gravely. 'Enjoy the rest of your holiday in Costa Rica, Tina.'

'I will.'

The Bowman family had started to leave when Dr. Cruz said, 'Oh, Tina, do you remember the lizard that bit you?'

'Uh-huh.'

'You remember its feet?'

'Uh-huh.'

'Did it have any toes?'

'Yes.'

'How many toes did it have?'

'Three,' she said.

'How do you know that?'

'Because I looked,' she said. 'Anyway, all the birds on the beach made marks in the sand with three toes, like this.' She held up her hand, middle three fingers spread wide. 'And the lizard made those kind of marks in the sand, too.'

'The lizard made marks like a bird?'

'Uh-huh,' Tina said. 'He walked like a bird, too. He jerked his head like this, up and down.' She took a few steps, bobbing her head.

After the Bowmans had departed, Dr. Cruz decided to report this conversation to Guitierrez, at the biological station.

'I must admit the girl's story is puzzling,' Guitierrez said. 'I have been doing some checking myself. I am no longer certain she was bitten by a basilisk. Not certain at all.'

'Then what could it be?'

'Well,' Guitierrez said, 'let's not speculate prematurely. By the way, have you heard of any other lizard bites at the hospital?'

'No, why?'

'Let me know, my friend, if you do.'

The Beach

Marty Guitierrez sat on the beach and watched the afternoon sun fall lower in the sky, until it sparkled harshly on the water of the bay, and its rays reached beneath the palm trees, to where he sat among the mangroves, on the beach of Cabo Blanco. As best he could determine, he was sitting near the spot where the American girl had been, two days before.

Although it was true enough, as he had told the Bowmans, that lizard bites were common, Guitierrez had never heard of a basilisk lizard biting anyone. And he had certainly never heard of anyone being hospitalized for a lizard bite. Then, too, the bite radius on Tina's arm appeared slightly too large for a basilisk. When he got back to the Carara station, he had checked the small research library there, but found no reference to basilisk lizard bites. Next he checked International BioSciences Services, a computer database in America. But he found no references to basilisk bites, or hospitalization for lizard bites.

He then called the medical officer in Amaloya, who confirmed that a nine-day-old infant, sleeping in its crib, had been bitten on the foot by an animal the grandmother – the only person actually to see it – claimed was a lizard. Subsequently the foot had become swollen and the infant had nearly died. The grandmother described the lizard as green with brown stripes. It had bitten the child several times before the woman frightened it away.

'Strange,' Guitierrez had said.

'No, like all the others,' the medical officer replied, adding that he had heard of other biting incidents: A child in Vásquez, the next village up the coast, had been bitten while sleeping. And another in Puerta Sotrero. All these incidents had occurred in the last two months. All had involved sleeping children and infants.

Such a new and distinctive pattern led Guitierrez to suspect the presence of a previously unknown species of lizard. This was particularly likely to happen in Costa Rica. Only seventy-five miles wide at its narrowest point, the country was smaller than the state of Maine. Yet, within its limited space, Costa Rica had a remarkable diversity of

18

biological habitats: sea-coasts on both the Atlantic and the Pacific; four separate mountain ranges, including twelve-thousand-foot peaks and active volcanoes; rain forests, cloud forests, temperate zones, swampy marshes, and arid deserts. Such ecological diversity sustained an astonishing diversity of plant and animal life. Costa Rica had three times as many species of birds as all of North America. More than a thousand species of orchids. More than five thousand species of insects.

New species were being discovered all the time at a pace that had increased in recent years, for a sad reason. Costa Rica was becoming deforested, and as jungle species lost their habitats, they moved to other areas, and sometimes changed behavior as well.

So a new species was perfectly possible. But along with the excitement of a new species was the worrisome possibility of new diseases. Lizards carried viral diseases, including several that could be transmitted to man. The most serious was central saurian encephalitis, or CSE, which caused a form of sleeping sickness in human beings and horses. Guitierrez felt it was important to find this new lizard, if only to test it for disease.

Sitting on the beach, he watched the sun drop lower, and sighed. Perhaps Tina Bowman had seen a new animal, and perhaps not. Certainly Guitierrez had not. Earlier that morning, he had taken the air pistol, loaded the clip with ligamine darts, and set out for the beach with high hopes. But the day was wasted. Soon he would have to begin the drive back up the hill from the beach; he did not want to drive that road in darkness.

Guitierrez got to his feet and started back up the beach. Farther along, he saw the dark shape of a howler monkey, ambling along the edge of the mangrove swamp. Guitierrez moved away, stepping out toward the water. If there was one howler, there would probably be others in the trees overhead, and howlers tended to urinate on intruders.

But this particular howler monkey seemed to be alone, and walking slowly, and pausing frequently to sit on its haunches. The monkey had something in its mouth. As Guitierrez came closer, he saw it was eating a lizard. The tail and the hind legs dropped from the monkey's jaws. Even from a distance, Guitierrez could see the brown stripes against the green.

Guitierrez dropped to the ground and aimed the pistol. The howler monkey, accustomed to living in a protected reserve, stared curiously. He did not run away, even when the first dart whined harmlessly past him. When the second dart struck deep in the thigh, the howler shrieked in anger and surprise, dropping the remains of its meal as it fled into the jungle.

Guitierrez got to his feet and walked forward. He wasn't worried about the monkey; the tranquilizer dose was too small to give it anything but a few minutes of dizziness. Already he was thinking of what to do with his new find. Guitierrez himself would write the preliminary report, but the remains would have to be sent back to the United States for final positive identification, of course. To whom should he send it? The acknowledged expert was Edward H. Simpson, emeritus professor of zoology at Columbia University, in New York. An elegant older man with swept-back white hair, Simpson was the world's leading authority on lizard taxonomy. Probably, Marty thought, he would send his lizard to Dr. Simpson.

New York

Dr. Richard Stone, head of the Tropical Diseases Laboratory of Columbia University Medical Center, often remarked that the name conjured up a grander place than it actually was. In the early twentieth century, when the laboratory occupied the entire fourth floor of the Biomedical Research Building, crews of technicians worked to eliminate the scourges of yellow fever, malaria, and cholera. But medical successes – and research laboratories in Nairobi and São Paulo – had left the TDL a much less important place than it once was. Now a fraction of its former size, it employed only two full-time technicians, and they were primarily concerned with diagnosing illnesses of New Yorkers who had traveled abroad. The lab's comfortable routine was unprepared for what it received that morning.

'Oh, very nice,' the technician in the Tropical Diseases Laboratory said, as she read the customs label. 'Partially masticated fragment of unidentified Costa Rican lizard.' She wrinkled her nose. 'This one's all yours, Dr. Stone.'

Richard Stone crossed the lab to inspect the new arrival. 'Is this the material from Ed Simpson's lab?'

'Yes,' she said. 'But I don't know why they'd send a lizard to *us*.'

'His secretary called,' Stone said. 'Simpson's on a field trip in Borneo for the summer, and because there's a question of communicable disease with this lizard, she asked our lab to take a look at it. Let's see what we've got.'

The white plastic cylinder was the size of a half-gallon milk container. It had locking metal latches and a screw top. It was labeled 'International Biological Specimen Container' and plastered with stickers and warnings in four languages. The warnings were intended to keep the cylinder from being opened by suspicious customs officials.

Apparently the warnings had worked; as Richard Stone swung the big light over, he could see the seals were still intact. Stone turned on the air handlers and pulled on plastic gloves and a face mask. After all, the lab had recently identified specimens contaminated with Venezuelan equine fever, Japanese B encephalitis, Kyasanur Forest virus, Langat virus, and Mayaro. Then he unscrewed the top.

There was the hiss of escaping gas, and white smoke boiled out. The cylinder turned frosty cold. Inside he found a plastic zip-lock sandwich bag, containing something green. Stone spread a surgical drape on the table and shook out the contents of the bag. A piece of frozen flesh struck the table with a dull thud.

'Huh,' the technician said. 'Looks eaten.'

'Yes, it does,' Stone said. 'What do they want with us?'

The technician consulted the enclosed documents. 'Lizard is biting local children. They have a question about identification of the species, and a concern about diseases transmitted from the bite.' She produced a child's picture of a lizard, signed TINA at the top. 'One of the kids drew a picture of the lizard.'

Stone glanced at the picture. 'Obviously we can't verify the species,' Stone said. 'But we can check diseases easily enough, if we can get any blood out of this fragment. What are they calling this animal?'

' "*Basiliscus amoratus* with three-toed genetic anomaly," ' she said, reading.

'Okay,' Stone said. 'Let's get started. While you're waiting for it to thaw, do an X-ray and take Polaroids for the record. Once we have blood, start running antibody sets until we get some matches. Let me know if there's a problem.'

Before lunchtime, the lab had its answer: the lizard blood showed no significant reactivity to any viral or bacterial antigen. They had run toxicity profiles as well, and they had found only one positive match: the blood was mildly reactive to the venom of the Indian king cobra. But such cross-reactivity was common among reptile species, and Dr. Stone did not think it noteworthy to include in the fax his technician sent to Dr. Martin Guitierrez that same evening.

There was never any question about identifying the lizard; that would await the return of Dr. Simpson. He was not due back for several weeks, and his secretary asked if the TDL would please store the lizard fragment in the meantime. Dr. Stone put it back in the zip-lock bag and stuck it in the freezer.

Martin Guitierrez read the fax from the Columbia Medical Center/Tropical Diseases Laboratory. It was brief:

SUBJECT: *Basiliscus amoratus* with genetic anomaly
(forwarded from Dr. Simpson's office)

MATERIALS: posterior segment, ? partially eaten animal

22

PROCEDURES PERFORMED: X-ray, microscopic, immunological RTX for viral, parasitic, bacterial disease.

FINDINGS: No histologic or immunologic evidence for any communicable disease in man in this *Basiliscus amoratus* sample.

(signed)
Richard A. Stone, M.D., director

Guitierrez made two assumptions based on the memo. First, that his identification of the lizard as a basilisk had been confirmed by scientists at Columbia University. And second, that the absence of communicable disease meant the recent episodes of sporadic lizard bites implied no serious health hazards for Costa Rica. On the contrary, he felt his original views were correct: that a lizard species had been driven from the forest into a new habitat, and was coming into contact with village people. Guitierrez was certain that in a few more weeks the lizards would settle down and the biting episodes would end.

The tropical rain fell in great drenching sheets, hammering the corrugated roof of the clinic in Bahía Anasco. It was nearly midnight; power had been lost in the storm, and the midwife Elena Morales was working by flashlight when she heard a squeaking, chirping sound. Thinking that it was a rat, she quickly put a compress on the forehead of the mother and went into the next room to check on the newborn baby. As her hand touched the doorknob, she heard the chirping again, and she relaxed. Evidently it was just a bird, flying in the window to get out of the rain. Costa Ricans said that when a bird came to visit a newborn child, it brought good luck.

Elena opened the door. The infant lay in a wicker bassinet, swaddled in a light blanket, only its face exposed. Around the rim of the bassinet, three dark-green lizards crouched like gargoyles. When they saw Elena, they cocked their heads and stared curiously at her, but did not flee. In the light of her flashlight Elena saw the blood dripping from their snouts. Softly chirping, one lizard bent down and, with a quick shake of its head, tore a ragged chunk of flesh from the baby.

Elena rushed forward, screaming, and the lizards fled into the darkness. But long before she reached the bassinet, she could see what had happened to the infant's face, and she knew the child must be dead. The lizards scattered into the rainy night, chirping and squealing, leaving behind only bloody three-toed tracks, like birds.

The Shape of the Data

Later, when she was calmer, Elena Morales decided not to report the lizard attack. Despite the horror she had seen, she began to worry that she might be criticized for leaving the baby unguarded. So she told the mother that the baby had asphyxiated, and she reported the death on the forms she sent to San José as SIDS: sudden infant death syndrome. This was a syndrome of unexplained death among very young children; it was unremarkable, and her report went unchallenged.

The university lab in San José that analyzed the saliva sample from Tina Bowman's arm made several remarkable discoveries. There was, as expected, a great deal of serotonin. But among the salivary proteins was a real monster: molecular mass of 1,980, one of the largest proteins known. Biological activity was still under study, but it seemed to be a neurotoxic poison related to cobra venom, although more primitive in structure.

The lab also detected trace quantities of the gamma-amino methionine hydrolase. Because this enzyme was a marker for genetic engineering, and not found in wild animals, technicians assumed it was a lab contaminant and did not report it when they called Dr. Cruz, the referring physician in Puntarenas.

The lizard fragment rested in the freezer at Columbia University, awaiting the return of Dr. Simpson, who was not expected for at least a month. And so things might have remained, had not a technician named Alice Levin walked into the Tropical Diseases Laboratory, seen Tina Bowman's picture, and said, 'Oh, whose kid drew the dinosaur?'

'What?' Richard Stone said, turning slowly toward her.

'The dinosaur. Isn't that what it is? My kid draws them all the time.'

'This is a lizard,' Stone said. 'From Costa Rica. Some girl down there drew a picture of it.'

'No,' Alice Levin said, shaking her head. 'Look at it. It's very clear. Big head, long neck, stands on its hind legs, thick tail. It's a dinosaur.'

'It can't be. It was only a foot tall.'

'So? There were little dinosaurs back then,' Alice said. 'Believe me,

I know. I have two boys, I'm an expert. The smallest dinosaurs were under a foot. Teenysaurus or something, I don't know. Those names are impossible. You'll never learn those names if you're over the age of ten.'

'You don't understand,' Richard Stone said. 'This is a picture of a contemporary animal. They sent us a fragment of the animal. It's in the freezer now.' Stone went and got it, and shook it out of the baggie.

Alice Levin looked at the frozen piece of leg and tail, and shrugged. She didn't touch it. 'I don't know,' she said. 'But that looks like a dinosaur to me.'

Stone shook his head. 'Impossible.'

'Why?' Alice Levin said. 'It could be a leftover or a remnant or whatever they call them.'

Stone continued to shake his head. Alice was uninformed; she was just a technician who worked in the bacteriology lab down the hall. And she had an active imagination. Stone remembered the time when she thought she was being followed by one of the surgical orderlies. . . .

'You know,' Alice Levin said, 'if this *is* a dinosaur, Richard, it could be a big deal.'

'It's not a dinosaur.'

'Has anybody checked it?'

'No,' Stone said.

'Well, take it to the Museum of Natural History or something,' Alice Levin said. 'You really should.'

'I'd be embarrassed.'

'You want me to do it for you?' she said.

'No,' Richard Stone said. 'I don't.'

'You're not going to do anything?'

'Nothing at all.' He put the baggie back in the freezer and slammed the door. 'It's not a dinosaur, it's a lizard. And whatever it is, it can wait until Dr. Simpson gets back from Borneo to identify it. That's final, Alice. This lizard's not going anywhere.'

Second Iteration

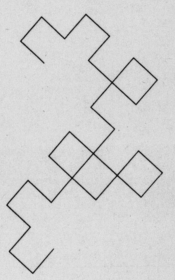

With subsequent drawings of the fractal curve, sudden changes may appear.

IAN MALCOLM

The Shore of the Inland Sea

Alan Grant crouched down, his nose inches from the ground. The temperature was over a hundred degrees. His knees ached, despite the rug-layer's pads he wore. His lungs burned from the harsh alkaline dust. Sweat dripped off his forehead onto the ground. But Grant was oblivious to the discomfort. His entire attention was focused on the six-inch square of earth in front of him.

Working patiently with a dental pick and an artist's camel brush, he exposed the tiny L-shaped fragment of jawbone. It was only an inch long, and no thicker than his little finger. The teeth were a row of small points, and had the characteristic medial angling. Bits of bone flaked away as he dug. Grant paused for a moment to paint the bone with rubber cement before continuing to expose it. There was no question that this was the jawbone from an infant carnivorous dinosaur. Its owner had died seventy-nine million years ago, at the age of about two months. With any luck, Grant might find the rest of the skeleton as well. If so, it would be the first complete skeleton of a baby carnivore –

'Hey, Alan!'

Alan Grant looked up, blinking in the sunlight. He pulled down his sunglasses, and wiped his forehead with the back of his arm.

He was crouched on an eroded hillside in the badlands outside Snakewater, Montana. Beneath the great blue bowl of sky, blunted hills, exposed outcroppings of crumbling limestone, stretched for miles in every direction. There was not a tree, or a bush. Nothing but barren rock, hot sun, and whining wind.

Visitors found the badlands depressingly bleak, but when Grant looked at this landscape, he saw something else entirely. This barren land was what remained of another, very different world, which had vanished eighty million years ago. In his mind's eye, Grant saw himself back in the warm, swampy bayou that formed the shoreline of a great inland sea. This inland sea was a thousand miles wide, extending all the way from the newly upthrust Rocky Mountains to the sharp, craggy peaks of the Appalachians. All of the American West was underwater.

At that time, there were thin clouds in the sky overhead, darkened by the smoke of nearby volcanoes. The atmosphere was denser, richer in carbon dioxide. Plants grew rapidly along the shoreline. There were no fish in these waters, but there were clams and snails. Pterosaurs swooped down to scoop algae from the surface. A few carnivorous dinosaurs prowled the swampy shores of the lake, moving among the palm trees. And offshore was a small island, about two acres in size. Ringed with dense vegetation, this island formed a protected sanctuary where herds of herbivorous duckbilled dinosaurs laid their eggs in communal nests, and raised their squeaking young.

Over the millions of years that followed, the pale green alkaline lake grew shallower, and finally vanished. The exposed land buckled and cracked under the heat. And the offshore island with its dinosaur eggs became the eroded hillside in northern Montana which Alan Grant was now excavating.

'Hey, *Alan!*'

He stood, a barrel-chested, bearded man of forty. He heard the chugging of the portable generator, and the distant clatter of the jack-hammer cutting into the dense rock on the next hill. He saw the kids working around the jackhammer, moving away the big pieces of rock after checking them for fossils. At the foot of the hill, he saw the six tipis of his camp, the flapping mess tent, and the trailer that served as their field laboratory. And he saw Ellie waving to him, from the shadow of the field laboratory.

'Visitor!' she called, and pointed to the east.

Grant saw the cloud of dust, and the blue Ford sedan bouncing over the rutted road toward them. He glanced at his watch: right on time. On the other hill, the kids looked up with interest. They didn't get many visitors in Snakewater, and there had been a lot of speculation about what a lawyer from the Environmental Protection Agency would want to see Alan Grant about.

But Grant knew that paleontology, the study of extinct life, had in recent years taken on an unexpected relevance to the modern world. The modern world was changing fast, and urgent questions about the weather, deforestation, global warming, or the ozone layer often seemed answerable, at least in part, with information from the past. Information that paleontologists could provide. He had been called as an expert witness twice in the past few years.

Grant started down the hill to meet the car.

The visitor coughed in the white dust as he slammed the car door. 'Bob Morris, EPA,' he said, extending his hand. 'I'm with the San Francisco office.'

Grant introduced himself and said, 'You look hot. Want a beer?'

'Jesus, yeah.' Morris was in his late twenties, wearing a tie, and pants from a business suit. He carried a briefcase. His wing-tip shoes crunched on the rocks as they walked toward the trailer.

'When I first came over the hill, I thought this was an Indian reservation,' Morris said, pointing to the tipis.

'No,' Grant said. 'Just the best way to live out here.' Grant explained that in 1978, the first year of the excavations, they had come out in North Slope octahedral tents, the most advanced available. But the tents always blew over in the wind. They tried other kinds of tents, with the same result. Finally they started putting up tipis, which were larger inside, more comfortable, and more stable in wind. 'These're Blackfoot tipis, built around four poles,' Grant said. 'Sioux tipis are built around three. But this used to be Blackfoot territory, so we thought . . .'

'Uh-huh,' Morris said. 'Very fitting.' He squinted at the desolate landscape and shook his head. 'How long you been out here?'

'About sixty cases,' Grant said. When Morris looked surprised, he explained, 'We measure time in beer. We start in June with a hundred cases. We've gone through about sixty so far.'

'Sixty-three, to be exact,' Ellie Sattler said, as they reached the trailer. Grant was amused to see Morris gaping at her. Ellie was wearing cut-off jeans and a workshirt tied at her midriff. She was twenty-four and darkly tanned. Her blond hair was pulled back.

'Ellie keeps us going,' Grant said, introducing her. 'She's very good at what she does.'

'What does she do?' Morris asked.

'Paleobotany,' Ellie said. 'And I also do the standard field preps.' She opened the door and they went inside.

The air conditioning in the trailer only brought the temperature down to eighty-five degrees, but it seemed cool after the midday heat. The trailer had a series of long wooden tables, with tiny bone specimens neatly laid out, tagged and labeled. Farther along were ceramic dishes and crocks. There was a strong odor of vinegar.

Morris glanced at the bones. 'I thought dinosaurs were big,' he said.

'They were,' Ellie said. 'But everything you see here comes from babies. Snakewater is important primarily because of the number of dinosaur nesting sites here. Until we started this work, there were hardly any infant dinosaurs known. Only one nest had ever been found, in the Gobi Desert. We've discovered a dozen different hadrosaur nests, complete with eggs and bones of infants.'

While Grant went to the refrigerator, she showed Morris the acetic acid baths, which were used to dissolve away the limestone from the delicate bones.

'They look like chicken bones,' Morris said, peering into the ceramic dishes.

'Yes,' she said. 'They're very bird-like.'

'And what about those?' Morris said, pointing through the trailer window to piles of large bones outside, wrapped in heavy plastic.

'Rejects,' Ellie said. 'Bones too fragmentary when we took them out of the ground. In the old days we'd just discard them, but nowadays we send them for genetic testing.'

'Genetic testing?' Morris said.

'Here you go,' Grant said, thrusting a beer into his hand. He gave another to Ellie. She chugged hers, throwing her long neck back. Morris stared.

'We're pretty informal here,' Grant said. 'Want to step into my office?'

'Sure,' Morris said. Grant led him to the end of the trailer, where there was a torn couch, a sagging chair, and a battered end-table. Grant dropped onto the couch, which creaked and exhaled a cloud of chalky dust. He leaned back, thumped his boots up on the endtable, and gestured for Morris to sit in the chair. 'Make yourself comfortable.'

Grant was a professor of paleontology at the University of Denver, and one of the foremost researchers in his field, but he had never been comfortable with social niceties. He saw himself as an outdoor man, and he knew that all the important work in paleontology was done outdoors, with your hands. Grant had little patience for the academics, for the museum curators, for what he called Teacup Dinosaur Hunters. And he took some pains to distance himself in dress and behavior from the Teacup Dinosaur Hunters, even delivering his lectures in jeans and sneakers.

Grant watched as Morris primly brushed off the seat of the chair before he sat down. Morris opened his briefcase, rummaged through his papers, and glanced back at Ellie, who was lifting bones with tweezers from the acid bath at the other end of the trailer, paying no attention to them. 'You're probably wondering why I'm here.'

Grant nodded. 'It's a long way to come, Mr. Morris.'

'Well,' Morris said, 'to get right to the point, the EPA is concerned about the activities of the Hammond Foundation. You receive some funding from them.'

'Thirty thousand dollars a year,' Grant said, nodding. 'For the last five years.'

'What do you know about the foundation?' Morris said.

Grant shrugged. 'The Hammond Foundation is a respected source of academic grants. They fund research all over the world, including several dinosaur researchers. I know they support Bob Kerry out of the Tyrrell in Alberta, and John Weller in Alaska. Probably more.'

'Do you know why the Hammond Foundation supports so much dinosaur research?' Morris asked.

'Of course. It's because old John Hammond is a dinosaur nut.'

'You've met Hammond?'

Grant shrugged. 'Once or twice. He comes here for brief visits. He's quite elderly, you know. And eccentric, the way rich people sometimes are. But always very enthusiastic. Why?'

'Well,' Morris said, 'the Hammond Foundation is actually a rather mysterious organization.' He pulled out a Xeroxed world map, marked with red dots, and passed it to Grant. 'These are the digs the foundation financed last year. Notice anything odd about them? Montana, Alaska, Canada, Sweden . . . They're all sites in the north. There's nothing below the forty-fifth parallel.' Morris pulled out more maps. 'It's the same, year after year. Dinosaur projects to the south, in Utah or Colorado or Mexico, never get funded. The Hammond Foundation only supports cold-weather digs. We'd like to know why.'

Grant shuffled through the maps quickly. If it was true that the foundation only supported cold-weather digs, then it was strange behavior, because some of the best dinosaur researchers were working in hot climates, and –

'And there are other puzzles,' Morris said. 'For example, what is the relationship of dinosaurs to amber?'

'Amber?'

'Yes. It's the hard yellow resin of dried tree sap –'

'I know what it is,' Grant said. 'But why are you asking?'

'Because,' Morris said, 'over the last five years, Hammond has purchased enormous quantities of amber in America, Europe, and Asia, including many pieces of museum-quality jewelry. The foundation has spent seventeen million dollars on amber. They now possess the largest privately held stock of this material in the world.'

'I don't get it,' Grant said.

'Neither does anybody else,' Morris said. 'As far as we can tell, it doesn't make any sense at all. Amber is easily synthesized. It has no commercial or defense value. There's no reason to stockpile it. But Hammond has done just that, over many years.'

'Amber,' Grant said, shaking his head.

'And what about his island in Costa Rica?' Morris continued. 'Ten years ago, the Hammond Foundation leased an island from the government of Costa Rica. Supposedly to set up a biological preserve.'

'I don't know anything about that,' Grant said, frowning.

'I haven't been able to find out much,' Morris said. 'The island is a hundred miles off the west coast. It's very rugged, and it's in an area of ocean where the combinations of wind and current make it almost perpetually covered in fog. They used to call it Cloud Island. Isla Nublar. Apparently the Costa Ricans were amazed that anybody would want it.' Morris searched in his briefcase. 'The reason I mention it,' he said, 'is that, according to the records, you were paid a consultant's fee in connection with this island.'

'I was?' Grant said.

Morris passed a sheet of paper to Grant. It was the Xerox of a check issued in March 1984 from InGen Inc., Farallon Road, Palo Alto, California. Made out to Alan Grant in the amount of twelve thousand dollars. At the lower corner, the check was marked CONSULTANT SERVICES/COSTA RICA/JUVENILE HYPERSPACE.

'Oh, sure,' Grant said. 'I remember that. It was weird as hell, but I remember it. And it didn't have anything to do with an island.'

Alan Grant had found the first clutch of dinosaur eggs in Montana in 1979, and many more in the next two years, but he hadn't gotten around to publishing his findings until 1983. His paper, with its report of a herd of ten thousand duckbilled dinosaurs living along the shore of a vast inland sea, building communal nests of eggs in the mud, raising their infant dinosaurs in the herd, made Grant a celebrity overnight. The notion of maternal instincts in giant dinosaurs – and the drawings of cute babies poking their snouts out of the eggs – had appeal around the world. Grant was besieged with requests for interviews, lectures, books. Characteristically, he turned them all down, wanting only to continue his excavations. But it was during those frantic days of the mid-1980s that he was approached by the InGen corporation with a request for consulting services.

'Had you heard of InGen before?' Morris asked.

'No.'

'How did they contact you?'

'Telephone call. It was a man named Gennaro or Gennino, something like that.'

Morris nodded. 'Donald Gennaro,' he said. 'He's the legal counsel for InGen.'

'Anyway, he wanted to know about eating habits of dinosaurs. And he offered me a fee to draw up a paper for him.' Grant drank his beer, set the can on the floor. 'Gennaro was particularly interested in young dinosaurs. Infants and juveniles. What they ate. I guess he thought I would know about that.'

'Did you?'

'Not really, no. I told him that. We had found lots of skeletal material, but we had very little dietary data. But Gennaro said he knew we hadn't published everything, and he wanted whatever we had. And he offered a very large fee. Fifty thousand dollars.'

Morris took out a tape recorder and set it on the endtable. 'You mind?'

'No, go ahead.'

'So Gennaro telephoned you in 1984. What happened then?'

'Well,' Grant said. 'You see our operation here. Fifty thousand would support two full summers of digging. I told him I'd do what I could.'

'So you agreed to prepare a paper for him.'

'Yes.'

'On the dietary habits of juvenile dinosaurs?'

'Yes.'

'You met Gennaro?'

'No. Just on the phone.'

'Did Gennaro say why he wanted this information?'

'Yes,' Grant said. 'He was planning a museum for children, and he wanted to feature baby dinosaurs. He said he was hiring a number of academic consultants, and named them. There were paleontologists like me, and a mathematician from Texas named Ian Malcolm, and a couple of ecologists. A systems analyst. Good group.'

Morris nodded, making notes. 'So you accepted the consultancy?'

'Yes. I agreed to send him a summary of our work: what we knew about the habits of the duckbilled hadrosaurs we'd found.'

'What kind of information did you send?' Morris asked.

'Everything: nesting behavior, territorial ranges, feeding behavior, social behavior. Everything.'

'And how did Gennaro respond?'

'He kept calling and calling. Sometimes in the middle of the night. Would the dinosaurs eat this? Would they eat that? Should the exhibit include this? I could never understand why he was so worked up. I mean, I think dinosaurs are important, too, but not *that* important. They've been dead sixty-five million years. You'd think his calls could wait until morning.'

'I see,' Morris said. 'And the fifty thousand dollars?'

Grant shook his head. 'I got tired of Gennaro and called the whole thing off. We settled up for twelve thousand. That must have been about the middle of '85.'

Morris made a note. 'And InGen? Any other contact with them?'

'Not since 1985.'

'And when did the Hammond Foundation begin to fund your research?'

'I'd have to look,' Grant said. 'But it was around then. Mid-eighties.'

'And you know Hammond as just a rich dinosaur enthusiast.'

'Yes.'

Morris made another note.

'Look,' Grant said. 'If the EPA is so concerned about John Hammond and what he's doing – the dinosaur sites in the north, the amber purchases, the island in Costa Rica – why don't you just ask him about it?'

'At the moment, we can't,' Morris said.

'Why not?' Grant said.

'Because we don't have any evidence of wrongdoing,' Morris said. 'But personally, I think it's clear John Hammond is evading the law.'

'I was first contacted,' Morris explained, 'by the Office of Technology Transfer. The OTT monitors shipments of American technology which might have military significance. They called to say that InGen had two areas of possible illegal technology transfer. First, InGen shipped three Cray XMPs to Costa Rica. InGen characterized it as transfer within corporate divisions, and said they weren't for resale. But OTT couldn't imagine why the hell somebody'd need that power in Costa Rica.'

'Three Crays,' Grant said. 'Is that a kind of computer?'

Morris nodded. 'Very powerful supercomputers. To put it in perspective, three Crays represent more computing power than any other privately held company in America. And InGen sent the machines to Costa Rica. You have to wonder why.'

'I give up. Why?' Grant said.

'Nobody knows. And the Hoods are even more worrisome,' Morris continued. 'Hoods are automated gene sequencers – machines that work out the genetic code by themselves. They're so new that they haven't been put on the restricted lists yet. But any genetic engineering lab is likely to have one, if it can afford the half-million-dollar price tag.' He flipped through his notes. 'Well, it seems InGen shipped *twenty-four* Hood sequencers to their island in Costa Rica.

'Again, they said it was a transfer within divisions and not an export,' Morris said. 'There wasn't much that OTT could do. They're not officially concerned with use. But InGen was obviously setting up one of the most powerful genetic engineering facilities in the world in an obscure Central American country. A country with no regulations. That kind of thing has happened before.'

There had already been cases of American bioengineering companies moving to another country so they would not be hampered by regulations and rules. The most flagrant, Morris explained, was the Biosyn rabies case.

In 1986, Genetic Biosyn Corporation of Cupertino tested a bioengineered rabies vaccine on a farm in Chile. They didn't inform the government of Chile, or the farm workers involved. They simply released the vaccine.

The vaccine consisted of live rabies virus, genetically modified to be nonvirulent. But the virulence hadn't been tested; Biosyn didn't know whether the virus could still cause rabies or not. Even worse, the virus had been modified. Ordinarily you couldn't contract rabies unless you were bitten by an animal. But Biosyn modified the rabies virus to cross the pulmonary alveoli; you could get an infection just inhaling it. Biosyn staffers brought this live rabies virus down to Chile in a carry-on bag on a commercial airline flight. Morris often wondered what would have happened if the capsule had broken open during the flight. Everybody on the plane might have been infected with rabies.

It was outrageous. It was irresponsible. It was criminally negligent. But no action was taken against Biosyn. The Chilean farmers who unwittingly risked their lives were ignorant peasants; the government of Chile had an economic crisis to worry about; and the American authorities had no jurisdiction. So Lewis Dodgson, the geneticist responsible for the test, was still working at Biosyn. Biosyn was still as reckless as ever. And other American companies were hurrying to set up facilities in foreign countries that lacked sophistication about genetic research. Countries that perceived genetic engineering to be like any other high-tech development, and thus welcomed it to their lands, unaware of the dangers posed.

'So that's why we began our investigation of InGen,' Morris said. 'About three weeks ago.'

'And what have you actually found?' Grant said.

'Not much,' Morris admitted. 'When I go back to San Francisco, we'll probably have to close the investigation. And I think I'm about finished here.' He started packing up his briefcase. 'By the way, what *does* "juvenile hyperspace" mean?'

'That's just a fancy label for my report,' Grant said. ' "Hyperspace" is a term for multidimensional space – like three-dimensional tic-tac-toe. If you were to take all the behaviors of an animal, its eating and movement and sleeping, you could plot the animal within the multidimensional space. Some paleontologists refer to the behavior of an animal as occurring in an ecological hyperspace. "Juvenile hyperspace" would just refer to the behavior of juvenile dinosaurs – if you wanted to be as pretentious as possible.'

At the far end of the trailer, the phone rang. Ellie answered it. She said, 'He's in a meeting right now. Can he call you back?'

· Morris snapped his briefcase shut and stood. 'Thanks for your help and the beer,' he said.

'No problem,' Grant said.

Grant walked with Morris down the trailer to the door at the far end. Morris said, 'Did Hammond ever ask for any physical materials from your site? Bones, or eggs, or anything like that?'

'No,' Grant said.

'Dr. Sattler mentioned you do some genetic work here. . . .'

'Well, not exactly,' Grant said. 'When we remove fossils that are broken or for some other reason not suitable for museum preservation, we send the bones out to a lab that grinds them up and tries to extract proteins for us. The proteins are then identified and the report is sent back to us.'

'Which lab is that?' Morris asked.

'Medical Biologic Services in Salt Lake.'

'How'd you choose them?'

'Competitive bids.'

'The lab has nothing to do with InGen?' Morris asked.

'Not that I know,' Grant said.

They came to the door of the trailer. Grant opened it, and felt the rush of hot air from outside. Morris paused to put on his sunglasses.

'One last thing,' Morris said. 'Suppose InGen wasn't really making a museum exhibit. Is there anything else they could have done with the information in the report you gave them?'

Grant laughed. 'Sure. They could feed a baby hadrosaur.'

Morris laughed, too. 'A baby hadrosaur. That'd be something to see. How big were they?'

'About so,' Grant said, holding his hands six inches apart. 'Squirrel-size.'

'And how long before they become full-grown?'

'Three years,' Grant said. 'Give or take.'

Morris held out his hand. 'Well, thanks again for your help.'

'Take it easy driving back,' Grant said. He watched for a moment as Morris walked back toward his car, and then closed the trailer door.

Grant said, 'What did you think?'

Ellie shrugged. 'Naïve.'

'You like the part where John Hammond is the evil arch-villain?'

Grant laughed. 'John Hammond's about as sinister as Walt Disney. By the way, who called?'

'Oh,' Ellie said, 'it was a woman named Alice Levin. She works at Columbia Medical Center. You know her?'

Grant shook his head. 'No.'

'Well, it was something about identifying some remains. She wants you to call her back right away.'

Skeleton

Ellie Sattler brushed a strand of blond hair back from her face and turned her attention to the acid baths. She had six in a row, at molar strengths from 5 to 30 percent. She had to keep an eye on the stronger solutions, because they would eat through the limestone and begin to erode the bones. And infant-dinosaur bones were so fragile. She marveled that they had been preserved at all, after eighty million years.

She listened idly as Grant said, 'Miss Levin? This is Alan Grant. What's this about a . . . You have what? A *what?*' He began to laugh. 'Oh, I doubt that very much, Miss Levin . . . No, I really don't have time, I'm sorry . . . Well, I'd take a look at it, but I can pretty much guarantee it's a basilisk lizard. But . . . yes, you can do that. All right. Send it now.' Grant hung up, and shook his head. 'These people.'

Ellie said, 'What's it about?'

'Some lizard she's trying to identify,' Grant said. 'She's going to fax me an X-ray.' He walked over to the fax and waited as the transmission came through. 'Incidentally, I've got a new find for you. A good one.'

'Yes?'

Grant nodded. 'Found it just before the kid showed up. On South Hill, horizon four. Infant velociraptor: jaw and complete dentition, so there's no question about identity. And the site looks undisturbed. We might even get a full skeleton.'

'That's fantastic,' Ellie said. 'How young?'

'Young,' Grant said. 'Two, maybe four months at most.'

'And it's definitely a velociraptor?'

'Definitely,' Grant said. 'Maybe our luck has finally turned.'

For the last two years at Snakewater, the team had excavated only duckbilled hadrosaurs. They already had evidence for vast herds of these grazing dinosaurs, roaming the Cretaceous plains in groups of ten or twenty thousand, as buffalo would later roam.

But increasingly the question that faced them was: where were the predators?

They expected predators to be rare, of course. Studies of predator/prey populations in the game parks of Africa and India suggested that, roughly speaking, there was one predatory carnivore for every four hundred herbivores. That meant a herd of ten thousand duckbills would support only twenty-five tyrannosaurs. So it was unlikely that they would find the remains of a large predator.

But where were the smaller predators? Snakewater had dozens of nesting sites – in some places, the ground was literally covered with fragments of dinosaur eggshells – and many small dinosaurs ate eggs. Animals like *Dromaeosaurus*, *Oviraptor*, *Velociraptor*, and *Coelurus* – predators three to six feet tall – must have been found here in abundance.

But they had discovered none so far.

Perhaps this velociraptor skeleton did mean their luck had changed. And an infant! Ellie knew that one of Grant's dreams was to study infant-rearing behavior in carnivorous dinosaurs, as he had already studied the behavior of herbivores. Perhaps this was the first step toward that dream. 'You must be pretty excited,' Ellie said.

Grant didn't answer.

'I said, you must be excited,' Ellie repeated.

'My God,' Grant said. He was staring at the fax.

Ellie looked over Grant's shoulder at the X-ray, and breathed out slowly. 'You think it's an *amassicus?*'

'Yes,' Grant said. 'Or a *triassicus*. The skeleton is so light.'

'But it's no lizard,' she said.

'No,' Grant said. 'This is not a lizard. No three-toed lizard has walked on this planet for two hundred million years.'

Ellie's first thought was that she was looking at a hoax – an ingenious, skillful hoax, but a hoax nonetheless. Every biologist knew that the threat of a hoax was omnipresent. The most famous hoax, the Piltdown man, had gone undetected for forty years, and its perpetrator was still unknown. More recently, the distinguished astronomer Fred Hoyle had claimed that a fossil winged dinosaur, *Archaeopteryx*, on display in the British Museum, was a fraud. (It was later shown to be genuine.)

The essence of a successful hoax was that it presented scientists with what they expected to see. And, to Ellie's eye, the X-ray image of the lizard was exactly correct. The three-toed foot was well balanced, with the medial claw smallest. The bony remnants of the fourth and fifth toes were located up near the metatarsal joint. The tibia was strong, and considerably longer than the femur. At the hip, the acetabulum was complete. The tail showed forty-five vertebrae. It was a *Procompsognathus*.

'Could this X-ray be faked?'

'I don't know,' Grant said. 'But it's almost impossible to fake an

X-ray. And *Procompsognathus* is an obscure animal. Even people familiar with dinosaurs have never heard of it.'

Ellie read the note. 'Specimen acquired on the beach of Cabo Blanco, July 16. . . . Apparently a howler monkey was eating the animal, and this was all that was recovered. Oh . . . and it says the lizard attacked a little girl.'

'I doubt that,' Grant said. 'But perhaps. *Procompsognathus* was so small and light we assume it must be a scavenger, only feeding off dead creatures. And you can tell the size' – he measured quickly – 'it's about twenty centimeters to the hips, which means the full animal would be about a foot tall. About as big as a chicken. Even a child would look pretty fearsome to it. It might bite an infant, but not a child.'

Ellie frowned at the X-ray image. 'You think this could really be a legitimate rediscovery?' she said. 'Like the coelacanth?'

'Maybe,' Grant said. The coelacanth was a five-foot-long fish thought to have died out sixty-five million years ago, until a specimen was pulled from the ocean in 1938. But there were other examples. The Australian mountain pygmy possum was known only from fossils until a live one was found in a garbage can in Melbourne. And a ten-thousand-year-old fossil fruit bat from New Guinea was described by a zoologist who not long afterward received a living specimen in the mail.

'But could it be real?' she persisted. 'What about the age?'

Grant nodded. 'The age is a problem.'

Most rediscovered animals were rather recent additions to the fossil record: ten or twenty thousand years old. Some were a few million years old; in the case of the coelacanth, sixty-five million years old. But the specimen they were looking at was much, much older than that. Dinosaurs had died out in the Cretaceous period, sixty-five million years ago. They had flourished as the dominant life form on the planet in the Jurassic, 190 million years ago. And they had first appeared in the Triassic, roughly 220 million years ago.

It was during the early Triassic period that *Procompsognathus* had lived – a time so distant that our planet didn't even look the same. All the continents were joined together in a single landmass, called Pangaea, which extended from the North to the South Pole – a vast continent of ferns and forests, with a few large deserts. The Atlantic Ocean was a narrow lake between what would become Africa and Florida. The air was denser. The land was warmer. There were hundreds of active volcanoes. And it was in this environment that *Procompsognathus* lived.

'Well,' Ellie said. 'We know animals have survived. Crocodiles are basically Triassic animals living in the present. Sharks are Triassic. So we know it has happened before.'

Grant nodded. 'And the thing is,' he said, 'how else do we explain it? It's either a fake – which I doubt – or else it's a rediscovery. What else could it be?'

The phone rang. 'Alice Levin again,' Grant said. 'Let's see if she'll send us the actual specimen.' He answered it and looked at Ellie, surprised. 'Yes, I'll hold for Mr. Hammond. Yes. Of course.'

'Hammond? What does he want?' Ellie said.

Grant shook his head, and then said into the phone, 'Yes, Mr. Hammond. Yes, it's good to hear your voice, too. . . . Yes . . .' He looked at Ellie. 'Oh, you did? Oh yes? Is that right?'

He cupped his hand over the mouthpiece and said, 'Still as eccentric as ever. You've got to hear this.'

Grant pushed the speaker button, and Ellie heard a raspy old-man's voice speaking rapidly: '– hell of an annoyance from some EPA fellow, seems to have gone off half cocked, all on his own, running around the country talking to people, stirring up things. I don't suppose anybody's come to see you way out there?'

'As a matter of fact,' Grant said, 'somebody did come to see me.'

Hammond snorted. 'I was afraid of that. Smart-ass kid named Morris?'

'Yes, his name was Morris,' Grant said.

'He's going to see all our consultants,' Hammond said. 'He went to see Ian Malcolm the other day – you know, the mathematician in Texas? That's the first I knew of it. We're having one hell of a time getting a handle on this thing, it's typical of the way government operates, there isn't any complaint, there isn't any charge, just harassment from some kid who's unsupervised and is running around at the taxpayers' expense. Did he bother you? Disrupt your work?'

'No, no, he didn't bother me.'

'Well, that's too bad, in a way,' Hammond said, 'because I'd try and get an injunction to stop him if he had. As it is, I had our lawyers call over at EPA to find out what the hell their problem is. The head of the office claims he didn't know there was any investigation! You figure that one out. Damned bureaucracy is all it is. Hell, I think this kid's trying to get down to Costa Rica, poke around, get onto our island. You know we have an island down there?'

'No,' Grant said, looking at Ellie, 'I didn't know.'

'Oh yes, we bought it and started our operation oh, four or five years ago now. I forget exactly. Called Isla Nublar – big island, hundred miles offshore. Going to be a biological preserve. Wonderful place. Tropical jungle. You know, you ought to see it, Dr. Grant.'

'Sounds interesting,' Grant said, 'but actually –'

43

'It's almost finished now, you know,' Hammond said. 'I've sent you some material about it. Did you get my material?'

'No, but we're pretty far from –'

'Maybe it'll come today. Look it over. The island's just beautiful. It's got everything. We've been in construction now thirty months. You can imagine. Big park. Opens in September next year. You really ought to go see it.'

'It sounds wonderful, but –'

'As a matter of fact,' Hammond said, 'I'm going to insist you see it, Dr. Grant. I know you'd find it right up your alley. You'd find it fascinating.'

'I'm in the middle of –' Grant said.

'Say, I'll tell you what,' Hammond said, as if the idea had just occurred to him. 'I'm having some of the people who consulted for us go down there this weekend. Spend a few days and look it over. At our expense, of course. It'd be terrific if you'd give us your opinion.'

'I couldn't possibly,' Grant said.

'Oh, just for a weekend,' Hammond said, with the irritating, cheery persistence of an old man. 'That's all I'm talking about, Dr. Grant. I wouldn't want to interrupt your work. I know how important that work is. Believe me, I know that. Never interrupt your work. But you could hop on down there this weekend, and be back on Monday.'

'No, I couldn't,' Grant said. 'I've just found a new skeleton and –'

'Yes, fine, but I still think you should come –' Hammond said, not really listening.

'And we've just received some evidence for a very puzzling and remarkable find, which seems to be a living procompsognathid.'

'A what?' Hammond said, slowing down. 'I didn't quite get that. You said a living procompsognathid?'

'That's right,' Grant said. 'It's a biological specimen, a partial fragment of an animal collected from Central America. A living animal.'

'You don't say,' Hammond said. 'A living animal? How extraordinary.'

'Yes,' Grant said. 'We think so, too. So, you see, this isn't the time for me to be leaving –'

'Central America, did you say?'

'Yes.'

'Where in Central America is it from, do you know?'

'A beach called Cabo Blanco, I don't know exactly where –'

'I see.' Hammond cleared his throat. 'And when did this, ah, specimen arrive in your hands?'

'Just today.'

'Today, I see. Today. I see. Yes.' Hammond cleared his throat again.

Grant looked at Ellie and mouthed, *What's going on?*

Ellie shook her head. *Sounds upset.*

Grant mouthed, *See if Morris is still here.*

She went to the window and looked out, but Morris's car was gone. She turned back.

On the speaker, Hammond coughed. 'Ah, Dr. Grant. Have you told anybody about it yet?'

'No.'

'Good, that's good. Well. Yes. I'll tell you frankly, Dr. Grant, I'm having a little problem about this island. This EPA thing is coming at just the wrong time.'

'How's that?' Grant said.

'Well, we've had our problems and some delays . . . Let's just say that I'm under a little pressure here, and I'd like you to look at this island for me. Give me your opinion. I'll be paying you the usual weekend consultant rate of twenty thousand a day. That'd be sixty thousand for three days. And if you can spare Dr. Sattler, she'll go at the same rate. We need a botanist. What do you say?'

Ellie looked at Grant as he said, 'Well, Mr. Hammond, that much money would fully finance our expeditions for the next two summers.'

'Good, good,' Hammond said blandly. He seemed distracted now, his thoughts elsewhere. 'I want this to be easy . . . Now, I'm sending the corporate jet to pick you up at that private airfield east of Choteau. You know the one I mean? It's only about two hours' drive from where you are. You be there at five p.m. tomorrow and I'll be waiting for you. Take you right down. Can you and Dr. Sattler make that plane?'

'I guess we can.'

'Good. Pack lightly. You don't need passports. I'm looking forward to it. See you tomorrow,' Hammond said, and he hung up.

Cowan, Swain and Ross

Midday sun streamed into the San Francisco law offices of Cowan, Swain and Ross, giving the room a cheerfulness that Donald Gennaro did not feel. He listened on the phone and looked at his boss, Daniel Ross, cold as an undertaker in his dark pinstripe suit.

'I understand, John,' Gennaro said. 'And Grant agreed to come? Good, good . . . yes, that sounds fine to me. My congratulations, John.' He hung up the phone and turned to Ross.

'We can't trust Hammond any more. He's under too much pressure. The EPA's investigating him, he's behind schedule on his Costa Rican resort, and the investors are getting nervous. There have been too many rumors of problems down there. Too many workmen have died. And now this business about a living procompsit-whatever on the mainland . . .'

'What does that mean?' Ross said.

'Maybe nothing,' Gennaro said. 'But Hamachi is one of our principal investors. I got a report last week from Hamachi's representative in San José, the capital of Costa Rica. According to the report, some new kind of lizard is biting children on the coast.'

Ross blinked. 'New lizard?'

'Yes,' Gennaro said. 'We can't screw around with this. We've got to inspect that island right away. I've asked Hammond to arrange independent site inspections every week for the next three weeks.'

'And what does Hammond say?'

'He insists nothing is wrong on the island. Claims he has all these security precautions.'

'But you don't believe him,' Ross said.

'No,' Gennaro said. 'I don't.'

Donald Gennaro had come to Cowan, Swain from a background in investment banking. Cowan, Swain's high-tech clients frequently needed capitalization, and Gennaro helped them find the money. One of his first assignments, back in 1982, had been to accompany John Hammond while the old man, then nearly seventy, put together the funding to start the InGen corporation. They eventually raised almost a billion dollars, and Gennaro remembered it as a wild ride.

'Hammond's a dreamer,' Gennaro said.

'A potentially dangerous dreamer,' Ross said. 'We should never have gotten involved. What is our financial position?'

'The firm,' Gennaro said, 'owns five percent.'

'General or limited?'

'General.'

Ross shook his head. 'We should never have done that.'

'It seemed wise at the time,' Gennaro said. 'Hell, it was eight years ago. We took it in lieu of some fees. And, if you remember, Hammond's plan was extremely speculative. He was really pushing the envelope. Nobody really thought he could pull it off.'

'But apparently he has,' Ross said. 'In any case, I agree that an inspection is overdue. What about your site experts?'

'I'm starting with experts Hammond already hired as consultants, early in the project.' Gennaro tossed a list onto Ross's desk. 'First group is a paleontologist, a paleobotanist, and a mathematician. They go down this weekend. I'll go with them.'

'Will they tell you the truth?' Ross said.

'I think so. None of them had much to do with the island, and one of them – the mathematician, Ian Malcolm – was openly hostile to the project from the start. Insisted it would never work, could never work.'

'And who else?'

'Just a technical person: the computer system analyst. Review the park's computers and fix some bugs. He should be there by Friday morning.'

'Fine,' Ross said. 'You're making the arrangements?'

'Hammond asked to place the calls himself. I think he wants to pretend that he's not in trouble, that it's just a social invitation. Showing off his island.'

'All right,' Ross said. 'But just make sure it happens. Stay on top of it. I want this Costa Rican situation resolved within a week.' Ross got up, and walked out of the room.

Gennaro dialed, heard the whining hiss of a radiophone. Then he heard a voice say, 'Grant here.'

'Hi, Dr. Grant, this is Donald Gennaro. I'm the general counsel for InGen. We talked a few years back, I don't know if you remember –'

'I remember,' Grant said.

'Well,' Gennaro said. 'I just got off the phone with John Hammond, who tells me the good news that you're coming down to our island in Costa Rica . . .'

'Yes,' Grant said. 'I guess we're going down there tomorrow.'

'Well, I just want to extend my thanks to you for doing this on short notice. Everybody at InGen appreciates it. We've asked Ian Malcolm, who like you was one of the early consultants, to come down as well. He's the mathematician at UT in Austin?'

'John Hammond mentioned that,' Grant said.

'Well, good,' Gennaro said. 'And I'll be coming, too, as a matter of fact. By the way, this specimen you have found of a pro . . . procom . . . what is it?'

'Procompsognathus,' Grant said.

'Yes. Do you have the specimen with you, Dr. Grant? The actual specimen?'

'No,' Grant said. 'I've only seen an X-ray. The specimen is in New York. A woman from Columbia University called me.'

'Well, I wonder if you could give me the details on that,' Gennaro said. 'Then I can run down that specimen for Mr. Hammond, who's very excited about it. I'm sure you want to see the actual specimen, too. Perhaps I can even get it delivered to the island while you're all down there,' Gennaro said.

Grant gave him the information. 'Well, that's fine, Dr. Grant,' Gennaro said. 'My regards to Dr. Sattler. I look forward to meeting you and him tomorrow.' And Gennaro hung up.

Plans

'This just came,' Ellie said the next day, walking to the back of the trailer with a thick manila envelope. 'One of the kids brought it back from town. It's from Hammond.'

Grant noticed the blue-and-white InGen logo as he tore open the envelope. Inside there was no cover letter, just a bound stack of paper. Pulling it out, he discovered it was blueprints. They were reduced, forming a thick book. The cover was marked: ISLA NUBLAR RESORT GUEST FACILITIES (FULL SET: SAFARI LODGE).

'What the hell is this?' he said.

As he flipped open the book, a sheet of paper fell out.

> Dear Alan and Ellie:
>> As you can imagine we don't have much in the way of formal promotional materials yet. But this should give you some idea of the Isla Nublar project. I think it's very exciting!
>> Looking forward to discussing this with you! Hope you can join us!
>
>> Regards,
>> John

'I don't get it,' Grant said. He flipped through the sheets. 'These are architectural plans.' He turned to the top sheet:

VISITOR CENTER/LODGE	ISLA NUBLAR RESORT
CLIENT	InGen Inc., Palo Alto, Calif.
ARCHITECTS	Dunning, Murphy & Associates, New York. Richard Murphy, design partner; Theodore Chen, senior designer; Sheldon James, administrative partner.
ENGINEERS	Harlow, Whitney & Fields, Boston, structural; A. T. Misikawa, Osaka, mechanical.

VISITOR CENTER/LODGE	ISLA NUBLAR RESORT
LANDSCAPING	Shepperton Rogers, London; A. Ashikiga, H. Ieyasu, Kanazawa.
ELECTRICAL	N. V. Kobayashi, Tokyo. A. R. Makasawa, senior consultant.
COMPUTER C/C	Integrated Computer Systems, Inc., Cambridge, Mass. Dennis Nedry, project supervisor.

Grant turned to the plans themselves. They were stamped INDUS-TRIAL SECRETS DO NOT COPY and CONFIDENTIAL WORK PRODUCT — NOT FOR DISTRIBUTION. Each sheet was numbered, and at the top: 'These plans represent the confidential creations of InGen Inc. You must have signed document 112/4A or you risk prosecution.'

'Looks pretty paranoid to me,' he said.

'Maybe there's a reason,' Ellie said.

The next page was a topographical map. It showed Isla Nublar as an inverted teardrop, bulging at the north, tapering at the south. The island was eight miles long, and the map divided it into several large sections.

The northern section was marked VISITOR AREA and it contained structures marked 'Visitor Arrivals,' 'Visitor Center/Administration,' 'Power/Desalinization/Support,' 'Hammond Res.,' and 'Safari Lodge.' Grant could see the outline of a swimming pool, the rectangles of tennis courts, and the round squiggles that represented planting and shrubbery.

'Looks like a resort, all right,' Ellie said.

There followed detail sheets for the Safari Lodge itself. In the elevation sketches, the lodge looked dramatic: a long low building with a series of pyramid shapes on the roof. But there was little about the other buildings in the visitor area.

And the rest of the island was even more mysterious. As far as Grant could tell, it was mostly open space. A network of roads, tunnels, and outlying buildings, and a long thin lake that appeared to be man-made, with concrete dams and barriers. But, for the most part, the island was divided into big curving areas with very little development at all. Each area was marked by codes:

/P/PROC/V/2A, /D/TRIC/L/5(4A+1), /LN/OTHN/C/4(3A+1), and /VV/HADR/X/11(6A+3+3DB).

'Is there an explanation for the codes?' she said.

Grant flipped the pages rapidly, but he couldn't find one.

'Maybe they took it out,' she said.

'I'm telling you,' Grant said. 'Paranoid.' He looked at the big curving divisions, separated from one another by the network of roads. There were only six divisions on the whole island. And each division was separated from the road by a concrete moat. Outside each moat was a fence with a little lightning sign alongside it. That mystified them until they were finally able to figure out it meant the fences were electrified.

'That's odd,' she said. 'Electrified fences at a resort?'

'Miles of them,' Grant said. 'Electrified fences and moats, together. And usually with a road alongside them as well.'

'Just like a zoo,' Ellie said.

They went back to the topographical map and looked closely at the contour lines. The roads had been placed oddly. The main road ran north-south, right through the central hills of the island, including one section of road that seemed to be literally cut into the side of a cliff, above a river. It began to look as if there had been a deliberate effort to leave these open areas as big enclosures, separated from the roads by moats and electric fences. And the roads were raised up above ground level, so you could see over the fences....

'You know,' Ellie said, 'some of these dimensions are enormous. Look at this. This concrete moat is thirty feet wide. That's like a military fortification.'

'So are these buildings,' Grant said. He had noticed that each open division had a few buildings, usually located in out-of-the-way corners. But the buildings were all concrete, with thick walls. In side-view elevations they looked like concrete bunkers with small windows. Like the Nazi pillboxes from old war movies.

At that moment, they heard a muffled explosion, and Grant put the papers aside. 'Back to work,' he said.

'*Fire!*'

There was a slight vibration, and then yellow contour lines traced across the computer screen. This time the resolution was perfect, and Alan Grant had a glimpse of the skeleton, beautifully defined, the long neck arched back. It was unquestionably an infant velociraptor, and it looked in perfect –

The screen went blank.

'I hate computers,' Grant said, squinting in the sun. 'What happened now?'

'Lost the integrator input,' one of the kids said. 'Just a minute.' The kid bent to look at the tangle of wires going into the back of the battery-powered portable computer. They had set the computer up on a beer carton on top of Hill Four, not far from the device they called Thumper.

Grant sat down on the side of the hill and looked at his watch. He said to Ellie, 'We're going to have to do this the old-fashioned way.'

One of the kids overheard. 'Aw, Alan.'

'Look,' Grant said, 'I've got a plane to catch. And I want the fossil protected before I go.'

Once you began to expose a fossil, you had to continue, or risk losing it. Visitors imagined the landscape of the badlands to be unchanging, but in fact it was continuously eroding, literally right before your eyes; all day long you could hear the clatter of pebbles rolling down the crumbling hillside. And there was always the risk of a rainstorm; even a brief shower would wash away a delicate fossil. Thus Grant's partially exposed skeleton was at risk, and it had to be protected until he returned.

Fossil protection ordinarily consisted of a tarp over the site, and a trench around the perimeter to control water runoff. The question was how large a trench the velociraptor fossil required. To decide that, they were using computer-assisted sonic tomography, or CAST. This was a new procedure, in which Thumper fired a soft lead slug into the ground, setting up shock waves that were read by the computer and assembled into a kind of X-ray image of the hillside. They had been using it all summer with varying results.

Thumper was twenty feet away now, a big silver box on wheels, with an umbrella on top. It looked like an ice-cream vendor's pushcart, parked incongruously on the badlands. Thumper had two youthful attendants loading the next soft lead pellet.

So far, the CAST program merely located the extent of finds, helping Grant's team to dig more efficiently. But the kids claimed that within a few years it would be possible to generate an image so detailed that excavation would be redundant. You could get a perfect image of the bones, in three dimensions, and it promised a whole new era of archaeology without excavation.

But none of that had happened yet. And the equipment that worked flawlessly in the university laboratory proved pitifully delicate and fickle in the field.

'How much longer?' Grant said.

'We got it now, Alan. It's not bad.'

Grant went to look at the computer screen. He saw the complete skeleton, traced in bright yellow. It was indeed a young specimen. The outstanding characteristic of *Velociraptor* – the single-toed claw, which in a full-grown animal was a curved, six-inch-long weapon capable of ripping open its prey – was in this infant no larger than the thorn on a rosebush. It was hardly visible at all on the screen. And *Velociraptor* was a lightly built dinosaur in any case, an animal as fine-boned as a bird, and presumably as intelligent.

Here the skeleton appeared in perfect order, except that the head and neck were bent back, toward the posterior. Such neck flexion was so common in fossils that some scientists had formulated a theory to explain it, suggesting that the dinosaurs had become extinct because they had been poisoned by the evolving alkaloids in plants. The twisted neck was thought to signify the death agony of the dinosaurs. Grant had finally put that one to rest, by demonstrating that many species of birds and reptiles underwent a postmortem contraction of posterior neck ligaments, which bent the head backward in a characteristic way. It had nothing to do with the cause of death; it had to do with the way a carcass dried in the sun.

Grant saw that this particular skeleton had also been twisted laterally, so that the right leg and foot were raised up above the backbone.

'It looks kind of distorted,' one of the kids said. 'But I don't think it's the computer.'

'No,' Grant said. 'It's just time. Lots and lots of time.'

Grant knew that people could not imagine geological time. Human life was lived on another scale of time entirely. An apple turned brown in a few minutes. Silverware turned black in a few days. A compost heap decayed in a season. A child grew up in a decade. None of these everyday human experiences prepared people to be able to imagine the meaning of eighty million years – the length of time that had passed since this little animal had died.

In the classroom, Grant had tried different comparisons. If you imagined the human lifespan of sixty years was compressed to an hour, then eighty million years would still be 3,652 years – older than the pyramids. The velociraptor had been dead a long time.

'Doesn't look very fearsome,' one of the kids said.

'He wasn't,' Grant said. 'At least, not until he grew up.' Probably this baby had scavenged, feeding off carcasses slain by the adults, after the big animals had gorged themselves, and lay basking in the sun. Carnivores could eat as much as 25 percent of their body weight in a single meal, and it made them sleepy afterward. The babies would chitter and scramble over the indulgent, somnolent bodies of the adults, and nip little bites from the dead animal. The babies were probably cute little animals.

But an adult velociraptor was another matter entirely. Pound for pound, a velociraptor was the most rapacious dinosaur that ever lived.

Although relatively small – about two hundred pounds, the size of a leopard – velociraptors were quick, intelligent, and vicious, able to attack with sharp jaws, powerful clawed forearms, and the devastating single claw on the foot.

Velociraptors hunted in packs, and Grant thought it must have been a sight to see a dozen of these animals racing at full speed, leaping onto the back of a much larger dinosaur, tearing at the neck and slashing at the ribs and belly. . . .

'We're running out of time,' Ellie said, bringing him back.

Grant gave instructions for the trench. From the computer image, they knew the skeleton lay in a relatively confined area; a ditch around a two-meter square would be sufficient. Meanwhile, Ellie lashed down the tarp that covered the side of the hill. Grant helped her pound in the final stakes.

'How did the baby die?' one of the kids asked.

'I doubt we'll know,' Grant replied. 'Infant mortality in the wild is high. In African parks, it runs seventy percent among some carnivores. It could have been anything – disease, separation from the group, anything. Or even attack by an adult. We know these animals hunted in packs, but we don't know anything about their social behavior in a group.'

The students nodded. They had all studied animal behavior, and they knew, for example, that when a new male took over a lion pride, the first thing he did was kill all the cubs. The reason was apparently genetic: the male had evolved to disseminate his genes as widely as possible, and by killing the cubs he brought all the females into heat, so that he could impregnate them. It also prevented the females from wasting their time nurturing the offspring of another male.

Perhaps the velociraptor hunting pack was also ruled by a dominant male. They knew so little about dinosaurs, Grant thought. After 150 years of research and excavation all around the world, they still knew almost nothing about what the dinosaurs had really been like.

'We've got to go,' Ellie said, 'if we're going to get to Choteau by five.'

Hammond

Gennaro's secretary bustled in with a new suitcase. It still had the sales tags on it. 'You know, Mr. Gennaro,' she said severely, 'when you forget to pack it makes me think you don't really want to go on this trip.'

'Maybe you're right,' Gennaro said. 'I'm missing my kid's birthday.' Saturday was Amanda's birthday, and Elizabeth had invited twenty screaming four-year-olds to share it, as well as Cappy the Clown and a magician. His wife hadn't been happy to hear that Gennaro was going out of town. Neither was Amanda.

'Well, I did the best I could on short notice,' his secretary said. 'There's running shoes your size, and khaki shorts and shirts, and a shaving kit. A pair of jeans and a sweatshirt if it gets cold. The car is downstairs to take you to the airport. You have to leave now to make the flight.'

She left. Gennaro walked down the hallway, tearing the sales tags off the suitcase. As he passed the all-glass conference room, Dan Ross left the table and came outside.

'Have a good trip,' Ross said. 'But let's be very clear about one thing. I don't know how bad this situation actually is, Donald. But if there's a problem on that island, burn it to the ground.'

'Jesus, Dan . . . We're talking about a big investment.'

'Don't hesitate. Don't think about it. Just do it. Hear me?'

Gennaro nodded. 'I hear you,' he said. 'But Hammond –'

'Screw Hammond,' Ross said.

'My boy, my boy,' the familiar raspy voice said. 'How have you been, my boy?'

'Very well, sir,' Gennaro replied. He leaned back in the padded leather chair of the Gulfstream II jet as it flew east, toward the Rocky Mountains.

'You never call me any more,' Hammond said reproachfully. 'I've missed you, Donald. How is your lovely wife?'

'She's fine. Elizabeth's fine. We have a little girl now.'

'Wonderful, wonderful. Children are such a delight. She'd get a kick out of our new park in Costa Rica.'

Gennaro had forgotten how short Hammond was; as he sat in the chair, his feet didn't touch the carpeting; he swung his legs as he talked. There was a childlike quality to the man, even though Hammond must now be . . . what? Seventy-five? Seventy-six? Something like that. He looked older than Cennaro remembered, but then, Gennaro hadn't seen him for almost five years.

Hammond was flamboyant, a born showman, and back in 1983 he had had an elephant that he carried around with him in a little cage. The elephant was nine inches high and a foot long, and perfectly formed, except his tusks were stunted. Hammond took the elephant with him to fund-raising meetings. Gennaro usually carried it into the room, the cage covered with a little blanket, like a tea cozy, and Hammond would give his usual speech about the prospects for developing what he called 'consumer biologicals.' Then, at the dramatic moment, Hammond would whip away the blanket to reveal the elephant. And he would ask for money.

The elephant was always a rousing success; its tiny body, hardly bigger than a cat's, promised untold wonders to come from the laboratory of Norman Atherton, the Stanford geneticist who was Hammond's partner in the new venture.

But as Hammond talked about the elephant, he left a great deal unsaid. For example, Hammond was starting a genetics company, but the tiny elephant hadn't been made by any genetic procedure; Atherton had simply taken a dwarf-elephant embryo and raised it in an artificial womb with hormonal modifications. That in itself was quite an achievement, but nothing like what Hammond hinted had been done.

Also, Atherton hadn't been able to duplicate his miniature elephant, and he'd tried. For one thing, everybody who saw the elephant wanted one. Then, too, the elephant was prone to colds, particularly during winter. The sneezes coming through the little trunk filled Hammond with dread. And sometimes the elephant would get his tusks stuck between the bars of the cage and snort irritably as he tried to get free; sometimes he got infections around the tusk line. Hammond always fretted that his elephant would die before Atherton could grow a replacement.

Hammond also concealed from prospective investors the fact that the elephant's behavior had changed substantially in the process of miniaturization. The little creature might look like an elephant, but he acted like a vicious rodent, quick-moving and mean-tempered. Hammond discouraged people from petting the elephant, to avoid nipped fingers.

And although Hammond spoke confidently of seven billion dollars in annual revenues by 1993, his project was intensely speculative. Hammond had vision and enthusiasm, but there was no certainty that his plan would work at all. Particularly since Norman Atherton, the brains behind the project, had terminal cancer – which was a final point Hammond neglected to mention.

Even so, with Gennaro's help, Hammond got his money. Between September of 1983 and November of 1985, John Alfred Hammond and his 'Pachyderm Portfolio' raised $870 million in venture capital to finance his proposed corporation, International Genetic Technologies, Inc. And they could have raised more, except Hammond insisted on absolute secrecy, and he offered no return on capital for at least five years. That scared a lot of investors off. In the end, they'd had to take mostly Japanese consortia. The Japanese were the only investors who had the patience.

Sitting in the leather chair of the jet, Gennaro thought about how evasive Hammond was. The old man was now ignoring the fact that Gennaro's law firm had forced this trip on him. Instead, Hammond behaved as if they were engaged in a purely social outing. 'It's too bad you didn't bring your family with you, Donald,' he said.

Gennaro shrugged. 'It's my daughter's birthday. Twenty kids already scheduled. The cake and the clown. You know how it is.'

'Oh, I understand,' Hammond said. 'Kids set their hearts on things.'

'Anyway, is the park ready for visitors?' Gennaro asked.

'Well, not officially,' Hammond said. 'But the hotel is built, so there is a place to stay. . . .'

'And the animals?'

'Of course, the animals are all there. All in their spaces.'

Gennaro said, 'I remember in the original proposal you were hoping for a total of twelve. . . .'

'Oh, we're far beyond that. We have two hundred and thirty-eight animals, Donald.'

'Two hundred and thirty-eight?'

The old man giggled, pleased at Gennaro's reaction. 'You can't imagine it. We have *herds* of them.'

'Two hundred and thirty-eight . . . How many species?'

'Fifteen different species, Donald.'

'That's incredible,' Gennaro said. 'That's fantastic. And what about all the other things you wanted? The facilities? The computers?'

'All of it, all of it,' Hammond said. 'Everything on that island is state-of-the-art. You'll see for yourself, Donald. It's perfectly wonderful. That's why this . . . *concern* . . . is so misplaced. There's absolutely no problem with the island.'

Gennaro said, 'Then there should be absolutely no problem with an inspection.'

'And there isn't,' Hammond said. 'But it slows things down. Everything has to stop for the official visit. . . .'

'You've had delays anyway. You've postponed the opening.'

'Oh, *that*.' Hammond tugged at the red silk handkerchief in the breast pocket of his sportcoat. 'It was bound to happen. Bound to happen.'

'Why?' Gennaro asked.

'Well, Donald,' Hammond said, 'to explain that, you have to go back to the initial concept of the resort. The concept of the most advanced amusement park in the world, combining the latest electronic and biological technologies. I'm not talking about rides. Everybody has *rides*. Coney Island has *rides*. And these days everybody has animatronic environments. The haunted house, the pirate den, the wild west, the earthquake - everyone has those things. So we set out to make biological attractions. *Living* attractions. Attractions so astonishing they would capture the imagination of the entire world.'

Gennaro had to smile. It was almost the same speech, word for word, that he had used on the investors, so many years ago. 'And we can never forget the ultimate object of the project in Costa Rica to make money,' Hammond said, staring out the windows of the jet. 'Lots and lots of money.'

'I remember,' Gennaro said.

'And the secret to making money in a park,' Hammond said, 'is to limit your personnel costs. The food handlers, ticket takers, cleanup crews, repair teams. To make a park that runs with minimal staff. That was why we invested in all the computer technology we automated wherever we could.'

'I remember. . . .'

'But the plain fact is,' Hammond said, 'when you put together all the animals and all the computer systems, you run into snags. Who ever got a major computer system up and running on schedule? Nobody I know.'

'So you've just had normal start-up delays?'

'Yes, that's right,' Hammond said. 'Normal delays.'

'I heard there were accidents during construction,' Gennaro said. 'Some workmen died. . . .'

'Yes, there were several accidents,' Hammond said. 'And a total of three deaths. Two workers died building the cliff road. One other died as a result of an earth-mover accident in January. But we haven't had any accidents for months now.' He put his hand on the younger man's arm. 'Donald,' he said, 'believe me when I tell you that everything on the island is going forward as planned. Everything on that island is perfectly *fine*.'

The intercom clicked. The pilot said, 'Seat belts, please. We're landing in Choteau.'

Choteau

Dry plains stretched away toward distant black buttes. The afternoon wind blew dust and tumbleweed across the cracked concrete. Grant stood with Ellie near the Jeep and waited while the sleek Grumman jet circled for a landing.

'I hate to wait on the money men,' Grant grumbled.

Ellie shrugged. 'Goes with the job.'

Although many fields of science, such as physics and chemistry, had become federally funded, paleontology remained strongly dependent on private patrons. Quite apart from his own curiosity about the island in Costa Rica, Grant understood that, if John Hammond asked for his help, he would give it. That was how patronage worked – how it had always worked.

The little jet landed and rolled quickly toward them. Ellie shouldered her bag. The jet came to a stop and a stewardess in a blue uniform opened the door.

Inside, he was surprised at how cramped it was, despite the luxurious appointments. Grant had to hunch over as he went to shake Hammond's hand.

'Dr. Grant and Dr. Sattler,' Hammond said. 'It's good of you to join us. Allow me to introduce my associate, Donald Gennaro.'

Gennaro was a stocky, muscular man in his mid-thirties wearing an Armani suit and wire-frame glasses. Grant disliked him on sight. He shook hands quickly. When Ellie shook hands, Gennaro said in surprise, 'You're a woman.'

'These things happen,' she said, and Grant thought: She doesn't like him, either.

Hammond turned to Gennaro. 'You know, of course, what Dr. Grant and Dr. Sattler do. They are paleontologists. They dig up dinosaurs.' And then he began to laugh, as if he found the idea very funny.

'Take your seats, please,' the stewardess said, closing the door. Immediately the plane began to move.

'You'll have to excuse us,' Hammond said, 'but we are in a bit of a rush. Donald thinks it's important we get right down there.'

The pilot announced four hours' flying time to Dallas, where they would refuel, and then go on to Costa Rica, arriving the following morning.

'And how long will we be in Costa Rica?' Grant asked.

'Well, that really depends,' Gennaro said. 'We have a few things to clear up.'

'Take my word for it,' Hammond said, turning to Grant. 'We'll be down there no more than forty-eight hours.'

Grant buckled his seat belt. 'This island of yours that we're going to – I haven't heard anything about it before. Is it some kind of secret?'

'In a way,' Hammond said. 'We have been very, very careful about making sure nobody knows about it, until the day we finally open that island to a surprised and delighted public.'

Target of Opportunity

The Biosyn Corporation of Cupertino, California, had never called an emergency meeting of its board of directors. The ten directors now sitting in the conference room were irritable and impatient. It was 8:00 p.m. They had been talking among themselves for the last ten minutes, but slowly had fallen silent. Shuffling papers. Looking pointedly at their watches.

'What are we waiting for?' one asked.

'One more,' Lewis Dodgson said. 'We need one more.' He glanced at his watch. Ron Meyer's office had said he was coming up on the six o'clock plane from San Diego. He should be here by now, even allowing for traffic from the airport.

'You need a quorum?' another director asked.

'Yes,' Dodgson said. 'We do.'

That shut them up for a moment. A quorum meant that they were going to be asked to make an important decision. And God knows they were, although Dodgson would have preferred not to call a meeting at all. But Steingarten, the head of Biosyn, was adamant. 'You'll have to get their agreement for this one, Lew,' he had said.

Depending on who you talked to, Lewis Dodgson was famous as the most aggressive geneticist of his generation, or the most reckless. Thirty-four, balding, hawk-faced, and intense, he had been dismissed by Johns Hopkins as a graduate student, for planning gene therapy on human patients without obtaining the proper FDA protocols. Hired by Biosyn, he had conducted the controversial rabies vaccine test in Chile. Now he was the head of product development at Biosyn, which supposedly consisted of 'reverse engineering': taking a competitor's product, tearing it apart, learning how it worked, and then making your own version. In practice, it involved industrial espionage, much of it directed toward the InGen corporation.

In the 1980s, a few genetic engineering companies began to ask, 'What is the biological equivalent of a Sony Walkman?' These companies weren't interested in pharmaceuticals or health; they were interested in entertainment, sports, leisure activities, cosmetics, and pets. The perceived demand for 'consumer biologicals' in the 1990s was high. InGen and Biosyn were both at work in this field.

Biosyn had already achieved some success, engineering a new, pale trout under contract to the Department of Fish and Game of the State of Idaho. This trout was easier to spot in streams, and was said to represent a step forward in angling. (At least, it eliminated complaints to the Fish and Game Department that there were no trout in the streams.) The fact that the pale trout sometimes died of sunburn, and that its flesh was soggy and tasteless, was not discussed. Biosyn was still working on that, and –

The door opened and Ron Meyer entered the room, slipped into a seat. Dodgson now had his quorum. He immediately stood.

'Gentlemen,' he said, 'we're here tonight to consider a target of opportunity: InGen.'

Dodgson quickly reviewed the background. InGen's start-up in 1983, with Japanese investors. The purchase of three Cray XMP supercomputers. The purchase of Isla Nublar in Costa Rica. The stockpiling of amber. The unusual donations to zoos around the world, from the New York Zoological Society to the Ranthapur Wildlife Park in India.

'Despite all these clues,' Dodgson said, 'we still had no idea where InGen might be going. The company seemed obviously focused on animals; and they had hired researchers with an interest in the past – paleobiologists, DNA phylogeneticists, and so on.

'Then, in 1987, InGen bought an obscure company called Millipore Plastic Products in Nashville, Tennessee. This was an agribusiness company that had recently patented a new plastic with the characteristics of an avian eggshell. This plastic could be shaped into an egg and used to grow chick embryos. Starting the following year, InGen took the entire output of this millipore plastic for its own use.'

'Dr. Dodgson, this is all very interesting –'

'At the same time,' Dodgson continued, 'construction was begun on Isla Nublar. This involved massive earthworks, including a shallow lake two miles long, in the center of the island. Plans for resort facilities were let out with a high degree of confidentiality, but it appears that InGen has built a private zoo of large dimensions on the island.'

One of the directors leaned forward and said, 'Dr. Dodgson. So what?'

'It's not an ordinary zoo,' Dodgson said. 'This zoo is unique in the world. It seems that InGen has done something quite extraordinary. They have managed to clone extinct animals from the past.'

'What animals?'

'Animals that hatch from eggs, and that require a lot of room in a zoo.'

'What animals?'

'Dinosaurs,' Dodgson said. 'They are cloning dinosaurs.'

The consternation that followed was entirely misplaced, in Dodgson's view. The trouble with money men was that they didn't keep up: they had invested in a field, but they didn't know what was possible.

In fact, there had been discussion of cloning dinosaurs in the technical literature as far back as 1982. With each passing year, the manipulation of DNA had grown easier. Genetic material had already been extracted from Egyptian mummies, and from the hide of a quagga, a zebra-like African animal that had become extinct in the 1880s. By 1985, it seemed possible that quagga DNA might be reconstituted, and a new animal grown. If so, it would be the first creature brought back from extinction solely by reconstruction of its DNA. If that was possible, what else was also possible? The mastodon? The saber-toothed tiger? The dodo?

Or even a dinosaur?

Of course, no dinosaur DNA was known to exist anywhere in the world. But by grinding up large quantities of dinosaur bones it might be possible to extract fragments of DNA. Formerly it was thought that fossilization eliminated all DNA. Now that was recognized as untrue. If enough DNA fragments were recovered, it might be possible to clone a living animal.

Back in 1982, the technical problems had seemed daunting. But there was no theoretical barrier. It was merely difficult, expensive, and unlikely to work. Yet it was certainly possible, if anyone cared to try.

InGen had apparently decided to try.

'What they have done,' Dodgson said, 'is build the greatest single tourist attraction in the history of the world. As you know, zoos are extremely popular. Last year, more Americans visited zoos than all professional baseball and football games combined. And the Japanese love zoos - there are fifty zoos in Japan, and more being built. And for this zoo, InGen can charge whatever they want. Two thousand dollars a day, ten thousand dollars a day ... And then there is the *merchandising*. The picture books, T-shirts, video games, caps, stuffed toys, comic books, and pets.'

'Pets?'

'Of course. If InGen can make full-size dinosaurs, they can also make pygmy dinosaurs as household pets. What child won't want a little dinosaur as a pet? A little patented animal for their very own. InGen will sell millions of them. And InGen will engineer them so that these pet dinosaurs can only eat InGen pet food. . . .'

'Jesus,' somebody said.

'Exactly,' Dodgson said. 'The zoo is the centerpiece of an enormous enterprise.'

'You said these dinosaurs will be patented?'

'Yes. Genetically engineered animals can now be patented. The Supreme Court ruled on that in favor of Harvard in 1987. InGen will own its dinosaurs, and no one else can legally make them.'

'What prevents us from creating our own dinosaurs?' someone said.

'Nothing, except that they have a five-year start. It'll be almost impossible to catch up before the end of the century.'

He paused. 'Of course, if we could obtain examples of their dinosaurs, we could reverse engineer them and make our own, with enough modifications in the DNA to evade their patents.'

'Can we obtain examples of their dinosaurs?'

Dodgson paused. 'I believe we can, yes.'

Somebody cleared his throat. 'There wouldn't be anything illegal about it. . . .'

'Oh no,' Dodgson said quickly. 'Nothing illegal. I'm talking about a legitimate source of their DNA. A disgruntled employee, or some trash improperly disposed of, something like that.'

'Do you have a legitimate source, Dr. Dodgson?'

'I do,' Dodgson said. 'But I'm afraid there is some urgency to the decision, because InGen is experiencing a small crisis, and my source will have to act within the next twenty-four hours.'

A long silence descended over the room. The men looked at the secretary, taking notes, and the tape recorder on the table in front of her.

'I don't see the need for a formal resolution on this,' Dodgson said. 'Just a sense of the room, as to whether you feel I should proceed. . . .'

Slowly the heads nodded.

Nobody spoke. Nobody went on record. They just nodded silently.

'Thank you for coming, gentlemen,' Dodgson said. 'I'll take it from here.'

Airport

Lewis Dodgson entered the coffee shop in the departure building of the San Francisco airport and looked around quickly. His man was already there, waiting at the counter. Dodgson sat down next to him and placed the briefcase on the floor between them.

'You're late, pal,' the man said. He looked at the straw hat Dodgson was wearing and laughed. 'What is this supposed to be, a disguise?'

'You never know,' Dodgson said, suppressing his anger. For six months, Dodgson had patiently cultivated this man, who had grown more obnoxious and arrogant with each meeting. But there was nothing Dodgson could do about that – both men knew exactly what the stakes were.

Bioengineered DNA was, weight for weight, the most valuable material in the world. A single microscopic bacterium, too small to see with the naked eye, but containing the genes for a heart-attack enzyme, streptokinase, or for 'ice-minus,' which prevented frost damage to crops, might be worth five billion dollars to the right buyer.

And that fact of life had created a bizarre new world of industrial espionage. Dodgson was especially skilled at it. In 1987, he convinced a disgruntled geneticist to quit Cetus for Biosyn, and take five strains of engineered bacteria with her. The geneticist simply put a drop of each on the fingernails of one hand, and walked out the door.

But InGen presented a tougher challenge. Dodgson wanted more than bacterial DNA; he wanted frozen embryos, and he knew InGen guarded its embryos with the most elaborate security measures. To obtain them, he needed an InGen employee who had access to the embryos, who was willing to steal them, and who could defeat the security. Such a person was not easy to find.

Dodgson had finally located a susceptible InGen employee earlier in the year. Although this particular person had no access to genetic material, Dodgson kept up the contact, meeting the man monthly at Carlos and Charlie's in Silicon Valley, helping him in small ways. And now that InGen was inviting contractors and advisers to visit the island, it was the moment that Dodgson had been waiting for – because it meant his man would have access to embryos.

'Let's get down to it,' the man said. 'I've got ten minutes before my flight.'

'You want to go over it again?' Dodgson said.

'Hell no, Dr. Dodgson,' the man said. 'I want to see the damn money.'

Dodgson flipped the latch on the briefcase and opened it a few inches. The man glanced down casually. 'That's all of it?'

'That's half of it. Seven hundred fifty thousand dollars.'

'Okay. Fine.' The man turned away, drank his coffee. 'That's fine, Dr. Dodgson.'

Dodgson quickly locked the briefcase. 'That's for all fifteen species, you remember.'

'I remember. Fifteen species, frozen embryos. And how am I going to transport them?'

Dodgson handed the man a large can of Gillette Foamy shaving cream. 'That's it?'

'That's it.'

'They may check my luggage. . . .'

Dodgson shrugged. 'Press the top,' he said.

The man pressed it, and white shaving cream puffed into his hand. 'Not bad.' He wiped the foam on the edge of his plate. 'Not bad.'

'The can's a little heavier than usual, is all.' Dodgson's technical team had been assembling it around the clock for the last two days. Quickly he showed him how it worked.

'How much coolant gas is inside?'

'Enough for thirty-six hours. The embryos have to be back in San José by then.'

'That's up to your guy in the boat,' the man said. 'Better make sure he has a portable cooler on board.'

'I'll do that,' Dodgson said.

'And let's just review the bidding. . . .'

'The deal is the same,' Dodgson said. 'Fifty thousand on delivery of each embryo. If they're viable, an additional fifty thousand each.'

'That's fine. Just make sure you have the boat waiting at the east dock of the island, Friday night. Not the north dock, where the big supply boats arrive. The east dock. It's a small utility dock. You got that?'

'I got it,' Dodgson said. 'When will you be back in San José?'

'Probably Sunday.' The man pushed away from the counter.

Dodgson fretted. 'You're sure you know how to work the –'

'I know,' the man said. 'Believe me, I know.'

'Also,' Dodgson said, 'we think the island maintains constant radio contact with InGen corporate headquarters in California, so –'

'Look, I've got it covered,' the man said. 'Just relax, and get the money ready. I want it all Sunday morning, in San José airport, in cash.'

'It'll be waiting for you,' Dodgson said. 'Don't worry.'

Malcolm

Shortly before midnight, he stepped on the plane at the Dallas airport, a tall, thin, balding man of thirty-five, dressed entirely in black: black shirt, black trousers, black socks, black sneakers.

'Ah, Dr. Malcolm,' Hammond said, smiling with forced graciousness.

Malcolm grinned. 'Hello, John. Yes, I am afraid your old nemesis is here.'

Malcolm shook hands with everyone, saying quickly, 'Ian Malcolm, how do you do? I do maths.' He struck Grant as being more amused by the outing than anything else.

Certainly Grant recognized his name. Ian Malcolm was one of the most famous of the new generation of mathematicians who were openly interested in 'how the real world works.' These scholars broke with the cloistered tradition of mathematics in several important ways. For one thing, they used computers constantly, a practice traditional mathematicians frowned on. For another, they worked almost exclusively with nonlinear equations, in the emerging field called chaos theory. For a third, they appeared to care that their mathematics described something that actually existed in the real world. And finally, as if to emphasize their emergence from academia into the world, they dressed and spoke with what one senior mathematician called 'a deplorable excess of personality.' In fact, they often behaved like rock stars.

Malcolm sat in one of the padded chairs. The stewardess asked him if he wanted a drink. He said, 'Diet Coke, shaken not stirred.'

Humid Dallas air drifted through the open door. Ellie said, 'Isn't it a little warm for black?'

'You're extremely pretty, Dr. Sattler,' he said. 'I could look at your legs all day. But no, as a matter of fact, black is an excellent color for heat. If you remember your black-body radiation, black is actually best in heat. Efficient radiation. In any case, I wear only two colors, black and gray.'

Ellie was staring at him, her mouth open.

'These colors are appropriate for any occasion,' Malcolm continued, 'and they go well together, should I mistakenly put on a pair of gray socks with my black trousers.'

'But don't you find it boring to wear only two colors?'

'Not at all. I find it liberating. I believe my life has value, and I don't want to waste it thinking about *clothing*,' Malcolm said. 'I don't want to think about *what I will wear* in the morning. Truly, can you imagine anything more boring than fashion? Professional sports, perhaps. Grown men swatting little balls, while the rest of the world pays money to applaud. But, on the whole, I find fashion even more tedious than sports.'

'Dr. Malcolm,' Hammond explained, 'is a man of strong opinions.'

'And mad as a hatter,' Malcolm said cheerfully. 'But you must admit, these are nontrivial issues. We live in a world of frightful givens. It is *given* that you will behave like this, *given* that you will care about that. No one thinks about the givens. Isn't it amazing? In the information society, nobody thinks. We expected to banish paper, but we actually banished thought.'

Hammond turned to Gennaro and raised his hands. 'You invited him.'

'And a lucky thing, too,' Malcolm said. 'Because it sounds as if you have a serious problem.'

'We have no problem,' Hammond said quickly.

'I always maintained this island would be unworkable,' Malcolm said. 'I predicted it from the beginning.' He reached into a soft leather briefcase. 'And I trust by now we all know what the eventual outcome is going to be. You're going to have to shut the thing down.'

'Shut it down!' Hammond stood angrily. 'This is ridiculous.'

Malcolm shrugged, indifferent to Hammond's outburst. 'I've brought copies of my original paper for you to look at,' he said. 'The original consultancy paper I did for InGen. The mathematics are a bit sticky, but I can walk you through it. Are you leaving now?'

'I have some phone calls to make,' Hammond said, and went into the adjoining cabin.

'Well, it's a long flight,' Malcolm said to the others. 'At least my paper will give you something to do.'

The plane flew through the night.

Grant knew that Ian Malcolm had his share of detractors, and he could understand why some found his style too abrasive, and his applications of chaos theory too glib. Grant thumbed through the paper, glancing at the equations.

Gennaro said, 'Your paper concludes that Hammond's island is bound to fail?'

'Correct.'

'Because of chaos theory?'

'Correct. To be more precise, because of the behavior of the system in phase space.'

Gennaro tossed the paper aside and said, 'Can you explain this in English?'

'Surely,' Malcolm said. 'Let's see where we have to start. You know what a nonlinear equation is?'

'No.'

'Strange attractors?'

'No.'

'All right,' Malcolm said. 'Let's go back to the beginning.' He paused, staring at the ceiling. 'Physics has had great success at describing certain kinds of behavior: planets in orbit, spacecraft going to the moon, pendulums and springs and rolling balls, that sort of thing. The regular movement of objects. These are described by what are called linear equations, and mathematicians can solve those equations easily. We've been doing it for hundreds of years.'

'Okay,' Gennaro said.

'But there is another kind of behavior, which physics handles badly. For example, anything to do with turbulence. Water coming out of a spout. Air moving over an airplane wing. Weather. Blood flowing through the heart. Turbulent events are described by nonlinear equations. They're hard to solve – in fact, they're usually impossible to solve. So physics has never understood this whole class of events. Until about ten years ago. The new theory that describes them is called chaos theory.

'Chaos theory originally grew out of attempts to make computer models of weather in the 1960s. Weather is a big complicated system, namely the earth's atmosphere as it interacts with the land and the sun. The behavior of this big complicated system always defied understanding. So naturally we couldn't predict weather. But what the early researchers learned from computer models was that, even if you could understand it, you still couldn't predict it. Weather prediction is absolutely impossible. The reason is that the behavior of the system is sensitively dependent on initial conditions.'

'You lost me,' Gennaro said.

'If I use a cannon to fire a shell of a certain weight, at a certain speed, and a certain angle of inclination – and if I then fire a second shell with almost the same weight, speed, and angle – what will happen?'

'The two shells will land at almost the same spot.'

'Right,' Malcolm said. 'That's linear dynamics.'

'Okay.'

'But if I have a weather system that I start up with a certain temperature and a certain wind speed and a certain humidity – and if I then repeat it with almost the same temperature, wind, and humidity – the second system will not behave almost the same. It'll wander off and rapidly will become *very* different from the first. Thunderstorms instead of sunshine. That's nonlinear dynamics. They are sensitive to initial conditions: tiny differences become amplified.'

'I think I see,' Gennaro said.

'The shorthand is the "butterfly effect." A butterfly flaps its wings in Peking, and weather in New York is different.'

'So chaos is all just random and unpredictable?' Gennaro said. 'Is that it?'

'No,' Malcolm said. 'We actually find hidden regularities within the complex variety of a system's behavior. That's why chaos has now become a very broad theory that's used to study everything from the stock market, to rioting crowds, to brain waves during epilepsy. Any sort of complex system where there is confusion and unpredictability. We can find an underlying order. Okay?'

'Okay,' Gennaro said. 'But what is this underlying order?'

'It's essentially characterized by the movement of the system within phase space,' Malcolm said.

'Jesus,' Gennaro said. 'All I want to know is why you think Hammond's island can't work.'

'I understand,' Malcolm said. 'I'll get there. Chaos theory says two things. First, that complex systems like weather have an underlying order. Second, the reverse of that – that simple systems can produce complex behavior. For example, pool balls. You hit a pool ball, and it starts to carom off the sides of the table. In theory, that's a fairly simple system, almost a Newtonian system. Since you can know the force imparted to the ball, and the mass of the ball, and you can calculate the angles at which it will strike the walls, you can predict the future behavior of the ball. In theory, you could predict the behavior of the ball far into the future, as it keeps bouncing from side to side. You could predict where it will end up three hours from now, in theory.'

'Okay.' Gennaro nodded.

'But in fact,' Malcolm said, 'it turns out you can't predict more than a few seconds into the future. Because almost immediately very small effects – imperfections in the surface of the ball, tiny indentations in the wood of the table – start to make a difference. And it doesn't take long before they overpower your careful calculations. So it turns out that this simple system of a pool ball on a table has unpredictable behavior.'

'Okay.'

'And Hammond's project,' Malcolm said, 'is another apparently simple system – animals within a zoo environment – that will eventually show unpredictable behavior.'

'You know this because of . . .'

'Theory,' Malcolm said.

'But hadn't you better see the island, to see what he's actually done?'

'No. That is quite unnecessary. The details don't matter. Theory tells me that the island will quickly proceed to behave in unpredictable fashion.'

'And you're confident of your theory.'

'Oh, yes,' Malcolm said. 'Totally confident.' He sat back in the chair. 'There is a problem with that island. It is an accident waiting to happen.'

Isla Nublar

With a whine, the rotors began to swing in circles overhead, casting shadows on the runway of San José airport. Grant listened to the crackle in his earphones as the pilot talked to the tower.

They had picked up another passenger in San José, a man named Dennis Nedry, who had flown in to meet them. He was fat and sloppy, eating a candy bar, and there was sticky chocolate on his fingers, and flecks of aluminum foil on his shirt. Nedry had mumbled something about doing computers on the island, and hadn't offered to shake hands.

Through the Plexi bubble Grant watched the airport concrete drop away beneath his feet, and he saw the shadow of the helicopter racing along as they went west, toward the mountains.

'It's about a forty-minute trip,' Hammond said, from one of the rear seats.

Grant watched the low hills rise up, and then they were passing through intermittent clouds, breaking out into sunshine. The mountains were rugged, though he was surprised at the amount of deforestation, acre after acre of denuded, eroded hills. 'Costa Rica,' Hammond said, 'has better population control than other countries in Central America. But, even so, the land is badly deforested. Most of this is within the last ten years.'

They came down out of the clouds on the other side of the mountains, and Grant saw the beaches of the west coast. They flashed over a small coastal village.

'Bahía Anasco,' the pilot said. 'Fishing village.' He pointed north. 'Up the coast there, you see the Cabo Blanco preserve. They have beautiful beaches.' The pilot headed straight out over the ocean. The water turned green, and then deep aquamarine. The sun shone on the water. It was about ten in the morning.

'Just a few minutes now,' Hammond said, 'and we should be seeing Isla Nublar.'

Isla Nublar, Hammond explained, was not a true island. Rather, it was a seamount, a volcanic upthrusting of rock from the ocean floor. 'Its volcanic origins can be seen all over the island,' Hammond said.

'There are steam vents in many places, and the ground is often hot underfoot. Because of this, and also because of prevailing currents, Isla Nublar lies in a foggy area. As we get there you will see – ah, there we are.'

The helicopter rushed forward, low to the water. Ahead Grant saw an island, rugged and craggy, rising sharply from the ocean.

'Christ, it looks like Alcatraz,' Malcolm said.

Its forested slopes were wreathed in fog, giving the island a mysterious appearance.

'Much larger, of course,' Hammond said. 'Eight miles long and three miles wide at the widest point, in total some twenty-two square miles. Making it the largest private animal preserve in North America.'

The helicopter began to climb, and headed toward the north end of the island. Grant was trying to see through the dense fog.

'It's not usually this thick,' Hammond said. He sounded worried.

At the north end of the island, the hills were highest, rising more than two thousand feet above the ocean. The tops of the hills were in fog, but Grant saw rugged cliffs and crashing ocean below. The helicopter climbed above the hills. 'Unfortunately,' Hammond said, 'we have to land on the island. I don't like to do it, because it disturbs the animals. And it's sometimes a bit thrilling –'

Hammond's voice cut off as the pilot said, 'Starting our descent now. Hang on, folks.' The helicopter started down, and immediately they were blanketed in fog. Grant heard a repetitive electronic beeping through his earphones, but he could see nothing at all; then he began dimly to discern the green branches of pine trees, reaching through the mist. Some of the branches were close.

'How the hell is he doing this?' Malcolm said, but nobody answered.

The pilot swung his gaze left, then right, looking at the pine forest. The trees were still close. The helicopter descended rapidly.

'Jesus,' Malcolm said.

The beeping was louder. Grant looked at the pilot. He was concentrating. Grant glanced down and saw a giant glowing fluorescent cross beneath the Plexi bubble at his feet. There were flashing lights at the corners of the cross. The pilot corrected slightly and touched down on a helipad. The sound of the rotors faded, and died.

Grant sighed, and released his seat belt.

'We have to come down fast, that way,' Hammond said, 'because of the wind shear. There is often bad wind shear on this peak, and . . . well, we're safe.'

Someone was running up to the helicopter. A man with a baseball cap and red hair. He threw open the door and said cheerfully, 'Hi, I'm

Ed Regis. Welcome to Isla Nublar, everybody. And watch your step, please.'

A narrow path wound down the hill. The air was chilly and damp. As they moved lower, the mist around them thinned, and Grant could see the landscape better. It looked, he thought, rather like the Pacific Northwest, the Olympic Peninsula.

'That's right,' Regis said. 'Primary ecology is deciduous rain forest. Rather different from the vegetation on the mainland, which is more classical rain forest. But this is a microclimate that only occurs at elevation, on the slopes of the northern hills. The majority of the island is tropical.'

Down below, they could see the white roofs of large buildings, nestled among the planting. Grant was surprised: the construction was elaborate. They moved lower, out of the mist, and now he could see the full extent of the island, stretching away to the south. As Regis had said, it was mostly covered in tropical forest.

To the south, rising above the palm trees, Grant saw a single trunk with no leaves at all, just a big curving stump. Then the stump moved, and twisted around to face the new arrivals. Grant realized that he was not seeing a tree at all.

He was looking at the graceful, curving neck of an enormous creature, rising fifty feet into the air.

He was looking at a dinosaur.

Welcome

'My God,' Ellie said softly. They were all staring at the animal above the trees. 'My *God*.'

Her first thought was that the dinosaur was extraordinarily beautiful. Books portrayed them as oversize, dumpy creatures, but this long-necked animal had a gracefulness, almost a dignity, about its movements. And it was quick – there was nothing lumbering or dull in its behavior. The sauropod peered alertly at them, and made a low trumpeting sound, rather like an elephant. A moment later, a second head rose above the foliage, and then a third, and a fourth.

'My God,' Ellie said again.

Gennaro was speechless. He had known all along what to expect – he had known about it for years – but he had somehow never believed it would happen, and now, he was shocked into silence. The awesome power of the new genetic technology, which he had formerly considered to be just so many words in an overwrought sales pitch – the power suddenly became clear to him. These animals were so big! They were enormous! Big as a house! And so many of them! Actual damned dinosaurs! Just as real as you could want.

Gennaro thought: We are going to make a fortune on this place. A *fortune*.

He hoped to God the island was safe.

Grant stood on the path on the side of the hill, with the mist on his face, staring at the gray necks craning above the palms. He felt dizzy, as if the ground were sloping away too steeply. He had trouble getting his breath. Because he was looking at something he had never expected to see in his life. Yet he was seeing it.

The animals in the mist were perfect apatosaurs, medium-size sauropods. His stunned mind made academic associations: North American herbivores, late Jurassic horizon. Commonly called 'brontosaurs.' First discovered by E. D. Cope in Montana in 1876. Specimens associated with Morrison formation strata in Colorado, Utah, and Oklahoma.

Recently Berman and McIntosh had reclassified it a diplodocus based on skull appearance. Traditionally, *Brontosaurus* was thought to spend most of its time in shallow water, which would help support its large bulk. Although this animal was clearly not in the water, it was moving much too quickly, the head and neck shifting above the palms in a very active manner – a surprisingly active manner –

Grant began to laugh.

'What is it?' Hammond said, worried. 'Is something wrong?'

Grant just shook his head, and continued to laugh. He couldn't tell them that what was funny was that he had seen the animal for only a few seconds, but he had already begun to accept it – and to use his observations to answer long-standing questions in the field.

He was still laughing as he saw a fifth and a sixth neck crane up above the palm trees. The sauropods watched the people arrive. They reminded Grant of oversize giraffes – they had the same pleasant, rather stupid gaze.

'I take it they're not animatronic,' Malcolm said. 'They're very life-like.'

'Yes, they certainly are,' Hammond said. 'Well, they should be, shouldn't they?'

From the distance, they heard the trumpeting sound again. First one animal made it, and then the others joined in.

'That's their call,' Ed Regis said. 'Welcoming us to the island.'

Grant stood and listened for a moment, entranced.

'You probably want to know what happens next,' Hammond was saying, continuing down the path. 'We've scheduled a complete tour of the facilities for you, and a trip to see the dinosaurs in the park later this afternoon. I'll be joining you for dinner, and will answer any remaining questions you may have then. Now, if you'll go with Mr. Regis . . .'

The group followed Ed Regis toward the nearest buildings. Over the path, a crude hand-painted sign read: 'Welcome to Jurassic Park.'

Third Iteration

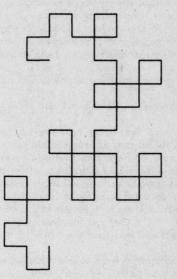

'Details emerge more clearly as the fractal curve is redrawn.

IAN MALCOLM

Jurassic Park

They moved into a green tunnel of overarching palms leading toward the main visitor building. Everywhere, extensive and elaborate planting emphasized the feeling that they were entering a new world, a prehistoric tropical world, and leaving the normal world behind.

Ellie said to Grant, 'They look pretty good.'

'Yes,' Grant said. 'I want to see them up close. I want to lift up their toe pads and inspect their claws and feel their skin and open their jaws and have a look at their teeth. Until then I don't know for sure. But yes, they look good.'

'I suppose it changes your field a bit,' Malcolm said.

Grant shook his head. 'It changes everything,' he said.

For 150 years, ever since the discovery of gigantic animal bones in Europe, the study of dinosaurs had been an exercise in scientific deduction. Paleontology was essentially detective work, searching for clues in the fossil bones and the trackways of the long-vanished giants. The best paleontologists were the ones who could make the most clever deductions.

And all the great disputes of paleontology were carried out in this fashion – including the bitter debate, in which Grant was a key figure, about whether dinosaurs were warm-blooded.

Scientists had always classified dinosaurs as reptiles, cold-blooded creatures drawing the heat they needed for life from the environment. A mammal could metabolize food to produce bodily warmth, but a reptile could not. Eventually a handful of researchers – led chiefly by John Ostrom and Robert Bakker at Yale – began to suspect that the concept of sluggish, cold-blooded dinosaurs was inadequate to explain the fossil record. In classic deductive fashion, they drew conclusions from several lines of evidence.

First was posture: lizards and reptiles were bent-legged sprawlers, hugging the ground for warmth. Lizards didn't have the energy to stand on their hind legs for more than a few seconds. But the dinosaurs stood on straight legs, and many walked erect on their hind legs. Among living animals, erect posture occurred only in warm-blooded mammals and birds. Thus dinosaur posture suggested warm-bloodedness.

Next they studied metabolism, calculating the pressure necessary to push blood up the eighteen-foot-long neck of a brachiosaur, and concluding that it could only be accomplished by a four-chambered, hot-blooded heart.

They studied trackways, fossil footprints left in mud, and concluded that dinosaurs ran as fast as a man; such activity implied warm blood. They found dinosaur remains above the Arctic Circle, in a frigid environment unimaginable for a reptile. And the new studies of group behavior, based largely on Grant's own work, suggested that dinosaurs had a complex social life and reared their young, as reptiles did not. Crocodiles and turtles abandon their eggs. But dinosaurs probably did not.

The warm-blooded controversy had raged for fifteen years, before a new perception of dinosaurs as quick-moving, active animals was accepted – but not without lasting animosities. At conventions, there were still colleagues who did not speak to one another.

But now, if dinosaurs could be cloned – why, Grant's field of study was going to change instantly. The paleontological study of dinosaurs was finished. The whole enterprise – the museum halls with their giant skeletons and flocks of echoing schoolchildren, the university laboratories with their bone trays, the research papers, the journals – all of it was going to end.

'You don't seem upset,' Malcolm said.

Grant shook his head. 'It's been discussed, in the field. Many people imagined it was coming. But not so soon.'

'Story of our species,' Malcolm said, laughing. 'Everybody knows it's coming, but not so soon.'

As they walked down the path, they could no longer see the dinosaurs, but they could hear them, trumpeting softly in the distance.

Grant said, 'My only question is, where'd they get the DNA?'

Grant was aware of serious speculation in laboratories in Berkeley, Tokyo, and London that it might eventually be possible to clone an extinct animal such as a dinosaur – if you could get some dinosaur DNA to work with. The problem was that all known dinosaurs were fossils, and the fossilization destroyed most DNA, replacing it with inorganic material. Of course, if a dinosaur was frozen, or preserved in a peat bog, or mummified in a desert environment, then its DNA might be recoverable.

But nobody had ever found a frozen or mummified dinosaur. So cloning was therefore impossible. There was nothing to clone *from*. All the modern genetic technology was useless. It was like having a Xerox copier but nothing to copy with.

Ellie said, 'You can't reproduce a real dinosaur, because you can't get real dinosaur DNA.'

'Unless there's a way we haven't thought of,' Grant said.

'Like what?' she said.

'I don't know,' Grant said.

Beyond a fence, they came to the swimming pool, which spilled over into a series of waterfalls and smaller rocky pools. The area was planted with huge ferns. 'Isn't this extraordinary?' Ed Regis said. 'Especially on a misty day, these plants really contribute to the prehistoric atmosphere. These are authentic Jurassic ferns, of course.'

Ellie paused to look more closely at the ferns. Yes, it was just as he said: *Serenna veriformans*, a plant found abundantly in fossils more than two hundred million years old, now common only in the wetlands of Brazil and Colombia. But whoever had decided to place this particular fern at poolside obviously didn't know that the spores of *veriformans* contained a deadly beta-carboline alkaloid. Even touching the attractive green fronds could make you sick, and if a child were to take a mouthful, he would almost certainly die – the toxin was fifty times more poisonous than oleander.

People were so naïve about plants, Ellie thought. They just chose plants for appearance, as they would choose a picture for the wall. It never occurred to them that plants were actually living things, busily performing all the living functions of respiration, ingestion, excretion, reproduction – and defense.

But Ellie knew that, in the earth's history, plants had evolved as competitively as animals, and in some ways more fiercely. The poison in *Serenna veriformans* was a minor example of the elaborate chemical arsenal of weapons that plants had evolved. There were terpenes, which plants spread to poison the soil around them and inhibit competitors; alkaloids, which made them unpalatable to insects and predators (and children); and pheromones, used for communication. When a Douglas fir tree was attacked by beetles, it produced an anti-feedant chemical – and so did other Douglas firs in distant parts of the forest. It happened in response to a warning alleochemical secreted by the trees that were under attack.

People who imagined that life on earth consisted of animals moving against a green background seriously misunderstood what they were seeing. That green background was busily alive. Plants grew, moved, twisted, and turned, fighting for the sun; and they interacted continuously with animals – discouraging some with bark and thorns; poisoning others; and feeding still others to advance their own reproduction, to spread their pollen and seeds. It was a complex, dynamic process which she never ceased to find fascinating. And which she knew most people simply didn't understand.

But if planting deadly ferns at poolside was any indication, then it was clear that the designers of Jurassic Park had not been as careful as they should have been.

'Isn't it just wonderful?' Ed Regis was saying. 'If you look up ahead, you'll see our Safari Lodge.' Ellie saw a dramatic, low building, with a series of glass pyramids on the roof. 'That's where you'll all be staying here in Jurassic Park.'

Grant's suite was done in beige tones, the rattan furniture in green jungle-print motifs. The room wasn't quite finished; there were stacks of lumber in the closet, and pieces of electrical conduit on the floor. There was a television set in the corner, with a card on top:

Channel 2: Hypsilophodont Highlands
Channel 3: Triceratops Territory
Channel 4: Sauropod Swamp
Channel 5: Carnivore Country
Channel 6: Stegosaurus South
Channel 7: Velociraptor Valley
Channel 8: Pterosaur Peak

He found the names irritatingly cute. Grant turned on the television but got only static. He shut it off and went into his bedroom, tossed his suitcase on the bed. Directly over the bed was a large pyramidal skylight. It created a tented feeling, like sleeping under the stars. Unfortunately the glass had to be protected by heavy bars, so that striped shadows fell across the bed.

Grant paused. He had seen the plans for the lodge, and he didn't remember bars on the skylight. In fact, these bars appeared to be a rather crude addition. A black steel frame had been constructed outside the glass walls, and the bars welded to the frame.

Puzzled, Grant moved from the bedroom to the living room. His window looked out on the swimming pool.

'By the way, those ferns are poison,' Ellie said, walking into his room. 'But did you notice anything about the rooms, Alan?'

'They changed the plans.'

'I think so, yes.' She moved around the room. 'The windows are small,' she said. 'And the glass is tempered, set in a steel frame. The doors are steel-clad. That shouldn't be necessary. And did you see the fence when we came in?'

Grant nodded. The entire lodge was enclosed within a fence, with bars of inch-thick steel. The fence was gracefully landscaped and painted flat black to resemble wrought iron, but no cosmetic effort could disguise the thickness of the metal, or its twelve-foot height.

'I don't think the fence was in the plans, either,' Ellie said. 'It looks to me like they've turned this place into a fortress.'

Grant looked at his watch. 'We'll be sure to ask why,' he said. 'The tour starts in twenty minutes.'

When Dinosaurs Ruled the Earth

They met in the visitor building: two stories high, and all glass with exposed black anodized girders and supports. Grant found it determinedly high-tech.

There was a small auditorium dominated by a robot *Tyrannosaurus rex*, poised menacingly by the entrance to an exhibit area labeled WHEN DINOSAURS RULED THE EARTH. Farther on were other displays: WHAT IS A DINOSAUR? and THE MESOZOIC WORLD. But the exhibits weren't completed; there were wires and cables all over the floor. Gennaro climbed up on the stage and talked to Grant, Ellie, and Malcolm, his voice echoing slightly in the room.

Hammond sat in the back, his hands folded across his chest.

'We're about to tour the facilities,' Gennaro said. 'I'm sure Mr. Hammond and his staff will show everything in the best light. Before we go, I wanted to review why we are here, and what I need to decide before we leave. Basically, as you all realize by now, this is an island in which genetically engineered dinosaurs have been allowed to move in a natural park-like setting, forming a tourist attraction. The attraction isn't open to tourists yet, but it will be in a year.

'Now, my question for you is a simple one. Is this island safe? Is it safe for visitors, and is it safely containing the dinosaurs?'

Gennaro turned down the room lights. 'There are two pieces of evidence which we have to deal with. First of all, there is Dr. Grant's identification of a previously unknown dinosaur on the Costa Rican mainland. This dinosaur is known only from a partial fragment. It was found in July of this year, after it supposedly bit an American girl on a beach. Dr. Grant can tell you more later. I've asked for the original fragment, which is in a lab in New York, to be flown here so that we can inspect it directly. Meanwhile, there is a second piece of evidence.

'Costa Rica has an excellent medical service, and it tracks all kinds of data. Beginning in March, there were reports of lizards biting infants in their cribs – and also, I might add, biting old people who were sleeping soundly. These lizard bites were sporadically reported in coastal villages from Ismaloya to Puntarenas. After March, lizard bites were no longer reported. However, I have this graph from the Public Health Service in San José of infant mortality in the towns of the west coast earlier this year.'

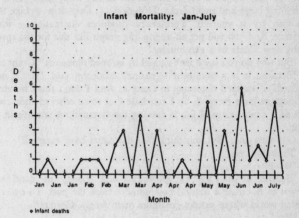

Infant Mortality: Jan-July

Month

• Infant deaths

'I direct your attention to two features of this graph,' Gennaro said. 'First, infant mortality is low in the months of January and February, then spikes in March, then it's low again in April. But from May onward, it is high, right through July, the month the American girl was bitten. The Public Health Service feels that something is now affecting infant mortality, and it is not being reported by the workers in the coastal villages. The second feature is the puzzling biweekly spiking, which seems to suggest some kind of alternating phenomenon is at work.'

The lights came back on. 'All right,' Gennaro said. 'That's the evidence I want explained. Now, are there any –'

'We can save ourselves a great deal of trouble,' Malcolm said. 'I'll explain it for you now.'

'You will?' Gennaro said.

'Yes,' Malcolm said. 'First of all, animals have very likely gotten off the island.'

'Oh balls,' Hammond growled, from the back.

'And second, the graph from the Public Health Service is almost certainly unrelated to any animals that have escaped.'

Grant said, 'How do you know that?'

'You'll notice that the graph alternates between high and low spikes,' Malcolm said. 'That is characteristic of many complex systems. For example, water dripping from a tap. If you turn on the faucet just a little, you'll get a constant drip, drip, drip. But if you open it a little more, so that there's a bit of turbulence in the flow, then you'll get alternating large and small drops. Drip drip . . . Drip drip . . . Like that. You can try it yourself. Turbulence produces alternation – it's a signature. And you will get an alternating graph like this for the spread of any new illness in a community.'

'But why do you say it isn't caused by escaped dinosaurs?' Grant said.

'Because it is a nonlinear signature,' Malcolm said. 'You'd need hundreds of escaped dinosaurs to cause it. And I don't think hundreds of dinosaurs have escaped. So I conclude that some other phenomenon, such as a new variety of flu, is causing the fluctuations you see in the graph.'

Gennaro said, 'But you think that dinosaurs have escaped?'

'Probably, yes.'

'Why?'

'Because of what you are attempting here. Look, this island is an attempt to re-create a natural environment from the past. To make an isolated world where extinct creatures roam freely. Correct?'

'Yes.'

'But from my point of view, such an undertaking is impossible. The mathematics are so self-evident that they don't need to be calculated. It's rather like my asking you whether, on a billion dollars in income, you had to pay tax. You wouldn't need to pull out your calculator to check. You'd know tax was owed. And, similarly, I know overwhelmingly that one cannot successfully duplicate nature in this way, or hope to isolate it.'

'Why not? After all, there are zoos. . . .'

'Zoos don't re-create nature,' Malcolm said. 'Let's be clear. Zoos take the nature that already exists and modify it *very* slightly, to create holding pens for animals. Even those minimal modifications often fail. The animals escape with regularity. But a zoo is not a model for this park. This park is attempting something far more ambitious than that. Something much more akin to making a space station on earth.'

Gennaro shook his head. 'I don't understand.'

'Well, it's very simple. Except for the air, which flows freely, everything about this park is meant to be isolated. Nothing gets in, nothing out. The animals kept here are never to mix with the greater ecosystems of earth. They are never to escape.'

'And they never have,' Hammond snorted.

'Such isolation is impossible,' Malcolm said flatly. 'It simply cannot be done.'

'It can. It's done all the time.'

'I beg your pardon,' Malcolm said. 'But you don't know what you are talking about.'

'You arrogant little snot,' Hammond said. He stood, and walked out of the room.

'Gentlemen, gentlemen,' Gennaro said.

'I'm sorry,' Malcolm said, 'but the point remains. What we call "nature" is in fact a complex system of far greater subtlety than we are willing to accept. We make a simplified image of nature and then we botch it up. I'm no environmentalist, but you have to understand what you don't understand. How many times must the point be made? How many times must we see the evidence? We build the Aswan Dam and claim it is going to revitalize the country. Instead, it destroys the fertile Nile Delta, produces parasitic infestation, and wrecks the Egyptian economy. We build the –'

'Excuse me,' Gennaro said. 'But I think I hear the helicopter. That's probably the sample for Dr. Grant to look at.' He started out of the room. They all followed.

At the foot of the mountain, Gennaro was screaming over the sound of the helicopter. The veins of his neck stood out. 'You did *what*? You invited *who*?'

'Take it easy,' Hammond said.

Gennaro screamed, 'Are you out of your goddamned *mind*?'

'Now, look here,' Hammond said, drawing himself up. 'I think we have to get something clear –'

'No,' Gennaro said. 'No, *you* get something clear. This is not a social outing. This is not a weekend excursion –'

'This is my island,' Hammond said, 'and I can invite whomever I want.'

'This is a serious investigation of your island because your investors are concerned that it's out of control. We think this is a very dangerous place, and –'

'You're not going to shut me down, Donald –'

'I will if I have to –'

'This is a safe place,' Hammond said, 'no matter what that damn mathematician is saying –'

'It's not –'

'And I'll demonstrate its safety –'

'And I want you to put them right back on that helicopter,' Gennaro said.

'Can't,' Hammond said, pointing toward the clouds. 'It's already leaving.' And, indeed, the sound of the rotors was fading.

'God damn it,' Gennaro said, 'don't you see you're needlessly risking –'

'Ah ah,' Hammond said. 'Let's continue this later. I don't want to upset the children.'

Grant turned, and saw two children coming down the hillside, led by Ed Regis. There was a bespectacled boy of about eleven, and a girl a few years younger, perhaps seven or eight, her blond hair pushed up under a Mets baseball cap, and a baseball glove slung over her shoulder. The two kids made their way nimbly down the path from the helipad, and stopped some distance from Gennaro and Hammond.

Low, under his breath, Gennaro said, '*Christ.*'

'Now, take it easy,' Hammond said. 'Their parents are getting a divorce, and I want them to have a fun weekend here.'

The girl waved tentatively.

'Hi, Grandpa,' she said. 'We're here.'

The Tour

Tim Murphy could see at once that something was wrong. His grandfather was in the middle of an argument with the younger, red-faced man opposite him. And the other adults, standing behind, looked embarrassed and uncomfortable. Alexis felt the tension, too, because she hung back, tossing her baseball in the air. He had to push her: 'Go on, Lex.'

'Go on yourself, Timmy.'

'Don't be a worm,' he said.

Lex glared at him, but Ed Regis said cheerfully, 'I'll introduce you to everybody, and then we can take the tour.'

'I have to go,' Lex said.

'I'll just introduce you first,' Ed Regis said.

'No, I have to go.'

But Ed Regis was already making introductions. First to Grandpa, who kissed them both, and then to the man he was arguing with. This man was muscular and his name was Gennaro. The rest of the introductions were a blur to Tim. There was a blond woman wearing shorts, and a man with a beard who wore jeans and a Hawaiian shirt. He looked like the outdoors type. Then a fat college kid who had something to do with computers, and finally a thin man in black, who didn't shake hands, but just nodded his head. Tim was trying to organize his impressions, and was looking at the blond woman's legs, when he suddenly realized that he knew who the bearded man was.

'Your mouth is open,' Lex said.

Tim said, 'I know him.'

'Oh *sure*. You just met him.'

'No,' Tim said. 'I have his book.'

The bearded man said, 'What book is that, Tim?'

'*Lost World of the Dinosaurs*,' Tim said.

Alexis snickered. 'Daddy says Tim has dinosaurs on the brain,' she said.

Tim hardly heard her. He was thinking of what he knew about Alan Grant. Alan Grant was one of the principal advocates of the theory that dinosaurs were warm-blooded. He had done lots of digging at the place called Egg Hill in Montana, which was famous because so many dinosaur eggs had been found there. Professor Grant had found most of the dinosaur eggs that had ever been discovered. He was also a good illustrator, and he drew the pictures for his own books.

'Dinosaurs on the brain?' the bearded man said. 'Well, as a matter of fact, I have that same problem.'

'Dad says dinosaurs are really stupid,' Lex said. 'He says Tim should get out in the air and play more sports.'

Tim felt embarrassed. 'I thought you had to go,' he said.

'In a minute,' Lex said.

'I thought you were in such a rush.'

'I'm the one who would know, don't you think, Timothy?' she said, putting her hands on her hips, copying her mother's most irritating stance.

'Tell you what,' Ed Regis said. 'Why don't we all just head on over to the visitor center, and we can begin our tour.' Everybody started walking. Tim heard Gennaro whisper to his grandfather, 'I could kill you for this,' and then Tim looked up and saw that Dr. Grant had fallen into step beside him.

'How old are you, Tim?'

'Eleven.'

'And how long have you been interested in dinosaurs?' Grant asked.

Tim swallowed. 'A while now,' he said. He felt nervous to be talking to Dr. Grant. 'We go to museums sometimes, when I can talk my family into it. My father.'

'Your father's not especially interested?'

Tim nodded, and told Grant about his family's last trip to the Museum of Natural History. His father had looked at a skeleton and said, 'That's a big one.'

Tim had said, 'No, Dad, that's a medium-size one, a camptosaurus.'

'Oh, I don't know. Looks pretty big to me.'

'It's not even full-grown, Dad.'

His father squinted at the skeleton. 'What is it, Jurassic?'

'Jeez. No. Cretaceous.'

'Cretaceous? What's the difference between Cretaceous and Jurassic?'

'Only about a hundred million years,' Tim said.

'Cretaceous is older?'

'No, Dad, Jurassic is older.'

'Well,' his father said, stepping back, 'it looks pretty damn big to me.' And he turned to Tim for agreement. Tim knew he had better agree with his father, so he just muttered something. And they went on to another exhibit.

Tim stood in front of one skeleton – a *Tyrannosaurus rex*, the mightiest predator the earth had ever known – for a long time. Finally his father said, 'What are you looking at?'

'I'm counting the vertebrae,' Tim said.

'The vertebrae?'

'In the backbone.'

'I know what vertebrae are,' his father said, annoyed. He stood there a while longer and then he said, 'Why are you counting them?'

'I think they're wrong. Tyrannosaurs should only have thirty-seven vertebrae in the tail. This has more.'

'You mean to tell me,' his father said, 'that the Museum of Natural History has a skeleton that's wrong? I can't believe that.'

'It's wrong,' Tim said.

His father stomped off toward a guard in the corner. 'What did you do now?' his mother said to Tim.

'I didn't do anything,' Tim said. 'I just said the dinosaur is wrong, that's all.'

And then his father came back with a funny look on his face, because of course the guard told him that the tyrannosaurus had too many vertebrae in the tail.

'How'd you know that?' his father asked.

'I read it,' Tim said.

'That's pretty amazing, son,' he said, and he put his hand on his shoulder, giving it a squeeze. 'You know how many vertebrae belong in that tail. I've never seen anything like it. You really *do* have dinosaurs on the brain.'

And then his father said he wanted to catch the last half of the Mets game on TV, and Lex said she did, too, so they left the museum. And Tim didn't see any other dinosaurs, which was why they had come there in the first place. But that was how things happened in his family.

How things *used* to happen in his family, Tim corrected himself. Now that his father was getting a divorce from his mother, things would probably be different. His father had already moved out, and even though it was weird at first, Tim liked it. He thought his mother had a boyfriend, but he couldn't be sure, and of course he would never mention it to Lex. Lex was heartbroken to be separated from her father, and in the last few weeks she had become so obnoxious that –

'Was it 5027?' Grant said.

'I'm sorry?' Tim said.

'The tyrannosaurus at the museum. Was it 5027?'

'Yes,' Tim said. 'How'd you know?'

Grant smiled. 'They've been talking about fixing it for years. But now it may never happen.'

'Why is that?'

'Because of what is taking place here,' Grant said, 'on your grandfather's island.'

Tim shook his head. He didn't understand what Grant was talking about. 'My mom said it was just a resort, you know, with swimming and tennis.'

'Not exactly,' Grant said. 'I'll explain as we walk along.'

Now I'm a damned babysitter, Ed Regis thought unhappily, tapping his foot as he waited in the visitor center. That was what the old man had told him: You watch my kids like a hawk, they're your responsibility for the weekend.

Ed Regis didn't like it at all. He felt degraded. He wasn't a damn babysitter. And, for that matter, he wasn't a damned tour guide, even for VIPs. He was the head of public relations for Jurassic Park, and he had much to prepare between now and the opening, a year away. Just to coordinate with the PR firms in San Francisco and London, and the agencies in New York and Tokyo, was a full-time job – especially since the agencies couldn't yet be told what the resort's real attraction was. The firms were all designing teaser campaigns, nothing specific, and they were unhappy. Creative people needed nurturing. They needed encouragement to do their best work. He couldn't waste his time taking scientists on tours.

But that was the trouble with a career in public relations – nobody saw you as a professional. Regis had been down here on the island off and on for the past seven months, and they were still pushing odd jobs on him. Like that episode back in January. Harding should have handled that. Harding, or Owens, the general contractor. Instead, it had fallen to Ed Regis. What did he know about taking care of some sick workman? And now he was a damn tour guide and babysitter. He turned back and counted the heads. Still one short.

Then, in the back, he saw Dr. Sattler emerge from the bathroom.

'All right, folks, let's begin our tour on the second floor.'

Tim went with the others, following Mr. Regis up the black suspended staircase to the second floor of the building. They passed a sign that read:

CLOSED AREA
AUTHORIZED PERSONNEL ONLY
BEYOND THIS POINT

Tim felt a thrill when he saw that sign. They walked down the second floor hallway. One wall was glass, looking out onto a balcony with palm trees in the light mist. On the other wall were stenciled doors, like offices: PARK WARDEN ... GUEST SERVICES ... GENERAL MANAGER ...

Halfway down the corridor they came to a glass partition marked with another sign:

BIOHAZARD

CAUTION
BIOLOGICAL
HAZARD

This Laboratory
Conforms to
USG P4/EK3
Genetic Protocols

Underneath were more signs:

CAUTION
Teratogenic Substances
Pregnant Women Avoid Exposure
To This Area

DANGER
Radioactive Isotopes In Use
Carcinogenic Potential

Tim grew more excited all the time. Teratogenic substances! Things that made monsters! It gave him a thrill, and he was disappointed to hear Ed Regis say, 'Never mind the signs, they're just up for legal reasons. I can assure you everything is perfectly safe.' He led them through the door. There was a guard on the other side. Ed Regis turned to the group.

'You may have noticed that we have a minimum of personnel on the island. We can run this resort with a total of twenty people. Of course, we'll have more when we have guests here, but at the moment there's only twenty. Here's our control room. The entire park is controlled from here.'

They paused before windows and peered into a darkened room that looked like a small version of Mission Control. There was a vertical glass see-through map of the park, and facing it a bank of glowing computer consoles. Some of the screens displayed data, but most of them showed video images from around the park. There were just two people inside, standing and talking.

'The man on the left is our chief engineer, John Arnold' – Regis pointed to a thin man in a button-down short-sleeve shirt and tie, smoking a cigarette – 'and next to him, our park warden, Mr. Robert Muldoon, the famous white hunter from Nairobi.' Muldoon was a burly man in khaki, sunglasses dangling from his shirt pocket. He glanced out at the group, gave a brief nod, and turned back to the computer screens. 'I'm sure you want to see this room,' Ed Regis said, 'but first, let's see how we obtain dinosaur DNA.'

The sign on the door said EXTRACTIONS and, like all the doors in the laboratory building, it opened with a security card. Ed Regis slipped the card in the slot; the light blinked; and the door opened.

Inside, Tim saw a small room bathed in green light. Four technicians in lab coats were peering into double-barreled stereo microscopes, or looking at images on high resolution video screens. The room was filled with yellow stones. The stones were in glass shelves; in cardboard boxes; in large pull-out trays. Each stone was tagged and numbered in black ink.

Regis introduced Henry Wu, a slender man in his thirties. 'Dr. Wu is our chief geneticist. I'll let him explain what we do here.'

Henry Wu smiled. 'At least I'll try,' he said. 'Genetics is a bit complicated. But you're probably wondering where our dinosaur DNA comes from.'

'It crossed my mind,' Grant said.

'As a matter of fact,' Wu said, 'there are two possible sources. Using the Loy antibody extraction technique, we can sometimes get DNA directly from dinosaur bones.'

'What kind of a yield?' Grant asked.

'Well, most soluble protein is leached out during fossilization, but twenty percent of the proteins are still recoverable by grinding up the bones and using Loy's procedure. Dr. Loy himself has used it to obtain

94

proteins from extinct Australian marsupials, as well as blood cells from ancient human remains. His technique is so refined it can work with a mere fifty nanograms of material. That's fifty-billionths of a gram.'

'And you've adapted his technique here?' Grant asked.

'Only as a backup,' Wu said. 'As you can imagine, a twenty percent yield is insufficient for our work. We need the entire dinosaur DNA strand in order to clone. And we get it here.' He held up one of the yellow stones. 'From amber – the fossilized resin of prehistoric tree sap.'

Grant looked at Ellie, then at Malcolm.

'That's really quite clever,' Malcolm said, nodding.

'I still don't understand,' Grant admitted.

'Tree sap,' Wu explained, 'often flows over insects and traps them. The insects are then perfectly preserved within the fossil. One finds all kinds of insects in amber – including biting insects that have sucked blood from larger animals.'

'Sucked the blood,' Grant repeated. His mouth fell open. 'You mean sucked the blood of dinosaurs . . .'

'Hopefully, yes.'

'And then the insects are preserved in amber . . .' Grant shook his head. 'I'll be damned – that just might work.'

'I assure you, it *does* work,' Wu said. He moved to one of the microscopes, where a technician positioned a piece of amber containing a fly under the microscope. On the video monitor, they watched as he inserted a long needle through the amber, into the thorax of the prehistoric fly.

'If this insect has any foreign blood cells, we may be able to extract them, and obtain paleo-DNA, the DNA of an extinct creature. We won't know for sure, of course, until we extract whatever is in there, replicate it, and test it. That is what we have been doing for five years now. It has been a long, slow process – but it has paid off.

'Actually, dinosaur DNA is somewhat easier to extract by this process than mammalian DNA. The reason is that mammalian red cells have no nuclei, and thus no DNA in their red cells. To clone a mammal, you must find a white cell, which is much rarer than red cells. But dinosaurs had nucleated red cells, as do modern birds. It is one of the many indications we have that dinosaurs aren't really reptiles at all. They are big leathery birds.'

Tim saw that Dr. Grant still looked skeptical, and Dennis Nedry, the messy fat man, appeared completely uninterested, as if he knew it all already. Nedry kept looking impatiently toward the next room.

'I see Mr. Nedry has spotted the next phase of our work,' Wu said. 'How we identify the DNA we have extracted. For that, we use powerful computers.'

They went through sliding doors into a chilled room. There was a loud humming sound. Two six-foot-tall round towers stood in the center of the room, and along the walls were rows of waist-high stainless-steel boxes. 'This is our high-tech laundromat,' Dr. Wu said. 'The boxes along the walls are all Hamachi-Hood automated gene sequencers. They are being run, at very high speed, by the Cray XMP supercomputers, which are the towers in the center of the room. In essence, you are standing in the middle of an incredibly powerful genetics factory.'

There were several monitors, all running so fast it was hard to see what they were showing. Wu pushed a button and slowed one image.

```
   1  GCGTTGCTGG CGTTTTTCCA TAGGCTCCGC CCCCCTGACG AGCATCACAA AAATCGACGC
  61  GGTGGCGAAA CCCGACAGGA CTATAAAGAT ACCAGGCGTT TCCCCCTGGA AGCTCCCTCG
 121  TGTTCCGACC CTGCCGCTTA CCGGATACCT GTCCGCCTTT CTCCCTTCGG GAAGCGTGGC
 181  TGCTCACGCT GTAGGTATCT CAGTTCGGTG TAGGTCGTTC GCTCCAAGCT GGGCTGTGTG
 241  CCGTTCAGCC CGACCGCTGC GCCTTATCCG GTAACTATCG TCTTGAGTCC AACCCGGTAA
 301  AGTAGGACAG GTGCCGGCAG CGCTCTGGGT CATTTTCGGC GAGGACCGCT TTCGCTGGAG
 361  ATCGGCCTGT CGCTTGCGGT ATTCGGAATC TTGCACGCCC TCGCTCAAGC CTTCGTCACT
 421  CCAAACGTTT CGGCGAGAAG CAGGCCATTA TCGCCGGCAT GGCGGCCGAC GCGCTGGGCT
 481  GGCGTTCGCG ACGCGAGGCT GGATGGCCTT CCCCATTATG ATTCTTCTCG CTTCCGGCGG
 541  CCCGCGTTGC AGGCCATGCT GTCCAGGCAG GTAGATGACG ACCATCAGGG ACAGCTTCAA
 601  CGGCTCTTAC CAGCCTAACT TCGATCACTG GACCGCTGAT CGTCACGGCG ATTTATGCCG
 661  CACATGGACG CGTTGCTGGC GTTTTTCCAT AGGCTCCGCC CCCCTGACGA GCATCACAAA
 721  CAAGTCAGAG GTGGCGAAAC CCGACAGGAC TATAAAGATA CCAGGCGTTT CCCCCTGGAA
 781  GCGCTCTCCT GTTCCGACCC TGCCGCTTAC CGGATACCTG TCCGCCTTTC TCCCTTCGGG
 841  CTTTCTCAAT GCTCACGCTG TAGGTATCTC AGTTCGGTGT AGGTCGTTCG CTCCAAGCTG
 901  ACGAACCCCC CGTTGCTGGC GACCGCTGCG CCTTATCCGG TAACTATCGT CTTGAGTCCA
 961  ACACGACTTA ACGGGTTGGC ATGGATTGTA GGCGCCGCCC TATACCTTGT CTGCCTCCCC
1021  GCGGTGCATG GAGCCGGGCC ACCTCGACCT GAATGGAAGC CGGCGGCACC TCGCTAACGG
1081  CCAAGAATTG GAGCCAATCA ATTCTTGCGG AGAACTGTGA ATGCGCAAAC CAACCCTTGG
1141  CCATCGCGTC CGCCATCTCC AGCAGCCGCA CGCGGCGCAT CTCGGGCAGC GTTGGGTCCT
1201  GCGCATGATC GTGCT ☇ CCTGTCGTTG AGGACCCGGC TAGGCTGGCG GGGTTGCCTT
1281  AGARTGAATC ACCGATACGC GAGCGAACGT GAAGCGACTG CTGCTGCAAA ACGTCTGCGA
1341  AACATGAATG GTCTTCGGTT TCCGTGTTTC GTAAAGTCTG GAAACGCGGA AGTCAGCGCC
```

'Here you see the actual structure of a small fragment of dinosaur DNA,' Wu said. 'Notice the sequence is made up of four basic compounds – adenine, thymine, guanine, and cytosine. This amount of DNA probably contains instructions to make a single protein – say, a hormone or an enzyme. The full DNA molecule contains *three billion* of these bases. If we looked at a screen like this once a second, for eight hours a day, it'd still take more than two years to look at the entire DNA strand. It's that big.'

He pointed to the image. 'This is a typical example, because you see the DNA has an error, down here in line 1201. Much of the DNA we extract is fragmented or incomplete. So the first thing we have to do is repair it – or rather, the computer has to. It'll cut the DNA, using what are called restriction enzymes. The computer will select a variety of enzymes that might do the job.'

```
  1  GCGTTGCTGGCGTTTTTCCATAGGCTCCGCCCCCCTGACGAGCATCACAAAAATCGACGC
 61  GGTGGCGAAACCCGACAGGACTATAAAGATACCAGGCGTTTCCCCCTGGAAGCGTCCCTCG
                  NspO4
121  TGTTCCGACCCTGCCGCTTACCGGATACCTGTCCGCCTTTCTCCCTTCGGGAAGCGTGGCC
181  TGCTCACGCTGTAGGTATCTCAGTTCGGTGTAGGTCGTTCGCTCCAAGCTGGGCTGTGTG
                                                      □    BrontIV
241  CCGTTCAGCCCGACCGCTGCGCCTTATCCGGTAACTATCGTCTTGAGTCCAACCCGGTAA
301  AGTAGGACAGGTGCCGGCAGCGCTCTGGGTCATTTTCGGCGGAGGACCGCTTTCGCTGGAG
              434 DnxTl             AoliBn
361  ATCGGCCTGTCGCTTGCGGTATTCGGAATCTTGCACGCCCTCGCTCAAGCCTTCGTCACT
421  CCAAACGTTTCGGCGAGAAGCAGGCCATTATCGCCGGCATGGCGGCCGACGCGCTGGGCT
481  GGCGTTCGCGACGCGAGGCTGGATGGCCTTCCCCATTATGATTCTTCTCGCTTCCGGCGG
541  CCCGCGTTGCAGGCCATGCTGTCCAGGCAGGTAGATGACGACCATCAGGGACAGCTTCAA
601  CGGCTCTTACCAGCCTAACTTCGATCACTGGACCGCTGATCGTCACGGCGATTTATGCCG
                                                    NspO4
661  CACATGGACGCGTTGCTGGCGTTTTTCCATAGGCTCCGCCCCCCTGACGAGCATCACAAA
721  CAAGTCAGAGGTGGCGAAACCCGACAGGACTATAAAGATACCAGGCGTTTCCCCCTGGAA
              924 Caol11             DinoLdn
781  GCGCTCTCCTGTTCCGACCCTGCCGCTTACCGGATACCTGTCCGCCTTTCTCCCTTCGGG
841  CTTTCTCAATGCTCACGCTGTAGGTATCTCAGTTCGGTGTAGGTCGTTCGCTCCAAGCTG
901  ACGAACCCCCCGTTCAGCCCGACCGCTGCGCCTTATCCGGTAACTATCGTCTTGAGTCCA
961  ACACGACTTAACGGGTTGGCATGGATTGTAGGCGCCGCCCTATACCTTGTCTGCCTCCCC
1021 GCGGTGCATGGAGCCGGGCCACCTCGACCTGAATGGAAGCCGGCGGCACCTCGCTAACGG
1081 CCAAGAATTGGAGCCAATCAATTCTTGCGGAGAACTGTGAATGCGCAAACCAACCCTTGG
1141 CCATCGCGTCCGCCATCTCCAGCAGCCGCACGGCGCGCATCTCGGGCAGCGTTGGGTCCT
              1416 DnxTl
              SSpd4
1201 GCGCATGATCGTGCT▉◫CCTGTCGTTGAGGACCCGGCTAGGCTGGCGGGGTTGGCCTTACT
1281 ATGAATCACCGATACGCGAGCGAACGTGAAGCGACTGCTGCTGCAAAACGTCTGCGACCTT
```

'Here is the same section of DNA, with the points of the restriction enzymes located. As you can see in line 1201, two enzymes will cut on either side of the damaged point. Ordinarily we let the computers decide which to use. But we also need to know what base pairs we should insert to repair the injury. For that, we have to align various cut fragments, like so

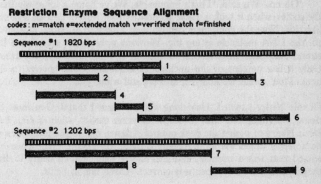

Restriction Enzyme Sequence Alignment

codes: m=match e=extended match v=verified match f=finished

Sequence #1   1820 bps

Sequence #2   1202 bps

'Now we are finding a fragment of DNA that overlaps the injury area, and will tell us what is missing. And you can see we can find it, and go ahead and make the repair. The dark bars you see are restriction fragments – small sections of dinosaur DNA, broken by enzymes and then analyzed. The computer is now recombining them, by searching for overlapping sections of code. It's a little bit like putting a puzzle together. The computer can do it very rapidly.'

```
   1  GCGTTGCTGGCGTTTTTCCATAGGCTCCGCCCCCCTGACGAGCATCACAAAAATCGACGC
  61  GGTGGCGAAACCCGACAGGACTATAAAGATACCAGGCGTTTCCCCCTGGAAGCTCCCTCG
 121  TGTTCCGACCCTGCCGCTTACCGGATACCTGTCCGCCTTTCTCCCTTCGGGAAGCGTGGC
 181  TGCTCACGCTGTAGGTATCTCAGTTCGGTGTAGGTCGTTCGCTCCAAGCTGGGCTGTGTG
 241  CCGTTCAGCCCGACCGCTGCGCCTTATCCGGTAACTATCGTCTTGAGTCCAACCCGGTAA
 301  AGTAGGACAGGTGCCGGCAGCGCTCTGGGTCATTTTCGGCGAGGACCGCTTTCGCTGGAG
 361  ATCGGCCTGTCGCTTGCGGTATTCGGAATCTTGCACGCCCTCGCTCAAGCCTTCGTCACT
 421  CCAAACGTTTCGGCGAGAAGCAGGCCATTATCGCCGGCATGGCGGCCGACGCGCTGGGCT
 481  GGCGTTCGCGACGCGAGGCTGGATGGCCTTCCCCATTATGATTCTTCTCGCTTCCGGCGG
 541  CCCGCGTTGCAGGCCATGCTGTCCAGGCAGGTAGATGACGACCATCAGGGACAGCTTCAA
 601  CGGCTCTTACCAGCCTAACTTCGATCACTGGACCGCTGATCGTCACGGCGATTTATGCCG
 661  CACATGGACGCGTTGCTGGCGTTTTTCCATAGGCTCCGCCCCCCTGACGAGCATCACAAA
 721  CAAGTCAGAGGTGGCGAAACCCGACAGGACTATAAAGATACCAGGCGTTTCCCCCTGGAA
 781  GCGCTCTCCTGTTCCGACCCTGCCGCTTACCGGATACCTGTCCGCCTTTCTCCCTTCGGG
 841  CTTTCTCAATGCTCACGCTGTAGGTATCTCAGTTCGGTGTAGGTCGTTCGCTCCAAGCTG
 901  ACGAACCCCCCGTTCAGCCCGACCGCTGCGCCTTATCCGGTAACTATCGTCTTGAGTCCA
 961  ACACGACTTAACGGGTTGGCATGGATTGTAGGCGCCGCCCTATACCTTGTCTGCCTCCCC
1021  GCGGTGCATGGAGCCGGGCACCTCGACCTGAATGGARGCCGGCGGCACCTCGCTAACGG
1081  CCARGAATTGGAGCCAATCAATTCTTGCGGAGAACTGTGAATGCGCAAACCAACCCTTGG
1141  CCATCGCGTCCGCCATCTCCAGCAGCCGCACGCGGCCGCATCTCGGGCAGCGTTGGGTCCT
1201  GCGCATGATCGTGCTAGCCTGTCGTTGAGGACCCGGCTAGGCTGGCGGGGTTGCCTTACT
1281  ATGAATCACCGATACGCGAGCGAACGTGAAGCGACTGCTGCTGCAAAACGTCTGCGACCT
1341  ATGAATGGTCTTCGGTTTCCGTGTTTCGTAAAGTCTGGAAACGCGGAAGTCAGCGCCCTG
```

'And here is the revised DNA strand, repaired by the computer. The operation you've witnessed would have taken months in a conventional lab, but we can do it in seconds.'

'Then are you working with the entire DNA strand?' Grant asked.

'Oh no,' Wu said. 'That's impossible. We've come a long way from the sixties, when it took a whole laboratory four *years* to decode a screen like this. Now the computers can do it in a couple of hours. But, even so, the DNA molecule is too big. We look only at the sections of the strand that differ from animal to animal, or from contemporary DNA. Only a few percent of the nucleotides differ from one species to the next. That's what we analyze, and it's still a big job.'

Dennis Nedry yawned. He'd long ago concluded that InGen must be doing something like this. A couple of years earlier, when InGen had hired Nedry to design the park control systems, one of the initial design parameters called for data records with 3×10^9 fields. Nedry just assumed that was a mistake, and had called Palo Alto to verify it. But they had told him the spec was correct. Three billion fields.

Nedry had worked on a lot of large systems. He'd made a name for himself setting up worldwide telephone communications for multinational corporations. Often those systems had millions of records. He was used to that. But InGen wanted something so much larger...

Puzzled, Nedry had gone to see Barney Fellows over at Symbolics, near the M.I.T. campus in Cambridge. 'What kind of a database has three billion records, Barney?'

'A mistake,' Barney said, laughing. 'They put in an extra zero or two.'

'It's not a mistake. I checked. It's what they want.'

'But that's crazy,' Barney said. 'It's not workable. Even if you had the fastest processors and blindingly fast algorithms, a search would still take days. Maybe weeks.'

'Yeah,' Nedry said. 'I know. Fortunately I'm not being asked to do algorithms. I'm just being asked to reserve storage and memory for the overall system. But still . . . what could the database be for?'

Barney frowned. 'You operating under an ND?'

'Yes,' Nedry said. Most of his jobs required nondisclosure agreements.

'Can you tell me anything?'

'It's a bioengineering firm.'

'Bioengineering,' Barney said. 'Well, there's the obvious . . .'

'Which is?'

'A DNA molecule.'

'Oh, come on,' Nedra said. 'Nobody could be analyzing a DNA molecule.' He knew biologists were talking about the Human Genome Project, to analyze a complete human DNA strand. But that would take ten years of coordinated effort, involving laboratories around the world. It was an enormous undertaking, as big as the Manhattan Project, which made the atomic bomb. 'This is a private company,' Nedry said.

'With three billion records,' Barney said. 'I don't know what else it could be. Maybe they're being optimistic designing their system.'

'Very optimistic,' Nedry said.

'Or maybe they're just analyzing DNA fragments, but they've got RAM-intensive algorithms.'

That made more sense. Certain database search techniques ate up a lot of memory.

'You know who did their algorithms?'

'No,' Nedry said. 'This company is very secretive.'

'Well, my guess is they're doing something with DNA,' Barney said. 'What's the system?'

'Multi-XMP.'

'*Multi*-XMP? You mean more than one Cray? Wow.' Barney was frowning, now, thinking that one over. 'Can you tell me anything else?'

'Sorry,' Nedry said. 'I can't.' And he had gone back and designed the control systems. It had taken him and his programming team more than a year, and it was especially difficult because the company wouldn't ever tell him what the subsystems were for. The instructions were simply 'Design a module for record keeping' or 'Design a module for visual display.' They gave him design parameters, but no details about use. He had been working in the dark. And now that the system was up and running, he wasn't surprised to learn there were bugs. What did they expect? And they'd ordered him down here in a panic, all hot and bothered about 'his' bugs. It was annoying, Nedry thought.

Nedry turned back to the group as Grant asked, 'And once the computer has analyzed the DNA, how do you know what animal it encodes?'

'We have two procedures,' Wu said. 'The first is phylogenetic mapping. DNA evolves over time, like everything else in an organism – hands or feet or any other physical attribute. So we can take an unknown piece of DNA and determine roughly, by computer, where it fits in the evolutionary sequence. It's time-consuming, but it can be done.'

'And the other way?'

Wu shrugged. 'Just grow it and find out what it is,' he said. 'That's what we usually do. I'll show you how that's accomplished.'

Tim felt a growing impatience as the tour continued. He liked technical things, but, even so, he was losing interest. They came to the next door, which was marked FERTILIZATION. Dr. Wu unlocked the door with his security card, and they went inside.

Tim saw still another room with technicians working at microscopes. In the back was a section entirely lit by blue ultraviolet light. Dr. Wu explained that their DNA work required the interruption of cellular mitosis at precise instants, and therefore they kept some of the most virulent poisons in the world. 'Helotoxins, colchicinoids, beta-alkaloids,' he said, pointing to a series of syringes set out under the UV light. 'Kill any living animal within a second or two.'

Tim would have liked to know more about the poisons, but Dr. Wu droned on about using unfertilized crocodile ova and replacing the DNA; and then Professor Grant asked some complicated questions. To one side of the room were big tanks marked LIQUID N_2. And there were big walk-in freezers with shelves of frozen embryos, each stored in a tiny silver-foil wrapper.

Lex was bored. Nedry was yawning. And even Dr. Sattler was losing interest. Tim was tired of looking at these complicated laboratories. He wanted to see the dinosaurs.

The next room was labeled HATCHERY. 'It's a little warm and damp in here,' Dr. Wu said. 'We keep it at ninety-nine degrees Fahrenheit and a relative humidity of one hundred percent. We also run a higher O_2 concentration. It's up to thirty-three percent.'

'Jurassic atmosphere,' Grant said.

'Yes. At least we presume so. If any of you feel faint, just tell me.'

Dr. Wu inserted his security card into the slot, and the outer door hissed open. 'Just a reminder: don't touch anything in this room. Some of the eggs are permeable to skin oils. And watch your heads. The sensors are always moving.'

He opened the inner door to the nursery, and they went inside. Tim faced a vast open room, bathed in deep infrared light. The eggs lay on long tables, their pale outlines obscured by the hissing low mist that covered the tables. The eggs were all moving gently, rocking.

'Reptile eggs contain large amounts of yolk but no water at all. The embryos must extract water from the surrounding environment. Hence the mist.'

Dr. Wu explained that each table contained 150 eggs, and represented a new batch of DNA extractions. The batches were identified by numbers at each table: STEG-458/2 or TRIC-390/4. Waist-deep in the mist, the workers in the nursery moved from one egg to the next, plunging their hands into the mist, turning the eggs every hour, and checking the temperatures with thermal sensors. The room was monitored by overhead TV cameras and motion sensors. An overhead thermal sensor moved from one egg to the next, touching each with a flexible wand, beeping, then going on.

'In this hatchery, we have produced more than a dozen crops of extractions, giving us a total of two hundred thirty-eight live animals. Our survival rate is somewhere around point four percent, and we naturally want to improve that. But by computer analysis we're working with something like five hundred variables: one hundred and twenty environmental, another two hundred intra-egg, and the rest from the genetic material itself. Our eggs are plastic. The embryos are mechanically inserted, and then hatched here.'

'And how long to grow?'

'Dinosaurs mature rapidly, attaining full size in two to four years. So we now have a number of adult specimens in the park.'

'What do the numbers mean?'

'Those codes,' Wu said, 'identify the various batch extractions of DNA. The first four letters identify the animals being grown. Over there, that TRIC means *Triceratops*. And the STEG means *Stegosaurus*, and so on.'

'And this table here?' Grant said.

The code said XXXX-0001/1. Beneath was scrawled 'Presumed Coelu.'

'That's a new batch of DNA,' Wu said. 'We don't know exactly what will grow out. The first time an extraction is done, we don't know for sure what the animal is. You can see it's marked "Presumed Coelu," so it is likely to be a coelurosaurus. A small herbivore, if I remember. It's hard for me to keep track of the names. There are something like three hundred genera of dinosaurs known so far.'

'Three hundred and forty-seven,' Tim said.

Grant smiled, then said, 'Is anything hatching now?'

'Not at the moment. The incubation period varies with each animal, but in general it runs about two months. We try to stagger hatchings, to make less work for the nursery staff. You can imagine how it is when we have a hundred and fifty animals born within a few days – though of course most don't survive. Actually, these X's are due any day now. Any other questions? No? Then we'll go to the nursery, where the newborns are.'

It was a circular room, all white. There were some incubators of the kind used in hospital nurseries, but they were empty at the moment. Rags and toys were scattered across the floor. A young woman in a white coat was seated on the floor, her back to them.

'What've you got here today, Kathy?' Dr. Wu asked.

'Not much,' she said. 'Just a baby raptor.'

'Let's have a look.'

The woman got to her feet and stepped aside. Tim heard Nedry say, 'It looks like a lizard.'

The animal on the floor was about a foot and a half long, the size of a small monkey. It was dark yellow with brown stripes, like a tiger. It had a lizard's head and long snout, but it stood upright on strong hind legs, balanced by a thick straight tail. Its smaller front legs waved in the air. It cocked its head to one side and peered at the visitors staring down at it.

'*Velociraptor*,' Alan Grant said, in a low voice.

'*Velociraptor mongoliensis*,' Wu said, nodding. 'A predator. This one's only six weeks old.'

'I just excavated a raptor,' Grant said, as he bent down for a closer look. Immediately the little lizard sprang up, leaping over Grant's head into Tim's arms.

'Hey!'

'They can jump,' Wu said. 'The babies can jump. So can the adults, as a matter of fact.'

Tim caught the velociraptor and held it to him. The little animal didn't weigh very much, a pound or two. The skin was warm and completely dry. The little head was inches from Tim's face. Its dark, beady eyes stared at him. A small forked tongue flicked in and out.

'Will he hurt me?'

'No. She's friendly.'

'Are you sure about that?' asked Gennaro, with a look of concern.

'Oh, quite sure,' Wu said. 'At least until she grows a little older. But, in any case, the babies don't have any teeth, even egg teeth.'

'Egg teeth?' Nedry said.

'Most dinosaurs are born with egg teeth – little horns on the tip of the nose, like rhino horns, to help them break out of the eggs. But raptors aren't. They poke a hole in the eggs with their pointed snouts, and then the nursery staff has to help them out.'

'You have to help them out,' Grant said, shaking his head. 'What happens in the wild?'

'In the wild?'

'When they breed in the wild,' Grant said. 'When they make a nest.'

'Oh, they can't do that,' Wu said. 'None of our animals is capable of breeding. That's why we have this nursery. It's the only way to replace stock in Jurassic Park.'

'Why can't the animals breed?'

'Well, as you can imagine, it's important that they not be able to breed,' Wu said. 'And whenever we faced a critical matter such as this, we designed redundant systems. That is, we always arranged at least two control procedures. In this case, there are two independent reasons why the animals can't breed. First of all, they're sterile, because we irradiate them with X-rays.'

'And the second reason?'

'All the animals in Jurassic Park are female,' Wu said, with a pleased smile.

Malcolm said, 'I should like some clarification about this. Because it seems to me that irradiation is fraught with uncertainty. The radiation dose may be wrong, or aimed at the wrong anatomical area of the animal –'

'All true,' Wu said. 'But we're quite confident we have destroyed gonadal tissue.'

'And as for them all being female,' Malcolm said, 'is that checked? Does anyone go out and, ah, lift up the dinosaurs' skirts to have a look? I mean, how does one determine the sex of a dinosaur, anyway?'

'Sex organs vary with the species. It's easy to tell on some, subtle on others. But, to answer your question, the reason we know all the animals are female is that we literally make them that way: we control their chromosomes, and we control the intra-egg developmental environment. From a bioengineering standpoint, females are easier to breed. You probably know that all vertebrate embryos are inherently female. We all start life as females. It takes some kind of added effect – such as a hormone at the right moment during development – to transform the growing embryo into a male. But, left to its own devices, the embryo will naturally become female. So our animals are all female. We tend to refer to some of them as male – such as the Tyrannosaurus rex; we all call it a "him" – but in fact, they're all female. And, believe me, they can't breed.'

The little velociraptor sniffed at Tim, and then rubbed her head against Tim's neck. Tim giggled.

'She wants you to feed her,' Wu said.

'What does she eat?'

'Mice. But she's just eaten, so we won't feed her again for a while.'

The little raptor leaned back, stared at Tim, and wiggled her forearms again in the air. Tim saw the small claws on the three fingers of each hand. Then the raptor burrowed her head against his neck again.

Grant came over, and peered critically at the creature. He touched the tiny three-clawed hand. He said to Tim, 'Do you mind?' and Tim released the raptor into his hands.

Grant flipped the animal onto its back, inspecting it, while the little lizard wiggled and squirmed. Then he lifted the animal high to look at its profile, and it screamed shrilly.

'She doesn't like that,' Regis said. 'Doesn't like to be held away from body contact. . . .'

The raptor was still screaming, but Grant paid no attention. Now he was squeezing the tail, feeling the bones. Regis said, 'Dr. Grant. If you please.'

'I'm not hurting her.'

'Dr. Grant. These creatures are not of our world. They come from a time when there were no human beings around to prod and poke them.'

'I'm not prodding and –'

'Dr. Grant. *Put her down*,' Ed Regis said.

'But —'

'*Now*.' Regis was starting to get annoyed.

Grant handed the animal back to Tim. It stopped squealing. Tim could feel its little heart beating rapidly against his chest.

'I'm sorry, Dr. Grant,' Regis said. 'But these animals are delicate in infancy. We have lost several from a postnatal stress syndrome, which we believe is adrenocortically mediated. Sometimes they die within five minutes.'

Tim petted the little raptor. 'It's okay, kid,' he said. 'Everything's fine now.' The heart was still beating rapidly.

'We feel it is important that the animals here be treated in the most humane manner,' Regis said. 'I promise you that you will have every opportunity to examine them later.'

But Grant couldn't stay away. He again moved toward the animal in Tim's arms, peering at it.

The little velociraptor opened her jaws and hissed at Grant, in a posture of sudden intense fury.

'Fascinating,' Grant said.

'Can I stay and play with her?' Tim said.

'Not right now,' Ed Regis said, glancing at his watch. 'It's three o'clock, and it's a good time for a tour of the park itself, so you can see all the dinosaurs in the habitats we have designed for them.'

Tim released the velociraptor, which scampered across the room, grabbed a cloth rag, put it in her mouth, and tugged at the end with her tiny claws.

Control

Walking back toward the control room, Malcolm said, 'I have one more question, Dr. Wu. How many different species have you made so far?'

'I'm not exactly sure,' Wu said. 'I believe the number at the moment is fifteen. Fifteen species. Do you know, Ed?'

'Yes, it's fifteen,' Ed Regis said, nodding.

'You don't know for *sure*?' Malcolm said, affecting astonishment.

Wu smiled. 'I stopped counting,' he said, 'after the first dozen. And you have to realize that sometimes we think we have an animal correctly made – from the standpoint of the DNA, which is our basic work – and the animal grows for six months and then something untoward happens. And we realize there is some error. A releaser gene isn't operating. A hormone not being released. Or some other problem in the developmental sequence. So we have to go back to the drawing board with that animal, so to speak.' He smiled. 'At one time, I thought I had more than twenty species. But now, only fifteen.'

'And is one of the fifteen species a –' Malcolm turned to Grant. 'What was the name?'

'*Procompsognathus*,' Grant said.

'You have made some procompsognathuses, or whatever they're called?' Malcolm asked.

'Oh yes,' Wu said immediately. 'Compys are very distinctive animals. And, we made an unusually large number of them.'

'Why is that?'

'Well, we want Jurassic Park to be as real an environment as possible – as authentic as possible – and the procompsognathids are actual scavengers from the Jurassic period. Rather like Jackals. So we wanted to have the compys around to clean up.'

'You mean to dispose of carcasses?'

'Yes, if there were any. But with only two hundred and thirty-odd animals in our total population, we don't have many carcasses,' Wu said. 'That wasn't the primary objective. Actually, we wanted the compys for another kind of waste management entirely.'

'Which was?'

'Well,' Wu said, 'we have some very big herbivores on this island. We have specifically tried not to breed the biggest sauropods, but even so, we've got several animals in excess of thirty tons walking around out there, and many others in the five- to ten-ton area. That gives us two problems. One is feeding them, and in fact we must import food to the island every two weeks. There is no way an island this small can support these animals for any time.

'But the other problem is waste. I don't know if you've ever seen elephant droppings,' Wu said, 'but they are substantial. Each spoor is roughly the size of a soccer ball. Imagine the droppings of a brontosaur, ten times as large. Now imagine the droppings of a *herd* of such animals, as we keep here. And the largest animals do not digest their food terribly well, so that they excrete a great deal. And in the sixty million years since dinosaurs disappeared, apparently the bacteria that specialize in breaking down their feces disappeared, too. At least, the sauropod feces don't decompose readily.'

'That's a problem,' Malcolm said.

'I assure you it is,' Wu said, not smiling. 'We had a hell of a time trying to solve it. You probably know that in Africa there is a specific insect, the dung beetle, which eats elephant feces. Many other large species have associated creatures that have evolved to eat their excrement. Well, it turns out that compys will eat the feces of large herbivores and redigest it. And the droppings of compys are readily broken down by contemporary bacteria. So, given enough compys, our problem was solved.'

'How many compys did you make?'

'I've forgotten exactly, but I think the target population was fifty animals. And we attained that, or very nearly so. In three batches. We did a batch every six months until we had the number.'

'Fifty animals,' Malcolm said, 'is a lot to keep track of.'

'The control room is built to do exactly that. They'll show you how it's done.'

'I'm sure,' Malcolm said. 'But if one of these compys were to escape from the island, to get away . . .'

'They can't get away.'

'I know that, but just supposing one did . . .'

'You mean like the animal that was found on the beach?' Wu said, raising his eyebrows. 'The one that bit the American girl?'

'Yes, for example.'

'I don't know what the explanation for that animal is,' Wu said. 'But I know it can't possibly be one of ours, for two reasons. First, the control procedures: our animals are counted by computer every few minutes. If one were missing, we'd know at once.'

'And the second reason?'

'The mainland is more than a hundred miles away. It takes almost a day to get there by boat. And in the outside world our animals will die within twelve hours,' Wu said.

'How do you know?'

'Because I've made sure that's precisely what will occur,' Wu said, finally showing a trace of irritation. 'Look, we're not fools. We understand these are prehistoric animals. They are part of a vanished ecology – a complex web of life that became extinct millions of years ago. They might have no predators in the contemporary world, no checks on their growth. We don't want them to survive in the wild. So I've made them lysine dependent. I inserted a gene that makes a single faulty enzyme in protein metabolism. As a result, the animals cannot manufacture the amino acid lysine. They must ingest it from the outside. Unless they get a rich dietary source of exogenous lysine – supplied by us, in tablet form – they'll go into a coma within twelve hours and expire. These animals are genetically engineered to be unable to survive in the real world. They can only live here in Jurassic Park. They are not free at all. They are essentially our prisoners.'

'Here's the control room,' Ed Regis said. 'Now that you know how the animals are made, you'll want to see the control room for the park itself, before we go out on the –'

He stopped. Through the thick glass window, the room was dark. The monitors were off, except for three that displayed spinning numbers and the image of a large boat.

'What's going on?' Ed Regis said. 'Oh hell, they're docking.'

'Docking?'

'Every two weeks, the supply boat comes in from the mainland. One of the things this island doesn't have is a good harbor, or even a good dock. It's a little hairy to get the ship in, when the seas are rough. Could be a few minutes.' He rapped on the window, but the men inside paid no attention. 'I guess we have to wait, then.'

Ellie turned to Dr. Wu. 'You mentioned before that sometimes you make an animal and it seems to be fine but, as it grows, it shows itself to be flawed. . . .'

'Yes,' Wu said. 'I don't think there's any way around that. We can duplicate the DNA, but there is a lot of timing in development, and we don't know if everything is working unless we actually see an animal develop correctly.'

Grant said, 'How do you know if it's developing correctly? No one has ever seen these animals before.'

Wu smiled. 'I have often thought about that. I suppose it is a bit of a paradox. Eventually, I hope, paleontologists such as yourself will compare our animals with the fossil record to verify the developmental sequence.'

Ellie said, 'But the animal we just saw, the velociraptor – you said it was a *mongoliensis*?'

'From the location of the amber,' Wu said. 'It is from China.'

'Interesting,' Grant said. 'I was just digging up an infant *antirrhopus*. Are there any full-grown raptors here?'

'Yes,' Ed Regis said without hesitation. 'Eight adult females. The females are the real hunters. They're pack hunters, you know.'

'Will we see them on the tour?'

'No,' Wu said, looking suddenly uncomfortable. And there was an awkward pause. Wu looked at Regis.

'Not for a while,' Regis said cheerfully. 'The velociraptors haven't been integrated into the park setting just yet. We keep them in a holding pen.'

'Can I see them there?' Grant said.

'Why, yes, of course. In fact, while we're waiting' – he glanced at his watch – 'you might want to go around and have a look at them.'

'I certainly would,' Grant said.

'Absolutely,' Ellie said.

'I want to go, too,' Tim said eagerly.

'Just go around the back of this building, past the support facility, and you'll see the pen. But don't get too close to the fence. Do you want to go, too?' he said to the girl.

'No,' Lex said. She looked appraisingly at Regis. 'You want to play a little pickle? Throw a few?'

'Well, sure,' Ed Regis said. 'Why don't you and I go downstairs and we'll do that, while we wait for the control room to open up?'

Grant walked with Ellie and Malcolm around the back of the main building, with the kid tagging along. Grant liked kids – it was impossible not to like any group so openly enthusiastic about dinosaurs. Grant used to watch kids in museums as they stared open-mouthed at the big skeletons rising above them. He wondered what their fascination really represented. He finally decided that children liked dinosaurs because these giant creatures personified the uncontrollable force of looming authority. They were symbolic parents. Fascinating and frightening, like parents. And kids loved them, as they loved their parents.

Grant also suspected that was why even young children learned the names of dinosaurs. It never failed to amaze him when a three-year-old shrieked: '*Stegosaurus!*' Saying these complicated names was a way of exerting power over the giants, a way of being in control.

'What do you know about *Velociraptor?*' Grant asked Tim. He was just making conversation.

'It's a small carnivore that hunted in packs, like *Deinonychus*,' Tim said.

'That's right,' Grant said, 'although the evidence for pack hunting is all circumstantial. It derives in part from the appearance of the animals, which are quick and strong, but small for dinosaurs – just a hundred and fifty to three hundred pounds each. We assume they hunted in groups if they were to bring down larger prey. And there are some fossil finds in which a single large prey animal is associated with several raptor skeletons, suggesting they hunted in packs. And, of course, raptors were large-brained, more intelligent than most dinosaurs.'

'How intelligent is that?' Malcolm asked.

'Depends on who you talk to,' Grant said. 'Just as paleontologists have come around to the idea that dinosaurs were probably warm-blooded, a lot of us are starting to think some of them might have been quite intelligent, too. But nobody knows for sure.'

They left the visitor area behind, and soon they heard the loud hum of generators, smelled the faint odor of gasoline. They passed a grove of palm trees and saw a large, low concrete shed with a steel roof. The noise seemed to come from there. They looked in the shed.

'It must be a generator,' Ellie said.

'It's big,' Grant said, peering inside.

The power plant actually extended two stories below ground level: a vast complex of whining turbines and piping that ran down in the earth, lit by harsh electric bulbs. 'They can't need all this just for a resort,' Malcolm said. 'They're generating enough power here for a small city.'

'Maybe for the computers?'

'Maybe.'

Grant heard bleating, and walked north a few yards. He came to an animal enclosure with goats. By a quick count, he estimated there were fifty or sixty goats.

'What's that for?' Ellie asked.

'Beats me.'

'Probably they feed 'em to the dinosaurs,' Malcolm said.

The group walked on, following a dirt path through a dense bamboo grove. At the far side, they came to a double-layer chain-link fence twelve feet high, with spirals of barbed wire at the top. There was an electric hum along the outer fence.

Beyond the fences, Grant saw dense clusters of large ferns, five feet high. He heard a snorting sound, a kind of snuffling. Then the sound of crunching footsteps, coming closer.

Then a long silence.

'I don't see anything,' Tim whispered, finally.

'Ssssh.'

Grant waited. Several seconds passed. Flies buzzed in the air. He still saw nothing.

Ellie tapped him on the shoulder, and pointed.

Amid the ferns, Grant saw the head of an animal. It was motionless, partially hidden in the fronds, the two large dark eyes watching them coldly.

The head was two feet long. From a pointed snout, a long row of teeth ran back to the hole of the auditory meatus which served as an ear. The head reminded him of a large lizard, or perhaps a crocodile. The eyes did not blink, and the animal did not move. Its skin was leathery, with a pebbled texture, and basically the same coloration as the infant's: yellow-brown with darker reddish markings, like the stripes of a tiger.

As Grant watched, a single forelimb reached up very slowly to part the ferns beside the animal's face. The limb, Grant saw, was strongly muscled. The hand had three grasping fingers, each ending in curved claws. The hand gently, slowly, pushed aside the ferns.

Grant felt a chill and thought, *He's hunting us.*

For a mammal like man, there was something indescribably alien about the way reptiles hunted their prey. No wonder men hated reptiles. The stillness, the coldness, the *pace* was all wrong. To be among alligators or other large reptiles was to be reminded of a different kind of life, a different kind of world, now vanished from the earth. Of course, this animal didn't realize that he had been spotted, that he –

The attack came suddenly, from the left and right. Charging raptors covered the ten yards to the fence with shocking speed. Grant had a blurred impression of powerful, six-foot-tall bodies, stiff balancing tails, limbs with curving claws, open jaws with rows of jagged teeth.

The animals snarled as they came forward, and then leapt bodily into the air, raising their hind legs with their big dagger-claws. Then they struck the fence in front of them, throwing off twin bursts of hot sparks.

The velociraptors fell backward to the ground, hissing. The visitors all moved forward, fascinated. Only then did the third animal attack, leaping up to strike the fence at chest level. Tim screamed in fright as the sparks exploded all around him. The creatures snarled, a low reptilian hissing sound, and leapt back among the ferns. Then they were gone, leaving behind a faint odor of decay, and hanging acrid smoke.

'*Holy shit*,' Tim said.

'It was so *fast*,' Ellie said.

'Pack hunters,' Grant said, shaking his head. 'Pack hunters for whom ambush is an instinct . . . Fascinating.'

'I wouldn't call them tremendously intelligent,' Malcolm said.

On the other side of the fence, they heard snorting in the palm trees. Several heads poked slowly out of the foliage. Grant counted three . . . four . . . five . . . The animals watched them. Staring coldly.

A black man in coveralls came running up to them. 'Are you all right?'

'We're okay,' Grant said.

'The alarms were set off.' The man looked at the fence, dented and charred. 'They attacked you?'

'Three of them did, yes.'

The black man nodded. 'They do that all the time. Hit the fence, take a shock. They never seem to mind.'

'Not too smart, are they?' Malcolm said.

The black man paused. He squinted at Malcolm in the afternoon light. 'Be glad for that fence, *señor*,' he said, and turned away.

From beginning to end, the entire attack could not have taken more than six seconds. Grant was still trying to organize his impressions. The speed was astonishing – the animals were so fast, he had hardly seen them move.

Walking back, Malcolm said, 'They are remarkably fast.'

'Yes,' Grant said. 'Much faster than any living reptile. A bull alligator can move quickly, but only over a short distance – five or six feet. Big lizards like the five-foot Komodo dragons of Indonesia have been clocked at thirty miles an hour, fast enough to run down a man. And they kill men all the time. But I'd guess the animal behind the fence was more than twice that fast.'

'Cheetah speed,' Malcolm said. 'Sixty, seventy miles an hour.'

'Exactly.'

'But they seemed to dart forward,' Malcolm said. 'Rather like birds.'

'Yes.' In the contemporary world, only very small mammals, like the cobra-fighting mongoose, had such quick responses. Small mammals, and of course birds. The snake-hunting secretary bird of Africa, or the cassowary. In fact, the velociraptor conveyed precisely the same impression of deadly, swift menace Grant had seen in the cassowary, the clawed ostrich-like bird of New Guinea.

'So these velociraptors look like reptiles, with the skin and general appearance of reptiles, but they move like birds, with the speed and predatory intelligence of birds. Is that about it?' Malcolm said.

'Yes,' Grant said. 'I'd say they display a mixture of traits.'

'Does that surprise you?'

'Not really,' Grant said. 'It's actually rather close to what paleontologists believed a long time ago.'

When the first giant bones were found in the 1820s and 1830s, scientists felt obliged to explain the bones as belonging to some oversize variant of a modern species. This was because it was believed that no species could ever become extinct, since God would not allow one of His creations to die.

Eventually it became clear that this conception of God was mistaken, and the bones belonged to extinct animals. But what kind of animals?

In 1842, Richard Owen, the leading British anatomist of the day, called them *Dinosauria*, meaning 'terrible lizards.' Owen recognized that dinosaurs seemed to combine traits of lizards, crocodiles, and birds. In particular, dinosaur hips were bird-like, not lizard-like. And, unlike lizards, many dinosaurs seemed to stand upright. Owen imagined dinosaurs to be quick-moving, active creatures, and his view was accepted for the next forty years.

But when truly gigantic finds were unearthed – animals that had weighed a hundred tons in life – scientists began to envision the dinosaurs as stupid, slow-moving giants destined for extinction. The image of the sluggish reptile gradually predominated over the image of the quick-moving bird. In recent years, scientists like Grant had begun to swing back toward the idea of more active dinosaurs. Grant's colleagues saw him as radical in his conception of dinosaur behavior. But now he had to admit his own conception had fallen far short of the reality of these large, incredibly swift hunters.

'Actually, what I was driving at,' Malcolm said, 'was this: Is it a persuasive animal to you? Is it in fact a dinosaur?'

'I'd say so, yes.'

'And the coordinated attack behavior . . .'

'To be expected,' Grant said. According to the fossil record, packs of velociraptors were capable of bringing down animals that weighed a thousand pounds, like *Tenontosaurus*, which could run as fast as a horse. Coordination would be required.

'How do they do that, without language?'

'Oh, language isn't necessary for coordinated hunting,' Ellie said. 'Chimpanzees do it all the time. A group of chimps will stalk a monkey and kill it. All communication is by eyes.'

'And were the dinosaurs in fact attacking us?'

'Yes.'

'They would kill us and eat us if they could?' Malcolm said.

'I think so.'

'The reason I ask,' Malcolm said, 'is that I'm told large predators such as lions and tigers are not born man-eaters. Isn't that true? These animals must learn somewhere along the way that human beings are easy to kill. Only afterward do they become man-killers.'

'Yes, I believe that's true,' Grant said.

'Well, these dinosaurs must be even more reluctant than lions and tigers. After all, they come from a time before human beings – or even large mammals – existed at all. God knows what they think when they see us. So I wonder: have they learned, somewhere along the line, that humans are easy to kill?'

The group fell silent as they walked.

'In any case,' Malcolm said, 'I shall be *extremely* interested to see the control room now.'

Version 4.4

'Was there any problem with the group?' Hammond asked.

'No,' Henry Wu said, 'there was no problem at all.'

'They accepted your explanation?'

'Why shouldn't they?' Wu said. 'It's all quite straightforward, in the broad strokes. It's only the details that get sticky. And I wanted to talk about the details with you today. You can think of it as a matter of aesthetics.'

John Hammond wrinkled his nose, as if he smelled something disagreeable. 'Aesthetics?' he repeated.

They were standing in the living room of Hammond's elegant bungalow, set back among palm trees in the northern sector of the park. The living room was airy and comfortable, fitted with a half-dozen video monitors showing the animals in the park. The file Wu had brought, stamped ANIMAL DEVELOPMENT: VERSION 4.4, lay on the coffee table.

Hammond was looking at him in that patient, paternal way. Wu, thirty-three years old, was acutely aware that he had worked for Hammond all his professional life. Hammond had hired him right out of graduate school.

'Of course, there are practical consequences as well,' Wu said. 'I really think you should consider my recommendations for phase two. We should go to version 4.4.'

'You want to replace all the current stock of animals?' Hammond said.

'Yes, I do.'

'Why? What's wrong with them?'

'Nothing,' Wu said, 'except that they're real dinosaurs.'

'That's what I asked for, Henry,' Hammond said, smiling. 'And that's what you gave me.'

'I know,' Wu said. 'But you see . . .' He paused. How could he explain this to Hammond? Hammond hardly ever visited the island. And it was a peculiar situation that Wu was trying to convey. 'Right now, as we stand here, almost no one in the world has ever seen an actual dinosaur. Nobody knows what they're really like.'

'Yes . . .'

'The dinosaurs we have now are real,' Wu said, pointing to the screens around the room, 'but in certain ways they are unsatisfactory. Unconvincing. I could make them better.'

'Better in what way?'

'For one thing, they move too fast,' Henry Wu said. 'People aren't accustomed to seeing large animals that are so quick. I'm afraid visitors will think the dinosaurs look speeded up, like film running too fast.'

'But, Henry, these are real dinosaurs. You said so yourself.'

'I know,' Wu said. 'But we could easily breed slower, more domesticated dinosaurs.'

'*Domesticated* dinosaurs?' Hammond snorted. 'Nobody wants domesticated dinosaurs, Henry. They want the real thing.'

'But that's my point,' Wu said. 'I don't think they do. They want to see their expectation, which is quite different.'

Hammond was frowning.

'You said yourself, John, this park is entertainment,' Wu said. 'And entertainment has nothing to do with reality. Entertainment is antithetical to reality.'

Hammond sighed. 'Now, Henry, are we going to have another one of those abstract discussions? You know I like to keep it simple. The dinosaurs we have now are real, and –'

'Well, not exactly,' Wu said. He paced the living room, pointed to the monitors. 'I don't think we should kid ourselves. We haven't *re-created* the past here. The past is gone. It can never be re-created. What we've done is *reconstruct* the past – or at least a version of the past. And I'm saying we can make a better version.'

'Better than real?'

'Why not?' Wu said. 'After all, these animals are already modified. We've inserted genes to make them patentable, and to make them lysine dependent. And we've done everything we can to promote growth, and accelerate development into adulthood.'

Hammond shrugged. 'That was inevitable. We didn't want to wait. We have investors to consider.'

'Of course. But I'm just saying, why stop there? Why not push ahead to make exactly the kind of dinosaur that we'd like to see? One that is more acceptable to visitors, and one that is easier for us to handle? A slower, more docile version for our park?'

Hammond frowned. 'But then the dinosaurs wouldn't be real.'

'But they're not real now,' Wu said. 'That's what I'm trying to tell you. There isn't any reality here.' He shrugged helplessly. He could see he wasn't getting through. Hammond had never been interested in technical details, and the essence of the argument was technical. How could he explain to Hammond about the reality of DNA dropouts, the patches, the gaps in the sequence that Wu had been obliged to fill in, making the best guesses he could, but still, making guesses. The DNA of the dinosaurs was like old photographs that had been retouched, basically the same as the original but in some places repaired and clarified, and as a result –

'Now, Henry,' Hammond said, putting his arm around Wu's shoulder. 'If you don't mind my saying so, I think you're getting cold feet. You've been working very hard for a long time, and you've done a hell of a job – a *hell* of a job – and it's finally time to reveal to some people what you've done. It's natural to be a little nervous. To have some doubts. But I am convinced, Henry, that the world will be entirely satisfied. Entirely satisfied.'

As he spoke, Hammond steered him toward the door.

'But, John,' Wu said. 'Remember back in '87, when we started to build the containment devices? We didn't have any full-grown adults yet, so we had to predict what we'd need. We ordered big taser shockers, cars with cattle prods mounted on them, guns that blow out electric nets. All built specially to our specifications. We've got a whole array of devices now – and they're all *too slow*. We've got to make some adjustments. You know that Muldoon wants military equipment: TOW missiles and laser-guided devices?'

'Let's leave Muldoon out of this,' Hammond said. 'I'm not worried. It's just a zoo, Henry.'

The phone rang, and Hammond went to answer it. Wu tried to think of another way to press his case. But the fact was that, after five long years, Jurassic Park was nearing completion, and John Hammond just wasn't listening to him any more.

There had been a time when Hammond listened to Wu very attentively. Especially when he had first recruited him, back in the days when Henry Wu was a twenty-eight-year-old graduate student getting his doctorate at Stanford in Norman Atherton's lab.

Atherton's death had thrown the lab into confusion as well as mourning; no one knew what would happen to the funding or the doctoral programs. There was a lot of uncertainty; people worried about their careers.

Two weeks after the funeral, John Hammond came to see Wu. Everyone in the lab knew that Atherton had had some association with Hammond, although the details were never clear. But Hammond had approached Wu with a directness Wu never forgot.

'Norman always said you're the best geneticist in his lab,' he said. 'What are your plans now?'

'I don't know. Research.'

'You want a university appointment?'

'Yes.'

'That's a mistake,' Hammond said briskly. 'At least, if you respect your talent.'

Wu had blinked. 'Why?'

'Because, let's face facts,' Hammond said. 'Universities are no longer the intellectual centers of the country. The very idea is preposterous. Universities are the backwater. Don't look so surprised. I'm not saying anything you don't know. Since World War II, all the really important discoveries have come out of private laboratories. The laser, the transistor, the polio vaccine, the microchip, the hologram, the personal computer, magnetic resonance imaging, CAT scans – the list goes on and on. Universities simply aren't where it's happening any more. And they haven't been for forty years. If you want to do something important in computers or genetics, you don't go to a *university*. Dear me, no.'

Wu found he was speechless.

'Good heavens,' Hammond said, 'what must you go through to start a new project? How many grant applications, how many forms, how many approvals? The steering committee? The department chairman? The university resources committee? How do you get more work space if you need it? More assistants if you need them? How long does all that take? A brilliant man can't squander precious time with forms and committees. Life is too short, and DNA too long. You want to make your mark. If you want to get something *done*, stay out of universities.'

In those days, Wu desperately wanted to make his mark. John Hammond had his full attention.

'I'm talking about *work*,' Hammond continued. 'Real accomplishment. What does a scientist need to work? He needs time, and he needs money. I'm talking about giving you a five-year commitment, and ten million dollars a year in funding. Fifty million dollars, and no one tells you how to spend it. You decide. Everyone else just *gets out of your way*.'

It sounded too good to be true. Wu was silent for a long time. Finally he said, 'In return for what?'

'For taking a crack at the impossible,' Hammond said. 'For trying something that probably can't be done.'

'What does it involve?'

'I can't give you details, but the general area involves cloning reptiles.'

'I don't think that's impossible,' Wu said. 'Reptiles are easier than mammals. Cloning's probably only ten, fifteen years off. Assuming some fundamental advances.'

'I've got five years,' Hammond said. 'And a lot of money, for somebody who wants to take a crack at it now.'

'Is my work publishable?'

'Eventually.'

'Not immediately?'

'No.'

'But eventually publishable?' Wu asked, sticking on this point.

Hammond had laughed. 'Don't worry. If you succeed, the whole world will know about what you've done, I promise you.'

And now it seemed the whole world would indeed know, Wu thought. After five years of extraordinary effort, they were just a year away from opening the park to the public. Of course, those years hadn't gone exactly as Hammond had promised. Wu had had some people telling him what to do, and many times fearsome pressures were placed on him. And the work itself had shifted – it wasn't even reptilian cloning, once they began to understand that dinosaurs were so similar to birds. It was avian cloning, a very different proposition. Much more difficult. And for the last two years, Wu had been primarily an administrator, supervising teams of researchers and banks of computer-operated gene sequencers. Administration wasn't the kind of work he relished. It wasn't what he had bargained for.

Still, he had succeeded. He had done what nobody really believed could be done, at least in so short a time. And Henry Wu thought that he should have some rights, some say in what happened, by virtue of his expertise and his efforts. Instead, he found his influence waning with each passing day. The dinosaurs existed. The procedures for obtaining them were worked out to the point of being routine. The technologies were mature. And John Hammond didn't need Henry Wu any more.

'That should be fine,' Hammond said, speaking into the phone. He listened for a while, and smiled at Wu. 'Fine. Yes. Fine.' He hung up. 'Where were we, Henry?'

'We were talking about phase two,' Wu said.

'Oh yes. We've gone over some of this before, Henry –'

'I know, but you don't realize –'

'Excuse me, Henry,' Hammond said, with an edge of impatience in his voice. 'I *do* realize. And I must tell you frankly, Henry. I see no reason to improve upon reality. Every change we've made in the genome has been forced on us by law or necessity. We may make other changes in the future, to resist disease, or for other reasons. But I don't think we should improve upon reality just because we think it's better that way. We have real dinosaurs out there now. That's what people want to see. And that's what they *should* see. That's our obligation, Henry. That's *honest*, Henry.'

And, smiling, Hammond opened the door for him to leave.

Control

Grant looked at all the computer monitors in the darkened control room, feeling irritable. Grant didn't like computers. He knew that this made him old-fashioned, dated as a researcher, but he didn't care. Some of the kids who worked for him had a real feeling for computers, an intuition. Grant never felt that. He found computers to be alien, mystifying machines. Even the fundamental distinction between an operating system and an application left him confused and disheartened, literally lost in a foreign geography he didn't begin to comprehend. But he noticed that Gennaro was perfectly comfortable, and Malcolm seemed to be in his element, making little sniffing sounds, like a bloodhound on a trail.

'You want to know about control mechanisms?' John Arnold said, turning in his chair in the control room. The head engineer was a thin, tense, chain-smoking man of forty-five. He squinted at the others in the room. 'We have *unbelievable* control mechanisms,' Arnold said, and lit another cigarette.

'For example,' Gennaro said.

'For example, animal tracking.' Arnold pressed a button on his console, and the vertical glass map lit up with a pattern of jagged blue lines. 'That's our juvenile T-rex. The little rex. All his movements within the park over the last twenty-four hours.' Arnold pressed the button again. 'Previous twenty-four.' And again. 'Previous twenty-four.'

The lines on the map became densely overlaid, a child's scribble. But the scribble was localized in a single area, near the southeast side of the lagoon.

'You get a sense of his home range over time,' Arnold said. 'He's young, so he stays close to the water. And he stays away from the big adult rex. You put up the big rex and the little rex, and you'll see their paths never cross.'

'Where is the big rex right now?' Gennaro asked.

Arnold pushed another button. The map cleared, and a single glowing spot with a code number appeared in the fields northwest of the lagoon. 'He's right there.'

'And the little rex?'

'Hell, I'll show you every animal in the park,' Arnold said. The map began to light up like a Christmas tree, dozens of spots of light, each tagged with a code number. 'That's two hundred thirty-eight animals as of this minute.'

'How accurate?'

'Within five feet.' Arnold puffed on the cigarette. 'Let's put it this way: you drive out in a vehicle and you will find the animals right there, exactly as they're shown on the map.'

'How often is this updated?'

'Every thirty seconds.'

'Pretty impressive,' Gennaro said. 'How's it done?'

'We have motion sensors all around the park,' Arnold said. 'Most of 'em hard-wired, some radio-telemetered. Of course, motion sensors won't usually tell you the species, but we get image recognition direct off the video. Even when we're not watching the video monitors, the computer is. And checking where everybody is.'

'Does the computer ever make a mistake?'

'Only with the babies. It mixes those up sometimes, because they're such small images. But we don't sweat that. The babies almost always stay close to herds of adults. Also you have the category tally.'

'What's that?'

'Once every fifteen minutes, the computer tallies the animals in all categories,' Arnold said. 'Like this.'

Total Animals	238		
Species	**Expected**	**Found**	**Ver**
Tyrannosaurs	2	2	4.1
Maiasaurs	21	21	3.3
Stegosaurs	4	4	3.9
Triceratops	8	8	3.1
Procompsognathids	49	49	3.9
Othnielia	16	16	3.1
Velociraptors	8	8	3.0
Apatosaurs	17	17	3.1
Hadrosaurs	11	11	3.1
Dilophosaurs	7	7	4.3
Pterosaurs	6	6	4.3
Hypsilophodontids	33	33	2.9
Euoplocephalids	16	16	4.0
Styracosaurs	18	18	3.9
Callovosaurs	22	22	4.1
Total	**238**	**238**	

'What you see here,' Arnold said, 'is an entirely separate counting procedure. It isn't based on the tracking data. It's a fresh look. The whole idea is that the computer can't make a mistake, because it compares two different ways of gathering the data. If an animal were missing, we'd know it within five minutes.'

'I see,' Malcolm said. 'And has that ever actually been tested?'

'Well, in a way,' Arnold said. 'We've had a few animals die. An othnielian got caught in the branches of a tree and strangled. One of the stegos died of that intestinal illness that keeps bothering them. One of the hypsilophodonts fell and broke his neck. And in each case, once the animal stopped moving, the numbers stopped tallying and the computer signaled an alert.'

'Within five minutes.'

'Yes.'

Grant said, 'What is the right-hand column?'

'Release version of the animals. The most recent are version 4.1 or 4.3. We're considering going to version 4.4.'

'Version numbers? You mean like software? New releases?'

'Well, yes,' Arnold said. 'It is like software, in a way. As we discover the glitches in the DNA, Dr. Wu's labs have to make a new version.'

The idea of living creatures' being numbered like software, being subject to updates and revisions, troubled Grant. He could not exactly say why – it was too new a thought – but he was instinctively uneasy about it. They were, after all, living creatures. . . .

Arnold must have noticed his expression, because he said, 'Look, Dr. Grant, there's no point getting starry-eyed about these animals. It's important for everyone to remember that these animals are *created*. Created by man. Sometimes there are bugs. So, as we discover the bugs, Dr. Wu's labs have to make a new version. And we need to keep track of what version we have out there.'

'Yes, yes, of course you do,' Malcolm said impatiently. 'But, going back to the matter of *counting* – I take it all the counts are based on motion sensors?'

'Yes.'

'And these sensors are everywhere in the park?'

'They cover ninety-two percent of the land area,' Arnold said. 'There are only a few places we can't use them. For example, we can't use them on the jungle river, because the movement of the water and the convection rising from the surface screws up the sensors. But we have them nearly everywhere else. And if the computer tracks an animal into an unsensed zone, it'll remember, and look for the animal to come out again. And if it doesn't, it gives us an alarm.'

'Now, then,' Malcolm said. 'You show forty-nine procompsogna-thids. Suppose I suspect that some of them aren't really the correct species. How would you show me that I'm wrong?'

'Two ways,' Arnold said. 'First of all, I can track individual movements against the other presumed compys. Compys are social animals, they move in a group. We have two compy groups in the park. So the individuals should be within either group A or group B.'

'Yes, but –'

'The other way is direct visual,' he said. He punched buttons and one of the monitors began to flick rapidly through images of compys, numbered from 1 to 49.

'These pictures are . . .'

'Current ID images. From within the last five minutes.'

'So you can see all the animals, if you want to?'

'Yes. I can visually review all the animals whenever I want.'

'How about physical containment?' Gennaro said. 'Can they get out of their enclosures?'

'Absolutely not,' Arnold said. 'These are expensive animals, Mr. Gennaro. We take very good care of them. We maintain multiple barriers. First, the moats.' He pressed a button, and the board lit up with a network of orange bars. 'These moats are never less than twelve feet deep, and water-filled. For bigger animals the moats may be thirty feet deep. Next, the electrified fences.' Lines of bright red glowed on the board. 'We have fifty miles of twelve-foot-high fencing, including twenty-two miles around the perimeter of the island. All the park fences carry ten thousand volts. The animals quickly learn not to go near them.'

'But if one *did* get out?' Gennaro said.

Arnold snorted, and stubbed out his cigarette.

'Just hypothetically,' Gennaro said. 'Supposing it happened?'

Muldoon cleared his throat. 'We'd go out and get the animal back,' he said. 'We have lots of ways to do that – taser shock guns, electrified nets, tranquilizers. All nonlethal, because – as Mr. Arnold says, these are expensive animals.'

Gennaro nodded. 'And if one got off the island?'

'It'd die in less than twenty-four hours,' Arnold said. 'These are genetically engineered animals. They're unable to survive in the real world.'

'How about this control system itself?' Gennaro said. 'Could anybody tamper with it?'

Arnold was shaking his head. 'The system is hardened. The computer is independent in every way. Independent power and independent backup power. The system does not communicate with the outside, so it cannot be influenced remotely by modem. The computer system is secure.'

There was a pause. Arnold puffed his cigarette. 'Hell of a system,' he said. 'Hell of a goddamned system.'

'Then I guess,' Malcolm said, 'your system works so well, you don't have any problems.'

'We've got endless problems here,' Arnold said, raising an eyebrow. 'But none of the things you worry about. I gather you're worried that the animals will escape, and will get to the mainland and raise hell. We haven't got any concern about that at all. We see these animals as fragile and delicate. They've been brought back after sixty-five million years to a world that's very different from the one they left, the one they were adapted to. We have a hell of a time caring for them.

'You have to realize,' Arnold continued, 'that men have been keeping mammals and reptiles in zoos for hundreds of years. So we know a lot about how to take care of an elephant or a croc. But nobody has ever tried to take care of a dinosaur before. They are new animals. And we just don't know. Diseases in our animals are the biggest concern.'

'Diseases?' Gennaro said, suddenly alarmed. 'Is there any way that a visitor could get sick?'

Arnold snorted again. 'You ever catch a cold from a zoo alligator, Mr. Gennaro? Zoos don't worry about that. Neither do we. What we *do* worry about is the animals' dying from their own illnesses, or infecting other animals. But we have programs to monitor that, too. You want to see the big rex's health file? His vaccination record? His dental record? That's something – you ought to see the vets scrubbing those big fangs so he doesn't get tooth decay. . . .'

'Not just now,' Gennaro said. 'What about your mechanical systems?'

'You mean the rides?' Arnold said.

Grant looked up sharply: *rides?*

'None of the rides are running yet,' Arnold was saying. 'We have the Jungle River Ride, where the boats follow tracks underwater, and we have the Aviary Lodge Ride, but none of it's operational yet. The park'll open with the basic dinosaur tour – the one that you're about to take in a few minutes. The other rides will come on line six, twelve months after that.'

'Wait a minute,' Grant said. 'You're going to have rides? Like an amusement park?'

Arnold said, 'This is a zoological park. We have tours of different areas, and we call them rides. That's all.'

Grant frowned. Again he felt troubled. He didn't like the idea of dinosaurs being used for an amusement park.

Malcolm continued his questions. 'You can run the whole park from this control room?'

'Yes,' Arnold said. 'I can run it single-handed, if I have to. We've got that much automation built in. The computer by itself can track the animals, feed them, and fill their water troughs for forty-eight hours without supervision.'

'This is the system Mr. Nedry designed?' Malcolm asked. Dennis Nedry was sitting at a terminal in the far corner of the room, eating a candy bar and typing.

'Yes, that's right,' Nedry said, not looking up from the keyboard.

'It's a hell of a system,' Arnold said proudly.

'That's right,' Nedry said absently. 'Just one or two minor bugs to fix.'

'Now,' Arnold said, 'I see the tour is starting, so unless you have other questions . . .'

'Actually, just one,' Malcolm said. 'Just a research question. You showed us that you can track the procompsognathids and you can visually display them individually. Can you do any studies of them as a group? Measure them, or whatever? If I wanted to know height or weight, or . . .'

Arnold was punching buttons. Another screen came up.

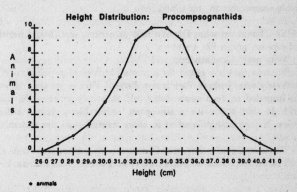

'We can do all of that, and very quickly,' Arnold said. 'The computer takes measurement data in the course of reading the video screens, so it is translatable at once. You see here we have a normal

Poisson distribution for the animal population. It shows that most of the animals cluster around an average central value, and a few are either larger or smaller than the average, at the tails of the curve.'

'You'd expect that kind of graph,' Malcolm said.

'Yes. Any healthy biological population shows this kind of distribution. Now, then,' Arnold said, lighting another cigarette, 'are there any other questions?'

'No,' Malcolm said. 'I've learned what I need to know.'

As they were walking out, Gennaro said, 'It looks like a pretty good system to me. I don't see how any animals could get off this island.'

'Don't you?' Malcolm said. 'I thought it was completely obvious.'

'Wait a minute,' Gennaro said. 'You think animals have gotten out?'

'I *know* they have.'

Gennaro said, 'But how? You saw for yourself. They can count all the animals. They can look at all the animals. They know where all the animals are at all times. How can one possibly escape?'

Malcolm smiled. 'It's quite obvious,' he said. 'It's just a matter of your assumptions.'

'Your assumptions,' Gennaro repeated, frowning.

'Yes,' Malcolm said. 'Look here. The basic event that has occurred in Jurassic Park is that the scientists and technicians have tried to make a new, complete biological world. And the scientists in the control room expect to see a natural world. As in the graph they just showed us. Even though a moment's thought reveals that nice, normal distribution is terribly worrisome on this island.'

'It is?'

'Yes. Based on what Dr. Wu told us earlier, one should never see a population graph like that.'

'Why not?' Gennaro said.

'Because that is a graph for a normal biological population. Which is precisely what Jurassic Park is not. Jurassic Park is not the real world. It is intended to be a controlled world that only imitates the natural world. In that sense, it's a true park, rather like a Japanese formal garden. Nature manipulated to be more natural than the real thing, if you will.'

'I'm afraid you've lost me,' Gennaro said, looking annoyed.

'I'm sure the tour will make everything clear,' Malcolm said.

The Tour

'This way, everybody, this way,' Ed Regis said. By his side, a woman was passing out pith helmets with 'Jurassic Park' labeled on the headband, and a little blue dinosaur logo.

A line of Toyota Land Cruisers came out of an underground garage beneath the visitor center. Each car pulled up, driverless and silent. Two black men in safari uniforms were opening the doors for passengers.

'Two to four passengers to a car, please, two to four passengers to a car,' a recorded voice was saying. 'Children under ten must be accompanied by an adult. Two to four passengers to a car, please . . .'

Tim watched as Grant, Sattler, and Malcolm got into the first Land Cruiser with the lawyer, Gennaro. Tim looked over at Lex, who was standing pounding her fist into her glove.

Tim pointed to the first car and said, 'Can I go with them?'

'I'm afraid they have things to discuss,' Ed Regis said. 'Technical things.'

'I'm interested in technical things,' Tim said. 'I'd rather go with them.'

'Well, you'll be able to hear what they're saying,' Regis said. 'We'll have a radio open between the cars.'

The second car came. Tim and Lex got in, and Ed Regis followed. 'These are electric cars,' Regis said. 'Guided by a cable in the roadway.'

Tim was glad he was sitting in the front seat, because mounted in the dashboard were two computer screens and a box that looked to him like a CD-ROM; that was a laser disk player controlled by a computer. There was also a portable walkie-talkie and some kind of a radio transmitter. There were two antennas on the roof, and some odd goggles in the map pocket.

The black men shut the doors of the Land Cruiser. The car started off with an electric hum. Up ahead, the three scientists and Gennaro were talking and pointing, clearly excited. Ed Regis said, 'Let's hear what they are saying.' An intercom clicked.

'I don't know what the hell you think you're doing here,' Gennaro said, over the intercom. He sounded very angry.

'I know quite well why I'm here,' Malcolm said.

'You're here to advise me, not play goddamned mind games. I've got five percent of this company and a responsibility to make sure that Hammond has done his job responsibly. Now you goddamn come here –'

Ed Regis pressed the intercom button and said, 'In keeping with the nonpolluting policies of Jurassic Park, these lightweight electric Land Cruisers have been specially built for us by Toyota in Osaka. Eventually we hope to drive among the animals – just as they do in African game parks – but, for now, sit back and enjoy the self-guided tour.' He paused. 'And, by the way, we can hear you back here.'

'Oh Christ,' Gennaro said. 'I have to be able to speak freely. I didn't ask for these damned kids to come –'

Ed Regis smiled blandly and pushed a button. 'We'll just begin the show, shall we?' They heard a fanfare of trumpets, and the interior screens flashed WELCOME TO JURASSIC PARK. A sonorous voice said, 'Welcome to Jurassic Park. You are now entering the lost world of the prehistoric past, a world of mighty creatures long gone from the face of the earth, which you are privileged to see for the first time.'

'That's Richard Kiley,' Ed Regis said. 'We spared no expense.'

The Land Cruiser passed through a grove of low, stumpy palm trees. Richard Kiley was saying, 'Notice, first of all, the remarkable plant life that surrounds you. Those trees to your left and right are called cycads, the prehistoric predecessors of palm trees. Cycads were a favorite food of the dinosaurs. You can also see bennettitaleans, and ginkgoes. The world of the dinosaur included more modern plants, such as pine and fir trees, and swamp cypresses. You will see these as well.'

The Land Cruiser moved slowly among the foliage. Tim noticed the fences and retaining walls were screened by greenery to heighten the illusion of moving through real jungle.

'We imagine the world of the dinosaurs,' said Richard Kiley's voice, 'as a world of huge vegetarians, eating their way through the giant swampy forests of the Jurassic and Cretaceous world, a hundred million years ago. But most dinosaurs were not as large as people think. The smallest dinosaurs were no bigger than a house cat, and the average dinosaur was about as big as a pony. We are first going to visit one of these average-size animals, called hypsilophodonts. If you look to your left, you may catch a glimpse of them now.'

They all looked to the left.

The Land Cruiser stopped on a low rise, where a break in the foliage provided a view to the east. They could see a sloping forested area which opened into a field of yellow grass that was about three feet high. There were no dinosaurs.

'Where are they?' Lex said.

Tim looked at the dashboard. The transmitter lights blinked and the CD-ROM whirred. Obviously the disk was being accessed by some automatic system. He guessed that the same motion sensors that tracked the animals also controlled the screens in the Land Cruiser. The screens now showed pictures of hypsilophodonts, and printed out data about them.

The voice said, 'Hypsilophodontids are the gazelles of the dinosaur world: small, quick animals that once roamed everywhere in the world, from England to Central Asia to North America. We think these dinosaurs were so successful because they had better jaws and teeth for chewing plants than their contemporaries did. In fact, the name "hypsilophodontid" means "high-ridge tooth," which refers to the characteristic self-sharpening teeth of these animals. You can see them in the plains directly ahead, and also perhaps in the branches of the trees.'

'In the *trees?*' Lex said. 'Dinosaurs in the trees?'

Tim was scanning with binoculars, too. 'To the right,' he said. 'Halfway up that big green trunk . . .'

In the dappled shadows of the tree a motionless, dark green animal about the size of a baboon stood on a branch. It looked like a lizard standing on its hind legs. It balanced itself with a long drooping tail.

'That's an othnielia,' Tim said.

'The small animals you see are called othnielia,' the voice said, 'in honor of the nineteenth-century dinosaur hunter Othniel Marsh of Yale.'

Tim spotted two more animals, on higher branches of the same tree. They were all about the same size. None of them were moving.

'Pretty boring,' Lex said. 'They're not doing anything.'

'The main herd of animals can be found in the grassy plain below you,' said the voice. 'We can rouse them with a simple mating call.' A loudspeaker by the fence gave a long nasal call, like the honking of geese.

From the field of grass directly to their left, six lizard heads poked up, one after another. The effect was comical, and Tim laughed.

The heads disappeared. The loudspeaker gave the call again, and once again the heads poked up – in exactly the same way, one after another. The fixed repetition of the behaviour was striking.

'Hypsilophodonts are not especially bright animals,' the voice explained. 'They have roughly the intelligence of a domestic cow.'

The heads were dull green, with a mottling of dark browns and blacks that extended down the slender necks. Judging from the size of the heads, Tim guessed their bodies were four feet long, about as large as deer.

Some of the hypsilophodonts were chewing, the jaws working. One reached up and scratched its head, with a five-fingered hand. The gesture gave the creature a pensive, thoughtful quality.

'If you see them scratching, that is because they have skin problems. The veterinary scientists here at Jurassic Park think it may be a fungus, or an allergy. But they're not sure yet. After all, these are the first dinosaurs in history ever to be studied alive.'

The electric motor of the car started, and there was a grinding of gears. At the unexpected sound, the herd of hypsilophodonts suddenly leapt into the air and bounded above the grass like kangaroos, showing their full bodies with massive hind limbs and long tails in the afternoon sunlight. In a few leaps, they were gone.

'Now that we've had a look at these fascinating herbivores, we will go on to some dinosaurs that are a little larger. Quite a bit larger, in fact.'

The Land Cruisers continued onward, moving south through Jurassic Park.

Control

'Gears are grinding,' John Arnold said, in the darkened control room. 'Have maintenance check the electric clutches on vehicles BB4 and BB5 when they come back.'

'Yes, Mr. Arnold,' replied the voice on the intercom.

'A minor detail,' Hammond said, walking in the room. Looking out, he could see the two Land Cruisers moving south through the park. Muldoon stood in the corner, silently watching.

Arnold pushed his chair back from the central console at the control panel. 'There are no minor details, Mr. Hammond,' he said, and he lit another cigarette. Nervous at most times, Arnold was especially edgy now. He was only too aware that this was the first time visitors had actually toured the park. In fact, Arnold's team didn't often go into the park. Harding, the vet, sometimes did. The animal handlers went to the individual feeding houses. But otherwise they watched the park from the control room. And now, with visitors out there, he worried about a hundred details.

John Arnold was a systems engineer who had worked on the Polaris submarine missile in the late 1960s, until he had his first child and the prospect of making weapons became too distasteful. Meanwhile, Disney had started to create amusement park rides of great technological sophistication, and they employed a lot of aerospace people. Arnold helped build Disney World in Orlando, and had gone on to implement major parks at Magic Mountain in California, Old Country in Virginia, and Astroworld in Houston.

His continuous employment at parks had eventually given him a somewhat skewed view of reality. Arnold contended, only half jokingly, that the entire world was increasingly described by the metaphor of the theme park. 'Paris is a theme park,' he once announced, after a vacation, 'although it's too expensive, and the park employees are unpleasant and sullen.'

For the past two years, Arnold's job had been to get Jurassic Park up and running. As an engineer, he was accustomed to long time schedules – he often referred to 'the September opening,' by which he meant September of the following year – and as the September opening approached, he was unhappy with the progress that had been made. He knew from experience that it sometimes took years to work the bugs out of a single park ride – let alone get a whole park running properly.

'You're just a worrier,' Hammond said.

'I don't think so,' Arnold said. 'You've got to realize that, from an engineering standpoint, Jurassic Park is by far the most ambitious theme park in history. Visitors will never think about it, but I do.'

He ticked the points off on his fingers.

'First, Jurassic Park has all the problems of any amusement park – ride maintenance, queue control, transportation, food handling, living accommodations, trash disposal, security.

'Second, we have all the problems of a major zoo – care of the animals; health and welfare; feeding and cleanliness; protection from insects, pests, allergies, and illnesses; maintenance of barriers; and all the rest.

'And, finally, we have the unprecedented problems of caring for a population of animals that no one has ever tried to maintain before.'

'Oh, it's not as bad as all that,' Hammond said.

'Yes, it is. You're just not here to see it,' Arnold said. 'The tyrannosaurs drink the lagoon water and sometimes get sick; we aren't sure why. The triceratops females kill each other in fights for dominance and have to be separated into groups smaller than six. We don't know why. The stegosaurs frequently get blisters on their tongues and diarrhea, for reasons no one yet understands, even though we've lost two. Hypsilophodonts get skin rashes. And the velociraptors –'

'Let's not start on the velociraptors,' Hammond said. 'I'm sick of hearing about the velociraptors. How they're the most vicious creatures anyone has ever seen.'

'They are,' Muldoon said, in a low voice. 'They should all be destroyed.'

'You wanted to fit them with radio collars,' Hammond said. 'And I agreed.'

'Yes. And they promptly chewed the collars off. But even if the raptors never get free,' Arnold said, 'I think we have to accept that Jurassic Park is inherently hazardous.'

'Oh *balls*,' Hammond said. 'Whose side are you on, anyway?'

'We now have fifteen species of extinct animals, and most of them are dangerous,' Arnold said. 'We've been forced to delay the Jungle River Ride because of the dilophosaurs; and the Pteratops Lodge in the aviary, because the pterodactyls are so unpredictable. These aren't engineering delays, Mr. Hammond. They're problems with control of the animals.'

'You've had plenty of engineering delays,' Hammond said. 'Don't blame it on the animals.'

'Yes, we have. In fact, it's all we could do to get the main attraction, Park Drive, working correctly, to get the CD-ROMs inside the cars to be controlled by the motion sensors. It's taken weeks of adjustment to get that working properly – and now the electric gearshifts on the cars are acting up! The gearshifts!'

'Let's keep it in perspective,' Hammond said. 'You get the engineering correct and the animals will fall into place. After all, they're trainable.'

From the beginning, this had been one of the core beliefs of the planners. The animals, however exotic, would fundamentally behave like animals in zoos anywhere. They would learn the regularities of their care, and they would respond.

'Meanwhile, how's the computer?' Hammond said. He glanced at Dennis Nedry, who was working at a terminal in the corner of the room. 'This damn computer has always been a headache.'

'We're getting there,' Nedry said.

'If you had done it right in the first place,' Hammond began, but Arnold put a restraining hand on his arm. Arnold knew there was no point in antagonizing Nedry while he was working.

'It's a large system,' Arnold said. 'There are bound to be glitches.'

In fact, the bug list now ran to more than 130 items, and included many odd aspects. For example:

The animal-feeding program reset itself every twelve hours, not every twenty-four hours, and would not record feedings on Sundays. As a result, the staff could not accurately measure how much the animals were eating.

The security system, which controlled all the security-card-operated doors, cut out whenever main power was lost, and did not come back on with auxiliary power. The security program only ran with main power.

The physical conservation program, intended to dim lights after 10:00 p.m., only worked on alternate days of the week.

The automated fecal analysis (called Auto Poop), designed to check for parasites in the animal stools, invariably recorded all specimens as having the parasite *Phagostomum venulosum*, although none did. The program then automatically dispensed medication into the animals' food. If the handlers dumped the medicine out of the hoppers to prevent its being dispensed, an alarm sounded which could not be turned off.

And so it went, page after page of errors.

When he had arrived, Dennis Nedry had been under the impression that he could make all the fixes himself over the weekend. He had paled when he saw the full listing. Now he was calling his office in Cambridge, telling his staff programmers they were going to have to cancel their weekend plans and work overtime until Monday. And he had told John Arnold that he would need to use every telephone link between Isla Nublar and the mainland just to transfer program data back and forth to his programmers.

While Nedry worked, Arnold punched up a new window in his own monitor. It allowed him to see what Nedry was doing at the corner console. Not that he didn't trust Nedry. But Arnold just liked to know what was going on.

He looked at the graphics display on his right-hand console, which showed the progress of the electric Land Cruisers. They were following the river, just north of the aviary, and the ornithischian paddock.

'If you look to your left,' said the voice, 'you will see the dome of the Jurassic Park aviary, which is not yet finished for visitors.' Tim saw sunlight glinting off aluminum struts in the distance. 'And directly below is our Mesozoic jungle river – where, if you are lucky, you just may catch a glimpse of a very rare carnivore. Keep your eyes peeled, everyone!'

Inside the Land Cruiser, the screens showed a bird-like head topped with a flaming red crest. But everyone in Tim's car was looking out the windows. The car was driving along a high ridge, overlooking a fast-moving river below. The river was almost enclosed by dense foliage on both sides.

'There they are now,' said the voice. 'The animals you see are called dilophosaurs.'

Despite what the recording said, Tim saw only one. The dilophosaur crouched on its hind legs by the river, drinking. It was built on the basic carnivore pattern, with a heavy tail, strong hind limbs, and a long neck. Its ten-foot-tall body was spotted yellow and black, like a leopard.

But it was the head that held Tim's attention. Two broad curving crests ran along the top of the head from the eyes to the nose. The crests met in the center, making a V shape above the dinosaur's head. The crests had red and black stripes, reminiscent of a parrot or toucan. The animal gave a soft hooting cry, like an owl.

'They're pretty,' Lex said.

'*Dilophosaurus*,' the tape said, 'is one of the earliest carnivorous dinosaurs. Scientists thought their jaw muscles were too weak to kill prey, and imagined they were primarily scavengers. But now we know they are poisonous.'

'Hey.' Tim grinned. 'All *right*.'

Again the distinctive hooting call of the dilophosaur drifted across the afternoon air toward them.

Lex shifted uneasily in her seat. 'Are they really poisonous, Mr. Regis?'

'Don't worry about it,' Ed Regis said.

'But are they?'

'Well, yes, Lex.'

'Along with such living reptiles as Gila monsters and rattlesnakes, *Dilophosaurus* secretes a hematotoxin from glands in its mouth. Unconsciousness follows within minutes of a bite. The dinosaur will then finish the victim off at its leisure – making *Dilophosaurus* a beautiful but deadly addition to the animals you see here at Jurassic Park.'

The Land Cruiser turned a corner, leaving the river behind. Tim looked back, hoping for a last glimpse of the dilophosaur. This was amazing! Poisonous dinosaurs! He wished he could stop the car, but everything was automatic. He bet Dr. Grant wanted to stop the car, too.

'If you look on the bluff to the right, you'll see Les Gigantes, the site of our superb three-star dining room. Chef Alain Richard hails from the world-famous Le Beaumanière in France. Make your reservations by dialing four from your hotel rooms.'

Tim looked up on the bluff, and saw nothing.

'Not for a while, though,' Ed Regis said. 'The restaurant won't even start construction until November.'

'Continuing on our prehistoric safari, we come next to the herbivores of the ornithischian group. If you look to your right, you can probably see them now.'

Tim saw two animals, standing motionless in the shade of a large tree. Triceratops: the size and gray color of an elephant, with the truculent stance of a rhino. The horns above each eye curved five feet into the air, looking almost like inverted elephant tusks. A third, rhino-like horn was located near the nose. And they had the beaky snout of a rhino.

'Unlike other dinosaurs,' the voice said, '*Triceratops serratus* can't see well. They're nearsighted, like the rhinos of today, and they tend to be surprised by moving objects. They'd charge our car if they were close enough to see it! But relax, folks – we're safe enough here.

'Triceratops have a fan-shaped crest behind their heads. It's made of solid bone, and it's very strong. These animals weigh about seven tons each. Despite their appearance, they are actually quite docile. They know their handlers, and they'll allow themselves to be petted. They particularly like to be scratched in the hindquarters.'

'Why don't they move?' Lex said. She rolled down her window. 'Hey! Stupid dinosaur! Move!'

'Don't bother the animals, Lex,' Ed Regis said.

'Why? It's stupid. They just sit there like a picture in a book,' Lex said.

The voice was saying, '– easygoing monsters from a bygone world stand in sharp contrast to what we will see next. The most famous predator in the history of the world: the mighty tyrant lizard, known as *Tyrannosaurus rex*.'

'Good, *Tyrannosaurus rex*,' Tim said.

'I hope he's better than these bozos,' Lex said, turning away from the triceratops.

The Land Cruiser rumbled forward.

Big Rex

'The mighty tyrannosaurs arose late in dinosaur history. Dinosaurs ruled the earth for a hundred and twenty million years, but there were tyrannosaurs for only the last fifteen million years of that period.'

The Land Cruisers had stopped at the rise of a hill. They overlooked a forested area sloping down to the edge of the lagoon. The sun was falling to the west, sinking into a misty horizon. The whole landscape of Jurassic Park was bathed in soft light, with lengthening shadows. The surface of the lagoon rippled in pink crescents. Farther south, they saw the graceful necks of the camarasaurs, standing at the water's edge, their bodies mirrored in the moving surface. It was quiet, except for the soft drone of cicadas. As they stared out at that landscape, it was possible to believe that they had really been transported millions of years back in time to a vanished world.

'It works, doesn't it?' they heard Ed Regis say, over the intercom. 'I like to come here sometimes, in the evening. And just sit.'

Grant was unimpressed. 'Where is T-rex?'

'Good question. You often see the little one down in the lagoon. The lagoon's stocked, so we have fish in there. The little one has learned to catch the fish. Interesting how he does it. He doesn't use his hands, but he ducks his whole head under the water. Like a bird.'

'The little one?'

'The little T-rex. He's a juvenile, two years old, and about a third grown now. Stands eight feet high, weighs a ton and a half. The other one's a full-grown tyrannosaur. But I don't see him at the moment.'

'Maybe he's down hunting the camarasaurs,' Grant said.

Regis laughed, his voice tinny over the radio. 'He would if he could, believe me. Sometimes he stands by the lagoon and stares at those animals, and wiggles those little forearms of his in frustration. But the T-rex territory is completely enclosed with trenches and fences. They're disguised from view, but believe me, he can't go anywhere.'

'Then where is he?'

'Hiding,' Regis said. 'He's a little shy.'

'Shy?' Malcolm said. 'Tyrannosaurus rex is *shy*?'

'Well, he conceals himself as a general rule. You almost never see him out in the open, especially in daylight.'

'Why is that?'

'We think it's because he has sensitive skin and sunburns easily.'

Malcolm began to laugh.

Grant sighed. 'You're destroying a lot of illusions.'

'I don't think you'll be disappointed,' Regis said. 'Just wait.'

They heard a soft bleating sound. In the center of a field, a small cage rose up into view, lifted on hydraulics from underground. The cage bars slid down, and the goat remained tethered in the center of the field, bleating plaintively.

'Any minute now,' Regis said again.

They stared out the window.

'Look at them,' Hammond said, watching the control room monitor. 'Leaning out of the windows, so eager. They can't wait to see it. They have come for the danger.'

'That's what I'm afraid of,' Muldoon said. He twirled the keys on his finger and watched the Land Cruisers tensely. This was the first time that visitors had toured Jurassic Park, and Muldoon shared Arnold's apprehension.

Robert Muldoon was a big man, fifty years old, with a steel-gray mustache and deep blue eyes. Raised in Kenya, he had spent most of his life as a guide for African big-game hunters, as had his father before him. But since 1980, he had worked principally for conservation groups and zoo designers as a wildlife consultant. He had become well known; an article in the London Sunday *Times* had said, 'What Robert Trent Jones is to golf courses, Robert Muldoon is to zoos: a designer of unsurpassed knowledge and skill.'

In 1986, he had done some work for a San Francisco company that was building a private wildlife park on an island in North America. Muldoon had laid out the boundaries for different animals, defining space and habitat requirements for lions, elephants, zebras, and hippos. Identifying which animals could be kept together, and which had to be separated. At the time, it had been a fairly routine job. He had been more interested in an Indian park called Tiger World in southern Kashmir.

Then, a year ago, he was offered a job as game warden of Jurassic Park. It coincided with a desire to leave Africa; the salary was excellent; Muldoon had taken it on for a year. He was astonished to discover the park was really a collection of genetically engineered prehistoric animals.

It was of course interesting work, but during his years in Africa,

Muldoon had developed an unblinking view of animals – an unromantic view – that frequently set him at odds with the Jurassic Park management in California, particularly the little martinet standing beside him in the control room. In Muldoon's opinion, cloning dinosaurs in a laboratory was one thing. Maintaining them in the wild was quite another.

It was Muldoon's view that some dinosaurs were too dangerous to be kept in a park setting. In part, the danger existed because they still knew so little about the animals. For example, nobody even suspected the dilophosaurs were poisonous until they were observed hunting indigenous rats on the island – biting the rodents and then stepping back, to wait for them to die. And even then nobody suspected the dilophosaurs could spit until one of the handlers was almost blinded by spitting venom.

After that, Hammond had agreed to study dilophosaur venom, which was found to contain seven different toxic enzymes. It was also discovered that the dilophosaurs could spit a distance of fifty feet. Since this raised the possibility that a guest in a car might be blinded, management decided to remove the poison sacs. The vets had tried twice, on two different animals, without success. No one knew where the poison was being secreted. And no one would ever know until an autopsy was performed on a dilophosaur – and management would not allow one to be killed.

Muldoon worried even more about the velociraptors. They were instinctive hunters, and they never passed up prey. They killed even when they weren't hungry. They killed for the pleasure of killing. They were swift: strong runners and astonishing jumpers. They had lethal claws on all four limbs; one swipe of a forearm would disembowel a man, spilling his guts out. And they had powerful tearing jaws that ripped flesh instead of biting it. They were far more intelligent than the other dinosaurs, and they seemed to be natural cage-breakers.

Every zoo expert knew that certain animals were especially likely to get free of their cages. Some, like monkeys and elephants, could undo cage doors. Others, like wild pigs, were unusually intelligent and could lift gate fasteners with their snouts. But who would suspect that the giant armadillo was a notorious cage-breaker? Or the moose? Yet a moose was almost as skillful with its snout as an elephant with its trunk. Moose were always getting free; they had a talent for it.

And so did velociraptors.

Raptors were at least as intelligent as chimpanzees. And, like chimpanzees, they had agile hands that enabled them to open doors and manipulate objects. They could escape with ease. And when, as

Muldoon had feared, one of them finally escaped, it killed two construction workers and maimed a third before being recaptured. After that episode, the visitor lodge had been reworked with heavy barred gates, a high perimeter fence, and tempered-glass windows. And the raptor holding pen was rebuilt with electronic sensors to warn of another impending escape.

Muldoon wanted guns as well. And he wanted shoulder-mounted TOW-missile launchers. Hunters knew how difficult it was to bring down a four-ton African elephant – and some of the dinosaurs weighed ten times as much. Management was horrified, insisting there be no guns anywhere on the island. When Muldoon threatened to quit, and to take his story to the press, a compromise was reached. In the end, two specially built laserguided missile launchers were kept in a locked room in the basement. Only Muldoon had keys to the room.

Those were the keys Muldoon was twirling now.

'I'm going downstairs,' he said.

Arnold, watching the control screens, nodded. The two Land Cruisers sat at the top of the hill, waiting for the T-rex to appear.

'Hey,' Dennis Nedry called, from the far console. 'As long as you're up, get me a Coke, okay?'

Grant waited in the car, watching quietly. The bleating of the goat became louder, more insistent. The goat tugged frantically at its tether, racing back and forth. Over the radio, Grant heard Lex say in alarm, 'What's going to happen to the goat? Is she going to eat the goat?'

'I think so,' someone said to her, and then Ellie turned the radio down. Then they smelled the odor, a garbage stench of putrefaction and decay that drifted up the hillside toward them.

Grant whispered, 'He's here.'

'She,' Malcolm said.

The goat was tethered in the center of the field, thirty yards from the nearest trees. The dinosaur must be somewhere among the trees, but for a moment Grant could see nothing at all. Then he realized he was looking too low: the animal's head stood twenty feet above the ground, half concealed among the upper branches of the palm trees.

Malcolm whispered, 'Oh, *my God*. . . . She's as large as a bloody building. . . .'

Grant stared at the enormous square head, five feet long, mottled reddish brown, with huge jaws and fangs. The tyrannosaur's jaws worked once, opening and closing. But the huge animal did not emerge from hiding.

Malcolm whispered: 'How long will it wait?'

'Maybe three or four minutes. Maybe –'

The tyrannosaur sprang silently forward, fully revealing her enormous body. In four bounding steps she covered the distance to the goat, bent down, and bit it through the neck. The bleating stopped. There was silence.

Poised over her kill, the tyrannosaur became suddenly hesitant. Her massive head turned on the muscular neck, looking in all directions. She stared fixedly at the Land Cruiser, high above on the hill.

Malcolm whispered, 'Can she see us?'

'Oh yes,' Regis said, on the intercom. 'Let's see if she's going to eat here in front of us, or if she's going to drag the prey away.'

The tyrannosaur bent down, and sniffed the carcass of the goat. A bird chirped: her head snapped up, alert, watchful. She looked back and forth, scanning in small jerking shifts.

'Like a bird,' Ellie said.

Still the tyrannosaur hesitated. 'What is she afraid of?' Malcolm whispered.

'Probably another tyrannosaur,' Grant whispered. Big carnivores like lions and tigers often became cautious after a kill, behaving as if suddenly exposed. Nineteenth-century zoologists imagined the animals felt guilty for what they had done. But contemporary scientists documented the effort behind a kill – hours of patient stalking before the final lunge – as well as the frequency of failure. The idea of 'nature, red in tooth and claw' was wrong; most often the prey got away. When a carnivore finally brought down an animal, it was watchful for another predator, who might attack it and steal its prize. Thus this tyrannosaur was probably fearful of another tyrannosaur.

The huge animal bent over the goat again. One great hind limb held the carcass in place as the jaws began to tear the flesh.

'She's going to stay,' Regis whispered. 'Excellent.'

The tyrannosaur lifted her head again, ragged chunks of bleeding flesh in her jaws. She stared at the Land Cruiser. She began to chew. They heard the sickening crunch of bones.

'Ewww,' Lex said, over the intercom. 'That's disgusting.'

And then, as if caution had finally gotten the better of her, the tyrannosaur lifted the remains of the goat in her jaws and carried it silently back among the trees.

'Ladies and gentlemen, *Tyrannosaurus rex*,' the tape said. The Land Cruisers started up, and moved silently off, through the foliage.

Malcolm sat back in his seat. 'Fantastic,' he said.

Gennaro wiped his forehead. He looked pale.

Control

Henry Wu came into the control room to find everyone sitting in the dark, listening to the voices on the radio.

'– Jesus, if an animal like that gets out,' Gennaro was saying, his voice tinny on the speaker, 'there'd be no stopping it.'

'No stopping it, no . . .'

'Huge, with no natural enemies . . .'

'My God, think of it . . .'

In the control room, Hammond said, 'Damn those people. They are so *negative*.'

Wu said, 'They're still going on about an animal escaping? I don't understand. They must have seen by now that we have everything under control. We've engineered the animals and engineered the resort. . . .' He shrugged.

It was Wu's deepest perception that the park was fundamentally sound, as he believed his paleo-DNA was fundamentally sound. Whatever problems might arise in the DNA were essentially point-problems in the code, causing a specific problem in the phenotype: an enzyme that didn't switch on, or a protein that didn't fold. Whatever the difficulty, it was always solved with a relatively minor adjustment in the next version.

Similarly, he knew that Jurassic Park's problems were not fundamental problems. They were not control problems. Nothing as basic, or as serious, as the possibility of an animal escaping. Wu found it offensive to think that anyone would believe him capable of contributing to a system where such a thing could happen.

'It's that Malcolm,' Hammond said darkly. 'He's behind it all. He was against us from the start, you know. He's got his theory that complex systems can't be controlled and nature can't be imitated. I don't know what his problem is. Hell, we're just making a zoo here. World's full of 'em, and they all work fine. But he's going to prove his theory or die trying. I just hope he doesn't panic Gennaro into trying to shut the park down.'

Wu said, 'Can he do that?'

'No,' Hammond said. 'But he can try. He can try and frighten the

Japanese investors, and get them to withdraw funds. Or he can make a stink with the San José government. He can make trouble.'

Arnold stubbed out his cigarette. 'Let's wait and see what happens,' he said. 'We believe in the park. Let's see how it plays out.'

Muldoon got off the elevator, nodded to the ground-floor guard, and went downstairs to the basement. He flicked on the lights. The basement was filled with two dozen Land Cruisers, arranged in neat rows. These were the electric cars that would eventually form an endless loop, touring the park, returning to the visitor center.

In the corner was a Jeep with a red stripe, one of two gasoline-powered vehicles – Harding, the vet, had taken the other that morning – which could go anywhere in the park, even among the animals. The Jeeps were painted with a diagonal red stripe because for some reason it discouraged the triceratops from charging the car.

Muldoon moved past the Jeep, toward the back. The steel door to the armaments room was unmarked. He unlocked it with his key, and swung the heavy door wide. Gun racks lined the interior. He pulled out a Randler Shoulder Launcher and a case of canisters. He tucked two gray rockets under his other arm.

After locking the door behind him, he put the gun into the back seat of the Jeep. As he left the garage, he heard the distant rumble of thunder.

'Looks like rain,' Ed Regis said, glancing up at the sky.

The Land Cruisers had stopped again, near the sauropod swamp. A large herd of apatosaurs was grazing at the edge of the lagoon, eating the leaves of the upper branches of the palm trees. In the same area were several duckbilled hadrosaurs, which in comparison looked much smaller.

Of course, Tim knew the hadrosaurs weren't really small. It was only that the apatosaurs were so much larger. Their tiny heads reached fifty feet into the air, extending out on their long necks.

'The big animals you see are commonly called *Brontosaurus*,' the recording said, 'but they are actually *Apatosaurus*. They weigh more than thirty tons. That means a single animal is as big as a whole herd of modern elephants. And you may notice that their preferred area, alongside the lagoon, is not swampy. Despite what the books say, brontosaurs avoid swamps. They prefer dry land.'

'*Brontosaurus* is the biggest dinosaur, Lex,' Ed Regis said. Tim didn't bother to contradict him. Actually, *Brachiosaurus* was three times as large. And some people thought *Ultrasaurus* and *Seismosaurus* were even larger than *Brachiosaurus*. *Seismosaurus* might have weighed a hundred tons!

Alongside the apatosaurs, the smaller hadrosaurs stood on their hind legs to get at foliage. They moved gracefully for such large creatures. Several infant hadrosaurs scampered around the adults, eating the leaves that dropped from the mouths of the larger animals.

'The dinosaurs of Jurassic Park don't breed,' the recording said. 'The young animals you see were introduced a few months ago, already hatched. But the adults nurture them anyway.'

There was the rolling growl of thunder. The sky was darker, lower, and menacing.

'Yeah, looks like rain, all right,' Ed Regis said.

The car started forward, and Tim looked back at the hadrosaurs. Suddenly, off to one side, he saw a pale yellow animal moving quickly. There were brownish stripes on its back. He recognized it instantly. 'Hey!' he shouted. 'Stop the car!'

'What is it?' Ed Regis said.

'Quick! *Stop the car!*'

'We move on now to see the last of our great prehistoric animals, the stegosaurs,' the recorded voice said.

'What's the matter, Tim?'

'I saw one! I saw one in the field out there!'

'Saw what?'

'A *raptor!* In that field!'

'The stegosaurs are a mid-Jurassic animal, evolving about a hundred and seventy million years ago,' the recording said. 'Several of these remarkable herbivores live here at Jurassic Park.'

'Oh, I don't think so, Tim,' Ed Regis said. 'Not a raptor.'

'I did! *Stop the car!*'

There was a babble on the intercom, as the news was relayed to Grant and Malcolm. 'Tim says he saw a raptor.'

'Where?'

'Back at the field.'

'Let's go back and look.'

'We can't go back,' Ed Regis said. 'We can only go forward. The cars are programmed.'

'We can't go back?' Grant said.

'No,' Regis said. 'Sorry. You see, it's kind of a ride –'

'Tim, this is Professor Malcolm,' said a voice cutting in on the intercom. 'I have just one question for you about this raptor. How old would you say it was?'

'Older than the baby we saw today,' Tim said. 'And younger than the big adults in the pen. The adults were six feet tall. This one was about half that size.'

'That's fine,' Malcolm said.

'I only saw it for a second,' Tim said.

'I'm sure it wasn't a raptor,' Ed Regis said. 'It couldn't possibly be a raptor. Must have been one of the othys. They're always jumping their fences. We have a hell of a time with them.'

'I know I saw a raptor,' Tim said.

'I'm hungry,' Lex said. She was starting to whine.

In the control room, Arnold turned to Wu. 'What do you think the kid saw?'

'I think it must have been an othy.'

Arnold nodded. 'We have trouble tracking othys, because they spend so much time in the trees.' The othys were an exception to the usual minute-to-minute control they maintained over the animals. The computers were constantly losing and picking up the othys, as they went into the trees and then came down again.

'What burns me,' Hammond said, 'is that we have made this wonderful park, this *fantastic* park, and our very first visitors are going through it like accountants, just looking for problems. They aren't experiencing the wonder of it at all.'

'That's their problem,' Arnold said. 'We can't make them experience wonder.' The intercom clicked, and Arnold heard a voice drawl, 'Ah, John, this is the *Anne B* over at the dock. We haven't finished offloading, but I'm looking at that storm pattern south of us. I'd rather not be tied up here if this chop gets any worse.'

Arnold turned to the monitor showing the cargo vessel, which was moored at the dock on the east side of the island. He pressed the radio button. 'How much left to do, Jim?'

'Just the three final equipment containers. I haven't checked the manifest, but I assume you can wait another two weeks for it. We're not well berthed here, you know, and we are one hundred miles offshore.'

'You requesting permission to leave?'

'Yes, John.'

'I want that equipment,' Hammond said. 'That's equipment for the labs. We need it.'

'Yes,' Arnold said. 'But you didn't want to put money into a storm barrier to protect the pier. So we don't have a good harbor. If the storm gets worse, the ship will be pounded against the dock. I've seen ships lost that way. Then you've got all the other expenses, replacement of the vessel plus salvage to clear your dock . . . and you can't use your dock until you do . . .'

Hammond gave a dismissing wave. 'Get them out of there.'

'Permission to leave, *Anne B*,' Arnold said, into the radio.

'See you in two weeks,' the voice said.

On the video monitor, they saw the crew on the decks, casting off the lines. Arnold turned back to the main console bank. He saw the Land Cruisers moving through fields of steam.

'Where are they now?' Hammond said.

'It looks like the south fields,' Arnold said. The southern end of the island had more volcanic activity than the north. 'That means they should be almost to the stegos. I'm sure they'll stop and see what Harding is doing.'

Stegosaur

As the Land Cruiser came to a stop, Ellie Sattler stared through the plumes of steam at the stegosaurus. It was standing quietly, not moving. A Jeep with a red stripe was parked alongside it.

'I have to admit, that's a funny-looking animal,' Malcolm said.

The stegosaurus was twenty feet long, with a huge bulky body and vertical armor plates along its back. The tail had dangerous-looking three-foot spikes. But the neck tapered to an absurdly small head with a stupid gaze, like a very dumb horse.

As they watched, a man walked around from behind the animal. 'That's our vet, Dr. Harding,' Regis said, over the radio. 'He's anesthetized the stego, which is why it's not moving. It's sick.'

Grant was already getting out of the car, hurrying toward the motionless stegosaur. Ellie got out and looked back as the second Land Cruiser pulled up and the two kids jumped out. 'What's he sick with?' Tim said.

'They're not sure,' Ellie said.

The great leathery plates along the stegosaur's spine drooped slightly. It breathed slowly, laboriously, making a wet sound with each breath.

'Is it contagious?' Lex said.

They walked toward the tiny head of the animal, where Grant and the vet were on their knees, peering into the stegosaur's mouth.

Lex wrinkled her nose. 'This thing sure is big,' she said. 'And *smelly.*'

'Yes, it is.' Ellie had already noticed the stegosaur had a peculiar odor, like rotting fish. It reminded her of something she knew, but couldn't quite place. In any case, she had never smelled a stegosaur before. Maybe this was its characteristic odor. But she had her doubts. Most herbivores did not have a strong smell. Nor did their droppings. It was reserved for the meat-eaters to develop a real stink.

'Is that because it's sick?' Lex asked.

'Maybe. And don't forget the vet's tranquilized it.'

'Ellie, have a look at this tongue,' Grant said.

The dark purple tongue drooped limply from the animal's mouth.

The vet shone a light on it so she could see the very fine silvery blisters. 'Microvesicles,' Ellie said. 'Interesting.'

'We've had a difficult time with these stegos,' the vet said. 'They're always getting sick.'

'What are the symptoms?' Ellie asked. She scratched the tongue with her fingernail. A clear liquid exuded from the broken blisters.

'Ugh,' Lex said.

'Imbalance, disorientation, labored breathing, and massive diarrhea,' Harding said. 'Seems to happen about once every six weeks or so.'

'They feed continuously?'

'Oh yes,' Harding said. 'Animal this size has to take in a minimum of five or six hundred pounds of plant matter daily just to keep going. They're constant foragers.'

'Then it's not likely to be poisoning from a plant,' Ellie said. Constant browsers would be constantly sick if they were eating a toxic plant. Not every six weeks.

'Exactly,' the vet said.

'May I?' Ellie asked. She took the flashlight from the vet. 'You have pupillary effects from the tranquilizer?' she said, shining the light in the stegosaur's eye.

'Yes. There's a miotic effect, pupils are constricted.'

'But these pupils are dilated,' she said.

Harding looked. There was no question: the stegosaur's pupil was dilated, and did not contract when light shone on it. 'I'll be damned,' he said. 'That's a pharmacological effect.'

'Yes.' Ellie got back on her feet and looked around. 'What is the animal's range?'

'About five square miles.'

'In this general area?' she asked. They were in an open meadow, with scattered rocky outcrops, and intermittent plumes of steam rising from the ground. It was late afternoon, and the sky was pink beneath the lowering gray clouds.

'Their range is mostly north and east of here,' Harding said. 'But when they get sick, they're usually somewhere around this particular area.'

It was an interesting puzzle, she thought. How to explain the periodicity of the poisoning? She pointed across the field. 'You see those low, delicate-looking bushes?'

'West Indian lilac.' Harding nodded. 'We know it's toxic. The animals don't eat it.'

'You're sure?'

'Yes. We monitor them on video, and I've checked droppings just to be certain. The stegos never eat the lilac bushes.'

Melia azedarach, called chinaberry or West Indian lilac, contained a number of toxic alkaloids. The Chinese used the plant as a fish poison.

'They don't eat it,' the vet said.

'Interesting,' Ellie said. 'Because otherwise I would have said that this animal shows all the classic signs of *Melia* toxicity: stupor, blistering of the mucous membranes, and pupillary dilatation.' She set off toward the field to examine the plants more closely, her body bent over the ground. 'You're right,' she said. 'Plants are healthy, no sign of being eaten. None at all.'

'And there's the six-week interval,' the vet reminded her.

'The stegosaurs come here how often?'

'About once a week,' he said. 'Stegos make a slow loop through their home-range territory, feeding as they go. They complete the loop in about a week.'

'But they're only sick once every six weeks.'

'Correct,' Harding said.

'This is boring,' Lex said.

'Ssshh,' Tim said. 'Dr. Sattler's trying to think.'

'Unsuccessfully,' Ellie said, walking farther out into the field.

Behind her, she heard Lex saying, 'Anybody want to play a little pickle?'

Ellie stared at the ground. The field was rocky in many places. She could hear the sound of the surf, somewhere to the left. There were berries among the rocks. Perhaps the animals were just eating berries. But that didn't make sense. West Indian lilac berries were terribly bitter.

'Finding anything?' Grant said, coming up to join her.

Ellie sighed. 'Just rocks,' she said. 'We must be near the beach, because all these rocks are smooth. And they're in funny little piles.'

'Funny little piles?' Grant said.

'All over. There's one pile right there.' She pointed.

As soon as she did, she realized what she was looking at. The rocks were worn, but it had nothing to do with the ocean. These rocks were heaped in small piles, almost as if they had been thrown down that way.

They were piles of gizzard stones.

Many birds and crocodiles swallowed small stones, which collected in a muscular pouch in the digestive tract, called the gizzard. Squeezed by the muscles of the gizzard, the stones helped crush tough plant food before it reached the stomach, and thus aided digestion. Some scientists thought dinosaurs also had gizzard stones. For one thing, dinosaur teeth were too small, and too little worn, to have been used for chewing food. It was presumed that dinosaurs swallowed their food whole and let the gizzard stones break down the plant fibers. And some skeletons had been found with an associated pile of small stones in the abdominal area. But it had never been verified, and –

'Gizzard stones,' Grant said.

'I think so, yes. They swallow these stones, and after a few weeks the stones are worn smooth, so they regurgitate them, leaving this little pile, and swallow fresh stones. And when they do, they swallow berries as well. And get sick.'

'I'll be damned,' Grant said. 'I'm sure you're right.'

He looked at the pile of stones, brushing through them with his hand, following the instinct of a paleontologist.

Then he stopped.

'Ellie,' he said. 'Take a look at this.'

'Put it there, babe! Right in the old mitt!' Lex cried, and Gennaro threw the ball to her.

She threw it back so hard that his hand stung. 'Take it easy! I don't have a glove!'

'You wimp!' she said contemptuously.

Annoyed, he fired the ball at her, and heard it *smack*! in the leather. 'Now that's more like it,' she said.

Standing by the dinosaur, Gennaro continued to play catch as he talked to Malcolm. 'How does this sick dinosaur fit into your theory?'

'It's predicted,' Malcolm said.

Gennaro shook his head. 'Is anything *not* predicted by your theory?'

'Look,' Malcolm said. 'It's nothing to do with me. It's chaos theory. But I notice nobody is willing to listen to the consequences of the mathematics. Because they imply very large consequences for human life. Much larger than Heisenberg's principle or Gödel's theorem, which everybody rattles on about. Those are actually rather academic considerations. Philosophical considerations. But chaos theory concerns everyday life. Do you know why computers were first built?'

'No,' Gennaro said.

'Burn it in there,' Lex yelled.

'Computers were built in the late 1940s because mathematicians like John von Neumann thought that if you had a computer – a machine to handle a lot of variables simultaneously – you would be able to predict the weather. Weather would finally fall to human understanding. And men believed that dream for the next forty years. They believed that prediction was just a function of keeping track of things. If you knew enough, you could predict anything. That's been a cherished scientific belief since Newton.'

'And?'

'Chaos theory throws it right out the window. It says that you can never predict certain phenomena at all. You can never predict the weather more than a few days away. All the money that has been spent on long-range forecasting – about half a billion dollars in the last few decades – is money wasted. It's a fool's errand. It's as pointless as trying to turn lead into gold. We look back at the alchemists and laugh at what they were trying to do, but future generations will laugh at us the same way. We've tried the impossible – and spent a lot of money doing it. Because in fact there are great categories of phenomena that are inherently unpredictable.'

'Chaos says that?'

'Yes, and it is astonishing how few people care to hear it,' Malcolm said. 'I gave all this information to Hammond long before he broke ground on this place. You're going to engineer a bunch of prehistoric animals and set them on an island? Fine. A lovely dream. Charming. But it won't go as planned. It is inherently unpredictable, just as the weather is.'

'You told him this?' Gennaro said.

'Yes. I also told him where the deviations would occur. Obviously the fitness of the animals to the environment was one area. This stegosaur is a hundred million years old. It isn't adapted to our world. The air is different, the solar radiation is different, the land is different, the insects are different, the sounds are different, the vegetation is different. Everything is different. The oxygen content is decreased. This poor animal's like a human being at ten thousand feet altitude. Listen to him wheezing.'

'And the other areas?'

'Broadly speaking, the ability of the park to control the spread of life forms. Because the history of evolution is that life escapes all barriers. Life breaks free. Life expands to new territories. Painfully, perhaps even dangerously. But life finds a way.' Malcolm shook his head. 'I don't mean to be philosophical, but there it is.'

Gennaro looked over. Ellie and Grant were across the field, waving their arms and shouting.

'Did you get my Coke?' Dennis Nedry asked, as Muldoon came back into the control room.

Muldoon didn't bother to answer. He went directly to the monitor and looked at what was happening. Over the radio he heard Harding's voice saying, '– the stego – finally – handle on – now –'

'What's that about?' Muldoon said.

'They're down by the south point,' Arnold said. 'That's why they're breaking up a little. I'll switch them to another channel. But they found out what's wrong with the stegos. Eating some kind of berry.'

Hammond nodded. 'I knew we'd solve that sooner or later,' he said.

'It's not very impressive,' Gennaro said. He held the white fragment, no larger than a postage stamp, up on his fingertip in the fading light. 'You sure about this, Alan?'

'Absolutely sure,' Grant said. 'What gives it away is the patterning on the interior surface, the interior curve. Turn it over and you will notice a faint pattern of raised lines, making roughly triangular shapes.'

'Yes, I see them.'

'Well, I've dug out two eggs with patterns like that at my site in Montana.'

'You're saying this is a piece of dinosaur eggshell?'

'Absolutely,' Grant said.

Harding shook his head. 'These dinosaurs can't breed.'

'Evidently they can,' Gennaro said.

'That must be a bird egg,' Harding said. 'We have literally dozens of species on the island.'

Grant shook his head. 'Look at the curvature. The shell is almost flat. That's from a very big egg. And notice the thickness of the shell. Unless you have ostriches on this island, it's a dinosaur egg.'

'But they can't possibly breed,' Harding insisted. 'All the animals are female.'

'All I know,' Grant said, 'is that this is a dinosaur egg.'

Malcolm said, 'Can you tell the species?'

'Yes,' Grant said. 'It's a velociraptor egg.'

Control

'Absolutely absurd,' Hammond said in the control room, listening to the report over the radio. 'It must be a bird egg. That's all it *can* be.'

The radio crackled. He heard Malcolm's voice. 'Let's do a little test, shall we? Ask Mr. Arnold to run one of his computer tallies.'

'Now?'

'Yes, right now. I understand you can transmit it to the screen in Dr. Harding's car. Do that, too, will you?'

'No problem,' Arnold said. A moment later, the screen in the control room printed out:

Total Animals	238		
Species	**Expected**	**Found**	**Ver**
Tyrannosaurs	2	2	4.1
Maiasaurs	21	21	3.3
Stegosaurs	4	4	3.9
Triceratops	8	8	3.1
Procompsognathids	49	49	3.9
Othnielia	16	16	3.1
Velociraptors	8	8	3.0
Apatosaurs	17	17	3.1
Hadrosaurs	11	11	3.1
Dilophosaurs	7	7	4.3
Pterosaurs	6	6	4.3
Hypsilophodontids	33	33	2.9
Euoplocephalids	16	16	4.0
Styracosaurs	18	18	3.9
Callovosaurs	22	22	4.1
Total	**238**	**238**	

'I hope you're satisfied,' Hammond said. 'Are you receiving it down there on your screen?'

'We see it,' Malcolm said.

'Everything accounted for, as always.' He couldn't keep the satisfaction out of his voice.

'Now then,' Malcolm said. 'Can you have the computer search for a different number of animals?'

'Like what?' Arnold said.

'Try two hundred thirty-nine.'

'Just a minute,' Arnold said, frowning. A moment later the screen printed:

Total Animals	239		
Species	**Expected**	**Found**	**Ver**
Tyrannosaurs	2	2	4.1
Maiasaurs	21	21	3.3
Stegosaurs	4	4	3.9
Triceratops	8	8	3.1
Procompsognathids	49	50	??
Othnielia	16	16	3.1
Velociraptors	8	8	3.0
Apatosaurs	17	17	3.1
Hadrosaurs	11	11	3.1
Dilophosaurs	7	7	4.3
Pterosaurs	6	6	4.3
Hypsilophodontids	33	33	2.9
Euoplocephalids	16	16	4.0
Styracosaurs	18	18	3.9
Callovosaurs	22	22	4.1
Total	**238**	**239**	

Hammond sat forward. 'What the hell is *that?*'

'We picked up another compy.'

'From *where?*'

'I don't know!'

The radio crackled. 'Now, then: can you ask the computer to search for, let us say, three hundred animals?'

'What is he talking about?' Hammond said, his voice rising. 'Three hundred animals? What's he talking about?'

'Just a minute,' Arnold said. 'That'll take a few minutes.' He punched buttons on the screen. The first line of the totals appeared:

Total Animals	239

'I don't understand what he's driving at,' Hammond said.

'I'm afraid I do,' Arnold said. He watched the screen. The numbers on the first line were clicking:

Total Animals	244

'Two hundred forty-four?' Hammond said. 'What's going on?'

'The computer is counting the animals in the park,' Wu said. '*All* the animals.'

'I thought that's what it always did.' He spun. 'Nedry! Have you screwed up again?'

'No,' Nedry said, looking up from his console. 'Computer allows the operator to enter an expected number of animals, in order to make the counting process faster. But it's a convenience, not a flaw.'

'He's right,' Arnold said. 'We just always used the base count of two hundred thirty-eight because we assumed there couldn't be more.'

Total Animals	262

'Wait a minute,' Hammond said. 'These animals can't breed. The computer must be counting field mice or something.'

'I think so, too,' Arnold said. 'It's almost certainly an error in the visual tracking. But we'll know soon enough.'

Hammond turned to Wu. 'They can't breed, can they?'

'No,' Wu said.

Total Animals	270

'Where are they coming from?' Arnold said.

'Damned if I know,' Wu said.

They watched the numbers climb.

Total Animals	283

Over the radio, they heard Gennaro say, 'Holy shit, how much more?'

And they heard the girl say, 'I'm getting hungry. When are we going home?'

'Pretty soon, Lex.'

On the screen, there was a flashing error message:

ERROR: Search Params: 300 Animals Not Found

'An error,' Hammond said, nodding. 'I *thought* so. I had the feeling all along there must be an error.'

But a moment later the screen printed:

Total Animals	292		
Species	**Expected**	**Found**	**Ver**
Tyrannosaurs	2	2	4.1
Maiasaurs	21	22	??
Stegosaurs	4	4	3.9
Triceratops	8	8	3.1
Procompsognathids	49	65	??
Othnielia	16	23	??
Velociraptors	8	37	??
Apatosaurs	17	17	3.1
Hadrosaurs	11	11	3.1
Dilophosaurs	7	7	4.3
Pterosaurs	6	6	4.3
Hypsilophodontids.	33	34	??
Euoplocephalids	16	16	4.0
Styracosaurs	18	18	3.9
Callovosaurs	22	22	4.1
Total	**238**	**292**	

The radio crackled. 'Now you see the flaw in your procedures,' Malcolm said. 'You only tracked the expected number of dinosaurs. You were worried about losing animals, and your procedures were designed to advise you instantly if you had less than the expected number. But that wasn't the problem. The problem was, you had *more* than the expected number.'

'Christ,' Arnold said.

'There can't be more,' Wu said. 'We know how many we've released. There can't be more than that.'

'Afraid so, Henry,' Malcolm said. 'They're breeding.'

'No.'

'Even if you don't accept Grant's eggshell, you can prove it with your own data. Take a look at the compy height graph. Arnold will put it up for you.'

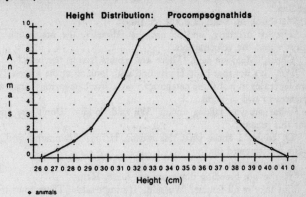

'Notice anything about it?' Malcolm said.

'It's a Poisson distribution,' Wu said. 'Normal curve.'

'But didn't you say you introduced the compys in three batches? At six-month intervals?'

'Yes . . .'

'Then you should get a graph with peaks for each of the three separate batches that were introduced,' Malcolm said, tapping the keyboard. 'Like this.'

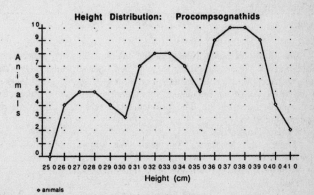

'But you didn't get this graph,' Malcolm said. 'The graph you actually got is a graph of a breeding population. Your compys are breeding.'

Wu shook his head. 'I don't see how.'

'They're breeding, and so are the othnielia, the maiasaurs, the hypsys – and the velociraptors.'

'Christ,' Muldoon said. 'There are raptors free in the park.'

'Well, it's not that bad,' Hammond said, looking at the screen. 'We have increases in just three categories – well, five categories. Very small increases in two of them . . .'

'What are you talking about?' Wu said, loudly. 'Don't you know what this means?'

'Of course I know what this means, Henry,' Hammond said. 'It means you screwed up.'

'Absolutely not.'

'You've got breeding dinosaurs out there, Henry.'

'But they're all female,' Wu said. 'It's impossible. There must be a mistake. And look at the numbers. A small increase in the big animals, the maiasaurs and the hypsys. And big increases in the number of small animals. It just doesn't make sense. It must be a mistake.'

The radio clicked. 'Actually not,' Grant said. 'I think these numbers confirm that breeding is taking place. In seven different sites around the island.'

Breeding Sites

The sky was growing darker. Thunder rumbled in the distance. Grant and the others leaned in the doors of the Jeep, staring at the screen on the dashboard. 'Breeding sites?' Wu said, over the radio.

'Nests,' Grant said. 'Assuming the average clutch is eight to twelve hatching eggs, these data would indicate the compys have two nests. The raptors have two nests. The othys have one nest. And the hypsys and the maias have one nest each.'

'Where are these nests?'

'We'll have to find them,' Grant said. 'Dinosaurs build their nests in secluded places.'

'But why are there so few big animals?' Wu said. 'If there is a maia nest of eight to twelve eggs, there should be eight to twelve new maias. Not just one.'

'That's right,' Grant said. 'Except that the raptors and the compys that are loose in the park are probably eating the eggs of the bigger animals — and perhaps eating the newly hatched young, as well.'

'But we've never seen that,' Arnold said, over the radio.

'Raptors are nocturnal,' he said. 'Is anyone watching the park at night?'

There was a long silence.

'I didn't think so,' Grant said.

'It still doesn't make sense,' Wu said. 'You can't support fifty additional animals on a couple of nests of eggs.'

'No,' Grant said. 'I assume they are eating something else as well. Perhaps small rodents. Mice and rats?'

There was another silence.

'Let me guess,' Grant said. 'When you first came to the island, you had a problem with rats. But as time passed, the problem faded away.'

'Yes. That's true. . . .'

'And you never thought to investigate why.'

'Well, we just assumed . . .' Arnold said.

'Look,' Wu said, 'the fact remains, all the animals are female. They can't breed.'

Grant had been thinking about that. He had recently learned of an intriguing West German study that he suspected held the answer. 'When you made your dinosaur DNA,' Grant said, 'you were working with fragmentary pieces, is that right?'

'Yes,' Wu said.

'In order to make a complete strand, were you ever required to include DNA fragments from other species?'

'Occasionally, yes,' Wu said. 'It's the only way to accomplish the job. Sometimes we included avian DNA, from a variety of birds, and sometimes reptilian DNA.'

'Any amphibian DNA? Specifically, frog DNA?'

'Possibly. I'd have to check.'

'Check,' Grant said. 'I think you'll find that holds the answer.'

Malcolm said, 'Frog DNA? Why frog DNA?'

Gennaro said impatiently, 'Listen, this is all very intriguing, but we're forgetting the main question: have any animals gotten off the island?'

Grant said, 'We can't tell from these data.'

'Then how are we going to find out?'

'There's only one way I know,' Grant said. 'We'll have to find the individual dinosaur nests, inspect them, and count the remaining egg fragments. From that we may be able to determine how many animals were originally hatched. And we can begin to assess whether any are missing.'

Malcolm said, 'Even so, you won't know if the missing animals are killed, or dead from natural causes, or whether they have left the island.'

'No,' Grant said, 'but it's a start. And I think we can get more information from an intensive look at the population graphs.'

'How are we going to find these nests?'

'Actually,' Grant said, 'I think the computer will be able to help us with that.'

'Can we go back now?' Lex said. 'I'm *hungry*.'

'Yes, let's go,' Grant said, smiling at her. 'You've been very patient.'

'You'll be able to eat in about twenty minutes,' Ed Regis said, starting toward the two Land Cruisers.

'I'll stay for a while,' Ellie said, 'and get photos of the stego with Dr. Harding's camera. Those vesicles in the mouth will have cleared up by tomorrow.'

'I want to get back,' Grant said. 'I'll go with the kids.'

'I will, too,' Malcolm said.

'I think I'll stay,' Gennaro said, 'and go back with Harding in his Jeep, with Dr. Sattler.'

'Fine, let's go.'

They started walking. Malcolm said, 'Why exactly is our lawyer staying?'

Grant shrugged. 'I think it might have something to do with Dr. Sattler.'

'Really? The shorts, you think?'

'It's happened before,' Grant said.

When they came to the Land Cruisers, Tim said, 'I want to ride in the front one this time, with Dr. Grant.'

Malcolm said, 'Unfortunately, Dr. Grant and I need to talk.'

'I'll just sit and listen. I won't say anything,' Tim said.

'It's a private conversation,' Malcolm said.

'Tell you what, Tim,' Ed Regis said. 'Let them sit in the rear car by themselves. We'll sit in the front car, and you can use the night-vision goggles. Have you ever used night-vision goggles, Tim? They're goggles with very sensitive CCDs that allow you to see in the dark.'

'Neat,' he said, and moved toward the first car.

'Hey!' Lex said. 'I want to use it, too.'

'No,' Tim said.

'No fair! No fair! You get to do everything, Timmy!'

Ed Regis watched them go and said to Grant, 'I can see what the ride back is going to be like.'

Grant and Malcolm climbed into the second car. A few raindrops spattered the windshield. 'Let's get going,' Ed Regis said. 'I'm about ready for dinner. And I could do with a nice banana daiquiri. What do you say, folks? Daiquiri sound good?' He pounded the metal panel of the car. 'See you back at camp,' he said, and he started running toward the first car, and climbed aboard.

A red light on the dashboard blinked. With a soft electric whirr, the Land Cruisers started off.

Driving back in the fading light, Malcolm seemed oddly subdued. Grant said, 'You must feel vindicated. About your theory.'

'As a matter of fact, I'm feeling a bit of dread. I suspect we are at a very dangerous point.'

'Why?'

'Intuition.'

'Do mathematicians believe in intuition?'

'Absolutely. Very important, intuition. Actually, I was thinking of fractals,' Malcolm said. 'You know about fractals?'

Grant shook his head. 'Not really, no.'

'Fractals are a kind of geometry, associated with a man named Mandelbrot. Unlike ordinary Euclidean geometry that everybody learns in school – squares and cubes and spheres – fractal geometry appears to describe real objects in the natural world. Mountains and clouds are fractal shapes. So fractals are probably related to reality. Somehow.

'Well, Mandelbrot found a remarkable thing with his geometric tools. He found that things looked almost identical at different scales.'

'At different scales?' Grant said.

'For example,' Malcolm said, 'a big mountain, seen from far away, has a certain rugged mountain shape. If you get closer, and examine a small peak of the big mountain, it will have the same mountain shape. In fact, you can go all the way down the scale to a tiny speck of rock, seen under a microscope – it will have the same basic fractal shape as the big mountain.'

'I don't really see why this is worrying you,' Grant said. He yawned. He smelled the sulfur fumes of the volcanic steam. They were coming now to the section of road that ran near the coastline, overlooking the beach and the ocean.

'It's a way of looking at things,' Malcolm said. 'Mandelbrot found a sameness from the smallest to the largest. And this sameness of scale also occurs for events.'

'Events?'

'Consider cotton prices,' Malcolm said. 'There are good records of cotton prices going back more than a hundred years. When you study fluctuations in cotton prices, you find that the graph of price fluctuations in the course of a day looks basically like the graph for a week, which looks basically like the graph for a year, or for ten years. And that's how things are. A day is like a whole life. You start out doing one thing, but end up doing something else, plan to run an errand, but never get there. . . . And at the end of your life, your whole existence has that same haphazard quality, too. Your whole life has the same shape as a single day.'

'I guess it's one way to look at things,' Grant said.

'No,' Malcolm said. 'It's the *only* way to look at things. At least, the only way that is true to reality. You see, the fractal idea of sameness carries within it an aspect of recursion, a kind of doubling back on itself, which means that events are unpredictable. That they can change suddenly, and without warning.'

'Okay . . .'

'But we have soothed ourselves into imagining sudden change as something that happens outside the normal order of things. An accident, like a car crash. Or beyond our control, like a fatal illness. We do not conceive of sudden, radical, irrational change as built into the very fabric of existence. Yet it is. And chaos theory teaches us,' Malcolm said, 'that straight linearity, which we have come to take for granted in everything from physics to fiction, simply does not exist. Linearity is an artificial way of viewing the world. Real life isn't a series of interconnected events occurring one after another like beads strung on a necklace. Life is actually a series of encounters in which one event may change those that follow in a wholly unpredictable, even devastating way.' Malcolm sat back in his seat, looking toward the other Land Cruiser, a few yards ahead. 'That's a deep truth about the structure of our universe. But, for some reason, we insist on behaving as if it were not true.'

At that moment, the cars jolted to a stop.

'What's happened?' Grant said.

Up ahead, they saw the kids in the car, pointing toward the ocean. Offshore, beneath lowering clouds, Grant saw the dark outline of the supply boat making its way back toward Puntarenas.

'Why have we stopped?' Malcolm said.

Grant turned on the radio and heard the girl saying excitedly, 'Look there, Timmy! You see it, it's there!'

Malcolm squinted at the boat. 'They talking about the boat?'

'Apparently.'

Ed Regis climbed out of the front car and came running back to their window. 'I'm sorry,' he said, 'but the kids are all worked up. Do you have binoculars here?'

'For what?'

'The little girl says she sees something on the boat. Some kind of animal,' Regis said.

Grant grabbed the binoculars and rested his elbows on the window ledge of the Land Cruiser. He scanned the long shape of the supply ship. It was so dark it was almost a silhouette; as he watched, the ship's running lights came on, brilliant in the dark purple twilight.

'Do you see anything?' Regis said.

'No,' Grant said.

'They're low down,' Lex said, over the radio. 'Look low down.'

Grant tilted the binoculars down, scanning the hull just above the water-line. The supply ship was broad-beamed, with a splash flange that ran the length of the ship. But it was quite dark now, and he could hardly make out details.

'No, nothing . . .'

'I can see them,' Lex said impatiently. 'Near the back. Look near the *back!*'

'How can she see anything in this light?' Malcolm said.

'Kids can see,' Grant said. 'They've got visual acuity we forgot we ever had.'

He swung the binoculars toward the stern, moving them slowly, and suddenly he saw the animals. They were playing, darting among the silhouetted stern structures. He could see them only briefly, but even in the fading light he could tell that they were upright animals, about two feet tall, standing with stiff balancing tails.

'You see them now?' Lex said.

'I see them,' he said.

'What are they?'

'They're raptors,' Grant said. 'At least two. Maybe more. Juveniles.'

'Jesus,' Ed Regis said. 'That boat's going to the mainland.'

Malcolm shrugged. 'Don't get excited. Just call the control room and tell them to recall the boat.'

Ed Regis reached in and grabbed the radio from the dashboard. They heard hissing static, and clicks as he rapidly changed channels. 'There's something wrong with this one,' he said. 'It's not working.'

He ran off to the first Land Cruiser. They saw him duck into it. Then he looked back at them. 'There's something wrong with both the radios,' he said. 'I can't raise the control room.'

'Then let's get going,' Grant said.

In the control room, Muldoon stood before the big windows that overlooked the park. At seven o'clock, the quartz floodlights came on all over the island, turning the landscape into a glowing jewel stretching away to the south. This was his favorite moment of the day. He heard the crackle of static from the radios.

'The Land Cruisers have started again,' Arnold said. 'They're on their way home.'

'But why did they stop?' Hammond said. 'And why can't we talk to them?'

'I don't know,' Arnold said. 'Maybe they turned off the radios in the cars.'

'Probably the storm,' Muldoon said. 'Interference from the storm.'

'They'll be here in twenty minutes,' Hammond said. 'You better call down and make sure the dining room is ready for them. Those kids are going to be hungry.'

Arnold picked up the phone and heard a steady monotonous hiss. 'What's this? What's going on?'

'Jesus, hang that up,' Nedry said. 'You'll screw up the data stream.'

'You've taken *all* the phone lines? Even the internal ones?'

'I've taken all the lines that communicate outside,' Nedry said. 'But your internal lines should still work.'

Arnold punched console buttons one after another. He heard nothing but hissing on all the lines.

'Looks like you've got 'em all.'

'Sorry about that,' Nedry said. 'I'll clear a couple for you at the end of the next transmission, in about fifteen minutes.' He yawned. 'Looks like a long weekend for me. I guess I'll go get that Coke now.' He picked up his shoulder bag and headed for the door. 'Don't touch my console, okay?'

The door closed.

'What a slob,' Hammond said.

'Yeah,' Arnold said. 'But I guess he knows what he's doing.'

Along the side of the road, clouds of volcanic steam misted rainbows in the bright quartz lights. Grant said into the radio, 'How long does it take the ship to reach the mainland?'

'Eighteen hours,' Ed Regis said. 'More or less. It's pretty reliable.' He glanced at his watch. 'It should arrive around eleven tomorrow morning.'

Grant frowned. 'You still can't talk to the control room?'

'Not so far.'

'How about Harding? Can you reach him?'

'No, I've tried. He may have his radio turned off.'

Malcolm was shaking his head. 'So we're the only ones who know about the animals on the ship.'

'I'm trying to raise somebody,' Ed Regis said. 'I mean, Christ, we don't want those animals on the mainland.'

'How long until we get back to the base?'

'From here, another sixteen, seventeen minutes,' Ed Regis said.

At night, the whole road was illuminated by big floodlights. It felt to Grant as if they were driving through a bright green tunnel of leaves. Large raindrops spattered the windshield.

Grant felt the Land Cruiser slow, then stop. 'Now what?'

Lex said, 'I don't want to stop. Why did we stop?'

And then, suddenly, all the floodlights went out. The road was plunged into darkness. Lex said, 'Hey!'

'Probably just a power outage or something,' Ed Regis said. 'I'm sure the lights'll be on in a minute.'

'What the hell?' Arnold said, staring at his monitors.

'What happened?' Muldoon said. 'You lose power?'

'Yeah, but only power on the perimeter. Everything in this building's working fine. But outside, in the park, the power is gone. Lights, TV cameras, everything.' His remote video monitors had gone black.

'What about the two Land Cruisers?'

'Stopped somewhere around the tyrannosaur paddock.'

'Well,' Muldoon said, 'call Maintenance and let's get the power back on.'

Arnold picked up one of his phones and heard hissing: Nedry's computers talking to each other. 'No phones. That damn Nedry. Nedry! Where the hell is he?'

Dennis Nedry pushed open the door marked FERTILIZATION. With the perimeter power out, all the security-card locks were disarmed. Every door in the building opened with a touch.

The problems with the security system were high on Jurassic Park's bug list. Nedry wondered if anybody ever imagined that it wasn't a bug – that Nedry had programmed it that way. He had built in a classic trap door. Few programmers of large computer systems could resist the temptation to leave themselves a secret entrance. Partly it was common sense: if inept users locked up the system – and then called you for help – you always had a way to get in and repair the mess. And partly it was a kind of signature: Kilroy was here.

And partly it was insurance for the future. Nedry was annoyed with the Jurassic Park project; late in the schedule, InGen had demanded extensive modifications to the system but hadn't been willing to pay for them, arguing they should be included under the original contract. Lawsuits were threatened; letters were written to Nedry's other clients, implying that Nedry was unreliable. It was blackmail, and in the end Nedry had been forced to eat his overages on Jurassic Park and to make the changes that Hammond wanted.

But later, when he was approached by Lewis Dodgson at Biosyn, Nedry was ready to listen. And able to say that he could indeed get past Jurassic Park security. He could get into any room, any system, anywhere in the park. Because he had programmed it that way. Just in case.

He entered the fertilization room. The lab was deserted; as he had anticipated, all the staff was at dinner. Nedry unzipped his shoulder bag and removed the can of Gillette shaving cream. He unscrewed the base, and saw the interior was divided into a series of cylindrical slots.

He pulled on a pair of heavy insulated gloves and opened the walk-in freezer marked CONTENTS VIABLE BIOLOGICAL MAINTAIN $-10°$ C MINIMUM. The freezer was the size of a small closet, with shelves from floor to ceiling. Most of the shelves contained reagents and liquids in plastic sacs. To one side he saw a smaller nitrogen cold box with a heavy ceramic door. He opened it, and a rack of small tubes slid out, in a cloud of white liquid-nitrogen smoke.

The embryos were arranged by species: Stegosaurus, Apatosaurus, Hadrosaurus, Tyrannosaurus. Each embryo in a thin glass container, wrapped in silver foil, stoppered with polylene. Nedry quickly took two of each, slipping them into the shaving cream can.

Then he screwed the base of the can shut and twisted the top. There was a hiss of releasing gas inside, and the can frosted in his hands. Dodgson had said there was enough coolant to last thirty-six hours. More than enough time to get back to San José.

Nedry left the freezer, returned to the main lab. He dropped the can back in his bag, zipped it shut.

He went back into the hallway. The theft had taken less than two minutes. He could imagine the consternation upstairs in the control room, as they began to realize what had happened. All their security codes were scrambled, and all their phone lines were jammed. Without his help, it would take hours to untangle the mess – but in just a few minutes Nedry would be back in the control room, setting things right.

And no one would ever suspect what he had done.

Grinning, Dennis Nedry walked down to the ground floor, nodded to the guard, and continued downstairs to the basement. Passing the neat lines of electric Land Cruisers, he went to the gasoline-powered Jeep parked against the wall. He climbed into it, noticing some odd gray tubing on the passenger seat. It looked almost like a rocket launcher, he thought, as he turned the ignition key and started the Jeep.

Nedry glanced at his watch. From here, into the park, and three minutes straight to the east dock. Three minutes from there back to the control room.

Piece of cake.

'Damn it!' Arnold said, punching buttons on the console. 'It's all screwed up.'

Muldoon was standing at the windows, looking out at the park. The lights had gone out all over the island, except in the immediate area around the main buildings. He saw a few staff personnel hurrying to get out of the rain, but no one seemed to realize anything was wrong. Muldoon looked over at the visitor lodge, where the lights burned brightly.

'Uh-oh,' Arnold said. 'We have real trouble.'

'What's that?' Muldoon said. He turned away from the window, and so he didn't see the Jeep drive out of the underground garage and head east along the maintenance road into the park.

'That idiot Nedry turned off the security systems,' Arnold said. 'The whole building's opened up. None of the doors are locked any more.'

'I'll notify the guards,' Muldoon said.

'That's the least of it,' Arnold said. 'When you turn off the security, you turn off all the peripheral fences as well.'

'The fences?' Muldoon said.

'The electrical fences,' Arnold said. 'They're off, all over the island.'

'You mean . . .'

'That's right,' Arnold said. 'The animals can get out now.' Arnold lit a cigarette. 'Probably nothing will happen, but you never know. . . .'

Muldoon started toward the door. 'I better drive out and bring in the people in those two Land Cruisers,' he said. 'Just in case.'

Muldoon quickly went downstairs to the garage. He wasn't really worried about the fences' going down. Most of the dinosaurs had been in their paddocks for nine months or more, and they had brushed up against the fences more than once, with notable results. Muldoon knew how quickly animals learned to avoid shock stimuli. You could train a laboratory pigeon with just two or three stimulation events. So it was unlikely the dinosaurs would now approach the fences.

Muldoon was more concerned about what the people in the cars would do. He didn't want them getting out of the Land Cruisers, because once the power came back on, the cars would start moving again, whether the people were inside them or not. They might be left behind. Of course, in the rain it was unlikely they would leave the cars. But, still . . . you never knew. . . .

He reached the garage and hurried toward the Jeep. It was lucky, he thought, that he had had the foresight to put the launcher in it. He could start right out, and be out there in –

It was gone!

'What the hell?' Muldoon stared at the empty parking space, astonished.

The Jeep was gone!

What the hell was happening?

Fourth Iteration

'Inevitably, underlying instabilities begin to appear.'

IAN MALCOLM

The Main Road

Rain drummed loudly on the roof of the Land Cruiser. Tim felt the night-vision goggles pressing heavily on his forehead. He reached for the knob near his ear and adjusted the intensity. There was a brief phosphorescent flare, and then, in shades of electronic green and black, he could see the Land Cruiser behind, with Dr. Grant and Dr. Malcolm inside. Neat!

Dr. Grant was staring out the front windshield toward him. Tim saw him pick up the radio from the dash. There was a burst of static, and then he heard Dr. Grant's voice: 'Can you see us back here?'

Tim picked up the radio from Ed Regis. 'I see you.'

'Everything all right?'

'We're fine, Dr. Grant.'

'Stay in the car.'

'We will. Don't worry.' He clicked the radio off.

Ed Regis snorted. 'It's pouring down rain. Of course we'll stay in the car,' he muttered.

Tim turned to look at the foliage at the side of the road. Through the goggles, the foliage was a bright electronic green, and beyond he could see sections of the green grid pattern of the fence. The Land Cruisers were stopped on the downslope of a hill, which must mean they were someplace near the tyrannosaur area. It would be amazing to see a tyrannosaur with these night-vision goggles. A real thrill. Maybe the tyrannosaur would come to the fence and look over at them. Tim wondered if its eyes would glow in the dark when he saw them. That would be neat.

But he didn't see anything, and eventually he stopped looking. Everyone in the cars fell silent. The rain thrummed on the roof of the car. Sheets of water streamed down over the sides of the windows. It was hard for Tim to see out, even with the goggles.

'How long have we been sitting here?' Malcolm asked.

'I don't know. Four or five minutes.'

'I wonder what the problem is.'

'Maybe a short circuit from the rain.'

'But it happened before the rain really started.'

There was another silence. In a tense voice, Lex said, 'But there's no lightning, right?' She had always been afraid of lightning, and she now sat nervously squeezing her leather mitt in her hands.

Dr. Grant said, 'What was that? We didn't quite read that.'

'Just my sister talking.'

'Oh.'

Tim again scanned the foliage, but saw nothing. Certainly nothing as big as a tyrannosaur. He began to wonder if the tyrannosaurs came out at night. Were they nocturnal animals? Tim wasn't sure if he had ever read that. He had the feeling that tyrannosaurs were all-weather, day or night animals. The time of day didn't matter to a tyrannosaur.

The rain continued to pour.

'Hell of a rain,' Ed Regis said. 'It's really coming down.'

Lex said, 'I'm hungry.'

'I know that, Lex,' Regis said, 'but we're stuck here, sweetie. The cars run on electricity in buried cables in the road.'

'Stuck for how long?'

'Until they fix the electricity.'

Listening to the sound of the rain, Tim felt himself growing sleepy. He yawned, and turned to look at the palm trees on the left side of the road, and was startled by a sudden thump as the ground shook. He swung back just in time to catch a glimpse of a dark shape as it swiftly crossed the road between the two cars.

'Jesus!'

'What was it?'

'It was huge, it was big as the car –'

'Tim! Are you there?'

He picked up the radio. 'Yes, I'm here.'

'Did you see it, Tim?'

'No,' Tim said. 'I missed it.'

'What the hell was it?' Malcolm said.

'Are you wearing the night-vision goggles, Tim?'

'Yes. I'll watch,' Tim said.

'Was it the tyrannosaur?' Ed Regis asked.

'I don't think so. It was in the road.'

'But you didn't see it?' Ed Regis said.

'No.'

Tim felt bad that he had missed seeing the animal, whatever it was. There was a sudden white crack of lightning, and his night goggles flared bright green. He blinked his eyes and started counting. 'One one thousand . . . two one thousand . . .'

The thunder crashed, deafeningly loud and very close.

Lex began to cry. 'Oh, *no . . .*'

'Take it easy, honey,' Ed Regis said. 'It's just lightning.'

Tim scanned the side of the road. The rain was coming down hard now, shaking the leaves with hammering drops. It made everything move. Everything seemed alive. He scanned the leaves . . .

He stopped. There was something beyond the leaves.

Tim looked up, higher.

Behind the foliage, beyond the fence, he saw a thick body with a pebbled, grainy surface like the bark of a tree. But it wasn't a tree . . . He continued to look higher, sweeping the goggles upward –

He saw the huge head of the tyrannosaurus. Just standing there, looking over the fence at the two Land Cruisers. The lightning flashed again, and the big animal rolled its head and bellowed in the glaring light. Then darkness, and silence again, and the pounding rain.

'Tim?'

'Yes, Dr. Grant.'

'You see what it is?'

'Yes, Dr. Grant.'

Tim had the sense that Dr. Grant was trying to talk in a way that wouldn't upset his sister.

'What's going on right now?'

'Nothing,' Tim said, watching the tyrannosaur through his night goggles. 'Just standing on the other side of the fence.'

'I can't see much from here, Tim.'

'I can see fine, Dr. Grant. It's just standing there.'

'Okay.'

Lex continued to cry, snuffling.

There was another pause. Tim watched the tyrannosaur. The head was huge! The animal looked from one vehicle to another. Then back again. It seemed to stare right at Tim.

In the goggles, the eyes glowed bright green.

Tim felt a chill, but then, as he looked down the animal's body, moving down from the massive head and jaws, he saw the smaller, muscular forelimb. It waved in the air and then it gripped the fence.

'Jesus Christ,' Ed Regis said, staring out the window.

The greatest predator the world has ever known. The most fearsome attack in human history. Somewhere in the back of his publicist's brain, Ed Regis was still writing copy. But he could feel his knees begin to shake uncontrollably, his trousers flapping like flags. Jesus, he was frightened. He didn't want to be here. Alone among all the people in the two cars, Ed Regis knew what a dinosaur attack was like. He knew what happened to people. He had seen the mangled bodies that resulted from a raptor attack. He could picture it in his mind. And this was a rex! Much, much bigger! The greatest meat-eater that ever walked the earth!

Jesus.

When the tyrannosaur roared it was terrifying, a scream from some other world. Ed Regis felt the spreading warmth in his trousers. He'd peed in his pants. He was simultaneously embarrassed and terrified. But he knew he had to do something. He couldn't just stay here. He had to do something. *Something.* His hands were shaking, trembling against the dash.

'Jesus Christ,' he said again.

'Bad language,' Lex said, wagging her finger at him.

Tim heard the sound of a door opening, and he swung his head away from the tyrannosaur – the night-vision goggles streaked laterally – in time to see Ed Regis stepping out through the open door, ducking his head in the rain.

'Hey,' Lex said, 'Where are you going?'

Ed Regis just turned and ran in the opposite direction from the tyrannosaur, disappearing into the woods. The door to the Land Cruiser hung open; the paneling was getting wet.

'He left!' Lex said. 'Where did he go? He left us alone!'

'Shut the door,' Tim said, but she had started to scream, 'He left us! He left us!'

'Tim, what's going on?' It was Dr. Grant, on the radio. 'Tim?'

Tim leaned forward and tried to shut the door. From the back seat, he couldn't reach the handle. He looked back at the tyrannosaur as lightning flashed again, momentarily silhouetting the huge black shape against the white-flaring sky.

'Tim, what's happening?'

'He left us, he left us!'

Tim blinked to recover his vision. When he looked again, the tyrannosaur was standing there, exactly as before, motionless and huge. Rain dripped from its jaws. The forelimb gripped the fence . . .

And then Tim realized: the tyrannosaur was holding on to the fence! The fence wasn't electrified any more!

'Lex, *close the door!*'

The radio crackled. 'Tim!'

'I'm here, Dr. Grant.'

'What's going on?'

'Regis ran away,' Tim said.

'He *what?*'

174

'He ran away. I think he saw that the fence isn't electrified,' Tim said.

'The fence isn't electrified?' Malcolm said, over the radio. 'Did he say the fence isn't electrified?'

'Lex,' Tim said, '*close the door.*' But Lex was screaming, 'He left us, he left us!' in a steady, monotonous wail, and there was nothing for Tim to do but climb out of the back door, into the slashing rain, and shut the door for her. Thunder rumbled, and the lightning flashed again. Tim looked up and saw the tyrannosaur crashing down the cyclone fence with a giant hind limb.

'Timmy!'

He jumped back in and slammed the door, the sound lost in the thunderclap.

The radio: 'Tim! Are you there?'

He grabbed the radio. 'I'm here.' He turned to Lex. 'Lock the doors. Get in the middle of the car. And *shut up.*'

Outside, the tyrannosaur rolled its head and took an awkward step forward. The claws of its feet had caught in the grid of the flattened fence. Lex saw the animal finally, and became silent, still. She watched with wide eyes.

Radio crackle. 'Tim.'

'Yes, Dr. Grant.'

'Stay in the car. Stay down. Be quiet. Don't move, and don't make noise.'

'Okay.'

'You should be all right. I don't think it can open the car.'

'Okay.'

'Just stay quiet, so you don't arouse its attention any more than necessary.'

'Okay.' Tim clicked the radio off. 'You hear that, Lex?'

His sister nodded, silently. She never took her eyes off the dinosaur. The tyrannosaur roared. In the glare of lightning, they saw it pull free of the fence and take a bounding step forward.

Now it was standing between the two cars. Tim couldn't see Dr. Grant's car any more, because the huge body blocked his view. The rain ran in rivulets down the pebbled skin of the muscular hind legs. He couldn't see the animal's head, which was high above the roofline.

The tyrannosaur moved around the side of their car. It went to the very spot where Tim had gotten out of the car. Where Ed Regis had gotten out of the car. The animal paused there. The big head ducked down, toward the mud.

Tim looked back at Dr. Grant and Dr. Malcolm in the rear car. Their faces were tense as they stared forward through the windshield.

The huge head raised back up, jaws open, and then stopped by the side windows. In the glare of lightning, they saw the beady, expressionless reptile eye moving in the socket.

It was looking in the car.

His sister's breath came in ragged, frightened gasps. He reached out and squeezed her arm, hoping she would stay quiet. The dinosaur continued to stare for a long time through the side window. Perhaps the dinosaur couldn't really see them, he thought. Finally the head lifted up, out of view again.

'Timmy . . .' Lex whispered.

'It's okay,' Tim whispered. 'I don't think it saw us.'

He was looking back toward Dr. Grant when a jolting impact rocked the Land Cruiser and shattered the windshield in a spiderweb as the tyrannosaur's head crashed against the hood of the Land Cruiser. Tim was knocked flat on the seat. The night-vision goggles slid off his forehead.

He got back up quickly, blinking in the darkness, his mouth warm with blood.

'Lex?'

He couldn't see his sister anywhere.

The tyrannosaur stood near the front of the Land Cruiser, its chest moving as it breathed, the forelimbs making clawing movements in the air.

'Lex!' Tim whispered. Then he heard her groan. She was lying somewhere on the floor under the front seat.

Then the huge head came down, entirely blocking the shattered windshield. The tyrannosaur banged again on the front hood of the Land Cruiser. Tim grabbed the seat as the car rocked on its wheels. The tyrannosaur banged down twice more, denting the metal.

Then it moved around the side of the car. The big raised tail blocked his view out of all the side windows. At the back, the animal snorted, a deep rumbling growl that blended with the thunder. It sank its jaws into the spare tire mounted on the back of the Land Cruiser and, in a single head shake, tore it away. The rear of the car lifted into the air for a moment; then it thumped down with a muddy splash.

'Tim!' Dr. Grant said. 'Tim, are you there?'

Tim grabbed the radio. 'We're okay,' he said. There was a shrill metallic scrape as claws raked the roof of the car. Tim's heart was pounding in his chest. He couldn't see anything out of the windows on the right side except pebbled leathery flesh. The tyrannosaur was leaning against the car, which rocked back and forth with each breath, the springs and metal creaking loudly.

Lex groaned again. Tim put down the radio, and started to crawl over into the front seat. The tyrannosaur roared and the metal roof dented downward. Tim felt a sharp pain in his head and tumbled to the floor, onto the transmission hump. He found himself lying alongside Lex, and he was shocked to see that the whole side of her head was covered in blood. She looked unconscious.

There was another jolting impact, and pieces of glass fell all around him. Tim felt rain. He looked up and saw that the front windshield had broken out. There was just a jagged rim of glass and, beyond, the big head of the dinosaur.

Looking down at him.

Tim felt a sudden chill and then the head rushed forward toward him, the jaws open. There was the squeal of metal against teeth, and he felt the hot stinking breath of the animal and a thick tongue stuck into the car through the windshield opening. The tongue slapped wetly around inside the car – he felt the hot lather of dinosaur saliva – and the tyrannosaur roared – a deafening sound inside the car –

The head pulled away abruptly.

Tim scrambled up, avoiding the dent in the roof. There was still room to sit on the front seat by the passenger door. The tyrannosaur stood in the rain near the front fender. It seemed confused by what had happened to it. Blood dripped freely from its jaws.

The tyrannosaur looked at Tim, cocking its head to stare with one big eye. The head moved close to the car, sideways, and peered in. Blood spattered on the dented hood of the Land Cruiser, mixing with the rain.

It can't get to me, Tim thought. It's too big.

Then the head pulled away, and in the flare of lightning he saw the hind leg lift up. And the world tilted crazily as the Land Cruiser slammed over on its side, the windows splatting in the mud. He saw Lex fall helplessly against the side window, and he fell down beside her, banging his head. Tim felt dizzy. Then the tyrannosaur's jaws clamped onto the window frame, and the whole Land Cruiser was lifted up into the air, and shaken.

'Timmy!' Lex shrieked, so near to his ear that it hurt. She was suddenly awake, and he grabbed her as the tyrannosaur crashed the car down again. Tim felt a stabbing pain in his side, and his sister fell on top of him. The car went up again, tilting crazily. Lex shouted '*Timmy!*' and he saw the door give way beneath her, and she fell out of the car into the mud, but Tim couldn't answer, because in the next instant everything swung crazily – he saw the trunks of the palm trees sliding downward past him – moving sideways through the air – he glimpsed the ground very far below – the hot roar of the tyrannosaur – the blazing eye – the tops of the palm trees –

And then, with a metallic scraping shriek, the car fell from the tyrannosaur's jaws, a sickening fall, and Tim's stomach heaved in the moment before the world became totally black, and silent.

In the other car, Malcolm gasped. 'Jesus! What happened to the car?'

Grant blinked his eyes as the lightning faded.

The other car was gone.

Grant couldn't believe it. He peered forward, trying to see through the rain-streaked windshield. The dinosaur's body was so large, it was probably just blocking –

No. In another flash of lightning, he saw clearly: the car was gone.

'What happened?' Malcolm said.

'I don't know.'

Faintly, over the rain, Grant heard the sound of the little girl screaming. The dinosaur was standing in darkness on the road up ahead, but they could see well enough to know that it was bending over now, sniffing the ground.

Or eating something on the ground.

'Can you see?' Malcolm said, squinting.

'Not much, no,' Grant said. The rain pounded on the roof of the car. He listened for the little girl, but he didn't hear her any more. The two men sat in the car, listening.

'Was it the girl?' Malcolm said, finally. 'It sounded like the girl.'

'It did, yes.'

'Was it?'

'I don't know,' Grant said. He felt a seeping fatigue overtake him. Blurred through the rainy windshield, the dinosaur was coming toward their car. Slow, ominous strides, coming right toward them.

Malcolm said, 'You know, at times like this one feels, well, perhaps extinct animals *should* be left extinct. Don't you have that feeling now?'

'Yes,' Grant said. He was feeling his heart pounding.

'Umm. Do you, ah, have any suggestions about what we do now?'

'I can't think of a thing,' Grant said.

Malcolm twisted the handle, kicked open the door, and ran. But even as he did, Grant could see he was too late, the tyrannosaur too close. There was another crack of lightning, and in that instant of glaring white light, Grant watched in horror as the tyrannosaur roared, and leapt forward.

Grant was not clear about exactly what happened next. Malcolm was running, his feet splashing in the mud. The tyrannosaur bounded alongside him and ducked its massive head, and Malcolm was tossed into the air like a small doll.

By then Grant was out of the car, too, feeling the cold rain slashing his face and body. The tyrannosaur had turned its back to him, the huge tail swinging through the air. Grant was tensing to run for the woods when suddenly the tyrannosaur spun back to face him, and roared.

Grant froze.

He was standing beside the passenger door of the Land Cruiser, drenched in rain. He was completely exposed, the tyrannosaur no more than eight feet away. The big animal roared again. At so close a range the sound was terrifyingly loud. Grant felt himself shaking with cold and fright. He pressed his trembling hands against the metal of the door panel to steady them.

The tyrannosaur roared once more, but it did not attack. It cocked its head, and looked with first one eye, then the other, at the Land Cruiser. And it did nothing.

It just stood there.

What was going on?

The powerful jaws opened and closed. The tyrannosaur bellowed angrily, and then the big hind leg came up and crashed down on the roof of the car; the claws slid off with a metal screech, barely missing Grant as he stood there, still unmoving.

The foot splashed in the mud. The head ducked down in a slow arc, and the animal inspected the car, snorting. It peered into the front windshield. Then, moving toward the rear, it banged the passenger door shut, and moved right toward Grant as he stood there. Grant was dizzy with fear, his heart pounding inside his chest. With the animal so close, he could smell the rotten flesh in the mouth, the sweetish blood-smell, the sickening stench of the carnivore...

He tensed his body, awaiting the inevitable.

The big head slid past him, toward the rear of the car. Grant blinked.

What had happened?

Was it possible the tyrannosaur hadn't seen him? It seemed as if it hadn't. But how could that be? Grant looked back to see the animal sniffing the rear-mounted tire. It nudged the tire with its snout, and then the head swung back. Again it approached Grant.

This time the animal stopped, the black flaring nostrils just inches away. Grant felt the animal's startling hot breath on his face. But the tyrannosaur wasn't sniffing like a dog. It was just breathing, and if anything it seemed puzzled.

No, the tyrannosaur couldn't see him. Not if he stood motionless.

And in a detached academic corner of his mind he found an explanation for that, a reason why –

The jaws opened before him, the massive head raised up. Grant squeezed his fists together, and bit his lip, trying desperately to remain motionless, to make no sound.

The tyrannosaur bellowed in the night air.

But by now Grant was beginning to understand. The animal couldn't see him, but it suspected he was there, somewhere, and was trying with its bellowing to frighten Grant into some revealing movement. So long as he stood his ground, Grant realized, he was invisible.

In a final gesture of frustration, the big hind leg lifted up and kicked the Land Cruiser over, and Grant felt searing pain and the surprising sensation of his own body flying through the air. It seemed to be happening very slowly, and he had plenty of time to feel the world turn colder, and watch the ground rush up to strike him in the face.

Return

'Oh damn,' Harding said. 'Will you look at that.'

They were sitting in Harding's gasoline-powered Jeep, staring forward past the *flick flick* of the windshield wipers. In the yellow flare of the headlamps, a big fallen tree blocked the road.

'Must have been the lightning,' Gennaro said. 'Hell of a tree.'

'We can't get past it,' Harding said. 'I better tell Arnold in control.'

He picked up the radio and twisted the channel dial. 'Hello, John. Are you there, John?'

There was nothing but steady hissing static. 'I don't understand,' he said. 'The radio lines seem to be down.'

'It must be the storm,' Gennaro said.

'I suppose,' Harding said.

'Try the Land Cruisers,' Ellie said.

Harding opened the other channels, but there was no answer.

'Nothing,' he said. 'They're probably back to camp by now, and outside the range of our little set. In any case, I don't think we should stay here. It'll be hours before Maintenance gets a crew out here to move that tree.'

He turned the radio off, and put the Jeep into reverse.

'What're you going to do?' Ellie said.

'Go back to the turnout, and get onto the maintenance road. Fortunately there's a second road system,' Harding explained. 'We have one road for visitors, and a second road for animal handlers and feed trucks and so on. We'll drive back on that maintenance road. It's a little longer. And not so scenic. But you may find it interesting. If the rain lets up, we'll get a glimpse of some of the animals at night. We should be back in thirty, forty minutes,' Harding said. 'If I don't get lost.'

He turned the Jeep around in the night, and headed south again.

Lightning flashed, and every monitor in the control room went black. Arnold sat forward, his body rigid and tense. Jesus, not now. Not now. That was all he needed – to have everything go out now in the storm. All the main power circuits were surge-protected, of course, but Arnold wasn't sure about the modems Nedry was using for his data transmission. Most people didn't know it was possible to blow an entire system through a modem – the lightning pulse climbed back into the computer through the telephone line, and – bang! – no more motherboard. No more RAM. No more file server. No more computer.

The screens flickered. And then, one by one, they came back on.

Arnold sighed, and collapsed back in his chair.

He wondered again where Nedry had gone. Five minutes ago, he'd sent guards to search the building for him. The fat bastard was probably in the bathroom reading a comic book. But the guards hadn't come back, and they hadn't called in.

Five minutes. If Nedry was in the building, they should have found him by now.

'Somebody took the damned Jeep,' Muldoon said as he came back in the room. 'Have you talked to the Land Cruisers yet?'

'Can't raise them on the radio,' Arnold said. 'I have to use this, because the main board is down. It's weak, but it ought to work. I've tried on all six channels. I know they have radios in the cars, but they're not answering.'

'That's not good,' Muldoon said.

'If you want to go out there, take one of the maintenance vehicles.'

'I would,' Muldoon said, 'but they're all in the east garage, more than a mile from here. Where's Harding?'

'I assume he's on his way back.'

'Then he'll pick up the people in the Land Cruisers on his way.'

'I assume so.'

'Anybody tell Hammond the kids aren't back yet?'

'Hell no,' Arnold said. 'I don't want that son of a bitch running around here, screaming at me. Everything's all right, for the moment. The Land Cruisers are just stuck in the rain. They can sit a while, until Harding brings them back. Or until we find Nedry, and make that little bastard turn the systems back on.'

'You can't get them back on?' Muldoon said.

Arnold shook his head. 'I've been trying. But Nedry's done something to the system. I can't figure out what, but if I have to go into the code itself, that'll take hours. We need Nedry. We've got to find the son of a bitch right away.'

Nedry

The sign said ELECTRIFIED FENCE 10,000 VOLTS DO NOT TOUCH, but Nedry opened it with his bare hand, and unlocked the gate, swinging it wide. He went back to the Jeep, drove through the gate, and then walked back to close it behind him.

Now he was inside the park itself, no more than a mile from the east dock. He stepped on the accelerator and hunched forward over the steering wheel, peering through the rain-slashed windshield as he drove the Jeep down the narrow road. He was driving fast – too fast – but he had to keep to his timetable. He was surrounded on all sides by black jungle, but soon he should be able to see the beach and the ocean off to his left.

This damned storm, he thought. It might screw up everything. Because if Dodgson's boat wasn't waiting for him at the east dock when Nedry got there, the whole plan would be ruined. Nedry couldn't wait very long, or he would be missed back at the control room. The whole idea behind the plan was that he could drive to the east dock, drop off the embryos, and be back in a few minutes, before anyone noticed. It was a good plan, a clever plan. Nedry'd worked on it carefully, refining every detail. This plan was going to make him a million and a half dollars, one point five meg. That was ten years of income in a single tax-free shot, and it was going to change his life. Nedry'd been damned careful, even to the point of making Dodgson meet him in the San Francisco airport at the last minute with an excuse about wanting to see the money. Actually, Nedry wanted to record his conversation with Dodgson, and mention him by name on the tape. Just so that Dodgson wouldn't forget he owed the rest of the money, Nedry was including a copy of the tape with the embryos. In short, Nedry had thought of everything.

Except this damned storm.

Something dashed across the road, a white flash in his headlights. It looked like a large rat. It scurried into the underbrush, dragging a fat tail. Possum. Amazing that a possum could survive here. You'd think the dinosaurs would get an animal like that.

Where was the damned dock?

He was driving fast, and he'd already been gone five minutes. He should have reached the east dock by now. Had he taken a wrong turn? He didn't think so. He hadn't seen any forks in the road at all.

Then where was the dock?

It was a shock when he came around a corner and saw that the road terminated in a gray concrete barrier, six feet tall and streaked dark with rain. He slammed on the brakes, and the Jeep fishtailed, losing traction in an end-to-end spin, and for a horrified moment he thought he was going to smash into the barrier – he knew he was going to smash – and he spun the wheel frantically, and the Jeep slid to a stop, the headlamps just a foot from the concrete wall.

He paused there, listening to the rhythmic flick of the wipers. He took a deep breath and exhaled slowly. He looked back down the road. He'd obviously taken a wrong turn somewhere. He could retrace his steps, but that would take too long.

He'd better try and find out where the hell he was.

He got out of the Jeep, feeling heavy raindrops spatter his head. It was a real tropical storm, raining so hard that it hurt. He glanced at his watch, pushing the button to illuminate the digital dial. Six minutes gone. Where the hell was he? He walked around the concrete barrier and on the other side, along with the rain, he heard the sound of gurgling water. Could it be the ocean? Nedry hurried forward, his eyes adjusting to the darkness as he went. Dense jungle on all sides. Raindrops slapping on the leaves.

The gurgling sound became louder, drawing him forward, and suddenly he came out of the foliage and felt his feet sink into soft earth and saw the dark currents of the river. The river! He was at the jungle river!

Damn, he thought. At the river *where?* The river ran for miles through the island. He looked at his watch again. Seven minutes gone. 'You have a problem, Dennis,' he said aloud.

As if in reply, there was a soft hooting cry of an owl in the forest.

Nedry hardly noticed; he was worrying about his plan. The plain fact was that time had run out. There wasn't a choice any more. He had to abandon his original plan. All he could do was go back to the control room, restore the computer, and somehow try to contact Dodgson, to set up the drop at the east dock for the following night. Nedry would have to scramble to make that work, but he thought he could pull it off. The computer automatically logged all calls; after Nedry got through to Dodgson, he'd have to go back into the computer and erase the record of the call. But one thing was sure – he couldn't stay out in the park any longer, or his absence would be noticed.

Nedry started back, heading toward the glow of the car's headlights. He was drenched and miserable. He heard the soft hooting cry once more, and this time he paused. That hadn't really sounded like an owl. And it seemed to be close by, in the jungle somewhere off to his right.

As he listened, he heard a crashing sound in the underbrush. Then silence. He waited, and heard it again. It sounded distinctly like something big, moving slowly through the jungle toward him.

Something big. Something near. A big dinosaur.

Get out of here.

Nedry began to run. He made a lot of noise as he ran, but even so he could hear the animal crashing through the foliage. And hooting.

It was coming closer.

Stumbling over tree roots in the darkness, clawing his way past dripping branches, he saw the Jeep ahead, and the lights shining around the vertical wall of the barrier made him feel better. In a moment he'd be in the car and then he'd get the hell out of here. He scrambled around the barrier and then he froze.

The animal was already there.

But it wasn't close. The dinosaur stood forty feet away, at the edge of the illumination from the headlamps. Nedry hadn't taken the tour, so he hadn't seen the different types of dinosaurs, but this one was strange-looking. The ten-foot-tall body was yellow with black spots, and along the head ran a pair of red V-shaped crests. The dinosaur didn't move, but again gave its soft hooting cry.

Nedry waited to see if it would attack. It didn't. Perhaps the headlights from the Jeep frightened it, forcing it to keep its distance, like a fire.

The dinosaur stared at him and then snapped its head in a single swift motion. Nedry felt something smack wetly against his chest. He looked down and saw a dripping glob of foam on his rain-soaked shirt. He touched it curiously, not comprehending. . . .

It was spit.

The dinosaur had spit on him.

It was creepy, he thought. He looked back at the dinosaur and saw the head snap again, and immediately felt another wet smack against his neck, just above the shirt collar. He wiped it away with his hand.

Jesus, it was disgusting. But the skin of his neck was already starting to tingle and burn. And his hand was tingling, too. It was almost like he had been touched with acid.

Nedry opened the car door, glancing back at the dinosaur to make sure it wasn't going to attack, and felt a sudden, excruciating pain in his eyes, stabbing like spikes into the back of his skull, and he squeezed his eyes shut and gasped with the intensity of it and threw up his hands to cover his eyes and felt the slippery foam trickling down both sides of his nose.

Spit.

The dinosaur had spit in his eyes.

Even as he realized it, the pain overwhelmed him, and he dropped to his knees, disoriented, wheezing. He collapsed onto his side, his cheek pressed to the wet ground, his breath coming in thin whistles through the constant, ever-screaming pain that caused flashing spots of light to appear behind his tightly shut eyelids.

The earth shook beneath him and Nedry knew the dinosaur was moving, he could hear its soft hooting cry, and despite the pain he forced his eyes open and still he saw nothing but flashing spots against black. Slowly the realization came to him.

He was blind.

The hooting was louder as Nedry scrambled to his feet and staggered back against the side panel of the car, as a wave of nausea and dizziness swept over him. The dinosaur was close now, he could *feel* it coming close, he was dimly aware of its snorting breath.

But he couldn't see.

He couldn't see anything, and his terror was extreme.

He stretched out his hands, waving them wildly in the air to ward off the attack he knew was coming.

And then there was a new, searing pain, like a fiery knife in his belly, and Nedry stumbled, reaching blindly down to touch the ragged edge of his shirt, and then a thick, slippery mass that was surprisingly warm, and with horror he suddenly knew he was holding his own intestines in his hands. The dinosaur had torn him open. His guts had fallen out.

Nedry fell to the ground and landed on something scaly and cold, it was the animal's foot, and then there was new pain on both sides of his head. The pain grew worse, and as he was lifted to his feet he knew the dinosaur had his head in its jaws, and the horror of that realization was followed by a final wish, that it would all be ended soon.

Bungalow

'More coffee?' Hammond asked politely.

'No, thank you,' Henry Wu said, leaning back in his chair. 'I couldn't eat anything more.' They were sitting in the dining room of Hammond's bungalow, in a secluded corner of the park not far from the labs. Wu had to admit that the bungalow Hammond had built for himself was elegant, with sparse, almost Japanese lines. And the dinner had been excellent, considering the dining room wasn't fully staffed yet.

But there was something about Hammond that Wu found troubling. The old man was different in some way ... subtly different. All during dinner, Wu had tried to decide what it was. In part, a tendency to ramble, to repeat himself, to retell old stories. In part, it was an emotional lability, flaring anger one moment, maudlin sentimentality the next. But all that could be understood as a natural concomitant of age. John Hammond was, after all, almost seventy-seven.

But there was something else. A stubborn evasiveness. An insistence on having his way. And, in the end, a complete refusal to deal with the situation that now faced the park.

Wu had been stunned by the evidence (he did not yet allow himself to believe the case was proved) that the dinosaurs were breeding. After Grant had asked about amphibian DNA, Wu had intended to go directly to his laboratory and check the computer records of the various DNA assemblies. Because, if the dinosaurs were in fact breeding, then everything about Jurassic Park was called into question – their genetic development methods, their genetic control methods, everything. Even the lysine dependency might be suspect. And if these animals could truly breed, and could also survive in the wild ...

Henry Wu wanted to check the data at once. But Hammond had stubbornly insisted Wu accompany him at dinner.

'Now then, Henry, you must save room for ice cream,' Hammond said, pushing back from the table. 'María makes the most wonderful ginger ice cream.'

'All right.' Wu looked at the beautiful, silent serving girl. His eyes followed her out of the room, and then he glanced up at the single video monitor mounted in the wall. The monitor was dark. 'Your monitor's out,' Wu said.

'Is it?' Hammond glanced over. 'Must be the storm.' He reached behind him for the telephone. 'I'll just check with John in control.'

Wu could hear the static crackle on the telephone line. Hammond shrugged, and set the receiver back in its cradle. 'Lines must be down,' he said. 'Or maybe Nedry's still doing data transmission. He has quite a few bugs to fix this weekend. Nedry's a genius in his way, but we had to press him quite hard, toward the end, to make sure he got things right.'

'Perhaps I should go to the control room and check,' Wu said.

'No, no,' Hammond said. 'There's no reason. If there were any problem, we'd hear about it. Ah.'

María came back into the room, with two plates of ice cream.

'You must have just a little, Henry,' Hammond said. 'It's made with fresh ginger, from the eastern part of the island. It's an old man's vice, ice cream. But still . . .'

Dutifully, Wu dipped his spoon. Outside, lightning flashed, and there was the sharp crack of thunder. 'That was close,' Wu said. 'I hope the storm isn't frightening the children.'

'I shouldn't think so,' Hammond said. He tasted the ice cream. 'But I can't help but hold some fears about this park, Henry.'

Inwardly, Wu felt relieved. Perhaps the old man was going to face the facts, after all. 'What kind of fears?'

'You know, Jurassic Park's really made for children. The children of the world love dinosaurs, and the children are going to delight – just *delight* – in this place. Their little faces will shine with the joy of finally seeing these wonderful animals. But I am afraid . . . I may not live to see it, Henry. I may not live to see the joy on their faces.'

'I think there are other problems, too,' Wu said, frowning.

'But none so pressing on my mind as this,' Hammond said, 'that I may not live to see their shining, delighted faces. This is our triumph, this park. We have done what we set out to do. And, you remember, our original intent was to use the newly emerging technology of genetic engineering to make money. A lot of money.'

Wu knew Hammond was about to launch into one of his old speeches. He held up his hand. 'I'm familiar with this, John –'

'If you were going to start a bioengineering company, Henry, what would you do? Would you make products to help mankind, to fight illness and disease? Dear me, no. That's a terrible idea. A very poor use of new technology.'

Hammond shook his head sadly. 'Yet, you'll remember,' he said, 'the original genetic engineering companies, like Genentech and Cetus, were all started to make pharmaceuticals. New drugs for mankind. Noble, noble purpose. Unfortunately, drugs face all kinds of barriers. FDA testing alone takes five to eight years – if you're lucky. Even worse, there are forces at work in the marketplace. Suppose you make a miracle drug for cancer or heart disease – as Genentech did. Suppose you now want to charge a thousand dollars or two thousand dollars a dose. You might imagine that is your privilege. After all, you invented the drug, you paid to develop and test it; you should be able to charge whatever you wish. But do you really think that the government will let you do that? No, Henry, they will not. Sick people aren't going to pay a thousand dollars a dose for needed medication – they won't be grateful, they'll be outraged. Blue Cross isn't going to pay it. They'll scream highway robbery. So something will happen. Your patent application will be denied. Your permits will be delayed. *Something* will force you to see reason – and to sell your drug at a lower cost. From a business standpoint, that makes helping mankind a very risky business. Personally, I would *never* help mankind.'

Wu had heard the argument before. And he knew Hammond was right; some new bioengineered pharmaceuticals had indeed suffered inexplicable delays and patent problems.

'Now,' Hammond said, 'think how different it is when you're making entertainment. Nobody *needs* entertainment. That's not a matter for government intervention. If I charge five thousand dollars a day for my park, who is going to stop me? After all, nobody needs to come here. And, far from being highway robbery, a costly price tag actually increases the appeal of the park. A visit becomes a status symbol, and all Americans love that. So do the Japanese, and of course they have far more money.'

Hammond finished his ice cream, and María silently took the dish away. 'She's not from here, you know,' he said. 'She's Haitian. Her mother is French. But in any case, Henry, you will recall that the original purpose behind pointing my company in this direction in the first place – was to have freedom from government intervention, anywhere in the world.'

'Speaking of the rest of the world . . .'

Hammond smiled. 'We have already leased a large tract in the Azores, for Jurassic Park Europe. And you know we long ago obtained an island near Guam, for Jurassic Park Japan. Construction on the next two Jurassic Parks will begin early next year. They will all be open within four years. At that time, direct revenues will exceed ten billion dollars a year, and merchandising, television, and ancillary rights should double that. I see no reason to bother with children's pets, which I'm told Lew Dodgson thinks we're planning to make.'

'Twenty billion dollars a year,' Wu said softly, shaking his head.

'That's speaking conservatively,' Hammond said. He smiled. 'There's no reason to speculate wildly. More ice cream, Henry?'

'Did you find him?' Arnold snapped, when the guard walked into the control room.

'No, Mr. Arnold.'

'*Find him.*'

'I don't think he's in the building, Mr. Arnold.'

'Then look in the lodge,' Arnold said, 'look in the maintenance building, look in the utility shed, look everywhere, but just *find him*.'

'The thing is . . .' The guard hesitated. 'Mr. Nedry's the fat man, is that right?'

'That's right,' Arnold said. 'He's fat. A fat slob.'

'Well, Jimmy down in the main lobby said he saw the fat man go into the garage.'

Muldoon spun around. 'Into the garage? When?'

'About ten, fifteen minutes ago.'

'Jesus,' Muldoon said.

The Jeep screeched to a stop. 'Sorry,' Harding said.

In the headlamps, Ellie saw a herd of apatosaurs lumbering across the road. There were six animals, each the size of a house, and a baby as large as a full-grown horse. The apatosaurs moved in unhurried silence, never looking toward the Jeep and its glowing headlamps. At one point, the baby stopped to lap water from a puddle in the road, then moved on.

A comparable herd of elephants would have been startled by the arrival of a car, would have trumpeted and circled to protect the baby. But these animals showed no fear. 'Don't they see us?' she said.

'Not exactly, no,' Harding said. 'Of course, in a literal sense they do see us, but we don't really *mean* anything to them. We hardly ever take cars out at night, and so they have no experience of them. We are just a strange, smelly object in their environment. Representing no threat, and therefore no interest. I've occasionally been out at night, visiting a sick animal, and on my way back these fellows blocked the road for an hour or more.'

'What do you do?'

Harding grinned. 'Play a recorded tyrannosaur roar. That gets them moving. Not that they care much about tyrannosaurs. These apatosaurs are so big they don't really have any predators. They can break a tyrannosaur's neck with a swipe of their tail. And they know it. So does the tyrannosaur.'

'But they do see us. I mean, if we were to get out of the car . . .'

Harding shrugged. 'They probably wouldn't react. Dinosaurs have excellent visual acuity, but they have a basic amphibian visual system: it's attuned to movement. They don't see unmoving things well at all.'

The animals moved on, their skin glistening in the rain. Harding put the car in gear. 'I think we can continue now,' he said.

Wu said, 'I suspect you may find there are pressures on your park, just as there are pressures on Genentech's drugs.' He and Hammond had moved to the living room, and they were now watching the storm lash the big glass windows.

'I can't see how,' Hammond said.

'The scientists may wish to constrain you. Even to stop you.'

'Well, they *can't do that*,' Hammond said. He shook his finger at Wu. 'You know why the scientists would try to do that? It's because they want to do research, of course. That's all they ever want to do, is research. Not to accomplish anything. Not to make any progress. Just do *research*. Well, they have a surprise coming to them.'

'I wasn't thinking of that,' Wu said.

Hammond sighed. 'I'm sure it would be *interesting* for the scientists, to do research. But you arrive at the point where these animals are simply too expensive to be used for research. This is wonderful technology, Henry, but it's also frightfully expensive technology. The fact is, it can only be supported as entertainment.' Hammond shrugged. 'That's just the way it is.'

'But if there are attempts to close down –'

'Face the damn facts, Henry,' Hammond said irritably. 'This isn't America. This isn't even Costa Rica. This is my island. I own it. And nothing is going to stop me from opening Jurassic Park to all the children of the world.' He chuckled. 'Or, at least, to the rich ones. And I tell you, they'll love it.'

In the back seat of the Jeep, Ellie Sattler stared out the window. They had been driving through rain-drenched jungle for the last twenty minutes, and had seen nothing since the apatosaurs crossed the road.

'We're near the jungle river now,' Harding said, as he drove. 'It's off there somewhere to our left.'

Abruptly he slammed on the brakes again. The car skidded to a stop in front of a flock of small green animals. 'Well, you're getting quite a show tonight,' he said. 'Those are compys.'

Procompsognathids, Ellie thought, wishing that Grant were here to see them. This was the animal they had seen in the fax, back in Montana. The little dark green procompsognathids scurried to the other side of the road, then squatted on their hind legs to look at the car, chittering briefly, before hurrying onward into the night.

'Odd,' Harding said. 'Wonder where they're off to? Compys don't usually move at night, you know. They climb up in a tree and wait for daylight.'

'Then why are they out now?' Ellie said.

'I can't imagine. You know compys are scavengers, like buzzards. They're attracted to a dying animal, and they have tremendously sensitive smell. They can smell a dying animal for miles.'

'Then they're going to a dying animal?'

'Dying, or already dead.'

'Should we follow them?' Ellie said.

'I'd be curious,' Harding said. 'Yes, why not? Let's go see where they're going.'

He turned the car around, and headed back toward the compys.

Tim

Tim Murphy lay in the Land Cruiser, his cheek pressed against the car door handle. He drifted slowly back to consciousness. He wanted only to sleep. He shifted his position, and felt the pain in his cheekbone where it lay against the metal door. His whole body ached. His arms and his legs and most of all his head – there was a terrible pounding pain in his head. All the pain made him want to go back to sleep.

He pushed himself up on one elbow, opened his eyes, and retched, vomiting all over his shirt. He tasted sour bile and wiped his mouth with the back of his hand. His head throbbed; he felt dizzy and seasick, as if the world were moving, as if he were rocking back and forth on a boat.

Tim groaned, and rolled onto his back, turning away from the puddle of vomit. The pain in his head made him breathe in short, shallow gasps. And he still felt sick, as if everything were moving. He opened his eyes and looked around, trying to get his bearings.

He was inside the Land Cruiser. But the car must have flipped over on its side, because he was lying on his back against the passenger door, looking up at the steering wheel and beyond, at the branches of a tree, moving in the wind. The rain had nearly stopped, but water drops still fell on him through the broken front windshield.

He stared curiously at the fragments of glass. He couldn't remember how the windshield had broken. He couldn't remember anything except that they had been parked on the road and he had been talking to Dr. Grant when the tyrannosaur came toward them. That was the last thing he remembered.

He felt sick again, and closed his eyes until the nausea passed. He was aware of a rhythmic creaking sound, like the rigging of a boat. Dizzy and sick to his stomach, he really felt as if the whole car were moving beneath him. But when he opened his eyes again, he saw it was true – the Land Cruiser *was* moving, lying on its side, swaying back and forth.

The whole car was moving.

Tentatively, Tim rose to his feet. Standing on the passenger door, he peered over the dashboard, looking out through the shattered windshield. At first he saw only dense foliage, moving in the wind. But here and there he could see gaps, and beyond the foliage, the ground was –

The ground was twenty feet below him.

He stared uncomprehendingly. The Land Cruiser was lying on its side in the branches of a large tree, twenty feet above the ground, swaying back and forth in the wind.

'Oh shit,' he said. What was he going to do? He stood on his tiptoes and peered out, trying to see better, grabbing the steering wheel for support. The wheel spun free in his hand, and with a loud *crack* the Land Cruiser shifted position, dropping a few feet in the branches of the tree. He looked down through the shattered glass of the passenger-door window at the ground below.

'Oh shit. Oh shit.' He kept repeating it. 'Oh shit. Oh shit.'

Another loud *crack* – the Land Cruiser jolted down another foot.

He had to get out of here.

He looked down at his feet. He was standing on the door handle. He crouched back down on his hands and knees to look at the handle. He couldn't see very well in the dark, but he could tell that the door was dented outward so the handle couldn't turn. He'd never get the door open. He tried to roll the window down, but the window was stuck, too. Then he thought of the back door. Maybe he could open that. He leaned over the front seat, and the Land Cruiser lurched with the shift in weight.

Carefully, Tim reached back and twisted the handle on the rear door.

It was stuck, too.

How was he going to get out?

He heard a snorting sound and looked down. A dark shape passed below him. It wasn't the tyrannosaur. This shape was tubby and it made a kind of snuffling as it waddled along. The tail flopped back and forth, and Tim could see the long spikes.

It was the stegosaur, apparently recovered from its illness. Tim wondered where the other people were: Gennaro and Sattler and the vet. He had last seen them near the stegosaur. How long ago was that? He looked at his watch, but the face was cracked; he couldn't see the numbers. He took the watch off and tossed it aside.

The stegosaur snuffled and moved on. Now the only sound was the wind in the trees, and the creaking of the Land Cruiser as it shifted back and forth.

He had to get out of here.

Tim grabbed the handle, tried to force it, but it was stuck solid. It wouldn't move at all. Then he realized what was wrong: the rear door was locked! Tim pulled up the pin and twisted the handle. The rear door swung open, downward – and came to rest against the branch a few feet below.

The opening was narrow, but Tim thought he could wriggle through it. Holding his breath, he crawled slowly back into the rear seat. The Land Cruiser creaked, but held its position. Gripping the doorposts on both sides, Tim slowly lowered himself down, through the narrow angled opening of the door. Soon he was lying flat on his stomach on the slanted door, his legs sticking out of the car. He kicked in the air – his feet touched something solid – a branch – and he rested his weight on it.

As soon as he did, the branch bent down and the door swung wider, spilling him out of the Land Cruiser, and he fell – leaves scratching his face – his body bouncing from branch to branch – a jolt – searing pain, bright light in his head –

He slammed to a stop, the wind knocked from him. Tim lay doubled over a large branch, his stomach burning pain.

Tim heard another *crack* and looked up at the Land Cruiser, a big dark shape five feet above him.

Another *crack*. The car shifted.

Tim forced himself to move, to climb down. He used to like to climb trees. He was a good tree-climber. And this was a good tree to climb, the branches spaced close together, almost like a staircase . . .

Crackkkk . . .

The car was definitely moving.

Tim scrambled downward, slipping over the wet branches, feeling sticky sap on his hands, hurrying. He had not descended more than a few feet when the Land Cruiser creaked a final time, and then slowly, very slowly, nosed over. Tim could see the big green grille and the front headlights swinging down at him, and then the Land Cruiser fell free, gaining momentum as it rushed toward him, slamming against the branch where Tim had just been –

And it stopped.

His face just inches from the dented grille, bent inward like an evil mouth, headlamps for eyes. Oil dripped on Tim's face.

He was still twelve feet above the ground. He reached down, found another branch, and moved down. Above, he saw the branch bending under the weight of the Land Cruiser, and then it cracked, and the Land Cruiser came rushing down toward him and he knew he could never escape it, he could never get down fast enough, so Tim just let go.

He fell the rest of the way.

Tumbling, banging, feeling pain in every part of his body, hearing

the Land Cruiser smashing down through the branches after him like
a pursuing animal, and then Tim's shoulder hit the soft ground, and he
rolled as hard as he could, and pressed his body against the trunk of
the tree as the Land Cruiser tumbled down with a loud metallic crash
and a sudden hot burst of electrical sparks that stung his skin and
sputtered and sizzled on the wet ground around him.

Slowly, Tim got to his feet. In the darkness he heard the snuffling, and
saw the stegosaur coming back, apparently attracted by the crash of the
Land Cruiser. The dinosaur moved dumbly, the low head thrust forward, and the big cartilaginous plates running in two rows along the
hump of the back. It behaved like an overgrown tortoise. Stupid like
that. And slow.

Tim picked up a rock and threw it.

'Get away!'

The rock thunked dully off the plates. The stegosaur kept coming.

'Go on! *Go!*'

He threw another rock, and hit the stegosaur in the head. The
animal grunted, turned slowly away, and shuffled off in the direction it
had come.

Tim leaned against the crumpled Land Cruiser and looked around
in the darkness. He had to get back to the others, but he didn't want
to get lost. He knew he was somewhere in the park, probably not far
from the main road. If he could only get his bearings. He couldn't see
much in the dark, but –

Then he remembered the goggles.

He climbed through the shattered front windshield into the Land
Cruiser and found the night-vision goggles, and the radio. The radio
was broken and silent, so he left it behind. But the goggles still worked.
He flicked them on, saw the reassuringly familiar phosphorescent green
image.

Wearing the goggles, he saw the battered fence off to his left, and
walked toward it. The fence was twelve feet high, but the tyrannosaur
had flattened it easily. Tim hurried across it, moved through an area
of dense foliage, and came out onto the main road.

Through his goggles, he saw the other Land Cruiser turned on its
side. He ran toward it, took a breath, and looked inside. The car was
empty. No sign of Dr. Grant and Dr. Malcolm.

Where had they gone?

Where had everybody gone?

He felt sudden panic, standing alone in the jungle road at night
with that empty car, and turned quickly in circles, seeing the bright

green world in the goggles swirl. Something pale by the side of the road caught his eye. It was Lex's baseball. He wiped the mud off it.

'Lex!'

Tim shouted as loud as he could, not caring if the animals heard him. He listened, but there was only the wind, and the plink of raindrops falling from the trees.

'Lex!'

He vaguely remembered that she had been in the Land Cruiser when the tyrannosaur attacked. Had she stayed there? Or had she gotton away? The events of the attack were confused in his mind. He wasn't exactly sure what had happened. Just to think of it made him uneasy. He stood in the road, gasping with panic.

'*Lex!*'

The night seemed to close in around him. Feeling sorry for himself, he sat in a cold rainy puddle in the road and whimpered for a while. When he finally stopped, he still heard whimpering. It was faint, and it was coming from somewhere farther up the road.

'How long has it been?' Muldoon said, coming back into the control room. He was carrying a black metal case.

'Half an hour.'

'Harding's Jeep should be back here by now.'

Arnold stubbed out his cigarette. 'I'm sure they'll arrive any minute now.'

'Still no sign of Nedry?' Muldoon said.

'No. Not yet.'

Muldoon opened the case, which contained six portable radios. 'I'm going to distribute these to people in the building.' He handed one to Arnold. 'Take the charger, too. These are our emergency radios, but nobody had them plugged in, naturally. Let it charge about twenty minutes, and then try and raise the cars.'

Henry Wu opened the door marked FERTILIZATION and entered the darkened lab. There was nobody here; apparently all the technicians were still at dinner. Wu went directly to the computer terminal and punched up the DNA logbooks. The logbooks had to be kept on computer. DNA was such a large molecule that each species required ten gigabytes of optical disk space to store details of all the iterations. He was going to have to check all fifteen species. That was a tremendous amount of information to search through.

He still wasn't clear about why Grant thought frog DNA was important. Wu himself didn't often distinguish one kind of DNA from another. After all, most DNA in living creatures was exactly the same. DNA was an incredibly ancient substance. Human beings, walking around in the streets of the modern world, bouncing their pink new babies, hardly stopped to think that the substance at the center of it all – the substance that began the dance of life – was a chemical almost as old as the earth itself. The DNA molecule was so old that its evolution had essentially finished more than two billion years ago. There had been little new since that time. Just a few recent combinations of the old genes – and not much of that.

When you compared the DNA of man and the DNA of a lowly bacterium, you found that only about 10 percent of the strands were different. This innate conservatism of DNA emboldened Wu to use whatever DNA he wished. In making his dinosaurs, Wu had manipulated the DNA as a sculptor might clay or marble. He had created freely.

He started the computer search program, knowing it would take two or three minutes to run. He got up and walked around the lab, checking instruments out of long-standing habit. He noted the recorder outside the freezer door, which tracked the freezer temperature. He saw there was a spike in the graph. That was odd, he thought. It meant somebody had been in the freezer. Recently, too – within the last half-hour. But who would go in there at night?

The computer beeped, signaling that the first of the data searches was complete. Wu went over to see what it had found, and when he saw the screen, he forgot all about the freezer and the graph spike. .

LEITZKE DNA SEARCH ALGORITHM
DNA: Version Search Criteria: RANA (all, fragment len > 0)

DNA Incorporating RANA Fragments	Versions
Maiasaurs	2.1–2.9
Procompsognathids	3.0–3.7
Othnielia	3.1–3.3
Velociraptors	1.0–3.0
Hypsilophodontids	2.4–2.7

The result was clear: all breeding dinosaurs incorporated *rana*, or frog, DNA. None of the other animals did. Wu still did not understand why this had caused them to breed. But he could no longer deny that Grant was right. The dinosaurs were breeding.

He hurried up to the control room.

Lex

She was curled up inside a big one-meter drainage pipe that ran under
the road. She had her baseball glove in her mouth and she was rocking
back and forth, banging her head repeatedly against the back of the
pipe. It was dark in there, but he could see her clearly with his goggles.
She seemed unhurt, and he felt a great burst of relief.

'Lex, it's me. Tim.'

She didn't answer. She continued to bang her head on the pipe.

'Come on out.'

She shook her head no. He could see she was badly frightened.

'Lex,' he said, 'if you come out, I'll let you wear these night goggles.'
She just shook her head.

'Look what I have,' he said, holding up his hand. She stared
uncomprehendingly. It was probably too dark for her to see. 'It's your
ball, Lex. I found your ball.'

'So what.'

He tried another approach. 'It must be uncomfortable in there.
Cold, too. Wouldn't you like to come out?'

She resumed banging her head against the pipe.

'Why not?'

'There's aminals out there.'

That threw him for a moment. She hadn't said 'aminals' for years.
'The aminals are gone,' he said.

'There's a big one. A Tyrannosaurus rex.'

'He's gone.'

'Where did he go?'

'I don't know, but he's not around here now,' Tim said, hoping it
was true.

Lex didn't move. He heard her banging again. Tim sat down in
the grass outside the pipe, where she could see him. The ground was
wet where he sat. He hugged his knees and waited. He couldn't think
of anything else to do. 'I'm just going to sit here,' he said. 'And rest.'

'Is Daddy out there?'

'No,' he said, feeling strange. 'He's back at home, Lex.'

'Is Mommy?'

'No, Lex.'

'Are there any grownups out there?' Lex said.

'Not yet. But I'm sure they'll come soon. They're probably on their way right now.'

Then he heard her moving inside the pipe, and she came out. Shivering with cold, and with dried blood on her forehead, but otherwise all right.

She looked around in surprise and said, 'Where's Dr. Grant?'

'I don't know.'

'Well, he was here before.'

'He was? When?'

'*Before*,' Lex said. 'I saw him when I was in the pipe.'

'Where'd he go?'

'How am I supposed to know?' Lex said, wrinkling her nose. She began to shout: 'Hellooo. Hell-oooo! Dr. Grant? Dr. Grant!'

Tim was uneasy at the noise she was making – it might bring back the tyrannosaur – but a moment later he heard an answering shout. It was coming from the right, over toward the Land Cruiser that Tim had left a few minutes before. With his goggles, Tim saw with relief that Dr. Grant was walking toward them. He had a big tear in his shirt at the shoulder, but otherwise he looked okay.

'Thank God,' he said. 'I've been looking for you.'

Shivering, Ed Regis got to his feet, and wiped the cold mud off his face and hands. He had spent a very bad half hour, wedged among big boulders on the slope of a hill below the road. He knew it wasn't much of a hiding place, but he was panicked and he wasn't thinking clearly. He had lain in this muddy cold place and he had tried to get hold of himself, but he kept seeing that dinosaur in his mind. That dinosaur coming toward him. Toward the car.

Ed Regis didn't remember exactly what had happened after that. He remembered that Lex had said something but he hadn't stopped, he *couldn't* stop, he had just kept running and running. Beyond the road he had lost his footing and tumbled down the hill and come to rest by some boulders, and it had seemed to him that he could crawl in among the boulders, and hide, there was enough room, so that was what he had done. Gasping and terrified, thinking of nothing except to get away from the tyrannosaur. And, finally, when he was wedged in there like a rat between the boulders, he had calmed down a little, and he had been overcome with horror and shame because he'd abandoned those kids, he had just run away, he had just saved himself. He knew he should go back up to the road, he should try to rescue them, because he had always imagined himself as brave and cool under pressure, but whenever he tried to get control of himself, to make himself go back up there – somehow he just couldn't. He started to feel panicky, and he had trouble breathing, and he didn't move.

He told himself it was hopeless, anyway. If the kids were still up there on the road they could never survive, and certainly there was nothing Ed Regis could do for them, and he might as well stay where he was. No one was going to know what had happened except him. And there was nothing he could do. Nothing he could have done. And so Regis had remained among the boulders for half an hour, fighting off panic, carefully not thinking about whether the kids had died, or about what Hammond would have to say when he found out.

What finally made him move was the peculiar sensation he noticed in his mouth. The side of his mouth felt funny, kind of numb and tingling, and he wondered if he had hurt it during the fall. Regis touched his face and felt swollen flesh on the side of his mouth. It was funny, but it didn't hurt at all. Then he realized the swollen flesh was a leech growing fat as it sucked his lips. *It was practically in his mouth.* Shivering with nausea, Regis pulled the leech away, feeling it tear from the flesh of his lips, feeling the gush of warm blood in his mouth. He spat, and flung it with disgust into the forest. He saw another leech on his forearm, and pulled it off, leaving a dark bloody streak behind. Jesus, he was probably covered with them. That fall down the hillside. These jungle hills were full of leeches. So were the dark rocky crevices. What did the workmen say? The leeches crawled up your underwear. They liked dark warm places. They liked to crawl right up your –

'Hellooo!'

He stopped. It was a voice, carried by the wind.

'Helloo! Dr. Grant!'

Jesus, *that was the little girl.*

Ed Regis listened to the tone of her voice. She didn't sound frightened, or in pain. She was just calling in her insistent way. And it slowly dawned on him that something else must have happened, that the tyrannosaur must have gone away – or at least hadn't attacked – and that the other people might still be alive. Grant and Malcolm. Everybody might be alive. And the realization made him pull himself together in an instant, the way you got sober in an instant when the cops pulled you over, and he felt better, because now he knew what he had to do. And as he crawled out from the boulders he was already formulating the next step, already figuring out what he would say, how to handle things from this point.

Regis wiped the cold mud off his face and hands, the evidence that he had been hiding. He wasn't embarrassed that he had been hiding, but now he had to take charge. He scrambled back up toward the road, but when he emerged from the foliage he had a moment of disorientation. He didn't see the cars at all. He was somehow at the bottom of the hill. The Land Cruisers must be at the top.

He started walking up the hill, back toward the Land Cruisers. It was very quiet. His feet splashed in the muddy puddles. He couldn't hear the little girl any more. Why had she stopped calling? As he walked, he began to think that maybe something had happened to her. In that case, he shouldn't walk back there. Maybe the tyrannosaur was still hanging around. Here he was, already at the bottom of the hill. That much closer to home.

And it was so quiet. Spooky, it was so quiet.

Ed Regis turned around, and started walking back toward the camp.

Alan Grant ran his hands over her limbs, squeezing the arms and legs briefly. She didn't seem to have any pain. It was amazing: aside from a cut on her head, she was fine. 'I *told* you I was,' she said.

'Well, I had to check.'

The boy was not quite so fortunate. Tim's nose was swollen and painful; Grant suspected it was broken. His right shoulder was badly bruised and swollen. But his legs seemed to be all right. Both kids could walk. That was the important thing.

Grant himself was all right except for a claw abrasion down his right chest, where the tyrannosaur had kicked him. It burned with every breath, but it didn't seem to be serious, and it didn't limit his movement.

He wondered if he had been knocked unconscious, because he had only dim recollections of events immediately preceding the moment he had sat up, groaning, in the woods ten yards from the Land Cruiser. At first his chest had been bleeding, so he had stuck leaves on the wound, and after a while it clotted. Then he had started walking around, looking for Malcolm and the kids. Grant couldn't believe he was still alive, and as scattered images began to come back to him, he tried to make sense of them. The tyrannosaur should have killed them all easily. Why hadn't it?

'I'm hungry,' Lex said.

'Me, too,' Grant said. 'We've got to get ourselves back to civilization. And we've got to tell them about the ship.'

'We're the only ones who know?' Tim said.

'Yes. We've got to get back and tell them.'

'Then let's walk down the road toward the hotel,' Tim said, pointing down the hill. 'That way we'll meet them when they come for us.'

Grant considered that. And he kept thinking about one thing: the dark shape that had crossed between the Land Cruisers even before the attack started. What animal had that been? He could think of only one possibility: the little tyrannosaur.

'I don't think so, Tim. The road has high fences on both sides,' Grant said. 'If one of the tyrannosaurs is farther down on the road, we'll be trapped.'

'Then should we wait here?' Tim said.

'Yes,' Grant said. 'Let's just wait here until someone comes.'

'I'm hungry,' Lex said.

'I hope it won't be very long,' Grant said.

'I don't want to stay here,' Lex said.

Then, from the bottom of the hill, they heard the sound of a man coughing.

'Stay here,' Grant said. He ran forward, to look down the hill.

'Stay here,' Tim said, and he ran forward after him.

Lex followed her brother. 'Don't leave me, don't leave me here, you guys –'

Grant clapped his hand over her mouth. She struggled to protest. He shook his head, and pointed over the hill, for her to look.

At the bottom of the hill, Grant saw Ed Regis, standing rigid, unmoving. The forest around them had become deadly silent. The steady background drone of cicadas and frogs had ceased abruptly. There was only the faint rustle of leaves, and the whine of the wind.

Lex started to speak, but Grant pulled her against the trunk of the nearest tree, ducking down among the heavy gnarled roots at the base. Tim came in right after them. Grant put his hands to his lips, signaling them to be quiet, and then he slowly looked around the tree.

The road below was dark, and as the branches of the big trees moved in the wind, the moonlight filtering through made a dappled, shifting pattern. Ed Regis was gone. It took Grant a moment to locate him. The publicist was pressed up against the trunk of a big tree, hugging it. Regis wasn't moving at all.

The forest remained silent.

Lex tugged impatiently at Grant's shirt; she wanted to know what was happening. Then, from somewhere very near, they heard a soft snorting exhalation, hardly louder than the wind. Lex heard it, too, because she stopped struggling.

The sound floated toward them again, soft as a sigh. Grant thought it was almost like the breathing of a horse.

Grant looked at Regis, and saw the moving shadows cast by the moonlight on the trunk of the tree. And then Grant realized there was another shadow, superimposed on the others, but not moving: a strong curved neck, and a square head.

The exhalation came again.

Tim leaned forward cautiously, to look. Lex did, too.

They heard a *crack* as a branch broke, and into the path stepped a tyrannosaur. It was the juvenile: about eight feet tall, and it moved with the clumsy gait of a young animal, almost like a puppy. The juvenile tyrannosaur shuffled down the path, stopping with every step to sniff the air before moving on. It passed the tree where Regis was hiding, and gave no indication that it had seen him. Grant saw Regis's body relax slightly. Regis turned his head, trying to watch the tyrannosaur on the far side of the tree.

The tyrannosaur was now out of view down the road. Regis started to relax, releasing his grip on the tree. But the jungle remained silent. Regis remained close to the tree trunk for another half a minute. Then the sounds of the forest returned: the first tentative croak of a tree frog, the buzz of one cicada, and then the full chorus. Regis stepped away from the tree, shaking his shoulders, releasing the tension. He walked into the middle of the road, looking in the direction of the departed tyrannosaur.

The attack came from the left.

The juvenile roared as it swung its head forward, knocking Regis flat to the ground. He yelled and scrambled to his feet, but the tyrannosaur pounced, and it must have pinned him with its hind leg, because suddenly Regis wasn't moving, he was sitting up in the path shouting at the dinosaur and waving his hands at it, as if he could scare it off. The young dinosaur seemed perplexed by the sounds and movement coming from its tiny prey. The juvenile bent its head over, sniffing curiously, and Regis pounded on the snout with his fists.

'Get away! Back off! Go on, back off!' Regis was shouting at the top of his lungs, and the dinosaur backed away, allowing Regis to get to his feet. Regis was shouting 'Yeah! You heard me! Back off! Get away!' as he moved away from the dinosaur. The juvenile continued to stare curiously at the odd, noisy little animal before it, but when Regis had gone a few paces, it lunged and knocked him down again.

It's playing with him, Grant thought.

'Hey!' Regis shouted as he fell, but the juvenile did not pursue him, allowing him to get to his feet. He jumped to his feet, and continued backing away. 'You stupid – back! Back! You heard me – back!' he shouted like a lion tamer.

The juvenile roared, but it did not attack, and Regis now edged toward the trees and high foliage to the right. In another few steps he would be in hiding. 'Back! You! Back!' Regis shouted, and then, at the last moment, the juvenile pounced, and knocked Regis flat on his back. 'Cut that out!' Regis yelled, and the juvenile ducked his head, and Regis began to scream. No words, just a high-pitched scream.

The scream cut off abruptly, and when the juvenile lifted his head, Grant saw ragged flesh in his jaws.

'Oh no,' Lex said, softly. Beside her, Tim had turned away, suddenly nauseated. His night-vision goggles slipped from his forehead and landed on the ground with a metallic clink.

The juvenile's head snapped up, and it looked toward the top of the hill.

Tim picked up his goggles as Grant grabbed both the children's hands and began to run.

Control

In the night, the compys scurried along the side of the road. Harding's Jeep followed a short distance behind. Ellie pointed farther up the road. 'Is that a light?'

'Could be,' Harding said. 'Looks almost like headlights.'

The radio suddenly hummed and crackled. They heard John Arnold say, '— you there?'

'Ah, there he is,' Harding said. 'Finally.' He pressed the button. 'Yes, John, we're here. We're near the river, following the compys. It's quite interesting.'

More crackling. Then: '— eed your car —'

'What'd he say?' Gennaro said.

'Something about a car,' Ellie said. At Grant's dig in Montana, Ellie was the one who operated the radiophone. After years of experience, she had become skilled at picking up garbled transmissions. 'I think he said he needs your car.'

Harding pressed the button. 'John? Are you there? We can't read you very well. John?'

There was a flash of lightning, followed by a long sizzle of radio static, then Arnold's tense voice. '— where are — ou —'

'We're one mile north of the hypsy paddock. Near the river, following some compys.'

'No — damn well — get back here — ow!'

'Sounds like he's got a problem,' Ellie said, frowning. There was no mistaking the tension in the voice. 'Maybe we should go back.'

Harding shrugged. 'John's frequently got a problem. You know how engineers are. They want everything to go by the book.' He pressed the button on the radio. 'John? Say again, please. . . .'

More crackling.

More static. The loud crash of lightning. Then: '— Muldoo — need your car — ow —'

Gennaro frowned. 'Is he saying Muldoon needs our car?'

'That's what it sounded like,' Ellie said.

'Well, that doesn't make any sense,' Harding said.

'— other — stuck — Muldoon wants — car —'

'I get it,' Ellie said. 'The other cars are stuck on the road in the storm, and Muldoon wants to go get them.'

Harding shrugged. 'Why doesn't Muldoon take the other car?' He pushed the radio button. 'John? Tell Muldoon to take the other car. It's in the garage.'

The radio crackled. '– not – listen – crazy bastards – car –'

Harding pressed the radio button. 'I said, it's in the garage, John. The car is in the garage.'

More static. '– edry has – ssing – one –'

'I'm afraid this isn't getting us anywhere,' Harding said. 'All right, John. We're coming in now.' He turned the radio off, and turned the car around. 'I just wish I understood what the urgency is.'

Harding put the Jeep in gear, and they rumbled down the road in the darkness. It was another ten minutes before they saw the welcoming lights of the Safari Lodge. And as Harding pulled to a stop in front of the visitor center, they saw Muldoon coming toward them. He was shouting, and waving his arms.

'God damn it, Arnold, you son of a bitch! God damn it, get this park back on track! *Now!* Get my grandkids back here! *Now!*' John Hammond stood in the control room, screaming and stamping his little feet. He had been carrying on this way for the last two minutes, while Henry Wu stood in the corner, looking stunned.

'Well, Mr. Hammond,' Arnold said, 'Muldoon's on his way out right now, to do exactly that.' Arnold turned away, and lit another cigarette. Hammond was like every other management guy Arnold had ever seen. Whether it was Disney or the Navy, management guy always behaved the same. They never understood the technical issues; and they thought that screaming was the way to make things happen. And maybe it was, if you were shouting at your secretaries to get you a limousine.

But screaming didn't make any difference at all to the problems that Arnold now faced. The computer didn't care if it was screamed at. The power network didn't care if it was screamed at. Technical systems were completely indifferent to all this explosive human emotion. If anything, screaming was counterproductive, because Arnold now faced the virtual certainty that Nedry wasn't coming back, which meant that Arnold himself had to go into the computer code and try and figure out what had gone wrong. It was going to be a painstaking job; he'd need to be calm and careful.

'Why don't you go downstairs to the cafeteria,' Arnold said, 'and get a cup of coffee? We'll call you when we have more news.'

'I don't want a Malcolm Effect here,' Hammond said.

'Don't worry about a Malcolm Effect,' Arnold said. 'Will you let me go to work?'

'God damn you,' Hammond said.

'I'll call you, sir, when I have news from Muldoon,' Arnold said. He pushed buttons on his console, and saw the familiar control screens change.

```
*/Jurassic Park Main Modules/
*/
*/ Call Libs
Include: biostat.sys
Include: sysrom.vst
Include: net.sys
Include: pwr.mdl
*/
*/Initialize
SetMain [42]2002/9A{total CoreSysop %4 [vig. 7*tty]}
if ValidMeter(mH) (**mH).MeterVis return
Term Call 909 c.lev {void MeterVis $303} Random(3#*MaxFid)
on SetSystem(!Dn) set shp-val.obj to lim(Val{d}SumVal
  if SetMeter(mH) (**mH).ValdidMeter(Vdd) return
  on SetSystem(!Telcom) set mxcpl.obj to lim(Val{pd})NextVal
```

Arnold was no longer operating the computer. He had now gone behind the scenes to look at the code – the line-by-line instructions that told the computer how to behave. Arnold was unhappily aware that the complete Jurassic Park program contained more than half a million lines of code, most of it undocumented, without explanation.

Wu came forward. 'What are you doing, John?'

'Checking the code.'

'By inspection? That'll take forever.'

'Tell me,' Arnold said. 'Tell me.'

The Road

Muldoon took the curve very fast, the Jeep sliding on the mud. Sitting beside him, Gennaro clenched his fists. They were racing along the cliff road, high above the river, now hidden below them in darkness. Muldoon accelerated forward. His face was tense.

'How much farther?' Gennaro said.

'Two, maybe three miles.'

Ellie and Harding were back at the visitor center. Gennaro had offered to accompany Muldoon. The car swerved. 'It's been an hour,' Muldoon said. 'An hour, with no word from the other cars.'

'But they have radios,' Gennaro said.

'We haven't been able to raise them,' Muldoon said.

Gennaro frowned. 'If I was sitting in a car for an hour in the rain, I'd sure try to use the radio to call for somebody.'

'So would I,' Muldoon said.

Gennaro shook his head. 'You really think something could have happened to them?'

'Chances are,' Muldoon said, 'that they're perfectly fine, but I'll be happier when I finally see them. Should be any minute now.'

The road curved, and then ran up a hill. At the base of the hill Gennaro saw something white, lying among the ferns by the side of the road. 'Hold it,' Gennaro said, and Muldoon braked. Gennaro jumped out and ran forward in the headlights of the Jeep to see what it was. It looked like a piece of clothing, but there was –

Gennaro stopped.

Even from six feet away, he could see clearly what it was. He walked forward more slowly.

Muldoon leaned out of the car and said, 'What is it?'

'It's a leg,' Gennaro said.

The flesh of the leg was pale blue-white, terminating in a ragged bloody stump where the knee had been. Below the calf he saw a white sock, and a brown slip-on shoe. It was the kind of shoe Ed Regis had been wearing.

By then Muldoon was out of the car, running past him to crouch over the leg. 'Jesus.' He lifted the leg out of the foliage, raising it into the light of the headlamps, and blood from the stump gushed down over his hand. Gennaro was still three feet away. He quickly bent over, put his hands on his knees, squeezed his eyes shut, and breathed deeply, trying not to be sick.

'Gennaro.' Muldoon's voice was sharp.

'What?'

'Move. You're blocking the light.'

Gennaro took a breath, and moved. When he opened his eyes he saw Muldoon peering critically at the stump. 'Torn at the joint line,' Muldoon said. 'Didn't bite it – twisted and ripped it. Just ripped his leg off.' Muldoon stood up, holding the severed leg upside down so the remaining blood dripped onto the ferns. His bloody hand smudged the white sock as he gripped the ankle. Gennaro felt sick again.

'No question what happened,' Muldoon was saying. 'The T-rex got him.' Muldoon looked up the hill, then back to Gennaro. 'You all right? Can you go on?'

'Yes,' Gennaro said. 'I can go on.'

Muldoon was walking back toward the Jeep, carrying the leg. 'I guess we better bring this along,' he said. 'Doesn't seem right to leave it here. Christ, it's going to make a mess of the car. See if there's anything in the back, will you? A tarp or newspaper . . .'

Gennaro opened the back door and rummaged around in the space behind the rear seat. He felt grateful to think about something else for a moment. The problem of how to wrap the severed leg expanded to fill his mind, crowding out all other thoughts. He found a canvas bag with a tool kit, a wheel rim, a cardboard box, and –

'Two tarps,' he said. They were neatly folded plastic.

'Give me one,' Muldoon said, still standing outside the car. Muldoon wrapped the leg and passed the now shapeless bundle to Gennaro. Holding it in his hand, Gennaro was surprised at how heavy it felt. 'Just put it in the back,' Muldoon said. 'If there's a way to wedge it, you know, so it doesn't roll around . . .'

'Okay.' Gennaro put the bundle in the back, and Muldoon got behind the wheel. He accelerated, the wheels spinning in the mud, then digging in. The Jeep rushed up the hill, and for a moment at the top the headlights still pointed upward into the foliage, and then they swung down, and Gennaro could see the road before them.

'Jesus,' Muldoon said.

Gennaro saw a single Land Cruiser, lying on its side in the center of the road. He couldn't see the second Land Cruiser at all. 'Where's the other car?'

Muldoon looked around briefly, pointed to the left. 'There.' The second Land Cruiser was twenty feet away, crumpled at the foot of a tree.

'What's it doing there?'

'The T-rex threw it.'

'*Threw* it?' Gennaro said.

Muldoon's face was grim. 'Let's get this over with,' he said, climbing out of the Jeep. They hurried forward to the second Land Cruiser. Their flashlights swung back and forth in the night.

As they came closer, Gennaro saw how battered the car was. He was careful to let Muldoon look inside first.

'I wouldn't worry,' Muldoon said. 'It's very unlikely we'll find anyone.'

'No?'

'No,' he said. He explained that, during his years in Africa, he had visited the scenes of a half-dozen animal attacks on humans in the bush. One leopard attack: the leopard had torn open a tent in the night and taken a three-year-old child. Then one buffalo attack in Amboseli; two lion attacks; one croc attack in the north, near Meru. In every case, there was surprisingly little evidence left behind.

Inexperienced people imagined horrific proofs of an animal attack – torn limbs left behind in the tent, trails of dripping blood leading away into the bush, bloodstained clothing not far from the campsite. But the truth was, there was usually nothing at all, particularly if the victim was small, an infant or a young child. The person just seemed to disappear, as if he had walked out into the bush and never come back. A predator could kill a child just by shaking it, snapping the neck. Usually there wasn't any blood.

And most of the time you never found any other remains of the victims. Sometimes a button from a shirt, or a silver of rubber from a shoe. But most of the time, nothing.

Predators took children – they preferred children – and they left nothing behind. So Muldoon thought it highly unlikely that they would ever find any remains of the children.

But as he looked in now, he had a surprise.

'I'll be damned,' he said.

Muldoon tried to put the scene together. The front windshield of the Land Cruiser was shattered, but there wasn't much glass nearby. He had noticed shards of glass back on the road. So the windshield must have broken back there, before the tyrannosaur picked the car up and threw it here. But the car had taken a tremendous beating. Muldoon shone his light inside.

'Empty?' Gennaro said, tensely.

'Not quite,' Muldoon said. His flashlight glinted off a crushed radio handset, and on the floor of the car he saw something else, something curved and black. The front doors were dented and jammed shut, but he climbed in through the back door and crawled over the seat to pick up the black object.

'It's a watch,' he said, peering at it in the beam of his flashlight. A cheap digital watch with a molded black rubber strap. The LCD face was shattered. He thought the boy might have been wearing it, though he wasn't sure. But it was the kind of watch a kid would have.

'What is it, a watch?' Gennaro said.

'Yes. And there's a radio, but it's broken.'

'Is that significant?'

'Yes. And there's something else . . .' Muldoon sniffed. There was a sour odor inside the car. He shone the light around until he saw the vomit dripping off the side door panel. He touched it: still fresh. 'One of the kids may still be alive,' Muldoon said.

Gennaro squinted at him. 'What makes you think so?'

'The watch,' Muldoon said. 'The watch proves it.' He handed the watch to Gennaro, who held it in the glow of the flashlight, and turned it over in his hands.

'Crystal is cracked,' Gennaro said.

'That's right,' Muldoon said. 'And the band is uninjured.'

'Which means?'

'The kid took it off.'

'That could have happened anytime,' Gennaro said. 'Anytime before the attack.'

'No,' Muldoon said. 'Those LCD crystals are tough. It takes a powerful blow to break them. The watch face was shattered during the attack.'

'So the kid took his watch off.'

'Think about it,' Muldoon said. 'If you were being attacked by a tyrannosaur, would you stop to take your watch off?'

'Maybe it was torn off.'

'It's almost impossible to tear a watch off somebody's wrist, without tearing the hand off, too. Anyway, the band is intact. No,' Muldoon said. 'The kid took it off himself. He looked at his watch, saw it was broken, and took it off. He had the time to do that.'

'When?'

'It could only have been after the attack,' Muldoon said. 'The kid must have been in this car, after the attack. And the radio was broken, so he left it behind, too. He's a bright kid, and he knew they weren't useful.'

'If he's so bright,' Gennaro said, 'where'd he go? Because I'd stay right here and wait to be picked up.'

'Yes,' Muldoon said. 'But perhaps he couldn't stay here. Maybe the tyrannosaur came back. Or some other animal. Anyway, something made him leave.'

'Then where'd he go?' Gennaro said.

'Let's see if we can determine that,' Muldoon said, and he strode off toward the main road.

Gennaro watched Muldoon peering at the ground with his flashlight. His face was just inches from the mud, intent on his search. Muldoon really believed he was on to something, that at least one of the kids was still alive. Gennaro remained unimpressed. The shock of finding the severed leg had left him with a grim determination to close the park, and destroy it. No matter what Muldoon said, Gennaro suspected him of unwarranted enthusiasm, and hopefulness, and –

'You notice these prints?' Muldoon asked, still looking at the ground.

'What prints?' Gennaro said.

'These footprints – see them, coming toward us from up the road? – and they're adult-size prints. Some kind of rubber-sole shoe. Notice the distinctive tread pattern . . .'

Gennaro saw only mud. Puddles catching the light from the flashlights.

'You can see,' Muldoon continued, 'the adult prints come to here, where they're joined by other prints. Small, and medium-size . . . moving around in circles, overlapping . . . almost as if they're standing together, talking . . . But now here they are, they seem to be running . . .' He pointed off. 'There. Into the park.'

Gennaro shook his head. 'You can see whatever you want in this mud.'

Muldoon got to his feet and stepped back. He looked down at the ground and sighed. 'Say what you like, I'll wager one of the kids survived. And maybe both. Perhaps even an adult as well, if these big prints belong to someone other than Regis. We've got to search the park.'

'Tonight?' Gennaro said.

But Muldoon wasn't listening. He had walked away, toward an embankment of soft earth, near a drainpipe for rain. He crouched again. 'What was that little girl wearing?'

'Christ,' Gennaro said. 'I don't know.'

Proceeding slowly, Muldoon moved farther toward the side of the road. And then they heard a wheezing sound. It was definitely an animal sound.

'Listen,' Gennaro said, feeling panic, 'I think we better –'

'Shhh,' Muldoon said.

He paused, listening.

'It's just the wind,' Gennaro said.

They heard the wheezing again, distinctly this time. It wasn't the wind. It was coming from the foliage directly ahead of him, by the side of the road. If didn't sound like an animal, but Muldoon moved forward cautiously. He waggled his light and shouted, but the wheezing did not change character. Muldoon pushed aside the fronds of a palm.

'What is it?' Gennaro said.

'It's Malcolm,' Muldoon said.

Ian Malcolm lay on his back, his skin gray-white, mouth slackly open. His breath came in wheezing gasps. Muldoon handed the flashlight to Gennaro, and then bent to examine the body. 'I can't find the injury,' he said. 'Head okay, chest, arms . . .'

Then Gennaro shone the light on the legs. 'He put a tourniquet on.' Malcolm's belt was twisted tight over the right thigh. Gennaro moved the light down the leg. The right ankle was bent outward at an awkward angle from the leg, the trousers flattened, soaked in blood. Muldoon touched the ankle gently, and Malcolm groaned.

Muldoon stepped back and tried to decide what to do next. Malcolm might have other injuries. His back might be broken. It might kill him to move him. But if they left him here, he would die of shock. It was only because he had had the presence of mind to put a tourniquet on that he hadn't already bled to death. And probably he was doomed. They might as well move him.

Gennaro helped Muldoon pick the man up, hoisting him awkwardly over their shoulders. Malcolm moaned, and breathed in ragged gasps. 'Lex,' he said. 'Lex . . . went . . . Lex . . .'

'Who's Lex?' Muldoon said.

'The little girl,' Gennaro said.

They carried Malcolm back to the Jeep, and wrested him into the back seat. Gennaro tightened the tourniquet around his leg. Malcolm groaned again. Muldoon slid the trouser cuff up and saw the pulpy flesh beneath, the dull white splinters of protruding bone.

'We've got to get him back,' Muldoon said.

'You going to leave here without the kids?' Gennaro said.

'If they went into the park, it's twenty square miles,' Muldoon said, shaking his head. 'The only way we can find anything out there is with the motion sensors. If the kids are alive and moving around, the motion sensors will pick them up, and we can go right to them and bring them back. But if we don't take Dr. Malcolm back right now, he'll die.'

'Then we have to go back,' Gennaro said.

'Yes, I think so.'

They climbed into the car. Gennaro said, 'Are you going to tell Hammond the kids are missing?'

'No,' Muldoon said. 'You are.'

Control

Donald Gennaro stared at Hammond, sitting in the deserted cafeteria. The man was spooning ice cream, calmly eating it. 'So Muldoon believes the children are somewhere in the park?'

'He thinks so, yes.'

'Then I'm sure we'll find them.'

'I hope so,' Gennaro said. He watched the old man deliberately eating, and he felt a chill.

'Oh, I am sure we'll find them. After all, I keep telling everyone, this park is made for kids.'

Gennaro said, 'Just so you understand that they're missing, sir.'

'*Missing?*' he snapped. 'Of course I know they're *missing*. I'm not senile.' He sighed, and changed tone again. 'Look, Donald,' Hammond said. 'Let's not get carried away. We've had a little breakdown from the storm or whatever, and as a result we've suffered a regrettable, unfortunate accident. And that's all that's happened. We're dealing with it. Arnold will get the computers cleaned up. Muldoon will pick up the kids, and I have no doubt he'll be back with them by the time we finish this ice cream. So let's just wait and see what develops, shall we?'

'Whatever you say, sir,' Gennaro said.

'Why?' Henry Wu said, looking at the console screen.

'Because I think Nedry did something to the code,' Arnold said. 'That's why I'm checking it.'

'All right,' Wu said. 'But have you tried your options?'

'Like what?' Arnold said.

'I don't know. Aren't the safety systems still running?' Wu said. 'Keychecks? All that?'

'Jesus,' Arnold said, snapping his fingers. 'They must be. Safety systems can't be turned off except at the main panel.'

'Well,' Wu said, 'if Keychecks is active, you can trace what he did.'

'I sure as hell can,' Arnold said. He started to press buttons. Why hadn't he thought of it before? It was so obvious. The computer system at Jurassic Park had several tiers of safety systems built into it. One of them was a keycheck program, which monitored all the keystrokes entered by operators with access to the system. It was originally installed as a debugging device, but it was retained for its security value.

In a moment, all the keystrokes that Nedry had entered into the computer earlier in the day were listed in a window on the screen:

```
13,42,121,32,88,77,19,13,122,13,44,52,77,90,13,99,13,100,13,109,55,103
144,13,99,87,60,13,44,12,09,13,43,63,13,46,57,89,103,122,13,44,52,88,9
31,13,21,13,57,98,100,102,103,13,112,13,146,13,13,13,77,67,88,23,13,13
system
nedry
goto command level
nedry
040/#xy/67&
mr goodbytes
security
keycheck off
safety off
sl off
security
whte_rbt.obj
```

'That's it?' Arnold said. 'He was screwing around here for hours, it seemed like.'

'Probably just killing time,' Wu said. 'Until he finally decided to get down to it.'

The initial list of numbers represented the ASCI keyboard codes for the keys Nedry had pushed at his console. Those numbers meant he was still within the standard user interface, like any ordinary user of the computer. So initially Nedry was just looking around, which you wouldn't have expected of the programmer who had designed the system.

'Maybe he was trying to see if there were changes, before he went in,' Wu said.

'Maybe,' Arnold said. Arnold was now looking at the list of commands, which allowed him to follow Nedry's progression through the system, line by line. 'At least we can see what he did.'

system was Nedry's request to leave the ordinary user interface and access the code itself. The computer asked for his name, and he replied: *nedry*. That name was authorized to access the code, so the computer allowed him into the system. Nedry asked to *goto command level*, the computer's highest level of control. The command level required extra security, and asked Nedry for his name, access number, and password.

nedry
040/#xy/67&.
mr goodbytes

Those entries got Nedry into the command level. From there he wanted *security*. And since he was authorized, the computer allowed him to go there. Once at the security level, Nedry tried three variations:

keycheck off
safety off
sl off

'He's trying to turn off the safety systems,' Wu said. 'He doesn't want anybody to see what he's about to do.'

'Exactly,' Arnold said. 'And apparently he doesn't know it's no longer possible to turn the systems off except by manually flipping switches on the main board.'

After three failed commands, the computer automatically began to worry about Nedry. But since he had gotten in with proper authorization, the computer would assume that Nedry was lost, trying to do something he couldn't accomplish from where he was. So the computer asked him again where he wanted to be, and Nedry said:

security. And he was allowed to remain there.

'Finally,' Wu said, 'here's the kicker.' He pointed to the last of the commands Nedry had entered.

whte-rbt.obj

'What the hell is that?' Arnold said. 'White rabbit? Is that supposed to be his private joke?'

'It's marked as an object,' Wu said. In computer terminology, an 'object' was a block of code that could be moved around and used, the way you might move a chair in a room. An object might be a set of commands to draw a picture, or to refresh the screen, or to perform a certain calculation.

'Let's see where it is in the code,' Arnold said. 'Maybe we can figure out what it does.' He went to the program utilities and typed:

FIND WHTE-RBT.OBJ

The computer flashed back:

OBJECT NOT FOUND IN LIBRARIES

'It doesn't exist,' Arnold said.

'Then search the code listing,' Wu said.

Arnold typed:

FIND/LISTINGS: WHTE-RBT.OBJ

The screen scrolled rapidly, the lines of code blurring as they swept past. It continued this way for almost a minute, and then abruptly stopped.

'There it is,' Wu said. 'It's not an object, it's a command.'

The screen showed an arrow pointing to a single line of code:

```
curV = GetHandl {ssm.dt} tempRgn {itm.dd2}.
curH = GetHandl {ssd.itl} tempRgn2 {itm.dd4}.
on DrawMeter(!gN) set shp_val.obj to lim(Val{d})-Xval.
if ValidMeter(mH) (**mH).MeterVis return.
if Meterhandl(vGT) ((DrawBack(tY)) return.
limitDat.4 = maxBits (%33) to {limit .04} set on.
limitDat.5 = setzero, setfive, 0 {limit .2-var(szh)}.
→on whte_rbt.obj call link.sst {security, perimeter} set to off.
vertRange = {maxRange+setlim} tempVgn(fdn-&bb + $404).
horRange = {maxRange-setlim/2} tempHgn(fdn-&dd + $105).
void DrawMeter send_screen.obj print.
```

'Son of a bitch,' Arnold said.

Wu shook his head. 'It isn't a bug in the code at all.'

'No,' Arnold said. 'It's a trap door. The fat bastard put in what looked like an object call, but it's actually a command that links the security and perimeter systems and then turns them off. Gives him complete access to every place in the park.'

'Then we must be able to turn them back on,' Wu said.

'Yeah, we must.' Arnold frowned at the screen. 'All we have to do is figure out the command. I'll run an execution trace on the link,' he said. 'We'll see where that gets us.'

Wu got up from his chair. 'Meanwhile,' he said, 'meanwhile, that somebody went into the freezer about an hour ago. I think I better go count my embryos.'

Ellie was in her room, about to change out of her wet clothes, when there was a knock on the door.

'Alan?' she said, but when she opened the door she saw Muldoon· standing there, with a plastic-wrapped package under his arm. Muldoon was also soaking wet, and there were streaks of dirt on his clothes.

'I'm sorry, but we need your help,' Muldoon said briskly. 'The Land Cruisers were attacked an hour ago. We brought Malcolm back, but he's in shock. He's got a very bad injury to his leg. He's still unconscious, but I put him in the bed in his room. Harding is on his way over.'

'Harding?' she said. 'What about the others?'

'We haven't found the others yet, Dr. Sattler,' Muldoon said. He was speaking slowly now.

'Oh, my God.'

'But we think that Dr. Grant and the children are still alive. We think they went into the park, Dr. Sattler.'

'Went into the park?'

'We think so. Meanwhile, Malcolm needs help. I've called Harding.'

'Shouldn't you call the doctor?'

'There's no doctor on the island. Harding's the best we have.'

'But surely you can call for a doctor –' she said.

'No.' Muldoon shook his head. 'Phone lines are down. We can't call out.' He shifted the package in his arm.

'What's that?' she said.

'Nothing. Just go to Malcolm's room, and help Harding, if you will.' And Muldoon was gone.

She sat on her bed, shocked. Ellie Sattler was not a woman disposed to unnecessary panic, and she had known Grant to get out of dangerous situations before. Once he'd been lost in the badlands for four days when a cliff gave way beneath him and his truck fell a hundred feet into a ravine. Grant's right leg was broken. He had no water. But he walked back on a broken leg.

On the other hand, the kids . . .

She shook her head, pushing the thought away. The kids were probably with Grant. And if Grant was out in the park, well . . . what better person to get them safely through Jurassic Park than a dinosaur expert?

In the Park

'I'm tired,' Lex said. 'Carry me, Dr. Grant.'

'You're too big to carry,' Tim said.

'But I'm *tired*,' she said.

'Okay, Lex,' Grant said, picking her up. 'Oof, you're heavy.'

It was almost 9:00 p.m. The full moon was blurred by drifting mist, and their blunted shadows led them across an open field, toward dark woods beyond. Grant was lost in thought, trying to decide where he was. Since they had originally crossed over the fence that the tyrannosaur had battered down, Grant was reasonably sure they were now somewhere in the tyrannosaur paddock. Which was a place he did not want to be. In his mind, he kept seeing the computer tracing of the tyrannosaur's home range, the tight squiggle of lines that traced his movements within a small area. He and the kids were in that area now.

But Grant also remembered that the tyrannosaurs were isolated from all the other animals, which meant they would know they had left the paddock when they crossed a barrier – a fence, or a moat, or both.

He had seen no barriers, so far.

The girl put her head on his shoulder, and twirled her hair in her fingers. Soon she was snoring. Tim trudged alongside Grant.

'How you holding up, Tim?'

'Okay,' he said. 'But I think we might be in the tyrannosaur area.'

'I'm pretty sure we are. I hope we get out soon.'

'You going to go into the woods?' Tim said. As they came closer, the woods seemed dark and forbidding.

'Yes,' Grant said. 'I think we can navigate by the numbers on the motion sensors.'

The motion sensors were green boxes set about four feet off the ground. Some were freestanding; most were attached to trees. None of them were working, because apparently the power was still off. Each sensor box had a glass lens mounted in the center, and a painted code number beneath that. Up ahead, in the mist-streaked moonlight, Grant could see a box marked T/S/04.

They entered the forest. Huge trees loomed on all sides. In the moonlight, a low mist clung to the ground, curling around the roots of the trees. It was beautiful, but it made walking treacherous. And Grant was watching the sensors. They seemed to be numbered in descending order. He passed T/S/03, and T/S/02. Eventually they reached T/S/01. He was tired from carrying the girl, and he had hoped this would coincide with a boundary for the tyrannosaur paddock, but it was just another box in the middle of the woods. The next box after that was marked T/N/01, followed by T/N/02. Grant realized the numbers must be arranged geographically around a central point, like a compass. They were going from south to north, so the numbers got smaller as they approached the center, then got larger again.

'At least we're going the right way,' Tim said.

'Good for you,' Grant said.

Tim smiled, and stumbled over vines in the mist. He got quickly to his feet. They walked on for a while. 'My parents are getting a divorce,' he said.

'Uh-huh,' Grant said.

'My dad moved out last month. He has his own place in Mill Valley now.'

'Uh-huh.'

'He never carries my sister any more. He never even picks her up.'

'And he says you have dinosaurs on the brain,' Grant said.

Tim sighed. 'Yeah.'

'You miss him?' Grant said.

'Not really,' Tim said. 'Sometimes. She misses him more.'

'Who, your mother?'

'No, Lex. My mom has a boyfriend. She knows him from work.'

They walked in silence for a while, passing T/N/03 and T/N/04. 'Have you met him?' Grant said.

'Yeah.'

'How is he?'

'He's okay,' Tim said. 'He's younger than my dad, but he's bald.'

'How does he treat you?'

'I don't know. Okay. I think he just tries to get on my good side. I don't know what's going to happen. Sometimes my mom says we'll have to sell the house and move. Sometimes he and my mom fight, late at night. I sit in my room and play with my computer, but I can still hear it.'

'Uh-huh,' Grant said.

'Are you divorced?'

'No,' Grant said. 'My wife died a long time ago.'

'And now you're with Dr. Sattler?'

Grant smiled in the darkness. 'No. She's my student.'

'You mean she's still in *school*?'

'Graduate school, yes.' Grant paused long enough to shift Lex to his other shoulder, and then they continued on, past T/N/05 and T/N/06. There was the rumble of thunder in the distance. The storm had moved to the south. There was very little sound in the forest except for the drone of cicadas and the soft croaking of tree frogs.

'You have children?' Tim asked.

'No,' Grant said.

'Are you going to marry Dr. Sattler?'

'No, she's marrying a nice doctor in Chicago sometime next year.'

'Oh,' Tim said. He seemed surprised to hear it. They walked along for a while. 'Then who are you going to marry?'

'I don't think I'm going to marry anybody,' Grant said.

'Me neither,' Tim said.

They walked for a while. Tim said, 'Are we going to walk all night?'

'I don't think I can,' Grant said. 'We'll have to stop, at least for a few hours.' He glanced at his watch. 'We're okay. We've got almost fifteen hours before we have to be back. Before the ship reaches the mainland.'

'Where are we going to stop?' Tim asked, immediately.

Grant was wondering the same thing. His first thought was that they might climb a tree, and sleep up there. But they would have to climb very high to get safely away from the animals, and Lex might fall out while she was asleep. And tree branches were hard; they wouldn't get any rest. At least, he wouldn't.

They needed someplace really safe. He thought back to the plans he had seen on the jet coming down. He remembered that there were outlying buildings for each of the different divisions. Grant didn't know what they were like, because plans for the individual buildings weren't included. And he couldn't remember exactly where they were, but he remembered they were scattered all around the park. There might be buildings somewhere nearby.

But that was a different requirement from simply crossing a barrier and getting out of the tyrannosaur paddock. Finding a building meant a search strategy of some kind. And the best strategies were –

'Tim, can you hold your sister for me? I'm going to climb a tree and have a look around.'

High in the branches, he had a good view of the forest, the tops of the trees extending away to his left and right. They were surprisingly near the edge of the forest – directly ahead the trees ended before a clearing, with an electrified fence and a pale concrete moat.

Beyond that, a large open field in what he assumed was the sauropod paddock. In the distance, more trees, and misty moonlight sparkling on the ocean.

Somewhere he heard the bellowing of a dinosaur, but it was far away. He put on Tim's night-vision goggles and looked again. He followed the gray curve of the moat, and then saw what he was looking for: the dark strip of a service road, leading to the flat rectangle of a roof. The roof was barely above ground level, but it was there. And it wasn't far. Maybe a quarter of a mile or so from the tree.

When he came back down, Lex was sniffling.

'What's the matter?'

'I heard an animal.'

'It won't bother us. Are you awake now? Come on.'

He led her to the fence. It was twelve feet high, with a spiral of barbed wire at the top. It seemed to stretch far above them in the moonlight. The moat was immediately on the other side.

Lex looked up at the fence doubtfully.

'Can you climb it?' Grant asked her.

She handed him her glove, and her baseball. 'Sure. Easy.' She started to climb. 'But I bet Timmy can't.'

Tim spun in fury: '*You shut up.*'

'Timmy's afraid of heights.'

'I am not.'

She climbed higher. 'Are so.'

'Am not.'

'Then come and get me.'

Grant turned to Tim, pale in the darkness. The boy wasn't moving. 'You okay with the fence, Tim?'

'Sure.'

'Want some help?'

'Timmy's a fraidy-cat,' Lex called.

'What a stupid jerk,' Tim said, and he started to climb.

'It's *freezing*,' Lex said. They were standing waist-deep in smelly water at the bottom of a deep concrete moat. They had climbed the fence without incident, except that Tim had torn his shirt on the coils of barbed wire at the top. Then they had all slid down into the moat, and now Grant was looking for a way out.

'At least I got Timmy over the fence for you,' Lex said. 'He really is scared most times.'

'Thanks for your help,' Tim said sarcastically. In the moonlight, he could see floating lumps on the surface. He moved along the moat, looking at the concrete wall on the far side. The concrete was smooth; they couldn't possibly climb it.

'Eww,' Lex said, pointing to the water.

'It won't hurt you, Lex.'

Grant finally found a place where the concrete had cracked and a vine grew down toward the water. He tugged on the vine, and it held his weight. 'Let's go, kids.' They started to climb the vine, back to the field above.

It took only a few minutes to cross the field to the embankment leading to the below-grade service road, and the maintenance building off to the right. They passed two motion sensors, and Grant noticed with some uneasiness that the sensors were still not working, nor were the lights. More than two hours had passed since the power first went out, and it was not yet restored.

Somewhere in the distance, they heard the tyrannosaur roar. 'Is he around here?' Lex said.

'No,' Grant said. 'We're in another section of park from him.' They slid down a grassy embankment and moved toward the concrete building. In the darkness it was forbidding, bunker-like.

'What is this place?' Lex said.

'It's safe,' Grant said, hoping that was true.

The entrance gate was large enough to drive a truck through. It was fitted with heavy bars. Inside, they could see, the building was an open shed, with piles of grass and bales of hay stacked among equipment.

The gate was locked with a heavy padlock. As Grant was examining it, Lex slipped sideways between the bars. 'Come on, you guys.'

Tim followed her. 'I think you can do it, Dr. Grant.'

He was right; it was a tight squeeze, but Grant was able to ease his body between the bars and get into the shed. As soon as he was inside, a wave of exhaustion struck him.

'I wonder if there's anything to eat,' Lex said.

'Just hay.' Grant broke open a bale, and spread it around on the concrete. The hay in the center was warm. They lay down, feeling the warmth. Lex curled up beside him, and closed her eyes. Tim put his arm around her. He heard the sauropods trumpeting softly in the distance.

Neither child spoke. They were almost immediately snoring. Grant raised his arm to look at his watch, but it was too dark to see. He felt the warmth of the children against his own body.

Grant closed his eyes, and slept.

Control

Muldoon and Gennaro came into the control room just as Arnold clapped his hands and said, 'Got you, you little son of a bitch.'

'What is it?' Gennaro said.

Arnold pointed to the screen:

```
Vg1 =  GetHandl {dat.dt} tempCall {itm.temp}
Vg2 =  GetHandl {dat.itl} tempCall {itm.temp}
if Link(Vg1,Vg2) set Lim(Vg1,Vg2) return
if Link(Vg2,Vg1) set Lim(Vg2,Vg1) return
→on whte_rbt.obj link set security (Vg1), perimeter (Vg2)
limitDat.1 = maxBits (%22) to {limit .04} set on
limitDat.2 = setzero, setfive, 0 {limit .2−var(dzh)}
→on fini.obj call link.sst {security, perimeter} set to on
→on fini.obj set link.sst {security, perimeter} restore
→on fini.obj delete line rf whte_rbt.obj, fini.obj
Vg1 = GetHandl {dat.dt} tempCall {itm.temp}
Vg2 = GetHandl {dat.itl} tempCall {itm.temp}
limitDat.4 = maxBits (%33) to {limit .04} set on
limitDat.5 = setzero, setfive, 0 {limit .2−var(szh)}
```

'That's it,' Arnold said, pleased.

'That's what?' Gennaro asked, staring at the screen.

'I finally found the command to restore the original code. The command called 'fini.obj' resets the linked parameters, namely the fence and the power.'

'Good,' Muldoon said.

'But it does something else,' Arnold said. 'It then erases the code lines that refer to it. It destroys all evidence it was ever there. Pretty slick.'

Gennaro shook his head. 'I don't know much about computers.' Although he knew enough to know what it meant when a high-tech company went back to the source code. It meant big, big problems.

'Well, watch this,' Arnold said, and he typed in the command:

FINI.OBJ

The screen flickered and immediately changed.

```
Vg1 = GetHandl {dat.dt} tempCall {itm.temp}
Vg2 = GetHandl {dat.itl} tempCall {itm.temp}
if Link(Vg1,Vg2) set Lim(Vg1,Vg2) return
if Link(Vg2,Vg1) set Lim(Vg2,Vg1) return
limitDat.1 = maxBits (%22) to {limit .04} set on
limitDat.2 = setzero, setfive, 0 {limit .2-var(dzh)}
Vg1 = GetHandl {dat.dt} tempCall {itm.temp}
Vg2 = GetHandl {dat.itl} tempCall {itm.temp}
limitDat.4 = maxBits (%33) to {limit .04} set on
limitDat.5 = setzero, setfive, 0 {limit .2-var(szh)}
```

Muldoon pointed to the windows. 'Look!' Outside, the big quartz lights were coming on throughout the park. They went to the windows and looked out.'

'Hot damn,' Arnold said.

Gennaro said, 'Does this mean the electrified fences are back on?'

'You bet it does,' Arnold said. 'It'll take a few seconds to get up to full power, because we've got fifty miles of fence out there, and the generator has to charge the capacitors along the way. But in half a minute we'll be back in business.' Arnold pointed to the vertical glass see-through map of the park.

On the map, bright red lines were snaking out from the power station, moving throughout the park, as electricity surged through the fences.

'And the motion sensors?' Gennaro said.

'Yes, them, too. It'll be a few minutes while the computer counts. But everything's working,' Arnold said. 'Half past nine, and we've got the whole damn thing back up and running.'

Grant opened his eyes. Brilliant blue light was streaming into the building through the bars of the gate. Quartz light: the power was back on! Groggily, he looked at his watch. It was just nine-thirty. He'd been asleep only a couple of minutes. He decided he could sleep a few minutes more, and then he would go back up to the field and stand in front of the motion sensors and wave, setting them off. The control room would spot him; they'd send a car out to pick him and the kids up, he'd tell Arnold to recall the supply ship, and they'd all finish the night in their own beds back in the lodge.

He would do that right away. In just a couple of minutes. He yawned, and closed his eyes again.

'Not bad,' Arnold said in the control room, staring at the glowing map. 'There's only three cutouts in the whole park. Much better than I hoped for.'

'Cutouts?' Gennaro said.

'The fence automatically cuts out short-circuited sections,' he explained. 'You can see a big one here, in sector twelve, near the main road.'

'That's where the rex knocked the fence down,' Muldoon said.

'Exactly. And another one is here in sector eleven. Near the sauropod maintenance building.'

'Why would that section be out?' Gennaro said.

'God knows,' Arnold said. 'Probably storm damage or a fallen tree. We can check it on the monitor in a while. The third one is over there by the jungle river. Don't know why that should be out, either.'

As Gennaro looked, the map became more complex, filling with green spots and numbers. 'What's all this?'

'The animals. The motion sensors are working again, and the computer's starting to identify the location of all the animals in the park. And anybody else, too.'

Gennaro stared at the map. 'You mean Grant and the kids . . .'

'Yes. We've reset our search number above four hundred. So, if they're out there moving around,' Arnold said, 'the motion sensors will pick them up as additional animals.' He stared at the map. 'But I don't see any additionals yet.'

'Why does it take so long?' Gennaro said.

'You have to realize, Mr. Gennaro,' Arnold said, 'that there's a lot of extraneous movement out there. Branches blowing in the wind, birds flying around, all kinds of stuff. The computer has to eliminate all the background movement. It may take – ah. Okay. Count's finished.'

Gennaro said, 'You don't see the kids?'

Arnold twisted in his chair, and looked back to the map. 'No,' he said, 'at the moment, there are no additionals on the map at all. Everything out there has been accounted for as a dinosaur. They're probably up in a tree, or somewhere else where we can't see them. I wouldn't worry yet. Several animals haven't shown up, like the big rex. That's probably because it's sleeping somewhere and not moving. The people may be sleeping, too. We just don't know.'

Muldoon shook his head. 'We better get on with it,' he said. 'We need to repair the fences, and get the animals back into their paddocks. According to that computer, we've got five to herd back to the proper paddocks. I'll take the maintenance crews out now.'

Arnold turned to Gennaro. 'You may want to see how Dr. Malcolm is doing. Tell Dr. Harding that Muldoon will need him in about an hour to supervise the herding. And I'll notify Mr. Hammond that we're starting our final cleanup.'

Gennaro passed through the iron gates and went in the front door of the Safari Lodge. He saw Ellie Sattler coming down the hallway, carrying towels and a pan of steaming water. 'There's a kitchen at the other end,' she said. 'We're using that to boil water for the dressings.'

'How is he?' Gennaro asked.

'Surprisingly good,' she said.

Gennaro followed Ellie down to Malcolm's room, and was startled to hear the sound of laughter. The mathematician lay on his back in the bed, with Harding adjusting an IV line.

'So the other man says, "I'll tell you frankly, I didn't like it, Bill. I went back to toilet paper!"'

Harding was laughing.

'It's not bad, is it?' Malcolm said, smiling. 'Ah, Mr. Gennaro. You've come to see me. Now you know what happens from trying to get a leg up on the situation.'

Gennaro came in, tentatively.

Harding said, 'He's on fairly high doses of morphine.'

'Not high enough, I can tell you,' Malcolm said. 'Christ, he's stingy with his drugs. Did they find the others yet?'

'No, not yet,' Gennaro said. 'But I'm glad to see you doing so well.'

'How else should I be doing,' Malcolm said, 'with a compound fracture of the leg that is likely septic and beginning to smell rather, ah, pungent? But I always say, if you can't keep a sense of humor...'

Gennaro smiled. 'Do you remember what happened?'

'*Of course* I remember,' Malcolm said. 'Do you think you could be bitten by a *Tyrannosaurus rex* and it would escape your mind? No indeed, I'll tell you, you'd remember it for the rest of your life. In my case, perhaps not a terribly long time. But, still – yes, I remember.'

Malcolm described running from the Land Cruiser in the rain, and being chased down by the rex. 'It was my own damned fault, he was too close, but I was panicked. In any case, he picked me up in his jaws.'

'How?' Gennaro said.

'Torso,' Malcolm said, and lifted his shirt. A broad semicircle of bruised punctures ran from his shoulder to his navel. 'Lifted me up in his jaws, shook me bloody hard, and threw me down. And I was fine – terrified of course, but, still and all, fine – right up to the moment he threw me. I broke the leg in the fall. But the bite was not half bad.' He sighed. 'Considering.'

Harding said, 'Most of the big carnivores don't have strong jaws.

The real power is in the neck musculature. The jaws just hold on, while they use the neck to twist and rip. But with a small creature like Dr. Malcolm, the animal would just shake him, and then toss him.'

'I'm afraid that's right,' Malcolm said. 'I doubt I'd have survived, except the big chap's heart wasn't in it. To tell the truth, he struck me as a rather clumsy attacker of anything less than an automobile or a small apartment building.'

'You think he attacked halfheartedly?'

'It pains me to say it,' Malcolm said, 'but I don't honestly feel I had his full attention. He had mine, of course. But, then, he weighs eight tons. I don't.'

Gennaro turned to Harding and said, 'They're going to repair the fences now. Arnold says Muldoon will need your help herding animals.'

'Okay,' Harding said.

'So long as you leave me Dr. Sattler, and ample morphine,' Malcolm said. 'And so long as we do not have a Malcolm Effect here.'

'What's a Malcolm Effect?' Gennaro said.

'Modesty forbids me,' Malcolm said, 'from telling you the details of a phenomenon named after me.' He sighed again, and closed his eyes. In a moment, he was sleeping.

Ellie walked out into the hallway with Gennaro. 'Don't be fooled,' she said. 'It's a great strain on him. When will you have a helicopter here?'

'A helicopter?'

'He needs surgery on that leg. Make sure they send for a helicopter, and get him off this island.'

The Park

The portable generator sputtered and roared to life, and the quartz floodlights glowed at the ends of their telescoping arms. Muldoon heard the soft gurgle of the jungle river a few yards to the north. He turned back to the maintenance van and saw one of the workmen coming out with a big power saw.

'No, no,' he said. 'Just the ropes, Carlos. We don't need to cut it.'

He turned back to look at the fence. They had difficulty finding the shorted section at first, because there wasn't much to see: a small protocarpus tree was leaning against the fence. It was one of several that had been planted in this region of the park, their feathery branches intended to conceal the fence from view.

But this particular tree had been tied down with guy wires and turnbuckles. The wires had broken free in the storm, and the metal turnbuckles had blown against the fence and shorted it out. Of course, none of this should have happened; grounds crews were supposed to use plastic-coated wires and ceramic turnbuckles near fences. But it had happened anyway.

In any case, it wasn't going to be a big job. All they had to do was pull the tree off the fence, remove the metal fittings, and mark it for the gardeners to fix in the morning. It shouldn't take more than twenty minutes. And that was just as well, because Muldoon knew the dilophosaurs always stayed close to the river. Even though the workmen were separated from the river by the fence, the dilos could spit right through it, delivering their blinding poison.

Ramón, one of the workmen, came over. 'Señor Muldoon,' he said, 'did you see the lights?'

'What lights?' Muldoon said.

Ramón pointed to the east, through the jungle. 'I saw it as we were coming out. It is there, very faint. You see it? It looks like the lights of a car, but it is not moving.'

Muldoon squinted. It probably was just a maintenance light. After all, power was back on. 'We'll worry about it later,' he said. 'Right now let's just get that tree off the fence.'

Arnold was in an expansive mood. The park was almost back in order. Muldoon was repairing the fences. Hammond had gone off to supervise the transfer of the animals with Harding. Although he was tired, Arnold was feeling good; he was even in a mood to indulge the lawyer, Gennaro. 'The Malcolm Effect?' Arnold said. 'You worried about that?'

'I'm just curious,' Gennaro said.

'You mean you want me to tell you why Ian Malcolm is wrong?'

'Sure.'

Arnold lit another cigarette. 'It's technical.'

'Try me.'

'Okay,' Arnold said. 'Chaos theory describes nonlinear systems. It's now become a very broad theory that's been used to study everything from the stock market, to rioting crowds, to brain waves during epilepsy. A very *fashionable* theory. Very trendy to apply it to any complex system where there might be unpredictability. Okay?'

'Okay,' Gennaro said.

'Ian Malcolm is a mathematician specializing in chaos theory. Quite amusing and personable, but basically what he does, besides wear black, is use computers to model the behavior of complex systems. And John Hammond loves the latest scientific fad, so he asked Malcolm to model the system at Jurassic Park. Which Malcolm did. Malcolm's models are all phase-space shapes on a computer screen. Have you seen them?'

'No,' Gennaro said.

'Well, they look like a weird twisted ship's propeller. According to Malcolm, the behavior of any system follows the surface of the propeller. You with me?'

'Not exactly,' Gennaro said.

Arnold held his hand in the air. 'Let's say I put a drop of water on the back of my hand. That drop is going to run off my hand. Maybe it'll run toward my wrist. Maybe it'll run toward my thumb, or down between my fingers. I don't know for sure where it will go, but I know it will run somewhere along the surface of my hand. It has to.'

'Okay,' Gennaro said.

'Chaos theory treats the behavior of a whole system like a drop of water moving on a complicated propeller surface. The drop may spiral down, or slip outward toward the edge. It may do many different things, depending. But it will always move along the surface of the propeller.'

'Okay.'

'Malcolm's models tend to have a ledge, or a sharp incline, where the drop of water will speed up greatly. He modestly calls this speeding-up movement the Malcolm Effect. The whole system could suddenly collapse. And that was what he said about Jurassic Park. That it had inherent instability.'

'Inherent instability,' Gennaro said. 'And what did you do when you got his report?'

'We disagreed with it, and ignored it, of course,' Arnold said.

'Was that wise?'

'It's self-evident,' Arnold said. 'We're dealing with living systems, after all. This is life, not computer models.'

In the harsh quartz lights, the hypsilophodont's green head hung down out of the sling, the tongue dangling, the eyes dull.

'Careful! Careful!' Hammond shouted, as the crane began to lift.

Harding grunted and eased the head back onto the leather straps. He didn't want to impede circulation through the carotid artery. the crane hissed as it lifted the animal into the air, onto the waiting flatbed truck. The hypsy was a small dryosaur, seven feet long, weighing about five hundred pounds. She was dark green with mottled brown spots. She was breathing slowly, but she seemed all right. Harding had shot her a few moments before with the tranquilizer gun, and apparently he had guessed the correct dose. There was always a tense moment dosing these big animals. Too little and they would run off into the forest, collapsing where you couldn't get to them. Too much and they went into terminal cardiac arrest. This one had taken a single bounding leap and keeled over. Perfectly dosed.

'Watch it! Easy!' Hammond was shouting to the workmen.

'Mr. Hammond,' Harding said. 'Please.'

'Well, they should be careful –'

'They *are* being careful,' Harding said. He climbed up onto the back of the flatbed as the hypsy came down, and he set her into the restraining harness. Harding slipped on the cardiogram collar that monitored heartbeat, then picked up the big electronic thermometer the size of a turkey baster and slipped it into the rectum. It beeped: 96.2 degrees.

'How is she?' Hammond asked fretfully.

'She's fine,' Harding said. 'She's only dropped a degree and a half.'

'That's too much,' Hammond said. 'Too deep.'

'You don't want her waking up and jumping off the truck,' Harding snapped.

Before coming to the park, Harding had been the chief of veterinary medicine at the San Diego Zoo, and the world's leading expert on avian care. He flew all over the world, consulting with zoos in Europe, India, and Japan on the care of exotic birds. He'd had no interest when this peculiar little man showed up, offering him a position in a private game park. But when he learned what Hammond had done . . . It was impossible to pass up. Harding had an academic bent, and the prospect of writing the first *Textbook of Veterinary Internal Medicine: Diseases of Dinosauria* was compelling. In the late twentieth century, veterinary medicine was scientifically advanced; the best zoos ran clinics little different from hospitals. New textbooks were merely refinements of old. For a world-class practitioner, there were no worlds left to conquer. But to be the first to care for a whole new class of animals: that was something!

And Harding had never regretted his decision. He had developed considerable expertise with these animals. And he didn't want to hear from Hammond now.

The hypsy snorted and twitched. She was still breathing shallowly; there was no ocular reflex yet. But it was time to get moving. 'All aboard,' Harding shouted. 'Let's get this girl back to her paddock.'

'Living systems,' Arnold said, 'are not like mechanical systems. Living systems are never in equilibrium. They are inherently unstable. They may seem stable, but they're not. Everything is moving and changing. In a sense, everything is on the edge of collapse.'

Gennaro was frowning. 'But lots of things don't change; body temperature doesn't change, all kinds of other −'

'Body temperature changes constantly,' Arnold said. '*Constantly*. It changes cyclically over twenty-four hours, lowest in the morning, highest in the afternoon. It changes with mood, with disease, with exercise, with outside temperature, with food. It continuously fluctuates up and down. Tiny jiggles on a graph. Because, at any moment, some forces are pushing temperature up, and other forces are pulling it down. It is inherently unstable. And every other aspect of living systems is like that, too.'

'So you're saying . . .'

'Malcolm's just another theoretician,' Arnold said. 'Sitting in his office, he made a nice mathematical model, and it never occurred to him that what he saw as defects were actually necessities. Look: when I was working on missiles, we dealt with something called 'resonant yaw.' Resonant yaw meant that, even though a missile was only slightly unstable off the pad, it was hopeless. It was inevitably going to go out of control, and it couldn't be brought back. That's a feature of mechanical systems. A little wobble can get worse until the whole system collapses. But those same little wobbles are essential to a living system. They mean the system is healthy and responsive. Malcolm never understood that.'

'Are you sure he didn't understand that? He seems pretty clear on the difference between living and nonliving –'

'Look,' Arnold said. 'The proof is right here.' He pointed to the screens. 'In less than an hour,' he said, 'the park will all be back on line. The only thing I've got left to clear is the telephones. For some reason, they're still out. But everything else will be working. And that's not theoretical. That's fact.'

The needle went deep into the neck, and Harding injected the medrine into the anesthetized female dryosaur as she lay on her side on the ground. Immediately the animal began to recover, snorting and kicking her powerful hind legs.

'Back, everybody,' Harding said, scrambling away. 'Get back.'

The dinosaur staggered to her feet, standing drunkenly. She shook her lizard head, stared at the people standing back in the quartz lights, and blinked.

'She's drooling,' Hammond said, worried.

'Temporary,' Harding said. 'It'll stop.'

The dryosaur coughed, and then moved slowly across the field, away from the lights.

'Why isn't she hopping?'

'She will,' Harding said. 'It'll take her about an hour to recover fully. She's fine.' He turned back to the car. 'Okay, boys, let's go deal with the stego.'

Muldoon watched as the last of the stakes was pounded into the ground. The lines were pulled taut, and the protocarpus tree was lifted clear. Muldoon could see the blackened, charred streaks on the silver fence where the short had occurred. At the base of the fence, several ceramic insulators had burst. They would have to be replaced. But before that could be done, Arnold would to have to shut down all the fences.

'Control. This is Muldoon. We're ready to begin repair.'

'All right,' Arnold said. 'Shutting out your section now.'

Muldoon glanced at his watch. Somewhere in the distance, he heard soft hooting. It sounded like owls, but he knew it was the dilophosaurs. He went over to Ramón and said, 'Let's finish this up. I want to get to those other sections of fence.'

An hour went by. Donald Gennaro stared at the glowing map in the control room as the spots and numbers flickered and changed. 'What's happening now?'

Arnold worked at the console. 'I'm trying to get the phones back. So we can call about Malcolm.'

'No, I mean out there.'

Arnold glanced up at the board. 'It looks as if they're about done with the animals, and the two sections. Just as I told you, the park is back in hand. With no catastrophic Malcolm Effect. In fact, there's just that third section of fence . . .'

'Arnold.' It was Muldoon's voice.

'Yes?'

'Have you seen this bloody fence?'

'Just a minute.'

On one of the monitors, Gennaro saw a high angle down on a field of grass, blowing in the wind. In the distance was a low concrete roof. 'That's the sauropod maintenance building,' Arnold explained. 'It's one of the utility structures we use for equipment, feed storage, and so on. We have them all around the park, in each of the paddocks.' On the monitor, the video image panned. 'We're turning the camera now to get a look at the fence . . .'

Gennaro saw a shining wall of metallic mesh in the light. One section had been trampled, knocked flat. Muldoon's Jeep and work crew were there.

'Huh,' Arnold said. 'Looks like the rex went into the sauropod paddock.'

Muldoon said, 'Fine dining tonight.'

'We'll have to get him out of there,' Arnold said.

'With what?' Muldoon said. 'We haven't got anything to use on a rex. I'll fix this fence, but I'm not going in there until daylight.'

'Hammond won't like it.'

'We'll discuss it when I get back,' Muldoon said.

'How many sauropods will the rex kill?' Hammond said, pacing around the control room.

'Probably just one,' Harding said. 'Sauropods are big; the rex can feed off a single kill for several days.'

'We have to go out and get him tonight,' Hammond said.

Muldoon shook his head. 'I'm not going in there until daylight.'

Hammond was rising up and down on the balls of his feet, the way he did whenever he was angry. 'Are you forgetting you work for me?'

'No, Mr. Hammond, I'm not forgetting. But that's a full-grown adult tyrannosaur out there. How do you plan to get him?'

'We have tranquilizer guns.'

'We have tranquilizer guns that shoot a twenty-cc dart,' Muldoon said. 'Fine for an animal that weighs four or five hundred pounds. That tyrannosaur weighs eight tons. It wouldn't even feel it.'

'You ordered a larger weapon . . .'

'I ordered three larger weapons, Mr. Hammond, but you cut the requisition, so we got only one. And it's gone. Nedry took it when he left.'

'That was pretty stupid. Who let that happen?'

'Nedry's not my problem, Mr. Hammond,' Muldoon said.

'You're saying,' Hammond said, 'that, as of this moment, there is no way to stop the tyrannosaur?'

'That's exactly what I'm saying,' Muldoon said.

'That's ridiculous,' Hammond said.

'It's your park, Mr. Hammond. You didn't want anybody to be able to injure your precious dinosaurs. Well, now you've got a rex in with the sauropods, and there's not a damned thing you can do about it.' He left the room.

'Just a minute,' Hammond said, hurrying after him.

Gennaro stared at the screens, and listened to the shouted argument in the hallway outside. He said to Arnold, 'I guess you don't have control of the park yet, after all.'

'Don't kid yourself,' Arnold said, lighting another cigarette. 'We have the park. It'll be dawn in a couple of hours. We may lose a couple of dinos before we get the rex out of there, but, believe me, we have the park.'

Dawn

Grant was awakened by a loud grinding sound, followed by a mechanical clanking. He opened his eyes and saw a bale of hay rolling past him on a conveyor belt, up toward the ceiling. Two more bales followed it. Then the clanking stopped as abruptly as it had begun, and the concrete building was silent again.

Grant yawned. He stretched sleepily, winced in pain, and sat up.

Soft yellow light came through the side windows. It was morning: he had slept the whole night! He looked quickly at his watch: 5:00 a.m. Still almost six hours to go before the boat had to be recalled. He rolled onto his back, groaning. His head throbbed, and his body ached as if he had been beaten up. From around the corner, he heard a squeaking sound, like a rusty wheel. And then Lex giggling.

Grant stood slowly, and looked at the building. Now that it was daylight, he could see it was some kind of a maintenance building, with stacks of hay and supplies. On the wall he saw a gray metal box and a stenciled sign: SAUROPOD MAINTENANCE BLDG (04). This must be the sauropod paddock, as he had thought. He opened the box and saw a telephone, but when he lifted the receiver he heard only hissing static. Apparently the phones weren't working yet.

'Chew your food,' Lex was saying. 'Don't be a piggy, Ralph.'

Grant walked around the corner and found Lex by the bars, holding out handfuls of hay to an animal outside that looked like a large pink pig and was making the squeaking sounds Grant had heard. It was actually an infant triceratops, about the size of a pony. The infant didn't have horns on its head yet, just a curved bony frill behind big soft eyes. It poked its snout through the bars toward Lex, its eyes watching her as she fed it more hay.

'That's better,' Lex said. 'There's plenty of hay, don't worry.' She patted the baby on the head. 'You like hay, don't you, Ralph?'

Lex turned back and saw him.

'This is Ralph,' Lex said. 'He's my friend. He likes hay.'

Grant took a step and stopped, wincing.

'You look pretty bad,' Lex said.

237

'I feel pretty bad.'

'Tim, too. His nose is all swollen up.'

'Where is Tim?'

'Peeing,' she said. 'You want to help me feed Ralph?'

The baby triceratops looked at Grant. Hay stuck out of both sides of its mouth, dropping on the floor as it chewed.

'He's a *very* messy eater,' Lex said. 'And he's very hungry.'

The baby finished chewing and licked its lips. It opened its mouth, waiting for more. Grant could see the slender sharp teeth, and the beaky upper jaw, like a parrot.

'Okay, just a minute,' Lex said, scooping up more straw from the concrete floor. 'Honestly, Ralph,' she said, 'You'd think your mother never fed you.'

'Why is his name Ralph?'

'Because he looks like Ralph. At school.'

Grant came closer and touched the skin of the neck gently.

'It's okay, you can pet him,' Lex said. 'He likes it when you pet him, don't you, Ralph?'

The skin felt dry and warm, with the pebbled texture of a football. Ralph gave a little squeak as Grant petted it. Outside the bars, its thick tail swung back and forth with pleasure.

'He's pretty tame.' Ralph looked from Lex to Grant as it ate, and showed no sign of fear. It reminded Grant that the dinosaurs didn't have ordinary responses to people. 'Maybe I can ride him,' Lex said.

'Let's not.'

'I bet he'd let me,' Lex said. 'It'd be fun to ride a dinosaur.'

Grant looked out the bars past the animal, to the open fields of the sauropod compound. It was growing lighter every minute. He should go outside, he thought, and set off one of the motion sensors on the field above. After all, it might take the people in the control room an hour to get out here to him. And he didn't like the idea that the phones were still down . . .

He heard a deep snorting sound, like the snort of a very large horse, and suddenly the baby became agitated. It tried to pull its head back through the bars, but got caught on the edge of its frill, and it squeaked in fright.

The snorting came again. It was closer this time.

Ralph reared up on its hind legs, frantic to get out from between the bars. It wriggled its head back and forth, rubbing against the bars.

'Ralph, take it easy,' Lex said.

'Push him out,' Grant said. He reached up to Ralph's head and leaned against it, pushing the animal sideways and backward. The frill popped free and the baby fell outside the bars, losing its balance and flopping on its side. Then the baby was covered in shadow, and a huge leg came into view, thicker than a tree trunk. The foot had five curved toenails, like an elephant's.

Ralph looked up and squeaked. A head came down into view: six feet long, with three long white horns, one above each of the large brown eyes and a smaller horn at the tip of the nose. It was a full-grown triceratops. The big animal peered at Lex and Grant, blinking slowly, and then turned its attention to Ralph. A tongue came out and licked the baby. Ralph squeaked and rubbed up against the big leg happily.

'Is that his mom?' Lex said.

'Looks like it,' Grant said.

'Should we feed the mom, too?' Lex said.

But the big triceratops was already nudging Ralph with her snout, pushing the baby away from the bars.

'Guess not.'

The infant turned away from the bars and walked off. From time to time, the big mother nudged her baby, guiding it away, as they both walked out into the fields.

'Goodbye, Ralph,' Lex said, waving. Tim came out of the shadows of the building.

'Tell you what,' Grant said. 'I'm going up on the hill to set off the motion sensors, so they'll know to come get us. You two stay here and wait for me.'

'No,' Lex said.

'Why? Stay here. It's safe here.'

'You're not leaving us,' she said. 'Right, Timmy?'

'Right,' Tim said.

'Okay,' Grant said.

They crawled through the bars, stepping outside.

It was just before dawn.

The air was warm and humid, the sky soft pink and purple. A white mist clung low to the ground. Some distance away, they saw the mother triceratops and the baby moving away toward a herd of large duckbilled hadrosaurs, eating foliage from trees at the edge of the lagoon.

Some of the hadrosaurs stood knee-deep in the water. They drank, lowering their flat heads, meeting their own reflections in the still water. Then they looked up again, their heads swiveling. At the water's edge, one of the babies ventured out, squeaked, and scrambled back while the adults watched indulgently.

Farther south, other hadrosaurs were eating the lower vegetation. Sometimes they reared up on their hind legs, resting their forelegs on the tree trunks, so they could reach the leaves on higher branches. And in the far distance, a giant apatosaur stood above the trees, the tiny head swiveling on the long neck. The scene was so peaceful Grant found it hard to imagine any danger.

'Yow!' Lex shouted, ducking. Two giant red dragonflies with six-foot wingspans hummed past them. 'What was that?'

'Dragonflies,' he said. 'The Jurassic was a time of huge insects.'

'Do they bite?' Lex said.

'I don't think so,' Grant said.

Tim held out his hand. One of the dragonflies lighted on it. He could feel the weight of the huge insect.

'He's going to bite you,' Lex warned.

But the dragonfly just slowly flapped its red-veined transparent wings, and then, when Tim moved his arm, flew off again.

'Which way do we go?' Lex said.

'There.'

They started walking across the field. They reached a black box mounted on a heavy metal tripod, the first of the motion sensors. Grant stopped and waved his hand in front of it back and forth, but nothing happened. If the phones didn't work, perhaps the sensors didn't work, either. 'We'll try another one,' he said, pointing across the field. Somewhere in the distance, they heard the roar of a large animal.

'Ah hell,' Arnold said. 'I just can't find it.' He sipped coffee and stared bleary-eyed at the screens. He had taken all the video monitors off line. In the control room, he was searching the computer code. He was exhausted; he'd been working for twelve straight hours. He turned to Wu, who had come up from the lab.

'Find what?'

'The phones are still out. I can't get them back on. I think Nedry did something to the phones.'

Wu lifted one phone, heard hissing. 'Sounds like a modem.'

'But it's not,' Arnold said. 'Because I went down into the basement and shut off all the modems. What you're hearing is just white noise that sounds like a modem transmitting.'

'So the phone lines are jammed?'

'Basically, yes. Nedry jammed them very well. He's inserted some kind of a lockout into the program code, and now I can't find it, because I gave that restore command which erased part of the program listings. But apparently the command to shut off the phones is still resident in the computer memory.'

Wu shrugged. 'So? Just reset: shut the system down and you'll clear memory.'

'I've never done it before,' Arnold said. 'And I'm reluctant to do it. Maybe all the systems will come back on start-up – but maybe they won't. I'm not a computer expert, and neither are you. Not really. And without an open phone line, we can't talk to anybody who is.'

'If the command is RAM-resident, it won't show up in the code. You can do a RAM dump and search that, but you don't know what you're searching for. I think all you can do is reset.'

Gennaro stormed in. 'We still don't have any telephones.'

'Working on it.'

'You've been working on it since midnight. And Malcolm is worse. He needs medical attention.'

'It means I'll have to shut down,' Arnold said. 'I can't be sure everything will come back on.'

Gennaro said, 'Look. There's a sick man over in that lodge. He needs a doctor or he'll die. You can't call for a doctor unless you have a phone. Four people have probably died already. Now, shut down and get the phones working!'

Arnold hesitated.

'Well?' Gennaro said.

'Well, it's just . . . the safety systems don't allow the computer to be shut down, and –'

'*Then turn the goddamn safety systems off!* Can't you get it through your head that he's going to die unless he gets help?'

'Okay,' Arnold said.

He got up and went to the main panel. He opened the doors, and uncovered the metal swing-latches over the safety switches. He popped them off, one after another. 'You asked for it,' Arnold said. 'And you got it.'

He threw the master switch.

The control room was dark. All the monitors were black. The three men stood there in the dark.

'How long do we have to wait?' Gennaro said.

'Thirty seconds,' Arnold said.

'P-U!' Lex said, as they crossed the field.

'What?' Grant said.

'That smell!' Lex said. 'It stinks like rotten garbage.'

Grant hesitated. He stared across the field toward the distant trees, looking for movement. He saw nothing. There was hardly a breeze to stir the branches. It was peaceful and silent in the early morning. 'I think it's your imagination,' he said.

'Is not –'

Then he heard the honking sound. It came from the herd of duckbilled hadrosaurs behind them. First one animal, then another and another, until the whole herd had taken up the honking cry. The duckbills were agitated, twisting and turning, hurrying out of the water, circling the young ones to protect them . . .

They smell it, too, Grant thought.

With a roar, the tyrannosaur burst from the trees fifty yards away, near the lagoon. It rushed out across the open field with huge strides. It ignored them, heading toward the herd of hadrosaurs.

'I told you!' Lex screamed. 'Nobody listens to me!'

In the distance, the duckbills were honking and starting to run. Grant could feel the earth shake beneath his feet. 'Come on, kids!' He grabbed Lex, lifting her bodily off the ground, and ran with Tim through the grass. He had glimpses of the tyrannosaur down by the lagoon, lunging at the hadrosaurs, which swung their big tails in defense and honked loudly and continuously. He heard the crashing of foliage and trees, and when he looked over again, the duckbills were charging.

In the darkened control room, Arnold checked his watch. Thirty seconds. The memory should be cleared by now. He pushed the main power switch back on.

Nothing happened.

Arnold's stomach heaved. He pushed the switch off, then on again. Still nothing happened. He felt sweat on his brow.

'What's wrong?' Gennaro said.

'Oh hell,' Arnold said. Then he remembered you had to turn the safety switches back on before you restarted the power. He flipped on the three safeties, and covered them again with the latch covers. Then he held his breath, and turned the main power switch.

The room lights came on.

The computer beeped.

The screens hummed.

'Thank God,' Arnold said. He hurried to the main monitor. There were rows of labels on the screen:

```
┌─────────────────────────────────────────────────────────────────────┐
│              JURASSIC PARK - SYSTEM STARTUP                           │
└─────────────────────────────────────────────────────────────────────┘
```

		STARTUP AB(O)			STARTUP CN/D	
Security Main	Monitor Main	Command Main	Electrical Main	Hydraulic Main	Master Main	Zoolog Main
SetGrids DNL	View VBB	Access TNL	Heating Cooling	Door Fold Interface	SAAG-Rnd	Repair Storage
Critical Locks	TeleCom VBB	Reset Revert	Emgency Illumin	GAS/VLD Main II	Common Interface	Status Main
Control Passthru	TeleCom RSD	Template Main	FNCC Params	Explosion Fire Hzd	Schematic Main	Safety / Health

Gennaro reached for the phone, but it was dead. No static hissing this time – just nothing at all. 'What's this?'

'Give me a second,' Arnold said. 'After a reset, all the system modules have to be brought on line manually.' Quickly, he went back to work.

'Why manually?' Gennaro said.

'Will you just let me work, for Christ's sake?'

Wu said, 'The system is not intended to ever shut down. So, if it does shut down, it assumes that there is a problem somewhere. It requires you to start up everything manually. Otherwise, if there were a short somewhere, the system would start up, short out, start up again, short out again, in an endless cycle.'

'Okay,' Arnold said. 'We're going.'

Gennaro picked up the phone and started to dial, when he suddenly stopped.

'Jesus, look at that,' he said. He pointed to one of the video monitors.

But Arnold wasn't listening. He was staring at the map, where a tight cluster of dots by the lagoon had started to move in a coordinated way. Moving fast, in a kind of swirl.

'What's happening?' Gennaro said.

'The duckbills,' Arnold said tonelessly. 'They've stampeded.'

The duckbills charged with surprising speed, their enormous bodies in a tight cluster, honking and roaring, the infants squealing and trying to stay out from underfoot. The herd raised a great cloud of yellow dust. Grant couldn't see the tyrannosaur.

The duckbills were running right toward them.

Still carrying Lex, he ran with Tim toward a rocky outcrop, with a stand of big conifers. They ran hard, feeling the ground shake beneath their feet. The sound of the approaching herd was deafening, like the sound of jets at an airport. It filled the air, and hurt their ears. Lex was shouting something, but he couldn't hear what she was saying, and as they scrambled onto the rocks, the herd closed in around them.

Grant saw the immense legs of the first hadrosaurs that charged past, each animal weighing five tons, and then they were enveloped in a cloud so dense he could see nothing at all. He had the impression of huge bodies, giant limbs, bellowing cries of pain as the animals wheeled and circled. One duckbill struck a boulder and it rolled past them, out into the field beyond.

In the dense cloud of dust, they could see almost nothing beyond the rocks. They clung to the boulders, listening to the screams and honks, the menacing roar of the tyrannosaur. Lex dug her fingers into Grant's shoulder.

Another hadrosaur slammed its big tail against the rocks, leaving a splash of hot blood. Grant waited until the sounds of the fighting had moved off to the left, and then he pushed the kids to start climbing the largest tree. They climbed swiftly, feeling for the branches, as the animals stampeded all around them in the dust. They went up twenty feet, and then Lex clutched at Grant and refused to go farther. Tim was tired, too, and Grant thought they were high enough. Through the dust, they could see the broad backs of the animals below as they wheeled and honked. Grant propped himself against the coarse bark of the trunk, coughed in the dust, closed his eyes, and waited.

Arnold adjusted the camera as the herd moved away. The dust slowly cleared. He saw that the hadrosaurs had scattered, and the tyrannosaur had stopped running, which could only mean it had made a kill. The tyrannosaur was now near the lagoon. Arnold looked at the video monitor and said, 'Better get Muldoon to go out there and see how bad it is.'

'I'll get him,' Gennaro said, and left the room.

The Park

A faint crackling sound, like a fire in a fireplace. Something warm and wet tickled Grant's ankle. He opened his eyes and saw an enormous beige head. The head tapered to a flat mouth shaped like the bill of a duck. The eyes, protruding above the flat duckbill, were gentle and soft like a cow's. The duck mouth opened and chewed branches on the limb where Grant was sitting. He saw large flat teeth in the cheek. The warm lips touched his ankle again as the animal chewed.

A duckbilled hadrosaur. He was astonished to see it up close. Not that he was afraid; all the species of duckbilled dinosaurs were herbivorous, and this one acted exactly like a cow. Even though it was huge, its manner was so calm and peaceful Grant didn't feel threatened. He stayed where he was on the branch, careful not to move, and watched as it ate.

The reason Grant was astonished was that he had a proprietary feeling about this animal: it was probably a maiasaur, from the late Cretaceous in Montana. With John Horner, Grant had been the first to describe the species. Maiasaurs had an upcurved lip, which gave them the appearance of smiling. The name meant 'good mother lizard'; maiasaurs were thought to protect their eggs until the babies were born and could take care of themselves.

Grant heard an insistent chirping, and the big head swung down. He moved just enough to see the baby hadrosaur scampering around the feet of the adult. The baby was dark beige with black spots. The adult bent her head low to the ground and waited, unmoving, while the baby stood up on its hind legs, resting its front legs on the mother's jaw, and ate the branches that protruded from the side of the mother's mouth.

The mother waited patiently until the baby had finished eating, and dropped back down to all fours again. Then the big head came back up toward Grant.

The hadrosaur continued to eat, just a few feet from him. Grant looked at the two elongated airholes on top of the flat upper bill. Apparently the dinosaur couldn't smell Grant. And even though the left eye was looking right at him, for some reason the hadrosaur didn't react to him.

He remembered how the tyrannosaur had failed to see him, the previous night. Grant decided on an experiment.

He coughed.

Instantly the hadrosaur froze, the big head suddenly still, the jaws no longer chewing. Only the eye moved, looking for the source of the sound. Then, after a moment, when there seemed to be no danger, the animal resumed chewing.

Amazing, Grant thought.

Sitting in his arms, Lex opened her eyes and said, 'Hey, what's *that?*'

The hadrosaur trumpeted in alarm, a loud resonant honk that so startled Lex that she nearly fell out of the tree. The hadrosaur pulled its head away from the branch and trumpeted again.

'Don't make her mad,' Tim said, from the branch above.

The baby chirped and scurried beneath the mother's legs as the hadrosaur stepped away from the tree. The mother cocked her head and peered inquisitively at the branch where Grant and Lex were sitting. With its upturned smiling lips, the dinosaur had a comical appearance.

'Is it dumb?' Lex said.

'No,' Grant said. 'You just surprised her.'

'Well,' Lex said, 'is she going to let us get down, or what?'

The hadrosaur had backed ten feet away from the tree. She honked again. Grant had the impression she was trying to frighten them away. But the dinosaur didn't really seem to know what to do. She acted confused and uneasy. They waited in silence, and after a minute the hadrosaur approached the branch again, jaws moving in anticipation. She was clearly going to resume eating.

'Forget it,' Lex said. 'I'm not staying *here*.' She started to climb down the branches. At her movement, the hadrosaur trumpeted in fresh alarm.

Grant was amazed. He thought, It really can't see us when we don't move. And after a minute it literally forgets that we're here. This was just like the tyrannosaur – another classic example of an amphibian visual cortex. Studies of frogs had shown that amphibians only saw moving things, like insects. If something didn't move, they literally didn't see it. The same thing seemed to be true of dinosaurs.

In any case, the maiasaur now seemed to find these strange creatures climbing down the tree too upsetting. With a final honk, she nudged her baby, and lumbered slowly away. She paused once, and looked back at them, then continued on.

They reached the ground. Lex shook herself off. Both children were covered in a layer of fine dust. All around them, the grass had been flattened. There were streaks of blood, and a sour smell.

Grant looked at his watch. 'We better get going, kids,' he said.

'Not me,' Lex said. 'I'm not walking out there *any more*.'

'We have to.'

'Why?'

'Because,' Grant said, 'we have to tell them about the boat. Since they can't seem to see us on the motion sensors, we have to go all the way back ourselves. It's the only way.'

'Why can't we take the raft?' Tim said.

'What raft?'

Tim pointed to the low concrete maintenance building with the bars, where they had spent the night. It was twenty yards away, across the field. 'I saw a raft back there,' he said.

Grant immediately understood the advantages. It was now seven o'clock in the morning. They had at least eight miles to go. If they could take a raft along the river, they would make much faster progress than going overland. 'Let's do it,' Grant said.

Arnold punched the visual search mode and watched as the monitors began to scan throughout the park, the images changing every two seconds. It was tiring to watch, but it was the fastest way to find Nedry's Jeep, and Muldoon had been adamant about that. He had gone out with Gennaro to look at the stampede, but now that it was daylight, he wanted the car found. He wanted the weapons.

His intercom clicked. 'Mr. Arnold, may I have a word with you, please?'

It was Hammond. He sounded like the voice of God.

'You want to come here, Mr. Hammond?'

'No, Mr. Arnold,' Hammond said. 'Come to me. I'm in the genetics lab with Dr. Wu. We'll be waiting for you.'

Arnold sighed, and stepped away from the screens.

Grant stumbled deep in the gloomy recesses of the building. He pushed past five-gallon containers of herbicide, tree-pruning equipment, spare tires for a Jeep, coils of cyclone fencing, hundred-pound fertilizer bags, stacks of brown ceramic insulators, empty motor-oil cans, work lights and cables.

'I don't see any raft.'

'Keep going.'

Bags of cement, lengths of copper pipe, green mesh . . . and two plastic oars hung on clips on the concrete wall.

'Okay,' he said, 'but where's the raft?'

'It must be here somewhere,' Tim said.

'You never saw a raft?'

'No, I just assumed it was here.'

Poking among the junk, Grant found no raft. But he did find a set of plans, rolled up and speckled with mold from humidity, stuck back in a metal cabinet on the wall. He spread the plans on the floor, brushing away a big spider. He looked at them for a long time.

'I'm hungry. . . .'

'Just a minute.'

They were detailed topographical charts for the main area of the island, where they now were. According to this, the lagoon narrowed into the river they had seen earlier, which twisted northward . . . right through the aviary . . . and on to within a half-mile of the visitor lodge.

He flipped back through the pages. How to get to the lagoon? According to the plans, there should be a door at the back of the building they were in. Grant looked up, and saw it, recessed back in the concrete wall. The door was wide enough for a car. Opening it, he saw a paved road running straight down toward the lagoon. The road was dug below ground level, so it couldn't be seen from above. It must be another service road. And it led to a dock at the edge of the lagoon. And clearly stenciled on the dock was RAFT STORAGE.

'Hey,' Tim said, 'look at this.' He held out a metal case to Grant.

Opening it, Grant found a compressed-air pistol and a cloth belt that held darts. There were six darts in all, each as thick as his finger. Labeled MORO-709.

'Good work, Tim.' He slung the belt around his shoulder, and stuck the gun in his trousers.

'Is it a tranquilizer gun?'

'I'd say so.'

'What about the boat?' Lex said.

'I think it's on the dock,' Grant said. They started down the road. Grant carried the oars on his shoulder. 'I hope it's a big raft,' Lex said, 'because I can't swim.'

'Don't worry,' he said.

'Maybe we can catch some fish,' she said.

They walked down the road with the sloping embankment rising up on both sides of them. They heard a deep rhythmic snorting sound, but Grant could not see where it was coming from.

'Are you sure there's a raft down here?' Lex said, wrinkling her nose.

'Probably,' Grant said.

The rhythmic snorting became louder as they walked, but they also heard a steady droning, buzzing sound. When they reached the end of the road, at the edge of the small concrete dock, Grant froze in shock.

The tyrannosaur was *right there.*

It was sitting upright in the shade of a tree, its hind legs stretched out in front. Its eyes were open but it was not moving, except for its head, which lifted and fell gently with each snorting sound. The buzzing came from the clouds of flies that surrounded it, crawling over its face and slack jaws, its bloody fangs, and the red haunch of a killed hadrosaur that lay on its side behind the tyrannosaur.

The tyrannosaur was only twenty yards away. Grant felt sure it must have seen him, but the big animal did not respond. It just sat there. It took him a moment to realize: the tyrannosaur was asleep. Sitting up, but asleep.

He signaled to Tim and Lex to stay where they were. Grant walked slowly forward onto the dock, in full view of the tyrannosaur. The big animal continued to sleep, snoring softly.

Near the end of the dock, a wooden shed was painted green to blend with the foliage. Grant quietly unlatched the door and looked inside. He saw a half-dozen orange life vests hanging on the wall, several rolls of wire-mesh fencing, some coils of rope, and two big rubber cubes sitting on the floor. The cubes were strapped tight with flat rubber belts.

Rafts.

He looked back at Lex.

She mouthed: *No boat.*

He nodded, *Yes.*

The tyrannosaur raised its forelimb to swipe at the flies buzzing around its snout. But otherwise it did not move. Grant pulled one of the cubes out onto the dock. It was surprisingly heavy. He freed the straps, found the inflation cylinder. With a loud hiss, the rubber began to expand, and then with a *hiss-whap!* it popped fully open on the dock. The sound was fearfully loud in their ears.

Grant turned, stared up at the dinosaur.

The tyrannosaur grunted, and snorted. It began to move. Grant braced himself to run, but the animal shifted its ponderous bulk and then it settled back against the tree trunk and gave a long, growling belch.

Lex looked disgusted, waving her hand in front of her face.

Grant was soaked in sweat from the tension. He dragged the rubber raft across the dock. It flopped into the water with a loud splash.

The dinosaur continued to sleep.

Grant tied the boat up to the dock, and returned to the shed to take out two life preservers. He put these in the boat, and then waved for the kids to come out onto the dock.

Pale with fear, Lex waved back, *No*.

He gestured: *Yes*.

The tyrannosaur continued to sleep.

Grant stabbed in the air with an emphatic finger. Lex came silently, and he gestured for her to get into the raft; then Tim got in, and they both put on their life vests. Grant got in and pushed off. The raft drifted silently out into the lagoon. Grant picked up his paddles and fitted them into the oarlocks. They moved farther from the dock.

Lex sat back, and sighed loudly with relief. Then she looked stricken, and put her hand over her mouth. Her body shook, with muffled sounds: she was suppressing a cough.

She *always* coughed at the wrong times!

'Lex,' Tim whispered fiercely, looking back toward the shore.

She shook her head miserably, and pointed to her throat. He knew what she meant: a tickle in her throat. What she needed was a drink of water. Grant was rowing, and Tim leaned over the side of the raft and scooped his hand in the lagoon, holding his cupped hand toward her.

Lex coughed loudly, explosively. In Tim's ears, the sound echoed across the water like a gunshot.

The tyrannosaur yawned lazily, and scratched behind its ear with its hind foot, just like a dog. It yawned again. It was groggy after its big meal, and it woke up slowly.

On the boat, Lex was making little gargling sounds.

'Lex, *shut up!*' Tim said.

'I can't help it,' she whispered, and then she coughed again. Grant rowed hard, moving the raft powerfully into the center of the lagoon.

On the shore, the tyrannosaur stumbled to its feet.

'I couldn't help it, Timmy!' Lex shrieked miserably. 'I couldn't help it!'

'Shhhh!'

Grant was rowing as fast as he could.

'Anyway, it doesn't matter,' she said. 'We're far enough away. He can't swim.'

'*Of course he can swim, you little idiot!*' Tim shouted at her. On the shore, the tyrannosaur stepped off the dock and plunged into the water. It moved strongly into the lagoon after them.

'Well, how should I know?' she said.

'Everybody knows tyrannosaurs can swim! It's in all the books! Anyway, all reptiles can swim!'

'Snakes can't.'

'*Of course* snakes can. You *idiot!*'

'Settle down,' Grant said. 'Hold on to something!' Grant was watching the tyrannosaur, noticing how the animal swam. The tyrannosaur was now chest-deep in the water, but it could hold its big head high above the surface. Then Grant realized the animal wasn't swimming, it was walking, because moments later only the very top of the head – the eyes and nostrils – protruded above the surface. By then it looked like a crocodile, and it swam like a crocodile, swinging its big tail back and forth, so the water churned behind it. Behind the head, Grant saw the hump of the back, and the ridges along the length of tail, as it occasionally broke the surface.

Exactly like a crocodile, he thought unhappily. The biggest crocodile in the world.

'I'm sorry, Dr. Grant!' Lex wailed. 'I didn't mean it!'

Grant glanced over his shoulder. The lagoon was no more than a hundred yards wide here, and they had almost reached the center. If he continued, the water would become shallow again. The tyrannosaur would be able to walk again, and he would move faster in shallow water. Grant swung the boat around, and began to row north.

'What are you *doing?*'

The tyrannosaur was now just a few yards away. Grant could hear its sharp snorting breaths as it came closer. Grant looked at the paddles in his hands, but they were light plastic – not weapons at all.

The tyrannosaur threw its head back and opened its jaws wide, showing rows of curved teeth, and then in a great muscular spasm lunged forward to the raft, just missing the rubber gunwale, the huge skull slapping down, the raft rocking away on the crest of the splash.

The tyrannosaur sank below the surface, leaving gurgling bubbles. The lagoon was still. Lex gripped the gunwale handles and looked back.

'Did he drown?'

'No,' Grant said. He saw bubbles – then a faint ripple along the surface – coming toward the boat –

'Hang on!' he shouted, as the head bucked up beneath the rubber, bending the boat and lifting it into the air, spinning them crazily before it splashed down again.

'Do something!' Alexis screamed. 'Do something!'

Grant pulled the air pistol out of his belt. It looked pitifully small in his hands, but there was the chance that, if he shot the animal in a sensitive spot, in the eye or the nose –.

The tyrannosaur surfaced beside the boat, opened its jaws, and roared. Grant aimed, and fired. The dart flashed in the light, and smacked into the cheek. The tyrannosaur shook its head, and roared again.

And suddenly they heard an answering roar, floating across the water toward them.

Looking back, Grant saw the juvenile T-rex on the shore, crouched over the killed sauropod, claiming the kill as its own. The juvenile slashed at the carcass, then raised its head high and bellowed. The big tyrannosaur saw it, too, and the response was immediate – it turned back to protect its kill, swimming strongly toward the shore.

'He's going away!' Lex squealed, clapping her hands. 'He's going away! Naah-naah-na-na-naah! Stupid dinosaur!'

From the shore, the juvenile roared defiantly. Enraged, the big tyrannosaur burst from the lagoon at full speed, water streaming from its enormous body as it raced up the hill past the dock. The juvenile ducked its head and fled, its jaws still filled with ragged flesh.

The big tyrannosaur chased it, racing past the dead sauropod, disappearing over the hill. They heard its final threatening bellow, and then the raft moved to the north, around a bend in the lagoon, to the river.

Exhausted from rowing, Grant collapsed back, his chest heaving. He couldn't catch his breath. He lay gasping in the raft.

'Are you okay, Dr. Grant?' Lex asked.

'From now on, will you just do what I tell you?'

'Oh-*kay*,' she sighed, as if he had just made the most unreasonable demand in the world. She trailed her arm in the water for a while. 'You stopped rowing,' she said.

'I'm tired,' Grant said.

'Then how come we're still moving?'

Grant sat up. She was right. The raft drifted steadily north. 'There must be a current.' The current was carrying them north, toward the hotel. He looked at his watch and was astonished to see it was fifteen minutes past seven. Only fifteen minutes had passed since he had last looked at his watch. It seemed like two hours.

Grant lay back against the rubber gunwales, closed his eyes, and slept.

Fifth Iteration

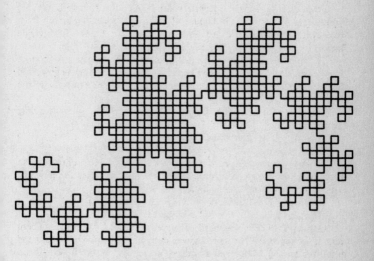

'Flaws in the system will now become severe.'

IAN MALCOLM

Search

Gennaro sat in the Jeep and listened to the buzzing of the flies, and stared at the distant palm trees wavering in the heat. He was astonished by what looked like a battleground: the grass was trampled flat for a hundred yards in every direction. One big palm tree was uprooted from the ground. There were great washes of blood in the grass, and on the rocky outcropping to their right.

Sitting beside him, Muldoon said, 'No doubt about it. Rexy's been among the hadrosaurs.' He took another drink of whiskey, and capped the bottle. 'Damn lot of flies,' he said.

They waited, and watched.

Gennaro drummed his fingers on the dashboard. 'What are we waiting for?'

Muldoon didn't answer immediately. 'The rex is out there somewhere,' he said, squinting at the landscape in the morning sun. 'And we don't have any weapons worth a damn.'

'We're in a Jeep.'

'Oh, he can outrun the Jeep, Mr. Gennaro,' Muldoon said, shaking his head. 'Once we leave this road and go onto open terrain, the best we can do in a four-wheel drive is thirty, forty miles an hour. He'll run us right down. No problem for him.' Muldoon sighed. 'But I don't see much moving out there now. You ready to live dangerously?'

'Sure,' Gennaro said.

Muldoon started the engine, and at the sudden sound, two small othnielians leapt up from the matted grass directly ahead. Muldoon put the car in gear. He drove in a wide circle around the trampled site, and then moved inward, driving in decreasing concentric circles until he finally came to the place in the field where the little othnielians had been. Then he got out and walked forward in the grass, away from the Jeep. He stopped as a dense cloud of flies lifted into the air.

'What is it?' Gennaro called.

'Bring the radio,' Muldoon said.

Gennaro climbed out of the Jeep and hurried forward. Even from a distance he could smell the sour-sweet odor of early decay. He saw a dark shape in the grass, crusted with blood, legs askew.

'Young hadrosaur,' Muldoon said, staring down at the carcass. 'The whole herd stampeded, and the young one got separated, and the T-rex brought it down.'

'How do you know?' Gennaro said. The flesh was ragged from many bites.

'You can tell from the excreta,' Muldoon said. 'See those chalky white bits there in the grass? That's hadro spoor. Uric acid makes it white. But you look there' – he pointed to a large mound, rising knee-high in the grass – 'that's tyrannosaur spoor.'

'How do you know the tyrannosaur didn't come later?'

'The bite pattern,' Muldoon said. 'See those little ones there?' He pointed along the belly. 'Those are from the othys. Those bites haven't bled. They're postmortem, from scavengers. Othys did that. But the hadro was brought down by a bite on the neck – you see the big slash there, above the shoulder blades – and that's the T-rex, no question.'

Gennaro bent over the carcass, staring at the awkward, trampled limbs with a sense of unreality. Beside him, Muldoon flicked on his radio. 'Control.'

'Yes,' John Arnold said, over the radio.

'We got another hadro dead. Juvenile.' Muldoon bent down among the flies and checked the skin on the sole of the right foot. A number was tattooed there. 'Specimen is number HD/09.'

The radio crackled. 'I've got something for you,' Arnold said.

'Oh? What's that?'

'I found Nedry.'

The Jeep burst through the line of palm trees along the east road and came out into a narrower service road, leading toward the jungle river. It was hot in this area of the park, the jungle close and fetid around them. Muldoon was fiddling with the computer monitor in the Jeep, which now showed a map of the resort with overlaid grid lines. 'They found him up on remote video,' he said. 'Sector 1104 is just ahead.'

Farther up the road, Gennaro saw a concrete barrier, and the Jeep parked alongside it. 'He must have taken the wrong turnoff,' Muldoon said. 'The little bastard.'

'What'd he take?' Gennaro asked.

'Wu says fifteen embryos. Know what that's worth?'

Gennaro shook his head.

'Somewhere between two and ten million,' Muldoon said. He shook his head. 'Big stakes.'

As they came closer, Gennaro saw the body lying beside the car. The body was indistinct and green – but then green shapes scattered away, as the Jeep pulled to a stop.

'Compys,' Muldoon said. 'The compys found him.'

A dozen procompsognathids, delicate little predators no larger than ducks, stood at the edge of the jungle, chittering excitedly as the men climbed out of the car.

Dennis Nedry lay on his back, the chubby boyish face now red and bloated. Flies buzzed around the gaping mouth and thick tongue. His body was mangled – the intestines torn open, one leg chewed through. Gennaro turned away quickly, to look at the little compys, which squatted on their hind legs a short distance away and watched the men curiously. The little dinosaurs had five-fingered hands, he noticed. They wiped their faces and chins, giving them an eerily human quality which –

'I'll be damned,' Muldoon said. 'Wasn't the compys.'

'What?'

Muldoon was shaking his head. 'See these blotches? On his shirt and his face? Smell that sweet smell like old, dried vomit?'

Gennaro rolled his eyes. He smelled it.

'That's dilo saliva,' Muldoon said. 'Spit from the dilophosaurs. You see the damage on the corneas, all that redness. In the eyes it's painful but not fatal. You've got about two hours to wash it out with the antivenin; we keep it all around the park, just in case. Not that it mattered to this bastard. They blinded him, then ripped him down the middle. Not a nice way to go. Maybe there's justice in the world after all.'

The procompsognathids squeaked and hopped up and down as Gennaro opened the back door and took out gray metal tubing and a stainless-steel case. 'It's all still there,' he said. He handed two dark cylinders to Gennaro.

'What're these?' Gennaro said.

'Just what they look like,' Muldoon said. 'Rockets.' As Gennaro backed away, he said, 'Watch it – you don't want to step in something.'

Gennaro stepped carefully over Nedry's body. Muldoon carried the tubing to the other Jeep, and placed it in the back. He climbed behind the wheel. 'Let's go.'

'What about him?' Gennaro said, pointing to the body.

'What about him?' Muldoon said. 'We've got things to do.' He put the car in gear. Looking back, Gennaro saw the compys resume their feeding. One jumped up and squatted on Nedry's open mouth as it nibbled the flesh of his nose.

The jungle river became narrower. The banks closed in on both sides until the trees and foliage overhanging the banks met high above to block out the sun. Tim heard the cry of birds, and saw small chirping dinosaurs leaping among the branches. But mostly it was silent, the air hot and still beneath the canopy of trees.

Grant looked at his watch. It was eight o'clock.

They drifted along peacefully, among dappled patches of light. If anything, they seemed to be moving faster than before. Awake now, Grant lay on his back and stared up at the branches overhead. In the bow, he saw her reaching up.

'Hey, what're you doing?' he said.

'You think we can eat these berries?' She pointed to the trees. Some of the overhanging branches were close enough to touch. Tim saw clusters of bright red berries on the branches.

'No,' Grant said.

'Why? Those little dinosaurs are eating them.' She pointed to small dinosaurs, scampering in the branches.

'No, Lex.'

She sighed, dissatisfied with his authority. 'I wish Daddy was here,' she said. 'Daddy always knows what to do.'

'What're you talking about?' Tim said. 'He *never* knows what to do.'

'Yes, he does,' she sighed. Lex stared at the trees as they slid past, their big roots twisting toward the water's edge. 'Just because you're not his favorite . . .'

Tim turned away, said nothing.

'But don't worry, Daddy likes you, too. Even if you're into computers and not sports.'

'Dad's a real sports nut,' Tim explained to Grant.

Grant nodded. Up in the branches, small pale yellow dinosaurs, barely two feet tall, hopped from tree to tree. They had beaky heads, like parrots. 'You know what they call those?' Tim said. 'Microceratops.'

'Big deal,' Lex said.

'I thought you might be interested.'

'Only very young boys,' she said, 'are interested in dinosaurs.'

'Says who?'

'Daddy.'

Tim started to yell, but Grant raised his hand. 'Kids,' he said, 'shut up.'

'Why?' Lex said. 'I can do what I want, if I –'

Then she fell silent, because she heard it, too. It was a bloodcurdling shriek, from somewhere downriver.

'Well, where the hell is the damn rex?' Muldoon said, talking into the radio. 'Because we don't see him here.' They were back at the sauropod compound, looking out at the trampled grass where the hadrosaurs had stampeded. The tyrannosaur was nowhere to be found.

'Checking now,' Arnold said, and clicked off.

Muldoon turned to Gennaro. 'Checking now,' he repeated sarcastically. 'Why the hell didn't he check before? Why didn't he keep track of him?'

'I don't know,' Gennaro said.

'He's not showing up,' Arnold said, a moment later.

'What do you mean, he's not showing up?'

'He's not on the monitors. Motion sensors aren't finding him.'

'Hell,' Muldoon said. 'So much for the motion sensors. You see Grant and the kids?'

'Motion sensors aren't finding them, either.'

'Well, what are we supposed to do now?' Muldoon said.

'Wait,' Arnold said.

'Look! Look!'

Directly ahead, the big dome of the aviary rose above them. Grant had seen it only from a distance; now he realized it was enormous – a quarter of a mile in diameter or more. The pattern of geodesic struts shone dully through the light mist, and his first thought was that the glass must weigh a ton. Then, as they came closer, he saw there wasn't any glass – just struts. A thin mesh hung inside the elements.

'It isn't finished,' Lex said.

'I think it's meant to be open like that,' Grant said.

'Then all the birds can fly out.'

'Not if they're *big* birds,' Grant said.

The river carried them beneath the edge of the dome. They stared upward. Now they were inside the dome, still drifting down the river. But within minutes the dome was so high above them that it was hardly visible in the mist. Grant said, 'I seem to remember there's a second lodge here.' Moments later, he saw the roof of a building over the tops of the trees to the north.

'You want to stop?' Tim said.

'Maybe there's a phone. Or motion sensors.' Grant steered toward the shore. 'We need to try to contact the control room. It's getting late.'

They clambered out, slipping on the muddy bank, and Grant hauled the raft out of the water. Then he tied the rope to a tree and they set off, through a dense forest of palm trees.

Aviary

'I just don't understand,' John Arnold said, speaking into the phone. 'I don't see the rex, and I don't see Grant and the kids anywhere, either.'

He sat in front of the consoles and gulped another cup of coffee. All around him, the control room was strewn with paper plates and half-eaten sandwiches. Arnold was exhausted. It was 8:00 a.m. on Saturday. In the fourteen hours since Nedry destroyed the computer that ran Jurassic Park, Arnold had patiently pulled systems back on line, one after another. 'All the park systems are back, and functioning correctly. The phones are working. I've called for a doctor for you.'

On the other end of the line, Malcolm coughed. Arnold was talking to him in his room at the lodge. 'But you're having trouble with the motion sensors?'

'Well, I'm not finding what I am looking for.'

'Like the rex?'

'He's not reading at all now. He started north about twenty minutes ago, following along the edge of the lagoon, and then I lost him. I don't know why, unless he's gone to sleep again.'

'And you can't find Grant and the kids?'

'No.'

'I think it's quite simple,' Malcolm said. 'The motion sensors cover an inadequate area.'

'Inadequate?' Arnold bristled. 'They cover ninety-two –'

'Ninety-two percent of the land area, I remember,' Malcolm said. 'But if you put the remaining areas up on the board, I think you'll find that the eight percent is topologically unified, meaning that those areas are contiguous. In essence, an animal can move freely anywhere in the park and escape detection, by following a maintenance road or the jungle river or the beaches or whatever.'

'Even if that were so,' Arnold said, 'the animals are too stupid to know that.'

'It's not clear how stupid the animals are,' Malcolm said.

'You think that's what Grant and the kids are doing?' Arnold said.

'Definitely not,' Malcolm said, coughing again. 'Grant's no fool. He clearly wants to be detected by you. He and the kids are probably waving at every motion sensor in sight. But maybe they have other problems we don't know about. Or maybe they're on the river.'

'I can't imagine they'd be on the river. The banks are very narrow. It's impossible to walk along there.'

'Would the river bring them all the way back here?'

'Yes, but it's not the safest way to go, because it passes through the aviary. . . .'

'Why wasn't the aviary on the tour?' Malcolm said.

'We've had problems setting it up. Originally the park was intended to have a treetop lodge built high above the ground, where visitors could observe the pterodactyls at flight level. We've got four dactyls in the aviary now – actually, they're cearadactyls, which are big fish-eating dactyls.'

'What about them?'

'Well, while we finished the lodge, we put the dactyls in the aviary to acclimate them. But that was a big mistake. It turns out our fish-hunters are territorial.'

'Territorial?'

'Fiercely territorial,' Arnold said. 'They fight among themselves for territory – and they'll attack any other animal that comes into the area they've marked out.'

'Attack?'

'It's impressive,' Arnold said. 'The dactyls glide to the top of the aviary, fold up their wings, and dive. A thirty-pound animal will strike a man on the ground like a ton of bricks. They were knocking the workmen unconscious, cutting them up pretty badly.'

'That doesn't injure the dactyls?'

'Not so far.'

'So, if those kids are in the aviary . . .'

'They're not,' Arnold said. 'At least, I hope they're not.'

'Is *that* the lodge?' Lex said. 'What a dump.'

Beneath the aviary dome, Pteratops Lodge was built high above the ground, on big wooden pylons, in the middle of a stand of fir trees. But the building was unfinished and unpainted; the windows were boarded up. The trees and the lodge were splattered with broad white streaks.

'I guess they didn't finish it, for some reason,' Grant said, hiding his disappointment. He glanced at his watch. 'Come on, let's go back to the boat.'

The sun came out as they walked along, making the morning more cheerful. Grant looked at the lattice work shadows on the ground from the dome above. He noticed that the ground and the foliage were spattered with broad streaks of the same white chalky substance that had been on the building. And there was a distinctive, sour odor in the morning air.

'Stinks here,' Lex said. 'What's all the white stuff?'

'Looks like reptile droppings. Probably from the birds.'

'How come they didn't finish the lodge?'

'I don't know.'

They entered a clearing of low grass, dotted with wild flowers. They heard a long, low whistle. Then an answering whistle, from across the forest.

'What's that?'

'I don't know.'

Then Grant saw the dark shadow of a cloud on the grassy field ahead. The shadow was moving fast. In moments, it had swept over them. He looked up and saw an enormous dark shape gliding above them, blotting out the sun.

'Yow!' Lex said. 'Is it a pterodactyl?'

'Yes,' Tim said.

Grant didn't answer. He was entranced by the sight of the huge flying creature. In the sky above, the pterodactyl gave a low whistle and wheeled gracefully, turning back toward them.

'How come they're not on the tour?' Tim said.

Grant was wondering the same thing. The flying dinosaurs were so beautiful, so graceful as they moved through the air. As Grant watched, he saw a second pterodactyl appear in the sky, and a third, and a fourth.

'Maybe because they didn't finish the lodge,' Lex said.

Grant was thinking these weren't ordinary pterodactyls. They were too large. They must be cearadactyls, big flying reptiles from the early Cretaceous. When they were high, these looked like small airplanes. When they came lower, he could see the animals had fifteen-foot wingspans, furry bodies, and heads like crocodiles'. They ate fish, he remembered. South America and Mexico.

Lex shaded her eyes and looked up at the sky. 'Can they hurt us?'

'I don't think so. They eat fish.'

One of the dactyls spiraled down, a flashing dark shadow that whooshed past them with a rush of warm air and a lingering sour odor.

'Wow!' Lex said. 'They're *really* big.' And then she said, 'Are you sure they can't hurt us?'

'Pretty sure.'

A second dactyl swooped down, moving faster than the first. It came from behind, streaked over their heads. Grant had a glimpse of its toothy beak and the furry body. It looked like a huge bat, he thought. But Grant was impressed with the frail appearance of the animals. Their huge wingspans – the delicate pink membranes stretched across them – so thin they were translucent – everything reinforced the delicacy of the dactyls.

'Ow!' Lex shouted, grabbing her hair. 'He bit me!'

'He what?' Grant said.

'He bit me! He bit me!' When she took her hand away, he saw blood on her fingers.

Up in the sky, two more dactyls folded their wings, collapsing into small dark shapes that plummeted toward the ground. They made a kind of scream as they hurtled downward.

'Come on!' Grant said, grabbing their hands. They ran across the meadow, hearing the approaching scream, and he flung himself on the ground at the last moment, pulling the kids down with him, as the two dactyls whistled and squeaked past them, flapping their wings. Grant felt claws tear the shirt along his back.

Then he was up, pulling Lex back onto her feet, and running with Tim a few feet forward while overhead two more birds wheeled and dove toward them, screaming. At the last moment, he pushed the kids to the ground, and the big shadows flapped past.

'Uck,' Lex said, disgusted. He saw that she was streaked with white droppings from the birds.

Grant scrambled to his feet. 'Come on!'

He was about to run when Lex shrieked in terror. He turned back and saw that one of the dactyls had grabbed her by the shoulders with its hind claws. The animal's huge leathery wings, translucent in the sunlight, flapped broadly on both sides of her. The dactyl was trying to take off, but Lex was too heavy, and while it struggled it repeatedly jabbed at her head with its long pointed jaw.

Lex was screaming, waving her arms wildly. Grant did the only thing he could think to do. He ran forward and jumped up, throwing himself against the body of the dactyl. He knocked it onto its back on the ground, and fell on top of the furry body. The animal screamed and snapped; Grant ducked his head away from the jaws and pushed back, as the giant wings beat around his body. It was like being in a tent in a windstorm. He couldn't see; he couldn't hear; there was nothing but the flapping and shrieking and the leathery membranes. The clawed legs scratched frantically at his chest. Lex was screaming. Grant pushed away from the dactyl and it squeaked and gibbered as it flapped its wings and struggled to turn over, to right itself. Finally it pulled in its wings like a bat and rolled over, lifted itself up on its little wing claws, and began to walk that way. He paused, astonished.

It could walk on its wings! Lederer's speculation was right! But then the other dactyls were diving down at them and Grant was dizzy, off balance, and in horror he saw Lex run away, her arms over her head . . . Tim shouting at the top of his lungs. . . .

The first of them swooped down and she threw something and suddenly the dactyl whistled and climbed. The other dactyls immediately climbed and chased the first into the sky. The fourth dactyl flapped awkwardly into the air to join the others. Grant looked upward, squinting to see what had happened. The three dactyls chased the first, screaming angrily.

They were alone in the field.

'What happened?' Grant said.

'They got my glove,' Lex said. 'My Darryl Strawberry special.'

They started walking again. Tim put his arm around her shoulders. 'Are you all right?'

'Of *course*, stupid,' she said, shaking him off. She looked upward. 'I hope they choke and die,' she said.

'Yeah,' Tim said. 'Me, too.'

Up ahead, they saw the boat on the shore. Grant looked at his watch. It was eight-thirty. He now had two and a half hours to get back.

Lex cheered as they drifted beyond the silver aviary dome. Then the banks of the river closed in on both sides, the trees meeting overhead once more. The river was narrower than ever, in some places only ten feet wide, and the current flowed very fast. Lex reached up to touch the branches as they went past.

Grant sat back in the raft and listened to the gurgle of the water through the warm rubber. They were moving faster now, the branches overhead slipping by more rapidly. It was pleasant. It gave a little breeze in the hot confines of the overhanging branches. And it meant they would get back that much sooner.

Grant couldn't guess how far they had come, but it must be several miles at least from the sauropod building where they had spent the night. Perhaps four or five miles. Maybe even more. That meant they might be only an hour's walk from the hotel, once they left the raft. But after the aviary, Grant was in no hurry to leave the river again. For the moment, they were making good time.

'I wonder how Ralph is,' Lex said. 'He's probably dead or something.'

'I'm sure he's fine.'

'I wonder if he'd let me ride him.' She sighed, sleepy in the sun. 'That would be fun, to ride Ralph.'

Tim said to Grant, 'Remember back at the stegosaurus? Last night?'

'Yes.'

'How come you asked them about frog DNA?'

'Because of the breeding,' Grant said. 'They can't explain why the dinosaurs are breeding, since they irradiate them, and since they're all females.'

'Right.'

'Well, irradiation is notoriously unreliable and probably doesn't work. I think that'll eventually be shown here. But there is still the problem of the dinosaurs' being female. How can they breed when they're all female?'

'Right,' Tim said.

'Well, across the animal kingdom, sexual reproduction exists in extraordinary variety.'

'Tim's very interested in sex,' Lex said.

They both ignored her. 'For example,' Grant said, 'many animals have sexual reproduction without ever having what we would call sex. The male releases a spermatophore, which contains the sperm, and the female picks it up at a later time. This kind of exchange does not require quite as much physical differentiation between male and female as we usually think exists. Male and female are more alike in some animals than they are in human beings.'

Tim nodded. 'But what about the frogs?'

Grant heard sudden shrieks from the trees above, as the microceratopsians scattered in alarm, shaking the branches. The big head of the tyrannosaur lunged through the foliage from the left, the jaws snapping at the raft. Lex howled in terror, and Grant paddled away toward the opposite bank, but the river here was only ten feet wide. The tyrannosaur was caught in the heavy growth; it butted and twisted its head, and roared. Then it pulled its head back.

Through the trees that lined the riverbank, they saw the huge dark form of the tyrannosaur, moving north, looking for a gap in the trees that lined the bank. The microceratopsians had all gone to the opposite bank, where they shrieked and scampered and jumped up and down. In the raft, Grant, Tim, and Lex stared helplessly as the tyrannosaur tried to break through again. But the trees were too dense along the banks of the river. The tyrannosaur again moved downstream, ahead of the boat, and tried again, shaking the branches furiously.

But again it failed.

Then it moved off, heading farther downstream.

'I *hate* him,' Lex said.

Grant sat back in the boat, badly shaken. If the tyrannosaur had broken through, there was nothing he could have done to save them. The river was so narrow that it was hardly wider than the raft. It was like being in a tunnel. The rubber gunwales often scraped on the mud as the boat was pulled along by the swift current.

He glanced at his watch. Almost nine. The raft continued downstream.

'Hey,' Lex said, 'listen!'

He heard snarling, interspersed by a repeated hooting cry. The cries were coming from beyond a curve, farther downriver. He listened, and heard the hooting again.

'What is it?' Lex said.

'I don't know,' Grant said. 'But there's more than one of them.' He paddled the boat to the opposite bank, grabbed a branch to stop the raft. The snarling was repeated. Then more hooting.

'It sounds like a bunch of owls,' Tim said.

Malcolm groaned. 'Isn't it time for more morphine yet?'

'Not yet,' Ellie said.

Malcolm sighed. 'How much water have we got here?'

'I don't know. There's plenty of running water from the tap –'

'No, I mean, how much stored? Any?'

Ellie shrugged. 'None.'

'Go into the rooms on this floor,' Malcolm said, 'and fill the bathtubs with water.'

Ellie frowned.

'Also,' Malcolm said, 'have we got any walkie-talkies? Flashlights? Matches? Sterno stoves? Things like that?'

'I'll look around. You planning for an earthquake?'

'Something like that,' Malcolm said. 'Malcolm Effect implies catastrophic changes.'

'But Arnold says all the systems are working perfectly.'

'That's when it happens,' Malcolm said.

Ellie said, 'You don't think much of Arnold, do you?'

'He's all right. He's an engineer. Wu's the same. They're both technicians. They don't have intelligence. They have what I call "thintelligence." They see the immediate situation. They think narrowly and they call it "being focused." They don't see the surround. They don't see the consequences. That's how you get an island like this. From thintelligent thinking. Because you cannot make an animal and not expect it to act *alive*. To be unpredictable. To escape. But they don't see that.'

'Don't you think it's just human nature?' Ellie said.

'God, no,' Malcolm said. 'That's like saying scrambled eggs and bacon for breakfast is human nature. It's nothing of the sort. It's uniquely Western training, and much of the rest of the world is nauseated by the thought of it.' He winced in pain. 'The morphine's making me philosophical.'

'You want some water?'

'No. I'll tell you the problem with engineers and scientists. Scientists have an elaborate line of bullshit about how they are seeking to know the truth about nature. Which is true, but that's not what drives them. Nobody is driven by abstractions like "seeking truth."

'Scientists are actually preoccupied with accomplishment. So they are focused on whether they can do something. They never stop to ask if they *should* do something. They conveniently define such considerations as pointless. If they don't do it, someone else will. Discovery, they believe, is inevitable. So they just try to do it first. That's the game in science. Even pure scientific discovery is an aggressive, penetrative act. It takes big equipment, and it literally changes the world afterward. Particle accelerators scar the land, and leave radioactive byproducts. Astronauts leave trash on the moon. There is always some proof that scientists were there, making their discoveries. Discovery is always a rape of the natural world. Always.

'The scientists want it that way. They have to stick their instruments in. They have to leave their mark. They can't just watch. They can't just appreciate. They can't just fit into the natural order. They have to make something unnatural happen. That is the scientist's job, and now we have whole societies that try to be scientific.' He sighed, and sank back.

Ellie said, 'Don't you think you're overstating —'

'What does one of your excavations look like a year later?'

'Pretty bad,' she admitted.

'You don't replant, you don't restore the land after you dig?'

'No.'

'Why not?'

She shrugged. 'There's no money, I guess. . . .'

'There's only enough money to dig, but not to repair?'

'Well, we're just working in the badlands. . . .'

'Just the badlands,' Malcolm said, shaking his head. 'Just trash. Just byproducts. Just side effects . . . I'm trying to tell you that scientists *want* it this way. They want byproducts and trash and scars and side effects. It's a way of reassuring themselves. It's built into the fabric of science, and it's increasingly a disaster.'

'Then what's the answer?'

'Get rid of the thintelligent ones. Take them out of power.'

'But then we'd lose all the advances —'

'What advances?' Malcolm said irritably. 'The number of hours women devote to housework has not changed since 1930, despite all the advances. All the vacuum cleaners, washer-dryers, trash compactors, garbage disposals, wash-and-wear fabrics . . . Why does it still take as long to clean the house as it did in 1930?'

Ellie said nothing.

'Because there haven't been any advances,' Malcolm said. 'Not really. Thirty thousand years ago, when men were doing cave paintings at Lascaux, they worked twenty hours a week to provide themselves with food and shelter and clothing. The rest of the time, they could play, or sleep, or do whatever they wanted. And they lived in a natural world, with clean air, clean water, beautiful trees and sunsets. Think about it. Twenty hours a week. Thirty thousand years ago.'

Ellie said, 'You want to turn back the clock?'

'No,' Malcolm said. 'I want people to wake up. We've had four hundred years of modern science, and we ought to know by now what it's good for, and what it's not good for. It's time for a change.'

'Before we destroy the planet?' she said.

He sighed, and closed his eyes. 'Oh dear,' he said. 'That's the *last* thing I would worry about.'

In the dark tunnel of the jungle river, Grant went hand over hand, holding branches, moving the raft cautiously forward. He still heard the sounds. And finally he saw the dinosaurs.

'Aren't those the ones that are poison?'

'Yes,' Grant said. '*Dilophosaurus.*'

Standing on the riverbank were two dilophosaurs. The ten-foot-tall bodies were spotted yellow and black. Underneath, the bellies were bright green, like lizards. Twin red curving crests ran along the top of the head from the eyes to the nose, making a V shape above the head. The bird-like quality was reinforced by the way they moved, bending to drink from the river, then rising to snarl and hoot.

Lex whispered, 'Should we get out and walk?'

Grant shook his head no. The dilophosaurs were smaller than the tyrannosaur, small enough to slip through the dense foliage at the banks of the river. And they seemed quick, as they snarled and hooted at each other.

'But we can't get past them in the boat,' Lex said. 'They're *poison.*'

'We have to,' Grant said. 'Somehow.'

The dilophosaurs continued to drink and hoot. They seemed to be interacting with each other in a strangely ritualistic, repetitive way. The animal on the left would bend to drink, opening its mouth to bare long rows of sharp teeth, and then it would hoot. The animal on the right would hoot in reply and bend to drink, in a mirror image of the first animal's movements. Then the sequence would be repeated, exactly the same way.

Grant noticed that the animal on the right was smaller, with smaller spots on its back, and its crest was a duller red –

'I'll be damned,' he said. 'It's a mating ritual.'

'Can we get past them?' Tim asked.

'Not the way they are now. They're right by the edge of the water.' Grant knew animals often performed such mating rituals for hours at a time. They went without food, they paid attention to nothing else. . . . He glanced at his watch. Nine-twenty.

'What do we do?' Tim said.

Grant sighed. 'I have no idea.'

He sat down in the raft, and then the dilophosaurs began to honk and roar repeatedly, in agitation. He looked up. The animals were both facing away from the river.

'What is it?' Lex said.

Grant smiled. 'I think we're finally getting some help.' He pushed off from the bank. 'I want you two kids to lie flat on the rubber. We'll go past as fast as we can. But just remember: whatever happens, don't say anything, and don't move. Okay?'

The raft began to drift downstream, toward the hooting dilophosaurs. It gained speed. Lex lay at Grant's feet, staring at him with frightened eyes. They were coming closer to the dilophosaurs, which were still turned away from the river. But he pulled out his air pistol, checked the chamber.

The raft continued on, and they smelled a peculiar odor, sweet and nauseating at the same time. It smelled like dried vomit. The hooting of the dilophosaurs was louder. The raft came around a final bend and Grant caught his breath. The dilophosaurs were just a few feet away, honking at the trees beyond the river.

As Grant had suspected, they were honking at the tyrannosaur. The tyrannosaur was trying to break through the foliage, and the dilos hooted and stomped their feet in the mud. The raft drifted past them. The smell was nauseating. The tyrannosaur roared, probably because it saw the raft. But in another moment . . .

A *thump*.

The raft stopped moving. They were aground, against the riverbank, just a few feet downstream from the dilophosaurs.

Lex whispered, 'Oh, *great*.'

There was a long slow scraping sound of the raft against the mud. Then the raft was moving again. They were going down the river. The tyrannosaur roared a final time and moved off; one dilophosaur looked surprised, then hooted. The other dilophosaur hooted in reply.

The raft floated downriver.

Tyrannosaur

The Jeep bounced along in the glaring sun. Muldoon was driving, with Gennaro at his side. They were in an open field, moving away from the dense line of foliage and palm trees that marked the course of the river, a hundred yards to the east. They came to a rise, and Muldoon stopped the car.

'Christ, it's hot,' he said, wiping his forehead with the back of his arm. He drank from the bottle of whiskey between his knees, then offered it to Gennaro.

Gennaro shook his head. He stared at the landscape shimmering in the morning heat. Then he looked down at the onboard computer and video monitor mounted in the dashboard. The monitor showed views of the park from remote cameras. Still no sign of Grant and the children. Or of the tyrannosaur.

The radio crackled. 'Muldoon.'

Muldoon picked up the handset. 'Yeah.'

'You got your onboards? I found the rex. He's in grid 442. Going to 443.'

'Just a minute,' Muldoon said, adjusting the monitor. 'Yeah. I got him now. Following the river.' The animal was slinking along the foliage that lined the banks of the river, going north.

'Take it easy with him. Just immobilize him.'

'Don't worry,' Muldoon said, squinting in the sun. 'I won't hurt him.'

'Remember,' Arnold said, 'the tyrannosaur's our main tourist attraction.'

Muldoon turned off his radio with a crackle of static. 'Bloody fool,' he said. 'They're still talking about tourists.' Muldoon started the engine. 'Let's go see Rexy and give him a dose.'

The Jeep jolted over the terrain.

'You're looking forward to this,' Gennaro said.

'I've wanted to put a needle in this big bastard for a while,' Muldoon said. 'And there he is.'

They came to a wrenching stop. Through the windshield, Gennaro saw the tyrannosaur directly ahead of them, moving among the palm trees along the river.

Muldoon drained the whiskey bottle and threw it in the back seat. He reached back for his tubing. Gennaro looked at the video monitor, which showed their Jeep and the tyrannosaur. There must be a closed-circuit camera in the trees somewhere behind.

'You want to help,' Muldoon said, 'you can break out those canisters by your feet.'

Gennaro bent over and opened a stainless-steel Halliburton case. It was padded inside with foam. Four cylinders, each the size of a quart milk bottle, were nestled in the foam. They were all labeled MORO-709. He took one out.

'You snap off the tip and screw on a needle,' Muldoon explained.

Gennaro found a plastic package of large needles, each the diameter of his fingertip. He screwed one onto the canister. The opposite end of the canister had a circular lead weight.

'That's the plunger. Compresses on impact.' Muldoon sat forward with the air rifle across his knees. It was made of heavy gray tubular metal and looked to Gennaro like a bazooka or a rocket launcher.

'What's MORO-709?'

'Standard animal trank,' Muldoon said. 'Zoos around the world use it. We'll try a thousand cc's to start.' Muldoon cracked open the chamber, which was large enough to insert his fist. He slipped the canister into the chamber and closed it.

'That should do it,' Muldoon said. 'Standard elephant gets about two hundred cc's, but they're only two or three tons each. *Tyrannosaurus rex* is eight tons, and a lot meaner. That matters to the dose.'

'Why?'

'Animal dose is partly body weight and partly temperament. You shoot the same dose of 709 into an elephant, a hippo, and a rhino – you'll immobilize the elephant, so it just stands there like a statue. You'll slow down the hippo, so it gets kind of sleepy but it keeps moving. And the rhino will just get fighting mad. But, on the other hand, you chase a rhino for more than five minutes in a car and he'll drop dead from adrenaline shock. Strange combination of tough and delicate.'

Muldoon drove slowly toward the river, moving closer to the tyrannosaur. 'But those are all mammals. We know a lot about handling mammals, because zoos are built around the big mammalian attractions – lions, tigers, bears, elephants. We know a lot less about reptiles. And nobody knows anything about dinosaurs. The dinosaurs are new animals.'

'You consider them reptiles?' Gennaro said.

'No,' Muldoon said, shifting gears. 'Dinosaurs don't fit existing categories.' He swerved to avoid a rock. 'Actually, what we find is, the dinosaurs were as variable as mammals are today. Some dinos are tame and cute, and some are mean and nasty. Some of them see well, and some of them don't. Some of them are stupid, and some of them are very, very intelligent.'

'Like the raptors?' Gennaro said.

Muldoon nodded. 'Raptors are smart. Very smart. Believe me, all the problems we have so far,' he said, 'are nothing compared with what we'd have if the raptors ever got out of their holding pen. Ah. I think this is as close as we can get to our Rexy.'

Up ahead, the tyrannosaur was poking its head through the branches, peering toward the river. Trying to get through. Then the animal moved a few yards downstream, to try again.

'Wonder what he sees in there?' Gennaro said.

'Hard to know,' Muldoon said. 'Maybe he's trying to get to the microceratopsians that scramble around in the branches. They'll run him a merry chase.'

Muldoon stopped the Jeep about fifty yards away from the tyrannosaur, and turned the vehicle around. He left the motor running. 'Get behind the wheel,' Muldoon said. 'And put your seat belt on.' He took another canister and hooked it onto his shirt. Then he got out.

Gennaro slid behind the wheel. 'You done this very often before?'

Muldoon belched. 'Never. I'll try to get him just behind the auditory meatus. We'll see how it goes from there.' He walked ten yards behind the Jeep and crouched down in the grass on one knee. He steadied the big gun against his shoulder, and flipped up the thick telescopic sight. Muldoon aimed at the tyrannosaur, which still ignored them.

There was a burst of pale gas, and Gennaro saw a white streak shoot forward in the air toward the tyrannosaur. But nothing seemed to happen.

Then the tyrannosaur turned slowly, curiously, to peer at them. It moved its head from side to side, as if looking at them with alternate eyes.

Muldoon had taken down the launcher, and was loading the second canister.

'You hit him?' Gennaro said.

Muldoon shook his head. 'Missed. Damn laser sights . . . See if there's a battery in the case.'

'A what?' Gennaro said.

'A battery,' Muldoon said. 'It's about as big as your finger. Gray markings.'

Gennaro bent over to look in the steel case. He felt the vibration of the Jeep, heard the motor ticking over. He didn't see a battery. The tyrannosaur roared. To Gennaro it was a terrifying sound, rumbling from the great chest cavity of the animal, bellowing out over the landscape. He sat up sharply and reached for the steering wheel, put his hand on the gearshift. On the radio, he heard a voice say, 'Muldoon. This is Arnold. Get out of there. Over.'

'I know what I'm doing,' Muldoon said.

The tyrannosaur charged.

Muldoon stood his ground. Despite the creature racing toward him, he slowly and methodically raised his launcher, aimed, and fired. Once again, Gennaro saw the puff of smoke, and the white streak of the canister going toward the animal.

Nothing happened. The tyrannosaur continued to charge.

Now Muldoon was on his feet and running, shouting, 'Go! Go!' Gennaro put the Jeep in gear and Muldoon threw himself onto the side door as the Jeep lurched forward. The tyrannosaur was closing rapidly, and Muldoon swung the door open and climbed inside.

'Go, damn it! Go!'

Gennaro floored it. The Jeep bounced precariously, the front end nosing so high they saw only sky through the windshield, then slamming down again toward the ground and racing forward again. Gennaro headed for a stand of trees to the left until, in the rearview mirror, he saw the tyrannosaur give a final roar and turn away.

Gennaro slowed the car. 'Jesus.'

Muldoon was shaking his head. 'I could have sworn I hit him the second time.'

'I'd say you missed,' Gennaro said.

'Needle must have broken off before the plunger injected.'

'Admit it, you missed.'

'Yeah,' Muldoon said. He sighed. 'I missed. Battery was dead in the damned laser sights. My fault. I should have checked it, after it was out all last night. Let's go back and get more canisters.'

The Jeep headed north, toward the hotel. Muldoon picked up the radio. 'Control.'

'Yes,' Arnold said.

'We're heading back to base.'

The river was now very narrow, and flowing swiftly. The raft was going faster all the time. It was starting to feel like an amusement park ride.

'Whee!' Lex yelled, holding on to the gunwale. 'Faster, faster!'

Grant squinted, looking forward. The river was still narrow and dark, but farther ahead he could see the trees ended, and there was bright sunlight beyond, and a distant roaring sound. The river seemed to end abruptly in a peculiar flat line ...

The raft was going still faster, rushing forward.

Grant grabbed for his paddles.

'What is it?'

'It's a waterfall,' Grant said.

The raft swept out of the overhanging darkness into brilliant morning sunlight, and raced forward on the swift current toward the lip of the waterfall. The roar was loud in their ears. Grant paddled as strongly as he could, but he only succeeded in spinning the boat in circles. It continued inexorably toward the lip.

Lex leaned toward him. 'I can't swim!' Grant saw that she did not have her life vest clasped, but there was nothing he could do about it; with frightening speed, they came to the edge, and the roar of the waterfall seemed to fill the world. Grant jammed his oar deep into the water, felt it catch and hold, right at the lip; the rubber raft shuddered in the current, but they did not go over. Grant strained against the oar and, looking over the edge, saw the sheer drop of fifty feet down to the surging pool below.

And standing in the surging pool, waiting for them, was the tyrannosaur.

Lex was screaming in panic, and then the boat spun, and the rear end dropped away, spilling them out into air and roaring water, and they fell sickeningly. Grant flailed his arms in the air, and the world went suddenly silent and slow.

It seemed to him he fell for long minutes; he had time to observe Lex, clutching her orange jacket, falling alongside him; he had time to observe Tim, looking down at the bottom; he had time to observe the frozen white sheet of the waterfall; he had time to observe the bubbling pool beneath him as he fell slowly, silently toward it.

Then, with a stinging slap, Grant plunged into cold water, surrounded by white boiling bubbles. He tumbled and spun and glimpsed the leg of the tyrannosaur as he was swirled past it, swept down through the pool and out into the stream beyond. Grant swam for the shore, clutched warm rocks, slipped off, caught a branch, and finally pulled himself out of the main current. Gasping, he dragged himself on his belly onto the rocks, and looked at the river just in time to see the brown rubber raft tumble past him. Then he saw Tim, battling the current, and he reached out and pulled him, coughing and shivering, onto the shore beside him.

Grant turned back to the waterfall, and saw the tyrannosaur plunge its head straight down into the water of the pool at his feet. The great head shook, splashing water to either side. It had something between its teeth.

And then the tyrannosaur lifted its head back up.

Dangling from the jaws was Lex's orange life vest.

A moment later, Lex bobbed to the surface beside the dinosaur's long tail. She lay face down in the water, her little body swept downstream by the current. Grant plunged into the water after her, was again immersed in the churning torrent. A moment later, he pulled her up onto the rocks, a heavy, lifeless weight. Her face was gray. Water poured from her mouth.

Grant bent over her to give her mouth-to-mouth but she coughed. Then she vomited yellow-green liquid and coughed again. Her eyelids fluttered. 'Hi,' she said. She smiled weakly. 'We did it.'

Tim started to cry. She coughed again. 'Will you stop it? What're you crying for?'

'Because.'

'We were worried about you,' Grant said. Small flecks of white were drifting down the river. The tyrannosaur was tearing up the life vest. Still turned away from them, facing the waterfall. But at any minute the animal might turn and see them. . . . 'Come on, kids,' he said.

'Where are we going?' Lex said, coughing.

'Come *on*.' He was looking for a hiding place. Downstream he saw only an open grassy plain, affording no protection. Upstream was the dinosaur. Then Grant saw a dirt path by the river. It seemed to lead up toward the waterfall.

And in the dirt he saw the clear imprint of a man's shoe. Leading up the path.

The tyrannosaur finally turned around, growling and looking out toward the grassy plain. It seemed to have figured out that they had gotten away. It was looking for them downstream. Grant and the kids ducked among the big ferns that lined the riverbanks. Cautiously, he led them upstream. 'Where are we going?' Lex said. 'We're going *back*.'

'I know.'

They were closer to the waterfall now, the roar much louder. The rocks became slippery, the path muddy. There was a constant hanging mist. It was like moving through a cloud. The path seemed to lead right into the rushing water, but as they came closer, they saw that it actually went behind the waterfall.

The tyrannosaur was still looking downstream, its back turned to them. They hurried along the path to the waterfall, and had almost moved behind the sheet of falling water when Grant saw the tyrannosaur turn. Then they were completely behind the waterfall, and Grant was unable to see out through the silver sheet.

Grant looked around in surprise. There was a little recess here, hardly larger than a closet, and filled with machinery: humming pumps and big filters and pipes. Everything was wet, and cold.

'Did he see us?' Lex said. She had to shout over the noise of the falling water. 'Where are we? What is this place? Did he see us?'

'Just a minute,' Grant said. He was looking at the equipment. This was clearly park machinery. And there must be electricity to run it, so perhaps there was also a telephone for communication. He poked among the filters and pipes.

'What are you doing?' Lex shouted.

'Looking for a telephone.' It was now nearly 10:00 a.m. They had just a little more than an hour to contact the ship before it reached the mainland.

In the back of the recess he found a metal door marked MAINT 04, but it was firmly locked. Next to it was a slot for a security card. Alongside the door he saw a row of metal boxes. He opened the boxes one after another, but they contained only switches and timers. No telephone. And nothing to open the door.

He almost missed the box to the left of the door. On opening it, he found a nine-button keypad, covered with spots of green mold. But it looked as if it was a way to open the door, and he had the feeling that on the other side of that door was a phone. Scratched in the metal of the box was the number 1023. He punched it in.

With a hiss, the door came open. Gaping darkness beyond, concrete steps leading downward. On the back wall he saw stenciled MAINT VEHICLE 04/22 CHARGER and an arrow pointing down the stairs. Could it really mean there was a car? 'Come on, kids.'

'Forget it,' Lex said. 'I'm not going in there.'

'Come on, Lex,' Tim said.

'Forget it,' Lex said. 'There's no lights or anything. I'm not going.'

'Never mind,' Grant said. There wasn't time to argue. 'Stay here, and I'll be right back.'

'Where're you going?' Lex said, suddenly alarmed.

Grant stepped through the door. It gave an electronic beep, and snapped shut behind him, on a spring.

Grant was plunged into total darkness. After a moment of surprise, he turned to the door and felt its damp surface. There was no knob, no latch. He turned to the walls on either side of the door, feeling for a switch, a control box, anything at all. . . .

There was nothing.

He was fighting panic when his fingers closed over a cold metal cylinder. He ran his hands over a swelling edge, a flat surface . . . a flashlight! He clicked it on, and the beam was surprisingly bright. He looked back at the door, but saw that it would not open. He would have to wait for the kids to unlock it. Meantime . . .

He started for the steps. They were damp and slippery with mold, and he went down carefully. Partway down the stairs, he heard a sniffing and the sound of claws scratching on concrete. He took out his dart pistol, and proceeded cautiously.

The steps bent around the corner, and as he shone his light, an odd reflection glinted back, and then, a moment later, he saw it: a car! It was an electric car, like a golf cart, and it faced a long tunnel that seemed to stretch away for miles. A bright red light glowed by the steering wheel of the car, so perhaps it was charged.

Grant heard the sniffing again, and he wheeled and saw a pale shape rise up toward him, leaping through the air, its jaws open, and without thinking Grant fired. The animal landed on him, knocking him down, and he rolled away in fright, his flashlight swinging wildly. But the animal didn't get up, and he felt foolish when he saw it.

It was a velociraptor, but very young, less than a year old. It was about two feet tall, the size of a medium dog, and it lay on the ground, breathing shallowly, the dart sticking from beneath its jaw. There was probably too much anesthetic for its body weight, and Grant pulled the dart out quickly. The velociraptor looked at him with slightly glazed eyes.

Grant had a clear feeling of intelligence from this creature, a kind of softness which contrasted strangely with the menace he had felt from the adults in the pen. He stroked the head of the velociraptor, hoping to calm it. He looked down at the body, which was shivering slightly as the tranquilizer took hold. And then he saw it was a male.

A young juvenile, and a male. There was no question what he was seeing. This velociraptor had been bred in the wild.

Excited by this development, he hurried back up the stairs to the door. With his flashlight, he scanned the flat, featureless surface of the door, and the interior walls. As he ran his hands over the door, it slowly dawned on him that he was locked inside, and unable to open it, unless the kids had the presence of mind to open it for him. He could hear them, faintly, on the other side of the door.

'Dr. Grant!' Lex shouted, pounding the door. 'Dr. Grant!'

'Take it easy,' Tim said. 'He'll be back.'

'But where did he go?'

'Listen, Dr. Grant knows what he's doing,' Tim said. 'He'll be back in a minute.'

'He should come back *now*,' Lex said. She bunched her fists on her hips, pushed her elbows wide. She stamped her foot angrily.

And then, with a roar, the tyrannosaur's head burst through the waterfall toward them.

Tim stared in horror as the big mouth gaped wide. Lex shrieked and threw herself on the ground. The head swung back and forth, and pulled out again. But Tim could see the shadow of the animal's head on the sheet of falling water.

He pulled Lex deeper into the recess, just as the jaws burst through again, roaring, the thick tongue flicking in and out rapidly. Water sprayed in all directions from the head. Then it pulled out again.

Lex huddled next to Tim, shivering. 'I *hate* him,' she said. She huddled back, but the recess was only a few feet deep, and crammed with machinery. There wasn't any place for them to hide.

The head came through the water again, but slowly this time, and the jaw came to rest on the ground. The tyrannosaur snorted, flaring its nostrils, breathing the air. But the eyes were still outside the sheet of water.

Tim thought: He can't see us. He knows we're in here, but he can't see through the water.

The tyrannosaur sniffed.

'What is he doing?' Lex said again.

'Sshhhh.'

With a low growl, the jaws slowly opened, and the tongue snaked out. It was thick and blue-black, with a little forked indentation at the tip. It was four feet long, and easily reached back to the far wall of the recess. The tongue slid with a rasping scrape over the filter cylinders. Tim and Lex pressed back against the pipes.

The tongue moved slowly to the left, then to the right, slapping wetly against the machinery. The tip curled around the pipes and valves, sensing them. Tim saw that the tongue had muscular movements, like an elephant's trunk. The tongue drew back along the right side of the recess. It dragged against Lex's legs.

'Eeww,' Lex said.

The tongue stopped. It curled, then began to rise like a snake up the side of her body –

'*Don't move*,' Tim whispered.

. . . past her face, then up along Tim's shoulder, and finally wrapping around his head. Tim squeezed his eyes shut as the slimy muscle covered his face. It was hot and wet and it stunk like urine.

Wrapped around him, the tongue began to drag him, very slowly, toward the open jaws.

'Timmy . . .'

Tim couldn't answer; his mouth was covered by the flat black tongue. He could see, but he couldn't talk. Lex tugged at his hand.

'Come on, Timmy!'

The tongue dragged him toward the snorting mouth. He felt the hot panting breath on his legs. Lex was tugging at him but she was no match for the muscular power that held him. Tim let go of her and pressed the tongue with both hands, trying to shove it over his head. He couldn't move it. He dug his heels into the muddy ground but he was dragged forward anyway.

Lex had wrapped her arms around his waist and was pulling backward, shouting to him, but he was powerless to do anything. He was beginning to see stars. A kind of peacefulness overcame him, a sense of peaceful inevitability as he was dragged along.

'Timmy?'

And then suddenly the tongue relaxed, and uncoiled. Tim felt it slipping off his face. His body was covered in disgusting white foamy slime, and the tongue fell limply to the ground. The jaws slapped shut, biting down on the tongue. Dark blood gushed out, mixing with the mud. The nostrils still snorted in ragged breaths.

'What's he doing?' Lex cried.

And then slowly, very slowly, the head began to slide backward, out of the recess, leaving a long scrape in the mud. And finally it disappeared entirely, and they could see only the silver sheet of falling water.

Control

'Okay,' Arnold said, in the control room. 'The rex is down.' He pushed back in his chair, and grinned as he lit a final cigarette and crumpled the pack. That did it: the final step in putting the park back in order. Now all they had to do was go out and move it.

'Son of a bitch,' Muldoon said, looking at the monitor. 'I got him after all.' He turned to Gennaro. 'It just took him an hour to feel it.'

Henry Wu frowned at the screen. 'But he could drown, in that position. . . .'

'He won't drown,' Muldoon said. 'Never seen an animal that was harder to kill.'

'I think we have to go out and move him,' Arnold said.

'We will,' Muldoon said. He didn't sound enthusiastic.

'That's a valuable animal.'

'I know it's a valuable animal,' Muldoon said.

Arnold turned to Gennaro. He couldn't resist a moment of triumph. 'I'd point out to you,' he said, 'that the park is now completely back to normal. Whatever Malcolm's mathematical model said was going to happen. We are completely under control again.'

Gennaro pointed to the screen behind Arnold's head and said, 'What's that?'

Arnold turned. It was the system status box, in the upper corner of the screen. Ordinarily it was empty. Arnold was surprised to see that it was now blinking yellow: AUX PWR LOW. For a moment, he didn't understand. Why should auxiliary power be low? They were running on main power, not auxiliary power. He thought perhaps it was just a routine status check on the auxiliary power, perhaps a check on the fuel tank levels or the battery charge. . . .

'Henry,' Arnold said to Wu. 'Look at this.'

Wu said, 'Why are you running on auxiliary power?'

'I'm not,' Arnold said.

'It looks like you are.'

'I can't be.'

'Print the system status log,' Wu said. The log was a record of the system over the last few hours.

Arnold pressed a button, and they heard the hum of a printer in the corner. Wu walked over to it.

Arnold stared at the screen. The box now turned from flashing yellow to red, and the message now read: AUX PWR FAIL. Numbers began to count backward from twenty.

'What the hell is going on?' Arnold said.

Cautiously, Tim moved a few yards out along the muddy path, into the sunshine. He peered around the waterfall, and saw the tyrannosaur lying on its side, floating in the pool of water below.

'I hope he's dead,' Lex said.

Tim could see he wasn't: the dinosaur's chest was still moving, and one forearm twitched in spasms. But something was wrong with him. Then Tim saw the white canister sticking in the back of the head, by the indentation of the ear.

'He's been shot with a dart,' Tim said.

'Good,' Lex said. 'He practically *ate* us.'

Tim watched the labored breathing. He felt unexpectedly distressed to see the huge animal humbled like this. He didn't want it to die. 'It's not his fault,' he said.

'Oh sure,' Lex said. 'He practically ate us and it's not his fault.'

'He's a carnivore. He was just doing what he does.'

'You wouldn't say that,' Lex said, 'if you were in his stomach right now.'

Then the sound of the waterfall changed. From a deafening roar, it became softer, quieter. The thundering sheet of water thinned, became a trickle . . .

And stopped.

'Timmy. The waterfall stopped,' Lex said.

It was now just dripping like a tap that wasn't completely turned off. The pool at the base of the waterfall was still. They stood near the top, in the cave-like indentation filled with machinery, looking down.

'Waterfalls aren't supposed to stop,' Lex said.

Tim shook his head. 'It must be the power. . . . Somebody turned off the power.' Behind them, all the pumps and filters were shutting down one after another, the lights blinking off, and the machinery becoming quiet. And then there was the *thunk* of a solenoid releasing, and the door marked MAINT 04 swung slowly open.

Grant stepped out, blinking in the light, and said, 'Good work, kids. You got the door open.'

'We didn't do anything,' Lex said.

'The power went out,' Tim said.

'Never mind that,' Grant said. 'Come and see what I've found.'

Arnold stared in shock.

One after another, the monitors went black, and then the room lights went out, plunging the control room into darkness and confusion. Everyone started yelling at once. Muldoon opened the blinds and let light in, and Wu brought over the printout.

'Look at this,' Wu said.

Time	Event	System Status	[Code]
05:12:44	Safety 1 Off	Operative	[AV12]
05:12:45	Safety 2 Off	Operative	[AV12]
05:12:46	Safety 3 Off	Operative	[AV12]
05:12:51	Shutdown Command	Shutdown	[-AV0]
05:13:48	Startup Command	Shutdown	[-AV0]
05:13:55	Safety 1 On	Shutdown	[-AV0]
05:13:57	Safety 2 On	Shutdown	[-AV0]
05:13:59	Safety 3 On	Shutdown	[-AV0]
05:14:08	Startup Command	Startup -Aux Power	[-AV1]
05:14:18	Monitor-Main	Operative -Aux Power	[AV04]
05:14:19	Security-Main	Operative -Aux Power	[AV05]
05:14:22	Command-Main	Operative -Aux Power	[AV06]
05:14:24	Laboratory-Main	Operative -Aux Power	[AV08]
05:14:29	TeleCom-VBB	Operative -Aux Power	[AV09]
05:14:32	Schematic-Main	Operative -Aux Power	[AV09]
05:14:37	View	Operative -Aux Power	[AV09]
05:14:44	Control Status Chk	Operative -Aux Power	[AV09]
05:14:57	Warning: Fence Status [NB]	Operative -Aux Power	[AV09]
09:11:37	Warning: Aux Fuel (20%)	Operative -Aux Power	[AVZZ]
09:33:19	Warning: Aux Fuel (10%)	Operative -Aux Power	[AVZ1]
09:53:19	Warning: Aux Fuel (1%)	Operative -Aux Power	[AVZ2]
09:53:39	Warning: Aux Fuel (0%)	Shutdown	[-AV0]

Wu said, 'You shut down at five-thirteen this morning, and when you started back up, you started with auxiliary power.'

'Jesus,' Arnold said. Apparently, main power had not been on since shutdown. When he powered back up, only the auxiliary power came on. Arnold was thinking that was strange, when he suddenly realized that that was *normal*. That was what was supposed to happen. It made perfect sense: the auxiliary generator fired up first, and it was used to turn on the main generator, because it took a heavy charge to start the main power generator. That was the way the system was designed.

But Arnold had never before had occasion to turn the main power off. And when the lights and screens came back on in the control room, it never occurred to him that main power hadn't also been restored.

But it hadn't, and all during the time since then, while they were looking for the rex, and doing one thing and another, the park had been running on auxiliary power. And that wasn't a good idea. In fact, the implications were just beginning to hit him –

'What does this line mean?' Muldoon said, pointing to the list.

05:14:57   Warning: Fence Status [NB]   Operative – Aux Power [AV09]

'It means a system status warning was sent to the monitors in the control room,' Arnold said. 'Concerning the fences.'

'Did you see that warning?'

Arnold shook his head. 'No. I must have been talking to you in the field. Anyway, no, I didn't see it.'

'What does it mean, "Warning: Fence Status"?'

'Well, I didn't know it at the time, but we were running on backup power,' Arnold said. 'And backup doesn't generate enough amperage to power the electrified fences, so they were automatically kept off.'

Muldoon scowled. 'The electrified fences were off?'

'Yes.'

'All of them? Since five this morning? For the last five hours?'

'Yes.'

'Including the velociraptor fences?'

Arnold sighed. 'Yes.'

'Jesus Christ,' Muldoon said. 'Five hours. Those animals could be out.'

And then, from somewhere in the distance, they heard a scream. Muldoon began to talk very fast. He went around the room, handing out the portable radios.

'Mr. Arnold is going to the maintenance shed to turn on main power. Dr. Wu, stay in the control room. You're the only other one who can work the computers. Mr. Hammond, go back to the lodge. Don't argue with me. Go now. Lock the gates, and stay behind them until you hear from me. I'll help Arnold deal with the raptors.' He turned to Gennaro. 'Like to live dangerously again?'

'Not really,' Gennaro said. He was very pale.

'Fine. Then go with the others to the lodge.' Muldoon turned away. 'That's it, everybody. Now *move*.'

Hammond whined, 'But what are you going to do to my animals?'

'That's not really the question, Mr. Hammond,' Muldoon said. 'The question is, what are they going to do to us?'

He went through the door, and hurried down the hall toward his office. Gennaro fell into step alongside him. 'Change your mind?' Muldoon growled.

'You'll need help,' Gennaro said.

'I might.' Muldoon went into the room marked ANIMAL SUPERVISOR, picked up the gray shoulder launcher, and unlocked a panel in the wall behind his desk. There were six cylinders and six canisters.

'The thing about these damn dinos,' Muldoon said, 'is that they have distributed nervous systems. They don't die fast, even with a direct hit to the brain. And they're built solidly; thick ribs make a shot to the heart dicey, and they're difficult to cripple in the legs or hindquarters. Slow bleeders, slow to die.' He was opening the cylinders one after another and dropping in the canisters. He tossed a thick webbed belt to Gennaro. 'Put that on.'

Gennaro tightened the belt, and Muldoon passed him the shells. 'About all we can hope to do is blow them apart. Unfortunately we've only got six shells here. There's eight raptors in that fenced compound. Let's go. Stay close. You have the shells.'

Muldoon went out and ran along the hallway, looking down over the balcony to the path leading toward the maintenance shed. Gennaro was puffing alongside him. They got to the ground floor and went out through the glass doors, and Muldoon stopped.

Arnold was standing with his back to the maintenance shed. Three raptors approached him. Arnold had picked up a stick, and he was waving it at them, shouting. The raptors fanned out as they came closer, one staying in the center, the other two moving to each side. Coordinated. Smooth. Gennaro shivered.

Pack behavior.

Muldoon was already crouching, setting the launcher on his shoulder. 'Load,' he said. Gennaro slipped the shell in the back of the launcher. There was an electric sizzle. Nothing happened. 'Christ, you've got it in backward,' Muldoon said, tilting the barrel so the shell fell into Gennaro's hands. Gennaro loaded again. The raptors were snarling at Arnold when the animal on the left simply exploded, the upper part of the torso flying into the air, blood spattering like a burst tomato on the walls of the building. The lower torso collapsed on the ground, the legs kicking in the air, the tail flopping.

'That'll wake 'em up,' Muldoon said.

Arnold ran for the door of the maintenance shed. The velociraptors turned, and started toward Muldoon and Gennaro. They fanned out as they came closer. In the distance, somewhere near the lodge, he heard screams.

Gennaro said, 'This could be a disaster.'

'Load,' Muldoon said.

Henry Wu heard the explosions and looked toward the door of the control room. He circled around the consoles, then paused. He wanted to go out, but he knew he should stay in the room. If Arnold was able to get the power back on – if only for a minute – then Wu could restart the main generator.

He had to stay in the room.

He heard someone screaming. It sounded like Muldoon.

Muldoon felt a wrenching pain in his ankle, tumbled down an embankment, and hit the ground running. Looking back, he saw Gennaro running in the other direction, into the forest. The raptors were ignoring Gennaro but pursuing Muldoon. They were now less than twenty yards away. Muldoon screamed at the top of his lungs as he ran, wondering vaguely where the hell he could go. Because he knew he had perhaps ten seconds before they got him.

Ten seconds.

Maybe less.

Ellie had to help Malcolm turn over as Harding jabbed the needle and injected morphine. Malcolm sighed and collapsed back. It seemed he was growing weaker by the minute. Over the radio, they heard tinny screaming, and muffled explosions coming from the visitor center.

Hammond came into the room and said, 'How is he?'

'He's holding,' Harding said. 'A bit delirious.'

'I am nothing of the sort,' Malcolm said. 'I am utterly clear.' They listened to the radio. 'It sounds like a war out there.'

'The raptors got out,' Hammond said.

'Did they,' Malcolm said, breathing shallowly. 'How could that possibly happen?'

'It was a system screwup. Arnold didn't realize that the auxiliary power was on, and the fences cut out.'

'Did they.'

'Go to hell, you supercilious bastard.'

'If I remember,' Malcolm said, 'I predicted fence integrity would fail.'

Hammond sighed, and sat down heavily. 'Damn it all,' he said, shaking his head. 'It must surely not have escaped your notice that at heart what we are attempting here is an extremely simple idea. My colleagues and I determined, several years ago, that it was possible to clone the DNA of an extinct animal, and to grow it. That seemed to us a wonderful idea, it was a kind of time travel – the only time travel in the world. Bring them back alive, so to speak. And since it was so exciting, and since it was possible to do it, we decided to go forward. We got this island, and we proceeded. It was all very simple.'

'Simple?' Malcolm said. Somehow he found the energy to sit up in the bed. 'Simple? You're a bigger fool than I thought you were. And I thought you were a very substantial fool.'

Ellie said, 'Dr. Malcolm,' and tried to ease him back down. But Malcolm would have none of it. He pointed toward the radio, the shouts and the cries.

'What is that, going on out there?' he said. 'That's your simple idea. *Simple.* You create new life forms, about which you know nothing at all. Your Dr. Wu does not even know the names of the things he is creating. He cannot be bothered with such details as *what the thing is called*, let alone what it *is*. You create many of them in a very short time, you never learn anything about them, yet you expect them to do your bidding, because you made them and you therefore think you own them; you forget that they are alive, they have an intelligence of their own, and they may not do your bidding, and you forget how little you know about them, how incompetent you are to do the things that you so frivolously call *simple* . . . Dear God . . .'

He sank back, coughing.

'You know what's wrong with scientific power?' Malcolm said. 'It's a form of inherited wealth. And you know what assholes congenitally rich people are. It never fails.'

Hammond said, 'What is he talking about?'

Harding made a sign, indicating delirium. Malcolm cocked his eye.

'I will tell you what I am talking about,' he said. 'Most kinds of power require a substantial sacrifice by whoever wants the power. There is an apprenticeship, a discipline lasting many years. Whatever kind of power you want. President of the company. Black belt in karate. Spiritual guru. Whatever it is you seek, you have to put in the time, the practice, the effort. You must give up a lot to get it. It has to be very important to you. And once you have attained it, it is your power. It can't be given away: it resides in you. It is literally the result of your discipline.

'Now, what is interesting about this process is that, by the time someone has acquired the ability to kill with his bare hands, he has also matured to the point where he won't use it unwisely. So that kind of power has a built-in control. The discipline of getting the power changes you so that you won't abuse it.

'But scientific power is like inherited wealth: attained without discipline. You read what others have done, and you take the next step. You can do it very young. You can make progress very fast. There is no discipline lasting many decades. There is no mastery: old scientists are ignored. There is no humility before nature. There is only a get-rich-quick, make-a-name-for-yourself-fast philosophy. Cheat, lie, falsify – it doesn't matter. Not to you, or to your colleagues. No one will criticize you. No one has any standards. They are all trying to do the same thing: to do something big, and do it fast.

'And because you can stand on the shoulders of giants, you can accomplish something quickly. You don't even know exactly what you have done, but already you have reported it, patented it, and sold it. And the buyer will have even less discipline than you. The buyer simply purchases the power, like any commodity. The buyer doesn't even conceive that any discipline might be necessary.'

Hammond said, 'Do you know what he is talking about?'

Ellie nodded.

'I haven't a clue,' Hammond said.

'I'll make it simple,' Malcolm said. 'A karate master does not kill people with his bare hands. He does not lose his temper and kill his wife. The person who kills is the person who has no discipline, no restraint, and who has purchased his power in the form of a Saturday night special. And that is the kind of power that science fosters, and permits. And that is why you think that to build a place like this is simple.'

'It *was* simple,' Hammond insisted.

'Then why did it go wrong?'

Dizzy with tension, John Arnold threw open the door to the maintenance shed and stepped into the darkness inside. Jesus, it was black. He should have realized the lights would be out. He felt the cool air, the cavernous dimensions of the space, extending two floors below him. He had to find the catwalk. He had to be careful, or he'd break his neck.

The catwalk.

He groped like a blind man until he realized it was futile. Somehow he had to get light into the shed. He went back to the door and cracked it open four inches. That gave enough light. But there was no way to keep the door open. Quickly he kicked off his shoe and stuck it in the door.

He went toward the catwalk, seeing it easily. He walked along the corrugated metal, hearing the difference in his feet, one loud, one soft. But at least he could see. Up ahead was the stairway leading down to the generators. Another ten yards.

Darkness.

The light was gone.

Arnold looked back to the door, and saw the light was blocked by the body of a velociraptor. The animal bent over, and carefully sniffed the shoe.

Henry Wu paced. He ran his hands over the computer consoles. He touched the screens. He was in constant movement. He was almost frantic with tension.

He reviewed the steps he would take. He must be quick. The first screen would come up, and he would press –

'Wu!' The radio hissed.

He grabbed for it. 'Yes. I'm here.'

'Got any bloody power yet?' It was Muldoon. There was something odd about his voice, something hollow.

'No,' Wu said. He smiled, glad to know Muldoon was alive.

'I think Arnold made it to the shed,' Muldoon said. 'After that, I don't know.'

'Where are you?' Wu said.

'I'm stuffed.'

'What?'

'Stuffed in a bloody pipe,' Muldoon said. 'And I'm very popular at the moment.'

Wedged in a pipe was more like it, Muldoon thought. There had been a stack of drainage pipes piled behind the visitor center, and he'd backed himself into the nearest one, scrambling like a poor bastard. Meter pipes, very tight fit for him, but they couldn't come in after him.

At least, not after he'd shot the leg off one, when the nosy bastard came too close to the pipe. The raptor had gone howling off, and the others were now respectful. His only regret was that he hadn't waited to see the snout at the end of the tube before he'd squeezed the trigger.

But he might still have his chance, because there were three or four outside, snarling and growling around him.

'Yes, very popular,' he said into the radio.

Wu said, 'Does Arnold have a radio?'

'Don't think so,' Muldoon said. 'Just sit tight. Wait it out.'

He hadn't seen what the other end of the pipe was like – he'd backed in too quickly – and he couldn't see now. He was wedged tight.

He could only hope that the far end wasn't open. Christ, he didn't like the thought of one of those bastards taking a bite of his hindquarters.

Arnold backed away down the catwalk. The velociraptor was barely ten feet away, stalking him, coming forward into the gloom. Arnold could hear the click of its deadly claws on the metal.

But he was going slowly. He knew the animal could see well, but the grille of the catwalk, the unfamiliar mechanical odors had made it cautious. That caution was his only chance, Arnold thought. If he could get to the stairs, and then move down to the floor below . . .

Because he was pretty sure velociraptors couldn't climb stairs. Certainly not narrow, steep stairs.

Arnold glanced over his shoulder. The stairs were just a few feet away. Another few steps . . .

He was there! Reaching back, he felt the railing, started scrambling down the almost vertical steps. His feet touched flat concrete. The raptor snarled in frustration, twenty feet above him on the catwalk.

'Too bad, buddy,' Arnold said. He turned away. He was now very close to the auxiliary generator. Just a few more steps and he would see it, even in this dim light . . .

There was a dull thump behind him.

Arnold turned.

The raptor was standing there on the concrete floor, snarling.

It had jumped down.

He looked quickly for a weapon, but suddenly he found he was slammed onto his back on the concrete. Something heavy was pressing on his chest, it was impossible to breathe, and he realized the animal was *standing on top of him*, and he felt the big claws digging into the flesh of his chest, and smelled the foul breath from the head moving above him, and he opened his mouth to scream.

Ellie held the radio in her hands, listening. Two more Tican workmen had arrived at the lodge; they seemed to know it was safe here. But there had been no others in the last few minutes. And it sounded quieter outside. Over the radio, Muldoon said, 'How long has it been?'

Wu said, 'Four, five minutes.'

'Arnold should have done it by now,' Muldoon said. 'If he's going to. You got any ideas?'

'No,' Wu said.

'We heard from Gennaro?'

Gennaro pressed the button. 'I'm here.'

'Where the hell are you?' Muldoon said.

'I'm going to the maintenance building,' Gennaro said. 'Wish me luck.'

Gennaro crouched in the foliage, listening.

Directly ahead he saw the planted pathway, leading toward the visitor center. Gennaro knew the maintenance shed was somewhere to the east. He heard the chirping of birds in the trees. A soft mist was blowing. One of the raptors roared, but it was some distance away. It sounded off to his right. Gennaro set out, leaving the path, plunging into the foliage.

Like to live dangerously?

Not really.

It was true, he didn't. But Gennaro thought he had a plan, or at least a possibility that might work. If he stayed north of the main complex of buildings, he could approach the maintenance shed from the rear. All the raptors were probably around the other buildings, to the south. There was no reason for them to be in the jungle.

At least, he hoped not.

He moved as quietly as he could, unhappily aware he was making a lot of noise. He forced himself to slow his pace, feeling his heart pound. The foliage here was very dense; he couldn't see more than six or seven feet ahead of him. He began to worry that he'd miss the maintenance shed entirely. But then he saw the roof to his right, above the palms.

He moved toward it, went around the side. He found the door, opened it, and slipped inside. It was very dark. He stumbled over something.

A man's shoe.

Gennaro frowned. He propped the door wide open and continued deeper into the building. He saw a catwalk directly ahead of him. Suddenly he realized he didn't know where to go. And he had left his radio behind.

Damn!

There might be a radio somewhere in the maintenance building. Or else he'd just look for the generator. He knew what a generator looked like. Probably it was somewhere down on the lower floor. He found a staircase leading down.

It was darker below, and it was difficult to see anything. He felt his way along among the pipes, holding his hands out to keep from banging his head.

He heard an animal snarl, and froze. He listened, but the sound did not come again. He moved forward cautiously. Something dripped on his shoulder, and his bare arm. It was warm, like water. He touched it in the darkness.

Sticky. He smelled it.

Blood.

He looked up. The raptor was perched on pipes, just a few feet above his head. Blood was trickling from its claws. With an odd sense of detachment, he wondered if it was injured. And then he began to run, but the raptor jumped onto his back, pushing him to the ground.

Gennaro was strong; he heaved up, knocking the raptor away, and rolled off across the concrete. When he turned back, he saw that the raptor had fallen on its side, where it lay panting.

Yes, it was injured. Its leg was hurt, for some reason.

Kill it.

Gennaro scrambled to his feet, looking for a weapon. The raptor was still panting on the concrete. He looked frantically for something – anything – to use as a weapon. When he turned back, the raptor was gone.

It snarled, the sound echoing in the darkness.

Gennaro turned in a full circle, feeling with his outstretched hands. And then he felt a sharp pain in his right hand.

Teeth.

It was biting him.

The raptor jerked his head, and Donald Gennaro was yanked off his feet, and he fell.

Lying in bed, soaked in sweat, Malcolm listened as the radio crackled.

'Anything?' Muldoon said. 'You getting anything?'

'No word,' Wu said.

'Hell,' Muldoon said.

There was a pause.

Malcolm sighed. 'I can't wait,' he said, 'to hear his new plan.'

'What I would like,' Muldoon said, 'is to get everybody to the lodge and regroup. But I don't see how.'

'There's a Jeep in front of the visitor center,' Wu said. 'If I drove over to you, could you get yourself into it?'

'Maybe. But you'd be abandoning the control room.'

'I can't do anything here anyway.'

'God knows that's true,' Malcolm said. 'A control room without electricity is not much of a control room.'

'All right,' Muldoon said. 'Let's try. This isn't looking good.'

Lying in his bed, Malcolm said, 'No, it's not looking good. It's looking like a disaster.'

Wu said, 'The raptors are going to follow us over there.'

'We're still better off,' Malcolm said. 'Let's go.'

The radio clicked off. Malcolm closed his eyes, and breathed slowly, marshaling his strength.

'Just relax,' Ellie said. 'Just take it easy.'

'You know what we are really talking about here,' Malcolm said. 'All this attempt to control ... We are talking about Western attitudes that are five hundred years old. They began at the time when Florence, Italy, was the most important city in the world. The basic idea of science – that there was a new way to look at reality, that it was objective, that it did not depend on your beliefs or your nationality, that it was *rational* – that idea was fresh and exciting back then. It offered promise and hope for the future, and it swept away the old medieval system, which was hundreds of years old. The medieval world of feudal politics and religious dogma and hateful superstitions fell before science. But, in truth, this was because the medieval world didn't really work any more. It didn't work economically, it didn't work intellectually, and it didn't fit the new world that was emerging.'

Malcolm coughed.

'But now,' he continued, 'science is the belief system that is hundreds of years old. And, like the medieval system before it, science is starting not to fit the world any more. Science has attained so much power that its practical limits begin to be apparent. Largely through science, billions of us live in one small world, densely packed and intercommunicating. But science cannot help us decide what to do with that world, or how to live. Science can make a nuclear reactor, but it cannot tell us not to use it. And our world starts to seem polluted in fundamental ways – air, and water, and land – because of ungovernable science.' He sighed. 'This much is obvious to everyone.'

There was a silence. Malcolm lay with his eyes closed, his breathing labored. No one spoke, and it seemed to Ellie that Malcolm had finally fallen asleep. Then he sat up again, abruptly.

'At the same time, the great intellectual justification of science has vanished. Ever since Newton and Descartes, science has explicitly offered us the vision of total control. Science has claimed the power to eventually control everything, through its understanding of natural laws. But in the twentieth century, that claim has been shattered beyond repair. First, Heisenberg's uncertainty principle set limits on what we could know about the subatomic world. Oh well, we say. None of us lives in a subatomic world. It doesn't make any practical difference as we go through our lives. Then Gödel's theorem set similar limits to mathematics, the formal language of science. Mathematicians used to think that their language had some special inherent trueness that derived from the laws of logic. Now we know that what we call 'reason' is just an arbitrary game. It's not special, in the way we thought it was.

'And now chaos theory proves that unpredictability is built into our daily lives. It is as mundane as the rainstorm we cannot predict. And so the grand vision of science, hundreds of years old – the dream of total control – has died, in our century. And with it much of the justification, the rationale for science to do what it does. And for us to listen to it. Science has always said that it may not know everything now but it will know, eventually. But now we see that isn't true. It is an idle boast. As foolish, and as misguided, as the child who jumps off a building because he believes he can fly.'

'This is very extreme,' Hammond said, shaking his head.

'We are witnessing the end of the scientific era. Science, like other outmoded systems, is destroying itself. As it gains in power, it proves itself incapable of handling the power. Because things are going very fast now. Fifty years ago, everyone was gaga over the atomic bomb. That was power. No one could imagine anything more. Yet, a bare decade after the bomb, we began to have genetic power. And genetic power is far more potent than atomic power. And it will be in everyone's hands. It will be in kits for backyard gardeners. Experiments for schoolchildren. Cheap labs for terrorists and dictators. And that will force everyone to ask the same question – What should I do with my power? – which is the very question science says it cannot answer.'

'So what will happen?' Ellie said.

Malcolm shrugged. 'A change.'

'What kind of change?'

'All major changes are like death,' he said. 'You can't see to the other side until you are there.' And he closed his eyes.

'The poor man,' Hammond said, shaking his head.

Malcolm sighed. 'Do you have any idea,' he said, 'how unlikely it is that you, or any of us, will get off this island alive?'

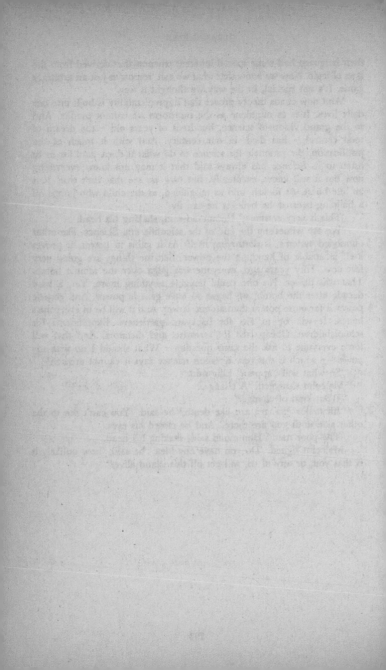

Sixth Iteration

'*System recovery may prove impossible.*'

IAN MALCOLM

Return

Its electric motor whirring, the cart raced forward down the dark underground tunnel. Grant drove, his foot to the floor. The tunnel was featureless except for the occasional air vent above, shaded to protect against rainfall, and thus permitting little light to enter. But he noticed that there were crusty white animal droppings in many places. Obviously lots of animals had been in here.

Sitting beside him in the cart, Lex shone the flashlight to the back, where the velociraptor lay. 'Why is it having trouble breathing?'

'Because I shot it with tranquilizer,' he said.

'Is it going to die?' she said.

'I hope not.'

'Why are we taking it?' Lex said.

'To prove to the people back at the center that the dinosaurs are really breeding,' Grant said.

'How do you know they're breeding?'

'Because this one is young,' Grant said. 'And because it's a boy dinosaur.'

'Is it?' Lex said, peering along the flashlight beam.

'Yes. Now shine that light forward, will you?' He held out his wrist, turning the watch to her. 'What does it say?'

'It says . . . ten-fifteen.'

'Okay.'

Tim said, 'That means we have only forty-five minutes to contact the boat.'

'We should be close,' Grant said. 'I figure we should be almost to the visitor center right now.' He wasn't sure, but he sensed the tunnel was gently tilting upward, leading them back to the surface, and –

'Wow!' Tim said.

They burst out into daylight with shocking speed. There was a light mist blowing, partially obscuring the building that loomed directly above them. Grant saw at once that it was the visitor center. They had arrived right in front of the garage!

'Yay!' Lex shouted. 'We did it! Yay!' She bounced up and down in

297

the seat as Grant parked the cart in the garage. Along one wall were stacked animal cages. They put the velociraptor in one, with a dish of water. Then they started climbing the stairs to the ground-floor entrance of the visitor center.

'I'm going to get a hamburger! And french fries! Chocolate milk shake! No more dinosaurs! Yay!' They came to the lobby, and they opened the door.

And they fell silent.

In the lobby of the visitor center, the glass doors had been shattered, and a cold gray mist blew through the cavernous main hall. A sign that read WHEN DINOSAURS RULED THE EARTH dangled from one hinge, creaking in the wind. The big tyrannosaur robot was upended and lay with its legs in the air, its tubing and metal innards exposed. Outside, through the glass, they saw rows of palm trees, shadowy shapes in the fog.

Tim and Lex huddled against the metal desk of the security guard. Grant took the guard's radio and tried all the channels. 'Hello, this is Grant. Is anybody there? Hello, this is Grant.'

Lex stared at the body of the guard, lying on the floor to the right. She couldn't see anything but his legs and feet.

'Hello, this is Grant. Hello.'

Lex was leaning forward, peering around the edge of the desk. Grant grabbed her sleeve. 'Hey. Stop that.'

'Is he dead? What's that stuff on the floor? Blood?'

'Yes.'

'How come it isn't real red?'

'You're morbid,' Tim said.

'What's "morbid"? I am not.'

The radio crackled. 'My God,' came a voice. 'Grant? Is that you?' And then: 'Alan? Alan?' It was Ellie.

'I'm here,' Grant said.

'Thank God,' Ellie said. 'Are you all right?'

'I'm all right, yes.'

'What about the kids? Have you seen them?'

'I have the kids with me,' Grant said. 'They're okay.'

'Thank God.'

Lex was crawling around the side of the desk. Grant slapped her ankle. 'Get back here.'

The radio crackled. ' – n where are you?'

'In the lobby. In the lobby of the main building.'

Over the radio, he heard Wu say, 'My God. They're *here*.'

'Alan, listen,' Ellie said. 'The raptors have gotten loose. They can open doors. They may be in the same building as you.'

'Great. Where are you?' Grant said.

'We're in the lodge.'

Grant said, 'And the others? Muldoon, everybody else?'

'We've lost a few people. But we got everybody else over to the lodge.'

'And are the telephones working?'

'No. The whole system is shut off. Nothing works.'

'How do we get the system back on?'

'We've been trying.'

'We have to get it back on,' Grant said, 'right away. If we don't, within half an hour the raptors will reach the mainland.'

He started to explain about the boat when Muldoon cut him off. 'I don't think you understand, Dr. Grant. We haven't got half an hour left, over here.'

'How's that?'

'Some of the raptors followed us. We've got two on the roof now.'

'So what? The building's impregnable.'

Muldoon coughed. 'Apparently not. It was never expected that animals would get up on the roof.' The radio crackled. ' – must have planted a tree too close to the fence. The raptors got over the fence, and onto the roof. Anyway, the steel bars on the skylight are supposed to be electrified, but of course the power's off. They're biting through the bars of the skylight.'

Grant said, 'Biting through the bars?' He frowned, trying to imagine it. 'How fast?'

'Yes,' Muldoon said, 'they have a bite pressure of fifteen thousand pounds a square inch. They're like hyenas, they can bite through steel and –' The transmission was lost for a moment.

'How fast?' Grant said again.

Muldoon said, 'I'd guess we've got another ten, fifteen minutes before they break through completely and come through the skylight into the building. And once they're in . . . Ah, just a minute, Dr. Grant.'

The radio clicked off.

In the skylight above Malcolm's bed, the raptors had chewed through the first of the steel bars. One raptor gripped the end of the bar and tugged, pulling it back. It put its powerful hind limb on the skylight and the glass shattered, glittering down on Malcolm's bed below. Ellie reached over and removed the largest fragments from the sheets.

'God, they're ugly,' Malcolm said, looking up.

Now that the glass was broken, they could hear the snorts and snarls of the raptors, the squeal of their teeth on the metal as they chewed the bars. There were silver thinned sections where they had chewed. Foamy saliva spattered onto the sheets, and the bedside table.

'At least they can't get in yet,' Ellie said. 'Not until they chew through another bar.'

Wu said, 'If Grant could somehow get to the maintenance shed . . .'

'Bloody hell,' Muldoon said. He limped around the room on his sprained ankle. 'He can't get there fast enough. He can't get the power on fast enough. Not to stop this.'

Malcolm coughed. 'Yes.' His voice was soft, almost a wheeze.

'What'd he say?' Muldoon said.

'Yes,' Malcolm repeated. 'Can . . .'

'Can what?'

'Distraction . . .' He winced.

'What kind of a distraction?'

'Go to . . . the fence. . . .'

'Yes? And do what?'

Malcolm grinned weakly. 'Stick . . . your hands through.'

'Oh Christ,' Muldoon said, turning away.

'Wait a minute,' Wu said. 'He's right. There are only two raptors here. Which means there are at least four more out there. We could go out and provide a distraction.'

'And then what?'

'And then Grant would be free to go to the maintenance building and turn on the generator.'

'And then go back to the control room and start up the system?'

'Exactly.'

'No time,' Muldoon said. 'No time.'

'But if we can lure the raptors down here,' Wu said, 'maybe even get them away from that skylight . . . It might work. Worth a try.'

'Bait,' Muldoon said.

'Exactly.'

'Who's going to be the bait? I'm no good. My ankle's shot.'

'I'll do it,' Wu said.

'No,' Muldoon said. 'You're the only one who knows what to do about the computer. You need to talk Grant through the start-up.'

'Then I'll do it,' Harding said.

'No,' Ellie said. 'Malcolm needs you. I'll do it.'

'Hell, I don't think so,' Muldoon said. 'You'd have raptors all around you, raptors on the roof. . . .'

But she was already bending over, lacing her running shoes. 'Just don't tell Grant,' she said. 'It'll make him nervous.'

The lobby was quiet, chilly fog drifting past them. The radio had been silent for several minutes. Tim said, 'Why aren't they talking to us?'

'I'm hungry,' Lex said.

'They're trying to plan,' Grant said.

The radio crackled. 'Grant, are you – nry Wu speaking. Are you there?'

'I'm here,' Grant said.

'Listen,' Wu said. 'Can you see to the rear of the visitor building from where you are?'

Grant looked through the rear glass doors, to the palm trees and the fog.

'Yes,' Grant said.

Wu said, 'There's a path straight through the palm trees to the maintenance building. That's where the power equipment and generators are. I believe you saw the maintenance building yesterday?'

'Yes,' Grant said. Though he was momentarily puzzled. Was it yesterday that he had looked into the building? It seemed like years ago.

'Now, listen,' Wu said. 'We think we can get all the raptors down here by the lodge, but we aren't sure. So be careful. Give us five minutes.'

'Okay,' Grant said.

'You can leave the kids in the cafeteria, and they should be all right. Take the radio with you when you go.'

'Okay.'

'Turn it off before you leave, so it doesn't make any noise outside. And call me when you get to the maintenance building.'

'Okay.'

Grant turned the radio off. Lex crawled back. 'Are we going to the cafeteria?' she said.

'Yes,' Grant said. They got up, and started walking through the blowing mist in the lobby.

'I want a hamburger,' Lex said.

'I don't think there's any electricity to cook with.'

'Then ice cream.'

'Tim, you'll have to stay with her and help her.'

'I will.'

'I've got to leave for a while,' Grant said.

'I know.'

They moved to the cafeteria entrance. On opening the door, Grant saw square dining-room tables and chairs, swinging stainless-steel doors beyond. Nearby, a cash register and a rack with gum and candy.

'Okay, kids. I want you to stay here no matter what. Got it?'

'Leave us the radio,' Lex said.

'I can't. I need it. Just stay here. I'll only be gone about five minutes. Okay?'

'Okay.'

Grant closed the door. The cafeteria became completely dark. Lex clutched his hand. 'Turn on the lights,' she said.

'I can't,' Tim said. 'There's no electricity.' But he pulled down his night-vision goggles.

'That's fine for you. What about me?'

'Just hold my hand. We'll get some food.' He led her forward. In phosphorescent green he saw the tables and chairs. To the right, the glowing green cash register, and the rack with gum and candy. He grabbed a handful of candy bars.

'I told you,' Lex said. 'I want ice cream, not candy.'

'Take these anyway.'

'Ice cream, Tim.'

'Okay, okay.'

Tim stuffed the candy bars in his pocket, and led Lex deeper into the dining room. She tugged on his hand. 'I can't see *spit*,' she said.

'Just walk with me. Hold my hand.'

'Then slow down.'

Beyond the tables and chairs was a pair of swinging doors with little round windows in them. They probably led to the kitchen. He pushed one door open and it held wide.

Ellie Sattler stepped outside the front door to the lodge, and felt the chilly mist on her face and legs. Her heart was thumping, even though she knew she was completely safe behind the fence. Directly ahead, she saw the heavy bars in the fog.

But she couldn't see much beyond the fence. Another twenty yards before the landscape turned milky white. And she didn't see any raptors at all. In fact, the gardens and trees were almost eerily silent. 'Hey!' she shouted into the fog, tentatively.

Muldoon leaned against the door frame. 'I doubt that'll do it,' he said. 'You've got to make a *noise*.' He hobbled out carrying a steel rod from the construction inside. He banged the rod against the bars like a dinner gong. 'Come and get it! Dinner is served!'

'Very amusing,' Ellie said. She glanced nervously toward the roof. She saw no raptors.

'They don't understand English.' Muldoon grinned. 'But I imagine they get the general idea. . . .'

She was still nervous, and found his humor annoying. She looked toward the visitor building, cloaked in the fog. Muldoon resumed banging on the bars. At the limit of her vision, almost lost in the fog, she saw a ghostly pale animal. A raptor.

'First customer,' Muldoon said.

The raptor disappeared, a white shadow, and then came back, but it did not approach any closer, and it seemed strangely incurious about the noise coming from the lodge. She was starting to worry. Unless she could attract the raptors to the lodge, Grant would be in danger.

'You're making too much noise,' Ellie said.

'Bloody hell,' Muldoon said.

'Well, you are.'

'I know these animals – '

'You're drunk,' she said. 'Let me handle it.'

'And how will you do that?'

She didn't answer him. She went to the gate. 'They say the raptors are intelligent.'

'They are. At least as intelligent as chimps.'

'They have good hearing?'

'Yes, excellent.'

'Maybe they'll know this sound,' she said, and opened the gate. The metal hinges, rusted from the constant mist, creaked loudly. She closed it again, opened it with another creak.

She left it open.

'I wouldn't do that,' Muldoon said. 'You're going to do that, let me get the launcher.'

'Get the launcher.'

He sighed, remembering. 'Gennaro has the shells.'

'Well, then,' she said. 'Keep an eye out.' And she went through the gate, stepping outside the bars. Her heart was pounding so hard she could barely feel her feet on the dirt. She moved away from the fence, and it disappeared frighteningly fast in the fog. Soon it was lost behind her.

Just as she expected, Muldoon began shouting to her in drunken agitation. 'God damn it, girl, don't you do that,' he bellowed.

'Don't call me "girl," ' she shouted back.

'I'll call you any damn thing I want,' Muldoon shouted.

She wasn't listening. She was turning slowly, her body tense, watching from all sides. She was at least twenty yards from the fence now, and she could see the mist drifting like a light rain past the foliage. She stayed away from the foliage. She moved through a world of shades of gray. The muscles in her legs and shoulders ached from the tension. Her eyes strained to see.

'Do you hear me, damn it?' Muldoon bellowed.

How good are these animals? she wondered. Good enough to cut off my retreat? There wasn't much distance back to the fence, not really –

They attacked.

There was no sound.

The first animal charged from the foliage at the base of a tree to the left. It sprang forward and she turned to run. The second attacked from the other side, clearly intending to catch her as she ran, and it leapt into the air, claws raised to attack, and she darted like a broken field runner, and the animal crashed down in the dirt. Now she was running flat out, not daring to look back, her breaths coming in deep gasps, seeing the bars of the fence emerge from the haze, seeing Muldoon throw the gate wide, seeing him reaching for her, shouting to her, grabbing her arm and pulling her through so hard she was yanked off her feet and fell to the ground. And she turned in time to see first one, then two – then three – animals hit the fence and snarl.

'Good work,' Muldoon shouted. He was taunting the animals now, snarling back, and it drove them wild. They flung themselves at the fence, leaping forward, and one of them nearly made it over the top. 'Christ, that was close! These bastards can jump!'

She got to her feet, looking at the scrapes and bruises, the blood running down her leg. All she could think was: three animals here. And two on the roof. That meant one was still missing, somewhere.

'Come on, help me,' Muldoon said. 'Let's keep 'em interested!'

Grant left the visitor center and moved quickly forward, into the mist. He found the path among the palm trees and followed it north. Up ahead, the rectangular maintenance shed emerged from the fog.

There was no door that he could see at all. He walked on, around the corner. At the back, screened by planting, Grant saw a concrete loading dock for trucks. He scrambled up to face a vertical rolling door of corrugated steel; it was locked. He jumped down again and continued around the building. Farther ahead, to his right, Grant saw an ordinary door. It was propped open with a man's shoe.

Grant stepped inside and squinted in the darkness. He listened, heard nothing. He picked up his radio and turned it on.

'This is Grant,' he said. 'I'm inside.'

Wu looked up at the skylight. The two raptors still peered down into Malcolm's room, but they seemed distracted by the noises outside. He went to the lodge window. Outside, the three velociraptors continued to charge the fence. Ellie was running back and forth, safely behind the bars. But the raptors no longer seemed to be seriously trying to get her. Now they almost seemed to be playing, circling back from the fence, rearing up and snarling, then dropping down low, to circle again and finally charge. Their behavior had taken on the distinct quality of display, rather than serious attack.

'Like birds,' Muldoon said. 'Putting on a show.'

Wu nodded. 'They're intelligent. They see they can't get her. They're not really trying.'

The radio crackled. ' – side.'

Wu gripped the radio. 'Say again, Dr. Grant?'

'I'm inside,' Grant said.

'Dr. Grant, you're in the maintenance building?'

'Yes,' Grant said. And he added, 'Maybe you should call me Alan.'

'All right, Alan. If you're standing just inside the east door, you see a lot of pipes and tubing.' Wu closed his eyes, visualizing it. 'Straight ahead is a big recessed well in the center of the building that goes two stories underground. To your left is a metal walkway with railings.'

'I see it.'

'Go along the walkway.'

'I'm going.' Faintly, the radio carried the clang of his footsteps on metal.

'After you go twenty or thirty feet, you will see another walkway going right.'

'I see it,' Grant said.

'Follow that walkway.'

'Okay.'

'As you continue,' Wu said, 'you will come to a ladder on your left. Going down into the pit.'

'I see it.'

'Go down the ladder.'

There was a long pause. Wu ran his fingers through his damp hair. Muldoon frowned tensely.

'Okay, I'm down the ladder,' Grant said.

'Good,' Wu said. 'Now, straight ahead of you should be two large yellow tanks that are marked "Flammable." '

'They say "In-flammable." And then something underneath. In Spanish.'

'Those are the ones,' Wu said. 'Those are the two fuel tanks for the generator. One of them has been run dry, and so we have to switch over to the other. If you look at the bottom of the tanks, you'll see a white pipe coming out.'

'Four-inch PVC?'

'Yes. PVC. Follow that pipe as it goes back.'

'Okay. I'm following it. . . . *Ow!*'

'What happened?'

'Nothing. I hit my head.'

There was a pause.

'Are you all right?'

'Yeah, fine. Just . . . hurt my head. Stupid.'

'Keep following the pipe.'

'Okay, okay,' Grant said. He sounded irritable. 'Okay. The pipe goes to a big aluminum box with air vents in the sides. Says "Honda." It looks like the generator.'

'Yes,' Wu said. 'That's the generator. If you walk around to the side, you'll see a panel with two buttons.'

'I see them. Yellow and red?'

'That's right,' Wu said. 'Press the yellow one first, and while you hold it down, press the red one.'

'Right.'

There was another pause. It lasted almost a minute. Wu and Muldoon looked at each other.

'Alan?'

'It didn't work,' Grant said.

'Did you hold down the yellow one first and then press the red?' Wu asked.

'Yes, I did,' Grant said. He sounded annoyed. 'I did exactly what you told me to do. There was a hum, and then a click, click, click, very fast, and then the hum stopped, and nothing after that.'

'Try it again.'

'I already did,' Grant said. 'It didn't work.'

'Okay, just a minute.' Wu frowned. 'It sounds like the generator is trying to fire up but it can't for some reason. Alan?'

'I'm here.'

'Go around to the back of the generator, to where the plastic pipe runs in.'

'Okay.' A pause; then Grant said, 'The pipe goes into a round black cylinder that looks like a fuel pump.'

'That's right,' Wu said. 'That's exactly what it is. It's the fuel pump. Look for a little valve at the top.'

'A valve?'

'It should be sticking up at the top, with a little metal tab that you can turn.'

'I found it. But it's on the side, not the top.'

'Okay. Twist it open.'

'Air is coming out.'

'Good. Wait until – '

'– now liquid is coming out. It smells like gas.'

'Okay. Close the valve.' Wu turned to Muldoon, shaking his head. 'Pump lost its prime. Alan?'

'Yes.'

'Try the buttons again.'

A moment later, Wu heard the faint coughing and sputtering as the generator turned over, and then the steady chugging sound as it caught. 'It's on,' Grant said.

'Good work, Alan! Good work!'

'Now what?' Grant said. He sounded flat, dull. 'The lights haven't even come on in here.'

'Go back to the control room, and I'll talk you through restoring the systems manually.'

'That's what I have to do now?'

'Yes.'

'Okay,' Grant said. 'I'll call you when I get there.'

There was a final hiss, and silence.

'Alan?'

The radio was dead.

Tim went through the swinging doors at the back of the dining room and entered the kitchen. A big stainless-steel table in the center of the room, a big stove with lots of burners to the left, and, beyond that, big walk-in refrigerators. Tim started opening the refrigerators, looking for ice cream. Smoke came out in the humid air as he opened each one.

'How come the stove is on?' Lex said, releasing his hand.

'It's not on.'

'They all have little blue flames.'

'Those're pilot lights.'

'What're pilot lights?' They had an electric stove at home.

'Never mind,' Tim said, opening another refrigerator. 'But it means I can cook you something.' In this next refrigerator, he found all kinds of stuff, cartons of milk, and piles of vegetables, and a stack of T-bone steaks, fish – but no ice cream.

'You still want ice cream?'

'I told you, didn't I?'

The next refrigerator was huge. A stainless steel door, with a wide horizontal handle. He tugged on the handle, pulled it open, and saw a walk-in freezer. It was a whole room, and it was freezing cold.

'Timmy . . .'

'Will you wait a minute?' he said, annoyed. 'I'm trying to find your ice cream.'

'Timmy . . . *something's here.*'

She was whispering, and for a moment the last two words didn't register. Then Tim hurried back out of the freezer, seeing the edge of the door wreathed in glowing green smoke. Lex stood by the steel worktable. She was looking back to the kitchen door.

He heard a low hissing sound, like a very large snake. The sound rose and fell softly. It was hardly audible. It might even be the wind, but he somehow knew it wasn't.

'Timmy,' she whispered, 'I'm scared. . . .'

He crept forward to the kitchen door and looked out.

In the darkened dining room, he saw the orderly green rectangular pattern of the tabletops. And moving smoothly among them, silent as a ghost except for the hissing of its breath, was a velociraptor.

In the darkness of the maintenance room, Grant felt along the pipes, moving back toward the ladder. It was difficult to make his way in the dark, and somehow he found the noise of the generator disorienting. He came to the ladder, and had started back up when he realized there was something else in the room besides generator noise.

Grant paused, listening.

It was a man shouting.

It sounded like Gennaro.

'Where are you?' Grant shouted.

'Over *here*,' Gennaro said. 'In the truck.'

Grant couldn't see any truck. He squinted in the darkness. He looked out of the corner of his eye. He saw green glowing shapes, moving in the darkness. Then he saw the truck, and he turned toward it.

Tim found the silence chilling.

The velociraptor was six feet tall, and powerfully built, although its strong legs and tail were hidden by the tables. Tim could see only the muscular upper torso, the two forearms held tightly alongside the body, the claws dangling. He could see the iridescent speckled pattern on the back. The velociraptor was alert; as it came forward, it looked from side to side, moving its head with abrupt, bird-like jerks. The head also bobbed up and down as it walked, and the long straight tail dipped, which heightened the impression of a bird.

A gigantic, silent bird of prey.

The dining room was dark, but apparently the raptor could see well enough to move steadily forward. From time to time, it would bend over, lowering its head below the tables. Tim heard a rapid sniffing sound. Then the head would snap up, alertly, jerking back and forth like a bird's.

Tim watched until he was sure the velociraptor was coming toward the kitchen. Was it following their scent? All the books said dinosaurs had a poor sense of smell, but this one seemed to do just fine. Anyway, what did books know? Here was the real thing.

Coming toward him.

He ducked back into the kitchen.

'Is something out there?' Lex said.

Tim didn't answer. He pushed her under a table in the corner, behind a large waste bin. He leaned close to her and whispered fiercely: '*Stay here!*' And then he ran for the refrigerator.

He grabbed a handful of cold steaks and hurried back to the door. He quietly placed the first of the steaks on the floor, then moved back a few steps, and put down the second. . . .

Through his goggles, he saw Lex peeping around the bin. He waved her back. He placed the third steak, and the fourth, moving deeper into the kitchen. ·

The hissing was louder, and then the clawed hand gripped the door, and the big head peered cautiously around.

The velociraptor paused at the entrance to the kitchen.

Tim stood in a half-crouch at the back of the room, near the far leg of the steel worktable. But he had not had time to conceal himself; his head and shoulders still protruded over the tabletop. He was in clear view of the velociraptor.

Slowly, Tim lowered his body, sinking beneath the table. . . . The velociraptor jerked its head around, looking directly at Tim.

Tim froze. He was still exposed, but he thought, *Don't move.*

The velociraptor stood motionless in the doorway.

Sniffing.

It's darker here, Tim thought. He can't see so well. It's making him cautious.

But now he could smell the musty odor of the big reptile, and through his goggles he saw the dinosaur silently yawn, throwing back its long snout, exposing rows of razor-sharp teeth. The velociraptor stared forward again, jerking its head from side to side. The big eyes swiveled in the bony sockets.

Tim felt his heart pounding. Somehow it was worse to be confronted by an animal like this in a kitchen, instead of the open forest. The size, the quick movements, the pungent odor, the hissing breath . . .

Up close, it was a much more frightening animal than the tyrannosaur. The tyrannosaur was huge and powerful, but it wasn't especially smart. The velociraptor was man-size, and it was clearly quick and intelligent; Tim feared the searching eyes almost as much as the sharp teeth.

The velociraptor sniffed. It stepped forward – moving directly toward Lex! It must smell her, somehow! Tim's heart thumped.

The velociraptor stopped. It bent over slowly.

He's found the steak.

Tim wanted to bend down, to look below the table, but he didn't dare move. He stood frozen in a half-crouch, listening to the crunching sound. The dinosaur was eating it. Bones and all.

The raptor raised its slender head, and looked around. It sniffed. It saw the second steak. It moved quickly forward. It bent down.

Silence.

The raptor didn't eat it.

The head came back up. Tim's legs burned from the crouch, but he didn't move.

Why hadn't the animal eaten the second steak? A dozen ideas flashed through his mind – it didn't like the taste of beef, it didn't like the coldness, it didn't like the fact that the meat wasn't alive, it smelled a trap, it smelled Lex, it smelled Tim, it saw Tim –

The velociraptor moved very quickly now. It found the third steak, dipped its head, looked up again, and moved on.

Tim held his breath. The dinosaur was now just a few feet from him. Tim could see the small twitches in the muscles of the flanks. He could see the crusted blood on the claws of the hand. He could see the fine pattern of striations within the spotted pattern, and the folds of skin in the neck below the jaw.

The velociraptor sniffed. It jerked its head, and looked right at Tim. Tim nearly gasped with fright. Tim's body was rigid, tense. He watched as the reptile eye moved, scanning the room. Another sniff.

He's got me, Tim thought.

Then the head jerked back to look forward, and the animal went on, toward the fifth steak. Tim thought, Lex please don't move please don't move whatever you do please don't . . .

The velociraptor sniffed the steak, and moved on. It was now at the open door to the freezer. Tim could see the smoke billowing out, curling along the floor toward the animal's feet. One big clawed foot lifted, then came down again, silently. The dinosaur hesitated. Too cold, Tim thought. He won't go in there, it's too cold, he won't go in he won't go in he won't go in . . .

The dinosaur went in.

The head disappeared, then the body, then the stiff tail.

Tim sprinted, flinging his weight against the stainless-steel door of the locker, slamming it shut. It slammed on the tip of the tail! The door wouldn't shut! The velociraptor roared, a terrifying loud sound. Inadvertently, Tim took a step back – the tail was gone! He slammed the door shut and heard it click! Closed!

'Lex! Lex!' he was screaming. He heard the raptor pounding against the door, felt it thumping the steel. He knew there was a flat steel knob inside, and if the raptor hit that, it would knock the door open. They had to get the door locked. 'Lex!'

Lex was by his side. 'What do you want!'

Tim leaned against the horizontal door handle, holding it shut. 'There's a pin! A little pin! Get the pin!'

The velociraptor roared like a lion, the sound muffled by the thick steel. It crashed its whole body against the door.

'I can't see anything!' Lex shouted.

The pin was dangling beneath the door handle, swinging on a little metal chain. 'It's right there!'

'I can't see it!' she screamed, and then Tim realized she wasn't wearing the goggles.

'Feel for it!'

He saw her little hand reaching up, touching his, groping for the pin, and with her so close to him he could feel how frightened she was, her breath in little panicky gasps as she felt for the pin, and the velociraptor slammed against the door and it opened – God, *it opened* – but the animal hadn't expected that and had already turned back for another try and Tim slammed the door shut again. Lex scrambled back, reached up in the darkness.

'I have it!' Lex cried, clutching the pin in her hand, and she pushed it through the hole. It slid out again.

'From the top, put it in *from the top!*'

She held it again, lifting it on the chain, swinging it over the handle, and down. Into the hole.

Locked.

The velociraptor roared. Tim and Lex stepped back from the door as the dinosaur slammed into it again. With each impact, the heavy steel wall hinges creaked, but they held. Tim didn't think the animal could possibly open the door.

The raptor was locked in.

He gave a long sigh. 'Let's go,' he said.

He took her hand, and they ran.

'You should have seen them,' Gennaro said, as Grant led him back out of the maintenance building. 'There must have been two dozen of them.

Compys. I had to crawl into the truck to get away from them. They were all over the windshield. Just squatting there, waiting like buzzards. But they ran away when you came over.'

'Scavengers,' Grant said. 'They won't attack anything that's moving or looks strong. They attack things that are dead, or almost dead. Anyway, unmoving.'

They were going up the ladder now, back toward the entrance door. 'What happened to the raptor that attacked you?' Grant said.

'I don't know,' Gennaro said.

'Did it leave?'

'I didn't see. I got away, I think because it was injured. I think Muldoon shot it in the leg and it was bleeding while it was in here. Then . . . I don't know. Maybe it went back outside. Maybe it died in here. I didn't see.'

'And maybe it's still in here,' Grant said.

Wu stared out the lodge window at the raptors beyond the fence. They still seemed playful, making mock attacks at Ellie. The behavior had continued for a long time now, and it occurred to him that it might be too long. It almost seemed as if they were trying to keep Ellie's attention, in the same way that she was trying to keep theirs.

The behavior of the dinosaurs had always been a minor consideration for Wu. And rightly so: behavior was a second-order effect of DNA, like protein enfolding. You couldn't really predict behavior, and you couldn't really control it, except in very crude ways, like making an animal dependent on a dietary substance by withholding an enzyme. But, in general, behavioral effects were simply beyond the reach of understanding. You couldn't look at a DNA sequence and predict behavior. It was impossible.

And that had made Wu's DNA work purely empirical. It was a matter of tinkering, the way a modern workman might repair an antique grandfather clock. You were dealing with something out of the past, something constructed of ancient materials and following ancient rules. You couldn't be certain why it worked as it did; and it had been repaired and modified many times already, by forces of evolution, over eons of time. So, like the workman who makes an adjustment and then sees if the clock runs any better, Wu would make an adjustment and then see if the animals behaved any better. And he only tried to correct gross behavior: uncontrolled butting of the electrical fences, or rubbing the skin raw on tree trunks. Those were the behaviors that sent him back to the drawing board.

And the limits of his science had left him with a mysterious feeling about the dinosaurs in the park. He was never sure, never really sure at all, whether the behavior of the animals was historically accurate or not. Were they behaving as they really had in the past? It was an open question, ultimately unanswerable.

And though Wu would never admit it, the discovery that the dinosaurs were breeding represented a tremendous validation of his work. A breeding animal was demonstrably effective in a fundamental way; it implied that Wu had put all the pieces together correctly. He had re-created an animal millions of years old, with such precision that the creature could even reproduce itself.

But, still, looking at the raptors outside, he was troubled by the persistence of their behavior. Raptors were intelligent, and intelligent animals got bored quickly. Intelligent animals also formed plans, and –

Harding came out into the hallway from Malcolm's room. 'Where's Ellie?'

'Still outside.'

'Better get her in. The raptors have left the skylight.'

'When?' Wu said, moving to the door.

'Just a moment ago,' Harding said.

Wu threw open the front door. 'Ellie! Inside, now!'

She looked over at him, puzzled. 'There's no problem, everything's under control . . .'

'Now!'

She shook her head. 'I know what I'm doing,' she said.

'Now, Ellie, damn it!'

Muldoon didn't like Wu standing there with the door open, and he was about to say so, when he saw a shadow descend from above, and he realized at once what had happened. Wu was yanked bodily out the door, and Muldoon heard Ellie screaming. Muldoon got to the door and looked out and saw that Wu was lying on his back, his body already torn open by the big claw, and the raptor was jerking its head, tugging at Wu's intestines even though Wu was still alive, still feebly reaching up with his hands to push the big head away, he was being eaten while he was still alive, and then Ellie stopped screaming and started to run along the inside of the fence, and Muldoon slammed the door shut, dizzy with horror. It had happened so fast!

Harding said, 'He jumped down from the roof?'

Muldoon nodded. He went to the window and looked out, and he saw that the three raptors outside the fence were now running away. But they weren't following Ellie.

They were going back, toward the visitor center.

Grant came to the edge of the maintenance building and peered forward, in the fog. He could hear the snarls of the raptors, and they seemed to be coming closer. Now he could see their bodies running past him. They were going to the visitor center.

He looked back at Gennaro.

Gennaro shook his head, no.

Grant leaned close and whispered in his ear. 'No choice. We've got to turn on the computer.'

Grant set out in the fog.

After a moment, Gennaro followed.

Ellie didn't stop to think. When the raptors dropped inside the fence to attack Wu, she just turned and ran, as fast as she could, toward the far end of the lodge. There was a space fifteen feet wide between the fence and the lodge. She ran, not hearing the animals pursuing her, just hearing her own breath. She rounded the corner, saw a tree growing by the side of the building, and leapt, grabbing a branch, swinging up. She didn't feel panic. She felt a kind of exhilaration as she kicked and saw her legs rise up in front of her face, and she hooked her legs over a branch farther up, tightened her gut, and pulled up quickly.

She was already twelve feet off the ground, and the raptors still weren't following her, and she was beginning to feel pretty good, when she saw the first animal at the base of the tree. Its mouth was bloody, and bits of stringy flesh hung from its jaws. She continued to go up fast, hand over hand, just reaching and going, and she could almost see the top of the building. She looked down again.

The two raptors were climbing the tree.

Now she was at the level of the rooftop, she could see the gravel only four feet away, and the glass pyramids of the skylights, sticking up in the mist. There was a door on the roof; she could get inside. In a single heaving effort she flung herself through the air, and landed sprawling on the gravel. She scraped her face, but somehow the only sensation was exhilaration, as if it were a kind of game she was playing, a game she intended to win. She ran for the door that led to the stairwell. Behind her, she could hear the raptors shaking the branches of the tree. They were still in the tree.

She reached the door, and twisted the knob.

The door was locked.

It took a moment for the meaning of that to cut through her euphoria. The door was locked. She was on the roof and she couldn't get down. *The door was locked.*

She pounded on the door in frustration, and then she ran for the far side of the roof, hoping to see a way down, but there was only the green outline of the swimming pool through the blowing mist. All around the pool was concrete decking. Ten, twelve feet of concrete. Too much for her to jump across. No other trees to climb down. No stairs. No fire escape. Nothing.

Ellie turned back, and saw the raptors jumping easily to the roof. She ran to the far end of the building, hoping there might be another door there, but there wasn't.

The raptors came slowly toward her, stalking her, slipping silently among the glass pyramids. She looked down. The edge of the pool was ten feet away.

Too far.

The raptors were closer, starting to move apart, and illogically she thought: *Isn't this always the way? Some little mistake screws it all up.* She still felt giddy, still felt exhilaration, and she somehow couldn't believe these animals were going to get her, she couldn't believe that now her life was going to end like this. It didn't seem possible. She was enveloped in a kind of protective cheerfulness. She just didn't believe it would happen.

The raptors snarled. Ellie backed away, moving to the far end of the roof. She took a breath, and then began to sprint toward the edge. As she raced toward the edge, she saw the swimming pool, and she knew it was too far away but she thought, *What the hell*, and leapt into space.

And fell.

And with a stinging shock, she felt herself enveloped in coldness. She was underwater. She had done it! She came to the surface and looked up at the roof, and saw the raptors looking down at her. And she knew that, if she could do it, the raptors could do it, too. She splashed in the water and thought, *Can raptors swim?* But she was sure they could. They could probably swim like crocodiles.

The raptors turned away from the edge of the roof. And then she heard Harding calling 'Sattler?' and she realized he had opened the roof door. The raptors were going toward him.

Hurriedly, she climbed out of the pool and ran toward the lodge.

Harding had gone up the steps to the roof two at a time, and he had flung open the door without thinking. 'Sattler!' he shouted. And then he stopped. Mist blew among the pyramids on the roof. The raptors were not in sight.

'Sattler!'

He was so preoccupied with Sattler that it was a moment before he realized his mistake. He should be able to see the animals, he thought. In the next instant the clawed forearm smashed around the side of the door, catching him in the chest with a tearing pain, and it took all of his effort to pull himself backward and close the door on the arm, and from downstairs he heard Muldoon shouting, 'She's here, she's already inside.'

From the other side of the door, the raptor snarled, and Harding slammed the door again, and the claws pulled back, and he closed the door with a metallic clang and sank coughing to the floor.

'Where are we going?' Lex said. They were on the second floor of the visitor center. A glass-walled corridor ran the length of the building.

'To the control room,' Tim said.

'Where's that?'

'Down here someplace.' Tim looked at the names stencilled on the doors as he went past them. These seemed to be offices: PARK WARDEN ... GUEST SERVICES ... GENERAL MANAGER ... COMPTROLLER ...

They came to a glass partition marked with a sign:

CLOSED AREA
AUTHORIZED PERSONNEL ONLY
BEYOND THIS POINT

There was a slot for a security card, but Tim just pushed the door open.

'How come it opened?'

'The power is out,' Tim said.

'Why're we going to the control room?' she asked.

'To find a radio. We need to call somebody.'

Beyond the glass door the hallway continued. Tim remembered this area; he had seen it earlier, during the tour. Lex trotted along at his side. In the distance, they heard the snarling of raptors. The animals seemed to be approaching. Then Tim heard them slamming against the glass downstairs.

'They're out there ...' Lex whispered.

'Don't worry.'

'What are they doing here?' Lex said.

'Never mind now.'

PARK SUPERVISOR ... OPERATIONS ... MAIN CONTROL ...

'Here,' Tim said. He pushed open the door. The main control room was as he had seen it before. In the center of the room was a console with four chairs and four computer monitors. The room was entirely dark except for the monitors, which all showed a series of colored rectangles.

'So where's a radio?' Lex said.

But Tim had forgotten all about a radio. He moved forward, staring at the computer screens. The screens were on! That could only mean −

'The power must be back on . . .'

'Ick,' Lex said, shifting her body.

'What.'

'I was standing on somebody's *ear*,' she said.

Tim hadn't seen a body when they came in. He looked back and saw there was just an ear, lying on the floor.

'That is really disgusting,' Lex said.

'Never mind.' He turned to the monitors.

'Where's the rest of him?' she said.

'Never mind that now.'

He peered closely at the monitor. There were rows of colored labels on the screen:

JURASSIC PARK – SYSTEM STARTUP

	STARTUP AB(0)				STARTUP CN/D		
Security Main	Monitor Main	Command Main	Electrical Main	Hydraulic Main	Master Main	Zoolog Main
SetGrids DNL	View VBB	Access TNL	Heating Cooling	Door Fold Interface	SAAG- Rnd	Repair Storage
Critical Locks	TeleCom VBB	Reset Revert	Emgency Illumin	GAS/VLD Main II	Common Interface	Status Main
Control Passthru	TeleCom RSD	Template Main	FNCC Params	Explosion Fire Hzd	Schematic Main	Safety / Health

'You better not fool around with that, Timmy,' she said.

'Don't worry, I won't.'

He had seen complicated computers before, like the ones that were installed in the buildings his father worked on. Those computers controlled everything from the elevators and security to the heating and cooling systems. They looked basically like this − a lot of colored labels − but they were usually simpler to understand. And almost always there was a help label, if you needed to learn about the system. But he saw no help label here. He looked again, to be sure.

But then he saw something else: numerals clicking in the upper left corner of the screen. They read 10:47:22. Then Tim realized it was the time. There were only thirteen minutes left for the boat − but he was more worried about the people in the lodge.

There was a static crackle. He turned, and saw Lex holding a radio.

She was twisting the knobs and dials. 'How does it work?' she said. 'I can't make it work.'

'Give me that!'

'It's mine! I found it!'

'Give it to me, Lex!'

'I get to use it first!'

'Lex!'

Suddenly, the radio crackled. '*What the hell is going on!*' said Muldoon's voice.

Surprised, Lex dropped the radio on the floor.

Grant ducked back, crouching among the palm trees. Through the mist ahead he could see the raptors hopping and snarling and butting their heads against the glass of the visitor center. But, between snarls, they would fall silent and cock their heads, as if listening to something distant. And then they would make little whimpering sounds.

'What're they doing?' Gennaro said.

'It looks like they're trying to get into the cafeteria,' Grant said.

'What's in the cafeteria?'

'I left the kids there . . .' Grant said.

'Can they break through that glass?'

'I don't think so, no.'

Grant watched, and now he heard the crackle of a distant radio, and the raptors began hopping in a more agitated way. One after another, they began jumping higher and higher, until finally he saw the first of them leap lightly onto the second-floor balcony, and from there move inside the second floor of the visitor center.

In the control room on the second floor, Tim snatched up the radio which Lex had dropped. He pressed the button. 'Hello? Hello?'

'–s that you, Tim?' It was Muldoon's voice.

'It's me, yes.'

'Where are you?'

'In the control room. The power is on!'

'That's great, Tim,' Muldoon said.

'If someone will tell me how to turn the computer on, I'll do it.'

There was a silence.

'Hello?' Tim said. 'Did you hear me?'

'Ah, we have a problem about that,' Muldoon said. 'Nobody, ah, who is here knows how to do that. How to turn the computer on.'

Tim said, 'What, are you kidding? Nobody knows?' It seemed incredible.

'No.' A pause. 'I think it's something about the main grid. Turning on the main grid ... You know anything about computers, Tim?'

Tim stared at the screen. Lex nudged him. 'Tell him no, Timmy,' she said.

'Yes, some. I know something,' Tim said.

'Might as well try,' Muldoon said. 'Nobody here knows what to do. And Grant doesn't know about computers.'

'Okay,' Tim said. 'I'll try.' He clicked off the radio and stared at the screen, studying it.

'Timmy,' Lex said. 'You don't know what to do.'

'Yes I do.'

'If you know, then do it,' Lex said.

'Just a minute.' As a way to get started, he pulled the chair close to the keyboard and pressed the cursor keys. Those were the keys that moved the cursor around on the screen. But nothing happened. Then he pushed other keys. The screen remained unchanged.

'Well?' she said.

'Something's wrong,' Tim said, frowning.

'You just don't know, Timmy,' she said.

He examined the computer again, looking at it carefully. The keyboard had a row of function keys at the top, just like a regular PC keyboard, and the monitor was big and in color. But the monitor housing was sort of unusual. Tim looked at the edges of the screen and saw lots of faint pinpoints of red light.

Red light, all around the borders of the screen ... What could that be? He moved his finger toward the light and saw the soft red glow on his skin.

He touched the screen and heard a beep.

JURASSIC PARK - SYSTEM STARTUP

STARTUP AB(0)				STARTUP CN/D		
Security Main	Monitor Main	Command Main	Electrical Main	Hydraulic Main	Master Main	Zoolog Main
SetGrids DNL	View VBB		Heating Cooling	Door Fold Interface	SAAG-Rnd	Repair Storage
Critical Locks	TeleCom	Reset	Emergcu	GAS/VLD	Common	Status Main
Control Passthru	RJD	Main	Params	Fire Hzd	Main	Safety / Health

You Already Have Access
Make Your Selection From The Main Screen

A moment later, the message box disappeared, and the original screen flashed back up.

'What happened?' Lex said. 'What did you do? You touched something.'

Of course! he thought. He had touched the screen. It was a touch screen! The red lights around the edges must be infrared sensors. Tim had never seen such a screen, but he'd read about them in magazines. He touched RESET/REVERT.

Instantly the screen changed. He got a new message:

> THE COMPUTER IS NOW RESET
> MAKE YOUR SELECTION FROM THE MAIN SCREEN

Over the radio, they heard the sound of raptors snarling. 'I want to see,' Lex said. 'You should try VIEW.'

'No, Lex.'

'Well, I want VIEW,' she said. And before he could grab her hand, she had pressed VIEW. The screen changed.

SUBROUTINES – VIEW VIDEO INTERFACE ENVIRONMENTAL WATCH			
REMOTE CLC VIDEO – H			REMOTE CLC VIDEO – P
Monitor Interval	Set	Hold	Monitor Interval
Monitor Control	Auto	Man	Monitor Control
Optimize Sequence Rotation	AO(19)	DD(33)	Optimize Sequence Rotation
Specify Remote Camera	Command Sequence		RGB Image Parameters

'Uh-oh,' she said.

'Lex, will you cut it out?'

'Look!' she said. 'It worked! Ha!'

Around the room, the monitors showed quickly changing views of different parts of the park. Most of the images were misty gray, because of the exterior fog, but one showed the outside of the lodge, with a raptor on the roof, and then another switched to an image in bright sunlight, showing the bow of a ship, bright sunlight –

'What was that?' Tim said, leaning forward.

'What?'

'That picture!'

But the image had already changed, and now they were seeing the inside of the lodge, one room after another, and then he saw Malcolm, lying in a bed –

'Stop it,' Lex said. 'I see them!'

Tim touched the screen in several places, and got submenus. Then more submenus.

'Wait,' Lex said. 'You're confusing it. . . .'

'Will you shut up! You don't know anything about computers!'

Now he had a list of monitors on the screen. One of them was marked SAFARI LODGE: LV2-4. Another was REMOTE: SHIPBOARD (VND). He pressed the screen several times.

Video images came up on monitors around the room. One showed the bow of the supply ship, and the ocean ahead. In the distance, Tim saw land – buildings along a shore, and a harbor. He recognized the harbor because he had flown over it in the helicopter the day before. It was Puntarenas. The ship seemed to be just minutes from landing.

But his attention was drawn by the next screen, which showed the roof of the safari lodge, in gray mist. The raptors were mostly hidden behind the pyramids, but their heads bobbed up and down, coming into view.

And then, on the third monitor, he could see inside a room. Malcolm was lying in a bed, and Ellie stood next to him. They were both looking upward. As they watched, Muldoon walked into the room, and joined them, looking up with an expression of concern.

'They see us,' Lex said.

'I don't think so.'

The radio crackled. On the screen, Muldoon lifted the radio to his lips. 'Hello, Tim?'

'I'm here,' Tim said.

'Ah, we haven't got a whole lot of time,' Muldoon said, dully. 'Better get that power grid on.' And then Tim heard the raptors snarl, and saw one of the long heads duck down through the glass, briefly entering the picture from the top, snapping its jaws.

'Hurry, Timmy!' Lex said. 'Get the power on!'

The Grid

Tim suddenly found himself lost in a tangled series of monitor control screens, as he tried to get back to the main screen. Most systems had a single button or a single command to return to the previous screen, or to the main menu. But this system did not – or at least he didn't know it. Also, he was certain that help commands had been built into the system, but he couldn't find them, either, and Lex was jumping up and down and shouting in his ear, making him nervous.

Finally he got the main screen back. He wasn't sure what he had done, but it was back. He paused, looking for a command.

'Do something, Timmy!'

'Will you shut up? I'm trying to get help.' He pushed TEMPLATE-MAIN. The screen filled with a complicated diagram, with interconnecting boxes and arrows.

No good. No good.

He pushed COMMON INTERFACE. The screen shifted:

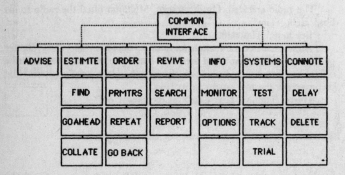

'What's that?' Lex said. 'Why aren't you turning on the power, Timmy?'

He ignored her. Maybe help on this system was called 'info.' He pushed INFO.

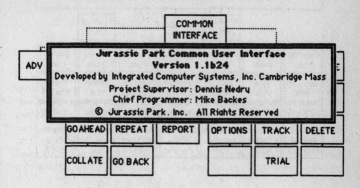

'Tim-ee,' Lex wailed, but he had already pushed FIND. He got another useless window. He pushed GO BACK.

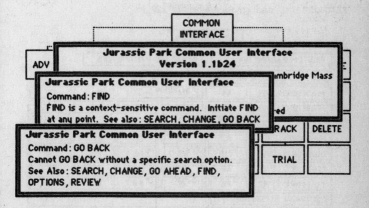

On the radio, he heard Muldoon say, 'How's it coming, Tim?' He didn't bother to answer. Frantic, he pushed buttons one after another. Suddenly, without warning, the main screen was back.

JURASSIC PARK – SYSTEM STARTUP

STARTUP AB(0)				STARTUP CN/D			
Security Main	Monitor Main	Command Main	Electrical Main	Hydraulic Main	Master Main	Zoolog Main
SetGrids DNL	View VBB	Access TNL	Heating Cooling	Door Fold Interface	SAAG-Rnd	Repair Storage
Critical Locks	TeleCom VBB	Reset Revert	Emgency Illumin	GAS/VLD Main II	Common Interface	Status Main
Control Passthru	TeleCom RSD	Template Main	FNCC Params	Explosion Fire Hzd	Schematic Main	Safety/Health

He studied the screen. ELECTRICAL MAIN and SETGRIDS DNL both looked like they might have something to do with grids. He noticed that SAFETY/HEALTH and CRITICAL LOCKS might be important, too. He heard the growl of the raptors. He had to make a choice. He pressed SETGRIDS DNL, and groaned when he saw it:

SET GRIDS DNL

CUSTOM PARAMETERS		STANDARD PARAMETERS		
ELECTRICAL SECONDARY (H)				
MAIN GRID LEVEL	A4	B4	C7	D4	E9
MAIN GRID LEVEL	C9	R5	D5	E3	G4
ELECTRICAL SECONDARY (P)				
MAIN GRID LEVEL	A2	B3	C6	D11	E2
MAIN GRID LEVEL	C9	R5	D5	E3	G4
MAIN GRID LEVEL	A8	B1	C8	D8	E8
MAIN GRID LEVEL	P4	R8	P4	E5	L6
ELECTRICAL SECONDARY (M)				
MAIN GRID LEVEL	A1	B1	C1	D2	E2
MAIN GRID LEVEL	C4	R4	D4	E5	G6

He didn't know what to do. He pushed STANDARD PARAMETERS.

STANDARD PARAMETERS

Park Grids	B4-C6	Outer Grids	C2-D2
Zoological Grids	BB-07	Pen Grids	R4-R4
Lodge Grids	F4-D4	Maint Grids	E5-L6
Main Grids	C4-G7	Sensor Grids	D5-G4
Utility Grids	AH-B5	Core Grids	A1-C1

Circuit Integrity Not Tested
Security Grids Remain Automatic

Tim shook his head in frustration. It took him a moment to realize that he had just gotten valuable information. He now knew the grid coordinates for the lodge! He pushed grid F4.

POWER GRID F4 (SAFARI LODGE)
COMMAND CANNOT BE EXECUTED. ERROR-505
(POWER INCOMPATIBLE WITH COMMAND ERROR.
Ref Manual Pages 4.09-4.11)

'It's not working,' Lex said.
'I know!' He pushed another button. The screen flashed again.

POWER GRID D4 (SAFARI LODGE)
COMMAND CANNOT BE EXECUTED. ERROR-505
(POWER INCOMPATIBLE WITH COMMAND ERROR.
Ref Manual Pages 4.09-4.11)

Tim tried to stay calm, to think it through. For some reason he was getting a consistent error message whenever he tried to turn on a grid. It was saying the power was incompatible with the command he was giving. But what did that mean? Why was power incompatible?

'Timmy...' Lex said, tugging at his arm.
'Not *now*, Lex.'
'*Yes, now*,' she said, and she pulled him away from the screen and the console. And then he heard the snarling of raptors.

It was coming from the hallway.

In the skylight above Malcolm's bed, the raptors had almost bitten through the second metal bar. They could now poke their heads entirely through the shattered glass, and lunge and snarl at the people below. Then after a moment they would pull back, and resume chewing on the metal.

Malcolm said, 'It won't be long now. Three, four minutes.' He pressed the button on the radio: 'Tim, are you there? Tim?'

There was no answer.

Tim slipped out the door and saw the velociraptor, down at the far end of the corridor, standing by the balcony. He stared in astonishment. How had it gotten out of the freezer?

Then, as he watched, a second raptor suddenly appeared on the balcony, and he understood. The raptor hadn't come from the freezer at all. It had come from outside. It had *jumped* from the ground below. The second raptor landed silently, perfectly balanced on the railing. Tim couldn't believe it. The big animal had jumped ten feet straight up. More than ten feet. Their legs must be incredibly powerful.

Lex whispered, 'I thought you said they couldn't −'

'Ssshh.' Tim was trying to think, but he watched with a kind of fascinated dread as the third raptor leapt to the balcony. The animals milled aimlessly in the corridor for a moment, and then they began to move forward in single file. Coming toward him and Lex.

Quietly, Tim pushed against the door at his back, to re-enter the control room. But the door was stuck. He pushed harder.

'We're locked out,' Lex whispered. 'Look.' She pointed to the slot for the security card alongside the door. A bright red dot glowed. Somehow the security doors had been activated. 'You idiot, you locked us out!'

Tim looked down the corridor. He saw several more doors, but each had a red light glowing alongside. That meant all the doors were locked. There was nowhere they could go.

Then he saw a slumped shape on the floor at the far end of the corridor. It was a dead guard. A white security card was clipped to his belt.

'Come on,' he whispered. They ran for the guard. Tim got the card, and turned back. But of course the raptors had seen them. They snarled, and blocked the way back to the control room. They began to spread apart, fanning out in the hallway to surround Tim and Lex. Their heads began to duck rhythmically.

They were going to attack.

Tim did the only thing he could do. Using the card, he opened the nearest door off the hallway and pushed Lex through. As the door began to close slowly behind them, the raptors hissed and charged.

Lodge

Ian Malcolm drew each breath as if it might be his last. He watched the raptors with dull eyes. Harding took his blood pressure, frowned, took it again. Ellie Sattler was wrapped in a blanket, shivering and cold. Muldoon sat on the floor, propped against the wall. Hammond was staring upward, not speaking. They all listened to the radio.

'What happened to Tim?' Hammond said. 'Still no word?'

'I don't know.'

Malcolm said, 'Ugly, aren't they. Truly ugly.'

Hammond shook his head. 'Who could have imagined it would turn out this way.'

Ellie said, 'Apparently Malcolm did.'

'I didn't imagine it,' Malcolm said. 'I *calculated* it.'

Hammond sighed. 'No more of this, please. He's been saying "I told you so" for hours. But nobody ever wanted this to happen.'

'It isn't a matter of wanting it or not,' Malcolm said, eyes closed. He spoke slowly, through the drugs. 'It's a matter of what you think you can accomplish. When the hunter goes out in the rain forest to seek food for his family, does he expect to control nature? No. He imagines that nature is beyond him. Beyond his understanding. Beyond his control. Maybe he prays to nature, to the fertility of the forest that provides for him. He prays because he knows he doesn't control it. He's at the mercy of it.

'But you decide you won't be at the mercy of nature. You decide you'll control nature, and from that moment on you're in deep trouble, because you can't do it. Yet you have made systems that require you to do it. And you can't do it – and you never have – and you never will. Don't confuse things. You can make a boat, but you can't make the ocean. You can make an airplane, but you can't make the air. Your powers are much less than your dreams of reason would have you believe.'

'He's lost me,' Hammond said, with a sigh. 'Where did Tim go? He seemed such a responsible boy.'

'I'm sure he's trying to get control of the situation,' Malcolm said. 'Like everybody else.'

'And Grant, too. What happened to Grant?'

Grant reached the rear door to the visitor center, the same door he had left twenty minutes before. He tugged on the handle: it was locked. Then he saw the little red light. The security doors were reactivated! Damn! He ran around to the front of the building, and went through the shattered front doors into the main lobby, stopping by the guard desk where he had been earlier. He could hear the dry hiss of his radio. He went to the kitchen, looking for the kids, but the kitchen door was open, the kids gone.

He went upstairs but came to the glass panel marked CLOSED AREA and the door was locked. He needed a security card to go farther.

Grant couldn't get in.

From somewhere inside the hallway, he heard the raptors snarling.

The leathery reptile skin touched Tim's face, the claws tore his shirt, and Tim fell onto his back, shrieking in fright.

'Timmy!' Lex yelled.

Tim scrambled to his feet again. The baby velociraptor perched on his shoulder, chirping and squeaking in panic. Tim and Lex were in the white nursery. There were toys on the floor: a rolling yellow ball, a doll, a plastic rattle.

'It's the baby raptor,' Lex said, pointing to the animal gripping Tim's shoulder.

The little raptor burrowed its head into Tim's neck. The poor thing was probably starving, Tim thought.

Lex came closer and the baby hopped onto her shoulder. It rubbed against her neck. 'Why is it doing that?' she said. 'Is it scared?'

'I don't know,' Tim said.

She passed the raptor back to Tim. The baby was chirping and squeaking, and hopping up and down on his shoulder excitedly. It kept looking around, head moving quickly. No doubt about it, the little thing was worked up and −

'Tim,' Lex whispered.

The door to the hallway hadn't closed behind them after they entered the nursery. Now the big velociraptors were coming through. First one, then a second one.

Clearly agitated, the baby chirped and bounced on Tim's shoulder. Tim knew he had to get away. Maybe the baby would distract them. After all, it was a baby raptor. He plucked the little animal from his shoulder and threw it across the room. The baby scurried between the legs of the adults. The first raptor lowered its snout, sniffed at the baby delicately.

Tim took Lex's hand, and pulled her deeper into the nursery. He had to find a door, a way to get out −

There was a high piercing shriek. Tim looked back to see the baby in the jaws of the adult. A second velociraptor came forward and tore at the limbs of the infant, trying to pull it from the mouth of the first. The two raptors fought over the baby as it squealed. Blood splattered in large drops onto the floor.

'They *ate* him,' Lex said.

The raptors fought over the remains of the baby, rearing back and butting heads. Tim found a door – it was unlocked – and went through, pulling Lex after him.

They were in another room, and from the deep green glow he realized it was the deserted DNA-extraction laboratory, the rows of stereo microscopes abandoned, the high-resolution screens showing frozen, giant black-and-white images of insects. The flies and gnats that had bitten dinosaurs millions of years ago, sucking the blood that now had been used to re-create dinosaurs in the park. They ran through the laboratory, and Tim could hear the snorts and snarls of the raptors, pursuing them, coming closer, and then he went to the back of the lab and through a door that must have had an alarm, because in the narrow corridor an intermittent siren sounded shrilly, and the lights overhead flashed on and off. Running down the corridor, Tim was plunged into darkness – then light again – then darkness. Over the sound of the alarm, he heard the raptors snort as they pursued him. Lex was whimpering and moaning. Tim saw another door ahead, with the blue biohazard sign, and he slammed into the door, and moved beyond it, and suddenly he collided with something big and Lex shrieked in terror.

'Take it easy, kids,' a voice said.

Tim blinked in disbelief. Standing above him was Dr. Grant. And next to him was Mr. Gennaro.

Outside in the hallway, it had taken Grant nearly two minutes to realize that the dead guard down in the lobby probably had a security card. He'd gone back and gotten it, and entered the upper corridor, moving quickly down the hallway. He had followed the sound of the raptors and found them fighting in the nursery. He was sure the kids would have gone to the next room, and had immediately run to the extractions lab.

And there he'd met the kids.

Now the raptors were coming toward them. The animals seemed momentarily hesitant, surprised by the appearance of more people.

Grant pushed the kids into Gennaro's arms and said, 'Take them back someplace safe.'

'But –'

'Through there,' Grant said, pointing over his shoulder to a far door. 'Take them to the control room, if you can. You should all be safe there.'

'What are you going to do?' Gennaro said.

The raptors stood near the door. Grant noticed that they waited until all the animals were together, and then they moved forward, as a group. Pack hunters. He shivered.

'I have a plan,' Grant said. 'Now go on.'

Gennaro led the kids away. The raptors continued slowly toward Grant, moving past the supercomputers, past the screens that still blinked endless sequences of computer-deciphered code. The raptors came forward without hesitation, sniffing the floor, repeatedly ducking their heads.

Grant heard the door click behind him and glanced over his shoulder. Everybody was standing on the other side of the glass door, watching him. Gennaro shook his head.

Grant knew what it meant. There was no door to the control room beyond. Gennaro and the kids were trapped in there.

It was up to him now.

Grant moved slowly, edging around the laboratory, leading the raptors away from Gennaro and the kids. He could see another door, nearer the front, which was marked TO LABORATORY. Whatever that meant. He had an idea, and he hoped he was right. The door had a blue biohazard sign. The raptors were coming closer. Grant turned and slammed into the door, and moved beyond it, into a deep, warm silence.

He turned.

Yes.

He was where he wanted to be, in the hatchery: beneath infrared lights, long tables, with rows of eggs and a low clinging mist. The rockers on the tables clicked and whirred in a steady motion. The mist poured over the sides of the tables and drifted to the floor, where it disappeared, evaporated.

Grant ran directly to the rear of the hatchery, into a glass-walled laboratory with ultraviolet light. His clothing glowed blue. He looked around at the glass reagents, beakers full of pipettes, glass dishes . . . all delicate laboratory equipment.

The raptors entered the room, cautiously at first, sniffing the humid air, looking at the long rocking tables of eggs. The lead animal wiped its bloody jaws with the back of its forearm. Silently the raptors passed between the long tables. The animals moved through the room in a coordinated way, ducking from time to time to peer beneath the tables.

They were looking for him.

Grant crouched, and moved to the back of the laboratory, looked up, and saw the metal hood marked with a skull and crossbones. A sign said CAUTION BIOGENIC TOXINS A4 PRECAUTIONS REQUIRED. Grant remembered that Regis had said they were powerful poisons. Only a few molecules would kill instantaneously . . .

The hood lay flush against the surface of the lab table. Grant could not slip his hand under it. He tried to open it, but there was no door, no handle, no way that he could see . . . Grant rose slowly, and glanced back at the main room. The raptors were still moving among the tables.

He turned to the hood. He saw an odd metal fixture sunk into the surface of the table. It looked like an outdoor electrical outlet with a round cover. He flipped up the cover, saw a button, pressed it.

With a soft hiss, the hood slid upward, to the ceiling.

He saw glass shelves above him, and rows of bottles marked with a skull and crossbones. He peered at the labels: CCK-55 . . . TETRA-ALPHA SECRETIN . . . THYMOLEVIN X-1612. . . . The fluids glowed pale green in the ultraviolet light. Nearby he saw a glass dish with syringes in it. The syringes were small, each containing a tiny amount of green glowing fluid. Crouched in the blue darkness, Grant reached for the dish of syringes. The needles on the syringes were capped in plastic. He removed one cap, pulling it off with his teeth. He looked at the thin needle.

He moved forward. Toward the raptors.

He had devoted his whole life to studying dinosaurs. Now he would see how much he really knew. Velociraptors were small carnivorous dinosaurs, like oviraptors and dromaeosaurs, animals that were long thought to steal eggs. Just as certain modern birds ate the eggs of other birds, Grant had always assumed that velociraptors would eat dinosaur eggs if they could.

He crept forward to the nearest egg table in the hatchery. Slowly he reached up into the mist and took a large egg from the rocking table. The egg was almost the size of a football, cream-colored with faint pink speckling. He held the egg carefully while he stuck the needle through the shell, and injected the contents of the syringe. The egg glowed faint blue.

Grant bent down again. Beneath the table, he saw the legs of the raptors, and the mist pouring down from the tabletops. He rolled the glowing egg along the floor, toward the raptors. The raptors looked up, hearing the faint rumble as the egg rolled, and jerked their heads around. Then they resumed their slow stalking search.

The egg stopped several yards from the nearest raptor.

Damn!

Grant did it all again: quietly reaching up for an egg, bringing it down, injecting it, and rolling it toward the raptors. This time, the egg came to rest by the foot of one velociraptor. It rocked gently, clicking against the big toe claw.

The raptor looked down in surprise at this new gift. It bent over and sniffed the glowing egg. It rolled the egg with its snout along the floor for a moment.

And ignored it.

The velociraptor stood upright again, and slowly moved on, continuing to search.

It wasn't working.

Grant reached for a third egg, and injected it with a fresh syringe. He held the glowing egg in his hands, and rolled it again. But he rolled this one fast, like a bowling ball. The egg rattled across the floor loudly.

One of the animals heard the sound – ducked down – saw it coming – and instinctively chased the moving object, gliding swiftly among the tables to intercept the egg as it rolled. The big jaws snapped down and bit into it, crushing the shell.

The raptor stood, pale albumen dripping from its jaws. It licked its lips noisily, and snorted. It bit again, and lapped the egg from the floor. But it didn't seem to be in the least distressed. It bent over to eat again from the broken egg. Grant looked down to see what would happen . . .

From across the room, the raptor saw him. *It was looking right at him.*

The velociraptor snarled menacingly. It moved toward Grant, crossing the room in long, incredibly swift strides. Grant was shocked to see it happening and froze in panic, when suddenly the animal made a gasping, gurgling sound and the big body pitched forward onto the ground. The heavy tail thumped the floor in spasms. The raptor continued to make choking sounds, punctuated by intermittent loud shrieks. Foam bubbled from its mouth. The head flopped back and forth. The tail slammed and thumped.

That's one, Grant thought.

But it wasn't dying very fast. It seemed to take forever to die. Grant reached up for another egg – and saw that the other raptors in the room were frozen in mid-action. They listened to the sound of the dying animal. One cocked its head, then another, and another. The first animal moved to look at the fallen raptor.

The dying raptor was now twitching, the whole body shaking on the floor. It made pitiful moans. So much foam bubbled from its mouth that Grant could hardly see the head any more. It flopped on the floor and moaned again.

The second raptor bent over the fallen animal, examining it. It appeared to be puzzled by these death throes. Cautiously, it looked at the foaming head, then moved down to the twitching neck, the heaving ribs, the legs . . .

And it took a bite from the hind leg.

The dying animal snarled, and suddenly lifted its head and twisted, sinking its teeth into the neck of its attacker.

That's two, Grant thought.

But the standing animal wrenched free. Blood flowed from its neck. It struck out with its hind claws, and with a single swift movement ripped open the belly of the fallen animal. Coils of intestine fell out like fat snakes. The screams of the dying raptor filled the room. The attacker turned away, as if fighting was suddenly too much trouble.

It crossed the room, ducked down, and came up with a glowing egg! Grant watched as the raptor bit into it, the glowing material dripping down its chin.

That makes two.

The second raptor was stricken almost instantly, coughing and pitching forward. As it fell, it knocked over a table. Dozens of eggs rolled everywhere across the floor. Grant looked at them in dismay.

There was still a third raptor left.

Grant had one more syringe. With so many eggs rolling on the floor, he would have to do something else. He was trying to decide what to do when the last animal snorted irritably. Grant looked up – the raptor had spotted him.

The final raptor did not move for a long time, it just stared. And then it slowly, quietly came forward. Stalking him. Bobbing up and down, looking first beneath the tables, then above them. It moved deliberately, cautiously, with none of the swiftness that it had displayed in a pack. A solitary animal now, it was careful. It never took its eyes off Grant. Grant looked around quickly. There was nowhere for him to hide. Nothing for him to do . . .

Grant's gaze was fixed on the raptor, moving slowly laterally. Grant moved, too. He tried to keep as many tables as he could between himself and the advancing animal. Slowly . . . slowly . . . he moved to the left . . .

The raptor advanced in the dark red gloom of the hatchery. Its breath came in soft hisses, through flared nostrils.

Grant felt eggs breaking beneath his feet, the yolk sticking to the soles of his shoes. He crouched down, felt the bulge of the radio in his pocket.

The radio.

He pulled it from his pocket and turned it on.

'Hello. This is Grant.'

'Alan?' Ellie's voice. 'Alan?'

'Listen,' he said softly. 'Just talk.'

'Alan, is that you?'

'*Talk*,' he said again, and he pushed the radio across the floor, away from him, toward the advancing raptor.

He crouched behind a table leg, and waited.

'Alan. Speak to me, please.'

Then a crackle, and silence. The radio remained silent. The raptor advanced. Soft hissing breath.

The radio was still silent.

What was the matter with her! Didn't she understand? In the darkness, the raptor came closer.

'. . . Alan?'

The tinny voice from the radio made the big animal pause. It sniffed the air, as if sensing someone else in the room.

'Alan, it's me. I don't know if you can hear me.'

The raptor now turned away from Grant, and moved toward the radio.

'Alan . . . please . . .'

Why hadn't he pushed the radio farther away? The raptor was going toward it, but it was close. The big foot came down very near him. Grant could see the pebbled skin, the soft green glow. The streaks of dried blood on the curved claw. He could smell the strong reptile odor.

'Alan, listen to me . . . Alan?'

The raptor bent over, poked at the radio on the floor, tentatively. Its body was turned away from Grant. The big tail was right above Grant's head. Grant reached up and jabbed the syringe deep into the flesh of the tail, and injected the poison.

The velociraptor snarled and jumped. With frightening speed it swung back toward Grant, jaws wide. It snapped, its jaws closing on the table leg, and jerked its head up. The table was knocked away, and Grant fell back, now completely exposed. The raptor loomed over him, rising up, its head banging into the infrared lights above, making them swing crazily.

'Alan?'

The raptor reared back, and lifted its clawed foot to kick. Grant rolled, and the foot slammed down, just missing him. He felt a searing sharp pain along his shoulder blades, the sudden warm flow of blood over his shirt. He rolled across the floor, crushing eggs, smearing his hands, his face. The raptor kicked again, smashing down on the radio, spattering sparks. It snarled in rage, and kicked a third time, and Grant came to the wall, nowhere else to go, and the animal raised its foot a final time.

And toppled backward.

The animal was wheezing. Foam came from its mouth.

Gennaro and the kids came into the room. Grant signaled them to stay back. The girl looked at the dying animal and said softly, 'Wow.'

Gennaro helped Grant to his feet. They all turned, and ran for the control room.

Control

Tim was astonished to find the screen in the control room was now flashing on and off. Lex said, 'What happened?'

JURASSIC PARK – SYSTEM STARTUP						
STARTUP AB(0)				STARTUP CN/D		
Security Main	Monitor Main	Command Main	Electrical Main	Hydraulic Main	Master Main	Cooling Main
Setbrid DNL	View VBB	Aux DNL	Heating Cooling	Door Fold Interface	SAAG-Rnd	Repair Storage
Critical Lock	TeleCom VBB	Reset Revert	Emgency Illumin	GAS/VLD Main II	Common Interface	Status Main
Control Passthru	TeleCom REC	Template Main	FNCC Params	Explosion Fire Hzd	Schematic Main	Safety Health

Tim saw Dr. Grant staring at the screen, and gingerly moving his hand toward the keyboard. 'I don't know about computers,' Grant said, shaking his head.

But Tim was already sliding into the seat. He touched the screen rapidly. On the video monitors, he could see the boat moving closer to Puntarenas. It was now only about two hundred yards from the dock. On the other monitor, he saw the lodge, with the raptors hanging down from the ceiling. On the radio, he heard their snarls.

'Do something, Timmy,' Lex said.

He pushed SETGRIDS DNL, even though it was flashing.

The screen answered:

WARNING: COMMAND EXECUTION ABORTED (AUX POWER LOW)

'What does that mean?' Tim said.

Gennaro snapped his fingers. 'That happened before. It means auxiliary power is low. You have to turn on main power.'

'I do?'

He pushed ELECTRICAL MAIN.

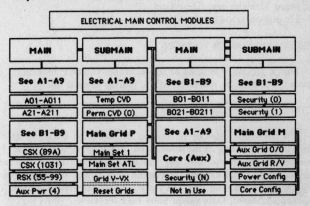

Tim groaned.

'What are you doing now?' Grant said. The whole screen was starting to flash.

Tim pushed MAIN.

Nothing happened. The screen continued to flash.

Tim pushed MAIN GRID P. He felt sick to his stomach with fear.

MAIN POWER GRID NOT ACTIVE/AUXILIARY POWER ONLY

The screen was still flashing. He pushed MAIN SET 1.

MAIN POWER ACTIVATED

All the lights in the room came on. All the monitor screens stopped flashing. 'Hey! All right!'

Tim pressed RESET GRIDS. Nothing happened for a moment. He glanced at the video monitors, then back at the main screen.

Which Grid Do You Want to Reset?				
Park	Maint	Security	Lodge	Other

Grant said something that Tim didn't hear, he only heard the tension in his voice. He was looking at Tim, worried.

Tim felt his heart thumping in his chest. Lex was yelling at him. He didn't want to look at the video monitor anymore. He could hear the sound of the bars bending in the lodge, and the raptors snarling. He heard Malcolm say, 'Dear God . . .'

He pushed LODGE.

SPECIFY GRID NUMBER TO RESET.

For a frozen interminable moment he couldn't remember the number, but then he remembered F4, and he pressed that.

ACTIVATING LODGE GRID F4 NOW.

On the video monitor he saw an explosion of sparks, sputtering down from the ceiling of the hotel room. The monitor flared white. Lex shouted 'What did you do!' but almost immediately the image came back and they could see that the raptors were caught between the bars, writhing and screaming in a hot cascade of sparks while Muldoon and the others cheered, their voices tinny over the radio.

'That's it,' Grant said, slapping Tim on the back. 'That's it! You did it!'

They were all standing and jumping up and down when Lex said, 'What about the ship?'

'The what?'

'The *ship*,' she said, and pointed to the screen.

On the monitor, the buildings beyond the bow of the ship were much larger, and moving to the right, as the ship turned left and prepared to dock. He saw crewmen heading out to the bow, preparing to tie up.

Tim scrambled back to his seat, and stared at the startup screen.

He studied the screen. TeleCom VBB and TeleCom RSD both looked like they might have something to do with telephones. He pressed TELECOM RSD.

YOU HAVE 23 WAITING CALLS AND/OR MESSAGES.
DO YOU WISH TO RECEIVE THEM NOW?

He pushed NO.

'Maybe the ship was one of the waiting calls,' Lex said. 'Maybe that way you could get the phone number!'

He ignored her.

ENTER THE NUMBER YOU WISH TO CALL OR PRESS F7 FOR DIRECTORY.

He pushed F7 and suddenly names and numbers spilled over the screen, an enormous directory. It wasn't alphabetical, and it took a while to scan it visually before he found what he was looking for:

> VSL ANNE B. (FREDDY) 708-3902

Now all he had to do was figure out how to dial. He pushed a row of buttons at the bottom of the screen:

DIAL NOW OR DIAL LATER?

He pushed DIAL NOW.

WE'RE SORRY, YOUR CALL CANNOT BE COMPLETED AS DIALED.
{ERROR-598}
PLEASE TRY AGAIN

He tried it again.

He heard a dial tone, then the tone of the numbers being automatically dialed in rapid succession.

'Is that it?' Grant said.

'Pretty good, Timmy,' Lex said. 'But they're almost there.' On the screen, they could see the prow of the ship closing on the Puntarenas dock. They heard a high-pitched squeal, and then a voice said, 'Ah, hello, John, this is Freddy. Do you read me, over?'

Tim picked up a phone on the console but heard only a dial tone.

'Ah, hello, John, this is Freddy, over?'

'*Answer it,*' Lex said.

Now they were all picking up phones, lifting every receiver in sight, but they heard only dial tones. Finally Tim saw a phone mounted on the side of the console with a blinking light.

'Ah, hello, control. This is Freddy. Do you read me, over?'

Tim grabbed the receiver. 'Hello, this is Tim Murphy, and I need you to –'

'Ah, say again, didn't get that, John.'

'Don't land the boat! Do you hear me?'

There was a pause. Then a puzzled voice said, 'Sounds like some damn kid.'

Tim said, 'Don't land the ship! Come back to the island!'

The voices sounded distant and scratchy. 'Did he – name was Murphy?' And another voice said, 'I didn't get – name.'

Tim looked frantically at the others. Gennaro reached for the phone. 'Let me do this. Can you get his name?'

There was the sharp crackle of static. '– got to be a joke or else – a – frigging ham operator – omething.'

Tim was working on the keyboard, there was probably some kind of a way to find out who Freddy was. . . .

'Can you hear me?' Gennaro said, into the phone. 'If you can hear me, answer me now, over.'

'Son,' came the drawled reply, 'we don't know who the hell you are, but you're not funny, and we're about to dock and we've got work to do. Now, identify yourself properly or get off this channel.'

Tim watched as the screen printed out FARRELL, FREDERICK D. (CAPT.).

'Try this for identification, Captain Farrell,' Gennaro said. 'If you don't turn that boat around and return to this island immediately, you will be found in violation of Section 509 of the Uniform Maritime Act, you will be subject to revocation of license, penalties in excess of fifty thousand dollars, and five years in jail. Do you hear that?'

There was a silence.

'Do you copy that, Captain Farrell?'

And then, distantly, they heard a voice say, 'I copy,' and another voice said, 'All ahead stern.' The boat began to turn away from the dock.

Lex began to cheer. Tim collapsed back in the chair, wiping the sweat from his forehead.

Grant said, 'What's the Uniform Maritime Act?'

'Who the hell knows?' Gennaro said.

They all watched the screen in satisfaction. The boat was definitely heading away from the shore.

'I guess the hard part's finished,' Gennaro said.

Grant shook his head. 'The hard part,' he said, 'is just beginning.'

Seventh Iteration

'Increasingly, the mathematics will demand the courage to face its implications.'

IAN MALCOLM

Seventh Iteration

Destroying the World

They moved Malcolm to another room in the lodge, to a clean bed. Hammond seemed to revive, and began bustling around, straightening up. 'Well,' he said, 'at least disaster is averted.'

'What disaster is that?' Malcolm said, sighing.

'Well,' Hammond said, 'they didn't get free and overrun the world.'

Malcolm sat up on one elbow. 'You were worried about that?'

'Surely that's what was at stake,' Hammond said. 'These animals, lacking predators, might get out and destroy the planet.'

'You egomaniacal *idiot*,' Malcolm said, in fury. 'Do you have any idea what you are talking about? You think you can destroy the planet? My, what intoxicating power you must have.' Malcolm sank back on the bed. 'You can't destroy this planet. You can't even come close.'

'Most people believe,' Hammond said stiffly, 'that the planet is in jeopardy.'

'Well, it's not,' Malcolm said.

'All the experts agree that our planet is in trouble.'

Malcolm sighed. 'Let me tell you about our planet,' he said. 'Our planet is four and a half billion years old. There has been life on this planet for nearly that long. Three point eight billion years. The first bacteria. And, later, the first multicellular animals, then the first complex creatures, in the sea, on the land. Then the great sweeping ages of animals – the amphibians, the dinosaurs, the mammals, each lasting millions upon millions of years. Great dynasties of creatures arising, flourishing, dying away. All this happening against a background of continuous and violent upheaval, mountain ranges thrust up and eroded away, cometary impacts, volcanic eruptions, oceans rising and falling, whole continents moving . . . Endless constant and violent change . . . Even today, the greatest geographical feature on the planet comes from two great continents colliding, buckling to make the Himalayan mountain range over millions of years. The planet has survived everything, in its time. It will certainly survive us.'

Hammond frowned. 'Just because it lasted a long time,' he said, 'doesn't mean it is permanent. If there was a radiation accident . . .'

'Suppose there was,' Malcolm said. 'Let's say we had a bad one, and all the plants and animals died, and the earth was clicking hot for a hundred thousand years. Life would survive somewhere – under the soil, or perhaps frozen in Arctic ice. And after all those years, when the planet was no longer inhospitable, life would again spread over the planet. The evolutionary process would begin again. It might take a few billion years for life to regain its present variety. And of course it would be very different from what it is now. But the earth would survive our folly. Life would survive our folly. Only we,' Malcolm said, 'think it wouldn't.'

Hammond said, 'Well, if the ozone layer gets thinner –'

'There will be more ultraviolet radiation reaching the surface. So what?'

'Well. It'll cause skin cancer.'

Malcolm shook his head. 'Ultraviolet radiation is good for life. It's powerful energy. It promotes mutation, change. Many forms of life will thrive with more UV radiation.'

'And many others will die out,' Hammond said.

Malcolm sighed. 'You think this is the first time such a thing has happened? Don't you know about oxygen?'

'I know it's necessary for life.'

'It is *now*,' Malcolm said. 'But oxygen is actually a metabolic poison. It's a corrosive gas, like fluorine, which is used to etch glass. And when oxygen was first produced as a waste product by certain plant cells – say, around three billion years ago – it created a crisis for all other life on our planet. Those plant cells were polluting the environment with a deadly poison. They were exhaling a lethal gas, and building up its concentration. A planet like Venus has less than one percent oxygen. On earth, the concentration of oxygen was going up rapidly – five, ten, eventually twenty-one percent! Earth had an atmosphere of pure poison! Incompatible with life!'

Hammond looked irritated. 'So what is your point? That modern pollutants will be incorporated, too?'

'No,' Malcolm said. 'My point is that life on earth can take care of itself. In the thinking of a human being, a hundred years is a long time. A hundred years ago, we didn't have cars and airplanes and computers and vaccines... It was a whole different world. But to the earth, a hundred years is *nothing*. A million years is *nothing*. This planet lives and breathes on a much vaster scale. We can't imagine its slow and powerful rhythms, and we haven't got the humility to try. We have been residents here for the blink of an eye. If we are gone tomorrow, the earth will not miss us.'

'And we very well might be gone,' Hammond said, huffing.

'Yes,' Malcolm said. 'We might.'

'So what are you saying? We shouldn't care about the environment?'

'No, of course not.'

'Then what?'

Malcolm coughed, and stared into the distance. 'Let's be clear. The planet is not in jeopardy. *We* are in jeopardy. We haven't got the power to destroy the planet – or to save it. But we might have the power to save ourselves.'

Under Control

Four hours had passed. It was afternoon; the sun was falling. The air conditioning was back on in the control room, and the computer was functioning properly. As near as they could determine, out of twenty-four people on the island, eight were dead and six more were missing. The visitor center and the Safari Lodge were both secure, and the northern perimeter seemed to be clear of dinosaurs. They had called authorities in San José for help. The Costa Rican National Guard was on its way, as well as an air ambulance to carry Malcolm to a hospital. But over the telephone, the Costa Rican guard had been distinctly cautious; undoubtedly calls would go back and forth between San José and Washington before help was finally sent to the island. And now it was growing late in the day; if the helicopters did not arrive soon, they would have to wait until morning.

In the meantime, there was nothing to do but wait. The ship was returning; the crew had discovered three young raptors scampering about in one of the aft holds, and had killed the animals. On Isla Nublar, the immediate danger appeared to have passed; everyone was in either the visitor center or the lodge. Tim had gotten quite good with the computer, and he flashed up a new screen.

Total Animals	292		
Species	**Expected**	**Found**	**Ver**
Tyrannosaurs	2	1	4.1
Maiasaurs	22	20	??
Stegosaurs	4	1	3.9
Triceratops	8	6	3.1
Procompsognathids	65	64	??
Othnielia	23	15	3.1
Velociraptors	37	27	??
Apatosaurs	17	12	3.1
Hadrosaurs	11	5	3.1
Dilophosaurs	7	4	4.3

Pterosaurs	6	5	4.3
Hypsilophodontids	34	14	??
Euoplocephalids	16	9	4.0
Styracosaurs	18	7	3.9
Callovosaurs	22	13	4.1
Total	**292**	**203**	

'What the hell is it doing now?' Gennaro said. 'Now it says there are *fewer* animals?'

Grant nodded. 'Probably.'

Ellie said, 'Jurassic Park is finally coming under control.'

'Meaning what?'

'Equilibrium.' Grant pointed to the monitors. On one of them, the hypsilophodonts leapt into the air as a pack of velociraptors entered the field from the west.

'The fences have been down for hours,' Grant said. 'The animals are mingling with each other. Populations reaching equilibrium – a true Jurassic equilibrium.'

'I don't think it was supposed to happen,' Gennaro said. 'The animals were never supposed to mix.'

'Well, they are.'

On another monitor, Grant saw a pack of raptors racing at full speed across an open field toward a four-ton hadrosaur. The hadrosaur turned to flee, and one of the raptors jumped onto its back, biting into the long neck, while others raced forward, circled around it, nipped at its legs, leapt up to slash at the belly with their powerful claws. Within minutes, six raptors had brought down the larger animal.

Grant stared, silently.

Ellie said, 'Is it the way you imagined?'

'I don't know what I imagined,' he said. He watched the monitor. 'No, not exactly.'

Muldoon said quietly, 'You know, it appears all the adult raptors are out right now.'

Grant didn't pay much attention at first. He just watched the monitors, the interaction of the great animals. In the south, the stegosaur was swinging its spiked tail, warily circling the baby tyrannosaur, which watched it, bemused, and occasionally lunged forward to nip ineffectually at the spikes. In the western quadrant, the adult triceratopsians were fighting among themselves, charging and locking horns. One animal already lay wounded and dying.

Muldoon said, 'We've got about an hour of good daylight left, Dr. Grant. If you want to try and find that nest.'

'Right,' Grant said. 'I do.'

'I was thinking,' Muldoon said, 'that, when the Costa Ricans come, they will probably imagine this island to be a military problem. Something to destroy as soon as possible.'

'Damn right,' Gennaro said.

'They'll bomb it from the air,' Muldoon said. 'Perhaps napalm, perhaps nerve gas as well. But from the air.'

'I hope they do,' Gennaro said. 'This island is too dangerous. Every animal on this island must be destroyed, and the sooner the better.'

Grant said, 'That's not satisfactory.' He got to his feet. 'Let's get started.'

'I don't think you understand, Alan,' Gennaro said. 'It's my opinion that this island is too dangerous. It must be destroyed. Every animal on this island must be destroyed, and that's what the Costa Rican guard will do. I think we should leave it in their capable hands. Do you understand what I'm saying?'

'Perfectly,' Grant said again.

'Then what's your problem?' Gennaro said. 'It's a military operation. Let them do it.'

Grant's back ached, where the raptor had clawed him. 'No,' he said. 'We have to take care of it.'

'Leave it to the experts,' Gennaro said.

Grant remembered how he had found Gennaro, just six hours earlier, huddled and terrified in the cab of a truck in the maintenance building. And suddenly he lost his temper and slammed the lawyer up against the concrete wall. 'Listen, you little bastard, you have a responsibility to this situation and you're going to start living up to it.'

'I am,' Gennaro said, coughing.

'No, you're not. You've shirked your responsibility all along, from the very beginning.'

'The hell —'

'You sold investors on an undertaking you didn't fully understand. You were part owner of a business you failed to supervise. You did not check the activities of a man whom you knew from experience to be a liar, and you permitted that man to screw around with the most dangerous technology in human history. I'd say you shirked your responsibility.'

Gennaro coughed again. 'Well, now I'm taking responsibility.'

'No,' Grant said. 'You're still shirking it. And you can't do that any more.' He released Gennaro, who bent over, gasping for breath. Grant turned to Muldoon. 'What have we got for weapons?'

Muldoon said, 'We've got some control nets, and shock prods.'

'How good are these shock prods?' Grant said.

'They're like bang sticks for sharks. They have an explosive capacitor tip, delivers a shock on contact. High voltage, low amps. Not fatal, but it's definitely incapacitating.'

'That's not going to do it,' Grant said. 'Not in the nest.'

'What nest?' Gennaro said, coughing.

'The raptor nest,' Ellie said.

'The *raptor nest*?'

Grant was saying, 'Have you got any radio collars?'

'I'm sure we do,' Muldoon said.

'Get one. And is there anything else that can be used for defense?'

Muldoon shook his head.

'Well, get whatever you can.'

Muldoon went away. Grant turned to Gennaro. 'Your island is a mess, Mr. Gennaro. Your experiment is a mess. It has to be cleaned up. But you can't do that until you know the extent of the mess. And that means finding the nests on the island. Especially the raptor nests. They'll be hidden. We have to find them, and inspect them, and count the eggs. We have to account for every animal born on this island. Then we can burn it down. But first we have a little work to do.'

Ellie was looking at the wall map, which now showed the animal ranges. Tim was working the keyboard. She pointed to the map. 'The raptors are localized in the southern area, down where the volcanic steam fields are. Maybe they like the warmth.'

'Is there any place to hide down there?'

'Turns out there is,' she said. 'There's massive concrete waterworks, to control flooding in the southern flatlands. Big underground area. Water and shade.'

Grant nodded. 'Then that's where they'll be.'

Ellie said, 'I think there's an entrance from the beach, too.' She turned to the consoles and said, 'Tim, show us the cutaways on the waterworks.' Tim wasn't listening. 'Tim?'

He was hunched over the keyboard. 'Just a minute,' he said. 'I found something.'

'What is it?'

'It's an unmarked storage room. I don't know what's there.'

'Then it might have weapons,' Grant said.

They were all behind the maintenance building, unlocking a steel storm door, lifting it up into the sunlight, to reveal concrete steps going down into the earth. 'Damned Arnold,' Muldoon said, as he hobbled down the steps. 'He must have known this was here all along.'

'Maybe not,' Grant said. 'He didn't try to go here.'

'Well, then, Hammond knew. Somebody knew.'

'Where is Hammond now?'

'Still in the lodge.'

They reached the bottom of the stairs, and came upon rows of gas masks hanging on the wall, in plastic containers. They shone their flashlights deeper into the room and saw several heavy glass cubes, two feet high, with steel caps. Grant could see small dark spheres inside the cubes. It was like being in a room full of giant pepper mills, he thought.

Muldoon opened the cap of one, reached in, and withdrew a sphere. He turned it in the light, frowning. 'I'll be damned.'

'What is it?' Grant said.

'MORO-12,' Muldoon said. 'It's an inhalation nerve gas. These are grenades. Lots and lots of grenades.'

'Let's get started,' Grant said grimly.

'It likes me,' Lex said, smiling. They were standing in the garage of the visitor center, by the little raptor that Grant had captured in the tunnel. She was petting the raptor through the cage bars. The animal rubbed up against her hand.

'I'd be careful there,' Muldoon said. 'They can give a nasty bite.'

'He likes me,' Lex said. 'His name is Clarence.'

'Clarence?'

'Yes,' Lex said.

Muldoon was holding the leather collar with the small metal box attached to it. Grant heard the high-pitched beeping in the headset. 'Is it a problem putting the collar on the animal?'

Lex was still petting the raptor, reaching through the cage. 'I bet he'll let me put it on him,' she said.

'I wouldn't try,' Muldoon said. 'They're unpredictable.'

'I bet he'll let me,' she said.

So Muldoon gave Lex the collar, and she held it out so the raptor could smell it. Then she slowly slipped it around the animal's neck. The raptor turned brighter green when Lex buckled it and closed the Velcro cover over the buckle. Then the animal relaxed, and turned paler again.

'I'll be damned,' Muldoon said.

'It's a chameleon,' Lex said.

'The other raptors couldn't do that,' Muldoon said, frowning. 'This wild animal must be different. By the way,' he said, turning to Grant, 'if they're all born females, how do they breed? You never explained that bit about the frog DNA.'

'It's not frog DNA,' Grant said. 'It's amphibian DNA. But the phenomenon happens to be particularly well documented in frogs. Especially West African frogs, if I remember.'

'What phenomenon is that?'

'Gender transition,' Grant said. 'Actually, it's just plain changing sex.' Grant explained that a number of plants and animals were known to have the ability to change their sex during life – orchids, some fish and shrimp, and now frogs. Frogs that had been observed to lay eggs were able to change, over a period of months, into complete males. They first adopted the fighting stance of males, they developed the mating whistle of males, they stimulated the hormones and grew the gonads of males, and eventually they successfully mated with females.

'You're kidding,' Gennaro said. 'And what makes it happen?'

'Apparently the change is stimulated by an environment in which all the animals are of the same sex. In that situation, some of the amphibians will spontaneously begin to change sex from female to male.'

'And you think that's what happened to the dinosaurs?'

'Until we have a better explanation, yes,' Grant said. 'I think that's what happened. Now, shall we find this nest?'

They piled into the Jeep, and Lex lifted the raptor from the cage. The animal seemed quite calm, almost tame in her hands. She gave it a final pat on the head, and released it.

The animal wouldn't leave.

'Go on, shoo!' Lex said. 'Go home!'

The raptor turned, and ran off into the foliage.

Grant held the receiver and wore the headphones. Muldoon drove. The car bounced along the main road, going south. Gennaro turned to Grant and said, 'What is it like, this nest?'

'Nobody knows,' Grant said.

'But I thought you'd dug them up.'

'I've dug up *fossil* dinosaur nests,' Grant said. 'But all fossils are distorted by the weight of millennia. We've made some hypotheses, some suppositions, but nobody really knows what the nests were like.'

Grant listened to the beeps, and signaled Muldoon to head farther west. It looked more and more as if Ellie had been correct: the nest was in the southern volcanic fields.

Grant shook his head. 'Not much about nesting behavior is clear,' he said. He found himself explaining about the modern reptiles, like crocodiles and alligators. Even their nesting behavior wasn't well understood. Actually, the American alligator was better studied than most, and in the case of alligators, only the female guarded the nest, and only until the time of birth. The male alligator had spent days in early spring lying beside the female in a mating pair, blowing bubbles on her cheeks and providing her with other signs of masculine attention designed to bring her to receptivity, causing her finally to lift her tail and allow him, as he lay beside her, to insert his penis. By the time the female built her nest, two months later, the male was long gone. And although the female guarded her cone-shaped, three-foot-high mud nest ferociously, her attention seemed to wane with time, and she generally abandoned her eggs by the time the hatchlings began to squeak and emerge from their shells. Thus, in the wild, a baby alligator began its life entirely on its own, and for that reason its belly was stuffed with egg yolk for nourishment in its early days.

'So the adult alligators don't protect the young?'

'Not as we imagine it,' Grant said. 'The biological parents both abandon the offspring. But there is a kind of group protection. Young alligators have a very distinctive distress cry, and it brings any adult who hears it – parent or not – to their assistance with a full-fledged, violent attack. Not a threat display. A full-on attack.'

'Oh.' Gennaro fell silent.

'But that's in all respects a distinctly reptile pattern,' Grant continued. 'For example, the alligator's biggest problem is to keep the eggs cool. The nests are always located in the shade. A temperature of ninety-eight point six degrees will kill an alligator egg, so the mother mostly guards her eggs to keep them cool.'

'And dinos aren't reptiles,' Muldoon said laconically.

'Exactly. The dinosaur nesting pattern could be much more closely related to that of any of a variety of birds.'

'So you actually mean you don't know,' Gennaro said, getting annoyed. 'You don't know what the nest is like?'

'No,' Grant said. 'I don't.'

'Well,' Gennaro said. 'So much for the damn experts.'

Grant ignored him. Already he could smell the sulfur. And up ahead he saw the rising steam of the volcanic fields.

The ground was hot, Gennaro thought, as he walked forward. It was actually *hot*. And here and there mud bubbled and spat up from the ground. And the reeking, sulfurous steam hissed in great shoulder-high plumes. He felt as if he were walking through hell.

He looked at Grant, walking along with the headset on, listening to the beeps. Grant in his cowboy boots and his jeans and his Hawaiian shirt, apparently very cool. Gennaro didn't feel cool. He was frightened to be in this stinking, hellish place, with the velociraptors somewhere around. He didn't understand how Grant could be so calm about it.

Or the woman. Sattler. She was walking along, too, just looking calmly around.

'Doesn't this bother you?' Gennaro said. 'I mean, worry you?'

'We've got to do it,' Grant said. He didn't say anything else.

They all walked forward, among the bubbling steam vents. Gennaro fingered the gas grenades that he had clipped to his belt. He turned to Ellie. 'Why isn't he worried about it?'

'Maybe he is,' she said. 'But he's also thought about this for his whole life.'

Gennaro nodded, and wondered what that would be like. Whether there was anything he had waited his whole life for. He decided there wasn't anything.

Grant squinted in the sunlight. Ahead, through veils of steam, an animal crouched, looking at them. Then it scampered away.

'Was that the raptor?' Ellie said.

'I think so. Or another one. Juvenile, anyway.'

She said, 'Leading us on?'

'Maybe.' Ellie had told him how the raptors had played at the fence to keep her attention while another climbed onto the roof. If true, such behavior implied a mental capacity that was beyond nearly all forms of life on earth. Classically, the ability to invent and execute plans was believed to be limited to only three species: chimpanzees, gorillas, and human beings. Now there was the possibility that a dinosaur might be able to do such a thing, too.

The raptor appeared again, darting into the light, then jumping away with a squeak. It really did seem to be leading them on.

Gennaro frowned. 'How smart are they?' he said.

'If you think of them as birds,' Grant said, 'then you have to wonder. Some new studies show the gray parrot has as much symbolic intelligence as a chimpanzee. And chimpanzees can definitely use language. Now researchers are finding that parrots have the emotional development of a three-year-old child, but their intelligence is unquestioned. Parrots can definitely reason symbolically.'

'But I've never heard of anybody killed by a parrot,' Gennaro grumbled.

Distantly, they could hear the sound of the surf on the island shore.

The volcanic fields were behind them now, and they faced a field of boulders. The little raptor climbed up onto one rock, and then abruptly disappeared.

'Where'd it go?' Ellie said.

Grant was listening to the earphones. The beeping stopped. 'He's gone.'

They hurried forward, and found in the midst of the rocks a small hole, like a rabbit hole. It was perhaps two feet in diameter. As they watched, the juvenile raptor reappeared, blinking in the light. Then it scampered away.

'No way,' Gennaro said. 'No way I'm going down there.'

Grant said nothing. He and Ellie began to plug in equipment. Soon he had a small video camera attached to a hand-held monitor. He tied the camera to a rope, turned it on, and lowered it down the hole.

'You can't see anything that way,' Gennaro said.

'Let it adjust,' Grant said. There was enough light along the upper tunnel for them to see smooth dirt walls, and then the tunnel opened out suddenly, abruptly. Over the microphone, they heard a squeaking sound. Then a lower, trumpeting sound. More noises, coming from many animals.

'Sounds like the nest, all right,' Ellie said.

'But you can't *see* anything,' Gennaro said. He wiped the sweat off his forehead.

'No,' Grant said. 'But I can hear.' He listened for a while longer, and then hauled the camera out, and set it on the ground. 'Let's get started.' He climbed up toward the hole. Ellie went to get a flashlight and a shock stick. Grant pulled the gas mask on over his face, and crouched down awkwardly, extending his legs backward.

'You can't be serious about going down there,' Gennaro said.

Grant nodded. 'It doesn't thrill me. I'll go first, then Ellie, then you come after.'

'Now, wait a minute,' Gennaro said, in sudden alarm. 'Why don't we drop these nerve-gas grenades down the hole, then go down afterward? Doesn't that make more sense?'

'Ellie, you got the flashlight?'

She handed the flashlight to Grant.

'What about it?' Gennaro said. 'What do you say?'

'I'd like nothing better,' Grant said. He backed down toward the hole. 'You ever seen anything die from poison gas?'

'No . . .'

'It generally causes convulsions. Bad convulsions.'

'Well, I'm sorry if it's unpleasant, but −'

'Look,' Grant said. 'We're going into this nest to find out how many animals have hatched. If you kill the animals first, and some of them fall on the nests in their spasms, that will ruin our ability to see what was there. So we can't do that.'

'But –'

'You made these animals, Mr. Gennaro.'

'*I* didn't.'

'Your money did. Your efforts did. You helped create them. They're your creation. And you can't just kill them because you feel a little nervous now.'

'I'm not a little nervous,' Gennaro said. 'I'm scared shi –'

'Follow me,' Grant said. Ellie handed him a shock stick. He pushed backward through the hole, and grunted. 'Tight fit.'

Grant exhaled, and extended his arms forward in front of him, and there was a kind of whoosh, and he was gone.

The hole gaped, empty and black.

'What happened to him?' Gennaro said, alarmed.

Ellie stepped forward and leaned close to the hole, listening at the opening. She clicked the radio, said softly, 'Alan?'

There was a long silence. Then they heard faintly: 'I'm here.'

'Is everything all right, Alan?'

Another long silence. When Grant finally spoke, his voice sounded distinctly odd, almost awestruck.

'Everything's fine,' he said.

Almost Paradigm

In the lodge, John Hammond paced back and forth in Malcolm's room. Hammond was impatient and uncomfortable. Since marshaling the effort for his last outburst, Malcolm had slipped into a coma, and now it appeared to Hammond that he might actually die. Of course a helicopter had been sent for, but God knows when it would arrive. The thought that Malcolm might die in the meantime filled Hammond with anxiety and dread.

And, paradoxically, Hammond found it all much worse because he disliked the mathematician so much. It was worse than if the man were his friend. Hammond felt that Malcolm's death, should it occur, would be the final rebuke, and that was more than Hammond could bear.

In any case, the smell in the room was quite ghastly. Quite ghastly. The rotten decay of human flesh.

'Everything . . . parad . . .' Malcolm said, tossing on the pillow.

'Is he waking up?' Hammond said.

Harding shook his head.

'What did he say? Something about paradise?'

'I didn't catch it,' Harding said.

Hammond paced some more. He pushed the window wider, trying to get some fresh air. Finally, when he couldn't stand it, he said, 'Is' there any problem about going outside?'

'I don't think so, no,' Harding said. 'I think this area is all right.'

'Well, look, I'm going outside for a bit.'

'All right,' Harding said. He adjusted the flow on the intravenous antibiotics.

'I'll be back soon.'

'All right.'

Hammond left, stepping out into the daylight, wondering why he had bothered to justify himself to Harding. After all, the man was his employee. Hammond had no need to explain himself.

He went through the gates of the fence, looking around the park. It was late afternoon, the time when the blowing mist was thinned, and the sun sometimes came out. The sun was out now, and Hammond took it as an omen. Say what they would, he knew that his park had promise. And even if that impetuous fool Gennaro decided to burn it to the ground, it would not make much difference.

Hammond knew that in two separate vaults at InGen headquarters in Palo Alto were dozens of frozen embryos. It would not be a problem to grow them again, on another island, elsewhere in the world. And if there had been problems here, then the next time they would solve those problems. That was how progress occurred. By solving problems.

As he thought about it, he concluded that Wu had not really been the man for the job. Wu had obviously been sloppy, too casual with his great undertaking. And Wu had been too preoccupied with the idea of making improvements. Instead of making dinosaurs, he had wanted to improve on them. Hammond suspected darkly that was the reason for the downfall of the park.

Wu was the reason.

Also, he had to admit that John Arnold was ill suited for the job of chief engineer. Arnold had impressive credentials, but at this point in his career he was tired, and he was a fretful worrier. He hadn't been organized, and he had missed things. Important things.

In truth, neither Wu nor Arnold had had the most important characteristic, Hammond decided. The characteristic of *vision*. That great sweeping act of imagination which evoked a marvelous park, where children pressed against the fences, wondering at the extraordinary creatures, come alive from their storybooks. Real *vision*. The ability to see the future. The ability to marshal resources to make that future vision a reality.

No, neither Wu nor Arnold was suited to that task.

And, for that matter, Ed Regis had been a poor choice, too. Harding was at best an indifferent choice. Muldoon was a drunk ...

Hammond shook his head. He would do better next time.

Lost in his thoughts, he headed toward his bungalow, following the little path that ran north from the visitor center. He passed one of the workmen, who nodded curtly. Hammond did not return the nod. He found the Tican workmen to be uniformly insolent. To tell the truth, the choice of this island off Costa Rica had also been unwise. He would not make such obvious mistakes again –

When it came, the roar of the dinosaur seemed frighteningly close. Hammond spun so quickly he fell on the path, and when he looked back he thought he saw the shadow of the juvenile T-rex, moving in the foliage beside the flagstone path, moving toward him.

What was the T-rex doing here? Why was it outside the fences?

Hammond felt a flash of rage: and then he saw the Tican workman, running for his life, and Hammond took the moment to get to his feet and dash blindly into the forest on the opposite side of the path. He was plunged in darkness; he stumbled and fell, his face mashed into wet leaves and damp earth, and he staggered back up to his feet, ran onward, fell again, and then ran once more. Now he was moving down a steep hillside, and he couldn't keep his balance. He tumbled helplessly, rolling and spinning over the soft ground, before finally coming to a stop at the foot of the hill. His face splashed into shallow tepid water, which gurgled around him and ran up his nose.

He was lying face down in a little stream.

He had panicked! What a fool! He should have gone to his bungalow! Hammond cursed himself. As he got to his feet, he felt a sharp pain in his right ankle that brought tears to his eyes. He tested it gingerly: it might be broken. He forced himself to put his full weight on it, gritting his teeth. Yes.

Almost certainly broken.

In the control room, Lex said to Tim, 'I wish they had taken us with them to the nest.'

'It's too dangerous for us, Lex,' Tim said. 'We have to stay here. Hey, listen to this one.' He pressed another button, and a recorded tyrannosaur roar echoed over the loudspeakers in the park.

'That's neat,' Lex said. 'That's better than the other one.'

'You can do it, too,' Tim said. 'And if you push this, you get reverb.'

'Let me try,' Lex said. She pushed the button. The tyrannosaur roared again. 'Can we make it last longer?' she said.

'Sure,' Tim said. 'We just twist this thing here . . .'

Lying at the bottom of the hill, Hammond heard the tyrannosaur roar, bellowing through the jungle.

Jesus.

He shivered, hearing that sound. It was terrifying, a scream from some other world. He waited to see what would happen. What would the tyrannosaur do? Had it already gotten that workman? Hammond waited, hearing only the buzz of the jungle cicadas, until he realized he was holding his breath, and let out a long sigh.

With his injured ankle, he couldn't climb the hill. He would have to wait at the bottom of the ravine. After the tyrannosaur had gone, he would call for help. Meanwhile, he was in no danger here.

Then he heard an amplified voice say, 'Come on, Timmy, I get to try it too. Come on. Let me make the noise.'

The kids!

The tyrannosaur roared again, but this time it had distinct musical overtones, and a kind of echo, persisting afterward.

'Neat one,' said the little girl. 'Do it again.'

Those damned kids!

He should never have brought those kids. They had been nothing but trouble from the beginning. Nobody wanted them around. Hammond had only brought them because he thought it would stop Gennaro from destroying the resort, but Gennaro was going to do it anyway. And the kids had obviously gotten into the control room and started fooling around – now, who had allowed that?

He felt his heart begin to race, and felt an uneasy shortness of breath. He forced himself to relax. There was nothing wrong. Although he could not climb the hill, he could not be more than a hundred yards from his own bungalow, and the visitor center. Hammond sat down in the damp earth, listening to the sounds in the jungle around him. And then, after a while, he began to shout for help.

Malcolm's voice was no louder than a whisper. 'Everything . . . looks different . . . on the other side,' he said.

Harding leaned close to him. 'On the other side?' He thought that Malcolm was talking about dying.

'When . . . shifts,' Malcolm said.

'Shifts?'

Malcolm didn't answer. His dry lips moved. 'Paradigm,' he said finally.

'Paradigm shifts?' Harding said. He knew about paradigm shifts. For the last two decades, they had been the fashionable way to talk about scientific change. 'Paradigm' was just another word for a model, but as scientists used it the term meant something more, a world view. A larger way of seeing the world. Paradigm shifts were said to occur whenever science made a major change in its view of the world. Such changes were relatively rare, occurring about once a century. Darwinian evolution had forced a paradigm shift. Quantum mechanics had forced a smaller shift.

'No,' Malcolm said. 'Not . . . paradigm . . . beyond . . .'

'Beyond paradigm?' Harding said.

'Don't care about . . . what . . . anymore . . .'

Harding sighed. Despite all efforts, Malcolm was rapidly slipping into a terminal delirium. His fever was higher, and they were almost out of his antibiotics.

'What don't you care about?'

'Anything,' Malcolm said. 'Because . . . everything looks different . . . on the other side.'

And he smiled.

Descent

'You're crazy,' Gennaro said to Ellie Sattler, watching as she squeezed backward into the rabbit hole, stretching her arms forward. 'You're crazy to do that!'

She smiled. 'Probably,' she said. She reached forward with her outstretched hands, and pushed backward against the sides of the hole. And suddenly she was gone.

The hole gaped black.

Gennaro began to sweat. He turned to Muldoon, who was standing by the Jeep. 'I'm not doing this,' he said.

'Yes, you are.'

'I can't do this. I can't.'

'They're waiting for you,' Muldoon said. 'You have to.'

'Christ only knows what's down there,' Gennaro said. 'I'm telling you, I can't do it.'

'You have to.'

Gennaro turned away, looked at the hole, looked back. 'I can't. You can't make me.'

'I suppose not,' Muldoon said. He held up the stainless-steel prod. 'Ever felt a shock stick?'

'No.'

'Doesn't do much,' Muldoon said. 'Almost never fatal. Generally knocks you flat. Perhaps loosens your bowels. But it doesn't usually have any permanent effect. At least, not on dinos. But, then, people are much smaller.'

Gennaro looked at the stick. 'You wouldn't.'

'I think you'd better go down and count those animals,' Muldoon said. 'And you better hurry.'

Gennaro looked back at the hole, at the black opening, a mouth in the earth. Then he looked at Muldoon, standing there, large and impassive.

Gennaro was sweating and lightheaded. He started walking toward the hole. From a distance it appeared small, but as he came closer it seemed to grow larger.

'That's it,' Muldoon said.

Gennaro climbed backward into the hole, but he began to feel too frightened to continue that way – the idea of backing into the unknown filled him with dread – so at the last minute he turned around and climbed head first into the hole, extending his arms forward and kicking his feet, because at least he would see where he was going. He pulled the gas mask over his face.

And suddenly he was rushing forward, sliding into blackness, seeing the dirt walls disappear into darkness before him, and then the walls became narrower – much narrower – terrifyingly narrow – and he was lost in the pain of a squeezing compression that became steadily worse and worse, that crushed the air out of his lungs, and he was only dimly aware that the tunnel tilted slightly upward, along the path, shifting his body, leaving him gasping and seeing spots before his eyes, and the pain was extreme.

And then suddenly the tunnel tilted downward again, and it became wider, and Gennaro felt rough surfaces, concrete, and cold air. His body was suddenly free, and bouncing, tumbling on concrete.

And then he fell.

Voices in the darkness. Fingers touching him, reaching forward from the whispered voices. The air was cold, like a cave.

'– okay?'

'He looks okay, yes.'

'He's breathing . . .'

'Fine.'

A female hand caressing his face. It was Ellie. 'Can you hear?' she whispered.

'Why is everybody whispering?' he said.

'Because.' She pointed.

Gennaro turned, rolled, got slowly to his feet. He stared as his vision grew accustomed to the darkness. But the first thing that he saw, gleaming in the darkness, was eyes. Glowing green eyes.

Dozens of eyes. All around him.

He was on a concrete ledge, a kind of embankment, about seven feet above the floor. Large steel junction boxes provided a makeshift hiding place, protecting them from the view of the two full-size velociraptors that stood directly before them, not five feet away. The animals were dark green with brownish tiger stripes. They stood upright, balancing on their stiff extended tails. They were totally silent, looking around watchfully with large dark eyes. At the feet of the adults, baby velociraptors skittered and chirped. Farther back, in the darkness, juveniles tumbled and played, giving short snarls and growls.

Gennaro did not dare to breathe.

Two raptors!

Crouched on the ledge, he was only a foot or two above the animals' head height. The raptors were edgy, their heads jerking nervously up and down. From time to time they snorted impatiently. Then they moved off, turning back toward the main group.

As his eyes adjusted, Gennaro could now see that they were in some kind of an enormous underground structure, but it was man-made – there were seams of poured concrete, and the nubs of protruding steel rods. And within this vast echoing space were many animals: Gennaro guessed at least thirty raptors. Perhaps more.

'It's a colony,' Grant said, whispering. 'Four or six adults. The rest juveniles and infants. At least two hatchings. One last year and one this year. These babies look about four months old. Probably hatched in April.'

One of the babies, curious, scampered up on the ledge, and came toward them, squeaking. It was now only ten feet away.

'Oh Jesus,' Gennaro said. But immediately one of the adults came forward, raised its head, and gently nudged the baby to turn back. The baby chittered a protest, then hopped up to stand on the snout of the adult. The adult moved slowly, allowing the baby to climb over its head, down its neck, onto its back. From that protected spot, the infant turned, and chirped noisily at the three intruders.

The adults still did not seem to notice them at all.

'I don't get it,' Gennaro whispered. 'Why aren't they attacking?'

Grant shook his head. 'They must not see us. And there aren't any eggs at the moment . . . Makes them more relaxed.'

'*Relaxed?*' Gennaro said. 'How long do we have to stay here?'

'Long enough to do the count,' Grant said.

As Grant saw it, there were three nests, attended by three sets of parents. The division of territory was centered roughly around the nests, although the offspring seemed to overlap, and run into different territories. The adults were benign with the young ones, and tougher with the juveniles, occasionally snapping at the older animals when their play got too rough.

At that moment, a juvenile raptor came up to Ellie and rubbed his head against her leg. She looked down and saw the leather collar with the black box. It was damp in one place. And it had chafed the skin of the young animal's neck.

The juvenile whimpered.

In the big room below, one of the adults turned curiously toward the sound.

'You think I can take it off?' she asked.

'Just do it quickly.'

'Oo-kay,' she said, squatting beside the small animal. It whimpered again.

The adults snorted, bobbed their heads.

Ellie petted the little juvenile, trying to soothe it, to silence its whimpering. She moved her hands toward the leather collar, lifted back the Velcro tab with a tearing sound. The adults jerked their heads.

Then one began to walk toward her.

'Oh *shit*,' Gennaro said, under his breath.

'Don't move,' Grant said. 'Stay calm.'

The adult walked past them, its long curved toes clicking on the concrete. The animal paused in front of Ellie, who stayed crouched by the juvenile, behind a steel box. The juvenile was exposed, and Ellie's hand was still on the collar. The adult raised its head, and sniffed the air. The adult's big head was very close to her hand, but it could not see her because of the junction box. A tongue flicked out, tentatively.

Grant reached for a gas grenade, plucked it from his belt, held his thumb on the pin. Gennaro put out a restraining hand, shook his head, nodded to Ellie.

She wasn't wearing her mask.

Grant set the grenade down, reached for the shock prod. The adult was still very close to Ellie.

Ellie eased the leather strap off. The metal of the buckle clinked on concrete. The adult's head jerked fractionally, and then cocked to one side, curious. It was moving forward again to investigate, when the little juvenile squeaked happily and scampered away. The adult remained by Ellie. Then finally it turned, and walked back to the center of the nest.

Gennaro gave a long exhalation. 'Jesus. Can we leave?'

'No,' Grant said. 'But I think we can get some work done now.'

In the phosphorescent green glow of the night-vision goggles, Grant peered down into the room from the ledge, looking at the first nest. It was made of mud and straw, formed into a broad, shallow basket shape. He counted the remains of fourteen eggs. Of course he couldn't count the actual shells from this distance, and in any case they were long since broken and scattered over the floor, but he was able to count the indentations in the mud. Apparently the raptors made their nests shortly before the eggs were laid, and the eggs left a permanent impression in the mud. He also saw evidence that at least one had broken. He credited thirteen animals.

The second nest had broken in half. But Grant estimated it had contained nine eggshells. The third nest had fifteen eggs, but it appeared that three eggs had been broken early.

'What's that total?' Gennaro said.

'Thirty-four born,' Grant said.

'And how many do you see?'

Grant shook his head. The animals were running all over the cavernous interior space, darting in and out of the light.

'I've been watching,' Ellie said, shining her light down at her notepad. 'You'd have to take photos to be sure, but the snout markings of the infants are all different. My count is thirty-three.'

'And juveniles?'

'Twenty-two. But, Alan – do you notice anything funny about them?'

'Like what?' Grant whispered.

'How they arrange themselves spatially. They're falling into some kind of a pattern or arrangement in the room.'

Grant frowned. He said, 'It's pretty dark . . .'

'No, look. Look for yourself. Watch the little ones. When they are playing, they tumble and run every which way. But in between, when the babies are standing around, notice how they orient their bodies. They face either that wall, or the opposite wall. It's like they line up.'

'I don't know, Ellie. You think there's a colony metastructure? Like bees?'

'No, not exactly,' she said. 'It's more subtle than that. It's just a tendency.'

'And the babies do it?'

'No. They all do it. The adults do it, too. Watch them. I'm telling you, they line up.'

Grant frowned. It seemed as if she was right. The animals engaged in all sorts of behavior, but during pauses, moments when they were watching or relaxing, they seemed to orient themselves in particular ways, almost as if there were invisible lines on the floor.

'Beats me,' Grant said. 'Maybe there's a breeze . . .'

'I don't feel one, Alan.'

'What are they doing? Some kind of social organization expressed as spatial structure?'

'That doesn't make sense,' she said. 'Because they all do it.'

Gennaro flipped up his watch. 'I knew this thing would come in handy one day.' Beneath the watch face was a compass.

Grant said, 'You have much use for that in court?'

'No.' Gennaro shook his head. 'My wife gave it to me,' he explained, 'for my birthday.' He peered at the compass. 'Well,' he said, 'they're not lined up according to anything . . . I guess they're sort of northeast-southwest, something like that.'

Ellie said, 'Maybe they're hearing something, turning their heads so they can hear . . .'

Grant frowned.

'Or maybe it's just ritual behavior,' she said, 'species-specific behavior that serves to identify them to one another. But maybe it doesn't have any broader meaning.' Ellie sighed. 'Or maybe they're weird. Maybe dinosaurs are weird. Or maybe it's a kind of communication.'

Grant was thinking the same thing. Bees could communicate spatially, by doing a kind of dance. Perhaps dinosaurs could do the same thing.

Gennaro watched them and said, 'Why don't they go outside?'

'They're nocturnal.'

'Yes, but it almost seems like they're hiding.'

Grant shrugged. In the next moment, the infants began to squeak and hop excitedly. The adults watched curiously for a moment. And then, with hoots and cries that echoed in the dark cavernous space, all the dinosaurs wheeled and ran, heading down the concrete tunnel, into the darkness beyond.

Hammond

John Hammond sat down heavily in the damp earth of the hillside and tried to catch his breath. Dear God, it was hot, he thought. Hot and humid. He felt as if he were breathing through a sponge.

He looked down at the streambed, now forty feet below. It seemed like hours since he had left the trickling water and begun to climb the hill. His ankle was now swollen and dark purple. He couldn't put any weight on it at all. He was forced to hop up the hill on his other leg, which now burned with pain from the exertion.

And he was thirsty. Before leaving the stream behind, he had drunk from it, even though he knew this was unwise. Now he felt dizzy, and the world sometimes swirled around him. He was having trouble with his balance. But he knew he had to climb the hill, and get back to the path above. Hammond thought he had heard footsteps on the path several times during the previous hour, and each time he had shouted for help. But somehow his voice hadn't carried far enough; he hadn't been rescued. And so, as the afternoon wore on, he began to realize that he would have to climb the hillside, injured leg or not. And that was what he was doing now.

Those damned kids.

Hammond shook his head, trying to clear it. He had been climbing for more than an hour, and he had gone only a third of the distance up the hill. And he was tired, panting like an old dog. His leg throbbed. He was dizzy. Of course, he knew perfectly well that he was in no danger – he was almost within sight of his bungalow, for God's sake – but he had to admit he was tired. Sitting on the hillside, he found he didn't really want to move any more.

And why shouldn't he be tired? he thought. He was seventy-six years old. That was no age to be climbing around hillsides. Even though Hammond was in peak condition for a man his age. Personally, he expected to live to be a hundred. It was just a matter of taking care of yourself, of taking care of things as they came up. Certainly he had plenty of reasons to live. Other parks to build. Other wonders to create –

He heard a squeaking, then a chittering sound. Some kind of small birds, hopping in the undergrowth. He'd been hearing small animals all afternoon. There were all kinds of things out here: rats, possums, snakes.

The squeaking got louder, and small bits of earth rolled down the hillside past him. Something was coming. Then he saw a dark green animal hopping down the hill toward him – and another – and another.

Compys, he thought with a chill.

Scavengers.

The compys didn't look dangerous. They were about as big as chickens, and they moved up and down with little nervous jerks, like chickens. But he knew they were poisonous. Their bites had a slow-acting poison that they used to kill crippled animals.

Crippled animals, he thought, frowning.

The first of the compys perched on the hillside, staring at him. It stayed about five feet away, beyond his reach, and just watched him. Others came down soon after, and they stood in a row. Watching. They hopped up and down and chittered and waved their little clawed hands.

'Shoo! Get out!' he said, and threw a rock.

The compys backed away, but only a foot or two. They weren't afraid. They seemed to know he couldn't hurt them.

Angrily, Hammond tore a branch from a tree and swiped at them with it. The compys dodged, nipped at the leaves, squeaked happily. They seemed to think he was playing a game.

He thought again about the poison. He remembered that one of the animal handlers had been bitten by a compy in a cage. The handler had said the poison was like a narcotic – peaceful, dreamy. No pain.

You just wanted to go to sleep.

The hell with that, he thought. Hammond picked up a rock, aimed carefully, and threw it, striking one compy flat in the chest. The little animal shrieked in alarm as it was knocked backward, and rolled over its tail. The other animals immediately backed away.

Better.

Hammond turned away, and started to climb the hill once more. Holding branches in both hands, he hopped on his left leg, feeling the ache in his thigh. He had not gone more than ten feet when one of the compys jumped onto his back. He flung his arms wildly, knocking the animal away, but lost his balance and slid back down the hillside. As he came to a stop, a second compy sprang forward, and took a tiny nip from his hand. He looked with horror, seeing the blood flow over his fingers. He turned and began to scramble up the hillside again.

Another compy jumped onto his shoulder, and he felt a brief pain as it bit the back of his neck. He shrieked and smacked the animal away. He turned to face the animals, breathing hard, and they stood all around him, hopping up and down and cocking their heads, watching him. From the bite on his neck, he felt warmth flow through his shoulders, down his spine.

Lying on his back on the hillside, he began to feel strangely relaxed, detached from himself. But he realized that nothing was wrong. No error had been made. Malcolm was quite incorrect in his analysis. Hammond lay very still, as still as a child in its crib, and he felt wonderfully peaceful. When the next compy came up and bit his ankle, he made only a half-hearted effort to kick it away. The little animals edged closer. Soon they were chittering all around him, like excited birds. He raised his head as another compy jumped onto his chest, the animal surprisingly light and delicate. Hammond felt only a slight pain, very slight, as the compy bent to chew his neck.

The Beach

Chasing the dinosaurs, following the curves and slopes of concrete, Grant suddenly burst out through a cavernous opening, and found himself standing on the beach, looking at the Pacific Ocean. All around him, the young velociraptors were scampering and kicking in the sand. But, one by one, the animals moved back into the shade of the palm trees at the edge of the mangrove swamp, and there they stood, lined up in their peculiar fashion, watching the ocean. They stared fixedly to the south.

'I don't get it,' Gennaro said.

'I don't, either,' Grant said, 'except that they clearly don't like the sun.' It wasn't very sunny on the beach; a light mist blew, and the ocean was hazy. But why had they suddenly left the nest? What had brought the entire colony to the beach?

Gennaro flipped up the dial on his watch, and looked at the way the animals were standing. 'Northeast-southwest. Same as before.'

Behind the beach, deeper in the woods, they heard the hum of the electric fence. 'At least we know how they get outside the fence,' Ellie said.

Then they heard the throb of marine diesels, and through the mist they saw a ship appearing in the south. A large freighter, it slowly moved north.

'So that's why they came out?' Gennaro said.

Grant nodded. 'They must have heard it coming.'

As the freighter passed, all the animals watched it, standing silent except for the occasional chirp or squeak. Grant was struck by the coordination of their behavior, the way they moved and acted as a group. But perhaps it was not really so mysterious. In his mind, he reviewed the sequence of events that had begun in the cave.

First the infants had been agitated. Then the adults had noticed. And finally all the animals had stampeded to the beach. That sequence seemed to imply that the younger animals, with keener hearing, had detected the boat first. Then the adults had led the troop out onto the beach. And as Grant looked, he saw that the adults were in charge now.

There was a clear spatial organization along the beach, and as the animals settled down, it was not loose and shifting, the way it had been inside. Rather, it was quite regular, almost regimented. The adults were spaced every ten yards or so, each adult surrounded by a cluster of infants. The juveniles were positioned between, and slightly ahead of, the adults.

But Grant also saw that all the adults were not equal. There was a female with a distinctive stripe along her head, and she was in the very center of the group as it ranged along the beach. That same female had stayed in the center of the nesting area, too. He guessed that, like certain monkey troops, the raptors were organized around a matriarchal pecking order, and that this striped animal was the alpha female of the colony. The males, he saw, were arranged defensively at the perimeter of the group.

But unlike monkeys, which were loosely and flexibly organized, the dinosaurs settled into a rigid arrangement – almost a military formation, it seemed. Then, too, there was the oddity of the northeast-southwest spatial orientation. That was beyond Grant. But, in another sense, he was not surprised. Paleontologists had been digging up bones for so long that they had forgotten how little information could be gleaned from a skeleton. Bones might tell you something about the gross appearance of an animal, its height and weight. They might tell you something about how the muscles attached, and therefore something about the crude behavior of the animal during life. They might give you clues to the few diseases that affected bone. But a skeleton was a poor thing, really, from which to try and deduce the total behavior of an organism.

Since bones were all the paleontologists had, bones were what they used. Like other paleontologists, Grant had become very expert at working with bones. And somewhere along the way, he had started to forget the unprovable possibilities – that the dinosaurs might be truly different animals, that they might possess behavior and social life organized along lines that were utterly mysterious to their later, mammalian descendants. That, since the dinosaurs were fundamentally birds –

'Oh, my God,' Grant said.

He stared at the raptors, ranged along the beach in a rigid formation, silently watching the boat. And he suddenly understood what he was looking at.

'Those animals,' Gennaro said, shaking his head, 'they sure are desperate to escape from here.'

'No,' Grant said. 'They don't want to escape at all.'

'They don't?'

'No,' Grant said. 'They want to migrate.'

Approaching Dark

'Migrating!' Ellie said. 'That's fantastic!'

'Yes,' Grant said. He was grinning.

Ellie said. 'Where do you suppose they want to go?'

'I don't know,' Grant said, and then the big helicopters burst through the fog, thundering and wheeling over the landscape, their underbellies heavy with armament. The raptors scattered in alarm as one of the helicopters circled back, following the line of the surf, and then moved in to land on the beach. A door was flung open and soldiers in olive uniforms came running toward them. Grant heard the rapid babble of voices in Spanish and saw that Muldoon was already aboard with the kids. One of the soldiers said in English, 'Please, you will come with us. Please, there is no time here.'

Grant looked back at the beach where the raptors had been, but they were gone. All the animals had vanished. It was as if they had never existed. The soldiers were tugging at him, and he allowed himself to be led beneath the thumping blades and climbed up through the big door. Muldoon leaned over and shouted in Grant's ear, 'They want us out of here now. They're going to do it now!'

The soldiers pushed Grant and Ellie and Gennaro into seats, and helped them clip on the harnesses. Tim and Lex waved to him and he suddenly saw how young they were, and how exhausted. Lex was yawning, leaning against her brother's shoulder.

An officer came toward Grant and shouted, '*Señor:* are you in charge?'

'No,' Grant said. 'I'm not in charge.'

'Who is in charge, please?'

'I don't know.'

The officer went on to Gennaro, and asked the same question: 'Are you in charge?'

'No,' Gennaro said.

The officer looked at Ellie, but said nothing to her. The door was left open as the helicopter lifted away from the beach, and Grant leaned out to see if he could catch a last look at the raptors, but then the helicopter was above the palm trees, moving north over the island.

Grant leaned to Muldoon, and shouted: 'What about the others?'

Muldoon shouted, 'They've already taken off Harding and some workmen. Hammond had an accident. Found him on the hill near his bungalow. Must have fallen.'

'Is he all right?' Grant said.

'No. Compys got him.'

'What about Malcolm?' Grant said.

Muldoon shook his head.

Grant was too tired to feel much of anything. He turned away, and looked back out the door. It was getting dark now, and in the fading light he could barely see the little rex, with bloody jaws, crouched over a hadrosaur by the edge of the lagoon and looking up at the helicopter and roaring as it passed by.

Somewhere behind them they heard explosions, and then ahead they saw another helicopter wheeling through the mist over the visitor center, and a moment later the building burst in a bright orange fireball, and Lex began to cry, and Ellie put her arm around her and tried to get her not to look.

Grant was staring down at the ground, and he had a last glimpse of the hypsilophodonts, leaping gracefully as gazelles, moments before another explosion flared bright beneath them. Their helicopter gained altitude, and then moved east, out over the ocean.

Grant sat back in his seat. He thought of the dinosaurs standing on the beach, and he wondered where they would migrate if they could, and he realized he would never know, and he felt sad and relieved in the same moment.

The officer came forward again, bending close to his face. 'Are you in charge?'

'No,' Grant said.

'Please, señor, who is in charge?'

'Nobody,' Grant said.

The helicopter gained speed as it headed toward the mainland. It was cold now, and the soldiers muscled the door closed. As they did, Grant looked back just once, and saw the island against a deep purple sky and sea, cloaked in a deep mist that blurred the white-hot explosions that burst rapidly, one after another, until it seemed the entire island was glowing, a diminishing bright spot in the darkening night.

Epilogue: San José

Days went by. The government was polite, and put them up in a nice hotel in San José. They were free to come and go, and to call whomever they wished. But they were not permitted to leave the country. Each day a young man from the American Embassy came to visit them, to ask if they needed anything, and to explain that Washington was doing everything it could to hasten their departure. But the plain fact was that many people had died in a territorial possession of Costa Rica. The plain fact was that an ecological disaster had been narrowly averted. The government of Costa Rica felt it had been misled and deceived by John Hammond and his plans for the island. Under the circumstances, the government was not disposed to release survivors in a hurry. They did not even permit the burial of Hammond or Ian Malcolm. They simply waited.

Each day it seemed to Grant he was taken to another government office, where he was questioned by another courteous, intelligent government officer. They made him go over his story, again and again. How Grant had met John Hammond. What Grant knew of the project. How Grant had received the fax from New York. Why Grant had gone to the island. What had happened at the island.

The same details, again and again, day after day. The same story.

For a long time, Grant thought they must believe he was lying to them, and that there was something they wanted him to tell, although he could not imagine what it was. Yet, in some odd way, they seemed to be waiting.

Finally, he was sitting around the swimming pool of the hotel one afternoon, watching Tim and Lex splash, when an American in khakis walked up.

'We've never met,' the American said. 'My name is Marty Guitierrez. I'm a researcher here, at the Carara station.'

Grant said, 'You were the one who found the original specimen of the *Procompsognathus*.'

'That's right, yes.' Guitierrez sat next to him. 'You must be eager to go home.'

'Yes,' Grant said. 'I have only a few days left to dig before the

373

winter sets in. In Montana, you know, the first snow usually comes in August.'

Guitierrez said, 'Is that why the Hammond Foundation supported northern digs? Because intact genetic material from dinosaurs was more likely to be recovered from cold climates?'

'That's what I presume, yes.'

Guitierrez nodded. 'He was a clever man, Mr. Hammond.'

Grant said nothing. Guitierrez sat back in the pool chair.

'The authorities won't tell you,' Guitierrez said finally. 'Because they are afraid, and perhaps also resentful of you, for what you have done. But something very peculiar is happening in the rural regions.'

'Biting the babies?'

'No, thankfully, that has stopped. But something else. This spring, in the Ismaloya section, which is to the north, some unknown animals ate the crops in a very peculiar manner. They moved each day, in a straight line – almost as straight as an arrow – from the coast, into the mountains, into the jungle.'

Grant sat upright.

'Like a migration,' Guitierrez said. 'Wouldn't you say?'

'What crops?' Grant said.

'Well, it was odd. They would only eat agama beans and soy, and sometimes chickens.'

Grant said, 'Foods rich in lysine. What happened to these animals?'

'Presumably,' Guitierrez said, 'they entered the jungles. In any case, they have not been found. Of course, it would be difficult to search for them in the jungle. A search party could spend years in the Ismaloya mountains, with nothing to show for it.'

'And we are being kept here because . . .'

Guitierrez shrugged. 'The government is worried. Perhaps there are more animals. More trouble. They are feeling cautious.'

'Do you think there are more animals?' Grant said.

'I can't say. Can you?'

'No,' Grant said. 'I can't say.'

'But you suspect?'

Grant nodded. 'Possibly there are. Yes.'

'I agree.'

Guitierrez pushed up from his chair. He waved to Tim and Lex, playing in the pool. 'Probably they will send the children home,' he said. 'There is no reason not to do that.' He put on his sunglasses. 'Enjoy your stay with us, Dr. Grant. It is a lovely country here.'

Grant said, 'You're telling me we're not going anywhere?'

'None of us is going anywhere, Dr. Grant,' Guitierrez said, smiling. And then he turned, and walked back toward the entrance of the hotel.

CONGO

For Bob Gottlieb

The more experience and insight I obtain into human nature, the more convinced do I become that the greater portion of a man is purely animal.

Henry Morton Stanely, 1887

The large male [gorilla] held my attention. . . . He gave an impression of dignity and restrained power, of absolute certainty in his majestic appearance. I felt a desire to communicate with him. . . . Never before had I had this feeling on meeting an animal. As we watched each other across the valley, I wondered if he recognized the kinship that bound us.

George B. Schaller, 1964

Contents

Introduction

Only prejudice, and a trick of the Mercator projection, prevents us from recognizing the enormity of the African continent. Covering nearly twelve million square miles, Africa is almost as large as North America and Europe combined. It is nearly twice the size of South America. As we mistake its dimensions, we also mistake its essential nature: the Dark Continent is mostly hot desert and open grassy plains.

In fact, Africa is called the Dark Continent for one reason only: the vast equatorial rain forests of its central region. This is the drainage basin of the Congo River, and one-tenth of the continent is given over to it – a million and a half square miles of silent, damp, dark forest, a single uniform geographical feature nearly half the size of the continental United States. This primeval forest has stood, unchanged and unchallenged, for more than sixty million years.

Even today, only half a million people inhabit the Congo Basin, and they are mostly clustered in villages along the banks of the slow muddy rivers that flow through the jungle. The great expanse of the forest remains inviolate, and to this day thousands of square miles are still unexplored.

This is true particularly of the northeastern corner of the Congo basin, where the rain forest meets the Virunga volcanoes, at the edge of the Great Rift Valley. Lacking established trade routes or compelling features of interest, Virunga was never seen by Western eyes until less than a hundred years ago.

The race to make 'the most important discovery of the 1980s' in the Congo took place during six weeks of 1979. This book recounts the thirteen days of the last American expedition to the Congo, in June, 1979 – barely a hundred years after Henry Morton Stanley first explored the Congo in 1874–77. A comparison of the two expeditions reveals much about the changing – and unchanging – nature of African exploration in the intervening century.

Stanley is usually remembered as the newsman who found Livingstone in 1871, but his real importance lay in later exploits. Moorehead calls him 'a new kind of man in Africa . . . a businessman-explorer. . . .

Stanley was not in Africa to reform the people nor to build an empire, and he was not impelled by any real interest in such matters as anthropology, botany or geology. To put it bluntly, he was out to make a name for himself.'

When Stanley set out again from Zanzibar in 1874, he was again handsomely financed by newspapers. And when he emerged from the jungle at the Atlantic Ocean 999 days later, having suffered incredible hardships and the loss of more than two-thirds of his original party, both he and his newspapers had one of the great stories of the century: Stanley had traveled the entire length of the Congo River.

But two years later, Stanley was back in Africa under very different circumstances. He traveled under an assumed name; he made diversionary excursions to throw spies off his trail; the few people who knew he was in Africa could only guess that he had in mind 'some grand commercial scheme.'

In fact, Stanley was financed by Leopold II of Belgium, who intended to acquire *personally* a large piece of Africa. 'It is not a question of Belgian colonies,' Leopold wrote Stanley. 'It is a question of creating a new State, as big as possible. . . . The King, as a private person, wishes to possess properties in Africa. Belgium wants neither a colony nor territories. Mr. Stanley must therefore buy lands or get them conceded to him. . . .'

This incredible plan was carried out. By 1885, one American said that Leopold 'possesses the Congo just as Rockefeller possesses Standard Oil.' The comparison was apt in more ways than one, for African exploration had become dominated by business.

It has remained so to this day. Stanley would have approved the 1979 American expedition, which was conducted in secrecy, with an emphasis on speed. But the differences would have astonished him. When Stanley passed near Virunga in 1875, it had taken him almost a year to get there; the Americans got their expedition on site in just over a week. And Stanley, who traveled with a small army of four hundred, would have been amazed at an expedition of only twelve – and one of them an ape. The territories through which the Americans moved a century later were autonomous political states; the Congo was now Zaire, and the Congo River the Zaire River. In fact, by 1979 the word 'Congo' technically referred only to the drainage basin of the Zaire River, although Congo was still used in geological circles as a matter of familiarity, and for its romantic connotations.

Despite these differences, the expeditions had remarkably similar outcomes. Like Stanley, the Americans lost two-thirds of their party, and emerged from the jungle as desperately as Stanley's men a century before. And like Stanley, they returned with incredible tales of cannibals and pygmies, ruined jungle civilizations, and fabulous lost treasures.

I would like to thank R. B. Travis, of Earth Resources Technology Services in Houston, for permission to use videotaped debriefings; Dr. Karen Ross, of ERTS, for further background on the expedition; Dr. Peter Elliot, of the Department of Zoology, University of California at Berkeley, and the Project Amy staff, including Amy herself; Dr. William Wens, of Kasai Mining & Manufacturing, Zaire; Dr. Smith Jefferson, of the Department of Medical Pathology, University of Nairobi, Kenya; and Captain Charles Munro, of Tangier, Morocco.

I am further indebted to Mark Warwick, of Nairobi, for his initial interest in this project; Alan Binks, of Nairobi, for graciously offering to take me into the Virunga region of Zaire; Joyce Small for arranging my transport, usually at short notice, to obscure parts of the world; and finally my special thanks to my assistant, Judith Lovejoy, whose untiring efforts through very difficult times were crucial to the completion of this book.

M.C.

Prologue: The Place of Bones

Dawn came to the Congo rain forest.

The pale sun burned away the morning chill and the clinging damp mist, revealing a gigantic silent world. Enormous trees with trunks forty feet in diameter rose two hundred feet overhead, where they spread their dense leafy canopy, blotting out the sky and perpetually dripping water to the ground below. Curtains of gray moss, and creepers and lianas, hung down in a tangle from the trees; parasitic orchids sprouted from the trunks. At ground level, huge ferns, gleaming with moisture, grew higher than a man's chest and held the low ground fog. Here and there was a spot of color: the red acanthema blossoms, which were deadly poison, and the blue dicindra vine, which only opened in early morning. But the basic impression was of a vast, oversized, gray-green world – an alien place, inhospitable to man.

Jan Kruger put aside his rifle and stretched his stiff muscles. Dawn came quickly at the equator; soon it was quite light, although the mist remained. He glanced at the expedition campsite he had been guarding: eight bright orange nylon tents, a blue mess tent, a supply tarp lashed over boxed equipment in a vain attempt to keep them dry. He saw the other guard, Misulu, sitting on a rock; Misulu waved sleepily. Nearby was the transmitting equipment: a silver dish antenna, the black transmitter box, the snaking coaxial cables running to the portable video camera mounted on the collapsible tripod. The Americans used this equipment to transmit daily reports by satellite to their home office in Houston.

Kruger was the *bwana mukubwa*, hired to take the expedition into the Congo. He had led expeditions before: oil companies, map-survey parties, timber-mining teams, and geological parties like this one. Companies sending teams into the field wanted someone who knew local customs and local dialects well enough to handle the porters and arrange the travel. Kruger was well suited for this job; he spoke Kiswahili as well as Bantu and a little Bagindi, and he had been to the Congo many times, although never to Virunga.

Kruger could not imagine why American geologists would want to go to the Virunga region of Zaire, in the northeast corner of the Congo rain forest. Zaire was the richest country in black Africa, in minerals – the world's largest producer of cobalt and industrial diamonds, the seventh largest producer of copper. In addition there were major deposits of gold, tin, zinc, tungsten and uranium. But most of the minerals were found in Shaba and Kasai, not in Virunga.

Kruger knew better than to ask why the Americans wanted to go to Virunga, and in any case he had his answer soon enough. Once the expedition passed Lake Kivu and entered the rain forest, the geologists began scouring river and streambeds. Searching placer deposits meant that they were looking for gold, or diamonds. It turned out to be diamonds.

But not just any diamonds. The geologists were after what they called Type IIb diamonds. Each new sample was immediately submitted to an electrical test. The resulting conversations were beyond Kruger – talk of dielectric gaps, lattice ions, resistivity. But he gathered that it was the electrical properties of the diamonds that mattered. Certainly the samples were useless as gemstones. Kruger had examined several, and they were all blue from impurities.

For ten days, the expedition had been tracing back placer deposits. This was standard procedure: if you found gold or diamonds in stream-beds, you moved upstream toward the presumed erosive source of the minerals. The expedition had moved to higher ground along the western slopes of the Virunga volcanic chain. It was all going routinely until one day around noon when the porters flatly refused to proceed further.

This part of Virunga, they said, was called *kanyamagufa*, which meant 'the place of bones.' The porters insisted that any men foolish enough to go further would have their bones broken, particularly their skulls. They kept touching their cheekbones, and repeating that their skulls would be crushed.

The porters were Bantu-speaking Arawanis from the nearest large town, Kisangani. Like most town-dwelling natives, they had all sorts of superstitions about the Congo jungle. Kruger called for the headman.

'What tribes are here?' Kruger asked, pointing to the jungle ahead.

'No tribes,' the headman said.

'No tribes at all? Not even Bambuti?' he asked, referring to the nearest group of pygmies.

'No men come here,' the headman said. 'This is *kanyamagufa*.'

'Then what crushes the skulls?'

'*Dawa*,' the headman said ominously, using the Bantu term for magical forces. 'Strong *dawa* here. Men stay away.'

Kruger sighed. Like many white men, he was thoroughly sick of hearing about *dawa*. *Dawa* was everywhere, in plants and rocks and storms and enemies of all kinds. But the belief in *dawa* was prevalent throughout much of Africa and strongly held in the Congo.

Kruger had been obliged to waste the rest of the day in tedious negotiation. In the end, he doubled their wages and promised them firearms when they returned to Kisangani, and they agreed to continue on. Kruger considered the incident an irritating native ploy. Porters could generally be counted on to invoke some local superstition to increase their wages, once an expedition was deep enough into the field to be dependent on them. He had budgeted for this eventuality and, having agreed to their demands, he thought no more about it.

Even when they came upon several areas littered with shattered fragments of bone – which the porters found frightening – Kruger was not concerned. Upon examination, he found the bones were not human but rather the small delicate bones of colobus monkeys, the beautiful shaggy black-and-white creatures that lived in the trees overhead. It was true that there were a lot of bones, and Kruger had no idea why they should be shattered, but he had been in Africa a long time, and he had seen many inexplicable things.

Nor was he any more impressed with the overgrown fragments of stone that suggested a city had once stood in this area. Kruger had come upon unexplored ruins before, too. In Zimbabwe, in Broken Hill, in Maniliwi, there were the remains of cities and temples that no twentieth-century scientist had ever seen and studied.

He camped the first night near the ruins.

The porters were panic-stricken, insisting that the evil forces would attack them during the night. Their fear was caught by the American geologists; to pacify them, Kruger had posted two guards that night, himself and the most trustworthy porter, Misulu. Kruger thought it was all a lot of rot, but it had seemed the politic thing to do.

And just as he expected, the night had passed quietly. Around midnight there had been some movement in the bush, and some low wheezing sounds, which he took to be a leopard. Big cats often had respiratory trouble, particularly in the jungle. Otherwise it was quiet, and now it was dawn: the night was over.

A soft beeping sound drew his attention. Misulu heard it too, and glanced questioningly at Kruger. On the transmitting equipment, a red light blinked. Kruger got up and crossed the campsite to the equipment. He knew how to operate it; the Americans had insisted that he learn, as an 'emergency procedure.' He crouched over the black transmitter box with its rectangular green LED.

He pressed buttons, and the screen printed TX HX, meaning a

transmission from Houston. He pressed the response code, and the screen printed CAMLOK. That meant that Houston was asking for video camera transmission. He glanced over at the camera on its tripod and saw that the red light on the case had blinked on. He pressed the carrier button and the screen printed SATLOK, which meant that a satellite transmission was being locked in. There would now be a six-minute delay, the time required to lock the satellite-bounced signal.

He'd better go wake Driscoll, the head geologist, he thought. Driscoll would need a few minutes before the transmission came through. Kruger found it amusing the way the Americans always put on a fresh shirt and combed their hair before stepping in front of the camera. Just like television reporters.

Overhead, the colobus monkeys shrieked and screamed in the trees, shaking the branches. Kruger glanced upward, wondering what had set them going. But it was normal for colobus monkeys to fight in the morning.

Something struck him lightly in the chest. At first he thought it was an insect but, glancing down at his khaki shirt, he saw a spot of red, and a fleshy bit of red fruit rolled down his shirt to the muddy ground. The damned monkeys were throwing berries. He bent over to pick it up. And then he realized that it was not a piece of fruit at all. It was a human eyeball, crushed and slippery in his fingers, pinkish white with a shred of white optic nerve still attached at the back.

He swung his gun around and looked over to where Misulu was sitting on the rock. Misulu was not there.

Kruger moved across the campsite. Overhead, the colobus monkeys fell silent. He heard his boots squish in the mud as he moved past the tents of sleeping men. And then he heard the wheezing sound again. It was an odd, soft sound, carried on the swirling morning mist. Kruger wondered if he had been mistaken, if it was really a leopard.

And he saw Misulu. Misulu lay on his back, in a kind of halo of blood. His skull had been crushed from the sides, the facial bones shattered, the face narrowed and elongated, the mouth open in an obscene yawn, the one remaining eye wide and bulging. The other eye had exploded outward with the force of the impact.

Kruger felt his heart pounding as he bent to examine the body. He wondered what could have caused such an injury. And then he heard the soft wheezing sound again, and this time he felt quite sure it was not a leopard. Then the colobus monkeys began their shrieking, and Kruger leapt to his feet and screamed.

DAY 1: HOUSTON
June 13, 1979

1. ERTS Houston

Ten thousand miles away, in the cold, windowless main data room of Earth Resources Technology Services, Inc., of Houston, Karen Ross sat hunched over a mug of coffee in front of a computer terminal, reviewing the latest Landsat images from Africa. Ross was the ERTS Congo Project Supervisor, and as she manipulated the satellite images in artificial contrast colors, blue and purple and green, she glanced at her watch impatiently. She was waiting for the next field transmission from Africa.

It was now 10:15 p.m. Houston time, but there was no indication of time or place in the room. Day or night, the main data facility of ERTS remained the same. Beneath banks of special kalon fluorescent lights, programming crews in sweaters worked at long rows of quietly clicking computer terminals, providing real-time inputs to the field parties that ERTS maintained around the world. This timeless quality was understood to be necessary for the computers, which required a constant temperature of 60 degrees, dedicated electrical lines, special color-corrected lights that did not interfere with circuitry. It was an environment made for machines; the needs of people were secondary.

But there was another rationale for the main facility design. ERTS wanted programmers in Houston to identify with said 'Karen Ross' for the voice monitors, and turned in a full circle for the scanners. There was a soft electronic bleep, and the door slid open at the third floor.

She emerged into a small square room with a ceiling video monitor, and faced the unmarked outer door of the Communications Control Room. She repeated 'Karen Ross,' and inserted her electronic identicard in the slot, resting her fingers on the metallic edge of the card so the computer could record galvanic skin potentials. (This was a refinement instituted three months earlier, after Travis learned that Army experiments with vocal cord surgery had altered voice characteristics precisely enough to false-positive Voiceident programs.) After a cycling pause, the door buzzed open. She went inside.

With its red night lights, Communications Control was like a soft, warm womb – an impression heightened by the cramped, almost claustrophobic quality of the room, packed with electronic equipment. From floor to ceiling, dozens of video monitors and LEDs flickered and glowed as the technicians spoke in hushed tones, setting dials and twisting knobs. The CCR was the electronic nerve center of ERTS: all communications from field parties around the world were routed through here. Everything in the CCR was recorded, not only incoming data but room voice responses, so the exact conversation on the night of June 13, 1979, is known.

One of the technicians said to her, 'We'll have the transponders hooked in in a minute. You want coffee?'

'No,' Ross said.

'You want to be out there, right?'

'I earned it,' she said. She stared at the video screens, at the bewildering display of rotating and shifting forms as the technicians began the litany of locking in the bird bounce, a transmission from satellite in orbit, 320 miles over their heads.

'Signal key.'

'Signal key. Password mark.'

'Password mark.'

'Carrier fix.'

'Carrier fix. We're rolling.'

She paid hardly any attention to the familiar phrases. She watched as the screens displayed gray fields of crackling static.

'Did we open or did they open?' she asked.

'We initiated,' a technician said. 'We had it down on the call sheet to check them at dawn local time. So when they didn't initiate, we did.'

'I wonder why they didn't initiate,' Ross said. 'Is something wrong?'

'I don't think so. We put out the initiation trigger and they picked it up and locked in within fifteen seconds, all the appropriate codes. Ah, here we go.'

At 6:22 a.m. Congo time, the transmission came through: there was a final blur of gray static and then the screens cleared. They were looking at a part of the camp in the Congo, apparently a view from a tripod-mounted video camera. They saw two tents, a low smoldering fire, the lingering wisps of a foggy dawn. There was no sign of activity, no people.

One of the technicians laughed. 'We caught them still sleeping. Guess they do need you there.' Ross was known for her insistence on formalities.

'Lock your remote,' she said.

The technician punched in the remote override. The field camera, ten thousand miles away, came under their control in Houston.

'Pan scan,' she said.

At the console, the technician used a joystick. They watched as the video images shifted to the left, and they saw more of the camp. The camp was destroyed: tents crushed and torn, supply tarp pulled away, equipment scattered in the mud. One tent burned brightly, sending up clouds of black smoke. They saw several dead bodies.

'Jesus,' one technician said.

'Back scan,' Ross said. 'Spot resolve to six-six.'

On the screens, the camera panned back across the camp. They looked at the jungle. They still saw no sign of life.

'Down pan. Reverse sweep.'

Onscreen, the camera panned down to show the silver dish of the portable antenna, and the black box of the transmitter. Nearby was another body, one of the geologists, lying on his back.

'Jesus, that's Roger. . . .'

'Zoom and T-lock,' Ross said. On the tape, her voice sounds cool, almost detached.

The camera zoomed in on the face. What they saw was grotesque, the head crushed and leaking blood from eyes and nose, mouth gaping toward the sky.

'What did *that*?'

At that moment, a shadow fell across the dead face onscreen. Ross jumped forward, grabbing the joystick and hitting the zoom control. The image widened swiftly; they could see the outline of the shadow now. It was a man. And he was moving.

'Somebody's there! Somebody's still alive!'

'He's limping. Looks wounded.'

Ross stared at the shadow. It did not look to her like a limping man; something was wrong, she couldn't put her finger on what it was. . . .

'He's going to walk in front of the lens,' she said. It was almost too much to hope for. 'What's that audio static?'

They were hearing an odd sound, like a hissing or a sighing.

'It's not static, it's in the transmission.'

'Resolve it,' Ross said. The technicians punched buttons, altering the audio frequencies, but the sound remained peculiar and indistinct. And then the shadow moved, and the man stepped in front of the lens.

'Diopter,' Ross said, but it was too late. The face had already appeared, very near the lens. It was too close to focus without a diopter. They saw a blurred, dark shape, nothing more. Before they could click in the diopter, it was gone.

'A native?'

'This region of the Congo is uninhabited,' Ross said.

'*Something* inhabits it.'

'Pan scan,' Ross said. 'See if you can get him onscreen again.'

The camera continued to pan. She could imagine it sitting on its tripod in the jungle, motor whirring as the lens head swung around. Then suddenly the image tilted and fell sideways.

'He knocked it over.'

'Damn!'

The video image crackled, shifting lines of static. It became very difficult to see.

'Resolve it! Resolve it!'

They had a final glimpse of a large face and a dark hand as the silver dish antenna was smashed. The image from the Congo shrank to a spot, and was gone.

2. Interference Signature

During June of 1979, Earth Resources Technology had field teams studying uranium deposits in Bolivia, copper deposits in Pakistan, agricultural field utilization in Kashmir, glacier advance in Iceland, timber resources in Malaysia, and diamond deposits in the Congo. This was not unusual for ERTS; they generally had between six and eight groups in the field at any time.

Since their teams were often in hazardous or politically unstable regions, they were vigilant in watching for the first signs of 'interference signatures.' (In remote-sensing terminology, a 'signature' is the characteristic appearance of an object or geological feature in a photograph or video image.) Most interference signatures were political. In 1977, ERTS had airlifted a team out of Borneo during a local Communist uprising, and again from Nigeria in 1978 during a military coup. Occasionally the signatures were geological; they had pulled a team from Guatemala in 1976 after the earthquake there.

In the opinion of R.B. Travis, called out of bed in the late hours of June 13, 1979, the videotapes from the Congo were 'the worst interference signature ever,' but the signature origin remained mysterious. All they knew was that the camp had been destroyed in a mere six minutes – the time between the signal initiation from Houston and the reception in the Congo. The rapidity was frightening; Travis's first instruction was to figure out 'what the hell happened out there.'

A heavyset man of forty-eight, Travis was accustomed to crises. By training he was an engineer with a background in satellite construction for RCA and later Rockwell; in his thirties he had shifted to management, becoming what aerospace engineers called a 'Rain Dancer.' Companies manufacturing satellites contracted eighteen to twenty-four months in advance for a launch rocket to put the satellite in orbit –

and then hoped that the satellite, with its half-million working parts, would be ready on the assigned day. If it was not, the only alternative was to pray for bad weather delaying the launch, to dance for rain.

Travis had managed to keep a sense of humor after a decade of high-tech problems; his management philosophy was summarized by a large sign mounted behind his desk, which read 'S.D.T.A.G.W.' It stood for 'Some Damn Thing Always Goes Wrong.'

But Travis was not amused on the night of June 13. His entire expedition had been lost, all the ERTS party killed – eight of his people, and however many local porters were with them. *Eight people!* The worst disaster in ERTS history, worse even than Nigeria in '78. Travis felt fatigued, mentally drained, as he thought of all the phone calls ahead of him. Not the calls he would make, but those he would receive. Would so-and-so be back in time for a daughter's graduation, a son's Little League playoff? Those calls would be routed to Travis, and he would have to listen to the bright expectation in the voices, the hopefulness, and his own careful answers – he wasn't sure, he understood the problem, he would do his best, of course, of course. . . . The coming deception exhausted him in advance.

Because Travis couldn't tell anyone what had happened for at least two weeks, perhaps a month. And then he would be making phone calls himself, and visits to the homes, and attending the memorial services where there would be no casket, a deadly blank space, a gap, and the inevitable questions from families and relatives that he couldn't answer while they scrutinized his face, looking for the least muscle twitch, or hesitation, or sign.

What could he tell them?

That was his only consolation – perhaps in a few weeks, Travis could tell them more. One thing was certain: if he were to make the dreadful calls tonight, he could tell the families nothing at all, for ERTS had no idea what had gone wrong. That fact added to Travis's sense of exhaustion. And there were details: Morris, the insurance auditor, came in and said 'What do you want to do about the terms?' ERTS took out term life insurance policies for every expedition member, and also for local porters. African porters received U.S. £15,000 each in insurance, which seemed trivial until one recognized that African per capita income averaged U.S. £180 per year. But Travis had always argued that local expedition people should share risk benefits – even if it meant paying widowed families a small fortune, in their terms. Even if it cost ERTS a small fortune for the insurance.

'Hold them,' Travis said.

'Those policies are costing us *per day* –'

'Hold them,' Travis said.

'For how long?'

'Thirty days,' Travis said.

'Thirty *more* days?'

'That's right.'

'But we know the holders are dead.' Morris could not reconcile himself to the waste of money. His actuarial mind rebelled.

'That's right,' Travis said. 'But you'd better slip the porters' families some cash to keep them quiet.'

'Jesus. How much are we talking about?'

'Five hundred dollars each.'

'How do we account that?'

'Legal fees,' Travis said. 'Bury it in legal, local disposition.'

'And the American team people that we've lost?'

'They have Master Charge,' Travis said. 'Stop worrying.'

Roberts, the British-born ERTS press liaison, came into his office. 'You want to open this can up?'

'No,' Travis said. 'I want to kill it.'

'For how long?'

'Thirty days.'

'Bloody hell. Your own staff will leak inside thirty days,' Roberts said. 'I promise you.'

'If they do, you'll squash it,' Travis said. 'I need another thirty days to make this contract.'

'Do we know what happened out there?'

'No,' Travis said. 'But we will.'

'How?'

'From the tapes.'

'Those tapes are a mess.'

'So far,' Travis said. And he called in the specialty teams of console hotdoggers. Travis had long since concluded that although ERTS could wake up political advisers around the world, they were most likely to get information in-house. 'Everything we know from the Congo field expedition,' he said, 'is registered on that final videotape. I want a sevenband visual and audio salvage, starting right now. Because that tape is all we have.'

The specialty teams went to work.

3. Recovery

ERTS referred to the process as 'data recovery,' or sometimes as 'data salvage.' The terms evoked images of deep-sea operations, and they were oddly appropriate.

To recover or salvage data meant that coherent meaning was pulled to the surface from the depths of massive electronic information storage. And, like salvage from the sea, it was a slow and delicate process, where a single false step meant the irretrievable loss of the very elements one was trying to bring up. ERTS had whole salvage crews skilled in the art of data recovery. One crew immediately went to work on the audio recovery, another on the visual recovery.

But Karen Ross was already engaged in a visual recovery. The procedures she followed were highly sophisticated, and only possible at ERTS.

Earth Resources Technology was a relatively new company, formed in 1975 in response to the explosive growth of information on the Earth and its resources. The amount of material handled by ERTS was staggering: just the Landsat imagery alone amounted to more than five hundred thousand pictures, and sixteen new images were acquired every hour, around the clock. With the addition of conventional and draped aerial photography, infrared photography, and artificial aperture side-looking radar, the total information available to ERTS exceeded two million images, with new input on the order of thirty images an hour. All this information had to be catalogued, stored, and made available for instantaneous retrieval. ERTS was like a library which acquired seven hundred new books a day. It was not surprising that the librarians worked at fever pitch around the clock.

Visitors to ERTS never seemed to realize that even with computers, such data-handling capacity would have been impossible ten years earlier. Nor did visitors understand the basic nature of the ERTS information – they assumed that the pictures on the screens were photographic, although they were not.

Photography was a nineteenth-century chemical system for recording information using light-sensitive silver salts. ERTS utilized a twentieth-century electrical system for recording information, analogous to chemical photographs, but very different. Instead of cameras, ERTS used multi-spectral scanners; instead of film, they used CCTs – computer compatible tapes. In fact, ERTS did not bother with 'pictures' as they were ordinarily understood from old-fashioned photographic technology. ERTS bought 'data scans' which they converted to 'data displays,' as the need arose.

Since the ERTS images were just electrical signals recorded on magnetic tape, a great variety of electrical image manipulation was possible. ERTS had 837 computer programs to alter imagery: to enhance it, to eliminate unwanted elements, to bring out details. Ross used fourteen programs on the Congo videotape – particularly on the static-filled section in which the hand and face appeared, just before the antenna was smashed.

First she carried out what was called a 'wash cycle,' getting rid of the static. She identified the static lines as occurring at specific scan positions, and having a specific gray-scale value. She instructed the computer to cancel those lines.

The resulting image showed blank spaces where the static was removed. So she did 'fill-in-the-blanks' – instructing the computer to introject imagery, according to what was around the blank spaces. In this operation the computer made a logical guess about what was missing.

She now had a static-free image, but it was muddy and indistinct, lacking definition. So she did a 'high-priced spread' – intensifying the image by spreading the gray-scale values. But for some reason she also got a phase distortion that she had to cancel, and that released spiking glitches previously suppressed, and to get rid of the glitches she had to run three other programs. . . .

Technical details preoccupied her for an hour, until suddenly the image 'popped,' coming up bright and clean. She caught her breath as she saw it. The screen showed a dark, brooding face with heavy brows, watchful eyes, a flattened nose, prognathous lips.

Frozen on the video screen was the face of a male gorilla.

Travis came over, shaking his head. 'We finished the audio recovery on that hissing noise. The computer confirms it as human breathing, with at least four separate origins. But it's damned strange. According to the analysis, the sound is coming from inhalation, not exhalation, the way people usually make sounds.'

'The computer is wrong,' Ross said. 'It's not human.' She pointed to the screen, and the face of the gorilla.

Travis showed no surprise. 'Artifact,' he said.

'It's no artifact.'

'You did fill-in-the-blanks, and you got an artifact. The tag team's been screwing around with the software at lunch again.' The tag team – the young software programmers – had a tendency to convert data to play highly sophisticated versions of pinball games. Their games sometimes got subrouted into other programs.

Ross herself had complained about it. 'But this image is real,' she insisted, pointing to the screen.

'Look,' Travis said, 'last week Harry did fill-in-the-blanks on the Karakorum Mountains and he got back a lunar landing game. You're supposed to land next to the McDonald's stand, all very amusing.' He walked off. 'You'd better meet the others in my office. We're setting advance times to get back in.'

'I'm leading the next team.'

Travis shook his head. 'Out of the question.'

'But what about this?' she said, pointing to the screen.

'I'm not buying that image,' Travis said. 'Gorillas don't behave that way. It's got to be an artifact.' He glanced at his watch. 'Right now, the only question I have is how fast we can put a team back in the Congo.'

4. Return Expedition

Travis had never had any doubts in his mind about going back in; from the first time he saw the videotapes from the Congo, the only question was how best to do it. He called in all the section heads: Accounts, Diplo, Remote, Geo, Logistics, Legal. They were all yawning and rubbing their eyes. Travis began by saying, 'I want us back in the Congo in ninety-six hours.'

Then he leaned back in his chair and let them tell him why it couldn't be done. There were plenty of reasons.

'We can't assemble the air cargo units for shipment in less than a hundred and sixty hours,' Cameron, the logistics man said.

'We can postpone the Himalaya team, and use their units,' Travis said.

'But that's a mountain expedition.'

'You can modify the units in nine hours,' Travis said.

'But we can't get equipment to fly it out,' Lewis, the transport master, said.

'Korean Airlines has a 747 cargo jet available at SFX. They tell me it can be down here in nine hours.'

'They have a plane just sitting there?' Lewis said, incredulous.

'I believe,' Travis said, 'that they had a last-minute cancellation from another customer.'

Irwin, the accountant, groaned. 'What'd that cost?'

'We can't get visas from the Zaire Embassy in Washington in time,'

Martin, the diplomatic man, said. 'And there is serious doubt they'd issue them to us at all. As you know, the first set of Congo visas were based on our mineral exploration rights with the Zaire government, and our MER are non-exclusive. We were granted permission to go in, and so were the Japanese, the Germans, and the Dutch, who've formed a mining consortium. But it's strictly first come, first served. First ore-body strike takes the contract. If Zaire finds out that our expedition is in trouble, they'll just cancel us out and let the Euro-Japanese consortium try their luck. There are three hundred Japanese trade officials in Kinshasa right now, spending yen like water.'

'I think that's right,' Travis said. 'If it became known that our expedition is in trouble.'

'It'll become known the minute we apply for visas.'

'We won't apply for them. As far as anybody knows,' Travis said, 'we still have an expedition in Virunga. If we put a second small team into the field fast enough, nobody will ever know that it wasn't the original team.'

'But what about the specific personnel visas to cross the borders, the manifests –'

'Details,' Travis said. 'That's what liquor is for,' referring to bribes, which were often liquor. In many parts of the world, expedition teams went in with crates of liquor and boxes of those perennial favorites, transistor radios and Polaroid cameras.

'Details? How're you going to cross the border?'

'We'll need a good man for that. Maybe Munro.'

'Munro? That's playing rough. The Zaire government hates Munro.'

'He's resourceful, and he knows the area.'

Martin, the diplomatic expert, cleared his throat and said, 'I'm not sure I should be here for this discussion. It looks to me as if you are proposing to enter a sovereign state with an illegal party led by a former Congo mercenary soldier. . . .'

'Not at all,' Travis said. 'I'm obliged to put a support party into the field to assist my people already there. Happens all the time. I have no reason to think anybody is in trouble; just a routine support party. I haven't got time to go through official channels. I may not be showing the best judgment in whom I hire, but it's nothing more serious than that.'

By 11:45 p.m. on the night of June 13, the main sequencing of the next ERTS expedition had been worked out and confirmed by the computer. A fully loaded 747 could leave Houston at 8 p.m. the following evening, June 14; the plane could be in Africa on June 15 to pick up Munro 'or someone like him'; and the full team could be in place in the Congo on June 17.

In ninety-six hours.

From the main data room, Karen Ross could look through the glass walls into Travis's office and see the arguments taking place. In her logical way, she concluded that Travis had 'Q'd' himself, meaning that he had drawn false conclusions from insufficient data, and had said Q.E.D. too soon. Ross felt there was no point in going back into the Congo until they knew what they were up against. She remained at her console, checking the image she had recovered.

Ross bought this image – but how could she make Travis buy it?

In the highly sophisticated data-processing world of ERTS, there was a constant danger that extracted information would begin to 'float' – that the images would cut loose from reality, like a ship cut loose from its moorings. This was true particularly when the database was put through multiple manipulations – when you were rotating 106 pixels in computer-generated hyper space.

So ERTS evolved other ways to check the validity of images they got back from the computer. Ross ran two check programs against the gorilla image. The first was called APNF, for Animation Predicted Next Frame.

It was possible to treat videotape as if it were movie film, a succession of stills. She showed the computer several 'stills' in succession, and then asked it to create the Predicted Next Frame. This PNF was then checked against the actual next frame.

She ran eight PNFs in a row, and they worked. If there was an error in the data handling, it was at least a consistent error.

Encouraged, she next ran a 'fast and dirty three-space.' Here the flat video image was assumed to have certain three-dimensional characteristics, based on gray-scale patterns. In essence, the computer decided that the shadow of a nose, or a mountain range, meant that the nose or mountain range protruded above the surrounding surface. Succeeding images could be checked against these assumptions. As the gorilla moved, the computer verified that the flat image was, indeed, three-dimensional and coherent.

This proved beyond a doubt that the image was real.

She went to see Travis.

'Let's say I buy this image,' Travis said, frowning. 'I still don't see why you should take the next expedition in.'

Ross said, 'What did the other team find?'

'The other team?' Travis asked innocently.

'You gave that tape to another salvage team to confirm my recovery,' Ross said.

Travis glanced at his watch. 'They haven't pulled anything out yet.' And he added, 'We all know you're fast with the database.'

Ross smiled. 'That's why you need me to take the expedition in,' she said. 'I know the database, because I generated the database. And if you intend to send another team in right away, before this gorilla thing is solved, the only hope you have is for the team leader to be fast onsite with the data. This time, you *need* a console hotdogger in the field. Or the next expedition will end up like the last one. Because you still don't know what happened to the last expedition.'

Travis sat behind his desk, and stared at her for a long time. She recognized his hesitation as a sign that he was weakening.

'And I want to go outside,' Ross said.

'To an outside expert?'

'Yes. Somebody on our grant list.'

'Risky,' Travis said. 'I hate to involve outside people at this point. You know the consortium is breathing down our necks. You up the leak ratios.'

'It's important,' Ross insisted.

Travis sighed. 'Okay, if you think it's important.' He sighed again. 'Just don't delay your team.'

Ross was already packing up her hard copy.

Alone, Travis frowned, turning over his decision in his mind. Even if they ran the next Congo expedition slam-bam, in and out in less than fifteen days, their fixed costs would still exceed three hundred thousand dollars. The Board was going to scream – sending an untried, twenty-four-year-old kid, a *girl*, into the field with this kind of responsibility. Especially on a project as important as this one, where the stakes were enormous, and where they had already fallen behind on every time-line and cost projection. And Ross was so cold, she was likely to prove a poor field leader, alienating the others in the team.

Yet Travis had a hunch about the Ross Glacier. His management philosophy, tempered in his rain-dancing days, was always to give the project to whoever had the most to gain from success – or the most to lose from failure.

He turned to face his console, mounted beside his desk. 'Travis,' he said, and the screen glowed.

'Psychograph file,' he said.

The screen showed call prompts.

'Ross, Karen,' Travis said.

The screen flashed THINKING A MOMENT. That was the programmed response which meant that information was being extracted. He waited.

Then the psychograph summary printed out across the screen. Every

ERTS employee underwent three days of intensive psychological testing to determine not only skills but potential biases. The assessment of Ross would, he felt, be reassuring to the Board.

HIGHLY INTELLIGENT / LOGICAL / FLEXIBLE / RESOURCEFUL / DATA INTUITIVE / THOUGHT PROCESSES SUITED TO RAPIDLY CHANGING REALTIME CONTEXTS / DRIVEN TO SUCCEED AT DEFINED GOALS / CAPABLE SUSTAINED MENTAL EFFORT /

It looked like the perfect description of the next Congo team leader. He scanned down the screen, looking for the negatives. These were less reassuring.

YOUTHFUL-RUTHLESS / TENUOUS HUMAN RAPPORT / DOMINEERING / INTELLECTUALLY ARROGANT / INSENSITIVE / DRIVEN TO SUCCEED AT ANY COST /

And there was a final 'flopover' notation. The very concept of personality flopover had been evolved through ERTS testing. It suggested that any dominant personality trait could be suddenly reversed under stress conditions: parental personalities could flop over and turn childishly petulant, hysterical personalities could become icy calm – or logical personalities could become illogical.

FLOPOVER MATRIX: DOMINANT {POSSIBLY UNDESIRABLE} OBJECTIVITY MAY BE LOST ONCE DESIRED GOAL IS PERCEIVED CLOSE AT HAND / DESIRE FOR SUCCESS MAY PROVOKE DANGEROUSLY ILLOGICAL RESPONSES / PARENTAL FIGURES WILL BE ESPECIALLY DENIGRATED / SUBJECT MUST BE MONITORED IN LATE STAGE GOAL-ORIENTED PROCEDURES /

Travis looked at the screen, and decided that such a circumstance was highly unlikely in the coming Congo expedition.

Karen Ross was exhilarated by her new authority. Shortly before midnight, she called up the grant lists on her office terminal. ERTS had animal experts in various areas whom they supported with nominal grants from a non-profit foundation called the Earth Resources Wildlife Fund. The grant lists were arranged taxonomically. Under 'Primates' she found fourteen names, including several in Borneo, Malaysia, and Africa as well as the United States. In the United States there was only one gorilla researcher available, a primatologist named Dr. Peter Elliot, at the University of California at Berkeley.

The file onscreen indicated that Elliot was twenty-nine years old, unmarried, an associate professor without tenure in the Department of Zoology. Principal Research Interest was listed as 'Primate Communications (Gorilla).' Funding was made to something called Project Amy.

She checked her watch. It was just midnight in Houston, 10 p.m. in California. She dialed the home number on the screen.

'Hello,' a wary male voice said.

'Dr. Peter Elliot?'

'Yes . . .' The voice was still cautious, hesitant. 'Are you a reporter?'

'No,' she said. 'This is Dr. Karen Ross in Houston; I'm associated with the Earth Resources Wildlife Fund, which supports your research.'

'Oh, yes . . .' The voice remained cautious. 'You're sure you're not a reporter? It's only fair to tell you I'm recording this telephone call as a potential legal document.'

Karen Ross hesitated. The last thing she needed was some paranoid academic recording ERTS developments. She said nothing.

'You're American?' he said.

'Of course.'

Karen Ross stared at the computer screens, which flashed VOICE IDENTIFICATION CONFIRMED: ELLIOT, PETER, 29 YEARS.

'State your business,' Elliot said.

'Well, we're about to send an expedition into the Virunga region of the Congo, and –'

'Really? When are you going?' The voice suddenly sounded excited, boyish.

'Well, as a matter of fact we're leaving in two days, and –'

'I want to go,' Elliot said.

Ross was so surprised she hardly knew what to say. 'Well, Dr. Elliot, that's not why I'm calling you, as a matter of fact –'

'I'm planning to go there anyway,' Elliot said. 'With Amy.'

'Who's Amy?'

'Amy is a gorilla,' Peter Elliot said.

DAY 2:
SAN FRANCISCO
June 14, 1979

1. Project Amy

It is unfair to suggest, as some primatologists later did, that Peter Elliot had to 'get out of town' in June, 1979. His motives, and the planning behind the decision to go to the Congo, are a matter of record. Professor Elliot and his staff had decided on an African trip at least two days before Ross called him.

But it is certainly true that Peter Elliot was under attack: from outside groups, the press, academic colleagues, and even members of his own department at Berkeley. Toward the end, Elliot was accused of being a 'Nazi criminal' engaged in the 'torture of dumb [sic] animals.' It is no exaggeration to say that Elliot had found himself, in the spring of 1979, fighting for his professional life.

Yet his research had begun quietly, almost accidentally. Peter Elliot was a twenty-three-year-old graduate student in the Department of Anthropology at Berkeley when he first read about a year-old gorilla with amoebic dysentery who had been flown from the Minneapolis zoo to the San Francisco School of Veterinary Medicine for treatment. That was in 1973, in the exciting early days of primate language research.

The idea that primates might be taught language was very old. In 1661, Samuel Pepys saw a chimpanzee in London and wrote in his diary that it was 'so much like a man in most things that . . . I do believe that it already understands much English, and I am of the mind it might be taught to speak or make signs.' Another seventeenth-century writer went further, saying, 'Apes and Baboons . . . can speak but will not for fear they should be imployed, and set to work.'

Yet for the next three hundred years attempts to teach apes to talk were notably unsuccessful. They culminated in an ambitious effort by a Florida couple, Keith and Kathy Hayes, who for six years in the early 1950s raised a chimpanzee named Vicki as if she were a human infant. During that time, Vicki learned four words – 'mama,' 'papa,' 'cup,' and 'up.' But her pronunciation was labored and her progress slow. Her difficulties seemed to support the growing conviction among scientists that man was the only animal capable of language. Typical was the pronouncement of George Gaylord Simpson: 'Language is . . . the most diagnostic single trait of man: all normal men have language; no other now living organisms do.'

This seemed so self-evident that for the next fifteen years nobody bothered to try teaching language to an ape. Then in 1966, a Reno, Nevada, couple named Beatrice and Allen Gardner reviewed movies of Vicki speaking. It seemed to them that Vicki was not so much incapable of language as incapable of speech. They noticed that while her lip movements were awkward, her hand gestures were fluid and expressive. The obvious conclusion was to try sign language.

In June, 1966, the Gardners began teaching American Sign Language (Ameslan), the standardized language of the deaf, to an infant chimpanzee named Washoe. Washoe's progress with ASL was rapid; by 1971, she had a vocabulary of 160 signs, which she used in conversation. She also made up new word combinations for things she had never seen before: when shown watermelon for the first time, she signed it 'water fruit.'

The Gardners' work was highly controversial; it turned out that many scientists had an investment in the idea that apes were incapable of language. (As one researcher said, 'My God, think of all those decades – and everyone agreeing that only man had language. What a mess.')

Washoe's skills provoked a variety of other experiments in teaching language. A chimpanzee named Lucy was taught to communicate through a computer; another, Sarah, was taught to use plastic markers on a board. Other apes were studied as well. An orangutan named Alfred began instruction in 1971; a lowland gorilla named Koko in 1972; and in 1973 Peter Elliot began with a mountain gorilla, Army.

At his first visit to the hospital to meet Amy, he found a pathetic little creature, heavily sedated, with restraining straps on her frail black arms and legs. He stroked her head and said gently, 'Hello, Amy, I'm Peter.'

Amy promptly bit his hand, drawing blood.

From this inauspicious beginning emerged a singularly successful research program. In 1973, the basic teaching technique, called molding, was well understood. The animal was shown an object and the researcher simultaneously molded the animal's hand into the correct sign, until the association was firmly made. Subsequent testing confirmed that the animal understood the meaning of the sign.

But if the basic methodology was accepted, the application was highly competitive. Researchers competed over the rate of sign acquisition, or vocabulary. (Among human beings, vocabulary was considered the best measure of intelligence.) The rate of sign acquisition could be taken as a measure of either the scientist's skill or the animal's intelligence.

It was by now clearly recognized that different apes had different personalities. As one researcher commented, 'Pongid studies are perhaps the only field in which academic gossip centers on the students and not the teachers.' In the increasingly competitive and disputatious world of primate research, it was said that Lucy was a drunk, that Koko was an ill-mannered brat, that Lana's head was turned by her celebrity ('she only works when there is an interviewer present'), and that Nim was so stupid he should have been named Dim.

At first glance, it may seem odd that Peter Elliot should have come under attack, for this handsome, rather shy man – the son of a Marin County dry cleaner – had avoided controversy during his years of work with Amy. Elliot's publications were modest and temperate; his progress with Amy was well documented; he showed no interest in publicity, and was not among those researchers who took their apes on the Carson or the Griffin show.

But Elliot's diffident manner concealed not only a quick intelligence, but a fierce ambition as well. If he avoided controversy, it was only because he didn't have time for it – he had been working nights and weekends for years, and driving his staff and Amy just as hard. He was very good at the business of science, getting grants; at all the animal behaviorist conferences, where others showed up in jeans and plaid lumberjack shirts, Elliot arrived in a three-piece suit. Elliot intended to be the foremost ape researcher, and he intended Amy to be the foremost ape.

Elliot's success in obtaining grants was such that by 1975 he employed four people working full time with Amy. By 1978, Project Amy had an annual budget of $160,000 and a staff of eight, including a child psychologist and a computer programmer. A staff member of the Bergren Institute later said that Elliot's appeal lay in the fact that he was 'a good investment; for example, Project Amy got fifty percent more computer time for our money because he went on line with his time-sharing terminal at night and on weekends, when the time was cheaper. He was very cost-effective. And dedicated, of course: Elliot obviously cared about nothing in life except his work with Amy. That made him a boring conversationalist but a very good bet, from our standpoint. It's hard to decide who's truly brilliant; it's easier to see who's driven, which in the long run may be more important. We anticipated great things from Elliot.'

Peter Elliot's difficulties began on the morning of February 2, 1979. Amy lived in a mobile home on the Berkeley campus; she spent nights there alone, and usually provided an effusive greeting the next day. However, on that morning the Project Amy staff found her in an uncharacteristic sullen mood; she was irritable and bleary-eyed, behaving as if she had been wronged in some fashion.

Elliot felt that something had upset her during the night. When asked, she kept making signs for 'sleep box,' a new word pairing he did not understand. That in itself was not unusual; Amy made up new word pairings all the time, and they were often hard to decipher. Just a few days before, she had bewildered them by talking about 'crocodile milk.' Eventually they realized that Amy's milk had gone sour, and that since she disliked crocodiles (which she had only seen in picture books), she somehow decided that sour milk was 'crocodile milk.'

Now she was talking about 'sleep box.' At first they thought she might be referring to her nestlike bed. It turned out she was using 'box' in her usual sense, to refer to the television set.

Everything in her trailer, including the television, was controlled on a twenty-four-hour cycle by the computer. They ran a check to see if the television had been turned on during the night, disturbing her sleep. Since Amy liked to watch television, it was conceivable that she had managed to turn it on herself. But Amy looked scornful as they examined the actual television in the trailer. She clearly meant something else.

Finally they determined that by 'sleep box' she meant 'sleep pictures.' When asked about these sleep pictures, Amy signed that they were 'bad pictures' and 'old pictures,' and that they 'make Amy cry.'

She was dreaming.

The fact that Amy was the first primate to report dreams caused tremendous excitement among Elliot's staff. But the excitement was short-lived. Although Amy continued to dream on succeeding nights, she refused to discuss her dreams; in fact, she seemed to blame the researchers for this new and confusing intrusion into her mental life. Worse, her waking behavior deteriorated alarmingly.

Her word acquisition rate fell from 2.7 words a week to 0.8 words a week, her spontaneous word formation rate from 1.9 to 0.3. Monitored attention span was halved. Mood swings increased; erratic and unmotivated behavior became commonplace; temper tantrums occurred daily. Amy was four and a half feet tall, and weighed 130 pounds. She was an immensely strong animal. The staff began to wonder if they could control her.

Her refusal to talk about her dreams frustrated them. They tried a variety of investigative approaches: they showed her pictures from books and magazines; they ran the ceiling-mounted video monitors around the clock, in case she signed something significant while alone (like young children, Amy often 'talked to herself'); they even administered a battery of neurological tests, including an EEG.

Finally they hit on finger painting.

This was immediately successful. Amy was enthusiastic about finger painting, and after they mixed cayenne pepper with the pigments, she stopped licking her fingers. She drew images swiftly and repetitively, and she seemed to become somewhat more relaxed, more her old self.

David Bergman, the child psychologist, noted that 'what Amy actually draws is a cluster of apparently related images: inverted crescent shapes, or semicircles, which are always associated with an area of vertical green streaks. Amy says the green streaks represent 'forest,' and she calls the semicircles 'bad houses' or 'old houses.' In addition she often draws black circles, which she calls "holes." '

Bergman cautioned against the obvious conclusion that she was drawing old buildings in the jungle. 'Watching her make drawings one after another, again and again, convinces me of the obsessive and private nature of the imagery. Amy is troubled by these pictures, and she is trying to get them out, to banish them to paper.'

In fact, the nature of the imagery remained mysterious to the Project Amy staff. By late April, 1979, they had concluded that her dreams could be explained in four ways. In order of seriousness, they were:

1. *The dreams are an attempt to rationalize events in her daily life.* This was the usual explanation of (human) dreams, but the staff doubted that it applied in Amy's case.

2. *The dreams are a transitional adolescent manifestation.* At seven years of age, Amy was a gorilla teenager, and for nearly a year she had shown many typical teenage traits, including rages and sulks, fussiness about her appearance, a new interest in the opposite sex.

3. *The dreams are a species-specific phenomenon.* It was possible that all gorillas had disturbing dreams, and that in the wild the resultant stresses were handled in some fashion by the behavior of the group. Although gorillas had been studied in the wild for the past twenty years, there was no evidence for this.

4. *The dreams are the first sign of incipient dementia.* This was the most feared possibility. To train an ape effectively, one had to begin with an infant; as the years progressed, researchers waited to see if their animal would grow up to be bright or stupid, recalcitrant or pliable, healthy or sickly. The health of apes was a constant worry; many programs collapsed after years of effort and expense when the apes died of physical or mental illness. Timothy, an Atlanta chimp, became psychotic in 1976 and committed suicide by coprophagia, choking to death on his own feces. Maurice, a Chicago orang, became intensely neurotic, developing phobias that halted work in 1977. For better or worse, the very intelligence that made apes worthwhile subjects for study also made them as unstable as human beings.

But the Project Amy staff was unable to make further progress. In May, 1979, they made what turned out to be a momentous decision: they decided to publish Amy's drawings, and submitted her images to the *Journal of Behavioral Sciences.*

2. Breakthrough

'Dream Behavior in a Mountain Gorilla' was never published. The paper was routinely forwarded to three scientists on the editorial board for review, and one copy somehow (it is still unclear just how) fell into the hands of the Primate Preservation Agency, a New York group formed in 1975 to prevent the 'unwarranted and illegitimate exploitation of intelligent primates in unnecessary laboratory research.'[*]

On June 3, the PPA began picketing the Zoology Department at Berkeley, and calling for the 'release' of Amy. Most of the demonstrators were women, and several young children were present; videotapes of an eight-year-old boy holding a placard with Amy's photograph and shouting 'Free Amy! Free Amy!' appeared on local television news.

In a tactical error, the Project Amy staff elected to ignore the protests except for a brief press release stating that the PPA was 'misinformed.' The release went out under the Berkeley Information Office letterhead.

On June 5, the PPA released comments on Professor Elliot's work from other primatologists around the country. (Many later denied the comments or claimed they were misquoted.) Dr. Wayne Turman, of the University of Oklahoma at Norman, was quoted as saying that Elliot's work was 'fanciful and unethical.' Dr. Felicity Hammond, of the Yerkes Primate Research Center in Atlanta, said that 'neither Elliot nor his research is of the first rank.' Dr. Richard Aronson at the University of Chicago called the research 'clearly fascist in nature.'

None of these scientists had read Elliot's paper before commenting; but the damage, particularly from Aronson, was incalculable. On June 8, Eleanor Vries, the spokesperson for the PPA, referred to the 'criminal research of Dr. Elliot and his Nazi staff'; she claimed Elliot's research caused Amy to have nightmares, and that Amy was being subjected to torture, drugs, and electroshock treatments.

Belatedly, on June 10, the Project Amy staff prepared a lengthy press release, explaining their position in detail and referring to the unpublished paper. But the University Information Office was now 'too busy' to issue the release.

[*] The following account of Elliot's persecution draws heavily on J. A. Peebles, 'Infringement of Academic Freedom by Press Innuendo and Hearsay: The Experience of Dr. Peter Elliot,' in the *Journal of Academic Law and Psychiatry* 52, no. 12 (1979): 19–38.

On June 11, the Berkeley faculty scheduled a meeting to consider 'issues of ethical conduct' within the University. Eleanor Vries announced that the PPA had hired the noted San Francisco attorney Melvin Belli 'to free Amy from subjugation.' Belli's office was not available for comment.

On the same day, the Project Amy staff had a sudden, unexpected breakthrough in their understanding of Amy's dreams.

Through all the publicity and commotion, the group had continued to work daily with Amy, and her continued distress – and flaring temper tantrums – was a constant reminder that they had not solved the initial problem. They persisted in their search for clues, although when the break finally came, it happened almost by accident.

Sarah Johnson, a research assistant, was checking prehistoric archaeological sites in the Congo, on the unlikely chance that Amy might have seen such a site ('old buildings in the jungle') in her infancy, before she was brought to the Minneapolis zoo. Johnson quickly discovered the pertinent facts about the Congo: the region had not been explored by Western observers until a hundred years ago; in recent times, hostile tribes and civil war had made scientific inquiry hazardous; and finally, the moist jungle environment did not lend itself to artifact preservation.

This meant remarkably little was known about Congolese prehistory, and Johnson completed her research in a few hours. But she was reluctant to return so quickly from her assignment, so she stayed on, looking at other books in the anthropology library – ethnographies, histories, early accounts. The earliest visitors to the interior of the Congo were Arab slave traders and Portuguese merchants, and several had written accounts of their travels. Because Johnson could read neither Arabic nor Portuguese, she just looked at the plates.

And then she saw a picture that, she said, 'sent a chill up my spine.'

It was a Portuguese engraving originally dated 1642 and reprinted in an 1842 volume. The ink was yellowing on frayed brittle paper, but clearly visible was a ruined city in the jungle, overgrown with creeper vines and giant ferns. The doors and windows were constructed with semicircular arches, exactly as Amy had drawn them.

'It was,' Elliot said later, 'the kind of opportunity that comes to a researcher once in his lifetime – if he's lucky. Of course we knew nothing about the picture; the caption was written in flowing script and included a word that looked like 'Zinj,' and the date 1642. We immediately hired translators skilled in archaic Arabic and seventeenth-century Portuguese, but that wasn't the point. The point was we had a chance to verify a major theoretical question. Amy's pictures seemed to be a clear case of specific genetic memory.'

Genetic memory was first proposed by Marais in 1911, and it had been vigorously debated ever since. In its simplest form, the theory proposed that the mechanism of genetic inheritance, which governed the transmission of all physical traits, was not limited to physical traits alone. Behavior was clearly genetically determined in lower animals, which were born with complex behavior that did not have to be learned. But higher animals had more flexible behavior, dependent on learning and memory. The question was whether higher animals, particularly apes and men, had any part of their psychic apparatus fixed from birth by their genes.

Now, Elliot felt, with Amy they had evidence for such a memory. Amy had been taken from Africa when she was only seven months old. Unless she had seen this ruined city in her infancy, her dreams represented a specific genetic memory which could be verified by a trip to Africa. By the evening of June 11, the Project Amy staff was agreed. If they could arrange it – and pay for it – they would take Amy back to Africa.

On June 12, the team waited for the translators to complete work on the source material. Checked translations were expected to be ready within two days. But a trip to Africa for Amy and two staff members would cost at least thirty thousand dollars, a substantial fraction of their total annual operating budget. And transporting a gorilla halfway around the world involved a bewildering tangle of customs regulations and bureaucratic red tape.

Clearly, they needed expert help, but they were not sure where to turn. And then, on June 13, a Dr. Karen Ross from one of their granting institutions, the Earth Resources Wildlife Fund, called from Houston to say that she was leading an expedition into the Congo in two days' time. And although she showed no interest in taking Peter Elliot or Amy with her, she conveyed – at least over the telephone – a confident familiarity with the way expeditions were assembled and managed in far-off places around the world.

When she asked if she could come to San Francisco to meet with Dr. Elliot, Dr. Elliot replied that he would be delighted to meet with her, at her convenience.

3. Legal Issues

Peter Elliot remembered June 14, 1979, as a day of sudden reverses. He began at 8 a.m. in the San Francisco law firm of Sutherland, Morton & O'Connell, because of the threatened custody suit from the PPA – a suit which became all the more important now that he was planning to take Amy out of the country.

He met with John Morton in the firm's wood-paneled library overlooking Grant Street. Morton took notes on a yellow legal pad. 'I think you're all right,' Morton began, 'but let me get a few facts. Amy is a gorilla?'

'Yes, a female mountain gorilla.'

'Age?'

'She's seven now.'

'So she's still a child?'

Elliot explained that gorillas matured in six to eight years, so that Amy was late adolescent, the equivalent of a sixteen-year-old human female.

Morton scratched notes on a pad. 'Could we say she's still a minor?'

'Do we want to say that?'

'I think so.'

'Yes, she's still a minor,' Elliot said.

'Where did she come from? I mean originally.'

'A woman tourist named Swenson found her in Africa, in a village called Bagimindi. Amy's mother had been killed by the natives for food. Mrs. Swenson bought her as an infant.'

'So she was not bred in captivity,' Morton said, writing on his pad.

'No. Mrs. Swenson brought her back to the States and donated her to the Minneapolis zoo.'

'She relinquished her interest in Amy?'

'I assume so,' Elliot said. 'We've been trying to reach Mrs. Swenson to ask about Amy's early life, but she's out of the country. Apparently she travels constantly; she's in Borneo. Anyway, when Amy was sent to San Francisco, I called the Minneapolis zoo to ask if I could keep her for study. The zoo said yes, for three years.'

'Did you pay any money?'

'No.'

'Was there a written contract?'

'No, I just called the zoo director.'

Morton nodded. 'Oral agreement . . .' he said, writing. 'And when the three years were up?'

'That was the spring of 1976. I asked the zoo for an extension of six years, and they gave it to me.'

'Again orally?'

'Yes. I called on the phone.'

'No correspondence?'

'No. They didn't seem very interested when I called. To tell you the truth, I think they had forgotten about Amy. The zoo has four gorillas, anyway.'

Morton frowned. 'Isn't a gorilla a pretty expensive animal? I mean, if you wanted to buy one for a pet or for the circus.'

'Gorillas are on the endangered list; you can't buy them as pets. But yes, they'd be pretty expensive.'

'How expensive?'

'Well, there's no established market value, but it would be twenty or thirty thousand dollars.'

'And all during these years, you have been teaching her language?'

'Yes,' Peter said. 'American Sign Language. She has a vocabulary of six hundred and twenty words now.'

'Is that a lot?'

'More than any known primate.'

Morton nodded, making notes. 'You work with her every day in ongoing research?'

'Yes.'

'Good,' Morton said. 'That's been very important in the animal custody cases so far.'

For more than a hundred years, there had been organized movements in Western countries to stop animal experimentation. They were led by the anti-vivisectionists, the RSPCA, the ASPCA. Originally these organizations were a kind of lunatic fringe of animal lovers, intent on stopping all animal research.

Over the years, scientists had evolved a standard defense acceptable to the courts. Researchers claimed that their experiments had the goal of bettering the health and welfare of mankind, a higher priority than animal welfare. They pointed out that no one objected to animals being used as beasts of burden or for agricultural work – a life of drudgery to which animals had been subjected for thousands of years. Using animals in scientific experiments simply extended the idea that animals were the servants of human enterprises.

In addition, animals were literally brutes. They had no self-awareness, no recognition of their existence in nature. This meant, in the words of philosopher George H. Mead, that 'animals have no rights. We are at liberty to cut off their lives; there is no wrong committed when an animal's life is taken away. He has not lost anything . . .'

Many people were troubled by these views, but attempts to establish guidelines quickly ran into logical problems. The most obvious concerned the perceptions of animals further down the phylogenetic scale. Few researchers operated on dogs, cats, and other mammals without anesthesia, but what about annelid worms, crayfish, leeches, and squid? Ignoring these creatures was a form of 'taxonomic discrimination.' Yet if these animals deserved consideration, shouldn't it also be illegal to throw a live lobster into a pot of boiling water?

The question of what constituted cruelty to animals was confused by the animal societies themselves. In some countries, they fought the extermination of rats; and in 1968 there was the bizarre Australian pharmaceutical case.* In the face of these ironies, the courts hesitated to interfere with animal experimentation. As a practical matter, researchers were free to do as they wished. The volume of animal research was extraordinary: during the 1970s, sixty-four million animals were killed in experiments in the United States each year.

But attitudes had slowly changed. Language studies with dolphins and apes made it clear that these animals were not only intelligent but self-aware; they recognized themselves in mirrors and photographs. In 1974, scientists themselves formed the International Primate Protection League to monitor research involving monkeys and apes. In March, 1978, the Indian government banned the export of rhesus monkeys to research laboratories around the world. And there were court cases which concluded that in some instances animals did, indeed, have rights.

The old view was analogous to slavery: the animal was the property of its owner, who could do whatever he wished. But now ownership became secondary. In February, 1977, there was a case involving a dolphin named Mary, released by a lab technician into the open ocean. The University of Hawaii prosecuted the technician, charging loss of a valuable research animal. Two trials resulted in hung juries; the case was dropped.

---

* A new pharmaceutical factory was built in Western Australia. In this factory all the pills came out on a conveyor belt; a person had to watch the belt, and press buttons to sort the pills into separate bins by size and color. A Skinnerian animal behaviorist pointed out that it would be simple to teach pigeons to watch the pills and peck colored keys to do the sorting process. Incredulous factory managers agreed to a test; the pigeons indeed performed reliably, and were duly placed on the assembly line. Then the RSPCA stepped in and put a stop to it on the grounds that it represented cruelty to animals; the job was turned over to a human operator, for whom it did not, apparently, represent cruelty.

In November, 1978, there was a custody case involving a chimpanzee named Arthur, who was fluent in sign language. His owner, Johns Hopkins University, decided to sell him and close the program. His trainer, William Levine, went to court and obtained custody on the grounds that Arthur knew language and thus was no longer a chimpanzee.

'One of the pertinent facts,' Morton said, 'was that when Arthur was confronted by other chimpanzees, he referred to them as "black things." And when Arthur was twice asked to sort photographs of people and photographs of chimps, he sorted them correctly except that both times he put his own picture in the stack with the people. He obviously did not consider himself a chimpanzee, and the court ruled that he should remain with his trainer, since any separation would cause him severe psychic distress.'

'Amy cries when I leave her,' Elliot said.

'When you conduct experiments, do you obtain her permission?'

'Always.' Elliot smiled. Morton obviously had no sense of day-to-day life with Amy. It was essential to obtain her permission for any course of action, even a ride in a car. She was a powerful animal, and she could be willful and stubborn.

'Do you keep a record of her acquiescence?'

'Videotapes.'

'Does she understand the experiments you propose?'

He shrugged. 'She says she does.'

'You follow a system of rewards and punishments?'

'All animal behaviorists do.'

Morton frowned. 'What forms do her punishments take?'

'Well, when she's a bad girl I make her stand in the corner facing the wall. Or else I send her to bed early without her peanut-butter-and-jelly snack.'

'What about torture and shock treatments?'

'Ridiculous.'

'You never physically punish the animal?'

'She's a pretty damn big animal. Usually I worry that she'll get mad and punish *me.*'

Morton smiled and stood. 'You're going to be all right,' he said. 'Any court will rule that Amy is your ward and that you must decide any ultimate disposition in her case.' He hesitated. 'I know this sounds strange, but could you put Amy on the stand?'

'I guess so,' Elliot said. 'Do you think it will come to that?'

'Not in this case,' Morton said, 'but sooner or later it will. You watch: within ten years, there will be a custody case involving a language-using primate, and the ape will be in the witness-box.'

Elliot shook his hand, and said as he was leaving, 'By the way, would I have any problem taking her out of the country?'

'If there *is* a custody case, you could have trouble taking her across state lines,' Morton said. 'Are you planning to take her out of the country?'

'Yes.'

'Then my advice is to do it fast, and don't tell anyone,' Morton said.

Elliot entered his office on the third floor of the Zoology Department building shortly after nine. His secretary, Carolyn, said: 'A Dr. Ross called from that Wildlife Fund in Houston; she's on her way to San Francisco. A Mr. Hakamichi called three times, says it's important. The Project Amy staff meeting is set for ten o'clock. And Windy is in your office.'

'Really?'

James Weldon was a senior professor in the Department, a weak, blustery man. 'Windy' Weldon was usually portrayed in departmental cartoons as holding a wet finger in the air: he was a master at knowing which way the wind was blowing. For the past several days, he had avoided Peter Elliot and his staff.

Elliot went into his office.

'Well, Peter my boy,' Weldon said, reaching out to give his version of a hearty handshake. 'You're in early.'

Elliot was instantly wary. 'I thought I'd beat the crowds,' he said. The picketers did not show up until ten o'clock, sometimes later, depending on when they had arranged to meet the TV news crews. That was how it worked these days: protest by appointment.

'They're not coming any more,' Weldon smiled.

He handed Elliot the late city edition of the *Chronicle*, a front-page story circled in black pen. Eleanor Vries had resigned her position as regional director of the PPA, pleading overwork and personal pressures; a statement from the PPA in New York indicated that they had seriously misconstrued the nature and content of Elliot's research.

'Meaning what?' Elliot asked.

'Belli's office reviewed your paper and Vries's public statements about torture, and decided that the PPA was exposed to a major libel suit,' Weldon said. 'The New York office is terrified. They'll be making overtures to you later today. Personally, I hope you'll be understanding.'

Elliot dropped into his chair. 'What about the faculty meeting next week?'

'Oh, that's essential,' Weldon said. 'There's no question that the faculty will want to discuss unethical conduct – on the part of the media, and issue a strong statement in your support. I'm drawing up a statement now, to come from my office.'

The irony of this was not lost on Elliot. 'You sure you want to go out on a limb?' he asked.

'I'm behind you one thousand percent, I hope you know that,' Weldon said. Weldon was restless, pacing around the office, staring at the walls, which were covered with Amy's finger paintings. Windy had something further on his mind. 'She's still making these same pictures?' he asked, finally.

'Yes,' Elliot said.

'And you still have no idea what they mean?'

Elliot paused; at best it was premature to tell Weldon what they thought the pictures meant. 'No idea,' he said.

'Are you sure?' Weldon asked, frowning. 'I think somebody knows what they mean.'

'Why is that?'

'Something very strange has happened,' Weldon said. 'Someone has offered to buy Amy.'

'To *buy* her? What are you talking about, to buy her?'

'A lawyer in Los Angeles called my office yesterday and offered to buy her for a hundred and fifty thousand dollars.'

'It must be some rich do-gooder,' Elliot said, 'trying to save Amy from torture.'

'I don't think so,' Weldon said. 'For one thing, the offer came from Japan. Someone named Hakamichi – he's in electronics in Tokyo. I found that out when the lawyer called back this morning, to increase his offer to two hundred and fifty thousand dollars.'

'Two hundred and fifty thousand dollars?' Elliot said. 'For Amy?' Of course it was out of the question. He would never sell her. But why would anyone offer so much money?

Weldon had an answer. 'This kind of money, a quarter of a million dollars, can only be coming from private enterprise. Industry. Clearly, Hakamichi has read about your work and found a use for speaking primates in an industrial context.' Windy stared at the ceiling, a sure sign he was about to wax eloquent. 'I think a new field might be opening up here, the training of primates for industrial applications in the real world.'

Peter Elliot swore. He was not teaching Amy language in order to put a hard hat on her head and a lunch pail in her hand, and he said so.

'You're not thinking it through,' Weldon said. 'What if we are on the verge of a new field of applied behavior for the great apes? Think what it means. Not only funding to the Department, and an opportunity for applied research. Most important, there would be a reason to keep these animals alive. You know that the great apes are becoming extinct. The chimps in Africa are greatly reduced in number. The orangs of Borneo are losing their natural habitat to the timber cutters and will be extinct in ten years. The gorilla is down to three thousand in the central African forests. These animals will all disappear in our lifetime – *unless there is a reason to keep them alive,* as species. You may provide that reason, Peter my boy. Think about it.'

Elliot did think about it, and he discussed it at the Project Amy staff meeting at ten o'clock. They considered possible industrial applications for apes, and possible advantages to employers, such as the lack of unions and fringe benefits. In the late twentieth century, these were major considerations. (In 1978, for each new automobile that rolled off the Detroit assembly lines, the cost of worker health benefits exceeded the cost of all the steel used to build the car.)

But they concluded that a vision of 'industrialized apes' was wildly fanciful. An ape like Amy was not a cheap and stupid version of a human worker. Quite the opposite: Amy was a highly intelligent and complex creature out of her element in the modern industrial world. She demanded a great deal of supervision; she was whimsical and unreliable; and her health was always at risk. It simply didn't make sense to use her in industry. If Hakamichi had visions of apes wielding soldering irons on a microelectronic assembly line, building TVs and hi-fi sets, he was sorely misinformed.

The only note of caution came from Bergman, the child psychologist. 'A quarter of a million is a lot of money,' he said, 'and Mr. Hakamichi is probably no fool. He must have learned about Amy through her drawings, which imply she is neurotic and difficult. If he's interested in her, I'd bet it's *because of her drawings.* But I can't imagine why those drawings should be worth a quarter of a million dollars.'

Neither could anyone else, and the discussion turned to the drawings themselves, and the newly translated texts. Sarah Johnson, in charge of research, started out with the flat comment 'I have bad news about the Congo.'*

For most of recorded history, she explained, nothing was known

* Johnson's principal reference was the definitive work by A. J. Parkinson, *The Congo Delta in Myth and History* (London: Peters, 1904).

421

about the Congo. The ancient Egyptians on the upper Nile knew only that their river originated far to the south, in a region they called the Land of Trees. This was a mysterious place with forests so dense they were as dark as night in the middle of the day. Strange creatures inhabited this perpetual gloom, including little men with tails, and animals half black and half white.

For nearly four thousand years afterward, nothing more substantial was learned about the interior of Africa. The Arabs came to East Africa in the seventh century A.D., in search of gold, ivory, spices, and slaves. But the Arabs were merchant seamen and did not venture inland. They called the interior Zinj – the Land of the Blacks – a region of fable and fantasy. There were stories of vast forests and tiny men with tails; stories of mountains that spewed fire and turned the sky black; stories of native villages overwhelmed by monkeys, which would have congress with the women; stories of great giants with hairy bodies and flat noses; stories of creatures half leopard, half man; stories of native markets where the fattened carcasses of men were butchered and sold as a delicacy.

Such stories were sufficiently forbidding to keep the Arabs on the coast, despite other stories equally alluring: mountains of shimmering gold, riverbeds gleaming with diamonds, animals that spoke the language of men, great jungle civilizations of unimaginable splendor. In particular, one story was repeated again and again in early accounts: the story of the Lost City of Zinj.

According to legend, a city known to the Hebrews of Solomonic times had been a source of inconceivable wealth in diamonds. The caravan route to the city had been jealously guarded, passed from father to son, as a sacred trust for generation after generation. But the diamond mines were exhausted and the city itself now lay in crumbling ruins, somewhere in the dark heart of Africa. The arduous caravan routes were long since swallowed up by jungle, and the last trader who remembered the way had carried his secret with him to the grave many hundreds of years before.

This mysterious and alluring place the Arabs called the Lost City of Zinj.* Yet despite its enduring fame, Johnson could find few detailed descriptions of the city. In 1187 Ibn Baratu, an Arab in Mombasa, recorded that 'the natives of the region tell . . . of a lost city far inland, called Zinj. There the inhabitants, who are black, once lived in wealth

---

* The fabled city of Zinj formed the basis for H. Rider Haggard's popular novel *King Solomon's Mines*, first published in 1885. Haggard, a gifted linguist, had served on the staff of the Governor of Natal in 1875, and he presumably heard of Zinj from the neighboring Zulus at that time.

and luxury, and even the slaves decorated themselves with jewels and especially blue diamonds, for a great store of diamonds is there.'

In 1292, a Persian named Mohammed Zaid stated that 'a large diamond [the size] of a man's clenched fist . . . was exhibited on the streets of Zanzibar, and all said it had come from the interior, where the ruins of a city called Zinj may be found, and it is here that such diamonds may be found in profusion, scattered upon the ground and also in rivers. . . .'

In 1334, another Arab, Ibn Mohammed, stated that 'our number made arrangements to seek out the city of Zinj, but quitted our quest upon learning that the city was long since abandoned, and much ruined. It is said that the aspect of the city is wondrous strange, for doors and windows are built in the curve of a half-moon, and the residences are now overtaken by a violent race of hairy men who speak in whispers no known language. . . .'

Then the Portuguese, those indefatigable explorers, arrived. By 1544, they were venturing inland from the west coast up the mighty Congo River, but they soon encountered all the obstacles that would prevent exploration of central Africa for hundreds of years to come. The Congo was not navigable beyond the first set of rapids, two hundred miles inland (at what was once Léopoldville, and is now Kinshasa). The natives were hostile and cannibalistic. And the hot steaming jungle was the source of disease – malaria, sleeping sickness, bilharzia, black-water fever – which decimated foreign intruders.

The Portuguese never managed to penetrate the central Congo. Neither did the English, under Captain Brenner, in 1644; his entire party was lost. The Congo would remain for two hundred years as a blank spot on the civilized maps of the world.

But the early explorers repeated the legends of the interior, including the story of Zinj. A Portuguese artist, Juan Diego de Valdez, drew a widely acclaimed picture of the Lost City of Zinj in 1642. 'But,' Sarah Johnson said, 'he also drew pictures of men with tails, and monkeys having carnal knowledge of native women.'

Somebody groaned.

'Apparently Valdez was crippled,' she continued. 'He lived all his life in the town of Setúbal, drinking with sailors and drawing pictures based on his conversations.'

Africa was not thoroughly explored until the mid-nineteenth century, by Burton and Speke, Baker and Livingstone, and especially Stanley. No trace of the Lost City of Zinj was found by any of them. Nor had any trace of the apocryphal city been found in the hundred years since.

The gloom that descended over the Project Amy staff meeting was profound. 'I told you it was bad news,' Sarah Johnson said.

'You mean,' Peter Elliot said, 'that this picture is based on a description, and we don't know whether the city actually exists or not.'

'I'm afraid so,' Sarah Johnson said. 'There is no proof that the city in the picture exists at all. It's just a story.'

4. Resolution

Peter Elliot's unquestioned reliance on twentieth-century hard data – facts, figures, graphs – left him unprepared for the possibility that the 1642 engraving, in all its detail, was merely the fanciful speculation of an uninhibited artist. The news came as a shock.

Their plans to take Amy to the Congo suddenly appeared childishly naïve; the resemblance of her sketchy, schematic drawings to the 1642 Valdez engraving was obviously coincidental. How could they ever have imagined that a Lost City of Zinj was anything but the stuff of ancient fable? In the seventeenth-century world of widening horizons and new wonders, the idea of such a city would have seemed perfectly reasonable, even compelling. But in the computerized twentieth century, the Lost City of Zinj was as unlikely as Camelot or Xanadu. They had been fools ever to take it seriously. 'The lost city doesn't exist,' he said.

'Oh, it exists, all right,' she said. 'There's no doubt about *that*.'

Elliot glanced up quickly, and then he saw that Sarah Johnson had not answered him. A tall gangly girl in her early twenties stood at the back of the room. She might have been considered beautiful except for her cold, aloof demeanor. This girl was dressed in a severe, businesslike suit, and she carried a briefcase, which she now set on the table, popping the latches.

'I'm Dr. Ross,' she announced, 'from the Wildlife Fund, and I'd like your opinion of these pictures.'

She passed around a series of photographs, which were viewed by the staff with an assortment of whistles and sighs. At the head of the table, Elliot waited impatiently until the photographs came down to him.

They were grainy black-and-white images with horizontal scanning line streaks, photographed off a video screen. But the image was unmistakable: a ruined city in the jungle, with curious inverted crescent-shaped doors and windows.

5. Amy

'By satellite?' Elliot repeated, hearing the tension in his voice.

'That's right, the pictures were transmitted by satellite from Africa two days ago.'

'Then you know the location of this ruin?'

'Of course.'

'And your expedition leaves in a matter of hours?'

'Six hours and twenty-three minutes, to be exact,' Ross said, glancing at her digital watch.

Elliot adjourned the meeting, and talked privately with Ross for more than an hour. Elliot later claimed that Ross had 'deceived' him about the purpose of the expedition and the hazards they would face. But Elliot was eager to go, and probably not inclined to be too fussy about the reasons behind Ross's coming expedition, or the dangers involved. As a skilled grantsman, he had long ago grown comfortable with situations where other peoples' money and his own motivations did not exactly coincide. This was the cynical side of academic life: how much pure research had been funded because it might cure cancer? A researcher promised anything to get his money.

Apparently it never occurred to Elliot that Ross might be using him as coldly as he was using her. From the start Ross was never entirely truthful; she had been instructed by Travis to explain the ERTS Congo mission 'with a little data dropout.' Data dropout was second nature to her; everyone at ERTS had learned to say no more than was necessary. Elliot treated her as if she were an ordinary funding agency, and that was a serious mistake.

In the final analysis, Ross and Elliot misjudged each other, for each presented a deceptive appearance, and in the same way. Elliot appeared so shy and retiring that one Berkeley faculty member commented, 'It's no wonder he's devoted his life to apes; he can't work up the nerve to talk to people.' But Elliot had been a tough middle linebacker in college, and his diffident academic demeanor concealed a head-crunching ambitious drive.

Similarly, Karen Ross, despite her youthful cheerleader beauty and soft, seductive Texas accent, possessed great intelligence and a deep inner toughness. (She had matured early, and a high-school teacher had once appraised her as 'the very flower of virile Texas womanhood.') Ross felt responsible for the previous ERTS expedition, and she was determined to rectify past errors. It was at least possible that Elliot and Amy could help her when she got onsite; that was reason enough to take them with her. Beyond that, Ross was concerned about the consortium, which was obviously seeking Elliot, since Hakamichi was calling. If she took Elliot and Amy with her, she removed a possible advantage to the consortium – again, reason enough to take them with her. Finally, she needed a cover in case her expedition was stopped at one of the borders – and a primatologist and an ape provided a perfect cover.

But in the end Karen Ross wanted only the Congo diamonds – and she was prepared to say anything, do anything, sacrifice anything to get them.

In photographs taken at San Francisco airport, Elliot and Ross appear as two smiling, youthful academics, embarking on a lark of an expedition to Africa. But in fact, their motivations were different, and grimly held. Elliot was reluctant to tell her how theoretical and academic his goals were – and Ross was reluctant to admit how pragmatic were hers.

In any case, by midday on June 14, Karen Ross found herself riding with Peter Elliot in his battered Fiat sedan along Hallowell Road, going past the University athletic field. She had some misgivings: they were going to meet Amy.

Elliot unlocked the door with its red sign DO NOT DISTURB ANIMAL EXPERIMENTATION IN PROGRESS. Behind the door, Amy was grunting and scratching impatiently. Elliot paused.

'When you meet her,' he said, 'remember that she is a gorilla and not a human being. Gorillas have their own etiquette. Don't speak loudly or make any sudden movements until she gets used to you. If you smile, don't show your teeth, because bared teeth are a threat. And keep your eyes downcast, because direct stares from strangers are considered hostile. Don't stand too close to me or touch me, because she's very jealous. If you talk to her, don't lie. Even though she uses sign language, she understands most human speech, and we usually just talk to her. She can tell when you're lying and she doesn't like it.'

'She doesn't like it?'

'She dismisses you, won't talk to you, and gets bitchy.'

'Anything else?'

'No, it should be okay.' He smiled reassuringly. 'We have this traditional greeting, even though she's getting a little big for it.' He opened the door, braced himself, and said, 'Good morning, Amy.'

A huge black shape came leaping out through the open door into his arms. Elliot staggered back under the impact. Ross was astonished by the size of the animal. She had been imagining something smaller and cuter. Amy was as large as an adult human female.

Amy kissed Elliot on the cheek with her large lips, her black head seeming enormous alongside his. Her breath steamed his glasses. Ross smelled a sweetish odor, and watched as he gently unwrapped her long arms from around his shoulders. 'Amy happy this morning?' he asked.

Amy's fingers moved quickly near her cheek, as if she were brushing away flies.

'Yes, I was late today,' Elliot said.

She moved her fingers again, and Ross realized that Amy was signing. The speed was surprising; she had expected something much slower and more deliberate. She noticed that Amy's eyes never left Elliot's face. She was extraordinarily attentive, focusing on him with total animal watchfulness. She seemed to absorb everything, his posture, his expression, his tone of voice, as well as his words.

'I had to work,' Elliot said. She sighed again quickly, like human gestures of dismissal. 'Yes, that's right, people work.' He led Amy back into the trailer, and motioned for Karen Ross to follow. Inside the trailer, he said, 'Amy, this is Dr. Ross. Say hello to Dr. Ross.'

Amy looked at Karen Ross suspiciously.

'Hello, Amy,' Karen Ross said, smiling at the floor. She felt a little foolish behaving this way, but Amy was large enough to frighten her.

Amy stared at Karen Ross for a moment, then walked away, across the trailer to her easel. She had been fingerpainting, and now resumed this activity, ignoring them.

'What's that mean?' Ross said. She distinctly felt she was being snubbed.

'We'll see,' Elliot said.

After a few moments, Amy ambled back, walking on her knuckles. She went directly to Karen Ross, sniffed her crotch, and examined her minutely. She seemed particularly interested in Ross's leather purse, which had a shiny brass clasp. Ross said later that 'it was just like any cocktail party in Houston. I was being checked out by another woman. I had the feeling that any minute she was going to ask me where I bought my clothes.'

That was not the outcome, however. Amy reached up and deliberately streaked globs of green finger paint on Ross's skirt.

'I don't think this is going too well,' Karen Ross said.

Elliot had watched the progress of this first meeting with more apprehension than he was willing to admit. Introducing new humans to Amy was often difficult, particularly if they were women.

Over the years, Elliot had come to recognize many distinctly 'feminine' traits in Amy. She could be coy, she responded to flattery, she was preoccupied with her appearance, loved makeup, and was very fussy about the color of the sweaters she wore in the winter. She preferred men to women, and she was openly jealous of Elliot's girl friends. He rarely brought them around to meet her, but sometimes in the morning she would sniff him for perfume, and she always commented if he had not changed his clothing overnight.

This situation might have been amusing if not for the fact that Amy made occasional unprovoked attacks on strange women. And an attack by Amy was never amusing.

Amy returned to the easel and signed, *No like woman no like Amy no like go away away.*

'Come on, Amy, be a good gorilla,' Peter said.

'What did she say?' Ross asked, going to the sink to wash the finger paint from her dress. Peter noticed that she did not squeal and shriek as many visitors did when they received an unfriendly greeting from Amy.

'She said she likes your dress,' he said.

Amy shot him a look, as she always did whenever Elliot mistranslated her. *Amy not lie. Peter not lie.*

'Be nice, Amy,' he said. 'Karen is a nice human person.'

Amy grunted, and returned to her work, painting rapidly.

'What happens now?' Karen Ross said.

'Give her time.' He smiled reassuringly. 'She needs time to adjust.'

He did not bother to explain that it was much worse with chimpanzees. Chimps threw feces at strangers, and even at workers they knew well; they sometimes attacked to establish dominance. Chimpanzees had a strong need to determine who was in charge. Fortunately, gorillas were much less formal in their dominance hierarchies, and less violent.

At that moment, Amy ripped the paper from the easel and shredded it noisily, flinging the pieces around the room.

'Is this part of the adjustment?' Karen Ross asked. She seemed more amused than frightened.

'Amy, cut it out,' Peter said, allowing his tone to convey irritation. 'Amy . . .'

Amy sat in the middle of the floor, surrounded by the paper. She tore it angrily and signed, *This woman. This woman.* It was classic displacement behavior. Whenever gorillas did not feel comfortable with direct aggression, they did something symbolic. In symbolic terms, she was now tearing Karen Ross apart.

And she was getting worked up, beginning what the Project Amy staff called 'sequencing.' Just as human beings first became red-faced, and then tensed their bodies, and then shouted and threw things before they finally resorted to direct physical aggression, so gorillas passed through a stereotyped behavioral sequence on the way to physical aggression. Tearing up paper, or grass, would be followed by lateral crablike movements and grunts. Then she would slap the ground, making as much noise as possible.

And then Amy would charge, if he didn't interrupt the sequence.

'Amy,' he said sternly. 'Karen button woman.'

Amy stopped shredding. In her world, 'button' was the acknowledged term for a person of high status.

Amy was extremely sensitive to individual moods and behavior, and she had no difficulty observing the staff and deciding who was superior to whom. But among strangers, Amy as a gorilla was utterly impervious to formal human status cues; the principal indicators – clothing, bearing, and speech – had no meaning to her.

As a young animal, she had inexplicably attacked policemen. After several biting episodes and threatened lawsuits, they finally learned that Amy found police uniforms with their shiny buttons clownlike and ridiculous; she assumed that anyone so foolishly dressed must be of inferior status and safe to attack. After they had taught her the concept of 'button,' she treated anyone in uniform with deference.

Amy now stared at 'button' Ross with new respect. Surrounded by the torn paper, she seemed suddenly embarrassed, as if she had made a social error. Without being told, she went and stood in the corner, facing the wall.

'What's that about?' Ross said.

'She knows she's been bad.'

'You make her stand in the corner, like a child? She didn't mean any harm.' Before Elliot could warn against it, she went over to Amy. Amy stared steadfastly at the corner.

Ross unshouldered her purse and set it on the floor within Amy's reach. Nothing happened for a moment. Then Amy took the purse, looked at Karen, then looked at Peter.

Peter said, 'She'll wreck whatever's inside.'

'That's all right.'

Amy immediately opened the brass clasp, and dumped the contents on the floor. She began sifting through, signing, *Lipstick lipstick, Amy like Amy want lipstick want.*

'She wants lipstick.'

Ross bent over and found it for her. Amy removed the cap and smeared a red circle on Karen's face. She then smiled and grunted happily, and crossed the room to her mirror, which was mounted on the floor. She applied lipstick.

'I think we're doing better,' Karen Ross said.

Across the room, Amy squatted by the mirror, happily making a mess of her face. She grinned at her smart image, then applied lipstick to her teeth. It seemed a good time to ask her the question. 'Amy want take trip?' Peter said.

Amy loved trips, and regarded them as special treats. After an especially good day, Elliot often took her for a ride to a nearby drive-in, where she would have an orange drink, sucking it through the straw and enjoying the commotion she caused among the other people there. Lipstick and an offer of a trip was almost too much pleasure for one morning. She signed, *Car trip?*

'No, not in the car. A long trip. Many days.'

Leave house?

'Yes, leave house. Many days.'

This made her suspicious. The only times she had left the house for many days had been during hospitalizations for pneumonia and urinary-tract infections; they had not been pleasant trips. She signed, *Where go trip?*

'To the jungle, Amy.'

There was a long pause. At first he thought she had not understood, but she knew the word for jungle, and she should be able to put it all together. Amy signed thoughtfully to herself, repetitively as she always did when she was mulling things over: *Jungle trip trip jungle go trip jungle go.* She set aside her lipstick. She stared at the bits of paper on the floor, and then she began to pick them up and put them in the wastebasket.

'What does that mean?' Karen Ross asked.

'That means Amy wants to take a trip,' Peter Elliot said.

6. Departure

The hinged nose of the Boeing 747 cargo jet lay open like a jaw, exposing the cavernous, brightly lit interior. The plane had been flown up from Houston to San Francisco that afternoon; it was now nine o'clock at night, and puzzled workers were loading on the large aluminum travel cage, boxes of vitamin pills, a portable potty, and cartons of toys. One workman pulled out a Mickey Mouse drinking cup and stared at it, shaking his head.

Outside on the concrete, Elliot stood with Amy, who covered her ears against the whine of the jet engines. She signed to Peter, *Birds noisy.*

'We fly bird, Amy,' he said.

Amy had never flown before, and had never seen an airplane at close hand. *We go car*, she decided, looking at the plane.

'We can't go by car. We fly.'

Fly where fly? Amy signed.

'Fly jungle.'

This seemed to perplex her, but he did not want to explain further. Like all gorillas, Amy had an aversion to water, refusing to cross even small streams. He knew she would be distressed to hear that they would be flying over large bodies of water. Changing the subject, he suggested they board the plane and look around. As they climbed the sloping ramp up the nose, Amy signed, *Where button woman?*

He had not seen Ross for the last five hours, and was surprised to discover that she was already on board, talking on a telephone mounted on a wall of the cargo hold, one hand cupped over her free ear to block the noise. Elliot overheard her say, 'Well, Irving seems to think it's enough. . . . Yes, we have four nine-oh-seven units and we are prepared to match and absorb. Two micro HUDs, that's all. . . . Yes, why not?' She finished the call, turned to Elliot and Amy.

'Everything okay?' he asked.

'Fine. I'll show you around.' She led him deeper into the cargo hold, with Amy at his side. Elliot glanced back and saw the chauffeur coming up the ramp with a series of numbered metal boxes marked INTEC, INC. followed by serial numbers.

'This,' Karen Ross said, 'is the main cargo hold.' It was filled with four-wheel-drive trucks, Land Cruisers, amphibious vehicles, inflatable boats, and racks of clothing, equipment, food – all tagged with computer codes, all loaded in modules. Ross explained that ERTS could outfit expeditions to any geographical and climatic condition in a matter of hours. She kept emphasizing the speed possible with computer assembly.

'Why the rush?' Elliot asked.

'It's business,' Karen Ross said. 'Four years ago, there were no companies like ERTS. Now there are nine around the world, and what they all sell is competitive advantage, meaning speed. Back in the sixties, a company – say, an oil company – might spend months or years investigating a possible site. But that's no longer competitive; business decisions are made in weeks or days. The pace of everything has speeded up. We're already looking to the nineteen-eighties, where we'll provide answers in *hours*. Right now the average ERTS contract runs a little under three weeks, or five hundred hours. But by 1990 there will be 'close of business' data – an executive can call us in the morning for information anywhere in the world, and have a complete report transmitted by computer to his desk before close of business that evening, say ten to twelve hours.'

As they continued the tour, Elliot noticed that although the trucks and vehicles caught the eye first, much of the aircraft storage space was given over to aluminum modules marked 'C31.'

'That's right,' Ross said. 'Command-Control Communications and

Intelligence. They're micronic components, the most expensive budget item we carry. When we started outfitting expeditions, twelve percent of the cost went to electronics. Now it's up to thirty-one percent, and climbing every year. It's field communications, remote sensing, defense, and so on.'

She led them to the rear of the plane, where there was a modular living area, nicely furnished, with a large computer console, and bunks for sleeping.

Amy signed, *Nice house.*

'Yes, it is nice.'

They were introduced to Jensen, a young bearded geologist, and to Irving Levine, who announced that he was the 'triple E.' The two men were running some kind of probability study on the computer but they paused to shake hands with Amy, who regarded them gravely, and then turned her attention to the screen. Amy was captivated by the colorful screen images and bright LEDs, and kept trying to punch the buttons herself. She signed, *Amy play box.*

'Not now, Amy,' Elliot said, and swatted her hands away.

Jensen asked, 'Is she always this way?'

'I'm afraid so,' Elliot said. 'She likes computers. She's worked around them ever since she was very young, and she thinks of them as her private property.' And then he added, 'What's a triple E?'

'Expedition electronics expert,' Irving said cheerfully. He was a short man with an impish quick smile. 'Doing the best I can. We picked up some stuff from Intec, that's about all. God knows what the Japs and the Germans will throw at us.'

'Oh, damn, there she goes,' Jensen said, laughing as Amy pushed the buttons.

Elliot said, 'Amy no!'

'It's just a game. Probably not interesting to apes,' Jensen said. And he added, 'She can't hurt anything.'

Amy signed, *Amy good gorilla,* and pushed the buttons on the computer again. She appeared relaxed, and Elliot was grateful for the distraction the computer provided. He was always amused by the sight of Amy's heavy dark form before a computer console. She would touch her lower lip thoughtfully before pushing the buttons, in what seemed a parody of human behavior.

Ross, practical as always, brought them back to mundane matters. 'Will Amy sleep on one of the bunks?'

Elliot shook his head. 'No. Gorillas expect to make a fresh bed each night. Give her some blankets, and she'll twist them into a nest on the floor and sleep there.'

Ross nodded. 'What about her vitamins and medications? Will she swallow pills?'

'Ordinarily you have to bribe her, or hide the pills in a piece of banana. She tends to gulp banana, without chewing it.'

'Without chewing.' Ross nodded as if that were important. 'We have a standard issue,' she said. 'I'll see that she gets them.'

'She takes the same vitamins that people do, except that she'll need lots of ascorbic acid.'

'We issue three thousand units a day. That's enough? Good. And she'll tolerate anti-malarials? We have to start them right away.'

'Generally speaking,' Elliot said, 'she has the same reaction to medication as people.'

Ross nodded. 'Will the cabin pressurization bother her? It's set at five thousand feet.'

Elliot shook his head. 'She's a mountain gorilla, and they live at five thousand to nine thousand feet, so she's actually altitude-adapted. But she's acclimated to a moist climate and she dehydrates quickly; we'll have to keep forcing fluids on her.'

'Can she use the head?'

'The seat's probably too high for her,' Elliot said, 'but I brought her potty.'

'She'll use her potty?'

'Sure.'

'I have a new collar for her; will she wear it?'

'If you give it to her as a gift.'

As they reviewed other details of Amy's requirements, Elliot realized that something had happened during the last few hours, almost without his knowing it: Amy's unpredictable, dream-driven neurotic behavior had fallen away. It was as if the earlier behavior was irrelevant; now that she was going on a trip, she was no longer moody and introspective, her interests were outgoing; she was once again a youthful female gorilla. He found himself wondering whether her dreams, her depression – finger paintings, everything – were a result of her confined laboratory environment for so many years. At first the laboratory had been agreeable, like a crib for young children. But perhaps in later years it pinched. Perhaps, he thought, Amy just needed a little excitement.

Excitement was in the air: as he talked with Ross, Elliot felt something remarkable was about to happen. This expedition with Amy was the first example of an event primate researchers had predicted for years – the Pearl thesis.

Frederick Pearl was a theoretical animal behaviorist. At a meeting of the American Ethnological Society in New York in 1972, he had said, 'Now that primates have learned sign language, it is only a matter of time until someone takes an animal into the field to assist the study of wild animals of the same species. We can imagine language-skilled primates acting as interpreters or perhaps even as ambassadors for mankind, in contact with wild creatures.'

Pearl's thesis attracted considerable attention, and funding from the U.S. Air Force, which had supported linguistic research since the 1960s. According to one story, the Air Force had a secret project called CONTOUR, involving possible contact with alien life forms. The official military position was that UFOs were of natural origin – but the military was covering its bets. Should alien contact occur, linguistic fundamentals were obviously critically important. And taking primates into the field was seen as an example of contact with 'alien intelligence'; hence the Air Force funding.

Pearl predicted that fieldwork would be undertaken before 1976, but in fact no one had yet done it. The reason was that on closer examination, no one could figure out quite what the advantages were – most language-using primates were as baffled by wild primates as human beings were. Some, like the chimpanzee Arthur, denied any association with their own kind, referring to them as 'black things.' (Amy, who had been taken to the zoo to view other gorillas, recognized them but was haughty, calling them 'stupid gorillas' once she found that when she signed to them, they did not reply.)

Such observations led another researcher, John Bates, to say in 1977 that 'we are producing an educated animal élite which demonstrates the same snobbish aloofness that a Ph.D. shows toward a truck driver . . . It is highly unlikely that the generation of language-using primates will be skillful ambassadors in the field. They are simply too disdainful.'

But the truth was that no one really knew what would happen when a primate was taken into the field. Because no one had done it: Amy would be the first.

At eleven o'clock, the ERTS cargo plane taxied down the runway at San Francisco International, lifted ponderously into the air, and headed east through the darkness toward Africa.

DAY 3: TANGIER
June 15, 1979

1. Ground Truth

Peter Elliot had known Amy since infancy. He prided himself on his ability to predict her responses, although he had only known her in a laboratory setting. Now, as she was faced with new situations, her behavior surprised him.

Elliot had anticipated Amy would be terrified of the take-off, and had prepared a syringe with Thoralen tranquilizer. But sedation proved unnecessary: Amy watched Jensen and Levine buckle their seat belts, and she immediately buckled herself in, too; she seemed to regard the procedure as an amusing, if simpleminded, game. And although her eyes widened when she heard the full roar of the engines, the human beings around her did not seem disturbed, and Amy imitated their bored indifference, raising her eyebrows and sighing at the tedium of it all.

Once airborne, however, Amy looked out the window and immediately panicked. She released her seat belt and scurried back and forth across the passenger compartment, moving from window to window, knocking people aside in whimpering terror while she signed, *Where ground ground where ground?* Outside, the ground was black and indistinct. *Where ground?* Elliot shot her with Thoralen and then began grooming her, sitting her down and plucking at her hair.

In the wild, primates devoted several hours each day to grooming one another, removing ticks and lice. Grooming behavior was important in ordering the group's social dominance structure – there was a pattern by which animals groomed each other, and with what frequency. And, like back rubs for people, grooming seemed to have a soothing, calming effect. Within minutes, Amy had relaxed enough to notice that the others were drinking, and she promptly demanded a 'green drop drink' – her term for a martini with an olive – and a cigarette. She was allowed this on special occasions such as departmental parties, and Elliot now gave her a drink and a cigarette.

But the excitement proved too much for her: an hour later, she was quietly looking out the window and signing *Nice picture* to herself when she vomited. She apologized abjectly, *Amy sorry Amy mess Amy Amy sorry.*

'It's all right, Amy,' Elliot assured her, stroking the back of her head. Soon afterward, signing *Amy sleep now*, she twisted the blankets into a nest on the floor and went to sleep, snoring loudly through her broad nostrils. Lying next to her, Elliot thought, how do other gorillas get to sleep with this racket?

Elliot had his own reaction to the journey. When he had first met Karen

Ross, he assumed she was an academic like himself. But this enormous airplane filled with computerized equipment, the acronymic complexity of the entire operation suggested that Earth Resources Technology had powerful resources behind it, perhaps even a military association.

Karen Ross laughed. 'We're much too organized to be military.' She then told him the background of the ERTS interest in Virunga. Like the Project Amy staff, Karen Ross had also stumbled upon the legend of the Lost City of Zinj. But she had drawn very different conclusions from the story.

During the last three hundred years, there had been several attempts to reach the lost city. In 1692, John Marley, an English adventurer, led an expedition of two hundred into the Congo; it was never heard from again. In 1744, a Dutch expedition went in; in 1804, another British party led by a Scottish aristocrat, Sir James Taggert, approached Virunga from the north, getting as far as the Rawana bend of the Ubangi River. He sent an advance party farther south, but it never returned.

In 1872, Stanley passed near the Virunga region but did not enter it; in 1899, a German expedition went in, losing more than half its party. A privately financed Italian expedition disappeared entirely in 1911. There had been no more recent searches for the Lost City of Zinj.

'So no one has ever found it,' Elliot said.

Ross shook her head. 'I think several expeditions found the city,' she said. 'But nobody ever got back out again.'

Such an outcome was not necessarily mysterious. The early days of African exploration were incredibly hazardous. Even carefully managed expeditions lost half of their party or more. Those who did not succumb to malaria, sleeping sickness, and blackwater fever faced rivers teeming with crocodiles and hippos, jungles with leopards and suspicious, cannibalistic natives. And, for all its luxuriant growth, the rain forest provided little edible food; a number of expeditions had starved to death.

'I began,' Ross said to Elliot, 'with the idea that the city existed, after all. Assuming it existed, where would I find it?'

The Lost City of Zinj was associated with diamond mines, and diamonds were found with volcanoes. This led Ross to look along the Great Rift Valley – an enormous geological fault thirty miles wide, which sliced vertically up the eastern third of the continent for a distance of fifteen hundred miles. The Rift Valley was so huge that its existence was not recognized until the 1890s, when a geologist named Gregory noticed that the cliff walls thirty miles apart were composed of the same rocks. In modern terms the Great Rift was actually an abortive attempt to form an ocean, for the eastern third of the continent had begun splitting off from the rest of the African land mass two hundred million years ago; for some reason, it had stopped before the break was complete.

On a map the Great Rift depression was marked by two features: a series of thin vertical lakes – Malawi, Tanganyika, Kivu, Mobutu – and a series of volcanoes, including the only active volcanoes in Africa at Virunga. Three volcanoes in the Virunga chain were active: Mukenko, Mubuti, and Kanagarawi. They rose 11,000–15,000 feet above the Rift Valley to the east, and the Congo Basin to the west. Thus Virunga seemed a good place to look for diamonds. Her next step was to investigate the ground truth.

'What's ground truth?' Peter asked.

'At ERTS, we deal mostly in remote sensing,' she explained. 'Satellite photographs, aerial run-bys, radar side scans. We carry millions of remote images, but there's no substitute for ground truth, the experience of a team actually on the site, finding out what's there. I started with the preliminary expedition we sent in looking for gold. They found diamonds as well.' She punched buttons on the console, and the screen images changed, glowing with dozens of flashing pinpoints of light.

'This shows the placer deposit locations in streambeds near Virunga. You see the deposits form concentric semicircles leading back to the volcanoes. The obvious conclusion is that diamonds were eroded from the slopes of the Virunga volcanoes, and washed down the streams to their present locations.'

'So you sent in a party to look for the source?'

'Yes.' She pointed to the screen. 'But don't be deceived by what you see here. This satellite image covers fifty thousand square kilometers of jungle. Most of it has never been seen by white men. It's hard terrain, with visibility limited to a few meters in any direction. An expedition could search that area for years, passing within two hundred meters of the city and failing to see it. So I needed to narrow the search sector. I decided to see if I could find the city.'

'Find the city? From satellite pictures?'

'Yes,' she said. 'And I found it.'

The rain forests of the world had traditionally frustrated remote-sensing technology. The great jungle trees spread an impenetrable canopy of vegetation, concealing whatever lay beneath. In aerial or satellite pictures, the Congo rain forest appeared as a vast, undulating carpet of featureless and monotonous green. Even large features, rivers fifty or a hundred feet wide, were hidden beneath this leafy canopy, invisible from the air.

So it seemed unlikely she would find any evidence for a lost city in aerial photographs. But Ross had a different idea: she would utilize the very vegetation that obscured her vision of the ground.

The study of vegetation was common in temperate regions, where the foliage underwent seasonal changes. But the equatorial rain forest was unchanging: winter or summer, the foliage remained the same. Ross turned her attention to another aspect, the differences in vegetation albedo.

Albedo was technically defined as the ratio of electromagnetic energy reflected by a surface to the amount of energy incident upon it. In terms of the visible spectrum, it was a measure of how 'shiny' a surface was. A river had a high albedo, since water reflected most of the sunlight striking it. Vegetation absorbed light, and therefore had a low albedo. Starting in 1977, ERTS developed computer programs which measured albedo precisely, making very fine distinctions.

Ross asked herself the question: If there was a lost city, what signature might appear in the vegetation? There was an obvious answer: late secondary jungle.

The untouched or virgin rain forest was called primary jungle. Primary jungle was what most people thought of when they thought of rain forests: huge hardwood trees, mahogany and teak and ebony, and underneath a lower layer of ferns and palms, clinging to the ground. Primary jungle was dark and forbidding, but actually easy to move through. However, if the primary jungle was cleared by man and later abandoned, an entirely different secondary growth took over. The dominant plants were softwoods and fast-growing trees, bamboo and thorny tearing vines, which formed a dense and impenetrable barrier.

But Ross was not concerned about any aspect of the jungle except its albedo. Because the secondary plants were different, secondary jungle had a different albedo from primary jungle. And it could be graded by age: unlike the hardwood trees of primary jungle, which lived hundreds of years, the softwoods of secondary jungle lived only twenty years or so. Thus as time went on, the secondary jungle was replaced by another form of secondary jungle, and later by still another form.

By checking regions where late secondary jungle was generally found – such as the banks of large rivers, where innumerable human settlements had been cleared and abandoned – Ross confirmed that the ERTS computers could, indeed, measure the necessary small differences in reflectivity.

She then instructed the ERTS scanners to search for albedo differences of .03 or less, with a unit signature size of a hundred meters or less, across the fifty thousand square kilometers of rain forest on the western slopes of the Virunga volcanoes. This job would occupy a team of fifty human aerial photographic analysts for thirty-one years. The computer scanned 129,000 satellite and aerial photographs in under nine hours.

And found her city.

In May, 1979, Ross had a computer image showing a very old secondary jungle pattern laid out in a geometric, gridlike form. The pattern was located 2 degrees north of the equator, longitude 30 degrees, on the western slopes of the active volcano Mukenko. The computer estimated the age of the secondary jungle at five hundred to eight hundred years.

'So you sent an expedition in?' Elliot said.

Ross nodded. 'Three weeks ago, led by a South African named Kruger. The expedition confirmed the placer diamond deposits, went on to search for the origin, and found the ruins of the city.'

'And then what happened?' Elliot asked.

He ran the videotape a second time.

Onscreen he saw black-and-white images of the camp, destroyed, smoldering. Several dead bodies with crushed skulls were visible. As they watched, a shadow moved over the dead bodies, and the camera zoomed back to show the outline of the lumbering shadow. Elliot agreed that it looked like the shadow of a gorilla, but he insisted, 'Gorillas couldn't do this. Gorillas are peaceful, vegetarian animals.'

They watched as the tape ran to the end. And then they reviewed her final computer-reconstituted image, which clearly showed the head of a male gorilla.

'That's ground truth,' Ross said.

Elliot was not so sure. He reran the last three seconds of videotape a final time, staring at the gorilla head. The image was fleeting, leaving a ghostly trail, but something was wrong with it. He couldn't quite identify what. Certainly this was atypical gorilla behavior, but there was something else. . . . He pushed the freeze-frame button and stared at the frozen image. The face and the fur were both gray: unquestionably gray.

'Can we increase contrast?' he asked Ross. 'This image is washed out.'

'I don't know,' Ross said, touching the controls. 'I think this is a pretty good image.' She was unable to darken it.

'It's very gray,' he said. 'Gorillas are much darker.'

'Well, this contrast range is correct for video.'

Elliot was sure this creature was too light to be a mountain gorilla. Either they were seeing a new race of animal, *or a new species*. A new species of great ape, gray in color, aggressive in behavior, discovered in the eastern Congo. . . . He had come on this expedition to verify Amy's dreams – a fascinating psychological insight – but now the stakes were suddenly much higher.

Ross said, 'You don't think this is a gorilla?'

'There are ways to test it,' he said. He stared at the screen, frowning, as the plane flew onward in the night.

2. B-8 Problems

'You want me to *what?*' Tom Seamans said, cradling the phone in his shoulder and rolling over to look at his bedside clock. It was 3 a.m.

'Go to the zoo,' Elliot repeated. His voice sounded garbled, as if coming from under water.

'Peter, where are you calling from?'

'We're somewhere over the Atlantic now,' Elliot said. 'On our way to Africa.'

'Is everything all right?'

'Everything is fine,' Elliot said. 'But I want you to go to the zoo first thing in the morning.'

'And do what?'

'Videotape the gorillas. Try to get them in movement. That's very important for the discriminant function, that they be moving.'

'I'd better write this down,' Seamans said. Seamans handled the computer programming for the Project Amy staff, and he was accustomed to unusual requests, but not in the middle of the night. 'What discriminant function?'

'While you're at it, run any films we have in the library of gorillas – any gorillas, wild or in zoos or whatever. The more specimens the better, so long as they're moving. And for a baseline, you'd better use chimps. Anything we have on chimps. Transfer it to tape and put it through the function.'

'What function?' Seamans yawned.

'The function you're going to write,' Elliot said. 'I want a multiple variable discriminant function based on total imagery –'

'You mean a pattern-recognition function?' Seamans had written pattern-recognition functions for Amy's language use, enabling them to monitor her signing around the clock. Seamans was proud of that program; in its own way, it was highly inventive.

'However you structure it,' Elliot said. 'I just want a function that'll discriminate gorillas from other primates like chimps. A species-differentiating function.'

'Are you kidding?' Seamans said. 'That's a B-8 problem.' In the developing field of pattern-recognition computer programs, so-called B-8 problems were the most difficult; whole teams of researchers had devoted years to trying to teach computers the difference between 'B' and '8' – precisely because the difference was so obvious. But what was obvious to the human eye was not obvious to the computer scanner. The scanner had to be told, and the specific instructions turned out to be far more difficult than anyone anticipated, particularly for handwritten characters.

Now Elliot wanted a program that would distinguish between similar visual images of gorillas and chimps. Seamans could not help asking, 'Why? It's pretty obvious. A gorilla is a gorilla, and a chimp is a chimp.'

'Just do it,' Elliot said.

'Can I use size?' On the basis of size alone, gorillas and chimps could be accurately distinguished. But visual functions could not determine size unless the distance from the recording instrument to the subject image was known, as well as the focal length of the recording lens.

'No, you can't use size,' Elliot said. 'Element morphology only.'

Seamans sighed. 'Thanks a lot. What resolution?'

'I need ninety-five-percent confidence limits on species assignment, to be based on less than three seconds of black-and-white scan imagery.'

Seamans frowned. Obviously, Elliot had three seconds of videotape imagery of some animal and he was not sure whether it was a gorilla or not. Elliot had seen enough gorillas over the years to know the difference: gorillas and chimps were utterly different animals in size, appearance, movement, and behaviour. They were as different as intelligent oceanic mammals – say, porpoises and whales. In making such discriminations, the human eye was far superior to any computer program that could be devised. Yet Elliot apparently did not trust his eye. What was he thinking of?

'I'll try,' Seamans said, 'but it's going to take a while. You don't write that kind of program overnight.'

'I need it overnight, Tom,' Elliot said. 'I'll call you back in twenty-four hours.'

3. Inside the Coffin

In one corner of the 747 living module was a sound-baffled fiberglass booth, with a hinged hood and a small CRT screen; it was called 'the coffin' because of the claustrophobic feeling that came from working inside it. As the airplane crossed the mid-Atlantic, Ross stepped inside the coffin. She had a last look at Elliot and Amy – both asleep, both snoring loudly – and Jensen and Levine playing 'submarine chase' on the computer console, as she lowered the hood.

Ross was tired, but she did not expect to get much sleep for the next two weeks, which was as long as she thought the expedition would last. Within fourteen days – 336 hours – Ross's team would either have beaten the Euro-Japanese consortium or she would have failed and the Zaire Virunga mineral exploration rights would be lost forever.

The race was already under way, and Karen Ross did not intend to lose it.

She punched Houston coordinates, including her own sender designation, and waited while the scrambler interlocked. From now on, there would be a signal delay of five seconds at both ends, because both she and Houston would be sending in coded burst transmissions to elude passive listeners.

The screen glowed: TRAVIS.

She typed back: ROSS. She picked up the telephone receiver.

'It's a bitch,' Travis said, although it was not Travis's voice, but a computer-generated flat audio signal, without expression.

'Tell me,' Ross said.

'The slants are rolling,' Travis's surrogate voice said.

She knew his slang: Travis called all competition 'slants'; in most instances during the past four years, the competition had been Japanese. (Travis was fond of saying, 'In the eighties, it's the Japs. In the nineties, it'll be the Chinks. Either way it's slants, and they all work Sundays and to hell with the football game. We gotta keep up.')

'Details,' Ross said, and waited for the five-second delay. She could imagine Travis in the CCR in Houston, hearing her own computer-generated voice. That flat voice required a change in speech patterns; what was ordinarily conveyed by phrasing and emphasis had to be made explicit.

'They know you're on your way,' Travis's voice whined. 'They are pushing their own schedule. The Germans are behind it – your friend Richter. I'm arranging a feeding in a matter of minutes. That's the good news.'

'And the bad news?'

'The Congo has gone to hell in the last ten hours,' Travis said. 'We have a nasty GPU.'

'Print,' she said.

On the screen, she saw printed GEOPOLITICAL UPDATE, followed by a dense paragraph. It read:

ZAIRE EMBASSY WASHINGTON STATES EASTERN BORDERS VIA RWANDA CLOSED / NO EXPLANATION / PRESUMPTION IDI AMIN TROOPS FLEEING TANZANIAN INVASION UGANDA INTO EASTERN ZAIRE / CONSEQUENT DISRUPTION / BUT FACTS DIFFER / LOCAL TRIBES {KIGANI} ON RAMPAGE / REPORTED ATROCITIES AND CANNIBALISM ETC / FOREST-DWELLING PYGMIES UNRELIABLE / KILLING ALL VISITORS CONGO RAIN FOREST / ZAIRE GOVERNMENT DISPATCHED GENERAL MUGURU {AKA BUTCHER OF STANLEYVILLE} / PUT DOWN KIGANI REBELLION 'AT ALL COSTS' / SITUATION HIGHLY UNSTABLE / ONLY LEGAL ENTRY INTO ZAIRE NOW WEST THROUGH KINSHASA / YOU ARE ON YOUR OWN / ACQUISITION WHITE HUNTER MUNRO NOW PARAMOUNT IMPORTANCE WHATEVER COST / KEEP HIM FROM CONSORTIUM WILL PAY ANYTHING / YOUR SITUATION EXTREME DANGER / MUST HAVE MUNRO TO SURVIVE /

She stared at the screen. It was the worst possible news. She said, 'Have you got a time course?'

EURO-JAPANESE CONSORTIUM NOW COMPRISES HAKAMICHI {JAPAN} / GERLICH {GERMANY} / VOORSTER {AMSTERDAM} / UNFORTUNATELY HAVE RESOLVED DIFFERENCES NOW IN COMPLETE ACCORD / MONITORING US CANNOT ANTICIPATE SECURE TRANSMISSIONS ANYTIME HENCEFORTH / ANTICIPATE ELECTRONIC COUNTERMEASURES AND WARFARE TACTICS IN PURSUIT OF TWO-B GOAL / THEY WILL ENTER CONGO {RELIABLE SOURCE} WITHIN 48 HOURS NOW SEEKING MUNRO /

'When will they reach Tangier?' she asked.

'In six hours. You?'

'Seven hours. And Munro?'

'We don't know about Munro,' Travis said. 'Can you booby him?'

'Absolutely,' Ross said. 'I'll arrange the booby now. If Munro doesn't see things our way, I promise you it'll be seventy-two hours before he's allowed out of the country.'

'What've you got?' Travis asked.

'Czech submachine guns. Found on the premises, with his prints on them, carefully applied. That should do it.'

'That should do it,' Travis agreed. 'What about your passengers?'
He was referring to Elliot and Amy.

'They're fine,' Ross said. 'They know nothing.'

'Keep it that way,' Travis said, and hung up.

4. Feeding Time

'It's feeding time,' Travis called cheerfully. 'Who's at the trough?'

'We've got five tap dancers on Beta dataline,' Rogers said. Rogers
was the electronic surveillance expert, the bug catcher.

'Anybody we know?'

'Know them all,' Rogers said, slightly annoyed. 'Beta line is our
main cross-trunk line in-house, so whoever wants to tap in to our system
will naturally plug in there. You get more bits and pieces that way. Of
course we aren't using Beta any more except for routine uncoded
garbage – taxes and payroll, that stuff.'

'We have to arrange a feed,' Travis said. A feed meant putting false
data out over a tapped line, to be picked up. It was a delicate operation.
'You have the slants on the line?'

'Sure. What do you want to feed them?'

'Coordinates for the lost city,' Travis said.

Rogers nodded, mopping his brow. He was a portly man who
sweated profusely. 'How good do you want it?'

'Damn good,' Travis said. 'You won't fool the slants with static.'

'You don't want to give them the actual co-ords?'

'God, no. But I want them reasonably close. Say, within two
hundred kilometers.'

'Can do,' Rogers said.

'Coded?' Travis said.

'Of course.'

'You have a code they can break in twelve to fifteen hours?'

Rogers nodded. 'We've got a dilly. Looks like hell, but then when
you work it, it pops out. Got an internal weakness in concealed lettering
frequency. At the other end, looks like we made a mistake, but it's very
breakable.'

'It can't be too easy,' Travis warned.

'Oh, no, they'll earn their yen. They'll never suspect a feed. We
ran it past the army and they came back all smiles, teaching us a lesson.
Never knew it was a setup.'

'Okay,' Travis said, 'put the data out, and let's feed them. I want something that'll give them a sense of confidence for the next forty-eight hours or more – until they figure out that we've screwed them.'

'Delighted,' Rogers said, and he moved off to Beta terminal.

Travis sighed. The feeding would soon begin, and he hoped it would protect his team in the field – long enough for them to get to the diamonds first.

5. Dangerous Signatures

The soft murmur of voices woke him.

'How unequivocal is that signature?'

'Pretty damn unequivocal. Here's the pissup, nine days ago, and it's not even epicentered.'

'That's cloud cover?'

'No, that's not cloud cover, it's too black. That's ejecta from the signature.'

'Hell.'

Elliot opened his eyes to see dawn breaking as a thin red line against blue-black through the windows of the passenger compartment. His watch read 5:11 – five in the morning, San Francisco time. He had slept only two hours since calling Seamans. He yawned and glanced down at Amy, curled up in her nest of blankets on the floor. Amy snored loudly. The other bunks were unoccupied.

He heard soft voices again, and looked toward the computer console. Jensen and Levine were staring at a screen and talking quietly. 'Dangerous signature. We got a computer projection on that?'

'Coming. It'll take a while. I asked for a five-year runback, as well as the other pissups.'

Elliot climbed out of his cot and looked at the screen. 'What're pissups?' he said.

'PSOPs are prior significant orbital passes by the satellite,' Jensen explained. 'They're called pissups because we usually ask for them when we're already pissing upwind. We've been looking at this volcanic signature here,' Jensen said, pointing to the screen. 'It's not too promising.'

'What volcanic signature?' Elliot asked.

They showed him the billowing plumes of smoke – dark green in artificial computer-generated colors – which belched from the mouth of Mukenko, one of the active volcanoes of the Virunga range. 'Mukenko erupts on the average of once every three years,' Levine said. 'The last eruption was March, 1977, but it looks like it's gearing up for another full eruption in the next week or so. We're waiting now for the probability assessment.'

'Does Ross know about this?'

They shrugged. 'She knows, but she doesn't seem worried. She got an urgent GPU – geopolitical update – from Houston about two hours ago, and she went directly into the cargo bay. Haven't seen her since.'

Elliot went into the dimly lit cargo bay of the jet. The cargo bay was not insulated and it was chilly: the trucks had a thin frost on metal and glass, and his breath hissed from his mouth. He found Karen Ross working at a table under low pools of light. Her back was turned to him, but when he approached, she dropped what she was doing and turned to face him.

'I thought you were asleep,' she said.

'I got restless. What's going on?'

'Just checking supplies. This is our advanced technology unit,' she said, lifting up a small backpack. 'We've developed a miniaturized package for field parties; twenty pounds of equipment contains everything a man needs for two weeks: food, water, clothing, everything.'

'Even water?' Elliot asked.

Water was heavy: seven-tenths of human body weight was water, and most of the weight of food was water; that was why dehydrated food was so light. But water was far more critical to human life than food. Men could survive for weeks without food, but they would die in a matter of hours without water. And water was heavy.

Ross smiled. 'The average man consumes four to six liters a day, which is eight to thirteen pounds of weight. On a two-week expedition to a desert region, we'd have to provide two hundred pounds of water for each man. But we have a NASA water-recycling unit which purifies all excretions, including urine. It weighs six ounces. That's how we do it.'

Seeing his expression, she said, 'It's not bad at all. Our purified water is cleaner than what you get from the tap.'

'I'll take your word for it.' Elliot picked up a pair of strange looking sunglasses. They were very dark and thick, and there was a peculiar lens mounted over the forehead bridge.

'Holographic night goggles,' Ross said. 'Employing thinfilm diffraction optics.' She then pointed out vibration-free camera lenses with optical systems that compensated for movement, strobe infrared lights, and miniature survey lasers no larger than a pencil eraser. There was also a series of small tripods with rapid-geared motors mounted on the top, and brackets to hold something, but she did not explain these devices beyond saying they were 'defensive units.'

Elliot drifted toward the far table, where he found six submachine guns set out under the lights. He picked one up; it was heavy, and gleaming with grease. Clips of ammunition lay stacked nearby. Elliot did not notice the lettering on the stock; the machine guns were Russian AK-47s manufactured under license in Czechoslovakia.

He glanced at Ross.

'Just precautions,' Ross said. 'We carry them on every expedition. It doesn't mean anything.'

Elliot shook his head. 'Tell me about your GPU from Houston,' he said.

'I'm not worried about it,' she said.

'I am,' Elliot said.

As Ross explained it, the GPU was just a technical report. The Zaire government had closed its eastern borders during the previous twenty-four hours; no tourist or commercial traffic could enter the country from Rwanda or Uganda; everyone now had to enter the country from the west, through Kinshasa.

No official reason was given for closing the eastern border, although sources in Washington speculated that Idi Amin's troops, fleeing across the Zaire border from the Tanzanian invasion of Uganda, might be causing 'local difficulties.' In central Africa, local difficulties usually meant cannibalism and other atrocities.

'Do you believe that?' Elliot asked. 'Cannibalism and atrocities?'

'No,' Ross said. 'It's all a lie. It's the Dutch and the Germans and the Japanese – probably your friend Hakamichi. The Euro-Japanese electronics consortium knows that ERTS is close to discovering important diamond reserves in Virunga. They want to slow us down as much as they can. They've got the fix in somewhere, probably in Kinshasa, and closed the eastern border. It's nothing more than that.'

'If there's no danger, why the machine guns?'

'Just precautions,' she said again. 'We'll never use machine guns on this trip, believe me. Now why don't you get some sleep? We'll be landing in Tangier soon.'

'Tangier?'

'Captain Munro is there.'

6. Munro

The name of 'Captain' Charles Munro was not to be found on the list of the expedition leaders employed by any of the usual field parties. There were several reasons for this, foremost among them his distinctly unsavory reputation.

Munro had been raised in the wild Northern Frontier Province of Kenya, the illegitimate son of a Scottish farmer and his handsome Indian housekeeper. Munro's father had the bad luck to be killed by Mau Mau guerillas in 1956.* Soon afterward, Munro's mother died of tuberculosis, and Munro made his way to Nairobi where in the late 1950s he worked as a white hunter, leading parties of tourists into the bush. It was during this time that Munro awarded himself the title of 'Captain,' although he had never served in the military.

Apparently, Captain Munro found humoring tourists uncongenial; by 1960, he was reported running guns from Uganda into the newly independent Congo. After Moise Tshombe went into exile in 1963, Munro's activities became politically embarrassing, and ultimately forced him to disappear from East Africa in late 1963.

He appeared again in 1964, as one of General Mobutu's white mercenaries in the Congo, under the leadership of Colonel 'Mad Mike' Hoare. Hoare assessed Munro as a 'hard, lethal customer who knew the jungle and was highly effective, when we could get him away from the ladies.' Following the capture of Stanleyville in Operation Dragon Rouge, Munro's name was associated with the mercenary atrocities at a village called Avakabi. Munro again disappeared for several years.

In 1968, he re-emerged in Tangier, where he lived splendidly and was something of a local character. The source of Munro's obviously substantial income was unclear, but he was said to have supplied Communist Sudanese rebels with East German light arms in 1971, to have assisted the royalist Ethiopians in their rebellion in 1974–1975, and to have assisted the French paratroopers who dropped into Zaire's Shaba province in 1978.

His mixed activities made Munro a special case in Africa in the 1970s; although he was *persona non grata* in a half-dozen African states, he traveled freely throughout the continent, using various passports. It

---

* Although more than nineteen thousand people were killed in the Mau Mau uprisings, only thirty-seven whites were killed during seven years of terrorism. Each dead white was properly regarded more as a victim of circumstances than of emerging black politics.

was a transparent ruse: every border official recognized him on sight, but these officials were equally afraid to let him enter the country or to deny him entry.

Foreign mining and exploration companies, sensitive to local feeling, were reluctant to hire Munro as an expedition leader for their parties. It was also true that Munro was by far the most expensive of the bush guides. Nevertheless, he had a reputation for getting tough, difficult jobs done. Under an assumed name, he had taken two German tin-mining parties into the Cameroons in 1974; and he had led one previous ERTS expedition into Angola during the height of the armed conflict in 1977. He quit another ERTS field group headed for Zambia the following year after Houston refused to meet his price: Houston had canceled the expedition.

In short, Munro was acknowledged as the best man for dangerous travel. That was why the ERTS jet stopped in Tangier.

At the Tangier airport, the ERTS cargo jet and its contents were bonded, but all ongoing personnel except Amy passed through customs, carrying their personal belongings. Jensen and Levine were pulled aside for searches; trace quantities of heroin were discovered in their hand baggage.

This bizarre event occurred through a series of remarkable coincidences. In 1977, United States customs agents began to employ neutron backscatter devices, as well as chemical vapor detectors, or sniffers. Both were hand-held electronic devices manufactured under contract by Hakamichi Electronics in Tokyo. In 1978, questions arose about the accuracy of these devices; Hakamichi suggested that they be tested at other ports of entry around the world, including Singapore, Bangkok, Delhi, Munich, and Tangier.

Thus Hakamichi Electronics knew the capabilities of the detectors at Tangier airport, and they also knew that a variety of substances, including ground poppy seeds and shredded turnip, would produce a false-positive registration on airport sensors. And the 'false-positive net' required forty-eight hours to untangle. (It was later shown that both men had somehow acquired traces of turnip on their briefcases.)

Both Irving and Jensen vigorously denied any knowledge of illicit material, and appealed to the local U.S. consular office. But the case could not be resolved for several days; Ross telephoned Travis in Houston, who determined that it was 'a slant plant' and a 'Dutch herring.' There was nothing to be done except to carry on, and continue with the expedition as best they could.

'They think this will stop us,' Travis said, 'but it won't.'

'Who's going to do the geology?' Ross asked.

'You are,' Travis said.

'And the electronics?'

'You're the certified genius,' Travis said. 'Just make sure you have Munro. He's the key to everything.'

The song of the muezzin floated over the pastel jumble of houses in the Tangier Casbah at twilight, calling the faithful to evening prayer. In the old days, the muezzin himself appeared in the minarets of the mosque, but now a recording played over loudspeakers: a mechanized call to the Muslim ritual of obeisance.

Karen Ross sat on the terrace of Captain Munro's house overlooking the Casbah and waited for her audience with the man himself. Beside her, Peter Elliot sat in a chair and snored noisily, exhausted from the long flight.

They had been waiting nearly three hours, and she was worried. Munro's house was of Moorish design, and open to the outdoors. From the interior she could hear voices, faintly carried by the breeze, speaking some Oriental language.

One of the graceful Moroccan servant girls that Munro seemed to have in infinite supply came onto the terrace carrying a telephone. She bowed formally. Ross saw that the girl had violet eyes; she was exquisitely beautiful, and could not have been more than sixteen. In careful English the girl said, 'This is your telephone to Houston. The bidding will now begin.'

Karen nudged Peter, who awoke groggily. 'The bidding will now begin,' she said.

Peter Elliot was surprised from the moment of his first entrance into Munro's house. He had anticipated a tough military setting and was amazed to see delicate carved Moroccan arches and soft gurgling fountains with sunlight sparkling on them.

Then he saw the Japanese and Germans in the next room, staring at him and at Ross. The glances were distinctly unfriendly, but Ross stood and said, 'Excuse me a moment,' and she went forward and embraced a young blond German man warmly. They kissed, chattered happily, and in general appeared to be intimate friends.

Elliot did not like this development, but he was reassured to see that the Japanese – identically dressed in black suits – were equally displeased. Noticing this, Elliot smiled benignly, to convey a sense of approval for the reunion.

But when Ross returned, he demanded, 'Who was that?'

'That's Richter,' she said. 'The most brilliant topologist in Western Europe; his field is *n*-space extrapolation. His work's extremely elegant.' She smiled. 'Almost as elegant as mine.'

'But he works for the consortium?'

'Naturally. He's German.'

'And you're talking with him?'

'I was delighted for the opportunity,' she said. 'Karl has a fatal limitation. He can only deal with pre-existing data. He takes what he is given, and does cartwheels with it in *n*-space. But he cannot imagine anything new at all. I had a professor at M.I.T. who was the same way. Tied to facts, a hostage to reality.' She shook her head.

'Did he ask about Amy?'

'Of course.'

'And what did you tell him?'

'I told him she was sick and probably dying.'

'And he believed that?'

'We'll see. There's Munro.'

Captain Munro appeared in the next room, wearing khakis, smoking a cigar. He was a tall, rugged-looking man with a mustache, and soft dark watchful eyes that missed nothing. He talked with the Japanese and Germans, who were evidently unhappy with what he was saying. Moments later, Munro entered their room, smiling broadly.

'So you're going to the Congo, Dr. Ross.'

'We are, Captain Munro,' she said.

Munro smiled. 'It seems as though everyone is going.'

There followed a rapid exchange which Elliot found incomprehensible. Karen Ross said, 'Fifty thousand U.S. in Swiss francs against point oh two of first-year adjusted extraction returns.'

Munro shook his head. 'A hundred in Swiss francs and point oh six of first-year return on the primary deposits, crude-grade accounting, no discounting.'

'A hundred in U.S. dollars against point oh one of the first-year return on all deposits, with full discounting from point of origin.'

'Point of origin? In the middle of the bloody Congo? I would want three years from point of origin: what if you're shut down?'

'You want a piece, you gamble. Mobutu's clever.'

'Mobutu's barely in control, and I am still alive because I am no gambler,' Munro said. 'A hundred against point oh four of first year on primary with front-load discount only. Or I'll take point oh two of yours.'

'If you're no gambler, I'll give you a straight buy-out for two hundred.'

Munro shook his head. 'You've paid more than that for your MER in Kinshasa.'

'Prices for everything are inflated in Kinshasa, including mineral exploration rights. And the current exploration limit, the computer CEL, is running well under a thousand.'

'If you say so.' He smiled, and headed back into the other room, where the Japanese and Germans were waiting for his return.

Ross said quickly, 'That's not for them to know.'

'Oh, I'm sure they know it anyway,' Munro said, and walked into the other room.

'Bastard,' she whispered to his back. She talked in low tones on the telephone. 'He'll never accept that. . . . No, no, he won't go for it . . . they want him bad. . . .'

Elliot said, 'You're bidding very high for his services.'

'He's the best,' Ross said, and continued whispering into the telephone. In the next room, Munro was shaking his head sadly, turning down an offer. Elliot noticed that Richter was very red in the face.

Munro came back to Karen Ross. 'What was your projected CEL?'

'Under a thousand.'

'So you say. Yet you know there's an ore intercept.'

'I don't know there's an ore intercept.'

'Then you're foolish to spend all this money to go to the Congo,' Munro said. 'Aren't you?'

Karen Ross made no reply. She stared at the ornate ceiling of the room.

'Virunga's not exactly a garden spot these days,' Munro continued. 'The Kigani are on the rampage, and they're cannibals. Pygmies aren't friendly any more either. Likely to find an arrow in your back for your troubles. Volcanoes always threatening to blow. Tsetse flies. Bad water. Corrupt officials. Not a place to go without a very good reason, hmm? Perhaps you should put off your trip until things settle down.'

Those were precisely Peter Elliot's sentiments, and he said so.

'Wise man,' Munro said, with a broad smile that annoyed Karen Ross.

'Evidently,' Karen Ross said, 'we will never come to terms.'

'That seems clear.' Munro nodded.

Elliot understood that negotiations were broken off. He got up to shake Munro's hand and leave – but before he could do that, Munro walked into the next room and conferred with the Japanese and Germans.

'Things are looking up,' Ross said.

'Why?' Elliot said. 'Because he thinks he's beaten you down?'

'No. Because he thinks we know more than they do about the site location and are more likely to hit an ore body and pay off.'

In the next room, the Japanese and Germans abruptly stood, and walked to the front door. At the door, Munro shook hands with the Germans, and bowed elaborately to the Japanese.

'I guess you're right,' Elliot said to Ross. 'He's sending them away.'

But Ross was frowning, her face grim. 'They can't do this,' she said. 'They can't just quit this way.'

Elliot was confused again. 'I thought you wanted them to quit.'

'Damn,' Ross said. 'We've been screwed.' She whispered into the telephone, talking to Houston.

Elliot didn't understand it at all. And his confusion was not resolved when Munro locked the door behind the last of the departing men, then came back to Elliot and Ross to say that supper was served.

They ate Moroccan-style, sitting on the floor and eating with their fingers. The first course was a pigeon pie, and it was followed by some sort of stew.

'So you sent the Japanese off?' Ross said. 'Told them no?'

'Oh, no,' Munro said. 'That would be impolite. I told them I would think about it. And I will.'

'Then why did they leave?'

Munro shrugged. 'Not my doing, I assure you. I think they heard something on the telephone which changed their whole plan.'

Karen Ross glanced at her watch, making a note of the time. 'Very good stew,' she said. She was doing her best to be agreeable.

'Glad you like it. It's *tajin*. Camel meat.'

Karen Ross coughed. Peter Elliot noticed that his own appetite had diminished. Munro turned to him. 'So you have the gorilla, Professor Elliot?'

'How did you know that?'

'The Japanese told me. The Japanese are fascinated by your gorilla. Can't figure the point of it, drives them mad. A young man with a gorilla, and a young woman who is searching for –'

'Industrial-grade diamonds,' Karen Ross said.

'Ah, industrial-grade diamonds.' He turned to Elliot. 'I enjoy a frank conversation. Diamonds, fascinating.' His manner suggested that he had been told nothing of importance.

Ross said, 'You've got to take us in, Munro.'

'World's full of industrial-grade diamonds,' Munro said. 'You can find them in Africa, India, Russia, Brazil, Canada, even in America –

Arkansas, New York, Kentucky – everywhere you look. But you're going to the Congo.'

The obvious question hung in the air.

'We are looking for Type IIb boron-coated blue diamonds,' Karen Ross said, 'which have semiconducting properties important to microelectronics applications.'

Munro stroked his mustache. 'Blue diamonds,' he said, nodding. 'It makes sense.'

Ross said that of course it made sense.

'You can't dope them?' Munro asked.

'No. It's been tried. There was a commercial boron-doping process, but it was too unreliable. The Americans had one and so did the Japanese. Everyone gave it up as hopeless.'

'So you've got to find a natural source.'

'That's right. I want to get there as soon as possible,' Ross said, staring at him, her voice flat.

'I'm sure you do,' Munro said. 'Nothing but business for our Dr. Ross, eh?' He crossed the room and, leaning against one of the arches, looked out on the dark Tangier night. 'I'm not surprised at all,' he said. 'As a matter of –'

At the first blast of machine-gun fire, Munro dived for cover, the glassware on the table splattered, one of the girls screamed, and Elliot and Ross threw themselves to the marble floor as the bullets whined around them, chipping the plaster overhead, raining plaster dust down upon them. The blast lasted thirty seconds or so, and it was followed by complete silence.

When it was over, they got up hesitantly, staring at one another.

'The consortium plays for keeps.' Munro grinned. 'Just my sort of people.'

Ross brushed plaster dust off her clothes. She turned to Munro. 'Five point two against the first two hundred, no deductions, in Swiss francs, adjusted.'

'Five point seven, and you have me.'

'Five point seven. Done.'

Munro shook hands with them, then announced that he would need a few minutes to pack his things before leaving for Nairobi.

'Just like that?' Ross asked. She seemed suddenly concerned, glancing again at her watch.

'What's your problem?' Munro asked.

'Czech AK-47s,' she said. 'In your warehouse.'

Munro showed no surprise. 'Better get them out,' he said. 'The consortium undoubtedly has something similar in the works, and we've got a lot to do in the next few hours.' As he spoke, they heard the police klaxons approaching from a distance. Munro said, 'We'll take the back stair.'

An hour later, they were airborne, heading toward Nairobi.

DAY 4: NAIROBI
June 16, 1979

1. Timeline

It was farther across Africa from Tangier to Nairobi than it was across the Atlantic Ocean from New York to London – 3,600 miles, an eight-hour flight. Ross spent the time at the computer console, working out what she called 'hyperspace probability lines.'

The screen showed a computer-generated map of Africa, with streaking multicolored lines across it. 'These are all timelines,' Ross said. 'We can weight them for duration and delay factors.' Beneath the screen was a total-elapsed-time clock, which kept shifting numbers.

'What's that mean?' Elliot asked.

'The computer's picking the fastest route. You see it's just identified a timeline that will get us on site in six days eighteen hours and fifty-one minutes. Now it's trying to beat that time.'

Elliot had to smile. The idea of a computer predicting *to the minute* when they would reach their Congo location seemed ludicrous to him. But Ross was totally serious.

As they watched, the computer clock shifted to 5 days 22 hours 24 minutes.

'Better,' Ross said, nodding. 'But still not very good.' She pressed another button and the lines shifted, stretching like rubber bands over the African continent. 'This is the consortium route,' she said, 'based on our assumptions about the expedition. They're going in big – thirty or more people, a full-scale undertaking. And they don't know the exact location of the city; at least, we don't think they know. But they have a substantial start on us, at least twelve hours, since their aircraft is already forming up in Nairobi.'

The clock registered total elapsed time: 5 days 09 hours 19 minutes. Then she pressed a button marked DATE and it shifted to 06 21 79 0814. 'According to this, the consortium will reach the Congo site a little after eight o'clock in the morning on June 21.'

The computer clicked quietly; the lines continued to stretch and pull, and the clock read a new date: 06 21 79 1224.

'Well,' she said, 'that's where we are now. Given maximum favorable movements for us and them, the consortium will beat us to the site by slightly more than four hours, five days from now.'

Munro walked past, eating a sandwich. 'Better lock another path,' he said. 'Or go radical.'

'I hesitate to go radical with the ape.'

Munro shrugged. 'Have to do something, with a timeline like that.'

Elliot listened to them with a vague sense of unreality: they were discussing a difference of hours, five days in the future. 'But surely,' Elliot said, 'over the next few days, with all the arrangements at Nairobi, and then getting into the jungle – you can't put too much faith in those figures.'

'This isn't like the old days of African exploration,' Ross said, 'where parties disappeared into the wilds for months. At most, the computer is off by minutes – say, roughly half an hour in the total five-day projection.' She shook her head. 'No. We have a problem here, and we've got to do something about it. The stakes are too great.'

'You mean the diamonds.'

She nodded, and pointed to the bottom of the screen, where the words BLUE CONTRACT appeared. He asked her what the Blue Contract was.

'One hell of a lot of money,' Ross said. And she added, 'I think.' For in truth she did not really know.

Each new contract at ERTS was given a code name. Only Travis and the computer knew the name of the company buying the contract; everyone else at ERTS, from computer programmers to field personnel, knew the projects only by their color-code names: Red contract, Yellow Contract, White Contract. This was a business protection for the firms involved. But the ERTS mathematicians could not resist a lively guessing game about contract sources, which was the staple of daily conversation in the company canteen.

The Blue Contract had come to ERTS in December, 1978. It called for ERTS to locate a natural source of industrial-grade diamonds in a friendly or neutralist country. The diamonds were to be Type IIb, 'nitrogen-poor' crystals. No dimensions were specified, so crystal size did not matter; nor were recoverable quantities specified: the contractor would take what he could get. And, most unusual, there was no UECL.

Nearly all contracts arrived with a unit extraction cost limit. It was not enough to find a mineral source; the minerals had to be extractable at a specified unit cost. This unit cost in turn reflected the richness of the ore body, its remoteness, the availability of local labor, political conditions, the possible need to build airfields, roads, hospitals, schools, mines, or refineries.

For a contract to come in without a UECL meant only one thing: somebody wanted blue diamonds so badly he didn't care what they cost.

Within forty-eight hours, the ERTS canteen had explained the Blue Contract. It turned out that Type IIb diamonds were blue from trace quantities of the element boron, which rendered them worthless as gemstones but altered their electronic properties, making them semiconductors with a resistivity on the order of 100 ohms centimeters. They also had light-transmissive properties.

Someone then found a brief article in *Electronic News* for November 17, 1978: 'McPhee Doping Dropped.' It explained that the Waltham, Massachusetts, firm of Silec, Inc., had abandoned the experimental McPhee technique to dope diamonds artificially with a monolayer boron coating. The McPhee process had been abandoned as too expensive and too unreliable to produce 'desirable semiconducting properties.' The article concluded that 'other firms have under-estimated problems in boron monolayer doping; Hakamichi (Tokyo) abandoned the Nagaura process in September of this year.' Working backward, the ERTS canteen fitted additional pieces of the puzzle into place.

Back in 1971, Intec, the Santa Clara microelectronics firm, had first predicted that diamond semiconductors would be important to a future generation of 'superconducting' computers in the 1980s.

The first generation of electronic computers, ENIAC and UNIVAC, built in the wartime secrecy of the 1940s, employed vacuum tubes. Vacuum tubes had an average life span of twenty hours, but with thousands of glowing hot tubes in a single machine, some computers shut down every seven to twelve minutes. Vacuum-tube technology imposed a limit on the size and power of planned second-generation computers.

But the second generation never used vacuum tubes. In 1947, the invention of the transistor – a thumbnail-sized sandwich of solid material which performed all the functions of a vacuum tube – ushered in an era of 'solid state' electronic devices which drew little power, generated little heat, and were smaller and more reliable than the tubes they replaced. Silicon technology provided the basis for three generations of increasingly compact, reliable, and cheap computers over the next twenty years.

But by the 1970s, computer designers began to confront the inherent limitations of silicon technology. Although circuits had been shrunk to microscopic dimensions, computation speed was still dependent on circuit length. To miniaturize circuits still more, where distances were already on the order of millionths of an inch, brought back an old problem: heat. Smaller circuits would literally melt from the heat produced. What was needed was some method to eliminate heat and reduce resistance at the same time.

It had been known since the 1950s that many metals when cooled to extremely low temperatures became 'superconducting,' permitting the unimpeded flow of electrons through them. In 1977, IBM announced it was designing an ultra-high-speed computer the size of a grapefruit, chilled with liquid nitrogen. The superconducting computer required a radically new technology, and a new range of low-temperature construction materials.

Doped diamonds would be used extensively throughout.

Several days later, the ERTS canteen came up with an alternative explanation. According to the new theory, the 1970s had been a decade of unprecedented growth in computers. Although the first computer manufacturers in the 1940s had predicted that four computers would do the computing work of the entire world for the foreseeable future, experts anticipated that by 1990 there would actually be *one billion* computers – most of them linked by communications networks to other computers. Such networks didn't exist, and might even be theoretically impossible. (A 1975 study by the Hanover Institute concluded there was insufficient metal in the earth's crust to construct the necessary computer transmission lines.)

According to Harvey Rumbaugh, the 1980s would be characterized by a critical shortage of computer data transmission systems: 'Just as the fossil fuel shortage took the industrialized world by surprise in the 1970s, so will the data transmission shortage take the world by surprise in the next ten years. People were denied *movement* in the 1970s; but they will be denied *information* in the 1980s, and it remains to be seen which shortage will prove more frustrating.'

Laser light represented the only hope for handling these massive data requirements, since laser channels carried twenty thousand times the information of an ordinary metal coaxial trunk line. Laser transmission demanded whole new technologies – including thin-spun fiber optics, and doped semi-conducting diamonds, which Rumbaugh predicted would be 'more valuable than oil' in the coming years.

Even further, Rumbaugh anticipated that within ten years *electricity itself would become obsolete*. Future computers would utilize only light circuits, and interface with light-transmission data systems. The reason was speed. 'Light,' Rumbaugh said, 'moves at the speed of light. Electricity doesn't. We are living in the final years of microelectronic technology.'

Certainly microelectronics did not look like a moribund technology. In 1979, microelectronics was a major industry throughout the industrialized world, accounting for eighty billion dollars annually in the United States alone; six of the top twenty corporations in the Fortune 500 were deeply involved in microelectronics. These companies had a history of extraordinary competition and advance, over a period of less than thirty years.

In 1958, a manufacturer could fit 10 electronic components onto a single silicon chip. By 1970, it was possible to fit 100 units onto a chip of the same size – a tenfold increase in slightly more than a decade.

But by 1972, it was possible to fit 1,000 units on a chip, and by 1974, 10,000 units. It was expected that by 1980, there would be one million units on a single chip the size of a thumbnail, but, using electronic photoprojection, this goal was actually realized in 1978. By the spring of 1979, the new goal was ten million units – or, even better, one billion units – on a single silicon chip by 1980. But nobody expected to wait past June or July of 1979 for this development.

Such advances within an industry are unprecedented. Comparison to older manufacturing technologies makes this clear. Detroit was content to make trivial product design changes at three-year intervals, but the electronics industry routinely expected *order of magnitude* advances in the same time. (To keep pace, Detroit would have had to increase automobile gas mileage from 8 miles ·per gallon in 1970 to 80,000,000 miles per gallon in 1979. Instead, Detroit went from 8 to 16 miles per gallon during that time, further evidence of the coming demise of the automotive industry as the center of the American economy.)

In such a competitive market, everyone worried about foreign powers, chiefly Japan, which since 1973 had maintained a Japanese Cultural Exchange in Santa Clara – actually a cover organization for blatant and well-financed industrial espionage.

The Blue Contract could only be understood in the light of an industry making major advances every few months. Travis had said that the Blue Contract was 'the biggest thing we'll see in the next ten years. Whoever finds those diamonds has a jump on the technology for at least five years. *Five years*. Do you know what that means?'

Ross knew what it meant. In an industry where competitive edges were measured in months, companies had made fortunes by beating competitors by a matter of weeks with some new technique or device; Syntel in California had been the first to make a 256K memory chip while everyone else was still making 16K chips and dreaming of 64K chips. Syntel kept their advantage for only sixteen weeks, but realized a profit of more than a hundred and thirty million dollars.

'And we're talking about *five years*,' Travis said. 'That's an advantage measured in billions of dollars, maybe tens of billions of dollars. If we can get to those diamonds.'

These were the reasons for the extraordinary pressure Ross felt as she continued to work with the computer. At the age of twenty-four, she was team leader in a high-technology race involving a half-dozen nations around the globe, all secretly pitting their business and industrial resources against one another.

The stakes made any conventional race seem ludicrous. Travis told her before she left, 'Don't be afraid when the pressure makes you crazy. You have *billions of dollars* riding on your shoulders. Just do the best you can.'

Doing the best she could, she managed to reduce the expedition timeline by another three hours and thirty-seven minutes – but they were still slightly behind the consortium projection. Not too far to make up the time, especially with Munro's cold-blooded shortcuts, but nevertheless behind – which could mean total disaster in a winner-take-all race.

And then she received bad news.

The screen printed PIGGYBACK SLURP/ALL BETS OFF.

'Hell,' Ross said. She felt suddenly tired. Because if there really had been a piggyback slurp, their chances of winning the race were vanishing – before any of them had even set foot in the rain forests of central Africa.

2. Piggyback Slurp

Travis felt like a fool.

He stared at the hard copy from Goddard Space Flight Center, Greenbelt, Maryland:

ERTS WHY ARE YOU SENDING US ALL THIS MUKENKO DATA WE DON'T REALLY CARE THANKS ANYWAY DESIST AT LEISURE.

That had arrived an hour ago from GSFC/Maryland, but it was already too late by more than five hours.

'Damn!' Travis said, staring at the telex.

The first indication to Travis that anything was wrong was when the Japanese and Germans broke off negotiations with Munro in Tangier. One minute they had been willing to pay anything; the next minute they could hardly wait to leave. The break-off had come abruptly, discontinuously; it implied the sudden introduction of new data into the consortium computer files.

New data from where?

There could be only one explanation – and now it was confirmed in the GSFC telex from Greenbelt.

ERTS WHY ARE YOU SENDING ALL THIS MUKENKO DATA

There was a simple answer to that: ERTS *wasn't* sending any data. At least, not willingly. ERTS and GSFC had an arrangement to exchange data updates – Travis had made that deal in 1978 to obtain cheaper satellite imagery from orbiting Landsats. Satellite imagery was his company's single greatest expense. In return for a look at derived ERTS data, GSFC agreed to supply satellite CCTs at 30 percent reduced gross cost.

It seemed like a good deal at the time, and the coded locks were specified in the agreement.

But now the potential drawbacks loomed large before Travis; his worst fears were confirmed. Once you put a line over two thousand miles from Houston to Greenbelt, you begged for a piggyback data slurp. Somewhere between Texas and Maryland someone had inserted a terminal linkup – probably in the carrier telephone lines – and had begun to slurp out data on a piggyback terminal. This was the form of industrial espionage they most feared.

A piggyback-slurp terminal tapped in between two legitimate terminals, monitoring the back and forth transmissions. After a time, the piggyback operator knew enough to begin making transmissions on line, slurping out data from both ends, pretending to be GSFC to Houston, and Houston to GSFC. The piggyback terminal could continue to function until one or both legitimate terminals realized that they were being slurped.

Now the question was how much data had been slurped out in the last seventy-two hours?

He had called for twenty-four-hour scanner checks, but they were disheartening. It looked as though the ERTS computer had yielded up not only original database elements, but also data-transformation histories – the sequence of operations performed on the data by ERTS over the last four weeks.

If that was true, it meant that the Euro-Japanese consortium piggyback knew what transformations ERTS had carried out on the Mukenko data – and therefore they knew where the lost city was located, with pinpoint accuracy. They now knew the location of the city as precisely as Ross did.

Timelines had to be adjusted, unfavorably to the ERTS team. And the updated computer projections were unequivocal – Ross or no Ross, the likelihood of the ERTS team reaching the site ahead of the Japanese and Germans was now almost nil.

From Travis's viewpoint, the entire ERTS expedition was now a futile exercise, and a waste of time. There was no hope of success. The only unfactorable element was the gorilla Amy, and Travis's instincts told him that a gorilla named Amy would not prove decisive in the discovery of mineral deposits in the northeastern Congo.

It was hopeless.

Should he recall the ERTS team? He stared at the console by his desk. 'Call cost-time,' he said.

The computer blinked COST-TIME AVAILABLE.

'Congo Field Survey,' he said.

The screen printed out numbers for the Congo Field Survey: expenditures by the hour, accumulated costs, committed future costs, cutoff points, future branch-point deletions.... The project was now just outside Nairobi, and was running an accumulated cost of slightly over $189,000.

Cancellation would cost $227,455.

'Factor BF,' he said.

The screen changed. BF. He now saw a series of probabilities. 'Factor BF' was *bona fortuna*, good luck – the imponderable in all expeditions, especially remote, dangerous expeditions.

THINKING A MOMENT, the computer flashed.

Travis waited. He knew that the computer would require several seconds to perform the computations to assign weights to random factors that might influence the expedition, still five or more days from the target site.

His beeper buzzed. Rogers, the tap dancer, said, 'We've traced the piggyback slurp. It's in Norman, Oklahoma, nominally at the North Central Insurance Corporation of America. NCIC is fifty-one percent owned by a Hawaiian holding company, Halekuli, Inc., which is in turn wholly owned by mainland Japanese interests. What do you want?'

'I want a very bad fire,' Travis said.

'Got you,' Rogers said. He hung up the phone.

The screen flashed ASSESSED FACTOR BF and a probability: .449. He was surprised: that figure meant that ERTS had an almost even chance of attaining the target site before the consortium. Travis didn't question the mathematics; .449 was good enough.

The ERTS expedition would continue to the Congo, at least for the time being. And in the meantime he would do whatever he could to slow down the consortium. Off the top of his head, Travis could think of one or two ideas to accomplish that.

3. Additional Data

The jet was moving south over Lake Rudolf in northern Kenya when Tom Seamans called Elliot.

Seamans had finished his computer analysis to discriminate gorillas from other apes, principally chimpanzees. He had then obtained from Houston a videotape of three seconds of a garbled video transmission which seemed to show a gorilla smashing a dish antenna and staring into a camera.

'Well?' Elliot said, looking at the computer screen. The data flashed up:

DISCRIMINANT FUNCTION GORILLA / CHIMP
FUNCTIONAL GROUPINGS DISTRIBUTED AS:
GORILLA: .9934
CHIMP: .1132
TEST VIDEOTAPE {HOUSTON}: .3349

'Hell,' Elliot said. At those figures, the study was equivocal, useless.

'Sorry about that,' Seamans said over the phone. 'But part of the trouble comes from the test material itself. We had to factor in the computer derivation of that image. The image has been cleaned up, and that means it's been regularized; the critical stuff has been lost. I'd like to work with the original digitized matrix. Can you get me that?'

Karen Ross was nodding yes. 'Sure,' Elliot said.

'I'll go another round with it,' Seamans said. 'But if you want my gut opinion, it is never going to turn out. The fact is that gorillas show a considerable individual variation in facial structure, just as people do. If we increase our sample base, we're going to get more variation, and a larger population interval. I think you're stuck. You can never prove it's not a gorilla – but for my money, it's not.'

'Meaning what?' Elliot asked.

'It's something new,' Seamans said. 'I'm telling you, if this was really a gorilla, it would have showed up .89 or .94, somewhere in there, on this function. But the image comes out at .39. That's just not good enough. It's not a gorilla, Peter.'

'Then what is it?'

'It's a transitional form. I ran a function to measure where the variation was. You know what was the major differential? Skin color. Even in black-and-white, it's not dark enough to be a gorilla, Peter. This is a whole new animal, I promise you.'

Elliot looked at Ross. 'What does this do to your timeline?'

'For the moment, nothing,' she said. 'Other elements are more critical, and this is unfactorable.'

The pilot clicked on the intercom. 'We are beginning our descent into Nairobi,' he said.

4. Nairobi

Five miles outside Nairobi, one can find the wild game of the East African savannah. And within the memory of many Nairobi residents the game could be found closer still – gazelles, buffalo, and giraffe wandering around backyards, and the occasional leopard slipping into one's bedroom. In those days, the city still retained the character of a wild colonial station; in its heyday, Nairobi was a fast-living place indeed: 'Are you married or do you live in Kenya?' went the standard question. The men were hard-drinking and rough, the women beautiful and loose, and the pattern of life no more predictable than the fox hunts that ranged over the rugged countryside each weekend.

But modern Nairobi is almost unrecognizable from the time of those freewheeling colonial days. The few remaining Victorian buildings lie stranded in a modern city of half a million, with traffic jams, stoplights, skyscrapers, supermarkets, same-day dry cleaners, French restaurants, and air pollution.

The ERTS cargo plane landed at Nairobi International Airport at dawn on the morning of June 16, and Munro contacted porters and assistants for the expedition. They intended to leave Nairobi within two hours – until Travis called from Houston to inform them that Peterson, one of the geologists on the first Congo expedition, had somehow made it back to Nairobi.

Ross was excited by the news. 'Where is he now?' she asked.

'At the morgue,' Travis said.

Elliot winced as he came close: the body on the stainless-steel table was a blond man his own age. The man's arms had been crushed; the skin was swollen, a ghastly purple color. He glanced at Ross. She seemed perfectly cool, not blinking or turning away. The pathologist stepped on a foot pedal, activating a microphone overhead. 'Would you state your name, please.'

'Karen Ellen Ross.'

'Your nationality and passport number?'

'American, F 1413649.'

'Can you identify the man before you, Miss Ross?'

'Yes,' she said. 'He is James Robert Peterson.'

'What is your relation to the deceased James Robert Peterson?'

'I worked with him,' she said dully. She seemed to be examining a geological specimen, scrutinizing it unemotionally. Her face showed no reaction.

The pathologist faced the microphone. 'Identity confirmed as James Robert Peterson, male Caucasian, twenty-nine years old, nationality American.' He turned back to Ross. 'When was the last time you saw Mr. Peterson?'

'In May of this year. He was leaving for the Congo.'

'You have not seen him in the last month?'

'No,' she said. 'What happened?'

The pathologist touched the puffy purple injuries on his arms. His fingertips sank in, leaving indentations like teeth in the flesh. 'Damned strange story,' the pathologist said.

The previous day, June 15, Peterson had been flown to Nairobi airport aboard a small charter cargo plane, in endstage terminal shock. He died several hours later without regaining consciousness. 'Extraordinary he made it at all. Apparently the aircraft made an unscheduled stop for a mechanical problem at Garona field, a dirt track in Zaire. And then this fellow comes stumbling out of the woods, collapsing at their feet.' The pathologist pointed out that the bones had been shattered in both arms. The injuries, he explained, were not new; they had occurred at least four days earlier, perhaps more. 'He must have been in incredible pain.'

Elliot said, 'What could cause that injury?'

The pathologist had never seen anything like it. 'Superficially, it resembles mechanical trauma, a crush injury from an automobile or truck. We see a good deal of those here; but mechanical crush injuries are never bilateral, as they are in this case.'

'So it wasn't a mechanical injury?' Karen Ross asked.

'Don't know what it was. It's unique in my experience,' the pathologist said briskly. 'We also found traces of blood under his nails, and a few strands of gray hair. We're running a test now.'

Across the room, another pathologist looked up from his microscope. 'The hair is definitely not human. Cross section doesn't match. Some kind of animal hair, close to human.'

'The cross section?' Ross said.

'Best index we have of hair origin,' the pathologist said. 'For instance, human pubic hair is more elliptical in cross section than other body hair, or facial hair. It's quite characteristic – admissible in court. But especially in this laboratory, we come across a great deal of animal hair, and we're expert in that as well.'

A large stainless-steel analyzer began pinging. 'Blood's coming through,' the pathologist said.

On a video screen they saw twin patterns of pastel-colored streaks. 'This is the electrophoresis pattern,' the pathologist explained. 'To check serum proteins. That's ordinary human blood on the left. On the right we have the blood sample from under the nails. You can see it's definitely not human blood.'

'Not human blood?' Ross said, glancing at Elliot.

'It's *close* to human blood,' the pathologist said, staring at the pattern. 'But it's not human. Could be a domestic or farm animal – a pig, perhaps. Or else a primate. Monkeys and apes are very close serologically to human beings. We'll have a computer analysis in a minute.'

On the screen, the computer printed ALPHA AND BETA SERUM GLOBULINS MATCH: GORILLA BLOOD.

The pathologist said, 'There's your answer to what he had under his nails. Gorilla blood.'

5. Examination

'She won't hurt you,' Elliot told the frightened orderly. They were in the passenger compartment of the 747 cargo jet. 'See, she's smiling at you.'

Amy was indeed giving her most winning smile, being careful not to expose her teeth. But the orderly from the private clinic in Nairobi was not familiar with these fine points of gorilla etiquette. His hands shook as he held the syringe.

Nairobi was the last opportunity for Amy to receive a thorough checkup. Her large, powerful body belied a constitutional fragility, as her heavy-browed, glowering face belied a meek, rather tender nature. In San Francisco, the Project Amy staff subjected her to a thorough medical regimen – urine samples every other day, stool samples checked weekly for occult blood, complete blood studies monthly, and a trip to the dentist every three months for removal of the black tartar that accumulated from her vegetarian diet.

Amy took it all in stride, but the terrified orderly did not know that. He approached her holding the syringe in front of him like a weapon. 'You sure he won't bite?'

Amy, trying to be helpful, signed *Amy promise no bite*. She was signing slowly, deliberately, as she always did when confronted by someone who did not know her language.

'She promises not to bite you,' Elliot said.

'So you say,' the orderly said. Elliot did not bother to explain that he hadn't said it; she had.

After the blood samples were drawn, the orderly relaxed a little. Packing up, he said, 'Certainly is an ugly brute.'

'You've hurt her feelings,' Elliot said.

And, indeed, Amy was signing vigorously, *What ugly?* 'Nothing, Amy,' Elliot said. 'He's just never seen a gorilla before.'

The orderly said, 'I beg your pardon?'

'You've hurt her feelings. You'd better apologize.'

The orderly snapped his medical case shut. He stared at Elliot and then at Amy. 'Apologize to *him?*'

'Her,' Elliot said. 'Yes. How would you like to be told you're ugly?'

Elliot felt strongly about this. Over the years, he had come to feel acutely the prejudices that human beings showed toward apes, considering chimpanzees to be cute children, oranges to be wise old men, and gorillas to be hulking, dangerous brutes. They were wrong in every case.

Each of these animals was unique, and did not fit the human

stereotypes at all. Chimps, for example, were much more callous than gorillas ever were. Because chimps were extroverts, an angry chimp was far more dangerous than an angry gorilla; at the zoo, Elliot would watch in amazement as human mothers pushed their children closer to look at the chimps, but recoiled protectively at the sight of the gorillas. These mothers obviously did not know that wild chimpanzees caught and ate human infants – something gorillas never did.

Elliot had witnessed repeatedly the human prejudice against gorillas, and had come to recognize its effect on Amy. Amy could not help the fact that she was huge and black and heavy-browed and squash-faced. Behind the face people considered so repulsive was an intelligent and sensitive consciousness, sympathetic to the people around her. It pained her when people ran away, or screamed in fear, or made cruel remarks.

The orderly frowned. 'You mean that he understands English?'

'Yes, *she* does.' The gender change was something else Elliot didn't like. People who were afraid of Amy always assumed she was male.

The orderly shook his head. 'I don't believe it.'

'Amy, show the man to the door.'

Amy lumbered over to the door and opened it for the orderly, whose eyes widened as he left. Amy closed the door behind him.

Silly human man, Amy signed.

'Never mind,' Elliot said. 'Come, Peter tickle Amy.' And for the next fifteen minutes, he tickled her as she rolled on the floor and grunted in deep satisfaction. Elliot never noticed the door open behind him, never noticed the shadow falling across the floor, until it was too late and he turned his head to look up and saw the dark cylinder swing down, and his head erupted with blinding white pain and everything went black.

6. Kidnapped

He awoke to a piercing electronic shriek.

'Don't move, sir,' a voice said.

Elliot opened his eyes and stared into a bright light shining down on him. He was still lying on his back in the aircraft; someone was bent over him.

'Look to the right . . . now to the left . . . Can you flex your fingers?'

He followed the instructions. The light was taken away and he saw a black man in a white suit crouched beside him. The man touched Elliot's head; his fingers came away red with blood. 'Nothing to be alarmed about,' the man said; 'it's quite superficial.' He looked off. 'How long would you estimate he was unconscious?'

'Couple of minutes, no more,' Munro said.

The high-pitched squeal came again. He saw Ross moving around the passenger section, wearing a shoulder pack, and holding a wand in front of her. There was another squeal. 'Damn,' she said, and plucked something from the molding around the window. 'That's five. They really did a job.'

Munro looked down at Elliot. 'How do you feel?' he asked.

'He should be put under observation for twenty-four hours,' the black man said. 'Just as a precaution.'

'Twenty-four hours!' Ross said, moving around the compartment.

Elliot said, 'Where is she?'

'They took her,' Munro said. 'They opened the rear door, inflated the pneumatic slide, and were gone before anyone realized what happened. We found this next to you.'

Munro gave him a small glass vial with Japanese markings. The sides of the vial were scratched and scored; at one end was a rubber plunger, at the other end a broken needle.

Elliot sat up.

'Easy there,' the doctor said.

'I feel fine,' Elliot said, although his head was throbbing. He turned the vial over in his hand. 'There was frost on it when you found it?'

Munro nodded. 'Very cold.'

'CO_2,' Elliot said. It was a dart from a gas gun. He shook his head. 'They broke the needle off in her.' He could imagine Amy's screams of outrage. She was unaccustomed to anything but the tenderest treatment. Perhaps that was one of the shortcomings of his work with her; he had not prepared her well enough for the real world. He sniffed the vial, smelled a pungent odor. 'Lobaxin. Fast-acting soporific, onset within fifteen seconds. It's what they'd use.' Elliot was angry. Lobaxin was not often used on animals because it caused liver damage. And they had broken the needle –

He got to his feet and leaned on Munro, who put his arm around him. The doctor protested.

'I'm fine,' Elliot said.

Across the room, there was another squeal, this one loud and prolonged. Ross was moving her wand over the medicine cabinet, past the bottles of pills and supplies. The sound seemed to embarrass her; quickly she moved away, shutting the cabinet.

She crossed the passenger compartment, and a squeal was heard again. Ross removed a small black device from the underside of one seat. 'Look at this. They must have brought an extra person just to plant the bugs. It'll take hours to sterilize the plane. We can't wait.'

She went immediately to the computer console and began typing.

Elliot said, 'Where are they now? The consortium?'

'The main party left from Kubala airport outside Nairobi six hours ago,' Munro said.

'Then they didn't take Amy with them.'

'Of course they didn't take her,' Ross said, sounding annoyed. 'They've got no use for her.'

'Have they killed her?' Elliot asked.

'Maybe,' Munro said quietly.

'Oh, *Jesus* . . .'

'But I doubt it,' Munro continued. 'They don't want any publicity, and Amy's famous – as famous in some circles as an ambassador or a head of state. She's a talking gorilla, and there aren't many of those. She's been on television news, she's had her picture in the newspapers . . . They'd kill you before they killed her.'

'Just so they don't kill her,' Elliot said.

'They won't,' Ross said, with finality. 'The consortium isn't interested in Amy. They don't even know why we brought her. They're just trying to blow our timeline – but they won't succeed.'

Something in her tone suggested that she planned to leave Amy behind. The idea appalled Elliot. 'We've got to get her back,' he said. 'Amy is my responsibility, I can't possibly abandon her here –'

'Seventy-two minutes,' Ross said, pointing to the screen. 'We have exactly one hour and twelve minutes, before we blow the timeline.' She turned to Munro. 'And we have to switch over to the second contingency.'

'Fine,' Munro said. 'I'll get the men working on it.'

'In a new plane,' Ross said. 'We can't take this one, it's contaminated.' She was punching in call letters to the computer console, her fingers clicking on the buttons. 'We'll take it straight to point M,' Ross said. 'Okay?'

'Absolutely,' Munro said.

Elliot said, 'I won't leave Amy. If you're going to leave her behind, you'll have to leave me as well –' Elliot stopped.

Printed on the screen was the message FORGET GORILLA PROCEED TO NEXT CHECKPOINT URGENT APE NOT SIGNIFICANT TIMELINE OUTCOME COMPUTER VERIFICATION REPEAT PROCEED WITHOUT AMY.

'You can't leave her behind,' Elliot said. 'I'll stay behind, too.'

'Let me tell you something,' Ross said. 'I never believed that Amy was important to this expedition – or you either. From the very beginning she was just a diversion. When I came to San Francisco, I was followed. You and Amy provided a diversion. You threw the consortium into a spin. It was worth it. Now it's not worth it. We'll leave you both behind if we have to. I couldn't care less.'

7. Bugs

'Well, goddam it,' Elliot began, 'do you mean to tell me that . . .'

'That's right,' Ross said coldly. 'You're expendable.' But even as she spoke, she grabbed his arm firmly and led him out of the airplane while she held her finger to her lips.

Elliot realized that she intended to pacify him in private, but he was determined not to back down from his position. Amy *was* his responsibility, and to hell with all the diamonds and international intrigue. Outside on the concrete runway he repeated stubbornly, 'I'm not leaving without Amy.'

'Neither am I.' Ross walked quickly across the runway toward a police helicopter.

Elliot hurried to catch up. 'What?'

'Don't you understand *anything*?' Ross said. 'That airplane's *not clean*. It's full of bugs, and the consortium's listening in. I made that speech for their benefit.'

'But who was following you in San Francisco?'

'Nobody. They're going to spend hours trying to figure out who was.'

'Amy and I weren't just a diversion?'

'Not at all,' she said. 'Look: we don't know what happened to the last ERTS Congo team, but no matter what you or Travis or anyone else says, *I* think gorillas were involved. And I think that Amy will help us when we get there.'

'As an ambassador?'

'We need information,' Ross said. 'And she knows more about gorillas than we do.'

'But can you find her in an hour and ten minutes?'

'Hell, no,' Ross said, checking her watch. 'This won't take more than twenty minutes.'

'Lower! Lower!'

Ross was shouting into her radio headset as she sat alongside the police helicopter pilot. The helicopter was circling the tower of Government House, turning and moving north, toward the Hilton.

'This is not acceptable, madam,' the pilot said politely. 'We fly below airspace limitations.'

'You're too damn high!' Ross said. She was looking at a box on her knees, with four compass-point digital readouts. She flicked switches quickly, while the radio crackled with angry complaints from Nairobi tower.

'East now, due east,' she instructed, and the helicopter tilted and moved east, toward the poor outskirts of the city.

In the back, Elliot felt his stomach twist with each banking turn of the helicopter. His head pounded and he felt awful, but he had insisted on coming. He was the only person knowledgeable enough to minister to Amy if she was in medical trouble.

Now, sitting alongside the pilot, Ross said, 'Got a reading,' and she pointed to the northeast. The helicopter thumped over crude shacks, junked automobile lots, dirt roads. 'Slower now, slower . . .'

The readouts glowed, the numbers shifting. Elliot saw them all go to zero, simultaneously.

'Down!' Ross shouted, and the helicopter descended in the center of a vast garbage dump.

The pilot remained with the helicopter; his final words were disquieting. 'Where there's garbage, there's rats,' he said.

'Rats don't bother me,' Ross said, climbing out with her box in her hand.

'Where there's rats, there's cobras,' the pilot said.

'Oh,' Ross said.

She crossed the dump with Elliot. There was a stiff breeze; papers and debris ruffled at their feet. Elliot's head ached, and the odors arising from the dump nauseated him.

'Not far now,' Ross said, watching the box. She was excited, glancing at her watch.

'Here!'

She bent over and picked through the trash, her hand making circles, digging deeper in frustration, elbow-deep in the trash.

Finally she came up with a necklace – a necklace she had given Amy when they first boarded the airplane in San Francisco. She turned it over, examining the plastic name tag on it, which Elliot noticed was unusually thick. There were fresh scratches on the back.

'Hell,' Ross said. 'Sixteen minutes shot.' And she hurried back to the waiting helicopter.

Elliot fell into step beside her. 'But how can you find her if they got rid of her necklace bug?'

'Nobody,' Ross said, 'plants only one bug. This was just a decoy, they were supposed to find it.' She pointed to the scratches on the back. 'But they're clever, they reset the frequencies.'

'Maybe they got rid of the second bug too,' Elliot said.

'They didn't,' Ross said. The helicopter lifted off, a thuddering whirr of blades, and the paper and trash of the dump swirled in circles beneath them. She pressed her mouthpiece to her lips and said to the pilot, 'Take me to the largest scrapmetal source in Nairobi.'

Within nine minutes, they had picked up another very weak signal, located within an automobile junkyard. The helicopter landed in the street outside, drawing dozens of shouting children. Ross went with Elliot into the junkyard, moving past the rusting hulks of cars and trucks.

'You're sure she's here?' Elliot said.

'No question. They have to surround her with metal, it's the only thing they can do.'

'Why?'

'Shielding.' She picked her way around the broken cars, pausing frequently to refer to her electronic box.

Then Elliot heard a grunt.

It came from inside an ancient rust-red Mercedes bus. Elliot climbed through the shattered doors, the rubber gaskets crumbling in his hands, into the interior. He found Amy on her back, tied with adhesive tape. She was groggy, but complained loudly when he tore the tape off her hair.

He located the broken needle in her right chest and plucked it out with forceps. Amy shrieked, then hugged him. He heard the far-off whine of a police siren.

'It's all right, Amy, it's all right,' he said. He set her down and examined her more carefully. She seemed to be okay.

And then he said, 'Where's the second bug?'

Ross grinned. 'She swallowed it.'

Now that Amy was safe, Elliot felt a wave of anger. 'You made her swallow it? An electronic bug? Don't you realize that she is a very delicate animal and her health is extremely precarious −'

'Don't get worked up,' Ross said. 'Remember the vitamins I gave you? You swallowed one, too.' She glanced at her watch. 'Thirty-two minutes,' she said. 'Not bad at all. We have forty minutes before we have to leave Nairobi.'

8. Present Point

Munro sat in the 747, punching buttons on the computer. He watched as the lines crisscrossed over the maps, ticking out datalines, timelines, information lock coordinates.

The computer ran through possible expedition routings quickly, testing a new one every ten seconds. After each data fit, outcomes were printed − cost, logistical difficulties, supply problems, total elapsed times from Houston, from Present Point (Nairobi), where they were now.

Looking for a solution.

It wasn't like the old days, Munro thought. Even five years ago, expeditions were still run on guesswork and luck. But now every expedition employed real-time computer planning; Munro had long since been forced to learn BASIC and TW/GESHUND and other major interactive languages. Nobody did it by the seat of the pants any more. The business had changed.

Munro had decided to join the ERTS expedition precisely because of those changes. Certainly he hadn't joined because of Karen Ross, who was stubborn and inexperienced. But ERTS had the most elaborate working database, and the most sophisticated planning programs. In the long run, he expected those programs to make the crucial difference. And he liked a smaller team; once the consortium was in the field, their working party of thirty was going to prove unwieldy.

But he had to find a faster timeline to get them in. Munro pressed the buttons, watching the data flash up. He set trajectories, intersections, junctions. Then, with a practiced eye, he began to eliminate alternatives.

He closed out pathways, shut down airfields, eliminated truck routes, avoided river crossings.

The computer kept coming back with reduced times, but from Present Point (Nairobi) the total elapsed times were always too long. The best projection beat the consortium by thirty-seven minutes – which was nothing to rely on. He frowned, and smoked a cigar. Perhaps if he crossed the Liko River at Mugana . . .

He punched the buttons.

It didn't help. Crossing the Liko was *slower*. He tried trekking through the Goroba Valley, even though it was probably too hazardous to execute.

PROPOSED ROUTING EXCESSIVELY HAZARDOUS.

'Great minds think alike,' Munro said, smoking his cigar. But it started him wondering: were there other, unorthodox approaches they had overlooked? And then he had an idea.

The others wouldn't like it, but it might work. . . .

Munro called the logistics equipment list. Yes, they were equipped for it. He punched in the routing, smiling as he saw the line streak straight across Africa, within a few miles of their destination. He called for outcomes.

PROPOSED ROUTING UNACCEPTABLE.

He pressed the override button, got the data outcomes anyway. It was just as he thought – they could beat the consortium by a full forty hours. Nearly two full days!

The computer went back to the previous statement:

PROPOSED ROUTING UNACCEPTABLE / ALTITUDE FACTORS / HAZARDS TO PERSONNEL EXCESSIVE / PROBABILITY SUCCESS UNDER LIMITS /

Munro didn't think that was true. He thought they could pull it off, especially if the weather was good. The altitude wouldn't be a problem, and the ground although rough would be reasonably yielding.

In fact, the more Munro thought about it, the more certain he was that it would work.

9. Departure

The little Fokker S-144 prop plane was pulled up alongside the giant 747 cargo jet, like an infant nursing at its mother's breast. Two cargo ramps were in constant motion as men transferred equipment from the larger plane to the smaller one. Returning to the airfield, Ross explained to Elliot that they would be taking the smaller plane, since the 747 had to be debugged, and since it was 'too large' for their needs now.

'But the jet must be faster,' Elliot said.

'Not necessarily,' Ross said, but she did not explain further.

In any case, things were now happening very fast, and Elliot had other concerns. He helped Amy aboard the Fokker, and checked her thoroughly. She seemed to be bruised all over her body – at least she complained that everything hurt when he touched her – but she had no broken bones, and she was in good spirits.

Several black men were loading equipment into the airplane, laughing and slapping each other on the back, having a fine time. Amy was intrigued with the men, demanding to know *What joke?* But they ignored her, concentrating on the work at hand. And she was still groggy from her medication. Soon she fell asleep.

Ross supervised the loading, and Elliot moved toward the rear of the plane, where she was talking with a jolly black man, whom she introduced as Kahega.

'Ah,' Kahega said, shaking Elliot's hand. 'Dr. Elliot. Dr. Ross and Dr. Elliot, two doctors, very excellent.'

Elliot was not sure why it was excellent.

Kahega laughed infectiously. 'Very good *cover*,' he announced. 'Not like the old days with Captain Munro. Now two doctors – a medical mission, yes? Very excellent. Where are the "medical supplies"?' He cocked an eyebrow.

'We have no medical supplies.' Ross sighed.

'Oh, very excellent, doctor, I like your manner,' Kahega said. 'You are American, yes? We take what, M-16s? Very good rifle, M-16. I prefer it myself.'

'Kahega thinks we are running guns,' Ross said. 'He just can't believe we aren't.'

Kahega was laughing. 'You are with Captain Munro!' he said, as if this explained everything. And then he went off to see about the other workmen.

'You sure we aren't running guns?' Elliot asked when they were alone.

'We're after something more valuable than guns,' Ross said. She was repacking the equipment, working quickly. Elliot asked if he could help, but she shook her head. 'I've got to do this myself. We have to get it down to forty pounds per person.'

'Forty pounds? For everything?'

'That's what the computer projection allows. Munro's brought in Kahega and seven other Kikuyu assistants. With the three of us, that makes eleven people all together, plus Amy – she gets her full forty pounds. But it means a total of four hundred eighty pounds.' Ross continued to weigh packs and parcels of food.

The news gave Elliot serious misgivings. The expedition was taking yet another turn, into still greater danger. His immediate desire to back out was checked by his memory of the video screen, and the gray gorillalike creature that he suspected was a new, unknown animal. That was a discovery worth risk. He stared out the window at the porters. 'They're Kikuyu?'

'Yes,' she said. 'They're good porters, even if they never shut up. Kikuyu tribesmen love to talk. They're all brothers, by the way, so be careful what you say. I just hope Munro didn't have to tell them too much.'

'The Kikuyu?'

'No, the NCNA.'

'The NCNA,' Elliot repeated.

'The Chinese. The Chinese are very interested in computers and electronic technology,' Ross said. 'Munro must be telling them something in exchange for the advice they're giving him.' She gestured to the window, and Elliot looked out. Sure enough, Munro stood under the shadow of the 747 wing, talking with four Chinese men.

'Here,' Ross said, 'stow these in that corner.' She pointed to three large Styrofoam cartons marked AMERICAN SPORT DIVERS, LAKE ELSINORE, CALIF.

'We doing underwater work?' Elliot asked, puzzled.

But Ross wasn't paying attention. 'I just wish I knew what he was telling them,' she said. But as it turned out, Ross needn't have worried, for Munro paid the Chinese in something more valuable to them than electronics information.

The Fokker lifted off from the Nairobi runway at 14:24 hours, three minutes ahead of their new timeline schedule.

During the sixteen hours following Amy's recovery, the ERTS expedition traveled 560 miles across the borders of four countries – Kenya, Tanzania, Rwanda, and Zaire – as they went from Nairobi to the Barawanda

Forest, at the edge of the Congo rain forest. The logistics of this complex move would have been impossible without the assistance of an outside ally. Munro said that he 'had friends in low places,' and in this case he had turned to the Chinese Secret Service, in Tanzania.

The Chinese had been active in Africa since the early 1960s, when their spy networks attempted to influence the course of the Congolese civil war because China wanted access to the Congo's rich supplies of uranium. Field operatives were run out of the Bank of China or, more commonly, the New China News Agency. Munro had dealt with a number of NCNA 'war correspondents' when he was running arms from 1963 to 1968, and he had never lost his contacts.

The Chinese financial commitment to Africa was considerable. In the late 1960s, more than half of China's two billion dollars in foreign aid went to African nations. An equal sum was spent secretly; in 1973, Mao Tse-tung complained publicly about the money he had wasted trying to overthrow the Zaire government of President Mobutu.

The Chinese mission in Africa was meant to counter the Russian influence, but since World War II the Chinese bore no great love for the Japanese, and Munro's desire to beat the Euro-Japanese consortium fell on sympathetic ears. To celebrate the alliance, Munro had brought three grease-stained cardboard cartons from Hong Kong.

The two chief Chinese operatives in Africa, Li T'ao and Liu Shu-wen, were both from Hunan province. They found their African posting tedious because of the bland African food, and gratefully accepted Munro's gift of a case of tree ears fungus, a case of hot bean sauce, and a case of chili paste with garlic. The fact that these spices came from neutral Hong Kong, and were not the inferior condiments produced in Taiwan, was a subtle point; in any case, the gift struck exactly the proper note for an informal exchange.

NCNA operatives assisted Munro with paperwork, some difficult-to-obtain equipment, and information. The Chinese possessed excellent maps, and remarkably detailed information about conditions along the northeast Zaire border – since they were assisting the Tanzanian troops invading Uganda. The Chinese had told him that the jungle rivers were flooding, and had advised him to procure a balloon for crossings. But Munro did not bother to take their advice; indeed, he seemed to have some plan to reach his destination without crossing any rivers at all. Although how, the Chinese could not imagine.

At 10 p.m. on June 16, the Fokker stopped to refuel at Rawamagena airport, outside Kigali in Rwanda. The local traffic control officer boarded the plane with a clipboard and forms, asking their next destination. Munro said that it was Rawamagena airport, meaning that the aircraft would make a loop, then return.

Elliot frowned. 'But we're going to land somewhere in the –'

'Sh-h-h,' Ross said, shaking her head. 'Leave it alone.'

Certainly the traffic officer seemed content with this flight plan; once the pilot signed the clipboard, he departed. Ross explained that flight controllers in Rwanda were accustomed to aircraft that did not file full plans. 'He just wants to know when the plane will be back at his field. The rest is none of his business.'

Rawamagena airport was sleepy; they had to wait two hours for petrol to be brought, yet the normally impatient Ross waited quietly. And Munro dozed, equally indifferent to the delay.

'What about the timeline?' Elliot asked.

'No problem,' she said. 'We can't leave for three hours anyway. We need the light over Mukenko.'

'That's where the airfield is?' Elliot asked.

'If you call it an airfield,' Munro said, and he pulled his safari hat down over his eyes and went back to sleep.

This worried Elliot until Ross explained to him that most outlying African airfields were just dirt strips cut into the bush. The pilots couldn't land at night, or in the foggy mornings, because there were often animals on the field, or encamped nomads, or another plane that had put down and was unable to take off again. 'We need the light,' she explained. 'That's why we're waiting. Don't worry: it's all factored in.'

Elliot accepted her explanation, and went back to check on Amy. Ross sighed. 'Don't you think we'd better tell him?' she asked.

'Why?' Munro said, not lifting his hat.

'Maybe there's a problem with Amy.'

'I'll take care of Amy,' Munro said.

'It's going to upset Elliot when he finds out,' Ross said.

'Of course it's going to upset him,' Munro said. 'But there's no point upsetting him until we have to. After all, what's this jump worth to us?'

'Forty hours, at least. It's dangerous, but it'll give us a whole new timeline. We could still beat them.'

'Well, there's your answer,' Munro said. 'Now keep your mouth shut, and get some rest.'

DAY 5: MORUTI
June 17, 1979

1. Zaire

Five hours out of Rawamagena, the landscape changed. Once past Goma, near the Zaire border, they found themselves flying over the easternmost fingers of the Congo rain forest. Elliot stared out the window, fascinated.

Here and there in the pale morning light, a few fragile wisps of fog clung like cotton to the canopy of trees. And occasionally they passed the dark snaking curve of a muddy river, or the straight deep red gash of a road. But for the most part they looked down upon an unbroken expanse of dense forest, extending away into the distance as far as the eye could see.

The view was boring, and simultaneously frightening – it was frightening to be confronted by what Stanley had called 'the indifferent immensity of the natural world.' As one sat in the air-conditioned comfort of an airplane seat, it was impossible not to recognize that this vast, monotonous forest was a giant creation of nature, utterly dwarfing in scale the greatest cities or other creations of mankind. Each individual green puff of a tree had a trunk forty feet in diameter, soaring two hundred feet into the air; a space the size of a Gothic cathedral was concealed beneath its billowing foliage. And Elliot knew that the forest extended to the west for nearly *two thousand miles*, until it finally stopped at the Atlantic Ocean, on the west coast of Zaire.

Elliot had been anticipating Amy's reaction to this first view of the jungle, her natural environment. She looked out the window with a fixed stare. She signed *Here jungle* with the same emotional neutrality that she named color cards, or objects spread out on her trailer floor in San Francisco. She was identifying the jungle, giving a name to what she saw, but she sensed no deeper recognition.

Elliot said to her, 'Amy like jungle?'

Jungle here, she signed. *Jungle is.*

He persisted, probing for the emotional context that he was sure must be there. Amy like jungle?

Jungle here. Jungle is. Jungle place here Amy see jungle here.

He tried another approach. 'Amy live jungle here?'

No. Expressionless.

'Where Amy live?'

Amy live Amy house. Referring to her trailer in San Francisco.

Elliot watched her loosen her seat belt, cup her chin on her hand as she stared lazily out the window. She signed, *Amy want cigarette.*

She had noticed Munro smoking.

'Later, Amy,' Elliot said.

At seven in the morning, they flew over the shimmering metal roofs of the tin and tantalum mining complex at Masisi. Munro, Kahega, and the other porters went to the back of the plane, where they worked on the equipment, chattering excitedly in Swahili.

Amy, seeing them go, signed, *They worried.*

'Worried about what, Amy?'

They worried men worry they worried problems. After a while, Elliot moved to the rear of the plane to find Munro's men half buried under great heaps of straw, stuffing equipment into oblong torpedo-shaped muslin containers, then packing straw around the supplies. Elliot pointed to the muslin torpedoes. 'What are these?'

'They're called Crosslin containers,' Munro said. 'Very reliable.'

'I've never seen equipment packed this way,' Elliot said, watching the men work. 'They seem to be protecting our supplies very carefully.'

'That's the idea,' Munro said. And he moved up the aircraft to the cockpit, to confer with the pilot.

Amy signed, *Nosehair man lie Peter.* 'Nosehair man' was her term for Munro, but Elliot ignored her. He turned to Kahega. 'How far to the airfield?'

Kahega glanced up. 'Airfield?'

'At Mukenko.'

Kahega paused, thinking it over. 'Two hours,' he said. And then he giggled. He said something in Swahili and all his brothers laughed, too.

'What's funny?' Elliot said.

'Oh, Doctor,' Kahega said, slapping him on the back. 'You are humorous by your nature.'

The airplane banked, making a slow wide circle in the air. Kahega and his brothers peered out the windows, and Elliot joined them. He saw only unbroken jungle – and then a column of green jeeps, moving down a muddy track far below. It looked like a military formation. He heard the word 'Muguru' repeated several times.

'What's the matter?' Elliot said. 'Is this Muguru?'

Kahega shook his head vigorously. 'No hell. This damn pilot, I warn Captain Munro, this damn pilot lost.'

'Lost?' Elliot repeated. Even the word was chilling.

Kahega laughed. 'Captain Munro set him right, give him dickens.'

The airplane now flew east, away from the jungle toward a wooded highland area, rolling hills and stands of deciduous trees. Kahega's brothers chattered excitedly, and laughed and slapped one another; they seemed to be having a fine time.

Then Ross came back, moving quickly down the aisle, her face tense. She unpacked cardboard boxes, withdrawing several basketball-sized spheres of tightly wrapped metal foil.

The foil reminded him of Christmas-tree tinsel. 'What's that for?' Elliot asked.

And then he heard the first explosion, and the Fokker shuddered in the air.

Running to the window, he saw a straight thin white vapor trail terminating in a black smoke cloud off to their right. The Fokker was banking, tilting toward the jungle. As he watched, a second trail streaked up toward them from the green forest below.

It was a missile, he realized. A guided missile.

'Ross!' Munro shouted.

'Ready!' Ross shouted back.

There was a bursting red explosion, and his view through the windows was obscured by dense smoke. The airplane shook with the blast, but continued the turn. Elliot couldn't believe it: *someone was shooting missiles at them.*

'Radar!' Munro shouted. 'Not optical! Radar!'

Ross gathered up the silver basketballs in her arms and moved back down the aisle. Kahega was opening the rear door, the wind whipping through the compartment.

'What the hell's happening?' Elliot said.

'Don't worry,' Ross said over her shoulder. 'We'll make up the time.' There was a loud whoosh, followed by a third explosion. With the airplane still banked steeply, Ross tore the wrappings from the basketballs and threw them out into the open sky.

Engines roaring, the Fokker swung eight miles to the south and climbed to twelve thousand feet, then circled the forest in a holding pattern. With each revolution, Elliot could see the foil strips hanging in the air like a glinting metallic cloud. Two more rockets exploded within the cloud. Even from a distance, the noise and the shock waves disturbed Amy; she was rocking back and forth in her seat, grunting softly.

'That's chaff,' Ross explained, sitting in front of her portable computer console, punching buttons. 'It confuses radar weapons systems. Those radar-guided SAMs read us as somewhere in the cloud.'

Elliot heard her words slowly, as if in a dream. It made no sense to him. 'But who's shooting at us?'

'Probably the FZA,' Munro said. 'Forces Zairoises Armoises – the Zaire army.'

'The Zaire army? Why?'

'It's a mistake,' Ross said, still punching buttons, not looking up.

'A mistake? They're shooting surface-to-air missiles at us and *it's a mistake*? Don't you think you'd better call them and tell them it's a mistake?'

'Can't,' Ross said.

'Why not?'

'Because,' Munro said, 'we didn't want to file a flight plan in Rawam-agena. That means we are technically in violation of Zaire airspace.'

'Jesus Christ,' Elliot said.

Ross said nothing. She continued to work at the computer console, trying to get the static to resolve on the screen, pressing one button after another.

'When I agreed to join this expedition,' Elliot said, beginning to shout, 'I didn't expect to get into a shooting war.'

'Neither did I,' Ross said. 'It looks as if we both got more than we bargained for.'

Before Elliot could reply, Munro put an arm around his shoulder and took him aside. 'It's going to be all right,' he told Elliot. 'They're outdated sixties SAMs and most of them are blowing up because the solid propellant's cracked with age. We're in no danger. Just look after Amy, she needs your help now. Let me work with Ross.'

Ross was under intense pressure. With the airplane circling eight miles from the chaff cloud, she had to make a decision quickly. But she had just been dealt a devastating – and wholly unexpected – setback.

The Euro-Japanese consortium had been ahead of them from the very start, by approximately eighteen hours and twenty minutes. On the ground in Nairobi, Munro had worked out a plan with Ross which would erase that difference and put the ERTS expedition on site *forty hours* ahead of the consortium team. This plan – which for obvious reasons she had not told Elliot – called for them to parachute onto the barren southern slopes of Mount Mukenko.

From Mukenko, Munro estimated it was thirty-six hours to the ruined city; Ross expected to jump at two o'clock that afternoon. Depending on cloud cover over Mukenko and the specific drop zone, they might reach the city as early as noon on June 19.

The plan was extremely hazardous. They would be jumping un-trained personnel into a wilderness area, more than three days' walk from the nearest large town. If anyone suffered a serious injury, the chances of survival were slight. There was also a question about the equipment: at altitudes of 8,000–10,000 feet on the volcanic slopes, air resistance was reduced, and the Crosslin packets might not provide enough protection.

Initially Ross had rejected Munro's plan as too risky, but he convinced her it was feasible. He pointed out that the parafoils were equipped with automated altimeter-release devices; that the upper volcanic scree was as yielding as a sandy beach; that the Crosslin containers could be overpacked; and that he could carry Amy down himself.

Ross had double-checked outcome probabilities from the Houston computer, and the results were unequivocal. The probability of a successful jump was .7980, meaning there was one chance in five that someone would be badly hurt. However, *given a successful jump*, the probability of expedition success was .9943, making it virtually certain they would beat the consortium to the site.

No alternate plan scored so high. She had looked at the data and said, 'I guess we jump.'

'I think we do,' Munro had said.

The jump solved many problems, for the geopolitical updates were increasingly unfavorable. The Kigani were now in full rebellion; the pygmies were unstable; the Zaire army had sent armored units into the eastern border area to put down the Kigani – and African field armies were notoriously trigger-happy. By jumping onto Mukenko, they expected to bypass all these hazards.

But that was before the Zaire army SAMs began exploding all around them. They were still eighty miles south of the intended drop zone, circling over Kigani territory, wasting time and fuel. It looked as if their daring plan, so carefully worked out and confirmed by computer, was suddenly irrelevant.

And to add to her difficulties, she could not confer with Houston; the computer refused to link up by satellite. She spent fifteen minutes working with the portable unit, boosting power and switching scrambler codes, until she finally realized that her transmission was being electronically jammed.

For the first time in her memory, Karen Ross wanted to cry.

'Easy now,' Munro said quietly, lifting her hands away from the buttons. 'One thing at a time, no point in getting upset.' Ross had been punching the buttons over and over again, unaware of what she was doing.

Munro was conscious of the deteriorating situation with both Elliot and Ross. He had seen it happen on expeditions before, particularly when scientists and technical people were involved. Scientists worked all day in laboratories where conditions could be rigorously regulated and monitored. Sooner or later, scientists came to believe that the outside world was just as controllable as their laboratories. Even though they knew better, the shock of discovering that the natural world followed its own rules and was indifferent to them represented a harsh psychic blow. Munro could read the signs.

'But this,' Ross said, 'is obviously a non-military aircraft, how can they do it?'

Munro stared at her. In the Congolese civil war, civilian aircraft had been routinely shot down by all sides. 'These things happen,' he said.

'And the jamming? Those bastards haven't got the capability to jam us. We're being jammed between our transmitter and our satellite transponder. To do that requires another satellite somewhere, and –' She broke off, frowning.

'You didn't expect the consortium to sit by idly,' Munro said. 'The question is, can you fix it? Have you got countermeasures?'

'Sure, I've got countermeasures,' Ross said. 'I can encode a burst bounce, I can transmit optically on an IR carrier, I can link a ground-base cable – but there's nothing I can put together in the next few minutes, and we need information now. Our plan is shot.'

'One thing at a time,' Munro repeated quietly. He saw the tension in her features, and he knew she was not thinking clearly. He also knew he could not do her thinking for her; he had to get her calm again.

In Munro's judgment, the ERTS expedition was already finished – they could not possibly beat the consortium to the Congo site. But he had no intention of quitting; he had led expeditions long enough to know that anything could happen, so he said, 'We can still make up the lost time.'

'Make it up? How?'

Munro said the first thing that came to mind: 'We'll take the Ragora north. Very fast river, no problem.'

'The Ragora's too dangerous.'

'We'll have to see,' Munro said, although he knew that she was right. The Ragora was much too dangerous, particularly in June. Yet he kept his voice calm, soothing, reassuring. 'Shall I tell the others?' he asked finally.

'Yes,' Ross said. In the distance, they heard another rocket explosion. 'Let's get out of here.'

Munro moved swiftly to the rear of the Fokker and said to Kahega, 'Prepare the men.'

'Yes, boss,' Kahega said. A bottle of whiskey was passed around, and each of the men took a long swallow.

Elliot said, 'What the hell is this?'

'The men are getting prepared,' Munro said.

'Prepared for what?' Elliot asked.

At that moment, Ross came back, looking grim. 'From here on, we'll continue on foot,' she said.

Elliot looked out the window. 'Where's the airfield?'

'There is no airfield,' Ross said.

'What do you mean?'

'I mean there is no airfield.'

'Is the plane going to put down in the fields?' Elliot asked.

'No,' Ross said. 'The plane is not going to put down at all.'

'Then how do we get down?' Elliot asked, but even as he asked the question, his stomach sank, because he knew the answer.

'Amy will be fine,' Munro said cheerfully, cinching Elliot's straps tightly around his chest. 'I gave her a shot of your Thoralen tranquilizer, and she'll be quite calm. No problem at all, I'll keep a good grip on her.'

'Keep a good grip on her?' Elliot asked.

'She's too small to fit a harness,' Munro said. 'I'll have to carry her down.' Amy snored loudly, and drooled on Munro's shoulder. He set Amy on the floor; she lay limply on her back, still snoring.

'Now, then,' Munro said. 'Your parafoil opens automatically. You'll find you have lines in both hands, left and right. Pull left to go left, right to go right, and −'

'What happens to her?' Elliot asked, pointing to Amy.

'I'll take her. Pay attention now. If anything goes wrong, your reserve chute is here, on your chest.' He tapped a cloth bundle with a small black digital box, which read 4757. 'That's your rate-of-fall altimeter. Automatically pops your reserve chute if you hit thirty-six hundred feet and are still falling faster than two feet per second. Nothing to worry about: whole thing's automatic.'

Elliot was chilled, drenched in sweat. 'What about landing?'

'Nothing to it.' Munro grinned. 'You'll land automatically too. Stay loose and relax, take the shock in the legs. Equivalent of jumping off a ten-foot ledge. You've done it a thousand times.'

Behind him Elliot saw the open door, bright sunlight glaring into the plane. The wind whipped and howled. Kahega's men jumped in quick succession, one after another. He glanced at Ross, who was ashen, her lower lip trembling as she gripped the doorway.

'Karen, you're not going to go along with −'

She jumped, disappearing into the sunlight. Munro said 'You're next.'

'I've never jumped before,' Elliot said.

'That's the best way. You won't be frightened.'

'But I *am* frightened.'

'I can help you with that,' Munro said, and he pushed Elliot out the plane.

Munro watched him fall away, his grin instantly gone. Munro had adopted his hearty demeanor only for Elliot's benefit. 'If a man has to do something dangerous,' he said later, 'it helps to be angry. It's for his own protection, really. Better he should hate someone than fall apart. I wanted Elliot to hate me all the way down.'

Munro understood the risks. The minute they left the aircraft, they also left civilization, and all the unquestioned assumptions of civilization. They were jumping not only through the air, but through time, backward into a more primitive and dangerous way of life – the eternal realities of the Congo, which had existed for centuries before them. 'Those were the facts of life,' Munro said, 'but I didn't see any reason to worry the others before they jumped. My job was to get those people into the Congo, not scare them to death. There was plenty of time for that.'

Elliot fell, scared to death.

His stomach jumped into his throat, and he tasted bile; the wind screamed around his ears and tugged at his hair; and the air was cold – he was instantly chilled and shivering. Below him the Barawana Forest lay spread across rolling hills. He felt no appreciation for the beauty before him, and in fact he closed his eyes, for he was plummeting at hideous speed toward the ground. But with his eyes shut he was more aware of the screaming wind.

Too much time had passed. Obviously the parafoil (whatever the hell that was) was not going to open. His life now depended on the parachute attached to his chest. He clutched it, a small tight bundle near his churning stomach. Then he pulled his hands away: he didn't want to interfere with its opening. He dimly remembered that people had died that way, when they interfered with the opening of their parachute.

The screaming wind continued; his body rushed sickeningly downward. *Nothing was happening.* He felt the fierce wind tugging at his feet, whipping his trousers, flapping his shirt against his arms. *Nothing was happening.* It had been at least three minutes since he'd jumped from the plane. He dared not open his eyes, for fear of seeing the trees rushing up close as his body crashed downward toward them in his final seconds of conscious life. . . .

He was going to throw up.

Bile dribbled from his mouth, but since he was falling head downward, the liquid ran up his chin to his neck and then inside his shirt. It was freezing cold. His shivering was becoming uncontrollable.

He snapped upright with a bone-twisting jolt.

For an instant he thought he had hit the ground, and then he realized that he was still descending through the air, but more slowly. He opened his eyes and stared at pale blue sky.

He looked down, and was shocked to see that he was still thousands of feet from the earth. Obviously he had only been falling a few seconds from the airplane above him –

Looking up, he could not see the plane. Directly overhead was a giant rectangular shape, with brilliant red, white, and blue stripes: the parafoil. Finding it easier to look up than down, he studied the parafoil intently. The leading edge was curved and puffy; the rear edge thin, fluttering in the breeze. The parafoil looked very much like an airplane wing, with cords running down to his body.

He took a deep breath and looked down. He was still very high over the landscape. There was some comfort in the slowness with which he was descending. It was really rather peaceful.

And then he noticed he wasn't moving down; he was moving sideways. He could see the other parafoils below, Kahega and his men and Ross; he tried to count them, and thought there were six, but he had difficulty concentrating. He appeared to be moving laterally away from them.

He tugged on the lines in his left hand, and he felt his body twist as the parafoil moved, taking him to the left.

Not bad, he thought.

He pulled harder on the left cords, ignoring the fact that this seemed to make him move faster. He tried to stay near the rectangles descending beneath him. He heard the scream of the wind in his ears. He looked up, hoping to see Munro, but all he could see was the stripes of his own parafoil.

He looked back down, and was astonished to find that the ground was a great deal closer. In fact, it seemed to be rushing up to him at brutal speed. He wondered where he had got the idea that he was drifting gently downward. There was nothing gentle about his descent at all. He saw the first of the parafoils crumple gently as Kahega touched ground, then the second, and the third.

It wouldn't be long before he landed. He was approaching the level of the trees, but his lateral movement was very fast. He realized that his left hand was rigidly pulling on the cords. He released his grip, and his lateral movement ceased. He drifted forward.

Two more parafoils crumpled on impact. He looked back to see Kahega and his men, already down, gathering up the cloth. They were all right; that was encouraging.

He was sliding right into a dense clump of trees. He pulled his cords and twisted to the right, his whole body tilting. He was moving very fast now. The trees could not be avoided. He was going to smash into them. The branches seemed to reach up like fingers, grasping for him.

He closed his eyes, and felt the branches scratching at his face and body as he crashed down, knowing that any second he was going to hit, that he was going to hit the ground and roll –

He never hit.

Everything became silent. He felt himself bobbing up and down. He opened his eyes and saw that he was swinging four feet above the ground. His parafoil had caught in the trees.

He fumbled with his harness buckles, and fell out onto the earth. As he picked himself up, Kahega and Ross came running over to ask if he was all right.

'I'm fine,' Elliot said, and indeed he felt extraordinarily fine, more alive than he could ever remember feeling. The next instant he fell over on rubber legs and promptly threw up.

Kahega laughed. 'Welcome to the Congo,' he said.

Elliot wiped his chin and said, 'Where is Amy?'

A moment later Munro landed, with a bleeding ear where Amy had bitten him in terror. But Amy was none the worse for the experience, and came running on her knuckles over to Elliot, making sure that he was all right, and then signing, *Amy fly no like.*

'Look out!'

The first of the torpedo-shaped Crosslin packets smashed down, exploding like a bomb when it hit the ground, spraying equipment and straw in all directions.

'There's the second one!'

Elliot dived for safety. The second bomb hit just a few yards away; he was pelted with foil containers of food and rice. Overhead, he heard the drone of the circling Fokker airplane. He got to his feet in time to see the final two Crosslin containers crash down, and Kahega's men running for safety, with Ross shouting, 'Careful, those have the lasers!'

It was like being in the middle of a blitz, but as swiftly as it had begun it was over. The Fokker above them flew off, and the sky was silent; the men began repacking the equipment and burying the parafoils, while Munro barked instructions in Swahili.

Twenty minutes later, they were moving single-file through the forest, starting a two-hundred-mile trek that would lead them into the unexplored eastern reaches of the Congo, to a fabulous reward.

If they could reach it in time.

2. Kigani

Once past the initial shock of his jump, Elliot enjoyed the walk through the Barawana Forest. Monkeys chattered in the trees, and birds called in the cool air; the Kikuyu porters were strung out behind them, smoking cigarettes and joking with one another in an exotic tongue. Elliot found all his emotions agreeable – the sense of freedom from a crass civilization; the sense of adventure, of unexpected events that might occur at any future moment; and finally the sense of romance, of a quest for the poignant past while omnipresent danger kept sensation at a peak of intense feeling. It was in this heightened mood that he listened to the forest animals around him, viewed the play of sunlight and shadow, felt the springy ground beneath his boots, and looked over at Karen Ross, whom he found beautiful and graceful in an utterly unexpected way.

Karen Ross did not look back at him.

As she walked, she twisted knobs on one of her black electronic boxes, trying to establish a signal. A second electronic box hung from a shoulder strap, and since she did not turn to look at him, he had time to notice that there was already a dark stain of sweat at her shoulder, and another running down the back of her shirt. Her dark blonde hair was damp, clinging unattractively to the back of her head. And he noticed that her trousers were wrinkled, streaked with dirt from the fall. She still did not look back.

'Enjoy the forest,' Munro advised him. 'This is the last time you'll feel cool and dry for quite a while.'

Elliot agreed that the forest was pleasant.

'Yes, very pleasant.' Munro nodded, with an odd expression on his face.

The Barawana Forest was not virginal. From time to time, they passed cleared fields and other signs of human habitation, although they never saw farmers. When Elliot mentioned that fact, Munro just shook his head. As they moved deeper into the forest Munro turned self-absorbed, unwilling to talk. Yet he showed an interest in the fauna, frequently pausing to listen intently to bird cries before signaling the expedition to continue on.

During these pauses, Elliot would look back down the line of porters with loads balanced on their heads, and feel acutely his kinship with Livingstone and Stanley and the other explorers who had ventured through Africa a century before. And in this, his romantic associations were accurate. Central African life was little changed since Stanley explored the Congo in the 1870s, and neither was the basic nature of expeditions to that region. Serious exploration was still carried out on foot; porters were still necessary; expenses were still daunting – and so were the dangers.

By midday, Elliot's boots had begun to hurt his feet, and he found that he was exceedingly tired. Apparently the porters were tired too, because they had fallen silent, no longer smoking cigarettes and shouting jokes to one another up and down the line. The expedition proceeded in silence until Elliot asked Munro if they were going to stop for lunch.

'No,' Munro said.

'Good,' Karen Ross said, glancing at her watch.

Shortly after one o'clock, they heard the thumping of helicopters. The reaction of Munro and the porters was immediate – they dived under a stand of large trees and waited, looking upwards. Moments later, two large green helicopters passed overhead; Elliot clearly read white stenciling: 'FZA.'

Munro squinted at the departing craft. They were American-made Hueys; he had not been able to see the armament. 'It's the army,' he said. 'They're looking for Kigani.'

An hour later, they arrived at a clearing where manioc was being grown. A crude wooden farmhouse stood in the center, with pale smoke issuing from a chimney and laundry on a wash line flapping in the gentle breeze. But they saw no inhabitants.

The expedition had circled around previous farm clearings, but this time Munro raised his hand to call for a halt. The porters dropped their loads and sat in the grass, not speaking.

The atmosphere was tense, although Elliot could not understand why. Munro squatted with Kahega at the edge of the clearing, watching the farmhouse and the surrounding fields. After twenty minutes, when there was still no sign of movement, Ross, who was crouched near Munro, became impatient. 'I don't see why we are –'

Munro clapped his hand over her mouth. He pointed to the clearing, and mouthed one word: Kigani.

Ross's eyes went wide. Munro took his hand away.

They all stared at the farmhouse. Still there was no sign of life. Ross made a circular movement with her arm, suggesting that they circle around the clearing and move on. Munro shook his head, and pointed to the ground, indicating that she should sit. Munro looked questioningly at Elliot, and pointed to Amy, who foraged in the tall grass off to one side. He seemed to be concerned that Amy would make noise. Elliot signed to Amy to be quiet, but it was not necessary. Amy had sensed the general tension, and glanced warily from time to time toward the farmhouse.

Nothing happened for several more minutes; they listened to the buzz of the cicadas in the hot midday sun, and they waited. They watched the laundry flutter in the breeze.

Then the thin wisp of blue smoke from the chimney stopped.

Munro and Kahega exchanged glances. Kahega slipped back to where the porters sat, opened one load, and brought out a machine gun. He covered the safety with his hand, muffling the click as he released it. It was incredibly quiet in the clearing. Kahega resumed his place next to Munro and handed him the gun. Munro checked the safety, then set the gun on the ground. They waited several minutes more. Elliot looked at Ross but she was not looking at him.

There was a soft creak as the farmhouse door opened. Munro picked up the machine gun.

No one came out. They all stared at the open door, waiting. And then finally the Kigani stepped into the sunlight.

Elliot counted twelve tall muscular men armed with bows and arrows, and carrying long *pangas* in their hands. Their legs and chests were streaked with white, and their faces were solid white, which gave their heads a menacing, skull-like appearance. As the Kigani moved off through the tall manioc, only their white heads were visible, looking around tensely.

Even after they were gone, Munro remained watching the silent clearing for another ten minutes. Finally he stood and sighed. When he spoke, his voice seemed incredibly loud. 'Those were Kigani,' Munro said.

'What were they doing?' Ross said.

'Eating,' Munro said. 'They killed the family in that house, and then ate them. Most farmers have left, because the Kigani are on the rampage.'

He signaled Kahega to get the men moving again, and they set off, skirting around the clearing. Elliot kept looking at the farmhouse, wondering what he would see if he went inside. Munro's statement had been so casual: *They killed the family . . . and then ate them.*

'I suppose,' Ross said, looking over her shoulder, 'that we should consider ourselves lucky. We're probably among the last people in the world to see these things.'

Munro shook his head. 'I doubt it,' he said. 'Old habits die hard.'

During the Congolese civil war in the 1960s, reports of widespread cannibalism and other atrocities shocked the Western world. But in fact cannibalism had always been openly practiced in central Africa.

In 1897, Sidney Hinde wrote that 'nearly all the tribes in the Congo Basin either are, or have been, cannibals; and among some of them the practice is on the increase.' Hinde was impressed by the undisguised nature of Congolese cannibalism: 'The captains of steamers have often assured me that whenever they try to buy goats from the natives, slaves are demanded in exchange; the natives often come aboard with tusks of ivory with the intention of buying a slave, complaining that *meat is now scarce in their neighborhood.*'

In the Congo, cannibalism was not associated with ritual or religion or war; it was a simple dietary preference. The Reverend Holman Bentley, who spent twenty years in the region, quoted a native as saying, 'You white men consider pork to be the tastiest of meat, but pork is not to be compared with human flesh.' Bentley felt that the natives 'could not understand the objections raised to the practice. "You eat fowls and goats, and we eat men; why not? What is the difference?" '

This frank attitude astonished observers, and led to bizarre customs. In 1910, Herbert Ward wrote of markets where slaves were sold 'piecemeal whilst still alive. Incredible as it may appear, captives are led from place to place in order that individuals may have the opportunity of indicating, by external marks on the body, the portion they desire to acquire. The distinguishing marks are generally made by means of coloured clay or strips of grass tied in a peculiar fashion. The astounding stoicism of the victims, who thus witness the bargaining for their limbs piecemeal, is only equalled by the callousness with which they walk forward to meet their fate.'

Such reports cannot be dismissed as late-Victorian hysteria, for all observers found the cannibals likable and sympathetic. Ward wrote that 'the cannibals are not schemers and they are not mean. In direct opposition to all natural conjectures, they are among the best types of men.' Bentley described them as 'merry, manly fellows, very friendly in conversation and quite demonstrative in their affection.'

Under Belgian colonial administration, cannibalism became much rarer – by the 1950s, there were even a few graveyards to be found – but no one seriously thought it had been eradicated. In 1956, H. C. Engert wrote, 'Cannibalism is far from being dead in Africa . . . I myself once lived in a cannibal village for a time, and found some [human] bones. The natives . . . were pleasant enough people. It was just an old custom which dies hard.'

Munro considered the 1979 Kigani uprising a political insurrection. The tribesmen were rebelling against the demand by the Zaire government that the Kigani change from hunting to farming, as if that were a simple matter. The Kigani were a poor and backward people; their knowledge of hygiene was rudimentary; their diet lacked proteins and vitamins, and they were prey to malaria, hookworm, bilharzia, and African sleeping sickness. One child in four died at birth, and few Kigani adults lived past the age of twenty-five. The hardships of their life required explanation, supplied by Angawa, or sorcerers. The Kigani believed that most deaths were supernatural: either the victim was under a sorcerer's spell, had broken some taboo, or was killed by vengeful spirits from the dead. Hunting also had a supernatural aspect: game was strongly influenced by the spirit world. In fact, the Kigani considered the supernatural world far more real than the day-to-day world, which they felt to be a 'waking dream,' and they attempted to control the supernatural through magical spells and potions, provided by the Angawa. They also carried out ritual body alterations, such as painting the face and hands white, to render an individual more powerful in battle. The Kigani believed that magic also resided in the bodies of their adversaries, and so to overcome spells cast by other Angawa they ate the bodies of their enemies. The magical power invested in the enemy thus became their own, frustrating enemy sorcerers.

These beliefs were very old, and the Kigani had long since settled on a pattern of response to threat, which was to eat other human beings. In 1890, they went on the rampage in the north, following the first visits by foreigners bearing firearms, which had frightened off the game. During the civil war in 1961, starving, they attacked and ate other tribes.

'And why are they eating people now?' Elliot asked Munro.

'They want their right to hunt,' Munro said. 'Despite the Kinshasa bureaucrats.'

In the early afternoon, the expedition mounted a hill from which they could overlook the valleys behind them to the south. In the distance they saw great billowing clouds of smoke and licking flames; there were the muffled explosions of air-to-ground rockets, and the helicopters wheeling like mechanical vultures over a kill.

'Those are Kigani villages,' Munro said, looking back, shaking his head. 'They haven't a prayer, especially since the men in those helicopters and the troops on the ground are all from the Abawe tribe, the traditional enemy of the Kigani.'

The twentieth-century world did not accommodate man-eating beliefs; indeed, the government in Kinshasa, two thousand miles away, had already decided to 'expunge the embarrassment' of cannibals within its borders. In June, the Zaire government dispatched five thousand armed troops, six rocket-armed American UH-2 helicopters, and ten armored personnel carriers to put down the Kigani rebellion. The military leader in charge, General Ngo Muguru, had no illusions about his directive. Muguru knew that Kinshasa wanted him to eliminate the Kigani as a tribe. And he intended to do exactly that.

During the rest of the day, they heard distant explosions of mortar and rockets. It was impossible not to contrast the modernity of this equipment with the bows and arrows of the Kigani they had seen. Ross said it was sad, but Munro replied that it was inevitable.

'The purpose of life,' Munro said, 'is to stay alive. Watch any animal in nature – all it tries to do is stay alive. It doesn't care about beliefs or philosophy. Whenever any animal's behavior puts it out of touch with the realities of its existence, it becomes extinct. The Kigani haven't seen that times have changed and their beliefs don't work. And they're going to be extinct.'

'Maybe there is a higher truth than merely staying alive,' Ross said.

'There isn't,' Munro said.

They saw several other parties of Kigani, usually from a distance of many miles. At the end of the day, after they had crossed the swaying wooden bridge over the Moruti Gorge, Munro announced that they were now beyond the Kigani territory and, at least for the time being, safe.

3. Moruti Camp

In a high clearing above Moruti, the 'place of soft winds,' Munro shouted Swahili instructions and Kahega's porters began to unpack their loads. Karen Ross looked at her watch. 'Are we stopping?'

'Yes,' Munro said.

'But it's only five o'clock. There's still two hours of light left.'

'We stop here,' Munro said. Moruti was located at 1,500 feet; another two hours' walking would put them down in the rain forest below. 'It's much cooler and more pleasant here.'

Ross said that she did not care about pleasantness.

'You will,' Munro said.

To make the best time, Munro intended to keep out of the rain forest wherever possible. Progress in the jungle was slow and uncomfortable; they would have more than enough experience with mud and leeches and fevers.

Kahega called to him in Swahili; Munro turned to Ross and said, 'Kahega wants to know how to pitch the tents.'

Kahega was holding a crumpled silver ball of fabric in his outstretched hand; the other porters were just as confused, rummaging through their loads, looking for familiar tent poles or stakes, finding none.

The ERTS camp had been designed under contract by a NASA team in 1977, based on the recognition that wilderness expedition equipment was fundamentally unchanged since the eighteenth century. 'Designs for modern exploration are long overdue,' ERTS said, and asked for state-of-the-art improvements in lightness, comfort, and efficiency of expedition gear. NASA had redesigned everything, from clothing and boots to tents and cooking gear, food and menus, first-aid kits, and communications systems for ERTS wilderness parties.

The redesigned tents were typical of the NASA approach. NASA had determined that tent weight consisted chiefly of the structural supports. In addition, single-ply tents were poorly insulated. If tents could be properly insulated, clothing and sleeping-bag weight could be reduced, as could the daily caloric requirements of expedition members. Since air was an excellent insulator, the obvious solution was an unsupported, pneumatic tent: NASA designed one that weighed six ounces.

Using a little hissing foot pump, Ross inflated the first tent. It was made from double-layer 20-mil silvered Mylar, and looked like a gleaming ribbed Quonset hut. The porters clapped their hands with delight;

Munro shook his head, amused; Kahega produced a small silver unit, the size of a shoebox. 'And this, Doctor? What is this?'

'We won't need that tonight. That's an air conditioner,' Ross said.

'Never go anywhere without one,' Munro said, still amused.

Ross glared at him. 'Studies show,' she said, 'that the single greatest factor limiting work efficiency is ambient temperature, with sleep deprivation as the second factor.'

'Really.'

Munro laughed and looked to Elliot, but Elliot was studiously examining the view of the rain forest in the evening sun. Amy came up and tugged at his sleeve.

Woman and nosehair man fight, she signed.

Amy had liked Munro from the beginning, and the feeling was mutual. Instead of patting her on the head and treating her like a child, as most people did, Munro instinctively treated her like a female. Then, too, he had been around enough gorillas to have a feeling for their behavior. Although he didn't know ASL, when Amy raised her arms, he understood that she wanted to be tickled, and would oblige her for a few moments, while she rolled grunting with pleasure on the ground.

But Amy was always distressed by conflict, and she was frowning now. 'They're just talking,' Elliot assured her.

She signed, *Amy want eat.*

'In a minute.' Turning back, he saw Ross setting up the transmitting equipment; this would be a daily ritual during the rest of the expedition, and one which never failed to fascinate Amy. Altogether, the equipment to send a transmission ten thousand miles by satellite weighed six pounds, and the electronic countermeasures, or ECM devices, weighed an additional three pounds.

First, Ross popped open the collapsed umbrella of the silver dish antenna, five feet in diameter. (Amy particularly liked this; as each day progressed, she would ask Ross when she would 'open metal flower.') Then Ross attached the transmitter box, plugging in the krylon-cadmium fuel cells. Next she linked the anti-jamming modules, and finally she hooked up the miniaturized computer terminal with its tiny keyboard and three-inch video screen.

This miniature equipment was highly sophisticated. Ross's computer had a 189K memory and all circuitry was redundant; housings were hermetically sealed and shockproof; even the keyboard was impedance-operated, so there were no moving parts to get gummed up, or admit water or dust.

And it was incredibly rugged. Ross remembered their 'field tests.' In the ERTS parking lot, technicians would throw new equipment against the wall, kick it across the concrete, and leave it in a bucket of muddy water overnight. Anything found working the next day was certified as field-worthy.

Now, in the sunset at Moruti, she punched in code co-ordinates to lock the transmission to Houston, checked signal strength, and waited the six minutes until the transponders matched up. But the little screen continued to show only gray static, with intermittent pulses of color. That meant someone was jamming them with a 'symphony.'

In ERTS slang, the simplest level of electronic jamming was called 'tuba.' Like a kid next door practicing his tuba, this jamming was merely annoying; it occurred within limited frequencies, and was often random or accidental, but transmissions could generally pass through it. At the next level was 'string quartet,' where multiple frequencies were jammed in an orderly fashion; next was 'big band,' where the electronic music covered a wider frequency range; and finally 'symphony,' where virtually the full transmission range was blocked.

Ross was now getting hit by a 'symphony.' To break through demanded coordination with Houston – which she was unable to arrange – but ERTS had several prearranged routines. She tried them one after another and finally broke the jamming with a technique called interstitial coding. (Interstitial coding utilized the fact that even dense music had periods of silence, or interstices, lasting microseconds. It was possible to monitor the jamming signals, identify regularities in the interstices, and then transmit in bursts during the silences.)

Ross was gratified to see the little screen glow in a multicolored image – a map of their position in the Congo. She punched in the field position lock, and a light blinked on the screen. Words appeared in 'shortline,' the compressed language devised for small-screen imagery. FILD TME-POSITN CHEK: PLS CONFRM LOCL TME 18:04 H6/17/79. She confirmed that it was indeed just after 6 p.m at their location. Immediately, overlaid lines produced a scrambled pattern as their Field Time-Position was measured against the computer simulation run in Houston before their departure.

Ross was prepared for bad news. According to her mental calculations, they had fallen some seventy-odd hours behind their projected timeline, and some twenty-odd hours behind the consortium.

Their original plan had called for them to jump onto the slopes of Mukenko at 2 p.m. on June 17, arriving at Zinj approximately thirty-six hours later, around midday of June 19. This would have put them onsite nearly two days before the consortium.

However, the SAM attack forced them to jump eighty miles south of their intended drop zone. The jungle terrain before them was varied, and they could expect to pick up time rafting on rivers, but it would still take a minimum of three days to go eighty miles.

That meant that they could no longer expect to beat the consortium to the site. Instead of arriving forty-eight hours ahead, they would be lucky if they arrived only twenty-four hours too late.

To her surprise, the screen blinked: FILD TME-POSITN CHEK: – 09:04 H WEL DUN. They were only nine hours off their simulation timeline.

'What does that mean?' Munro asked, looking at the screen.

There was only one possible conclusion. 'Something has slowed the consortium,' Ross said.

On the screen they read EURO/NIPON CONSRTIM LEGL TRUBL GOMA AIRPRT ZAIR THEIR AIRCRFT FOUND RADIOACTIVE TUF LUK FOR THEM.

'Travis has been working back in Houston,' Ross said. She could imagine what it must have cost ERTS to put in the fix at the rural airport in Goma. 'But it means we can still do it, if we can make up the nine hours.'

'We can do it,' Munro said.

In the light of the setting equatorial sun, Moruti camp gleamed like a cluster of dazzling jewels – a silver dish antenna, and five silver-domed tents, all reflecting the fiery sun. Peter Elliot sat on the hilltop with Amy and stared at the rain forest spread out below them. As night fell, the first hazy strands of mist appeared; and as the darkness deepened and water vapor condensed in the cooling air, the forest became shrouded in dense, darkening fog.

DAY 6: LIKO
June 18, 1979

1. Rain Forest

The next morning they entered the humid perpetual gloom of the Congo rain forest.

Munro noted the return of old feelings of oppression and claustrophobia, tinged with a strange, overpowering lassitude. As a Congo mercenary in the 1960s, he had avoided the jungle wherever possible. Most military engagements had occurred in open spaces – in the Belgian colonial towns, along riverbanks, beside the red dirt roads. Nobody wanted to fight in the jungle; the mercenaries hated it, and the superstitious Simbas feared it. When the mercenaries advanced, the rebels often fled into the bush, but they never went very far, and Munro's troops never pursued them. They just waited for them to come out again.

Even in the 1960s the jungle remained *terra incognita*, an unknown land with the power to hold the technology of mechanized warfare beyond its periphery. And with good reason, Munro thought. Men just did not belong there. He was not pleased to be back.

Elliot, never having been in a rain forest, was fascinated. The jungle was different from the way he had imagined it to be. He was totally unprepared for the scale – the gigantic trees soaring over his head, the trunks as broad as a house, the thick snaking moss-covered roots. To move in the vast space beneath these trees was like being in a very dark cathedral: the sun was completely blocked, and he could not get an exposure reading on his camera.

He had also expected the jungle to be much denser than it was. Their party moved through it freely; in a surprising way it seemed barren and silent – there were occasional birdcalls and cries from monkeys, but otherwise a profound stillness settled over them. And it was oddly monotonous: although he saw every shade of green in the foliage and the clinging creeper vines, there were few flowers or blooms. Even the occasional orchids seemed pale and muted.

He had expected rotting decay at every turn, but that was not true either. The ground underfoot was often firm, and the air had a neutral smell. But it was incredibly hot, and it seemed as though everything was wet – the leaves, the ground, the trunks of the trees, the oppressively still air itself, trapped under the overhanging trees.

Elliot would have agreed with Stanley's description from a century before: 'Overhead the wide-spreading branches absolutely shut out the daylight . . . We marched in a feeble twilight . . . The dew dropped and pattered on us incessantly. . . . Our clothes were heavily saturated with it. . . . Perspiration exuded from every pore, for the atmosphere was stifling. . . . What a forbidding aspect had the Dark Unknown which confronted us!'

Because Elliot had looked forward to his first experience of the equatorial African rain forest, he was surprised at how quickly he felt oppressed – and how soon he entertained thoughts of leaving again. Yet the tropical rain forests had spawned most new life forms, including man. The jungle was not one uniform environment but many different micro-environments, arranged vertically like a layer cake. Each micro-environment supported a bewildering profusion of plant and animal life, but there were typically few members of each species. The tropical jungle supported four times as many species of animal life as a comparable temperate forest. As he walked through the forest, Elliot found himself thinking of it as an enormous hot, dark womb, a place where new species were nourished in unchanging conditions until they were ready to migrate out to the harsher and more variable temperate zones. That was the way it had been for millions of years.

Amy's behavior immediately changed as she entered the vast humid darkness of her original home. In retrospect, Elliot believed he could have predicted her reaction, had he thought it through clearly.

Amy no longer kept up with the group.

She insisted on foraging along the trail, pausing to sit and chew tender shoots and grasses. She could not be budged or hurried, and ignored Elliot's requests that she stay with them. She ate lazily, a pleasant, rather vacant expression on her face. In shafts of sunlight, she would lie on her back, and belch, and sigh contentedly.

'What the hell is this all about?' Ross asked, annoyed. They were not making good time.

'She's become a gorilla again,' Elliot said. 'Gorillas are vegetarians, and they spend nearly all day eating; they're large animals, and they need a lot of food.' Amy had immediately reverted to these traits.

'Well, can't you make her keep up with us?'

'I'm trying. She won't pay attention to me.' And he knew why – Amy was finally back in a world where Peter Elliot was irrelevant, where she herself could find food and security and shelter, and everything else that she wanted.

'School's out,' Munro said, summarizing the situation. But he had a solution. 'Leave her,' he said crisply, and he led the party onward. He took Elliot firmly by the elbow. 'Don't look back,' he said. 'Just walk on. Ignore her.'

They continued for several minutes in silence.

Elliot said, 'She may not follow us.'

'Come, come, Professor,' Munro said. 'I thought you knew about gorillas.'

'I do,' Elliot said.

'Then you know there are none in this part of the rain forest.'

Elliot nodded; he had seen no nests or spoor. 'But she has everything she needs here.'

'Not everything,' Munro said. 'Not without other gorillas around.'

Like all higher primates, gorillas were social animals. They lived in a group, and they were not comfortable – or safe – in isolation. In fact, most primatologists assumed that there was a need for social contact as strongly perceived as hunger, thirst, or fatigue.

'We're her troop,' Munro said. 'She won't let us get far.'

Several minutes later, Amy came crashing through the underbrush fifty yards ahead. She watched the group, and glared at Peter.

'Now come here, Amy,' Munro said, 'and I'll tickle you.' Amy bounded up and lay on her back in front of him. Munro tickled her.

'You see, Professor? Nothing to it.'

Amy never strayed far from the group again.

If Elliot had an uncomfortable sense of the rain forest as the natural domain of his own animal, Karen Ross viewed it in terms of earth resources – in which it was poor. She was not fooled by the luxuriant, oversized vegetation, which she knew represented an extraordinarily efficient ecosystem built in virtually barren soil.*

The developing nations of the world did not understand this fact; once cleared, the jungle soil yielded disappointing crops. Yet the rain forests were being cleared at the incredible rate of fifty acres a minute, day and night. The rain forests of the world had circled the equator in a green belt for at least sixty million years – but man would have cleared them within twenty years.

This widespread destruction had caused some alarm Ross did not share. She doubted that the world climate would change or the atmospheric oxygen be reduced. Ross was not an alarmist, and not impressed by the calculations of those who were. The only reason she felt uneasy was that the forest was so little understood. A clearing rate of fifty acres a minute meant that plant and animal species were becoming extinct at the incredible rate of *one species per hour*. Life forms that had evolved

---

* The rain forest ecosystem is an energy utilization complex far more efficient than any energy conversion system developed by man. See C. F. Higgins et al., *Energy Resources and Ecosystem Utilization* (Englewood Cliffs, N.J.: Prentice Hall, 1977), pp. 232–255.

for millions of years were being wiped out every few minutes, and no one could predict the consequences of this stupendous rate of destruction. The extinction of species was proceeding much faster than anybody recognized, and the publicized lists of 'endangered' species told only a fraction of the story; the disaster extended all the way down the animal phyla to insects, worms, and mosses.

The reality was that entire ecosystems were being destroyed by man without a care or a backward glance. And these ecosystems were for the most part mysterious, poorly understood. Karen Ross felt herself plunged into a world entirely different from the exploitable world of mineral resources; this was an environment in which plant life reigned supreme. It was no wonder, she thought, that the Egyptians called this the Land of Trees. The rain forest provided a hothouse environment for plant life, an environment in which gigantic plants were much superior to – and much favored over – mammals, including the insignificant human mammals who were now picking their way through its perpetual darkness.

The Kikuyu porters had an immediate reaction to the forest: they began to laugh and joke and make as much noise as possible. Ross said to Kahega, 'They certainly are jolly.'

'Oh, no,' Kahega said. 'They are warning.'

'Warning?'

Kahega explained that the men made noise to warn off the buffalo and leopards. And the *tembo*, he added, pointing to the trail.

'Is this a *tembo* trail?' she asked.

Kahega nodded.

'The *tembo* live nearby?'

Kahega laughed. 'I hope no,' Kahega said. '*Tembo*. Elephant.'

'So this is a game trail. Will we see elephants?'

'Maybe yes, maybe no,' Kahega said. 'I hope no. They are very big, elephants.'

There was no arguing with his logic. Ross said, 'They tell me these are your brothers,' nodding down the line of porters.

'Yes, they are my brothers.'

'Ah.'

'But you mean that my brothers, we have the same mother?'

'Yes, you have the same mother.'

'No,' Kahega said.

Ross was confused. 'You are not real brothers?'

'Yes, we are real brothers. But we do not have the same mother.'

'Then why are you brothers?'

'Because we live in the same village.'

514

'With your father and mother?'

Kahega looked shocked. '*No*,' he said emphatically. 'Not the same village.'

'A different village, then?'

'Yes, of course – we are Kikuyu.'

Ross was perplexed. Kahega laughed.

Kahega offered to carry the electronic equipment that Ross had slung over her shoulder, but she declined. Ross was obliged to try and link up with Houston at intervals throughout the day, and at noon she found a clear window, probably because the consortium jamming operator took a break for lunch. She managed to link through and register another Field Time-Position.

The console read: FILD TME-POSITN CHEK – 10:03 H

They had lost nearly an hour since the previous check the night before. 'We've got to go faster,' she told Munro.

'Perhaps you'd prefer to jog,' Munro said. 'Very good exercise.' And then, because he decided he was being too hard on her, he added, 'A lot can happen between here and Virunga.'

They heard the distant growl of thunder and minutes later were drenched in a torrential rain, the drops so dense and heavy that they actually hurt. The rain fell solidly for the next hour, then stopped as abruptly as it had begun. They were all soaked and miserable, and when Munro called a halt for food, Ross did not protest.

Amy promptly went off into the forest to forage; the porters cooked curried meat gravy on rice; Munro, Ross, and Elliot burned leeches off their legs with cigarettes. The leeches were swollen with blood. 'I didn't even notice them,' Ross said.

'Rain makes 'em worse,' Munro said. Then he looked up sharply, glancing at the jungle.

'Something wrong?'

'No, nothing,' Munro said, and he went into an explanation of why leeches had to be burned off; if they were pulled off, a part of the head remained lodged in the flesh and caused an infection.

Kahega brought them food, and Munro said in a low voice, 'Are the men all right?'

'Yes,' Kahega said. 'The men are all right. They will not be afraid.'

'Afraid of what?' Elliot said.

'Keep eating. Just be natural,' Munro said.

Elliot looked nervously around the little clearing.

'Eat!' Munro whispered. 'Don't insult them. You're not supposed to know they're here.'

The group ate in silence for several minutes. And then the nearby brush rustled and a pygmy stepped out.

2. The Dancers of God

He was a light-skinned man about four and a half feet tall, barrel-chested, wearing only a loincloth, with a bow and arrow over his shoulder. He looked around the expedition, apparently trying to determine who was the leader.

Munro stood, and said something quickly in a language that was not Swahili. The pygmy replied. Munro gave him one of the cigarettes they had been using to burn off the leeches. The pygmy did not want it lit; instead he dropped it into a small leather pouch attached to his quiver. A brief conversation followed. The pygmy pointed off into the jungle several times.

'He says a white man is dead in their village,' Munro said. He picked up his pack, which contained the first-aid kit. 'I'll have to hurry.'

Ross said, 'We can't afford the time.'

Munro frowned at her.

'Well, the man's dead anyway.'

'He's not *completely* dead,' Munro said. 'He's not dead-for-ever.'

The pygmy nodded vigorously. Munro explained that pygmies graded illness in several stages. First a person was hot, then he was with fever, then ill, then dead, then completely dead – and finally dead-for-ever.

From the bush, three more pygmies appeared. Munro nodded. 'Knew he wasn't alone,' he said. 'These chaps never are alone. Hate to travel alone. The others were watching us; if we'd made a wrong move, we'd get an arrow for our trouble. See those brown tips? Poison.'

Yet the pygmies appeared relaxed now – at least until Amy came crashing back through the underbrush. Then there were shouts and swiftly drawn bows; Amy was terrified and ran to Peter, jumping up on him and clutching his chest – and making him thoroughly muddy.

The pygmies engaged in a lively discussion among themselves, trying to decide what Amy's arrival meant. Several questions were asked of Munro. Finally, Elliot set Amy back down on the ground and said to Munro, 'What did you tell them?'

'They wanted to know if the gorilla was yours, and I said yes. They wanted to know if the gorilla was female, and I said yes. They wanted to know if you had relations with the gorilla; I said no. They said that was good, that you should not become too attached to the gorilla, because that would cause you pain.'

'Why pain?'

'They said when the gorilla grows up, she will either run away into the forest and break your heart or kill you.'

Ross still opposed making a detour to the pygmy village, which was several miles away on the banks of the Liko River. 'We're behind on our timeline,' she said, 'and slipping further behind every minute.'

For the first and last time during the expedition, Munro lost his temper. 'Listen, Doctor,' he said, 'this isn't down-town Houston, this is the middle of the goddamn Congo and it's no place to be injured. We have medicines. That man may need it. You don't leave him behind. You just don't.'

'If we go to that village,' Ross said, 'we blow the rest of the day. It puts us nine or ten hours further back. Right now we can still make it. With another delay, we won't have a chance.'

One of the pygmies began talking quickly to Munro. He nodded, glancing several times at Ross. Then he turned to the others.

'He says that the sick white man has some writing on his shirt pocket. He's going to draw the writing for us.'

Ross glanced at her watch and sighed.

The pygmy picked up a stick and drew large characters in the muddy earth at their feet. He drew carefully, frowning in concentration as he reproduced the alien symbols: E R T S.

'Oh, God,' Ross said softly.

The pygmies did not walk through the forest: they ran at a brisk trot, slipping through the forest vines and branches, dodging rain puddles and gnarled tree roots with deceptive ease. Occasionally they glanced over their shoulders and giggled at the difficulties of the three white people who followed.

For Elliot, it was a difficult pace – a succession of roots to stumble over, tree limbs to strike his head on, thorny vines to tear at his flesh. He was gasping for breath, trying to keep up with the little men who padded effortlessly ahead of him. Ross was doing no better than he, and even Munro, although surprisingly agile, showed signs of fatigue.

Finally they came to a small stream and a sunlit clearing. The pygmies paused on the rocks, squatting and turning their faces up to the sun. The white people collapsed, panting and gasping. The pygmies seemed to find this hilarious, their laughter good-natured.

The pygmies were the earliest human inhabitants of the Congo rain forest. Their small size, distinctive manner, and deft agility had made them famous centuries before. More than four thousand years ago, an Egyptian commander named Herkouf entered the great forest west of the Mountains of the Moon; there he found a race of tiny men who sang and danced to their god. Herkouf's amazing report had the ring of fact, and Herodotus and later Aristotle insisted that these stories of the tiny men were true, and not fabulous. The Dancers of God inevitably acquired mythical trappings as the centuries passed.

As late as the seventeenth century, Europeans remained unsure whether tiny men with tails who had the power to fly through the trees, make themselves invisible, and kill elephants actually existed. That skeletons of chimpanzees were sometimes mistaken for pygmy skeletons added to the confusion. Colin Turnbull notes that many elements of the fable are actually true: the pounded-bark loincloths hang down and look like tails; the pygmies can blend into the forest and become virtually invisible; and they have always hunted and killed elephants.

The pygmies were laughing now as they got to their feet and padded off again. Sighing, the white people struggled up and lumbered after them. They ran for another half hour, never pausing or hesitating, and then Elliot smelled smoke and they came into a clearing beside a stream where the village was located.

He saw ten low rounded huts no more than four feet high, arranged in a semicircle. The villagers were all outside in the afternoon light, the women cleaning mushrooms and berries picked during the day, or cooking grubs and turtles on crackling fires; children tottered around, bothering the men who sat before their houses and smoked tobacco while the women worked.

At Munro's signal, they waited at the edge of the camp until they were noticed, and then they were led in. Their arrival provoked great interest; the children giggled and pointed; the men wanted tobacco from Munro and Elliot; the women touched Ross's blonde hair, and argued about it. A little girl crawled between Ross's legs, peering up her trousers. Munro explained that the women were uncertain whether Ross painted her hair, and the girl had taken it upon herself to settle the question of artifice.

'Tell them it's natural,' Ross said, blushing.

Munro spoke briefly to the women. 'I told them it was the color of your father's hair,' he told Ross. 'But I'm not sure they believe it.' He gave Elliot cigarettes to pass out, one to each man; they were received with broad smiles and odd girlish giggles.

Preliminaries concluded, they were taken to a newly constructed house at the far end of the village where the dead white man was said to be. They found a filthy, bearded man of thirty, sitting cross-legged in the small doorway, staring outward. After a moment Elliot realized the man was catatonic – he was not moving at all.

'Oh, my God,' Ross said. 'It's Bob Driscoll.'

'You know him?' Munro said.

'He was a geologist on the first Congo expedition.' She leaned close to him, waved her hand in front of his face. 'Bobby, it's me, Karen. Bobby, what happened to you?'

Driscoll did not respond, did not even blink. He continued to stare forward.

One of the pygmies offered an explanation to Munro. 'He came into their camp four days ago,' Munro said. 'He was wild and they had to restrain him. They thought he had black-water fever, so they made a house for him and gave him some medicines, and he was not wild any more. Now he lets them feed him, but he never speaks. They think perhaps he was captured by General Muguru's men and tortured, or else he is *agudu* – a mute.'

Ross moved back in horror.

'I don't see what we can do for him,' Munro said. 'Not in his condition. Physically he's okay, but . . .' He shook his head.

'I'll give Houston the location,' Ross said, 'and they'll send help from Kinshasa.'

During all this, Driscoll never moved. Elliot leaned forward to look at his eyes, and as he approached, Driscoll wrinkled his nose. His body tensed. He broke into a high-pitched wail – 'Ah-ah-ah-ah' – like a man about to scream.

Appalled, Elliot backed off, and Driscoll relaxed, falling silent again. 'What the hell was that all about?'

One of the pygmies whispered to Munro. 'He says,' Munro said, 'that you smell like gorilla.'

3. Ragora

Two hours later, they were reunited with Kahega and the others, led by a pygmy guide across the rain forest south of Gabutu. They were all sullen, uncommunicative – and suffering from dysentery.

The pygmies had insisted they stay for an early dinner, and Munro felt they had no choice but to accept. The meal was mostly a slender wild potato called *kitsombe*, which looked like a shriveled asparagus; forest onions, called *otsa*; and *modoke*, wild manioc leaves, along with several kinds of mushrooms. There were also small quantities of sour, tough turtle meat and occasional grasshoppers, caterpillars, worms, frogs, and snails.

This diet actually contained twice as much protein by weight as beefsteak, but it did not sit well on unaccustomed stomachs. Nor was the news around the campfire likely to improve their spirits.

According to the pygmies, General Muguru's men had established a supply camp up at the Makran escarpment, which was where Munro was headed. It seemed wise to avoid the troops. Munro explained there was no Swahili word for chivalry or sportsmanship, and the same was true of the Congolese variant, Lingala. 'In this part of the world, it's kill or be killed. We'd best stay away.'

Their only alternate route took them west, to the Ragora River. Munro frowned at his map, and Ross frowned at her computer console.

'What's wrong with the Ragora River?' Elliot asked.

'Maybe nothing,' Munro said. 'Depends on how hard it's rained lately.'

Ross glanced at her watch. 'We're now twelve hours behind,' she said. 'The only thing we can do is continue straight through the night on the river.'

'I'd do that anyway,' Munro said.

Ross had never heard of an expedition guide leading a party through a wilderness area at night. 'You would? Why?'

'Because,' Munro said, 'the obstacles on the lower river will be much easier at night.'

'What obstacles?'

'We'll discuss them when we come to them,' Munro said.

A mile before they reached the Ragora, they heard the distant roar of powerful water. Amy was immediately anxious, signing *What water?* again and again. Elliot tried to reassure her, but he was not inclined to do much; Amy was going to have to put up with the river, despite her fears.

But when they got to the Ragora they found that the sound came from tumbling cataracts somewhere upstream; directly before them, the river was fifty feet wide and a placid muddy brown.

'Doesn't look too bad,' Elliot said.

'No,' Munro said, 'it doesn't.'

But Munro understood about the Congo. The fourth largest river in the world (after the Nile, the Amazon, and the Yangtze) was unique in many ways. It twisted like a giant snake across the face of Africa, twice crossing the equator – the first time going north, toward Kisangani, and later going south, at Mbandaka. This fact was so remarkable that even a hundred years ago geographers did not believe it was true. Because the Congo flowed both north and south of the equator, there was always a rainy season somewhere along its path; the river was not subject to the seasonal fluctuations that characterized rivers such as the Nile. The Congo poured a steady 1,500,000 cubic feet of water every second into the Atlantic Ocean, a flow greater than any river except the Amazon.

But this tortuous course also made the Congo the least navigable of the great rivers. Serious disruptions began with the rapids of Stanley Pool, three hundred miles from the Atlantic. Two thousand miles inland, at Kisangani, where the river was still a mile wide, the Wagenia Cataract blocked all navigation. And as one moved farther upriver along the fan of tributaries, the impediments became even more pronounced, for above Kisangani the tributaries were descending rapidly into the low jungle from their sources – the highland savannahs to the south, and the 16,000-foot snow-capped Ruwenzori Mountains to the east.

The tributaries cut a series of gorges, the most striking of which was the Portes d'Enfer – the Gates of Hell – at Kongolo. Here the placid Lualaba River funneled through a gorge half a mile deep and a hundred yards wide.

The Ragora was a minor tributary of the Lualaba, which it joined near Kisangani. The tribes along the river referred to it as *baratawani*, 'the deceitful road,' for the Ragora was notoriously changeable. Its principal feature was the Ragora Gorge, a limestone cut two hundred feet deep and in places only ten feet wide. Depending on recent rainfall, the Ragora Gorge was either a pleasant scenic spectacle or a boiling whitewater nightmare.

At Abutu, they were still fifteen miles upriver from the gorge, and conditions on the river told them nothing about conditions within the gorge. Munro knew all that, but he did not feel it necessary to explain it to Elliot, particularly since at the moment Elliot was fully occupied with Amy.

Amy had watched with growing uneasiness as Kahega's men inflated the two Zodiac rafts. She tugged Elliot's sleeve and demanded to know *What balloons?*

'They're boats, Amy,' he said, although he sensed she had already figured that out, and was being euphemistic. 'Boat' was a word she had learned with difficulty; since she disliked water, she had no interest in anything intended to ride upon it.

Why boat? she asked.

'We ride boat now,' Elliot said.

Indeed, Kahega's men were pushing the boats to the edge of the water, and loading the equipment on, lashing it to the rubber stanchions at the gunwales.

Who ride? she asked.

'We all ride,' Elliot said.

Amy watched a moment longer. Unfortunately, everyone was nervous, Munro barking orders, the men working hastily. As she had often shown, Amy was sensitive to the moods of those around her. Elliot always remembered how she had insisted that something was wrong with Sarah Johnson for days before Sarah finally told the Project Amy staff that she had split up with her husband. Now Elliot was certain that Amy sensed their apprehension. *Cross water in boat?* she asked.

'No, Amy,' he said. 'Not cross. Ride boat.'

No, Amy signed, stiffening her back, tightening her shoulders.

'Amy,' he said, 'we can't leave you here.'

She had a solution for that. *Other people go. Peter stay Amy.*

'I'm sorry, Amy,' he said. 'I have to go. You have to go.'

No, she signed. *Amy no go.*

'Yes, Amy.' He went to his pack and got his syringe and a bottle of Thoralen.

With her body stiff and angry, she tapped the underside of her chin with a clenched fist.

'Watch your language, Amy,' he warned her.

Ross came over with orange life vests for him and Amy. 'Something wrong?'

'She's swearing,' Elliot said. 'Better leave us alone.' Ross took one look at Amy's tense, rigid body, and left hurriedly.

Amy signed Peter's name, then tapped the underside of her chin again. This was the Ameslan sign politely translated in scholarly reports as 'dirty,' although it was most often employed by apes when they needed to go to the potty. Primate investigators were under no illusions about what the animals really meant. Amy was saying, *Peter shitty.*

Nearly all language-skilled primates swore, and they employed a variety of words for swearing. Sometimes the pejorative seemed to be chosen at random, 'nut' or 'bird' or 'wash.' But at least eight primates in different laboratories had independently settled on the clenched-fist sign to signify extreme displeasure. The only reason this remarkable coincidence hadn't been written up was that no investigator was willing to try and explain it. It seemed to prove that apes, like people, found bodily excretions suitable terms to express denigration and anger.

Peter shitty, she signed again.

'Amy . . .' He doubled the Thoralen dose he was drawing into the syringe.

Peter shitty boat shitty people shitty.

'Amy, cut it out.' He stiffened his own body and hunched over, imitating a gorilla's angry posture; that often made her back off, but this time it had no effect.

Peter no like Amy. Now she was sulking, turned away from him, signing to nobody.

'Don't be ridiculous,' Elliot said, approaching her with the syringe held ready. 'Peter like Amy.'

She backed away and would not let him come close to her. In the end he was forced to load the CO_2 gun and shoot a dart into her chest. He had only done this three or four times in all their years together. She plucked out the dart with a sad expression. *Peter no like Amy.*

'Sorry,' Peter Elliot said, and ran forward to catch her as her eyes rolled back and she collapsed into his arms.

Amy lay on her back in the second boat at Elliot's feet, breathing shallowly. Ahead, Elliot saw Munro standing in the first boat, leading the way as the Zodiacs slid silently downstream.

Munro had divided the expedition into two rafts of six each; Munro went in the first, and Elliot, Ross, and Amy went in the second, under Kahega's command. As Munro put it, the second boat would 'learn from our misfortunes.'

But for the first two hours on the Rangora, there were no misfortunes. It was an extraordinarily peaceful experience to sit in the front of the boat and watch the jungle on both sides of the river glide past them in timeless, hypnotic silence. It was idyllic, and very hot; Ross began to trail her hand over the side in the muddy water, until Kahega put a stop to it.

'Where there is water, there is always *mamba*,' he said.

Kahega pointed to the muddy banks, where crocodiles basked in the sunshine, indifferent to their approach. Occasionally one of the huge reptiles yawned, lifting jagged jaws into the air, but for the most part they seemed sluggish, hardly noticing the boats.

Elliot was secretly disappointed. He had grown up on the jungle movies where the crocodiles slithered menacingly into the water at the first approach of boats. 'Aren't they going to bother us?' he asked.

'Too hot,' Kahega said. '*Mamba* sleepy except at cool times, eat morning and night, not now. In daytime, Kikuyu say *mamba* have joined army, one-two-three-four.' And he laughed.

It took some explaining before it was clear that Kahega's tribesmen had noticed that during the day the crocodiles did pushups, periodically lifting their heavy bodies off the ground on their stubby legs in a movement that reminded Kahega of army calisthenics.

'What is Munro so worried about?' Elliot asked. 'The crocodiles?'

'No,' Kahega said.

'The Ragora Gorge?'

'No,' Kahega said.

'Then what?'

'*After* the gorge,' Kahega said.

Now the Ragora twisted, and they came around a bend, and they heard the growing roar of the water. Elliot felt the boat gathering speed, the water rippling along the rubber gunwales. Kahega shouted, 'Hold fast, Doctors!'

And they were into the gorge.

Afterward, Elliot had only fragmented, kaleidoscopic impressions: the churning muddy water that boiled white in the sunlight; the erratic wrenching of his own boat, and the way Munro's boat up ahead seemed to reel and upend, yet miraculously remain upright.

They were moving so fast it was hard to focus on the passing blur of craggy red canyon walls, bare rock except for sparse green clinging scrub; the hot humid air and the shockingly cold muddy water that smashed over them, drenching them time and again; the pure white surge of water boiling around the black protruding rocks, like the bald heads of drowned men.

Everything was happening too fast.

Ahead, Munro's boat was often lost from sight for minutes at a time, concealed by giant standing waves of leaping, roaring muddy water. The roar echoed off the rock walls, reverberating, becoming a constant feature of their world; in the depths of the gorge, where the afternoon sun did not reach the narrow strip of dark water, the boats moved through a rushing, churning inferno, careening off rocky walls, spinning end around end, while the boatmen shouted and cursed and fended off the rock walls with paddles.

Amy lay on her back, lashed to the side of the boat, and Elliot was in constant fear that she would drown from the muddy waves that crashed over the gunwales. Not that Ross was doing much better; she kept repeating 'Oh my God oh my God oh my God' over and over, in a low monotone, as the water smashed down on them in successive waves, soaking them to the skin.

Other indignities were forced upon them by nature. Even in the boiling, pounding heart of the gorge, black clouds of mosquitoes hung in the air, stinging them again and again. Somehow it did not seem possible that there could be mosquitoes in the midst of the roaring chaos of the Ragora Gorge, but they were there. The boats moved with gut-wrenching fury through the standing waves, and in the growing darkness the passengers baled out the boats and slapped at the mosquitoes with equal intensity.

And then suddenly the river broadened, the muddy water slowed, and the walls of the canyon moved apart. The river became peaceful again. Elliot slumped back in the boat, exhausted, feeling the fading sun on his face and the water moving beneath the inflated rubber of the boat.

'We made it,' he said.

'So far,' Kahega said. 'But we Kikuyu say no one escapes from life alive. No relaxing now, Doctors!'

'Somehow,' Ross said wearily, 'I believe him.'

They drifted gently downstream for another hour, and the rock walls receded farther away on each side, until finally they were in flat African rain forest once more. It was as if the Ragora Gorge had never existed; the river was wide and sluggish gold in the descending sun.

Elliot stripped off his soaking shirt and changed it for a pullover, for the evening air was chilly. Amy snored at his feet, covered with a towel so she would not get too cold. Ross checked her transmitting equipment, making sure it was all right. When she was finished, the sun had set and it was rapidly growing dark. Kahega broke out a shotgun and inserted yellow stubby shells.

'What's that for?' Elliot said.

'*Kiboko*,' Kahega said. 'I do not know the word in English.' He shouted, '*Mzee! Nini maana kiboko?*'

In the lead boat, Munro glanced back. 'Hippopotamus,' he said.

'Hippo,' Kahega said.

'Are they dangerous?' Elliot asked.

'At night, we hope no,' Kahega said. 'But me, I think yes.'

The twentieth century had been a period of intensive wildlife study, which overturned many long-standing conceptions about animals. It was now recognized that the gentle, soft-eyed deer actually lived in a ruthless, nasty society, while the supposedly vicious wolf was devoted to family and offspring in exemplary fashion. And the African lion – the proud king of beasts – was relegated to the status of slinking scavenger, while the loathed hyena assumed new dignity. (For decades, observers had come upon a dawn kill to find lions feeding on the carcass, while the scavenging hyenas circled at the periphery, awaiting their chance. Only after scientists began night tracking the animals did a new interpretation emerge: hyenas actually made the kill, only to be driven off by opportunistic and lazy lions; hence the traditional dawn scene. This coincided with the discovery that lions were in many ways erratic and mean, while the hyenas had a finely developed social structure – yet another instance of long-standing human prejudice toward the natural world of animals.)

But the hippopotamus remained a poorly understood animal. Herodotus's 'river horse' was the largest African mammal after the elephant, but its habit of lying in the water with just eyes and nostrils protruding made it difficult to study. Hippos were organized around a male. A mature male had a harem of several females and their offspring, a group of eight to fourteen animals altogether.

Despite their obese, rather humorous appearance, hippos were capable of unusual violence. The bull hippopotamus was a formidable creature, fourteen feet long and weighing nearly ten thousand pounds. Charging, he moved with extraordinary speed for such a large animal, and his four stubby, blunted tusks were actually razor sharp on the sides. A hippo attacked by slashing, moving his cavernous mouth from side to side, rather than biting. And, unlike most animals, a fight between bulls often resulted in the death of one animal from deep slashing wounds. There was nothing symbolic about a hippopotamus fight.

The animal was dangerous to man, as well. In river areas where herds were found, half of native deaths were attributed to hippos; elephants and predatory cats accounted for the remainder. The hippopotamus was vegetarian, and at night the animals came onto the land, where they ate enormous quantities of grass to sustain their great bulk. A hippo separated from the water was especially dangerous; anyone finding himself between a landed hippo and the river he was rushing to return to did not generally survive the experience.

But the hippo was essential to Africa's river ecology. His fecal matter, produced in prodigious quantities, fertilized the river grasses, which in turn allowed river fish and other creatures to live. Without the hippopotamus African rivers would be sterile, and where they had been driven away, the rivers died.

This much was known, and one thing more. The hippopotamus was fiercely territorial. Without exception, the male defended his river against any intruder. And as had been recorded on many occasions, intruders included other hippos, crocodiles, and passing boats. And the people in them.

DAY 7: MUKENKO
June 19, 1979

1. Kiboko

Munro's intention in continuing through the night was twofold. First, he hoped to make up precious time, for all the computer projections assumed that they would stop each night. But it took no effort to ride the river in the moonlight; most of the party could sleep, and they would advance themselves another fifty or sixty miles by dawn.

But more important, he hoped to avoid the Ragora hippos, which could easily destroy their flimsy rubber boats. During the day, the hippos were found in pools beside the riverbanks, and the bulls would certainly attack any passing boat. At night, when the animals went ashore to forage, the expedition could slip down the river and avoid a confrontation entirely.

It was a clever plan, but it ran into trouble for an unexpected reason – their progress on the Ragora was too rapid. It was only nine o'clock at night when they reached the first hippo areas, too early for the animals to be eating. The hippos would attack the boats – but they would attack in the dark.

The river twisted and turned in a series of curves. At each curve there was a still pool, which Kahega pointed out as the kind of quiet water that hippos liked to inhabit. And he pointed to the grass on the banks, cut short as if the banks had been mown.

'Soon now,' Kahega said.

They heard a low grunting '*Haw-huh-huh-huh.*' It sounded like an old man trying to clear his throat of phlegm. Munro tensed in the lead boat. They drifted around another curve, carried smoothly in the flow of current. The two boats were now about ten yards apart. Munro held his loaded shot-gun ready.

The sound came again, this time in a chorus: '*Haw-huh-huh-huh.*'

Kahega plunged his paddle into the water. It struck bottom quickly. He pulled it out; only three feet of it was wet. 'Not deep,' he said, shaking his head.

'Is that bad?' Ross said.

'Yes, I think it is bad.'

They came around the next bend, and Elliot saw a half-dozen partially submerged black rocks near the shore, gleaming in the moonlight. Then one of the 'rocks' crashed upward and he saw an enormous creature lift entirely out of the shallow water so that he could see the four stubby legs, and the hippo churned forward toward Munro's boat.

Munro fired a low magnesium flare as the animal charged; in the harsh white light Elliot saw a gigantic mouth, four huge glistening blunted teeth, the head lifted upward as the animal roared. And then the hippo was engulfed in a cloud of pale yellow gas. The gas drifted back, and stung their eyes.

'He's using tear gas,' Ross said.

Munro's boat had already moved on. With a roar of pain the male hippo had plunged down into the water and disappeared from sight. In the second boat, they blinked back tears and watched for him as they approached the pool. Overhead, the magnesium flare sizzled and descended, lengthening sharp shadows, glaring off the water.

'Perhaps he's given up,' Elliot said. They could not see the hippo anywhere. They drifted in silence.

And suddenly the front of the boat bucked up, and the hippo roared and Ross screamed. Kahega toppled backward, discharging his gun into the air. The boat slapped down with a wrenching crash and a spray of water over the sides, and Elliot scrambled to his feet to check Amy and found himself staring into a huge pink cavernous mouth and hot breath. The mouth came down with a lateral slash on the side of the rubber boat, and the air began to hiss and sizzle in the water.

The mouth opened again, and the hippo grunted, but then Kahega had got to his feet and fired a stinging cloud of gas. The hippo backed off and splashed down, rocking the boat and propelling them onward, down the river. The whole right side of the boat was collapsing swiftly as the air leaked out of the huge cuts in the rubber. Elliot tried to pull them shut with his hands; the hissing continued unabated. They would sink within a minute.

Behind them, the bull hippo charged, racing down the shallow river like a powerboat, churning water in a wake from both sides of his body, bellowing in anger.

'Hold on, hold on!' Kahega shouted, and fired again. The hippo disappeared behind a cloud of gas, and the boat drifted around another curve. When the gas cleared the animal was gone. The magnesium flare sputtered into the water and they were plunged into darkness again. Elliot grabbed Amy as the boat sank, and they found themselves standing knee-deep in the muddy water.

They managed to beach the Zodiac on the dark riverbank. In the lead boat, Munro paddled over, surveyed the damage, and announced that they would inflate another boat and go on. He called for a rest, and they all lay in the moonlight on the river's edge swatting mosquitoes away.

Their reverie was interrupted by the screaming whine of ground-to-air rockets, blossoming explosions in the sky overhead. With each explosion, the riverbank glowed bright red, casting long shadows, then fading black once more.

'Muguru's men firing from the ground,' Munro said, reaching for his field glasses.

'What're they shooting at?' Elliot said, staring up into the ky.

'Beats me,' Munro said.

Amy touched Munro's arm, and signed, *Bird come.* But they heard no sound of an aircraft, only the bursting of rockets in the sky.

Munro said, 'You think she hears something?'

'Her hearing is very acute.'

And then they heard the drone of a distant aircraft, approaching from the south. As it came into view, they saw it twist, maneuvering among the brilliant yellow-red explosions that burst in the moonlight and glinted off the metal body of the aircraft.

'Those poor bastards are trying to make time,' Munro said, scanning the plane through field glasses. 'That's a C-130 transport with Japanese markings on the tail. Supply plane for the consortium base camp – if it makes it through.'

As they watched, the transport twisted left and right, running a zigzag course through the bursting fireballs of exploding missiles.

'Breaking a snake's back,' Munro said. 'The crew must be terrified; they didn't buy into this.'

Elliot felt a sudden sympathy for the crew; he imagined them staring out the windows as the fireballs exploded with brilliant light, illuminating the interior of the plane. Were they chattering in Japanese? Wishing they had never come?

A moment later, the aircraft droned onward to the north, out of sight, a final missile with a red-hot tail chasing after it, but it was gone over the jungle trees, and he listened to the distant explosion of the missile.

'Probably got through,' Munro said, standing. 'We'd better move on.' And he shouted in Swahili for Kahega to put the men on the river once more.

2. Mukenko

Elliot shivered, zipped his parka tighter, and waited for the hailstorm to stop. They were huddled beneath a stand of evergreen trees above 8,000 feet on the alpine slopes of Mount Mukenko. It was ten o'clock in the morning, and the air temperature was 38 degrees. Five hours before, they had left the river behind and begun their pre-dawn climb in 100-degree steaming jungle.

Alongside him, Amy watched the golfball-sized white pellets bounce on the grass and slap the branches of the tree over their heads. She had never seen hail before.

She signed, *What name?*

'Hail,' he told her.

Peter make stop.

'I wish I could, Amy.'

She watched the hail for a moment, then signed, *Amy want go home.*

She had begun talking about going home the night before. Although the Thoralen had worn off, she remained depressed and withdrawn. Elliot had offered her some food to cheer her up. She signed that she wanted milk. When he told her they had none (which she knew perfectly well), she signed that she wanted a banana. Kahega had produced a bunch of small, slightly sour jungle bananas. Amy had eaten them without objection on previous days, but she now threw them into the water contemptuously, signing she wanted 'real bananas.'

When Elliot told her that they had no real bananas, she signed, *Amy want go home.*

'We can't go home now, Amy.'

Amy good gorilla Peter take Amy home.

She had only known him as the person in charge, the final arbiter of her daily life in the experimental setting of Project Amy. He could think of no way to make clear to her that he was no longer in charge, and that he was not punishing her by keeping her here.

In fact, they were all discouraged. Each of the expedition members had looked forward to escaping the oppressive heat of the rain forest, but now that they were climbing Mukenko, their enthusiasm had quickly faded. 'Christ,' Ross said. 'From hippos to hail.'

As if on cue, the hail stopped. 'All right,' Munro said, 'let's get moving.'

Mukenko had never been climbed until 1933. In 1908, a German party under von Ranke ran into storms and had to descend; a Belgian team in 1913 reached 10,000 feet but could not find a route to the summit; and another German team was forced to quit in 1919 when two team members fell and died, above 12,000 feet. Nevertheless Mukenko was classified as a fairly easy (non-technical) climb by most mountaineers, who generally devoted a day to the ascent; after 1943, a new route up the southeast was found which was frustratingly slow but not dangerous, and it was this route that most climbers followed.

Above 9,000 feet, the pine forest disappeared and they crossed weak grassy fields cloaked in chilly mist; the air was thinner, and they called frequently for a rest. Munro had no patience with the complaints of his charges. 'What did you expect?' he demanded. 'It's a mountain. Mountains are high.' He was especially merciless with Ross, who seemed the most easily fatigued. 'What about your timetable?' he would ask her. 'We're not even to the difficult part. It's not even interesting until eleven thousand feet. You quit now and we'll never make it to the summit before nightfall, and that means we lose a full day.'

'I don't care,' Ross said finally, dropping to the ground, gasping for breath.

'Just like a woman,' Munro said scornfully, and smiled when Ross glared at him. Munro humiliated them, chided them, encouraged them – and somehow kept them moving.

Above 10,000 feet, the grass disappeared and there was only mossy ground cover; they came upon the solitary peculiar fat-leafed lobelia trees, emerging suddenly from the cold gray mist. There was no real cover between 10,000 feet and the summit, which was why Munro pushed them; he did not want to get caught in a storm on the barren upper slopes.

The sun broke out at 11,000 feet, and they stopped to position the second of the directional lasers for the ERTS laser-fix system. Ross had already set the first laser several miles to the south that morning, and it had taken thirty minutes.

The second laser was more critical, since it had to be matched to the first. Despite the electronic jamming, the transmitting equipment had to be connected with Houston, in order that the little laser – it was the size of a pencil eraser, mounted on a tiny steel tripod – could be accurately aimed. The two lasers on the volcano were positioned so that their beams crossed many miles away, above the jungle. And if Ross's calculations were correct, that intersection point was directly over the city of Zinj.

Elliot wondered if they were inadvertently assisting the consortium, but Ross said no. 'Only at night,' she said, 'when they aren't moving. During the day, they won't be able to lock on our beacons – that's the beauty of the system.'

Soon they smelled sulfurous volcanic fumes drifting down from the summit, now 1,500 feet above them. Up here there was no vegetation at all, only bare hard rock and scattered patches of snow tinged yellow from the sulfur. The sky was clear dark blue, and they had spectacular views of the south Virunga range – the great cone of Nyiragongo, rising steeply from the deep green of the Congo forests, and, beyond that, Mukenko, shrouded in fog.

The last thousand feet were the most difficult, particularly for Amy, who had to pick her way barefoot among the sharp lava rocks. Above 12,000 feet, the ground was loose volcanic scree. They reached the summit at five in the afternoon, and gazed over the eight-mile-wide lava lake and smoking crater of the volcano. Elliot was disappointed in the landscape of black rock and gray steam clouds. 'Wait until night,' Munro said.

That night the lava glowed in a network of hot red through the broken dark crust; hissing red steam slowly lost its color as it rose into the sky. On the crater rim, their little tents reflected the red glow of the lava. To the west scattered clouds were silver in the moonlight, and beneath them the Congo jungle stretched away for miles. They could see the straight green laser beams, intersecting over the black forest. With any luck they would reach that intersection tomorrow.

Ross connected her transmitting equipment to make the nightly report to Houston. After the regular six-minute delay, the signal linked directly through to Houston, without interstitial encoding or other evasive techniques.

'Hell,' Munro said.

'But what does it mean?' Elliot asked.

'It means,' Munro said gloomily, 'the consortium has stopped jamming us.'

'Isn't that good?'

'No,' Ross said. 'It's bad. They must already be on the site, and they've found the diamonds.' She shook her head, and adjusted the video screen:

HUSTN CONFRMS CONSRTUM ONSITE ZINJ PROBABILTY 1.000. TAK NO FURTHR RSKS. SITUTN HOPELSS.

'I can't believe it,' Ross said. 'It's all over.'

Elliot sighed. 'My feet hurt,' he said.

'I'm tired,' Munro said.

'The hell with it,' Ross said.

Utterly exhausted, they all went to bed.

DAY 8: KANYAMAGUFA
June 20, 1979

1. Descent

Everyone slept late on the morning of June 20. They had a leisurely breakfast, taking the time to cook a hot meal. They relaxed in the sun, and played with Amy, who was delighted by this unexpected attention. It was past ten o'clock before they started down Mukenko to the jungle.

Because the western slopes of Mukenko are sheer and impassable, they descended inside the smoking volcanic crater to a depth of half a mile. Munro led the way, carrying a porter's load on his head; Asari, the strongest porter, had to carry Amy, because the rocks were much too hot for her bare feet.

Amy was terrified, and regarded the human persons trekking single-file down the steep inner cone to be mad. Elliot was not sure she was wrong: the heat was intense; as they approached the lava lake, the acrid fumes made eyes water and nostrils burn; they heard the lava pop and crackle beneath the heavy black crust.

Then they reached the formation called Naragema – the Devil's Eye. It was a natural arch 150 feet high, and so smooth it appeared polished on the inside. Through this arch a fresh breeze blew, and they saw the green jungle below. They paused to rest in the arch, and Ross examined the smooth inner surface. It was part of a lava tube formed in some earlier eruption; the main body of the tube had been blown away, leaving just the slender arch.

'They call it the Devil's Eye,' Munro said, 'because from below, during an eruption, it glows like a red eye.'

From the Devil's Eye they descended rapidly through an alpine zone, and from there across the unworldly jagged terrain of a recent lava flow. Here they encountered black craters of scorched earth, some as deep as five or six feet. Munro's first thought was that the Zaire army had used this field for mortar practice. But on closer examination, they saw a scorched pattern etched into the rock, extending like tentacles outward from the craters. Munro had never seen anything like it; Ross immediately set up her antenna, hooked in the computer, and got in touch with Houston. She seemed very excited.

The party rested while she reviewed the data on the little screen. Munro said, 'What are you asking them?'

'The date of the last Mukenko eruption, and the local weather. It was in March – Do you know somebody named Seamans?'

'Yes,' Elliot said. 'Tom Seamans is the computer programmer for Project Amy. Why?'

'There's a message for you,' she said, pointing to the screen.

Elliot came around to look: SEMNS MESG FOR ELYT STNDBY.

'What's the message?' Elliot asked.

'Push the transmit button,' she said.

He pushed the button and the message flashed: REVUWD ORGNL TAPE HUSTN NU M.

'I don't understand,' Elliot said. Ross explained that the 'M' meant that there was more message, and he had to press the transmit button again. He pushed the button several times before he got the message, which in its entirely read:

REVUWD ORGNL TAPE HUSTN NU FINDNG RL AURL SIGNL INFO-COMPUTR ANLYSS COMPLTE THNK ITS LNGWGE.

Elliot found he could read the compressed shortline language by speaking it aloud: 'Reviewed original tape Houston, new finding regarding aural signal information, computer analysis complete think it's language.' He frowned. 'Language?'

Ross said, 'Didn't you ask him to review Houston's original tape material from the Congo?'

'Yes, but that was for visual identification of the animal on the screen. I never said anything to him about aural information.' Elliot shook his head. 'I wish I could talk to him.'

'You can,' Ross said. 'If you don't mind waking him up.' She pushed the interlock button, and fifteen minutes later Elliot typed, Hello Tom How Are You? The screen printed HLO TOM HOWRU.

'We don't usually waste satellite time with that kind of thing,' Ross said.

The screen printed SLEPY WHRERU.

He typed, Virunga. VIRNGA.

'Travis is going to scream when he sees this transcript,' Ross said. 'Do you realize what the transmission costs are?' But Ross needn't have worried; the conversation soon became technical:

RECVD MESG AURL INFO PLS XPLN.

AXIDENTL DISKVRY VRY XCITNG-DISCRIMNT FUNXN COMPTR ANLSS 99 CONFDNCE LIMTS TAPD AURL INFO {BRETHNG SOUNS} DEMNSTRTS CHRCTRISTX SPECH.

SPSFY CHRCTRISTX.

REPETNG ELMNTS-ARBTRARY PATRN-STRXRAL RLATNSHPS-PROBLY THRFOR SPOKN LNGWGE.

KN U TRNSLTE?

NOT SOFR.

WHT RESN?

COMPUTR HAS INSFSNT INFO IN AURL MESG-WNT MOR DATA-STL WORKNG-MAYB MOR TOMORO-FINGRS X.

RLY THNK GORILA LNGWGE?
YES IF GORILA.

'I'll be damned,' Elliot said. He ended the satellite transmission, but the final message from Seamans remained on the screen, glowing bright green:

YES IF GORILA.

2. The Hairy Men

Within two hours of receiving this unexpected news, the expedition had its first contact with gorillas.

They were by now back in the darkness of the equatorial rain forest. They proceeded directly toward the site, following the overhead laser beams. They could not see these beams directly, but Ross had brought a wired optical track guide, a cadmium photocell filtered to record the specific laser wavelength emission. Periodically during the day, she inflated a small helium balloon, attached the track guide with a wire, and released it. Lifted by the helium, the guide rose into the sky above the trees. There it rotated, sighted one of the laser lines, and transmitted coordinates down the wire to the computer. They followed the track of diminishing laser intensity from a single beam, and waited for the 'blip reading,' the doubled intensity value that would signal the intersection of two beams above them.

This was a slow job and their patience was wearing thin when, toward midday, they came upon the characteristic three-lobed feces of gorilla, and they saw several nests made of eucalyptus leaves on the ground and in the trees.

Fifteen minutes later, the air was shattered by a deafening roar. 'Gorilla,' Munro announced. 'That was a male telling somebody off.'

Amy signed, *Gorilla say go away.*

'We have to continue, Amy,' he said.

Gorilla no want human people come.

'Human people won't harm gorillas,' Elliot assured her. But Amy just looked blank at this, and shook her head, as if Elliot had missed the point.

Days later he realized that he had indeed missed the point. Amy was not telling him that the gorillas were afraid of being harmed by people. She was saying that the gorillas were afraid that the people would be harmed, by gorillas.

They had progressed halfway across a small jungle clearing when the large silverback male reared above the foliage and bellowed at them.

Elliot was leading the group, because Munro had gone back to help one of the porters with his pack. He saw six animals at the edge of the clearing, dark black shapes against the green, watching the human intruders. Several of the females cocked their heads and compressed their lips in a kind of disapproval. The dominant male roared again.

He was a large male with silver hair down his back. His massive head stood more than six feet above the ground, and his barrel chest indicated that he weighed more than four hundred pounds. Seeing him, Elliot understood why the first explorers to the Congo had believed gorillas to be 'hairy men,' for this magnificent creature looked like a gigantic man, both in size and shape.

At Elliot's back Ross whispered, 'What do we do?'

'Stay behind me,' Elliot said, 'and don't move.'

The silverback male dropped to all fours briefly, and began a soft *ho-ho-ho* sound, which grew more intense as he leapt to his feet again, grabbing handfuls of grass as he did so. He threw the grass in the air, and then beat his chest with flat palms, making a hollow thumping sound.

'Oh, no,' Ross said.

The chest-beating lasted five seconds, and then the male dropped to all fours again. He ran sideways across the grass, slapping the foliage and making as much noise as possible, to frighten the intruders off. Finally he began the *ho-ho-ho* sound once more.

The male stared at Elliot, expecting that this display would send him running. When it did not, the male leapt to his feet, pounded his chest, and roared with even greater fury.

And then he charged.

With a howling scream he came crashing forward at frightening speed, directly toward Elliot. Elliot heard Ross gasp behind him. He wanted to turn and run, his every bodily instinct screamed that he should run, but he forced himself to stand absolutely still – and to look down at the ground.

Staring at his feet while he listened to the gorilla crashing through the tall grass toward him, he had the sudden sensation that all his abstract book knowledge was wrong, that everything that scientists around the world thought about gorillas was wrong. He had a mental image of the huge head and the deep chest and the long arms swinging wide as the powerful animal rushed toward an easy kill, a stationary target foolish enough to believe all the academic misinformation sanctified by print. . . .

There was silence.

The gorilla (who must have been quite close) made a snorting noise, and Elliot could see his heavy shadow on the grass near his feet. But he did not look up until the shadow moved away.

When Elliot raised his head, he saw the male gorilla retreating backward, toward the far edge of the clearing. There the male turned, and scratched his head in a puzzled way, as if wondering why his terrifying display had not driven off the intruders. He slapped the ground a final time, and then he and the rest of the troop melted away into the tall grass. It was silent in the clearing until Ross collapsed into Elliot's arms.

'Well,' Munro said as he came up, 'it seems you know a thing or two about gorillas after all.' Munro patted Ross's arm. 'It's all right. They don't do anything unless you run away. Then they bite you on the ass. That's the native mark for cowardice in these regions – because it means you ran away.'

Ross was sobbing quietly, and Elliot discovered that his own knees were shaky; he went to sit down. It had all happened so fast that it was a few moments before he realized that these gorillas had behaved in exactly the textbook manner, which included not making any verbalizations even remotely like speech.

3. The Consortium

An hour later they found the wreckage of the C-130 transport. The largest airplane in the world appeared in correct scale as it lay half buried in the jungle, the gigantic nose crushed against equally gigantic trees, the enormous tail section twisted toward the ground, the massive wings buckled casting shadows on the jungle floor.

Through the shattered cockpit windshield, they saw the body of the pilot, covered with black flies. The flies buzzed and thumped against the glass as they peered in. Moving aft, they tried to look into the fuselage windows, but even on crumpled landing gear the body of the plane stood too high above the jungle floor.

Kahega managed to climb an overturned tree, and from there moved onto one wing and looked into the interior. 'No people,' he said.

'Supplies?'

'Yes, many supplies. Boxes and containers.'

Munro left the others, walking beneath the crushed tail section to examine the far side of the plane. The port wing, concealed from their view, was blackened and shattered, the engines gone. That explained why the plane had crashed – the last FZA missile had found its target, blowing away most of the port wing. Yet the wreck remained oddly mysterious to Munro; something about its appearance was wrong. He looked along the length of the fuselage, from the crushed nose, down the line of windows, past the stump of wing, past the rear exit doors. . . .

'I'll be damned,' Munro said softly.

He hurried back to the others, who were sitting on one of the tires, in the shadow of the starboard wing. The tire was so enormous that Ross could sit on it and swing her feet in the air without touching the ground.

'Well,' Ross said, with barely concealed satisfaction. 'They didn't get their damn supplies.'

'No,' Munro said. 'And we saw this plane the night before last, which means it's been down at least thirty-six hours.'

Munro waited for Ross to figure it out.

'Thirty-six hours?'

'That's right. Thirty-six hours.'

'And they never came back to get their supplies. . . .'

'They didn't even *try* to get them,' Munro said. 'Look at the main cargo doors, fore and aft – no one has tried to open them. I wonder why they never came back?'

In a section of dense jungle, the ground underfoot crunched and crackled. Pushing aside the palm fronds, they saw a carpeting of shattered white bones.

'*Kanyamagufa*,' Munro said. The place of bones. He glanced quickly at the porters to see what their reaction was, but they showed only puzzlement, no fear. They were East African Kikuyu and they had none of the superstitions of the tribes that bordered the rain forest.

Amy lifted her feet from the sharp bleached fragments. She signed, *Ground hurt.*

Elliot signed, What place this?

We come bad place.

What bad place?

Amy had no reply.

'These are bones!' Ross said, staring down at the ground.

'That's right,' Munro said quickly, 'but they're not human bones. Are they, Elliot?'

Elliot was also looking at the ground. He saw bleached skeletal remains from several species, although he could not immediately identify any of them.

'Elliot? Not human?'

'They don't look human,' Elliot agreed, staring at the ground. The first thing he noticed was that the majority of the bones came from distinctly small animals – birds, monkeys, and tiny forest rodents. Other small pieces were actually fragments from larger animals, but how large was hard to say. Perhaps large monkeys – but there weren't any large monkeys in the rain forest.

Chimpanzees? There were no chimps in this part of the Congo. Perhaps they might be gorillas: he saw one fragment from a cranium with heavy supraorbital ridging; he picked it up and turned it over in his hands.

It was a fragment of gorilla skull, no question. He felt the thickness of bone over the frontal sinuses, and he saw the beginning of the characteristic sagittal crest.

'Elliot?' Munro said, his voice tense, insistent. 'Non-human?'

'Definitely non-human,' Elliot said, staring. *What could shatter a gorilla skull?* It must have happened after death, he decided. A gorilla had died and after many years the bleached skeleton had been crushed in some fashion. Certainly it could not have happened during life.

'Not human,' Munro said, looking at the ground. 'Hell of a lot of bones, but nothing human.' As he walked past Elliot, he gave him a look. *Keep your mouth shut.* 'Kahega and his men know that you are expert in these matters,' Munro said, looking at him steadily.

What had Munro seen? Certainly he had been around enough death to know a human skeleton when he saw one. Elliot's glance fell on a curved bone. It looked a bit like a turkey wishbone, only much larger and broader, and white with age. He picked it up. It was a fragment of the zygomatic arch from a human skull. A cheekbone, from beneath the eye.

He turned the fragment in his hands. He looked back at the jungle floor, and the creepers that spread reaching tentacles over the white carpet of bones. He saw many very fragile bones, some so thin they were translucent – bones that he assumed had come from small animals.

Now he was not sure.

A question from graduate school returned to him. What seven bones compose the orbit of the human eye? Elliot tried to remember. The zygoma, the nasal, the inferior orbital, the sphenoid – that was four – the ethmoid, five – something must come from beneath, from the mouth – the palatine, six – one more to go – he couldn't think of the last bone. Zygoma, nasal, inferior orbital, sphenoid, ethmoid, palatine . . . delicate bones, translucent bones, small bones.

Human bones.

'At least these aren't human bones,' Ross said.

'No,' Elliot agreed. He glanced at Amy.

Amy signed, *People die here.*

'What did she say?'

'She said people don't benefit from the air here.'

'Let's push on,' Munro said.

Munro led him a little distance ahead of the others. 'Well done,' he said. 'Have to be careful about the Kikuyu. Don't want to panic them. What'd your monkey say?'

'She said people died there.'

'That's more than the others know,' Munro said, nodding grimly. 'Although they suspect.'

Behind them, the party walked single-file, nobody talking.

'What the hell happened back there?' Elliot said.

'Lot of bones,' Munro said. 'Leopard, colobus, forest rat, maybe a bush baby, human . . .'

'And gorilla,' Elliot said.

'Yes,' Munro said. 'I saw that, too. Gorilla.' He shook his head. 'What can kill a gorilla, Professor?'

Elliot had no answer.

The consortium camp lay in ruins, the tents shredded and shattered, the dead bodies covered with dense black clouds of flies. In the humid air, the stench was overpowering, the buzzing of the flies an angry monotonous sound. Everybody except Munro hung back at the edge of the camp.

'No choice,' he said. 'We've got to know what happened to these –' He went inside the camp itself, stepping over the flattened fence.

As Munro moved inside, the perimeter defenses were set off, emitting a screaming high-frequency signal. Outside the fence, the others cupped their hands over their ears and Amy snorted her displeasure.

Bad noise.

Munro glanced back at them. 'Doesn't bother me,' he said. 'That's what you get for staying outside.' Munro went to one dead body, turning it over with his foot. Then he bent down, swatting away the cloud of buzzing flies, and carefully examined the head.

Ross glanced over at Elliot. He seemed to be in shock, the typical scientist, immobilized by disaster. At his side, Amy covered her ears and winced. But Ross was not immobilized; she took a deep breath and crossed the perimeter. 'I have to know what defenses they installed.'

'Fine,' Elliot said. He felt detached, light-headed, as if he might faint; the sight and the smells made him dizzy. He saw Ross pick her way across the compound, then lift up a black box with an odd baffled cone. She traced a wire back toward the center of the camp. Soon afterward the high-frequency signal ceased; she had turned it off at the source.

Amy signed, *Better now.*

With one hand, Ross rummaged through the electronics equipment in the center of the units in the camp, while with the other she held her nose against the stench.

Kahega said, 'I'll see if they have guns, Doctor,' and he, too, moved into the camp. Hesitantly, the other porters followed him.

Alone, Elliot remained with Amy. She impassively surveyed the destruction, although she reached up and took his hand. He signed, *Amy what happen this place?*

Amy signed, *Things come.*

What things?

Bad things.

What things?

Bad things come things come bad.

What things?

Bad things.

Obviously he would get nowhere with this line of questioning. He told her to remain outside the camp, and went in himself, moving among the bodies and the buzzing flies.

Ross said, 'Anybody find the leader?'

Across the camp, Munro said, 'Menard.'

'Out of Kinshasa?'

Munro nodded. 'Yeah.'

'Who's Menard?' Elliot asked.

'He's got a good reputation, knows the Congo.' Ross picked her way through the debris. 'But he wasn't good enough.' A moment later she paused.

Elliot went over to her. She stared at a body lying face down on the ground.

'Don't turn it over,' she said. 'It's Richter.'

Elliot did not understand how she could be sure. The body was covered with black flies. He bent over.

'Don't touch him!'

'Okay,' Elliot said.

'Kahega,' Munro shouted, raising a green plastic twenty-liter can. The can sloshed with liquid in his hand. 'Let's get this done.'

Kahega and his men moved swiftly, splashing kerosene over the tents and dead bodies. Elliot smelled the sharp odor.

Ross, crouched under a torn nylon supply tent, shouted, 'Give me a minute!'

'Take all the time you want,' Munro said. He turned to Elliot, who was watching Amy outside the camp.

Amy was signing to herself: *People bad. No believe people bad things come.*

'She seems very calm about it,' Munro said.

'Not really,' Elliot said. 'I think she knows what took place here.'

'I hope she'll tell us,' Munro said. 'Because all these men died in the same way. Their skulls were crushed.'

The flames from the consortium camp licked upward into the air, and the black smoke billowed as the expedition moved onward through the jungle. Ross was silent, lost in thought. Elliot said, 'What did you find?'

'Nothing good,' she said. 'They had a perfectly adequate peripheral system, quite similar to our ADP – animal defense perimeter. Those cones I found are audio-sensing units, and when they pick up a signal, they emit an ultra-high-frequency signal that is very painful to auditory systems. Doesn't work for reptiles, but it's damn effective on mammalian systems. Send a wolf or a leopard running for the hills.'

'But it didn't work here,' Elliot said.

'No,' Ross said. 'And it didn't bother Amy very much.'

Elliot said, 'What does it do to human auditory systems?'

'You felt it. It's annoying, but that's all.' She glanced at Elliot. 'But there aren't any human beings in this part of the Congo. Except us.'

Munro asked, 'Can we make a better perimeter defense?'

'Damn right we can,' Ross said. 'I'll give you the next generation perimeter – it'll stop anything except elephants and rhinos.' But she didn't sound convinced.

Late in the afternoon, they came upon the remains of the first ERTS Congo camp. They nearly missed it, for during the intervening eight days the jungle vines and creepers had already begun to grow back over it, obliterating all traces. There was not much left – a few shreds of orange nylon, a dented aluminum cooking pan, the crushed tripod, and the broken video camera, its green circuit boards scattered across the ground. They found no bodies, and since the light was fading they pressed on.

Amy was distinctly agitated. She signed, *No go.*

Peter Elliot paid no attention.

Bad place old place no go.

'We go, Amy,' he said.

Fifteen minutes later they came to a break in the overhanging trees. Looking up, they saw the dark cone of Mukenko rising above the forest, and the faint crossed green beams of the lasers glinting in the humid air. And directly beneath the beams were the moss-covered stone blocks, half concealed in jungle foliage, of the Lost City of Zinj.

Elliot turned to look at Amy.

Amy was gone.

4. Weird

He could not believe it.

At first he thought she was just punishing him, running off to make him sorry for shooting the dart at her on the river. He explained to Munro and Ross that she was capable of such things, and they spent the next half hour wandering through the jungle, calling her name. But there was no response, just the eternal silence of the rain forest. The half hour became an hour, then almost two hours.

Elliot was panic-stricken.

When she still did not emerge from the foliage, another possibility had to be considered. 'Maybe she ran off with the last group of gorillas,' Munro said.

'Impossible,' Elliot said.

'She's seven, she's near maturity.' Munro shrugged. 'She *is* a gorilla.'

'Impossible,' Elliot insisted.

But he knew what Munro was saying. Inevitably, people who raised apes found at a certain point they could no longer keep them. With maturity the animals became too large, too powerful, too much their own species to be controllable. It was no longer possible to put them in diapers and pretend they were cute humanlike creatures. Their genes coded inevitable differences that ultimately became impossible to overlook.

'Gorilla troops aren't closed,' Munro reminded him. 'They accept strangers, particularly female strangers.'

'She wouldn't do that,' Elliot insisted. 'She couldn't.'

Amy had been raised from infancy among human beings. She was much more familiar with the Westernized world of freeways and drive-ins than she was with the jungle. If Elliot drove his car past her favorite drive-in, she was quick to tap his shoulder and point out his error. What did she know of the jungle? It was as alien to her as it was to Elliot himself. And not only that –

'We'd better make camp,' Ross said, glancing at her watch. 'She'll come back – if she wants to. After all,' she said, 'we didn't leave her. She left us.'

They had brought a bottle of Dom Pérignon champagne but nobody was in a mood to celebrate. Elliot was remorseful over the loss of Amy; the others were horrified by what they had seen of the earlier camp; with night rapidly falling, there was much to do to set up the ERTS system known as WEIRD (wilderness environment intruder response defenses).

The exotic WEIRD technology recognized the fact that perimeter defenses were traditional throughout the history of Congo exploration. More than a century before, Stanley observed that 'no camp is to be considered complete until it is fenced around by bush or trees.' In the years since there was little reason to alter the essential nature of that instruction. But defensive technology had changed, and the WEIRD system incorporated all the latest innovations.

Kahega and his men inflated the silvered Mylar tents, arranging them close together. Ross directed the placement of the tubular infrared night lights on telescoping tripods. These were positioned shining outward around the camp.

Next the perimeter fence was installed. This was a light-weight metalloid mesh, more like cloth than wire. Attached to stakes, it completely enclosed the campsite, and when hooked to the transformer carried 10,000 volts of electrical current. To reduce drain on the fuel cells, the current was pulsed at four cycles a second, creating a throbbing, intermittent hum.

Dinner on the night of June 21 was rice with rehydrated Creole shrimp sauce. The shrimps did not rehydrate well, remaining little cardboard-tasting chunks in the mix, but nobody complained about this failure of twentieth-century technology as they glanced around them at the deepening jungle darkness.

Munro positioned the sentries. They would stand four-hour watches; Munro announced that he, Kahega, and Elliot would take the first watch.

With night goggles in place, the sentries looked like mysterious grasshoppers peering out at the jungle. The night goggles intensified ambient light and overlaid this on the pre-existing imagery, rimming it in ghostly green. Elliot found the goggles heavy, and the electronic view through them difficult to adjust to. He pulled them off after several minutes, and was astonished to see that the jungle was inky black around him. He put them back on hastily.

The night passed quietly, without incident.

DAY 9: ZINJ
June 21, 1979

1. Tiger Tail

Their entrance into the Lost City of Zinj on the morning of June 21 was accomplished with none of the mystery and romance of nineteenth-century accounts of similar journeys. These twentieth-century explorers sweated and grunted under a burdensome load of technical equipment – optical range finders, data-lock compasses, RF directionals with attached transmitters, and microwave transponders – all deemed essential to the modern high-speed evaluation of a ruined archaeological site.

They were only interested in diamonds. Schliemann had been only interested in gold when he excavated Troy, and he had devoted three years to it. Ross expected to find her diamonds in three days.

According to the ERTS computer simulation the best way to do this was to draw up a ground plan of the city. With a plan in hand, it would be relatively simple to deduce mine locations from the arrangement of urban structures.

They expected a usable plan of the city within six hours. Using RF transponders, they had only to stand in each of the four corners of a building, pressing the radio beeper at each corner. Back in camp, two widely spaced receivers recorded their signals so that their computer could plot them in two dimensions. But the ruins were extensive, covering more than three square kilometers. A radio survey would separate them widely in dense foliage – and, considering what had happened to the previous expedition, this seemed unwise.

Their alternative was what ERTS called the non-systematic survey, or 'the tiger-tail approach.' (It was a joke at ERTS that one way to find a tiger was to keep walking until you stepped on its tail.) They moved through the ruined buildings, avoiding slithering snakes and giant spiders that scurried into dark recesses. The spiders were the size of a man's hand, and to Ross's astonishment made a loud clicking noise.

They noticed that the stonework was of excellent quality, although the limestone in many places was pitted and crumbling. And everywhere they saw the half-moon curve of doors and windows, which seemed to be a cultural design motif.

But aside from that curved shape, they found almost nothing distinctive about the rooms they passed through. In general, the rooms were rectangular and roughly the same size; the walls were bare, lacking decoration. After so many intervening centuries they found no artifacts at all – although Elliot finally came upon a pair of disc-shaped stone paddles, which they presumed had been used to grind spices or grain.

The bland, characterless quality of the city grew more disturbing as they continued; it was also inconvenient, since they had no way to refer to one place or another; they began assigning arbitrary names to different buildings. When Karen Ross found a series of cubby holes carved into the wall of one room, she announced that this must be a post office, and from then on it was referred to as 'the post office.'

They came upon a row of small rooms with postholes for wooden bars. Munro thought these were cells of a jail, but the cells were extremely small. Ross said that perhaps the people were small, or perhaps the cells were intentionally small for punishment. Elliot thought perhaps they were cages for a zoo. But in that case, why were all the cages of the same size? And Munro pointed out there was no provision for viewing the animals; he repeated his conviction that it was a jail, and the rooms became known as 'the jail.'

Near to the jail they found an open court they called 'the gymnasium.' It was apparently an athletic field or training ground. There were four tall stone stakes with a crumbling stone ring at the top; evidently these had been used for some kind of game like tetherball. In a corner of the court stood a horizontal overhead bar, like a jungle gym, no more than five feet off the ground. The low bar led Elliot to conclude that this was a playground for children. Ross repeated her belief that the people were small. Munro wondered if the gymnasium was a training area for soldiers.

As they continued their search, they were all aware that their reactions simply mirrored their preoccupations. The city was so neutral, so uninformative, that it became a kind of Rorschach for them. What they needed was objective information about the people who had built the city, and their life.

It was there all along, although they were slow to realize it. In many rooms, one wall or another was overgrown with blackgreen mold. Munro noticed that this mold did not grow in relation to light from a window, or air currents, or any other factor they could identify. In some rooms, the mold grew thickly halfway down a wall, only to stop in a sharp horizontal line, as if cut by a knife.

'Damn strange,' Munro said, peering at the mold, rubbing his finger against it. His finger came away with traces of blue paint.

That was how they discovered the elaborate bas-reliefs, once painted, that appeared throughout the city. However, the overgrowth of mold on the irregular carved surface and the pitting of the limestone made any interpretation of the images impossible.

At lunch, Munro mentioned that it was too bad they hadn't brought along a group of art historians to recover the bas-relief images. 'With

all their lights and machines, they could see what's there in no time,'
he said.

It gave Ross an idea.

The most recent examination techniques for artwork, as devised by
Degusto and others, employed infrared light and image intensification,
and the Congo expedition had the necessary equipment to contrive such
a method on the spot. At least it was worth a try. After lunch they
returned to the ruins, lugging in the video camera, one of the infrared
night lights, and the tiny computer display screen.

After an hour of fiddling they had worked out a system. By shining
infrared light on the walls and recording the image with the video
camera – and then feeding that image via satellite through the digitizing
computer programs in Houston, and returning it back to their portable
display unit – they were able to reconstitute the pictures on the walls.

Seeing the bas-reliefs in this way reminded Peter Elliot of the night
goggles. If you looked directly at the walls, you saw nothing but dark
moss and lichen and pitted stone. But if you looked at the little computer
screen, you saw the original painted scenes, vibrant and lifelike. It was,
he remembered, 'very peculiar. There we were in the middle of the
jungle, but we could only examine our environment indirectly, with
the machines. We used goggles to see at night, and video to see during
the day. We were using machines to see what we could not see otherwise,
and we were totally dependent on them.'

He also found it odd that the information recorded by the video
camera had to travel more than twenty thousand miles before returning
to the display screen, only a few feet away. It was, he said later, the
'world's longest spinal cord,' and it produced an odd effect. Even at the
speed of light, the transmission required a tenth of a second, and since
there was a short processing time in the Houston computer, the images
did not appear on the screen instantaneously, but arrived about half a
second late. The delay was just barely noticeable. The scenes they saw
provided them with their first insight into the city and its inhabitants.

The people of Zinj were relatively tall blacks, with round heads and
muscular bodies; in appearance they resembled the Bantu-speaking
people who had first entered the Congo from the highland savannahs
to the north, two thousand years ago. They were depicted here as lively
and energetic: despite the climate, they favored elaborately decorated,
colorful long robes; their attitudes and gestures were expansive; in all
ways they contrasted sharply with the bland and crumbling structures,
now all that remained of their civilization.

The first decoded frescoes showed marketplace scenes: sellers squatted on the ground beside beautiful woven baskets containing round objects, while buyers stood and bargained with them. At first they thought the round objects were fruit, but Ross decided they were stones.

'Those are uncut diamonds in a surrounding matrix,' she said, staring at the screen. 'They're selling diamonds.'

The frescoes led them to consider what had happened to the inhabitants of the city of Zinj, for the city was clearly abandoned, not destroyed – there was no sign of war or invaders, no evidence of any cataclysm or natural disaster.

Ross, voicing her deepest fears, suspected the diamond mines had given out, turning this city into a ghost town like so many other mining settlements in history. Elliot thought that a plague or disease had overcome the inhabitants. Munro said he thought the gorillas were responsible.

'Don't laugh,' he said. 'This is a volcanic area. Eruptions, earthquakes, drought, fires on the savannah – the animals go berserk, and don't behave in the ordinary way at all.'

'Nature on the rampage?' Elliot asked, shaking his head. 'There are volcanic eruptions here every few years, and we know this city existed for centuries. It can't be that.'

'Maybe there was a palace revolution, a coup.'

'What would that matter to gorillas?' Elliot laughed.

'It happens,' Munro said. 'In Africa, the animals always get strange when there's a war on, you know.' He then told them stories of baboons attacking farmhouses in South Africa and buses in Ethiopia.

Elliot was unimpressed. These ideas of nature mirroring the affairs of man were very old – at least as old as Aesop, and about as scientific. 'The natural world is indifferent to man,' he said.

'Oh, no question,' Munro said, 'but there isn't much natural world left.'

Elliot was reluctant to agree with Munro, but in fact a well-known academic thesis argued just that. In 1955, the French anthropologist Maurice Cavalle published a controversial paper entitled 'The Death of Nature.' In it he said:

One million years ago the earth was characterized by a pervasive wildness which we may call 'nature.' In the midst of this wild nature stood small enclaves of human habitation. Whether caves with artificial fire to keep men warm, or later cities with dwellings and artificial fields of cultivation, these enclaves were distinctly unnatural. In the succeeding millennia, the area of untouched nature surrounding artificial human enclaves progressively declined, although for centuries the trend remained invisible.

Even 300 years ago in France or England, the great cities of man were isolated by hectares of wilderness in which untamed beasts roamed, as they had for thousands of years before. And yet the expansion of man continued inexorably.

One hundred years ago, in the last days of the great European explorers, nature had so radically diminished that it was a novelty: it is for this reason that African explorations captured the imagination of nineteenth-century man. To enter a truly natural world was exotic, beyond the experience of most mankind, who lived from birth to death in entirely man-made circumstances.

In the twentieth century the balance has shifted so far that for all practical purposes one may say that nature has disappeared. Wild plants are preserved in hot-houses, wild animals in zoos and game parks: artificial settings created by man as a souvenir of the once-prevalent natural world. But an animal in a zoo or a game park does not live its natural life, any more than a man in a city lives a natural life.

Today we are surrounded by man and his creations. Man is inescapable, everywhere on the globe, and nature is a fantasy, a dream of the past, long gone.

Ross called Elliot away from his dinner. 'It's for you,' she said, pointing to the computer next to the antenna. 'That friend of yours again.'

Munro grinned. 'Even in the jungle, the phone never stops ringing.'

Elliot went over to look at the screen: COMPUTR LNGWAGE ANALYSS NG REQUIR MOR INPUT KN PROVIDE?

WHT INPUT? Elliot typed back.

MOR AURL INPUT-TRNSMIT RECORDNGS.

Elliot typed back, Yes If Occurs. YES IF OCRS.

RCORD FREQNCY 22–50,000 CYCLS-CRITICL

Elliot typed back, Understood. UNDRSTOD.

There was a pause, then the screen printed: HOWS AMY?

Elliot hesitated. FINE.

STAF SNDS LOV came the reply, and the transmission was momentarily interrupted.

HOLD TRSNMSN.

There was a long pause.

INCREDIBL NWZ, Seamans printed. HAV FOUND MRS SWENSN.

2. Swensn NWZ

For a moment Elliot did not recognize the name. Swensn? Who was Swensn? A transmission error? And then he realized: *Mrs. Swenson!* Amy's discoverer, the woman who had brought her from Africa and had donated her to the Minneapolis zoo. The woman who had been in Borneo all these weeks. IF WE HAD ONLY KNON AMY MOTHR NOT KILD BY NATIVS.

Elliot waited impatiently for the next message from Seamans.

Elliot stared at the message. He had always been told that Amy's mother had been killed by natives in a village called Bagimindi. The mother had been killed for food, and Amy was orphaned. . . .

WHT MEANS?

MOTHR ALREDY DED NOT EATN.

The natives hadn't killed Amy's mother? She was already dead?

XPLN.

SWENSN HAS PICTR CAN TRANSMT?

Hastily, Elliot typed, his fingers fumbling at the keyboard.

TRANSMT.

There was a pause that seemed interminable, and then the video screen received the transmission, scanning it from top to bottom. Long before the picture filled the screen, Elliot realized what it showed.

A crude snapshot of a gorilla corpse with a crushed skull. The animal lay on its back in a packed-earth clearing, presumably in a native village.

In that moment Elliot felt as if the puzzle that preoccupied him, that had caused so much anguish for so many months, was explained. If only they had been able to reach her before. . . .

The glowing electronic image faded to black.

Elliot was confronted by a rush of sudden questions. Crushed skulls occurred in the remote – and supposedly uninhabited – region of the Congo, *kanyamagufa*, the place of bones. But Bagimindi was a trading village on the Lubula River, more than a hundred miles away. How had Amy and her dead mother reached Bagimindi?

Ross said, 'Got a problem?'

'I don't understand the sequence. I need to ask –'

'Before you do,' she said, 'review the transmission. It's all in memory.' She pressed a button marked REPEAT.

The earlier transmitted conversation was repeated on the screen. As Elliot watched Seaman's answers, one line struck him: MOTHR ALREDY DED NOT EATN.

Why wasn't the mother eaten? Gorilla meat was an acceptable – indeed a prized – food in this part of the Congo basin. He typed in a question:

WHY MOTHR NOT EATN.
MOTHR / INFNT FWND BY NATIV ARMY PATRL DOWN FRM SUDAN CARRIED CRPSE / INFNT 5 DAYS TO BAGMINDI VILLAG FOR SALE TOURISTS. SWENSN THERE.

Five days! Quickly, Elliot typed the important question:
WHER FWND?
The answer came back: UNKNWN AREA CONGO.
SPECFY.
NO DETAILS. A short pause, then: THERS MOR PICTRS.
SND, he typed back.
The screen went blank, and then filled once more, from top to bottom. Now he saw a closer view of the female gorilla's crushed skull. And alongside the huge skull, a small black creature lying on the ground, hands and feet clenched, mouth open in a frozen scream.
Amy.

Ross repeated the transmission several times, finishing on the image of Amy as an infant – small, black, screaming.

'No wonder she's been having nightmares,' Ross said. 'She probably saw her mother killed.'

Elliot said, 'Well, at least we can be sure it wasn't gorillas. They don't kill each other.'

'Right now,' Ross said, 'we can't be sure of anything at all.'

The night of June 21 was so quiet that by ten o'clock they switched off the infrared night lights to save power. Almost at once they became aware of movement in the foliage outside the compound. Munro and Kahega swung their guns around. The rustling increased, and they heard an odd sighing sound, a sort of wheeze.

Elliot heard it too, and felt a chill: it was the same wheezing that had been recorded on the tapes from the first Congo expedition. He turned on the tape recorder, and swung the microphone around. They were all tense, alert, waiting.

But for the next hour nothing further happened. The foliage moved all around them, but they saw nothing. Then shortly before midnight the electrified perimeter fence erupted in sparks. Munro swung his gun around and fired; Ross hit the switch for the night lights and the camp was bathed in deep red.

'Did you see it?' Munro said. 'Did you see what it was?'

They shook their heads. Nobody had seen anything. Elliot checked his tapes; he had only the harsh rattle of gunfire, and the sound of sparks. No breathing.

The rest of the night passed uneventfully.

DAY 10: ZINJ
June 22, 1979

1. Return

The morning of June 22 was foggy and gray. Peter Elliot awoke at 6 a.m. to find the camp already up and active. Munro was stalking around the perimeter of the camp, his clothing soaked to the chest by the wet foliage. He greeted Elliot with a look of triumph, and pointed to the ground.

There, on the ground, were fresh footprints. They were deep and short, rather triangular-shaped, and there was a wide space between the big toe and the other four toes – as wide as the space between a human thumb and fingers.

'Definitely not human,' Elliot said, bending to look closely.

Munro said nothing.

'Some kind of primate.'

Munro said nothing.

'It can't be a gorilla,' Elliot finished, straightening. His video communication from the night before had hardened his belief that gorillas were not involved. Gorillas did not kill other gorillas as Amy's mother had been killed. 'It can't be a gorilla,' he repeated.

'It's a gorilla, all right,' Munro said. 'Have a look at this.' He pointed to another area of the soft earth. There were four indentations in a row. 'Those are the knuckles, when they walk on their hands.'

'But gorillas,' Elliot said, 'are shy animals that sleep at night and avoid contact with men.'

'Tell the one that made this print.'

'It's small for a gorilla,' Elliot said. He examined the fence nearby, where the electrical short had occurred the night before. Bits of gray fur clung to the fence. 'And gorillas don't have gray fur.'

'Males do,' Munro said. 'Silverbacks.'

'Yes, but the silverback coloring is whiter than this. This fur is distinctly gray.' He hesitated. 'Maybe it's a *kakundakari.*'

Munro looked disgusted.

The *kakundakari* was a disputed primate in the Congo. Like the yeti of the Himalayas and bigfoot of North America, he had been sighted but never captured. There were endless native stories of a six-foot-tall hairy ape that walked on his hind legs and otherwise behaved in a manlike fashion.

Many respected scientists believed the *kakundakari* existed; perhaps they remembered the authorities who had once denied the existence of the gorilla.

In 1774, Lord Monboddo wrote of the gorilla that 'this wonderful and frightful production of nature walks upright like man; is from 7 to

9 feet high . . . and amazingly strong; covered with longish hair, jet black over the body, but longer on the head; the face more like the human than the Chimpenza, but the complexion black; and has no tail.'

Forty years later, Bowditch described an African ape 'generally five feet high, and four across the shoulders; its paw was said to be even more disproportionate than its breadth, and one blow of it to be fatal.' But it was not until 1847 that Thomas Savage, an African missionary, and Jeffries Wyman, a Boston anatomist, published a paper describing 'a second species in Africa . . . not recognized by naturalists,' which they proposed to call *Troglodytes gorilla*. Their announcement caused enormous excitement in the scientific world, and a rush in London, Paris, and Boston to procure skeletons; by 1855, there was no longer any doubt – a second, very large ape existed in Africa.

Even in the twentieth century, new animal species were discovered in the rain forest: the blue pig in 1944, and the red-breasted grouse in 1961. It was perfectly possible that a rare, reclusive primate might exist in the jungle depths. But there was still no hard evidence for the *kakundakari*.

'This print is from a gorilla,' Munro insisted. 'Or rather a group of gorillas. They're all around the perimeter fence. They've been scouting our camp.'

'Scouting our camp,' Elliot repeated, shaking his head.

'That's right,' Munro said. 'Just look at the bloody prints.'

Elliot felt his patience growing short. He said something about white-hunter campfire tales, to which Munro said something unflattering about people who knew everything from books.

At that point, the colobus monkeys in the trees overhead began to shriek and shake the branches.

They found Malawi's body just outside the compound. The porter had been going to the stream to get water when he had been killed; the collapsible buckets lay on the ground nearby. The bones of his skull had been crushed; the purple, swelling face was distorted, the mouth open.

The group was repelled by the manner of death; Ross turned away, nauseated; the porters huddled with Kahega, who tried to reassure them; Munro bent to examine the injury. 'You notice these flattened areas of compression, as if the head was squeezed between something. . . .'

Munro then called for the stone paddles that Elliot had found in the city the day before. He glanced back at Kahega.

Kahega stood at his most erect and said, 'We go home now, boss.'

'That's not possible,' Munro said.

'We go home. We must go home, one of our brothers is dead, we must make ceremony for his wife and his children, boss.'

'Kahega...'

'Boss, we must go now.'

'Kahega, we will talk.' Munro straightened, put his arm over Kahega and led him some distance away, across the clearing. They talked in low voices for several minutes.

'It's awful,' Ross said. She seemed genuinely affected with human feeling and instinctively Elliot turned to comfort her, but she continued, 'The whole expedition is falling apart. It's awful. We have to hold it together somehow, or we'll *never* find the diamonds.'

'Is that all you care about?'

'Well, they *do* have insurance....'

'For Christ's sake,' Elliot said.

'You're just upset because you've lost your damned monkey,' Ross said. 'Now get hold of yourself. They're watching us.'

The Kikuyu were indeed watching Ross and Elliot, trying to sense the drift of sentiment. But they all knew that the real negotiations were between Munro and Kahega, standing off to one side. Several minutes later Kahega returned, wiping his eyes. He spoke quickly to his remaining brothers, and they nodded. He turned back to Munro.

'We stay, boss.'

'Good,' Munro said, immediately resuming his former imperious tone. 'Bring the paddles.'

When they were brought, Munro placed the paddles to either side of Malawi's head. They fitted the semicircular indentations on the head perfectly.

Munro then said something quickly to Kahega in Swahili, and Kahega said something to his brothers, and they nodded. Only then did Munro take the next horrible step. He raised his arms wide, and then swung the paddles back hard against the already crushed skull. The dull sound was sickening; droplets of blood spattered over his shirt, but he did not further damage the skull.

'A man hasn't the strength to do this,' Munro said flatly. He looked up at Peter Elliot. 'Care to try?'

Elliot shook his head.

Munro stood. 'Judging by the way he fell, Malawi was standing when it happened.' Munro faced Elliot, looking him in the eye. 'Large animal, the size of a man. Large, strong animal. A gorilla.'

Elliot had no reply.

There is no doubt that Peter Elliot felt a personal threat in these developments, although not a threat to his safety. 'I simply couldn't accept it,' he said later. 'I knew my field, and I simply couldn't accept the idea of some unknown, radically violent behavior displayed by gorillas in the wild. And in any case, it didn't make sense. Gorillas making stone paddles that they used to crush human skulls? It was impossible.'

After examining the body, Elliot went to the stream to wash the blood from his hands. Once alone, away from the others, he found himself staring into the clear running water and considering the possibility that he might be wrong. Certainly primate researchers had a long history of misjudging their subjects.

Elliot himself had helped eradicate one of the most famous misconceptions – the brutish stupidity of the gorilla. In their first description, Savage and Wyman had written, 'This animal exhibits a degree of intelligence inferior to that of the Chimpanzee; this might be expected from its wider departure from the organization of the human subject.' Later observers saw the gorilla as 'savage, morose, and brutal.' But now there was abundant evidence from field and laboratory studies that the gorilla was in many ways brighter than the chimpanzee.

Then, too, there were the famous stories of chimpanzees kidnapping and eating human infants. For decades, primate researchers had dismissed such native tales as 'wild and superstitious fantasy.' But there was no longer any doubt that chimpanzees occasionally kidnapped – and ate – human infants; when Jane Goodall studied Gombe chimpanzees, she locked away her own infant to prevent his being taken and killed by the chimps.

Chimpanzees hunted a variety of animals, according to a complicated ritual. And field studies by Dian Fossey suggested that gorillas also hunted from time to time, killing small game and monkeys, whenever –

He heard a rustling in the bushes across the stream, and an enormous silverback male gorilla reared up in chest-high foliage. Peter was startled, although as soon as he got over his fright he realized that he was safe. Gorillas never crossed open water, even a small stream. Or was that a misconception, too?

The male stared at him across the water. There seemed to be no threat in his gaze, just a kind of watchful curiosity. Elliot smelled the musty odor of the gorilla, and he heard the breath hiss through his flattened nostrils. He was wondering what he should do when suddenly the gorilla crashed noisily away through the underbrush, and was gone.

This encounter perplexed him, and he stood, wiping the sweat from his face. Then he realized that there was still movement in the foliage across the stream. After a moment, another gorilla rose up, this one smaller: a female, he thought, though he couldn't be sure. The new gorilla gazed at him as implacably as the first. Then the hand moved.

Peter come give tickle.

'Amy!' he shouted, and a moment later he had splashed across the stream, and she had leapt into his arms, hugging him and delivering sloppy wet kisses and grunting happily.

Amy's unexpected return to camp nearly got her shot by the jumpy Kikuyu porters. Only by blocking her body with his own did Elliot prevent gunfire. Twenty minutes later, however, everyone had adjusted to her presence – and Amy promptly began making demands.

She was unhappy to learn that they had not acquired milk or cookies in her absence, but when Munro produced the bottle of warm Dom Pérignon, she agreed to accept champagne instead.

They all sat around her, drinking champagne from tin cups. Elliot was glad for the mitigating presence of the others, for now that Amy was sitting there, safely restored to him, calmly sipping her champagne and signing *Tickle drink Amy like*, he found himself overcome with anger toward her.

Munro grinned at Elliot as he gave him his champagne. 'Calmly, Professor, calmly. She's just a child.'

'The hell she is,' Elliot said. He conducted the subsequent conversation entirely in sign language, not speaking.

Amy, he signed. Why Amy leave?

She buried her nose in her cup, signing *tickle drink good drink.*

Amy, he signed. Amy tell Peter why leave.

Peter not like Amy.

Peter like Amy.

Peter hurt Amy Peter fly ouch pin Amy no like Peter no like Amy Amy sad sad.

In a detached corner of his mind, he thought he would have to remember that 'ouch pin' had now been extended to the Thoralen dart. Her generalization pleased him, but he signed sternly, Peter like Amy. Amy know Peter like Amy. Amy tell Peter why –

Peter no tickle Amy Peter not nice Amy Peter not nice human person Peter like woman no like Amy Peter not like Amy Amy sad Amy sad.

This increasingly rapid signing was itself an indication that she was upset. Where Amy go?

Amy go gorillas good gorillas. Amy like.

Curiosity overcame his anger. Had she joined a troop of wild gorillas for several days? If so, it was an event of major importance, a crucial moment in modern primate history – a language-skilled primate had joined a wild troop and had come back again. He wanted to know more.

Gorillas nice to Amy?

With a smug look: *Yes.*

Amy tell Peter.

She stared off into the distance, not answering.

To catch her attention Elliot snapped his fingers. She turned to him slowly, her expression bored.

Amy tell Peter, Amy stay gorillas?

Yes.

In her indifference was the clear recognition that Elliot was desperate to learn what she knew. Amy was always very astute at recognizing when she had the upper hand – and she had it now.

Amy tell Peter, he signed as calmly as he could.

Good gorillas like Amy Amy good gorilla.

That told him nothing at all. She was composing phrases by rote: another way of ignoring him.

Amy.

She glanced at him.

Amy tell Peter. Amy come see gorillas?

Yes.

Gorillas do what?

Gorillas sniff Amy.

All gorillas?

Big gorillas white back gorillas sniff Amy baby sniff Amy all gorillas sniff gorillas like Amy.

So silverback males had sniffed her, then infants, then all the members of the troop. That much was clear – remarkably clear, he thought, making a mental note of her extended syntax. Afterward had she been accepted in the troop? He signed, What happen Amy then?

Gorillas give food.

What food?

No name Amy food give food.

Apparently they had shown her food. Or had they actually fed her? Such a thing had never been reported in the wild, but then no one had ever witnessed the introduction of a new animal into a troop. She was a female, and nearly of reproductive age. . . .

What gorillas give food?

All give food Amy take food Amy like.

Apparently it was not males, or not males exclusively. But what had caused her acceptance? Granted that gorilla troops were not as closed to outsiders as monkey troops – what actually had happened?

Amy stay with gorillas?

Gorillas like Amy.

Yes. What Amy do?

Amy sleep Amy eat Amy live gorillas gorillas good gorillas Amy like.

So she had joined in the life of the troop, living the daily existence. Had she been totally accepted?

Amy like gorillas?
Gorillas dumb.
Why dumb?
Gorillas no talk.
No talk sign talk?
Gorillas no talk.

Evidently she had experienced frustration with the gorillas because they did not know her sign language. (Language-using primates were commonly frustrated and annoyed when thrown among animals who did not understand the signs.)

Gorillas nice to Amy?
Gorillas like Amy Amy like gorillas like Amy like gorillas.
Why Amy come back?
Want milk cookies.

'Amy,' he said, 'you know we don't have any damn milk or cookies.' His sudden verbalization startled the others. They looked questioningly at Amy.

For a long time she did not answer. *Amy like Peter. Amy sad want Peter.* He felt like crying.

Peter good human person.

Blinking his eyes he signed, Peter tickle Amy. She jumped into his arms.

Later, he questioned her in more detail. But it was a painstakingly slow process, chiefly because of Amy's difficulty in handling concepts of time.

Amy distinguished past, present, and future – she remembered previous events, and anticipated future promises – but the Project Amy staff had never succeeded in teaching her exact differentiations. She did not, for example, distinguish yesterday from the day before. Whether this reflected a failing in teaching methods or an innate feature of Amy's conceptual world was an open question. (There was evidence for a conceptual difference. Amy was particularly perplexed by spatial metaphors for time, such as 'that's behind us' or 'that's coming up.' Her trainers conceived of the past as behind them and the future ahead. But Amy's behavior seemed to indicate that she conceived of the past as in front of her – because she could see it – and the future behind her – because it was still invisible. Whenever she was impatient for the promised arrival of a friend, she repeatedly looked over her shoulder, even if she was facing the door.)

In any case, the time problem was a difficulty in talking to her now, and Elliot phrased his questions carefully. He asked, 'Amy, what happened at night? With the gorillas?'

She gave him the look she always gave him when she thought a question was obvious. *Amy sleep night.*

'And the other gorillas?'

Gorillas sleep night.

'All the gorillas?'

She disdained to answer.

'Amy,' he said, 'gorillas come to our camp at night.'

Come this place?

'Yes, this place. Gorillas come at night.'

She thought that over. *No.*

Munro said, 'What did she say?'

Elliot said, 'She said "No." Yes, Amy, they come.'

She was silent a moment, and then she signed, *Things come.*

Munro again asked what she had said.

'She said, "Things come." ' Elliot translated the rest of her responses for them.

Ross asked, 'What things, Amy?'

Bad things.

Munro said, 'Were they gorillas, Amy?'

Not gorillas. Bad things. Many bad things come forest come. Breath talk. Come night come.

Munro said, 'Where are they now, Amy?'

Amy looked around at the jungle. *Here. This bad old place things come.*

Ross said, 'What things, Amy? Are they animals?'

Elliot told them that Amy could not abstract the category 'animals.' 'She thinks people are animals,' he explained. 'Are the bad things people, Amy? Are they human persons?'

No.

Munro said, 'Monkeys?'

No. Bad things, not sleep night.

Munro said, 'Is she reliable?'

What means?

'Yes,' Elliot said. 'Perfectly.'

'She knows what gorillas are?'

Amy good gorilla, she signed.

'Yes, you are,' Elliot said. 'She's saying she's a good gorilla.'

Munro frowned. 'So she knows what gorillas are, but she says these things are not gorillas?'

'That's what she says.'

2. Missing Elements

Elliot got Ross to set up the video camera at the outskirts of the city, facing the campsite. With the videotape running he led Amy to the edge of the camp to look at the ruined buildings. Elliot wanted to confront Amy with the lost city, the reality behind her dreams – and he wanted a record of her responses to that moment. What happened was totally unexpected.

Amy had no reaction at all.

Her face remained impassive, her body relaxed. She did not sign. If anything she gave the impression of boredom, of suffering through another of Elliot's enthusiasms that she did not share. Elliot watched her carefully. She wasn't displacing; she wasn't repressing; she wasn't doing anything. She stared at the city with equanimity.

'Amy know this place?'

Yes.

'Amy tell Peter what place.'

Bad place old place.

'Sleep pictures?'

This bad place.

'Why is it bad, Amy?'

Bad place old place.

'Yes but why, Amy?'

Amy fear.

She showed no somatic indication of fear. Squatting on the ground alongside him she gazed forward, perfectly calm.

'Why Amy fear?'

Amy want eat.

'Why Amy fear?'

She would not answer, in the way that she did not deign to answer him whenever she was completely bored; he could not provoke her to discuss her dreams further. She was as closed on the subject as she had been in San Francisco. When he asked her to accompany them into the ruins, she calmly refused to do so. On the other hand, she did not seem distressed that Elliot was going into the city, and she cheerfully waved goodbye before going to demand more food from Kahega.

Only after the expedition was concluded and Elliot had returned to Berkeley did he find the explanation to this perplexing event – in Freud's *Interpretation of Dreams*, first published in 1887.

It may happen on rare occasions that a patient may be

confronted by the reality behind his dreams. Whether a physical edifice, a person, or a situation that has the tenor of deep familiarity, the subjective response of the dreamer is uniformly the same. The emotive content held in the dream – whether frightening, pleasurable, or mysterious – is drained away upon sight of the reality.... We may be certain that the apparent boredom of the subject does not prove the dream-content is false. Boredom may be most strongly felt when the dream-content is *real*. The subject recognizes on some deep level his inability to alter the conditions that he feels, and so finds himself overcome by fatigue, boredom, and indifference, to conceal from him *his fundamental helplessness in the face of a genuine problem which must be rectified*.

Months later, Elliot would conclude that Amy's bland reaction only indicated the depth of her feeling, and that Freud's analysis was correct; it protected her from a situation that had to be changed, but that Amy felt powerless to alter, especially considering whatever infantile memories remained from the traumatic death of her mother.

Yet at the time, Elliot felt disappointment with Amy's neutrality. Of all the possible reactions he had imagined when he first set out for the Congo, boredom was the least expected, and he utterly failed to grasp its significance – that the city of Zinj was so fraught with danger that Amy felt obliged in her own mind to push it aside, and to ignore it.

Elliot, Munro, and Ross spent a hot, difficult morning hacking their way through the dense bamboo and the clinging, tearing vines of secondary jungle growth to reach new buildings in the heart of the city. By midday, their efforts were rewarded as they entered structures unlike any they had seen before. These buildings were impressively engineered, enclosing vast cavernous spaces descending three and four stories beneath the ground.

Ross was delighted by the underground constructions, for it proved to her that the Zinj people had evolved the technology to dig into the earth, as was necessary for diamond mines. Munro expressed a similar view: 'These people,' he said, 'could do anything with earthworks.'

Despite their enthusiasm, they found nothing of interest in the depths of the city. They ascended to higher levels later in the day, coming upon a building so filled with reliefs that they termed it 'the gallery.' With the video camera hooked to the satellite linkup, they examined the pictures in the gallery.

These showed aspects of ordinary city life. There were domestic scenes of women cooking around fires, children playing a ball game with sticks, scribes squatting on the ground as they kept records on clay tablets. A whole wall of hunting scenes, the men in brief loincloths, armed with spears. And finally scenes of mining, men carrying baskets of stones from tunnels in the earth.

In this rich panorama, they noticed certain missing elements. The people of Zinj had dogs, used for hunting, and a variety of civet cat, kept as household pets – yet it had apparently never occurred to them to use animals as beasts of burden. All manual labor was done by human slaves. And they apparently never discovered the wheel for there were no carts or rolling vehicles. Everything was carried by hand in baskets.

Munro looked at the pictures for a long time and finally said 'Something else is missing.'

They were looking at a scene from the diamond mines, the dark pits in the ground from which men emerged carrying baskets heaped with gems.

'Of course!' Munro said, snapping his fingers. 'No police!'

Elliot suppressed a smile: he considered it only too predictable that a character like Munro would wonder about police in this long-dead society.

But Munro insisted his observation was significant. 'Look here,' he said. 'This city existed because of its diamond mines. It had no other reason for being, out here in the jungle. Zinj was a mining civilization – its wealth, its trade, its daily life, everything depended upon mining. It was a classic one-crop economy – and yet they didn't guard it, didn't regulate it, didn't control it?'

Elliot said, 'There are other things we haven't seen – pictures of people eating, for example. Perhaps it was taboo to show the guards.'

'Perhaps,' Munro said, unconvinced. 'But in every other mining complex in the world guards are ostentatiously prominent, as proof of control. Go to the South African diamond mines or the Bolivian emerald mines and the first thing you are made aware of is the security. But here,' he said, pointing to the reliefs, '*there are no guards.*'

Karen Ross suggested that perhaps they didn't need guards, perhaps the Zinjian society was orderly and peaceful. 'After all, it was a long time ago,' she said.

'Human nature doesn't change,' Munro insisted.

When they left the gallery, they came to an open courtyard, overgrown with tangled vines. The courtyard had a formal quality, heightened by the pillars of a temple-like building to one side. Their attention was immediately drawn to the courtyard floor. Strewn across the ground were dozens of stone paddles, of the kind Elliot had previously found.

'I'll be damned,' Elliot said. They picked their way through this field of paddles, and entered the building they came to call 'the temple.'

It consisted of a single large square room. The ceiling had been broken in several places, and hazy shafts of sunlight filtered down. Directly ahead, they saw an enormous mound of vines perhaps ten feet high, a pyramid of vegetation. Then they recognized that it was a statue.

Elliot climbed up on the statue and began stripping away the clinging foliage. It was hard work; the creepers had dug tenaciously into the stone. He glanced back at Munro. 'Better?'

'Come and look,' Munro said, with an odd expression on his face.

Elliot climbed down, stepped back to look. Although the statue was pitted and discolored, he could clearly see an enormous standing gorilla, the arms fierce, the arms stretched wide. In each hand, the gorilla held stone paddles like cymbals, ready to swing them together.

'My God.' Peter Elliot said.

'Gorilla,' Munro said with satisfaction.

Ross said, 'It's all clear now. These people worshiped gorillas. It was their religion.'

'But why would Amy say they weren't gorillas?'

'Ask her,' Munro said, glancing at his watch. 'I have to get us ready for tonight.'

3. Attack

They dug a moat outside the perimeter fence with collapsible metalloid shovels. The work continued long after sundown; they were obliged to turn on the red night lights while they filled the moat with water diverted from the nearby stream. Ross considered the moat a trivial obstacle – it was only a few inches deep and a foot wide. A man could step easily across it. In reply, Munro stood outside the moat and said, 'Amy, come here, I'll tickle you.'

With a delighted grunt, Amy came bounding toward him, but stopped abruptly on the other side of the water. 'Come on, I'll tickle you,' Munro said again, holding out his arms. 'Come on, girl.'

Still she would not cross. She signed irritably; Munro stepped over and lifted her across. 'Gorillas hate water,' he told Ross. 'I've seen them refuse to cross a stream smaller than this.' Amy was reaching up and scratching under his arms, then pointing to herself. The meaning was perfectly clear. 'Women,' Munro sighed, and bent over and tickled her vigorously. Amy rolled on the ground, grunting and snuffling and smiling broadly. When he stopped, she lay expectantly on the ground, waiting for more.

'That's all,' Munro said.

She signed to him.

'Sorry, I don't understand. No,' he laughed, 'signing slower doesn't help.' And then he understood what she wanted, and he carried her back across the moat again, into the camp. She kissed him wetly on the cheek.

'Better watch your monkey,' Munro said to Elliot as he sat down to dinner. He continued in this light bantering fashion, aware of the need to loosen everybody up; they were all nervous, crouching around the fire. But when the dinner was finished, and Kahega was off setting out the ammunition and checking the guns, Munro took Elliot aside and said, 'Chain her in your tent. If we start shooting tonight, I'd hate to have her running around in the dark. Some of the lads may not be too particular about telling one gorilla from another. Explain to her that it may get very noisy from the guns but she should not be frightened.'

'Is it going to get very noisy?' Elliot said.

'I imagine,' Munro said.

He took Amy into his tent and put on the sturdy chain leash she often wore in California. He tied one end to his cot, but it was a symbolic gesture; Amy could move it easily if she chose to. He made her promise to stay in the tent.

She promised. He stepped to the tent entrance, and she signed, *Amy like Peter*.

'Peter like Amy,' he said, smiling. 'Everything's going to be fine.'

He emerged into another world.

The red night lights had been doused, but in the flickering glow of the campfire he saw the goggle-eyed sentries in position around the compound. With the low throbbing pulse of the electrified fence, this sight created an unearthly atmosphere. Peter Elliot suddenly sensed the precariousness of their position – a handful of frightened people deep in the Congo rain forest, more than two hundred miles from the nearest human habitation.

Waiting.

He tripped over a black cable on the ground. Then he saw a network of cables, snaking over the compound, running to the guns of each sentry. He noticed then that the guns had an unfamiliar shape – they were somehow too slender, too insubstantial – and that the black cables ran from the guns to squat, snub-nosed mechanisms mounted on short tripods at intervals around the camp.

He saw Ross near the fire, setting up the tape recorder. 'What the hell is all this?' he whispered, pointing to the cables.

'That's a LATRAP. For laser-tracking projectile,' she whispered. 'The LATRAP system consists of multiple LGSDs attached to sequential RFSDs.'

She told him that the sentries held guns which were actually laser-guided sight devices, linked to rapid-firing sensor devices on tripods. 'They lock onto the target,' she said, 'and do the actual shooting once the target is identified. It's a jungle warfare system. The RFSDs have marlan-baffle silencers so the enemy won't know where the firing is coming from. Just make sure you don't step in front of one, because they automatically lock onto body heat.'

Ross gave him the tape recorder, and went off to check the fuel cells powering the perimeter fence. Elliot glanced at the sentries in the outer darkness; Munro waved cheerfully to him. Elliot realized that the sentries with their grasshopper goggles and their acronymic weapons could see him far better that he could see them. They looked like beings from another universe, dropped into the timeless jungle.

Waiting.

The hours passed. The jungle perimeter was silent except for the murmur of water in the moat. Occasionally the porters called to one another softly, making some joke in Swahili; but they never smoked because of the heat-sensing machinery. Eleven o'clock passed, and then midnight, and then one o'clock.

He heard Amy snoring in his tent, her noisy rasping audible above the throb of the electrified fence. He glanced over at Ross sleeping on the ground, her finger on the switch for the night lights. He looked at his watch and yawned; nothing was going to happen tonight; Munro was wrong.

Then he heard the breathing sound.

The sentries heard it too, swinging their guns in the darkness. Elliot pointed the recorder microphone toward the sound but it was hard to determine its exact location. The wheezing sighs seemed to come from all parts of the jungle at once, drifting with the night fog, soft and pervasive.

He watched the needles wiggle on the recording gauges. And then the needles bounced into the red, as Elliot heard a dull thud, and the gurgle of water. Everyone heard it; the sentries clicked off their safeties.

Elliot crept with his tape recorder toward the perimeter fence and looked out at the moat. Foliage moved beyond the fence. The sighing grew louder. He heard the gurgle of water and saw a dead tree trunk lying across the moat.

That was what the slapping sound had been: a bridge being placed across the moat. In that instant Elliot realized they had vastly underestimated whatever they were up against. He signaled Munro to come and look, but Munro was waving him away from the fence and pointing emphatically to the squat tripod on the ground near his feet. Before Elliot could move, the colobus monkeys began to shriek in the trees overhead – and the first of the gorillas silently charged.

He had a glimpse of an enormous animal, distinctly gray in color, racing up to him as he ducked down; a moment later, the gorilla hit the electrified fence with a shower of spitting sparks and the odor of burning flesh.

It was the start of an eerie, silent battle.

Emerald laser beams flashed through the air; the tripod-mounted machine guns made a soft *thew-thew-thew* as the bullets spit outward, the aiming mechanisms whining as the barrels spun and fired, spun and fired again. Every tenth bullet was a white phosphorus tracer; the air was crisscrossed green and white over Elliot's head.

The gorillas attacked from all directions; six of them simultaneously hit the fence and were repelled in a crackling burst of sparks. Still more charged, throwing themselves on the flimsy perimeter mesh, yet the sizzle of sparks and the shriek of the colobus monkeys was the loudest sound they heard. And then he saw gorillas in the trees overhanging the campsite. Munro and Kahega began firing upward, silent laser beams streaking into the foliage. He heard the sighing sound again.

Elliot turned and saw more gorillas tearing at the fence, which had gone dead – there were no more sparks.

And he realized that this swift, sophisticated equipment was not holding the gorillas back – they needed the noise. Munro had the same thought, because he shouted in Swahili for the men to hold their fire, and called to Elliot, 'Pull the silencers! The silencers!'

Elliot grabbed the black barrel on the first tripod mechanism and plucked it away, swearing – it was very hot. Immediately as he stepped away from the tripod, a stuttering sound filled the air, and two gorillas fell heavily from the trees, one still alive. The gorilla charged him as he pulled away the silencer from the second tripod. The stubby barrel swung around and blasted the gorilla at very close range; warm liquid spattered Elliot's face. He pulled the silencer from the third tripod and threw himself to the ground.

Deafening machine-gun fire and clouds of acrid cordite had an immediate effect on the gorillas; they backed off in disorder. There was a period of silence, although the sentries fired laser shots that sent the tripod machines scanning rapidly across the jungle landscape, whirring back and forth, searching for a target.

Then the machines stopped hunting, and paused. The jungle around them was still.

The gorillas were gone.

DAY 11: ZINJ
June 23, 1979

1. Gorilla Elliotensis

The gorilla corpses lay stretched on the ground, the bodies already stiffening in the morning warmth. Elliot spent two hours examining the animals, both adult males in the prime of life.

The most striking feature was the uniform gray color. The two known races of gorilla, the mountain gorilla in Virunga, and the lowland gorilla near the coast, both had black hair. Infants were often brown with a white tuft of hair at the rump, but their hair darkened within the first five years. By the age of twelve, adult males had developed the silver patch along their back and rump, the sign of sexual maturity.

With age, gorillas turned gray – as did people – in much the same way. Male gorillas first developed a spot of gray above each ear, and as the years passed more body hair turned gray. Old animals in their late twenties and thirties sometimes turned entirely gray except for their arms, which remained black.

But from their teeth Elliot estimated that these males were no more than ten years old. All their pigmentation seemed lighter, eye and skin color as well as hair. Gorilla skin was black, and eyes were dark brown. But here the pigmentation was distinctly gray, and the eyes were light yellow brown.

As much as anything it was the eyes that set him thinking.

Next Elliot measured the bodies. The crown-heel length was 139.2 and 141.7 centimeters. Male mountain gorillas had been recorded from 147 to 205 centimeters, with an average height of 175 centimeters – five feet eight inches. But these animals stood about four feet six inches tall. They were distinctly small for gorillas. He weighed them: 255 pounds and 347 pounds. Most mountain gorillas weighed between 280 and 450 pounds.

Elliot recorded thirty additional skeletal measurements for later analysis by the computer back in San Francisco. Because now he was convinced that he was onto something. With a knife, he dissected the head of the first animal, cutting away the gray skin to reveal the underlying muscle and bone. His interest was the sagittal crest, the bony ridge running along the center of the skull from the forehead to the back of the neck. The sagittal crest was a distinctive feature of gorilla skull architecture not found in other apes or man; it was what gave gorillas a pointy-headed look.

Elliot determined that the sagittal crest was poorly developed in these males. In general, the cranial musculature resembled a chimpanzee's far more than a gorilla's. Elliot made additional measurements of the molar cusps, the jaw, the simian shelf, and the brain case.

By midday, his conclusion was clear: this was at least a new race of gorilla, equal to the mountain and lowland gorilla – and it was possibly a new species of animal entirely.

'Something happens to the man who discovers a new species of animal,' wrote Lady Elizabeth Forstmann in 1879. 'At once he forgets his family and friends, and all those who were near and dear to him; he forgets colleagues who supported his professional efforts; most cruelly he forgets parents and children; in short, he abandons all who knew him prior to his insensate lust for fame at the hands of the demon called Science.'

Lady Forstmann understood, for her husband had just left her after discovering the Norwegian blue-crested grouse in 1878. 'In vain,' she observed, 'does one ask what it matters that another bird or animal is added to the rich panoply of God's creations, which already number – by Linnaean reckoning – in the millions. There is no response to such a question, for the discoverer has joined the ranks of the immortals, at least as he imagines it, and he lies beyond the power of mere people to dissuade him from his course.'

Certainly Peter Elliot would have denied that his own behavior resembled that of the dissolute Scottish nobleman.* Nevertheless he found he was bored by the prospect of further exploration of Zinj; he had no interest in diamonds, or Amy's dreams; he wished only to return home with a skeleton of the new ape, which would astonish colleagues around the world. He suddenly remembered he did not own a tuxedo, and he found himself preoccupied with matters of nomenclature; he imagined in future three species of African apes:

> *Pan troglodytes*, the chimpanzee.
> *Gorilla gorilla*, the gorilla.
> *Gorilla elliotensis*, a new species of gray gorilla.

Even if the species category and name were ultimately rejected, he would have accomplished far more than most scientists studying primates could ever hope to achieve.

Elliot was dazzled by his own prospects.

In retrospect, no one was thinking clearly that morning. When Elliot said he wanted to transmit the recorded breathing sounds to Houston,

---

* Sir Antony Forstmann died of gambling debts and syphilis in 1880.

Ross replied it was a trivial detail that could wait. Elliot did not press her; they both later regretted their decision.

And when they heard booming explosions like distant artillery fire that morning, they paid no attention. Ross assumed it was General Muguru's men fighting the Kigani. Munro told her that the fighting was at least fifty miles away, too far for the sound to carry, but offered no alternative explanation for the noise.

And because Ross skipped the morning transmission to Houston, she was not informed of new geological changes that might have given new significance to the explosive detonations.

They were seduced by the technology employed the night before, secure in their sense of indomitable power. Only Munro remained immune. He had checked their ammunition supplies with discouraging results. 'That laser system is splendid but it uses up bullets like there's no tomorrow,' Munro said. 'Last night consumed half of our total ammunition.'

'What can we do?' Elliot asked.

'I was hoping you'd have an answer for that,' Munro said. 'You examined the bodies.'

Elliot stated his belief that they were confronted with a new species of primate. He summarized the anatomical findings, which supported his beliefs.

'That's all well and good,' Munro said. 'But I'm interested in how they act, not how they look. You said it yourself – gorillas are usually diurnal animals, and these are nocturnal. Gorillas are usually shy and avoid men, while these are aggressive and attack men fearlessly. Why?'

Elliot had to admit that he didn't know.

'Considering our ammunition supplies, I think we'd better find out,' Munro said.

2. The Temple

The logical place to begin was the temple, with its enormous, menacing gorilla statue. They returned that afternoon, and found behind the statue a succession of small cubicle-like rooms. Ross thought that priests who worshiped the cult of the gorilla lived here.

She had an elaborate explanation: 'The gorillas in the surrounding jungle terrorized the people of Zinj, who offered sacrifices to appease the gorillas. The priests were a separate class, secluded from society. Look here, at the entrance to the line of cubicles, there is this little room. A guard stayed here to keep people away from the priests. It was a whole system of belief.'

Elliot was not convinced, and neither was Munro. 'Even religion is practical,' Munro said. 'It's supposed to benefit you.'

'People worship what they fear,' Ross said, 'hoping to control it.'

'But how could they control the gorillas?' Munro asked. 'What could they do?'

When the answer finally came it was startling, for they had it all backward.

They moved past the cubicles to a series of long corridors, decorated with bas-reliefs. Using their infrared computer system, they were able to see the reliefs, which were scenes arranged in a careful order like a picture textbook.

The first scene showed a series of caged gorillas. A black man stood near the cages holding a stick in his hand.

The second picture showed an African standing with two gorillas, holding ropes around their necks.

A third showed an African instructing the gorillas in a courtyard. The gorillas were tethered to vertical poles, each with a ring at the top.

The final picture showed the gorillas attacking a line of straw dummies, which hung from an overhead stone support. They now knew the meaning of what they had found in the courtyard of the gymnasium, and the jail.

'My God,' Elliot said. 'They *trained* them.'

Munro nodded. 'Trained them as guards to watch over the mines. An animal élite, ruthless and incorruptible. Not a bad idea when you think about it.'

Ross looked at the building around her again, realizing it wasn't a temple but a school. An objection occurred to her: these pictures were hundreds of years old, the trainers long gone. Yet the gorillas were still here. 'Who teaches them now?'

'They do,' Elliot said. 'They teach each other.'

'Is that possible?'

'Perfectly possible. Conspecific teaching occurs among primates.'

This had been a longstanding question among researchers. But Washoe, the first primate in history to learn sign language, taught ASL to her offspring. Language-skilled primates freely taught other animals in captivity; for that matter, they would teach people, signing slowly and repeatedly until the stupid uneducated human person got the point.

So it was possible for a primate tradition of language and behavior to be carried on for generations. 'You mean,' Ross said, 'that the people in this city have been gone for centuries, but the gorillas they trained are still here?'

'That's the way it looks,' Elliot said.

'And they use stone tools?' she asked. 'Stone paddles?'

'Yes,' Elliot said. The idea of tool use was not as farfetched as it first seemed. Chimpanzees were capable of elaborate tool use, of which the most striking example was 'termite fishing.' Chimps would make a twig, carefully bending it to their specifications, and then spend hours over a termite mound, fishing with the stick to catch succulent grubs.

Human observers labeled this activity 'primitive tool use' until they tried it themselves. It turned out that making a satisfactory twig and catching termites was not primitive at all; at least it proved to be beyond the ability of people who tried to duplicate it. Human fishermen quit, with a new respect for the chimpanzees, and a new observation – they now noticed that younger chimps spent days watching their elders make sticks and twirl them in the mound. Young chimps literally *learned* how to do it, and the learning process extended over a period of years.

This began to look suspiciously like culture; the apprenticeship of young Ben Franklin, printer, was not so different from the apprenticeship of young Chimpanzee, termite fisher. Both learned their skills over a period of years by observing their elders; both made mistakes on the way to ultimate success.

Yet manufactured stone tools implied a quantum jump beyond twigs and termites. The privileged position of stone tools as the special province of mankind might have remained sacrosanct were it not for a single iconoclastic researcher. In 1971, the British scientist R. V. S. Wright decided to teach an ape to make stone tools. His pupil was a five-year-old orangutan named Abang in the Bristol zoo. Wright presented Abang with a box containing food, bound with a rope; he showed Abang how to cut the rope with a flint chip to get the food. Abang got the point in an hour.

Wright then showed Abang how to make a stone chip by striking a pebble against a flint core. This was a more difficult lesson; over a period of weeks, Abang required a total of three hours to learn to grasp the flint core between his toes, strike a sharp chip, cut the rope, and get the food.

The point of the experiment was not that apes used stone tools, but that the ability to make stone tools was literally within their grasp. Wright's experiment was one more reason to think that human beings were not as unique as they had previously imagined themselves to be.

'But why would Amy say they weren't gorillas?'

'Because they're not,' Elliot said. 'These animals don't look like gorillas and they don't act like gorillas. They are physically and behaviorally different.' He went on to voice his suspicion that not only had these animals been trained, they had been *bred* – perhaps interbred with chimpanzees or, more strangely still, with men.

They thought he was joking. But the facts were disturbing. In 1960, the first blood protein studies quantified the kinship between man and ape. Biochemically man's nearest relative was the chimpanzee, much closer than the gorilla. In 1964, chimpanzee kidneys were successfully transplanted into men; blood transfusions were also possible.

But the degree of similarity was not fully known until 1975, when biochemists compared the DNA of chimps and men. It was discovered that chimps differed from men by only 1 percent of their DNA strands. And almost no one wanted to acknowledge one consequence: with modern DNA hybridization techniques and embryonic implantation, ape-ape crosses were certain, and man-ape crosses were possible.

Of course, the fourteenth-century inhabitants of Zinj had no way to mate DNA strands. But Elliot pointed out that they had consistently underestimated the skills of the Zinj people, who at the very least had managed, five hundred years ago, to carry out sophisticated animal-training procedures only duplicated by Western scientists within the last ten years.

And as Elliot saw it, the animals the Zinjians had trained presented an awesome problem.

'We have to face the realities,' he said. 'When Amy was given a human IQ test, she scored ninety-two. For all practical purposes, Amy is as smart as a human being, and in many ways she is smarter – more perceptive and sensitive. She can manipulate us at least as skillfully as we can manipulate her.

'These gray gorillas possess that same intelligence, yet they have been single-mindedly bred to be the primate equivalent of Doberman pinschers – guard animals, attack animals, trained for cunning and viciousness. But they are much brighter and more resourceful than dogs. And they will continue their attacks until they succeed in killing us all, as they have killed everyone who has come here before.'

3. Looking Through the Bars

In 1975, the mathematician S. L. Berensky reviewed the literature on primate language and reached a startling conclusion. 'There is no doubt,' he announced, 'that primates are far superior in intelligence to man.'

In Berensky's mind, 'The salient question – which every human visitor to the zoo intuitively asks – is, who is behind the bars? Who is caged, and who is free? . . . On both sides of the bars primates can be observed making faces at each other. It is too facile to say that man is superior because he has made the zoo. We impose our special horror of barred captivity – a form of punishment among our species – and assume that other primates feel as we do.'

Berensky likened primates to foreign ambassadors. 'Apes have for centuries managed to get along with human beings, as ambassadors from their species. In recent years, they have even learned to communicate with human beings using sign language. But it is a one-sided diplomatic exchange; no human being has attempted to live in ape society, to master their language and customs, to eat their food, to live as they do. The apes have learned to talk to us, but we have never learned to talk to them. Who, then, should be judged the greater intellect?'

Berensky added a prediction. 'The time will come,' he said, 'when circumstances may force some human beings to communicate with a primate society on its own terms. Only then human beings will become aware of their complacent egotism with regard to other animals.'

The ERTS expedition, isolated deep in the Congo rain forest, now faced just such a problem. Confronted by a new species of gorilla-like animal, they somehow had to deal with it on its own terms.

During the evening, Elliot transmitted the taped breath sounds to Houston, and from there they were relayed to San Francisco. The transcript which followed the transmission was brief:

Seamans wrote: RECVD TRNSMISN. SHLD HELP.

IMPORTNT-NEED TRNSLATION SOON, Elliot typed back. WHN HAVE? COMPUTR ANALYSS DIFICLT-PROBLMS XCEED MGNITUDE CSL / JSL TRNSLATN.

'What does that mean?' Ross said.

'He's saying that the translation problems exceed the problem of translating Chinese or Japanese sign language.'

She hadn't known there was a Chinese or Japanese sign language, but Elliot explained that there were sign languages for all major languages, and each followed its own rules. For instance, BSL, British sign language, was totally different from ASL, American sign language, even though spoken and written English language was virtually identical in the two countries.

Different sign languages had different grammar and syntax, and even obeyed different sign traditions. Chinese sign language used the middle finger pointing outward for several signs, such as TWO WEEKS FROM NOW and BROTHER, although this configuration was insulting and unacceptable in American sign language.

'But this is a spoken language,' Ross said.

'Yes,' Elliot said, 'but it's a complicated problem. We aren't likely to get it translated soon.'

By nightfall, they had two additional pieces of information. Ross ran a computer simulation through Houston which came back with a probability course of three days and a standard deviation of two days to find the diamond mines. That meant they should be prepared for five more days at the site. Food was not a problem, but ammunition was: Munro proposed to use tear gas.

They expected the gray gorillas to try a different approach, and they did, attacking immediately after dark. The battle on the night of June 23 was punctuated by the coughing explosions of canisters and the sizzling hiss of the gas. The strategy was effective; the gorillas were driven away, and did not return again that night.

Munro was pleased. He announced that they had enough tear gas to hold off the gorillas for a week, perhaps more. For the moment, their problems appeared to be solved.

DAY 12: ZINJ
June 24, 1979

1. The Offensive

Shortly after dawn, they discovered the bodies of Mulewe and Akari near their tent. Apparently the attack the night before had been a diversion, allowing one gorilla to enter the compound, kill the porters, and slip out again. Even more disturbing, they could find no clue to how the gorilla had got through the electrified fence and back out again.

A careful search revealed a section of fence torn near the bottom. A long stick lay on the ground nearby. The gorillas had used the stick to lift the bottom of the fence, enabling one to crawl through. And before leaving, the gorillas had carefully restored the fence to its original condition.

The intelligence implied by such behavior was hard to accept. 'Time and again,' Elliot said later, 'we came up against our prejudices about animals. We kept expecting the gorillas to behave in stupid, stereotyped ways but they never did. We never treated them as flexible and responsive adversaries, though they had already reduced our numbers by one fourth.'

Munro had difficulty accepting the calculated hostility of the gorillas. His experience had taught him that animals in nature were indifferent to man. Finally he concluded that 'these animals had been trained by men, and I had to think of them as men. The question became what would I do if they were men?'

For Munro the answer was clear: take the offensive.

Amy agreed to lead them into the jungle where she said the gorillas lived. By ten o'clock that morning, they were moving up the hillsides north of the city armed with machine guns. It was not long before they found gorilla spoor – quantities of dung, and nests on the ground and in the trees. Munro was disturbed by what he saw; some trees held twenty or thirty nests, suggesting a large population of animals.

Ten minutes later, they came upon a group of ten gray gorillas feeding on succulent vines: four males and three females, a juvenile, and two scampering infants. The adults were lazy, basking in the sun, eating in desultory fashion. Several other animals slept on their backs, snoring loudly. They all seemed remarkably unguarded.

Munro gave a hand signal; the safeties clicked off the guns. He prepared to fire into the group when Amy tugged at his trouser leg. He looked off and 'had the shock of my bloody life. Up the slope was another group, perhaps ten or twelve animals – and then I saw another group – and another – and another still. There must have been three hundred or more. The hillside was *crawling* with gray gorillas.'

The largest gorilla group ever sighted in the wild had been thirty-one individuals, in Kabara in 1971, and even that sighting was disputed. Most researchers thought it was actually two groups seen briefly together, since the usual group size was ten to fifteen individuals. Elliot found three hundred animals 'an awesome sight.' But he was even more impressed by the behavior of the animals. As they browsed and fed in the sunlight, they behaved very much like ordinary gorillas in the wild, but there were important differences.

'From the first sighting, I never had any doubt that they had language. Their wheezing vocalizations were striking and clearly constituted a form of language. In addition they used sign language, although nothing like what we knew. Their hand gestures were delivered with outstretched arms in a graceful way, rather like Thai dancers. These hand movements seemed to complement or add to the sighing vocalizations. Obviously the gorillas had been taught, or had elaborated on their own, a language system far more sophisticated than the pure sign language of laboratory apes in the twentieth century.'

Some abstract corner of Elliot's mind considered this discovery tremendously exciting, while at the same time he shared the fear of the others around him. Crouched behind the dense foliage they held their breath and watched the gorillas feed on the opposite hillside. Although the gorillas seemed peaceful, the humans watching them felt a tension approaching panic at being so close to such great numbers of them. Finally, at Munro's signal, they slipped back down the trail, and returned to the camp.

The porters were digging graves for Akari and Mulewe in camp. It was a grim reminder of their jeopardy as they discussed their alternatives. Munro said to Elliot, 'They don't seem to be aggressive during the day.'

'No,' Elliot said. 'Their behavior looks quite typical – if anything, it's more sluggish than that of ordinary gorillas in daytime. Probably most of the males are sleeping during the day.'

'How many animals on the hillside are males?' Munro asked. They had already concluded that only male animals participated in the attacks; Munro was asking for odds.

Elliot said, 'Most studies have found that adult males constitute fifteen percent of gorilla groupings. And most studies show that isolated observations underestimate troop size by twenty-five percent. There are more animals than you see at any given moment.'

The arithmetic was disheartening. They had counted three hundred gorillas on the hillside, which meant there were probably four hundred, of which 15 percent were males. That meant that there were sixty attacking animals – and only nine in their defending group.

'Hard,' Munro said, shaking his head.

Amy had one solution. She signed, *Go now.*

Ross asked what she said and Elliot told her, 'She wants to leave. I think she's right.'

'Don't be ridiculous,' Ross said. 'We haven't found the diamonds. We can't leave now.'

Go *now*, Amy signed again.

They looked at Munro. Somehow the group had decided that Munro would make the decision of what to do next. 'I want the diamonds as much as anyone,' he said. 'But they won't be much use to us if we're dead. We have no choice. We must leave if we can.'

Ross swore, in florid Texan style.

Elliot said to Munro, 'What do you mean, if we can?'

'I mean,' Munro said, 'that they may not let us leave.'

2. Departure

Following Munro's instructions, they carried only minimal supplies of food and ammunition. They left everything else – the tents, the perimeter defenses, the communications equipment, everything, in the sunlit clearing at midday.

Munro glanced back over his shoulder and hoped he was doing the right thing. In the 1960s, the Congo mercenaries had had an ironic rule: 'Don't leave home.' It had multiple meanings, including the obvious one that none of them should ever have come to the Congo in the first place. It also meant that once established in a fortified camp or colonial town you were unwise to step out into the surrounding jungle, whatever the provocation. Several of Munro's friends had bought it in the jungle because they had foolishly left home. The news would come to them: 'Digger bought it last week outside Stanleyville.' 'Outside? Why'd he leave home?'

Munro was leading the expedition outside now, and home was the little silver camp with its perimeter defense behind them. Back in that camp, they were sitting ducks for the attacking gorillas. The mercenaries had had something to say about that, too: 'Better a sitting duck than a dead duck.'

`As they marched through the rain forest, Munro was painfully aware of the single-file column strung out behind him, the least defensible formation. He watched the jungle foliage move in as their path narrowed. He did not remember this track being so narrow when they had come to the city. Now they were hemmed in by close ferns and spreading palms. The gorillas might be only a few feet away, concealed in the dense foliage, and they wouldn't know it until it was too late.

They walked on.

Munro thought if they could reach the eastern slopes of Mukenko, they would be all right. The gray gorillas were localized near the city, and would not follow them far. One or two hours' walking, and they would be beyond danger.

He checked his watch: they had been gone ten minutes.

And then he heard the sighing sound. It seemed to come from all directions. He saw the foliage moving before him, shifting as if blown by a wind. Only there was no wind. He heard the sighing grow louder.

The column halted at the edge of a ravine, which followed a streambed past sloping jungle walls on both sides. It was the perfect spot for an ambush. Along the line he heard the safeties click on the machine guns. Kahega came up. 'Captain, what do we do?'

Munro watched the foliage move, and heard the sighing. He could only guess at the numbers concealed in the bush. Twenty? Thirty? Too many, in any case.

Kahega pointed up the hillside to a track that ran above the ravine. 'Go up there?'

For a long time, Munro did not answer. Finally, he said, 'No, not up there.'

'Then where, Captain?'

'Back,' Munro said. 'We go back.'

When they turned away from the ravine, the sighing faded and the foliage ceased its movement. When he looked back over his shoulder for a last glimpse, the ravine appeared an ordinary passage in the jungle, without threat of any kind. But Munro knew the truth. They could not leave.

3. Return

Elliot's idea came in a flash of insight. 'In the middle of the camp,' he later related, 'I was looking at Amy signing to Kahega. Amy was asking him for a drink, but Kahega didn't know Ameslan, and he kept shrugging helplessly. It occurred to me that the linguistic skill of the gray gorillas was both their great advantage and their Achilles' heel.'

Elliot proposed to capture a single gray gorilla, learn its language, and use that language to establish communication with the other animals. Under normal circumstances it would take several months to learn a new ape language, but Elliot thought he could do it in a matter of hours.

Seamans was already at work on the gray-gorilla verbalizations; all he needed was further input. But Elliot had decided that the gray gorillas employed a combination of spoken sounds and sign language. And the sign language would be easy to work out.

Back at Berkeley, Seamans had developed a computer program called APE, for animal pattern explanation. APE was capable of observing Amy and assigning meanings to her signs. Since the APE program utilized declassified army software subroutines for code-breaking, it was capable of identifying new signs, and translating these as well. Although APE was intended to work with Amy in ASL, there was no reason why it would not work with an entirely new language.

If they could forge satellite links from the Congo to Houston to Berkeley, they could feed video data from a captive animal directly into the APE program. And APE promised a speed of translation far beyond the capacity of any human observer. (The army software was designed to break enemy codes in minutes.)

Elliot and Ross were convinced it would work; Munro was not. He made some disparaging comments about interrogating prisoners of war. 'What do you intend to do,' he said, 'torture the animal?'

'We will employ situational stress,' Elliot said, 'to elicit language usage.' He was laying out test materials on the ground: a banana, a bowl of water, a piece of candy, a stick, a succulent vine, stone paddles. 'We'll scare the hell out of her if we have to.'

'Her?'

'Of course,' Elliot said, loading the Thoralen dart gun. 'Her.'

4. Capture

He wanted a female without an infant. An infant would create difficulties.

Pushing through waist-high undergrowth, he found himself on the edge of a sharp ridge and saw nine animals grouped below him: two males, five females, and two juveniles. They were foraging through the jungle twenty feet below. He watched the group long enough to be sure that all the females used language, and that there were no infants concealed in the foliage. Then he waited for his chance.

The gorillas fed casually among the ferns, plucking up tender shoots, which they chewed lazily. After several minutes, one female moved up from the group to forage nearer the top of the ridge where he was crouching. She was separated from the rest of the group by more than ten yards.

Elliot raised the dart pistol in both hands and squinted down the sight at the female. She was perfectly positioned. He watched, squeezed the trigger slowly – and lost his footing on the ridge. He fell crashing down the slope, right into the midst of the gorillas.

Elliot lay unconscious on his back, twenty feet below, but his chest was moving, and his arm twitched; Munro felt certain that he was all right. Munro was only concerned about the gorillas.

The gray gorillas had seen Elliot fall and now moved toward the body. Eight or nine animals clustered around him, staring impassively, signing.

Munro slipped the safety off his gun.

Elliot groaned, touched his head, and opened his eyes. Munro saw Elliot stiffen as he saw the gorillas, but he did not move. Three mature males crouched very close to him, and he understood the precariousness of his situation. Elliot lay motionless on the ground for nearly a minute. The gorillas whispered and signed, but they did not come any closer.

Finally Elliot sat up on one elbow, which caused a burst of signing but no direct threatening behavior.

On the hillside above, Amy tugged at Munro's sleeve, signing emphatically. Munro shook his head: he did not understand; he raised his machine gun again, and Amy bit his kneecap. The pain was excruciating. It was all Munro could do to keep from screaming.

Elliot, lying on the ground below, tried to control his breathing. The gorillas were very close – close enough for him to touch them, close enough to smell the sweet, musty odor of their bodies. They were agitated; the males had started grunting, a rhythmic *ho-ho-ho*.

He decided he had better get to his feet, slowly and methodically. He thought that if he could put some distance between himself and the animals, their sense of threat would be reduced. But as soon as he began to move the grunting grew louder, and one of the males began a sideways crablike movement, slapping the ground with his flat palms.

Immediately Elliot lay back down. The gorillas relaxed, and he decided he had done the correct thing. The animals were confused by this human being crashing down in their midst; they apparently did not expect contact with men in foraging areas.

He decided to wait them out, if necessary remaining on his back for several hours until they lost interest and moved off. He breathed slowly, regularly, aware that he was sweating. Probably he smelled of fear – but like men, gorillas had a poorly developed sense of smell. They did not react to the odor of fear. He waited. The gorillas were sighing and signing swiftly, trying to decide what to do. Then one male abruptly resumed his crabwise movements, slapping the ground and staring at Elliot. Elliot did not move. In his mind, he reviewed the stages of attack behavior: grunting, sideways movement, slapping, tearing up grass, beating chest –

Charging.

The male gorilla began tearing up grass. Elliot felt his heart pounding. The gorilla was a huge animal, easily three hundred pounds. He reared up on his hind legs and beat his chest with flat palms, making a hollow sound. Elliot wondered what Munro was doing above. And then he heard a crash, and he looked up to see Amy tumbling down the hillside, breaking her fall by grabbing at branches and ferns. She landed at Elliot's feet.

The gorillas could not have been more surprised. The large male ceased beating his chest, dropped down from his upright posture, and glowered at Amy.

Amy grunted.

The large male moved menacingly toward Peter, but he never took his eyes off Amy. Amy watched him without response. It was a clear test of dominance. The male moved closer and closer, without hesitation –

Amy bellowed, a deafening sound; Elliot jumped in surprise. He had only heard her do it once or twice before in moments of extreme rage. It was unusual for females to roar, and the other gorillas were alarmed. Amy's forearms stiffened, her back went rigid, her face became tense. She stared aggressively at the male and roared again.

The male paused, tilted his head to one side. He seemed to be thinking it over. Finally he backed off, rejoining the semicircle of gray apes around Elliot's head.

Amy deliberately rested her hand on Elliot's leg, establishing possession. A juvenile male, four or five years old, impulsively scurried forward, baring his teeth. Amy slapped him across the face, and the juvenile whined and scrambled back to the safety of his group.

Amy glowered at the other gorillas. And then she began signing. *Go away leave Amy go away.*

The gorillas did not respond.

Peter good human person. But she seemed to be aware that the gorillas did not understand, for she then did something remarkable: she sighed, making the same wheezing sound that the gorillas made.

The gorillas were startled, and stared at one another.

But if Amy was speaking their language, it was without effect: they remained where they were. And the more she sighed, the more their reaction diminished, until finally they stared blandly at her.

She was not getting through to them.

Amy now came alongside Peter's head and began to groom him, plucking at his beard and scalp. The gray gorillas signed rapidly. Then the male began his rhythmic *ho-ho-ho* once more. When she saw this Amy turned to Peter and signed, *Amy hug Peter.* He was surprised: Amy never volunteered to hug Peter. Ordinarily she only wanted Peter to hug and tickle Amy.

Elliot sat up and she immediately pulled him to her chest, pressing his face into her hair. At once the male gorilla ceased grunting. The gray gorillas began to backpedal, as if they had committed some error. In that moment, Elliot understood: *she was treating him like her infant.*

This was classic primate behavior in aggressive situations. Primates carried strong inhibitions against harming infants, and this inhibition was invoked by adult animals in many contexts. Male baboons often ended their fight when one male grabbed an infant and clutched it to his chest; the sight of the small animal inhibited further attack. Chimpanzees showed more subtle variations of the same thing. If juvenile chimp play turned too brutal, a male would grab one juvenile and clutch it maternally, even though in this case both parent and child were symbolic. Yet the posture was sufficient to evoke the inhibition against further violence. In this case Amy was not only halting the male's attack but protecting Elliot as well, by treating him as an infant – if the gorillas would accept a bearded six-foot-tall infant.

They did.

They disappeared back into the foliage. Amy released Elliot from her fierce grip. She looked at him and signed, *Dumb things.*

'Thank you, Amy,' he said and kissed her.

Peter tickle Amy Amy good gorilla.

'You bet,' he said, and he tickled her for the next several minutes, while she rolled on the ground, grunting happily.

It was two o'clock in the afternoon when they returned to camp. Ross said, 'Did you get a gorilla?'

'No,' Elliot said.

'Well, it doesn't matter,' Ross said, 'because I can't raise Houston.'

Elliot was stunned: 'More electronic jamming?'

'Worse than that,' Ross said. She had spent an hour trying to establish a satellite link with Houston, and had failed. Each time the link was broken within seconds. Finally, after confirming that there was no fault with her equipment, she had checked the date. 'It's June 24,' she said. 'And we had communications trouble with the last Congo expedition on May 28. That's twenty-seven days ago.'

When Elliot still didn't get it, Munro said, 'She's telling you it's solar.'

'That's right,' Ross said. 'This is an ionospheric disturbance of solar origin.' Most disruptions of the earth's ionosphere – the thin layer of ionized molecules 50–250 miles up – were caused by phenomena such as sunspots on the surface of the sun. Since the sun rotated every twenty-seven days, these disturbances often recurred a month later.

'Okay,' Elliot said, 'it's solar. How long will it last?'

Ross shook her head. 'Ordinarily, I would say a few hours, a day at most. But this seems to be a severe disturbance and it's come up very suddenly. Five hours ago we had perfect communications – and now we have none at all. Something unusual is going on. It could last a week.'

'No communications for a week? No computer tie-ins, no nothing?'

'That's right,' Ross said evenly. 'From this moment on, we are entirely cut off from the outside world.'

5. Isolation

The largest solar flare of 1979 was recorded on June 24, by the Kitt Peak Observatory near Tucson, Arizona, and duly passed on to the Space Environment Services Center in Boulder, Colorado. At first the SESC did not believe the incoming data: even by the gigantic standards of solar astronomy, this flare, designated 78/06/414aa, was a monster.

The cause of solar flares in unknown, but they are generally associated with sunspots. In this case the flare appeared as an extremely bright spot ten thousand miles in diameter, affecting not only alpha hydrogen and ionized calcium spectral lines but also the white light spectrum from the sun. Such a 'continuous spectrum' flare was extremely rare.

Nor could the SESC believe the computed consequences. Solar flares release an enormous amount of energy; even a modest flare can double the amount of ultraviolet radiation emitted by the entire solar surface. But flare 78/06/414aa was almost *tripling* ultraviolet emissions. Within 8.3 minutes of its first appearance along the rotating rim – the time it takes light to reach the earth from the sun – this surge of ultraviolet radiation began to disrupt the ionosphere of the earth.

The consequence of the flare was that radio communications on a planet ninety-three million miles away were seriously disrupted. This was especially true for radio transmissions which utilized low signal strengths. Commercial radio stations generating kilowatts of power were hardly inconvenienced, but the Congo Field Survey, transmitting signals on the order of twenty thousand watts, was unable to establish satellite links. And since the solar flare also ejected X-rays and atomic particles which would not reach the earth for a full day, the radio disruption would last at least one day, and perhaps longer. At ERTS in Houston, technicians reported to Travis that the SESC predicted a time course of ionic disruption of four to eight days.

'You mean we're going to be out of contact with them for four to eight days?' Travis said.

'That's how it looks. Ross'll probably figure it out,' the technician said, 'when she can't re-establish today.'

'They need that computer hookup,' Travis said. The ERTS staff had run five computer simulations and the outcome was always the same – short of airlifting in a small army, Ross's expedition was in serious trouble. Survival projections were running 'point two four four and change' – only one chance in four that the Congo expedition would get out alive, assuming the help of the computer link which was now broken.

Travis wondered if Ross and the others realized how grave their situation was. 'Any new Band Five on Mukenko?' Travis asked.

Band 5 on Landsat satellites recorded infrared data. On its last pass over the Congo, Landsat had acquired significant new information on Mukenko. The volcano had become much hotter in the nine days since the previous Landsat pass; the temperature increase was on the order of 8 degrees.

'Nothing new,' the technician said. 'And the computers don't project an eruption. Four degrees of orbital change are within sensor error on that system, and the additional four degrees have no predictive value.'

'Well, that's something,' Travis said. 'But what are they going to do about the apes now that they're cut off from the computer?'

That was the question the Congo Field Survey had been asking themselves for the better part of an hour. With communications disrupted the only computers available were the computers in their own heads. And those computers were not powerful enough.

Elliot found it strange to think that his own brain was inadequate. 'We had all become accustomed to the availability of computing power,' he said later. 'In any decent laboratory you can get all the memory and all the computation speed you could want, day or night. We were so used to it we had come to take it for granted.'

Of course they could have eventually worked out the ape language, but they were up against a time factor: they didn't have months to puzzle it out; they had hours. Cut off from the APE program their situation was ominous. Munro said that they could not survive another night of frontal attack, and they had every reason to expect an attack that night.

Amy's rescue of Elliot suggested their plan. Amy had shown some ability to communicate with the gorillas; perhaps she could translate for them as well. 'It's worth a try,' Elliot insisted.

Unfortunately, Amy herself denied that this was possible. In response to the question 'Amy talk thing talk?' she signed, *No talk.*

'Not at all?' Elliot said, remembering the way she had sighed. 'Peter see Amy talk thing talk.'

No talk. Make noise.

He concluded from this that she was able to mimic the gorilla verbalizations but had no knowledge of their meaning. It was now past two; they had only four or five hours until nightfall.

Munro said, 'Give it up. She obviously can't help us.' Munro preferred to break camp and fight their way out in daylight. He was convinced that they could not survive another night among the gorillas.

But something nagged at Elliot's mind.

After years of working with Amy, he knew she had the maddening literal-mindedness of a child. With Amy, especially when she was feeling uncooperative, it was necessary to be exact to elicit the appropriate response. Now he looked at Amy and said, 'Amy talk thing talk?'

No talk.

'Amy understand thing talk?'

Amy did not answer. She was chewing on vines, preoccupied.

'Amy, listen to Peter.'

She stared at him.

'Amy understand thing talk?'

Amy understand thing talk, she signed back. She did it so matter-of-factly that at first he wondered if she realized what he was asking her.

'Amy watch thing talk, Amy understand talk?'

Amy understand.

'Amy sure?'

Amy sure.

'I'll be goddamned,' Elliot said.

Munro was shaking his head. 'We've only got a few hours of daylight left,' he said. 'And even if you do learn their language, how are you going to talk to them?'

6. Amy Talk Thing Talk

At 3 p.m., Elliot and Amy were completely concealed in the foliage along the hillside. The only sign of their presence was the slender cone of the microphone that protruded through the foliage. The microphone was connected to the videotape recorder at Elliot's feet, which he used to record the sounds of the gorillas on the hills beyond.

The only difficulty was trying to determine which gorilla the directional microphone had focused on – and which gorilla Amy had focused on, and whether they were the same gorilla. He could never be quite sure that Amy was translating the verbal utterances of the same animal that he was recording. There were eight gorillas in the nearest group and Amy kept getting distracted. One female had a six-month-old infant, and at one point, when the baby was bitten by a bee, Amy signed, *Baby mad*. But Elliot was recording a male.

Amy, he signed. Pay attention.

Amy pay attention. Amy good gorilla.

Yes, he signed. Amy good gorilla. Amy pay attention man thing.

Amy not like.

He swore silently, and erased half an hour of translations from Amy. She had obviously been paying attention to the wrong gorilla. When he started the tape again, he decided that this time he would record whatever Amy was watching. He signed, What thing Amy watch?

Amy watch baby.

That wouldn't work, because the baby didn't speak. He signed, Amy watch woman thing.

Amy like watch baby.

This dependency on Amy was like a bad dream. He was in the hands of an animal whose thinking and behavior he barely understood; he was cut off from the wider society of human beings and human machinery, thus increasing his dependency on the animal; and yet he had to trust her.

After another hour, with the sunlight fading, he took Amy back down the hillside to the camp.

Munro had planned as best he could.

First he dug a series of holes like elephant traps outside the camp; they were deep pits lined with sharp stakes, covered with leaves and branches.

He widened the moat in several places, and cleared away dead trees and underbrush that might be used as bridges.

He cut down the low tree branches overhanging the camp, so that if gorillas went into the trees, they would be kept at least thirty feet above the ground – too high to jump down.

He gave three of the remaining porters, Muzezi, Amburi, and Harawi, shotguns along with a supply of tear-gas canisters.

With Ross, he boosted power on the perimeter fence to almost 200 amps. This was the maximum the thin mesh could handle without melting; they had been obliged to reduce the pulses from four to two per second. But the additional current changed the fence from a deterrent to a lethal barrier. The first animals to hit that fence would be immediately killed, although the likelihood of shorts and a dead fence was considerably increased.

At sunset, Munro made his most difficult decision. He loaded the stubby tripod-mounted RFSDs with half their remaining ammunition. When that was gone, the machines would simply stop firing. From that point on, Munro was counting on Elliot and Amy and their translation.

And Elliot did not look very happy when he came back down the hill.

7. Final Defense

'How long until you're ready?' Munro asked him.

'Couple of hours, maybe more.' Elliot asked Ross to help him, and Amy went to get food from Kahega. She seemed very proud of herself, and behaved like an important person in the group.

Ross said, 'Did it work?'

'We'll know in a minute,' Elliot said. His first plan was to run the only kind of internal check on Amy that he could, by verifying repetitions of sounds. If she had consistently translated sounds in the same way, they would have a reason for confidence.

But it was painstaking work. They had only the half-inch VTR and the small pocket tape recorder; there were no connecting cables. They called for silence from the others in the camp and proceeded to run the checks, taping, retaping, listening to the whispering sounds.

At once they found that their ears simply weren't capable of discriminating the sounds – everything sounded the same. Then Ross had an idea.

'These sounds taped,' she said, 'as electrical signals.'

'Yes . . .'

'Well, the linkup transmitter has a 256K memory.'

'But we can't link up to the Houston computer.'

'I don't mean that,' Ross said. She explained that the satellite link-up was made by having the 256K computer onsite match an internally generated signal – like a video test pattern – to a transmitted signal from Houston. That was how they locked on. The machine was built that way, but they could use the matching program for other purposes.

'You mean we can use it to compare these sounds?' Elliot said.

They could, but it was incredibly slow. They had to transfer the taped sounds to the computer memory, and rerecord it in the VTR, on another portion of the tape bandwidth. Then they had to input that signal into the computer memory, and run a second comparison tape on the VTR. Elliot found that he was standing by, watching Ross shuffle tape cartridges and mini floppy discs. Every half hour, Munro would wander over to ask how it was coming; Ross became increasingly snappish and irritable. 'We're going as fast as we can,' she said.

It was now eight o'clock.

But the first results were encouraging: Amy was indeed consistent in her translations. By nine o'clock they had quantified matching on almost a dozen words:

FOOD	.9213	.112
EAT	.8844	.334
WATER	.9978	.004
DRINK	.7743	.334
{AFFIRMATION} YES	.6654	.441
{NEGATION} NO	.8883	.220
COME	.5459	.440
GO	.5378	.404
SOUND COMPLEX: ? AWAY	.5444	.343
SOUND COMPLEX: ? HERE	.6344	.344
SOUND COMPLEX: ? ANGER		
? BAD	.4232	.477

Ross stepped away from the computer. 'All yours,' she said to Elliot.

Munro paced across the compound. This was the worst time. Everyone waiting, on edge, nerves shot. He would have joked with Kahega and the other porters, but Ross and Elliot needed silence for their work. He glanced at Kahega.

Kahega pointed to the sky and rubbed his fingers together.

Munro nodded.

He had felt it too, the heavy dampness in the air, the almost palpable feeling of electrical charge. Rain was coming. That was all they needed, he thought. During the afternoon, there had been more booming and distant explosions, which he had thought were far-off lightning storms. But the sound was not right; these were sharp, single reports, more like a sonic boom than anything else. Munro had heard them before, and he had an idea about what they meant.

He glanced up at the dark cone of Mukenko, and the faint glow of the Devil's Eye. He looked at the crossed green laser beams overhead. And he noticed one of the beams was moving where it struck foliage in the trees above.

At first he thought it was an illusion, that the leaf was moving and not the beam. But after a moment he was sure: the beam itself was quivering, shifting up and down in the night air.

Munro knew this was an ominous development, but it would have to wait until later; at the moment, there were more pressing concerns. He looked across the compound at Elliot and Ross bent over their equipment, talking quietly and in general behaving as if they had all the time in the world.

Elliot actually was going as fast as he could. He had eleven reliable vocabulary words recorded on tape. His problem now was to compose an unequivocal message. This was not as easy as it first appeared.

For one thing, the gorilla language was not a pure verbal language. The gorillas used sign and sound combinations to convey information. This raised a classic problem in language structure – how was the information actually conveyed? (L. S. Verinski once said that if alien visitors watched Italians speaking they would conclude that Italian was basically a gestural sign language, with sounds added for emphasis only.) Elliot needed a simple message that did not depend on accompanying hand signs.

But he had no idea of gorilla syntax, which could critically alter meaning in most circumstances – the difference between 'me beat' and 'beat me.' And even a short message could be ambiguous in another language. In English, 'Look out!' generally meant the opposite of its literal meaning.

Faced with these uncertainties, Elliot considered broadcasting a single word. But none of the words on his list was suitable. His second choice was to broadcast several short messages, in case one was inadvertently ambiguous. He eventually decided on three messages: GO AWAY, NO COME, and BAD HERE; two of these combinations had the virtue of being essentially independent of word order.

By nine o'clock, they had already isolated the specific sound components. But they still had a complicated task ahead. What Elliot needed was a loop, repeating the sounds over and over. The closest they would come was the VCR, which rewound automatically to play its message again. He could hold the six sounds in the 256K memory and play them out, but the timing was critical. For the next hour, they frantically punched buttons, trying to bring the word combinations close enough together to sound – to their ears – correct.

By then it was after ten.

Munro came over with his laser gun. 'You think all this will work?'

Elliot shook his head. 'There's no way to know.' A dozen objections had come to mind. They had recorded a female voice, but would the gorillas respond to a female? Would they accept voice sounds without accompanying hand signals? Would the message be clear? Would the spacing of the sounds be acceptable? Would the gorillas pay attention at all?

There was no way to know. They would simply have to try.

Equally uncertain was the problem of broadcasting. Ross had made a speaker, removing the tiny speaker from the pocket tape recorder and gluing it to an umbrella on a collapsible tripod. This makeshift speaker produced surprisingly loud volume, but reproduction was muffled and unconvincing.

Shortly afterward, they heard the first sighing sounds.

Munro swung the laser gun through the darkness, the red activation light glowing on the electronic pod at the end of the barrel. Through his night goggles he surveyed the foliage. Once again, the sighing came from all directions; and although he heard the jungle foliage shifting, he saw no movement close to the camp. The monkeys overhead were silent. There was only the soft, ominous sighing. Listening now, Munro was convinced that the sounds represented a language of some form, and –

A single gorilla appeared and Kahega fired, his laser beam streaking arrow-straight through the night. The RFSD chattered and the foliage snapped with bullets. The gorilla ducked silently back into a stand of dense ferns.

Munro and the others quickly took positions along the perimeter, crouching tensely, the infrared night lights casting their shadows on the mesh fence and the jungle beyond.

The sighing continued for several minutes longer, and then slowly faded away, until all was silent again.

'What was that about?' Ross said.

Munro frowned. 'They're waiting.'

'For what?'

Munro shook his head. He circled the compound, looking at the other guards, trying to work it out. Many times he had anticipated the behavior of animals – a wounded leopard in the bush, a cornered buffalo – but this was different. He was forced to admit he didn't know what to expect. Had the single gorilla been a scout to look at their defenses? Or had an attack actually begun, only for some reason to be halted? Was it a maneuver designed to fray nerves? Munro had watched parties of hunting chimpanzees make brief threatening forays toward baboons, to raise the anxiety level of the entire troop before the actual assault, isolating some young animal for killing.

Then he heard the rumble of thunder. Kahega pointed to the sky, shaking his head. That was their answer.

'Damn,' Munro said.

At 10:30 a torrential tropical rain poured down on them. Their fragile speaker was immediately soaked and drooping. The rain shorted the electrical cables and the perimeter fence went dead. The night lights flickered, and two bulbs exploded. The ground turned to mud; visibility was reduced to five yards. And worst of all, the rain splattering the foliage was so noisy they had to shout to each other. The tapes were unfinished; the loudspeaker probably would not work, and certainly would not carry over the rain. The rain would interfere with the lasers and prevent the dispersal of tear gas. Faces in camp were grim.

Five minutes later, the gorillas attacked.

The rain masked their approach; they seemed to burst out of nowhere, striking the fence from three directions simultaneously. From that first moment, Elliot realized the attack would be unlike the others. The gorillas had learned from the earlier assaults, and now were intent on finishing the job.

Primate attack animals, trained for cunning and viciousness: even though that was Elliot's own assessment, he was astonished to see the proof in front of him. The gorillas charged in waves, like disciplined shock troops. Yet he found it more horrifying than an attack by human troops. To them we are just animals, he thought. An alien species, for which they have no feeling. We are just pests to be eliminated.

These gorillas did not care why human beings were there, or what reasons had brought them to the Congo. They were not killing for food, or defense, or protection of their young. They were killing because they were trained to kill.

The attack proceeded with stunning swiftness. Within seconds, the gorillas had breached the perimeter and trampled the mesh fence into the mud. Unchecked, they rushed into the compound, grunting and roaring. The driving rain matted their hair, giving them a sleek, menacing appearance in the red night lights. Elliot saw ten or fifteen animals inside the compound, trampling the tents and attacking the people. Azizi was killed immediately, his skull crushed between paddles.

Munro, Kahega, and Ross all fired laser bursts, but in the confusion and poor visibility their effectiveness was limited. The laser beams fragmented in the slashing rain; the tracer bullets hissed and sputtered. One of the RFSDs went haywire, the barrel swinging in wide arcs, bullets spitting out in all directions, while everyone dived into the mud. Several gorillas were killed by the RFSD bursts, clutching their chests in a bizarre mimicry of human death.

Elliot turned back to the recording equipment and Amy flung herself on him, panicked, grunting in fear. He pushed her away and switched on the tape replay.

By now the gorillas had overwhelmed everyone in the camp. Munro lay on his back, a gorilla on top of him. Ross was nowhere to be seen. Kahega had a gorilla clinging to his chest as he rolled in the mud. Elliot was hardly aware of the hideous scratching sounds now emanating from the loudspeaker, and the gorillas themselves paid no attention.

Another porter, Muzezi, screamed as he stepped in front of a firing RFSD; his frame shook with the impact of the bullets and he fell backward to the ground, his body smoking from the tracers. At least a dozen gorillas were dead or lying wounded in the mud, groaning. The haywire RFSD had run out of ammunition; the barrel swung back and forth, the empty chamber clicking. A gorilla kicked it over, and it lay writhing on its side in the mud like a living thing as the barrel continued to swing.

Elliot saw one gorilla crouched over, methodically tearing a tent apart, shredding the silver Mylar into strips. Across the camp, another arrival banged aluminum cook pans together, as if they were metal paddles. More gorillas poured into the compound, ignoring the rasping broadcast sounds. He saw a gorilla pass beneath the loudspeaker, very close, and pay no attention at all. Elliot had the sickening realization that their plan had failed.

They were finished; it was only a matter of time.

A gorilla charged him, bellowing in rage, swinging stone paddles wide. Terrified, Amy threw her hands over Elliot's eyes. 'Amy!' he shouted, pulling her fingers away, expecting to feel at any moment the impact of the paddles and the instant of blinding pain.

He saw the gorilla bearing down on him. He tensed his body. Six feet away, the charging gorilla stopped so abruptly that he literally skidded in the mud and fell backward. He sat there surprised, cocking his head, listening.

Then Elliot realized that the rain had nearly stopped, that there was now only a light drizzle sifting down over the campsite. Looking across the compound, Elliot saw another gorilla stop to listen – then another – and another – and another. The compound took on the quality of a frozen tableau, as the gorillas stood silent in the mist.

They were listening to the broadcast sounds.

He held his breath, not daring to hope. The gorillas seemed uncertain, confused by the sounds they heard. Yet Elliot sensed that at any moment they could arrive at some group decision and resume their attack with the same intensity as before.

That did not happen. The gorillas stepped away from the people, listening. Munro scrambled to his feet, raising his gun from the mud. But he did not shoot; the gorilla standing over him seemed to be in a trance, to have forgotten all about the attack.

In the gentle rain, with the flickering night lights, the gorillas moved away, one by one. They seemed perplexed, off balance. The rasping continued over the loudspeaker.

The gorillas left, moving back across the trampled perimeter fence, disappearing once more into the jungle. And then the expedition members were alone, staring at each other, shivering in the misty rain. The gorillas were gone.

Twenty minutes later, as they were trying to rebuild their shattered campsite, the rain poured down again with unabated fury.

DAY 13: MUKENKO
June 25, 1979

1. Diamonds

In the morning a fine layer of black ash covered the campsite, and in the distance Mukenko was belching great quantities of black smoke. Amy tugged at Elliot's sleeve.

Leave now, she signed insistently.

'No, Amy,' he said.

Nobody in the expedition was in a mood to leave, including Elliot. Upon arising, he found himself thinking of additional data he needed before leaving Zinj. Elliot was no longer satisfied with a skeleton of one of these creatures; like men, their uniqueness went beyond the details of physical structure to their behavior. Elliot wanted videotapes of the gray apes, and more recordings of verbalizations. And Ross was more determined than ever to find the diamonds, with Munro no less interested.

Leave now.

'Why leave now?' he asked her.

Earth bad. Leave now.

Elliot had no experience with volcanic activity, but what he saw did not impress him. Mukenko was more active than it had been in previous days, but the volcano had ejected smoke and gas since their first arrival in Virunga.

He asked Munro, 'Is there any danger?'

Munro shrugged. 'Kahega thinks so, but he probably just wants an excuse to go home.'

Amy came running over to Munro raising her arms, slapping them down on the earth in front of him. Munro recognized this as her desire to play; he laughed and began to tickle Amy. She signed to him.

'What's she saying?' Munro asked. 'What are you saying, you little devil?'

Amy grunted with pleasure, and continued to sign.

'She says leave now,' Elliot translated.

Munro stopped tickling her. 'Does she?' he asked sharply. 'What *exactly* does she say?'

Elliot was surprised at Munro's seriousness – although Amy accepted his interest in her communication as perfectly proper. She signed again, more slowly, for Munro's benefit, her eyes on his face.

'She says the earth is bad.'

'Hmm,' Munro said. 'Interesting.' He glanced at Amy and then at his watch.

Amy signed, *Nosehair man listen Amy go home now.*

'She says you listen to her and go home now,' Elliot said.

Munro shrugged. 'Tell her I understand.'

Elliot translated. Amy looked unhappy, and did not sign again.

'Where is Ross?' Munro asked.

'Here,' Ross said.

'Let's get moving,' Munro said, and they headed for the lost city. Now they had another surprise – Amy signed she was coming with them, and she hurried to catch up with them.

This was their final day in the city, and all the participants in the Congo expedition described a similar reaction: the city, which had been so mysterious before, was somehow stripped of its mystery. On this morning, they saw the city for what it was: a cluster of crumbling old buildings in a hot stinking uncomfortable jungle.

They all found it tedious, except for Munro. Munro was worried.

Elliot was bored, talking about verbalizations and why he wanted tape recordings, and whether it was possible to preserve a brain from one of the apes to take back with them. It seemed there was some academic debate about where language came from; people used to think language was a development of animal cries, but now they knew that animal barks and cries were controlled by the limbic system of the brain, and that real language came from some other part of the brain called Broca's area.... Munro couldn't pay attention. He kept listening to the distant rumbling of Mukenko.

Munro had firsthand experience with volcanoes; he had been in the Congo in 1968, when Mbuti, another of the Virunga volcanoes, erupted. When he had heard the sharp explosions the day before, he had recognized them as brontides, the unexplained accompaniments of coming earthquakes. Munro had assumed that Mukenko would soon erupt, and when he had seen the flickering laser beam the night before, he had known there was new rumbling activity on the upper slopes of the volcano.

Munro knew that volcanoes were unpredictable – as witnessed by the fact that this ruined city at the base of an active volcano had been untouched after more than five hundred years. There were recent lava fields on the mountain slopes above, and others a few miles to the south, but the city itself was spared. This in itself was not so remarkable – the configuration of Mukenko was such that most eruptions occurred on the gentle south slopes. But it did not mean that they were now in any less danger. The unpredictability of volcanic eruptions meant that they could become life-threatening in a matter of minutes. The danger was not from lava, which rarely flowed faster than a man could walk; it would take hours for lava to flow down from Mukenko's summit. The real danger from volcanic eruptions was ash and gas.

Just as most people killed by fires actually died from smoke inhalation, most deaths from volcanoes were caused by asphyxiation from dust and carbon monoxide. Volcanic gases were heavier than air; the Lost City of Zinj, located in a valley, could be filled in minutes with a heavy, poisonous atmosphere, should Mukenko discharge a large quantity of gas.

The question was how rapidly Mukenko was building toward a major eruptive phase. That was why Munro was so interested in Amy's reactions: it was well known that primates could anticipate geological events such as earthquakes and eruptions. Munro was surprised that Elliot, babbling away about freezing gorilla brains, didn't know about that. And he was even more surprised that Ross, with her extensive geological knowledge, did not regard the morning ashfall as the start of a major volcanic eruption.

Ross knew a major eruption was building. That morning, she had routinely tried to establish contact with Houston; to her surprise, the transmission keys immediately locked through. After the scrambler notations registered, she began typing in field updates, but the screen went blank, and flashed:

HUSTN STATN OVRIDE CLR BANX.

This was an emergency signal; she had never seen it before on a field expedition. She cleared the memory banks and pushed the transmit button. There was a burst transmission delay, then the screen printed:

COMPUTR DESIGNATN MAJR ERUPTN SIGNATR MUKENKO ADVIS LEAV SITE NOW EXPEDN JEPRDY DANGR REPET ALL LEAV SITE NOW.

Ross glanced across the campsite. Kahega was making breakfast; Amy squatted by the fire, eating a roasted banana (she had got Kahega to make special treats for her); Munro and Elliot were having coffee. Except for the black ashfall, it was a perfectly normal morning at the camp. She looked back at the screen.

MAJR ERUPTN SIGNATR MUKENKO ADVIS LEAV SITE NOW.

Ross glanced up at the smoking cone of Mukenko. The hell with it, she thought. She wanted the diamonds, and she had gone too far to quit now.

The screen blinked: PLS SIGNL REPLY.
Ross turned the transmitter off.

As the morning progressed they felt several sharp jolting earth tremors, which released clouds of dust from the crumbling buildings. The rumblings of Mukenko became more frequent. Ross paid no attention. 'It just means this is elephant country,' she said. That was an old geological adage: 'If you're looking for elephants, go to elephant country.' Elephant country meant a likely spot to find whatever minerals you were looking for. 'And if you want diamonds,' Ross said, shrugging, 'you go to volcanoes.'

The association of diamonds with volcanoes had been recognized for more than a century, but it was still poorly understood. Most theories postulated that diamonds, crystals of pure carbon, were formed in the intense heat and pressure of the upper mantle one thousand miles beneath the earth's surface. The diamonds remained inaccessible at this depth except in volcanic areas where rivers of molten magma carried them to the surface.

But this did not mean that you went to erupting volcanoes to catch diamonds being spewed out. Most diamond mines were at the site of extinct volcanoes, in fossilized cones called kimberlite pipes, named for the geological formations in Kimberley, South Africa. Virunga, near the geologically unstable Rift Valley, showed evidence of continuous volcanic activity for more than fifty million years. They were now looking for the same fossil volcanoes which the earlier inhabitants of Zinj had found.

Shortly before noon they found them, halfway up the hills east of the city – a series of excavated tunnels running into the mountain slopes of Mukenko.

Elliot felt disappointed. 'I don't know what I was expecting,' he said later, 'but it was just a brown-colored tunnel in the earth, with occasional bits of dull brown rock sticking out. I couldn't understand why Ross got so excited.' Those bits of dull brown rock were diamonds; when cleaned, they had the transparency of dirty glass.

'They thought I was crazy,' Ross said, 'because I began jumping up and down. But they didn't know what they were looking at.'

In an ordinary kimberlite pipe, diamonds were distributed sparsely in the rock matrix. The average mine recovered only thirty-two karats – a fifth of an ounce – for every hundred tons of rock removed. When you looked down a diamond mineshaft, you saw no diamonds at all. But the Zinj mines were lumpy with protruding stones. Using his machete, Munro dug out six hundred karats. And Ross saw six or seven stones protruding from the wall, each as large as the one Munro had removed. 'Just looking,' she said later, 'I could see easily four or five thousand karats. With no further digging, no separation, nothing. Just sitting there. It was a richer mine than the Premier in South Africa. It was *unbelievable*.'

Elliot asked the question that had already formed in Ross's own mind. 'If this mine is so damn rich,' he said, 'why was it abandoned?'

'The gorillas got out of control,' Munro said. 'They staged a coup.' He was laughing, plucking diamonds out of the rock.

Ross had considered that, as she had considered Elliot's earlier suggestion that the city had been wiped out by disease. She thought a less exotic explanation was likely. 'I think,' she said, 'that as far as they were concerned, the diamond mines had dried up.' Because as gemstones, these crystals were very poor indeed – blue, streaked with impurities.

The people of Zinj could not have imagined that five hundred years in the future these same worthless stones would be more scarce and desirable than any other mineral resources on the planet.

'What makes these blue diamonds so valuable?'

'They are going to change the world,' Ross said, in a soft voice. 'They are going to end the nuclear age.'

2. War at the Speed of Light

In January, 1979, testifying before the Senate Armed Services Subcommittee, General Franklin F. Martin of the Pentagon Advanced Research Project Agency said, 'In 1939, at the start of World War II, the most important country in the world to the American military effort was the Belgian Congo.' Martin explained that as a kind of 'accident of geography' the Congo, now Zaire, has for forty years remained vital to American interests – and will assume even more importance in the future. (Martin said bluntly that 'this country will go to war over Zaire before we go to war over any Arab oil state.')

During World War II, in three highly secret shipments, the Congo supplied the United States with uranium used to build the atomic bombs exploded over Japan. By 1960 the U.S. no longer needed uranium, but copper and cobalt were strategically important. In the 1970s the emphasis shifted to Zaire's reserves of tantalum, wolframite, germanium – substances vital to semiconducting electronics. And in the 1980s, 'so-called Type IIb blue diamonds will constitute the most important military resource in the world' – and the presumption was that Zaire had such diamonds. In General Martin's view, blue diamonds were essential because 'we are entering a time when the brute destructive power of a weapon will be less important than its speed and intelligence.'

For thirty years, military thinkers had been awed by intercontinental ballistic missiles. But Martin said that 'ICBMs are crude weapons. They do not begin to approach the theoretical limits imposed by physical laws. According to Einsteinian physics, nothing can happen faster than the speed of light, 186,000 miles a second. We are now developing high-energy pulsed lasers and particle beam weapons systems which operate *at the speed of light*. In the face of such weapons, ballistic missiles travelling a mere 17,000 miles an hour are slow-moving dinosaurs from a previous era, as inappropriate as cavalry in World War I, and as easily eliminated.'

Speed-of-light weapons were best suited to space, and would first appear in satellites. Martin noted that the Russians had made a 'kill' of the American spy satellite VV/02 as early as 1973; in 1975, Hughes Aircraft developed a rapid aiming and firing system which locked onto multiple targets, firing eight high-energy pulses in less than one second. By 1978, the Hughes team had reduced response time to fifty nanoseconds – fifty billionths of a second – and increased beam accuracy to five hundred missile knockdowns in less than one minute. Such developments presaged the end of the ICBM as a weapon.

'Without the gigantic missiles, miniature, high-speed computers will be vastly more important in future conflicts than nuclear bombs, and their speed of computation will be the single most important factor determining the outcome of World War III. Computer speed now stands at the center of the armament race, as megaton power once held the center twenty years ago.

'We will shift from electronic circuit computers to light circuit computers simply because of speed – the Fabry-Perot Interferometer, the optical equivalent of a transistor, can respond in 1 picosecond (10^{-12} seconds), at least 1,000 times faster than the fastest Josephson junctions.' The new generation of optical computers, Martin said, would be dependent on the availability of Type IIb boron-coated diamonds.

Elliot recognized at once the most serious consequence of the speed-of-light weapons – they were much too fast for human comprehension. Men were accustomed to mechanized warfare, but a future war would be a war of machines in a startlingly new sense: machines would actually govern the moment-to-moment course of a conflict which lasted only minutes from start to finish.

In 1956, in the waning years of the strategic bomber, military thinkers imagined an all-out nuclear exchange lasting 12 hours. By 1963, ICBMs had shrunk the time course to 3 hours. By 1974, military theorists were predicting a war that lasted just 30 minutes, yet this 'half-hour war' was vastly more complex than any earlier war in human history.

In the 1950s, if the Americans and the Russians launched all their bombers and rockets at the same moment, there would still be no more than 10,000 weapons in the air, attacking and counterattacking. Total weapons interaction events would peak at 15,000 in the second hour. This represented the impressive figure of 4 weapons interactions every second around the world.

But given diversified tactical warfare, the number of weapons and 'systems elements' increased astronomically. Modern estimates imagined 400 million computers in the field, with total weapons interactions at more than 15 billion in the first half hour of war. This meant there would be 8 million weapons interactions every second, in a bewildering ultrafast conflict of aircraft, missiles, tanks, and ground troops.

Such a war was only manageable by machines; human response times were simply too slow. World War III would not be a push-button war because as General Martin said, 'It takes too long for a man to push the button – at least 1.8 seconds, which is an eternity in modern warfare.'

This fact created what Martin called the 'rock problem.' Human responses were geologically slow, compared to a highspeed computer. 'A modern computer performs 2,000 calculations in the time it takes a man to blink. Therefore, from the point of view of computers fighting the next war, human beings will be essentially fixed and unchanging elements, like rocks. Human wars have never lasted long enough to take into account the rate of geological change. In the future, computer wars will not last long enough to take into account the rate of human change.'

Since human beings responded too slowly, it was necessary for them to relinquish decision-making control of the war to the faster intelligence of computers. 'In the coming war, we must abandon any hope of regulating the course of the conflict. If we decide to "run" the war at human speed, we will almost surely lose. Our only hope is to put our trust in machines. This makes human judgment, human values, human thinking utterly superfluous. World War III will be war by proxy: a pure war of machines, over which we dare exert no influence for fear of so slowing the decision-making mechanism as to cause our defeat.' And the final, crucial transition – the transition from computers working at nanoseconds to computers working at picoseconds – was dependent on Type IIb diamonds.

Elliot was appalled by this prospect of turning control over to the creations of men.

Ross shrugged. 'It's inevitable,' she said. 'In Olduvai Gorge in Tanzania, there are traces of a house two million years old. The hominid creature wasn't satisfied with caves and other natural shelters; he created his own accommodations. Men have always altered the natural world to suit their purposes.'

'But you can't give up control,' Elliot said.

'We've been doing it for centuries,' Ross said. 'What's a domesticated animal – or a pocket calculator – except an attempt to give up control? We don't want to plow fields or do square roots so we turn the job over to some other intelligence, which we've trained or bred or created.'

'But you can't let your creations take over.'

'We've been doing it for centuries,' Ross repeated. 'Look: even if we refused to develop faster computers, the Russians would. They'd be in Zaire right now looking for diamonds, if the Chinese weren't keeping them out. You can't stop technological advances. As soon as we know something is possible, we have to carry it out.'

'No,' Elliot said. 'We can make our own decisions. I won't be a part of this.'

'Then leave,' she said. 'The Congo's no place for academics, anyway.'

She began unpacking her rucksack, taking out a series of white ceramic cones, and a number of small boxes with antennae. She attached a box to each ceramic cone, then entered the first tunnel, placing the cones flat against the walls, moving deeper into darkness.

Peter not happy Peter.

'No,' Elliot said.

Why not happy?

'It's hard to explain, Amy,' he said.

Peter tell Amy good gorilla.

'I know, Amy.'

Karen Ross emerged from one tunnel, and disappeared into the second. Elliot saw the glow of her flashlight as she placed the cones, and then she was hidden from view.

Munro came out into the sunlight, his pockets bulging with diamonds. 'Where's Ross?'

'In the tunnels.'

'Doing what?'

'Some kind of explosive test, looks like.' Elliot gestured to three remaining ceramic cones on the ground near her pack.

Munro picked up one cone, and turned it over. 'Do you know what these are?' he asked.

Elliot shook his head.

'They're RCs,' Munro said, 'and she's out of her mind to place them here. She could blow the whole place apart.'

Resonant conventionals, or RCs, were timed explosives, a potent marriage of microelectronics and explosive technology. 'We used RCs two years ago on bridges in Angola,' Munro explained. 'Properly sequenced, six ounces of explosive can bring down fifty tons of braced structural steel. You need one of those sensors' – he gestured to a control box lying near her pack – 'which monitors shock waves from the early charges, and detonates the later charges in the timed sequence to set up resonating waves which literally shake the structure to pieces. Very impressive to see it happen.' Munro glanced up at Mukenko, smoking above them.

At that moment, Ross emerged from the tunnel, all smiles. 'We'll soon have our answers,' she said.

'Answers?'

'About the extent of the kimberlite deposits. I've set twelve seismic charges, which is enough to give us definitive readings.'

'You've set twelve *resonant* charges,' Munro said.

'Well, they're all I brought. We've got to make do.'

'They'll do,' Munro said. 'Perhaps too well. That volcano' – he pointed upwards – 'is in an eruptive phase.'

'I've placed a total of eight hundred grams of explosive,' Ross said. 'That's less than a pound and a half. It can't make the slightest difference.'

'Let's not find out.'

Elliot listened to their argument with mixed feelings. On the face of it, Munro's objections seemed absurd – a few trivial explosive charges, however timed, could not possibly trigger a volcanic eruption. It was ridiculous; Elliot wondered why Munro was so adamant about the dangers. It was almost as if Munro knew something that Elliot and Ross did not – and could not even imagine.

3. DOD/ARPD/VULCAN 7021

In 1978, Munro had led a Zambia expedition which included Robert Perry, a young geologist from the University of Hawaii. Perry had worked on PROJECT VULCAN, the most advanced program financed under the Department of Defense Advanced Research Project Division.

VULCAN was so controversial that during the 1975 House Armed Services Subcommittee hearings, project DOD/ARPD/VULCAN 7021 was carefully buried among 'miscellaneous long-term fundings of national security significance.' But the following year, Congressman David Inaga (D., Hawaii) challenged DOD/ARPD/VULCAN, demanding to know 'its exact military purpose, and why it should be funded entirely within the state of Hawaii.'

Pentagon spokesmen explained blandly that VULCAN was a 'tsunami warning system' of value to the residents of the Hawaiian islands, as well as to military installations there. Pentagon experts reminded Inaga that in 1948 a tsunami had swept across the Pacific Ocean, first devastating Kauai, but moving so swiftly along the Hawaiian island chain that when it struck Oahu and Pearl Harbor twenty minutes later, no effective warning had been given.

'That tsunami was triggered by an underwater volcanic avalanche off the coast of Japan,' they said. 'But Hawaii has its own active volcanoes, and now Honolulu is a city of half a million, and naval presence valued at more than thirty-five billion dollars, the ability to predict tsunami activity secondary to eruptions by Hawaiian volcanoes assumes major long-term significance.'

In truth, PROJECT VULCAN was not long-term at all; it was intended to be carried out at the next eruption of Mauna Loa, the largest active volcano in the world, located on the big island of Hawaii. The designated purpose of VULCAN was to control volcanic eruptions as they progressed; Mauna Loa was chosen because its eruptions were relatively mild and gentle.

Although it rose to an altitude of only 13,500 feet, Mauna Loa was the largest mountain in the world. Measured from its origin at the depths of the ocean floor, Mauna Loa had more than twice the cubic volume of Mount Everest; it was a unique and extraordinary geological formation. And Mauna Loa had long since become the most carefully studied volcano in history, having a permanent scientific observation station on its crater since 1928. It was also the most interfered-with volcano in history, since the lava that flowed down its slopes at three-year intervals had been diverted by everything from aerial bombers to local crews with shovels and sandbags.

VULCAN intended to alter the course of a Mauna Loa eruption by 'venting' the giant volcano, releasing the enormous quantities of molten magma by a series of timed, non-nuclear explosions detonated along fault lines in the shield. In October, 1978, VULCAN was carried out in secret, using navy helicopter teams experienced in detonating high-explosive resonant conic charges. The VULCAN project lasted two days; on the third day, the civilian Mauna Loa Volcanic Laboratory publicly announced that 'the October eruption of Mauna Loa has been milder than anticipated, and no further eruptive episodes are expected.'

PROJECT VULCAN was secret but Munro had heard all about it one drunken night around the campfire near Bangazi. And he remembered it now as Ross was planning a resonant explosive sequence in the region of a volcano in its eruptive phase. The basic tenet of VULCAN was that enormous, pent-up geological forces – whether the forces of an earthquake, or a volcano, or a Pacific typhoon – could be devastatingly unleashed by a relatively small energy trigger.

Ross prepared to fire her conical explosives.

'I think,' Munro said, 'that you should try again to contact Houston.'

'That's not possible,' Ross said, supremely confident. 'I'm required to decide on my own – and I've decided to assess the extent of diamond deposits in the hillsides now.'

As the argument continued, Amy moved away. She picked up the detonating device lying alongside Ross's pack. It was a tiny handheld device with six glowing LEDs, more than enough to fascinate Amy. She raised her fingers to push the buttons.

Karen Ross looked over. 'Oh God.'

Munro turned. 'Amy,' he said softly. 'Amy, no. No. Amy no good.'

Amy good gorilla Amy good.

Amy held the detonating device in her hand. She was captivated by the winking LEDs. She glanced over at the humans.

'No, Amy,' Munro said. He turned to Elliot. 'Can't you stop her?'

'Oh, what the hell,' Ross said. 'Go ahead, Amy.'

A series of rumbling explosions blasted gleaming diamond dust from the mine shafts, and then there was silence. 'Well,' Ross said finally, 'I hope you're satisfied. It's perfectly clear that such a minimal explosive charge could not affect the volcano. In the future you can leave the scientific aspects to me, and –'

And then Mukenko rumbled, and the earth shook so hard that they were all knocked to the ground.

4. ERTS Houston

At 1 a.m. Houston time, R.B. Travis frowned at the computer monitor in his office. He had just received the latest photosphere imagery from Kitt Peak Observatory, via GSFC telemetry. GSFC had kept him waiting all day for the data, which was only one of several reasons why Travis was in a bad humor.

The photospheric imagery was negative – the sphere of the sun appeared black on the screen, with a glowing white chain of sunspots. There were at least fifteen major sunspots across the sphere, one of which originated the massive solar flare that was making his life hell.

For two days now, Travis had been sleeping at ERTS. The entire operation had gone to hell. ERTS had a team in northern Pakistan, not far from the troubled Afghan border; another in central Malaysia, in an area of Communist insurrection; and the Congo team, which was facing rebelling natives and some unknown group of gorilla-like creatures.

Communications with all teams around the world had been cut off by the solar flare for more than twenty-four hours. Travis had been running computer simulations on all of them with six-hour updates. The results did not please him. The Pakistan team was probably all right, but would run six days over schedule and cost them an additional two hundred thousand dollars; the Malaysia team was in serious jeopardy; and the Congo team was classified CANNY – ERTS computer slang for 'can not estimate.' Travis had had two CANNY teams in the past – in the Amazon in 1976, and in Sri Lanka in 1978 – and he had lost people from both groups.

Things were going badly. Yet this latest GSFC was much better than the previous report. They had – it seemed – managed a brief transmission contact with the Congo several hours earlier, although there was no verification response from Ross. He wondered whether the team had received the warning or not. He stared at the black sphere with frustration.

Richards, one of the main data programmers, stuck his head in the door. 'I have something relevant to the CFS.'

'Fire away,' Travis said. Any news relevant to the Congo Field Survey was of interest.

'The South African seismological station at the University of Jo'burg reports tremors initiating at twelve oh four p.m. local time. Estimated epicenter coordinates are consistent with Mount Mukenko in the Virunga chain. The tremors are multiple, running Richter five to eight.'

'Any confirmation?' Travis asked.

'Nairobi is the nearest station, and they're computing a Richter six to nine, or a Morelli Nine, with heavy downfall of ejecta from the cone. They are also predicting that the LAC, the local atmospheric conditions, are conducive to severe electrical discharges.'

Travis glanced at his watch. 'Twelve oh four local time is nearly an hour ago,' he said. 'Why wasn't I informed?'

Richards said, 'It didn't come in from the African stations until now. I guess they figure it's no big deal, another volcano.'

Travis sighed. That was the trouble – volcanic activity was now recognized as a common phenomenon on the earth's surface. Since 1965, the first year that global records were kept, there had been twenty-two major eruptions each year, roughly one eruption every two weeks. Outlying stations were in no hurry to report such 'ordinary' occurrences – to delay was proof of fashionable boredom.

'But they have problems,' Richards said. 'With the satellites disrupted by the sunspots, everybody has to transmit surface cable. And I guess as far as they're concerned, the northeast Congo is uninhabited.'

Travis said, 'How bad is a Morelli Nine?'

Richards paused. 'It's pretty bad, Mr. Travis.'

5. 'Everything Was Moving'

In the Congo, earth movement was Richter scale 8, a Morelli scale IX. At this severity, the earth shakes so badly a man has difficulty standing. There are lateral shifts in the earth and rifts open up; trees and even steel-frame buildings topple.

For Elliot, Ross, and Munro, the five minutes following the onset of the eruption were a bizarre nightmare. Elliot recalled that '*everything was moving*. We were all literally knocked off our feet; we had to crawl on our hands and knees, like babies. Even after we got away from mine-shaft tunnels, the city swayed like a wobbling toy. It was quite a while – maybe half a minute – before the buildings began to collapse. Then everything came down at once: walls caving in, ceilings collapsing, big blocks of stone crashing down into the jungle. The trees were swaying too, and pretty soon they began falling over.'

The noise of this collapse was incredible, and added to that was the sound from Mukenko. The volcano wasn't rumbling any more; they heard staccato explosions of lava blasting from the cone. These explosions produced shock waves; even when the earth was solid under their feet, they were knocked over without warning by blasts of hot air. 'It was,' Elliot recalled, 'just like being in the middle of a war.'

Amy was panic-stricken. Grunting in terror, she leapt into Elliot's arms – and promptly urinated on his clothes – as they began to run back toward the camp.

A sharp tremor brought Ross to the ground. She picked herself up, and stumbled onward, acutely aware of the humidity and the dense ash and dust ejected by the volcano. Within minutes, the sky above them was dark as night, and the first flashes of lightning cracked through the boiling clouds. It had rained the night before; the jungle surrounding them was wet, the air supersaturated with moisture. In short, they had all the requisites for a lightning storm. Ross felt herself torn between the perverse desire to watch this unique theoretical phenomenon and the desire to run for her life.

In a searing burst of blue-white light, the lightning storm struck. Bolts of electricity crackled all around them like rain; Ross later estimated there were two hundred bolts within the first minute – nearly three every second. The familiar shattering crack of lightning was not punctuation but a continuous sound, a roar like a waterfall. The booming thunder caused sharp ear pains, and the accompanying shock waves literally knocked them backward.

Everything happened so fast that they had little chance to absorb sensations. Their ordinary expectations were turned upside down. One of the porters, Amburi, had come back toward the city to find them. They saw him standing in a clearing, waving them ahead when a lightning bolt crashed *up* through a nearby tree into the sky. Ross had known that the lightning flash came after the invisible downward flow of electrons and actually ran upward from the ground to the clouds above. But to see it! The explosive flash lifted Amburi off his feet and tossed him through the air toward them; he scrambled to his feet, shouting hysterically in Swahili.

All around them trees were cracking, splitting and hissing clouds of moisture as the lightning bolts shot upward through them. Ross later said, 'The lightning was everywhere, the blinding flashes were continuous, with this terrible sizzling sound. That man [Amburi] was screaming and the next instant the lightning grounded through him. I was close enough to touch him but there was very little heat, just white light. He went rigid and there was this terrible smell as his whole body burst into flame, and he fell to the ground. Munro rolled on him to put out the fire but he was dead, and we ran on. There was no time to react; we kept falling down from the [earthquake] tremors. Soon we were all half-blinded from the lightning. I remember hearing somebody screaming but I didn't know who it was. I was sure we would all die.'

Near camp, a gigantic tree crashed down before them, presenting an obstacle as broad and high as a three-story building. As they clambered through it, lightning sizzled through the damp branches, stripping off bark, glowing and scorching. Amy howled when a white bolt streaked across her hand as she gripped a wet branch. Immediately she dived to the ground, burying her head in the low foliage, refusing to move. Elliot had to drag her the remaining distance to the camp.

Munro was the first to reach camp. He found Kahega trying to pack the tents for their departure, but it was impossible with the tremors and the lightning crashing down through the dark ashen sky. One Mylar tent burst into flames. They smelled the harsh burning plastic. The dish antenna, resting on the ground, was struck and split apart, sending metal fragments flying.

'Leave!' Munro shouted. 'Leave!'

'*Ndio mzee!*' Kahega shouted, grabbing his pack hastily. He glanced back toward the others, and in that moment Elliot stumbled out of the black gloom with Amy clinging to his chest. He had injured his ankle and was limping slightly. Amy quickly dropped to the ground.

'Leave!' Munro shouted.

As Elliot moved on, Ross emerged from the darkness of the ashen atmosphere, coughing, bent double. The left side of her body was scorched and blackened, and the skin of her left hand was burned. She had been struck by lightning, although she had no later memory of it. She pointed to her nose and throat, coughing, 'Burns . . . hurts . . .'

'It's the gas,' Munro shouted. He put his arm around her and half-lifted her from her feet, carrying her away. 'We have to get uphill!'

An hour later, on higher ground, they had a final view of the city engulfed with smoke and ash. Farther up on the slopes of the volcano, they saw a line of trees burst into flames as an unseen dark wave of lava came sliding down the mountainside. They heard agonized bellows of pain from the gray gorillas on the hillside as hot lava rained down on them. As they watched, the foliage collapsed closer and closer to the city, until finally the city itself crumbled under a darkly descending cloud, and disappeared.

The Lost City of Zinj was buried forever.

Only then did Ross realize that her diamonds were buried forever as well.

6. Nightmare

They had no food, no water, and very little ammunition. They dragged themselves through the jungle, clothes burned and torn, faces haggard, exhausted. They did not speak to one another, but silently pressed on. Elliot said later they were 'living through a nightmare.'

The world through which they passed was grim and colorless. Sparkling white waterfalls and streams now ran black with soot, splashing into scummy pools of gray foam. The sky was dark gray, with occasional red flashes from the volcano. The very air became filmy gray; they coughed and stumbled through a world of black soot and ash.

They were all covered with ash – their packs gritty on their backs, their faces grimy when they wiped them, their hair many shades darker. Their noses and eyes burned. There was nothing to do about it; they could only keep going.

As Ross trudged through the dark air, she was aware of an ironic ending to her personal quest. Ross had long since acquired the expertise to tap into any ERTS databank she wanted, including the one that held her own evaluation. She knew her assigned qualities by heart:

YOUTHFUL-ARROGANT (probably) /TENUOUS HUMAN RAPPORT (she particularly resented that one) /DOMINEERING (maybe) / INTELLEC-

TUALLY ARROGANT (only natural) /INSENSITIVE (whatever that meant) /DRIVEN TO SUCCEED AT ANY COST (was that so bad?)

And she knew her late-stage conclusions. All that flopover matrix garbage about parental figures and so on. And the last line of her report: SUBJECT MUST BE MONITORED IN LATE STAGE GOAL ORIENTED PROCEDURES.

But none of that was relevant. She had gone after the diamonds only to be beaten by the worst volcanic eruption in Africa in a decade. Who could blame her for what had happened? It wasn't her fault. She would prove that on her next expedition. . . .

Munro felt the frustration of a gambler who has placed every bet correctly but still loses. He had been correct to avoid the Euro-Japanese consortium; he had been correct to go with ERTS; and yet he was coming out empty-handed. Well, he reminded himself, feeling the diamonds in his pockets, not *quite* empty handed . . .

Elliot was returning without photographs, videotapes, sound recordings, or the skeleton of a gray gorilla. Even his measurements had been lost. Without such proofs, he dared not claim a new species – in fact, he would be unwise even to discuss the possibility. A great opportunity had slipped away from him, and now, walking through the dark landscape, he had only a sense of the natural world gone mad: birds fell screeching from the sky, flopping at their feet, asphyxiated by the gases in the air above; bats skittered through the midday air; distant animals shrieked and howled. A leopard, fur burning on its hindquarters, ran past them at noon. Somewhere in the distance, elephants trumpeted with alarm.

They were trudging lost souls in a grim sooty world that seemed like a description of hell; perpetual fire and darkness, where tormented souls screamed in agony. And behind them Mukenko spat cinders and glowing rain. At one point, they were engulfed in a shower of red-hot embers that sizzled as they struck the damp canopy overhead, then turned the wet ground underfoot smoky, burning holes in their clothing, scorching their skin, setting hair smoldering as they danced in pain and finally sought shelter beneath tall trees, huddled together, awaiting the end of the fiery rain from the skies.

Munro planned from the first moments of the eruption to head directly for the wrecked C-130 transport, which would afford them shelter and supplies. He estimated they would reach the aircraft in two hours. In fact, six hours passed before the gigantic ash-covered hulk of the plane emerged from the murky afternoon darkness.

One reason it had taken them so long to move away from Mukenko was that they were obliged to avoid General Muguru and his troops. Whenever they came across jeep tracks, Munro led them farther west, into the depths of the jungle. 'He's not a fellow you want to meet,' Munro said. 'And neither are his boys. And they'd think nothing of cutting your liver out and eating it raw.'

Dark ash on wings and fuselage made the giant transport look as if it had crashed in black snow. Off one bent wing, a kind of waterfall of ash hissed over the metal down to the ground. Far in the distance, they heard the soft beating of Kigani drums, and thumping mortar from Muguru's troops. Otherwise it was ominously quiet.

Munro waited in the forest beyond the wreckage, watching the airplane. Ross took the opportunity to try to transmit on the computer, continuously brushing ash from the video screen, but she could not reach Houston.

Finally Munro signaled, and they all began to move forward. Amy, panicked, tugged at Munro's sleeve. *No go*, she signed. *People there*.

Munro frowned at her, glanced at Elliot. Elliot pointed to the airplane. Moments later, there was a crash, and two white-painted Kigani warriors emerged from the aircraft, onto the high wing. They were carrying cases of whiskey and arguing about how to get them down to the jungle floor below. After a moment, five more Kigani appeared beneath the wing, and the cases were passed to them. The two men above jumped down, and the group moved off.

Munro looked at Amy and smiled.

Amy good gorilla, she signed.

They waited another twenty minutes, and when no further Kigani appeared, Munro led the group to the airplane. They were just outside the cargo doors when a rain of white arrows began to whistle down on them.

'Inside!' Munro shouted, and hurried them all up the crumpled landing gear, onto the upper wing surface, and from there into the airplane. He slammed the emergency door; arrows clattered on the outer metal surface.

Inside the transport it was dark; the floor tilted at a crazy angle. Boxes of equipment had slid across the aisles, toppled over, and smashed. Broken glassware crunched underfoot. Elliot carried Amy to a seat, and then noticed that the Kigani had defecated on the seats.

Outside, they heard drums, and the steady rain of arrows on the metal and windows. Looking out through the dark ash, they glimpsed dozens of white-painted men, running through the trees, slipping under the wing.

'What are we going to do?' Ross asked.

'Shoot them,' Munro said briskly, breaking open their supplies, removing machine-gun clips. 'We aren't short of ammunition.'

'But there must be a hundred men out there.'

'Yes, but only one man is important. Kill the Kigani with red streaks painted beneath his eyes. That'll end the attack right away.'

'Why?' Elliot asked.

'Because he's the *Angawa* sorcerer,' Munro said, moving forward to the cockpit. 'Kill him and we're off the hook.'

Poison-tipped arrows clattered on the plastic windows and rang against the metal; the Kigani also threw feces, which thudded dully against the fuselage. The drums beat constantly.

Amy was terrified, and buckled herself into a seat, signing, *Amy leave now bird fly*.

Elliot found two Kigani concealed in the rear passenger compartment. To his own amazement he killed both without hesitation, firing the machine gun which bucked in his hands, blasting the Kigani back into the passenger seats, shattering windows, crumpling their bodies.

'Very good, Doctor.' Kahega grinned, although by then Elliot was shaking uncontrollably. He slumped into a seat next to Amy.

People attack bird fly now bird fly Amy want go.

'Soon, Amy,' he said, hoping it would prove true.

By now, the Kigani had abandoned their frontal assault; they were attacking from the rear, where there were no windows. Everyone could hear the sound of bare feet moving over the tail section and up onto the fuselage above their heads. Two warriors managed to climb through the open aft cargo door. Munro, who was in the cockpit, shouted, 'If they get you, they eat you!'

Ross fired at the rear door, and blood spattered on her clothes as the intruding Kigani were knocked out backward.

Amy no like, she signed. *Amy want go home.* She clutched her seat belt.

'There's the son of a bitch,' Munro shouted, and fired his machine gun. A young man of about twenty, his eyes smeared with red, fell onto his back, shuddering with machine-gun fire. 'Got him,' Munro said. 'Got the *Angawa*.' He sat back and allowed the warriors to remove the body.

It was then the Kigani attack ended, the warriors retreating into the silent bush. Munro bent over the slumped body of the pilot and stared out at the jungle.

'What happens now?' Elliot asked. 'Have we won?'

Munro shook his head. 'They'll wait for nightfall. Then they'll come back to kill us all.'

Elliot said, 'What will we do then?'

Munro had been thinking about that. He saw no possibility of their leaving the aircraft for a least twenty-four hours. They needed to defend themselves at night and they needed a wider clearing around the plane during the day. The obvious solution was to burn the waist-high bush in the immediate vicinity of the plane – if they could do that without exploding the residual fuel in the airplane tanks.

'Look for flamethrowers,' he told Kahega, 'or gas canisters.' And he began to check for documents that would tell him tank locations on the C-130.

Ross approached him. 'We're in trouble, aren't we.'

'Yes,' Munro said. He didn't mention the volcano.

'I suppose I made a mistake.'

'Well, you can atone,' Munro said, 'by thinking of some way out.'

'I'll see what I can do,' she said seriously, and went aft. Fifteen minutes later, she screamed.

Munro spun back into the passenger compartment, his machine gun raised to fire. But he saw that Ross had collapsed into a seat, laughing hysterically. The others stared at her, not sure what to do. He grabbed her shoulders and shook her: 'Get a grip on yourself,' he said, but she just went on laughing.

Kahega stood next to a gas cylinder marked PROPANE. 'She see this, and she ask how many more, I tell her six more, she begins to laugh.'

Munro frowned. The cylinder was large, 20 cubic feet. 'Kahega, what'd they carry that propane for?'

Kahega shrugged. 'Too big for cooking. They need only five, ten cubic feet for cooking.'

Munro said, 'And there are six more like this?'

'Yes, boss. Six.'

'That's a hell of a lot of gas,' Munro said, and then he realized that Ross with her instinct for planning would have grasped at once the significance of all that propane, and Munro also knew what it meant, and he broke into a grin.

Annoyed, Elliot said, 'Will someone please tell us what this means?'

'It means,' Munro said through his laughter, 'it means things are looking up.'

Buoyed by 50,000 pounds of heated air from the propane gas ring, the gleaming plastic sphere of the consortium balloon lifted off from the jungle floor, and climbed swiftly into the darkening night air.

The Kigani came running from the forest, the warriors brandishing spears and arrows. Pale white arrows sliced up in the fading light, but they fell short, arcing back down to the ground again. The balloon rose steadily into the sky.

At an altitude of 2,000 feet, the sphere caught an easterly wind which carried it away from the dark expanse of the Congo forest, over the smoking red volcanic heart of Mount Mukenko, and across the sharp depression of the Rift Valley, vertical walls shimmering in the moonlight.

From there, the balloon slid across the Zaire border, moving southeast toward Kenya – and civilization.

Epilogue: the Place of Fire

On September 18, 1979, the Landsat 3 satellite, at a nominal altitude of 918 kilometers, recorded a 185-kilometer-wide scan on Band 6 (.7–.8 millimicrons in the infrared spectrum) over central Africa. Penetrating cloud cover over the rain forest, the acquired image clearly showed the eruption of Mount Mukenko still continuing after three months. A computer projection of ejecta estimated 6–8 cubic kilometers of debris dispersed into the atmosphere, and another 2–3 cubic kilometers of lava released down the western flanks of the mountain. The natives called it *Kanyalifeka*, 'the place of fire.'

On October 1, 1979, R. B. Travis formally canceled the Blue Contract, reporting that no natural source of Type IIb diamonds could be anticipated in the foreseeable future. The Japanese electronics firm of Hakamichi revived interest in the Nagaura artificial boron-doping process. American firms had also begun work on doping; it was expected that the process would be perfected by 1984.

On October 23, Karen Ross resigned from ERTS to work for the U.S. Geological Survey EDC in Sioux Falls, South Dakota, where no military work was conducted, and no fieldwork was possible. She has since married John Bellingham, a scientist at EDC.

Peter Elliot took an indefinite leave of absence from the Berkeley Department of Zoology on October 30. A press release cited 'Amy's increasing maturity and size . . . making further laboratory research difficult . . .' Project Amy was formally disbanded, although most of the staff accompanied Elliot and Amy to the Institut d'Etudes Ethnologiques at Bukama, Zaire. Here Amy's interaction with wild gorillas continues to be studied in the field. In November, 1979, she was thought to be pregnant; by then she was spending most of her time with a local gorilla troop, so it was difficult to be sure. She disappeared in May 1980.*

The institute conducted a census of mountain gorillas from March to August 1980. The estimate was five thousand animals in all, approxi-

---

* In May, 1980, Amy disappeared for four months, but in September she returned with a male infant clinging to her chest. Elliot signed to her, and had the unexpected satisfaction of seeing the infant sign back to him *Amy like Peter like Peter*. The signing was crisp and correct and has been recorded on videotape. Amy would not approach closely with her infant; when the infant moved toward Elliot, Amy grabbed him to her chest, disappearing into the bush. She was later sighted among a troop of twelve gorillas on the slopes of Mt. Kyambara in northeastern Zaire.

mately half the estimate of George Schaller, field biologist, twenty years before. These data confirm that the mountain gorilla is disappearing rapidly. Zoo reproduction rates have increased, and gorillas are unlikely to become technically extinct, but their habitats are shrinking under the press of mankind, and researchers suspect that the gorilla will vanish as a wild, free-roaming animal in the next few years.

Kahega returned to Nairobi in 1979, working in a Chinese restaurant which went bankrupt in 1980. He then joined the National Geographic Society expedition to Botswana to study hippos.

Aki Ubara, the eldest son of the porter Marawani and a radio astronomer at Cambridge, England, won the Herskovitz Prize in 1980 for research on X-ray emissions from the galactic source M322.

At a handsome profit, Charles Munro sold 31 karats of blue Type IIb diamonds on the Amsterdam *bourse* in late 1979; the diamonds were purchased by Intel, Inc., an American micronics company. Subsequently he was stabbed by a Russian agent in Antwerp in January, 1980; the agent's body was later recovered in Brussels. Munro was arrested by an armed border patrol in Zambia in March, 1980, but charges were dropped. He was reported in Somalia in May, but there is no confirmation. He still resides in Tangier.

A Landsat 3 image acquired on January 8, 1980, showed that the eruption of Mount Mukenko had ceased. The faint signature of crossed laser beams, recorded on some earlier satellite passes, was no longer visible. The projected intersection point now marked a field of black quatermain lava with an average depth of eight hundred meters – nearly half a mile – over the Lost City of Zinj.

References

BALANDIER, GEORGES. *Daily Life in the Kingdom of the Kongo from the Sixteenth to the Eighteenth Century.* New York: Pantheon, 1968.

BANCHOFF, THOMAS F., and STRAUSS, CHARLES M. 'Real-Time Computer Graphics Analysis of Figures in Four-Space.' In *Hypergraphics*, edited by David W. Brisson, pp. 159–169. AAAS Selected Symposium 24. Boulder, Colo.: Westview Press, 1978.

BLEIBTREU, JOHN N. *The Parable of the Beast.* New York: Macmillan, 1967.

BROWN, HARRISON; BONNER, JAMES; and WEIR, JOHN. *The Next Hundred Years.* New York: Viking Press, 1963.

BURCHETT, WILFRED, and ROEBUCK, DEREK. *The Whores of War.* Harmondsworth, England: Penguin, 1977.

CAPLAN, ARTHUR L. 'Ethics, Evolution and the Milk of Human Kindness.' In *The Sociobiology Debate*, edited by Arthur L. Caplan, pp. 304–314. New York: Harper & Row, 1978.

CHURCHMAN, C. WEST. *The Systems Approach and Its Enemies.* New York: Basic Books, 1979.

CLARK, W. E. *The Antecedents of Man.* Edinburgh: University of Edinburgh Press, 1962.

COX, KEITH G. 'Kimberlite Pipes.' *Scientific American* 238, no. 4 (1978): pp. 120–134.

DEACON, RICHARD. *The Chinese Secret Service.* New York: Taplinger, 1974.

DERJAGUIN, B. V., and FEDOSEEV, D. B. 'The Synthesis of Diamonds at Low Pressure.' *Scientific American* 233, no. 5 (1975): pp. 102–110.

DESMOND, ADRIAN J. *The Ape's Reflexion.* New York: Dial, 1979.

DOUGLAS-HAMILTON, IAIN and ORIA. *Among the Elephants.* New York: Viking, 1975.

EVANS-PRITCHARD, E. E. 'The Morphology and Function of Magic: A Comparative Study of Trobriand and Zande Ritual and Spells.' In *Magic, Witchcraft and Curing*, edited by John Middleton, pp. 1–22. Garden City, N.Y.: Natural History Press, 1967.

——. *Witchcraft, Oracles and Magic Among the Azande.* Oxford: Clarendon Press, 1937.

FORBATH, PETER. *The River Congo.* New York: Harper & Row, 1977.

FOUTS, ROGER S. 'Sign Language in Chimpanzees: Implications of the Visual Mode and the Comparative Approach.' In *Sign Language and Language Acquisition in Man and Ape: New Dimensions in Comparative Pedolinguistics*, edited by Fred C. C. Peng, pp. 121–137. AAAS Selected Symposium 16. Boulder, Colo.: Westview Press, 1978.

FRANCIS, PETER. *Volcanoes.* Harmondsworth, England: Penguin, 1976.

GOLD, THOMAS, and SOTER, STEVEN. 'Brontides: Natural Explosive Noises.' *Science* 204, no. 4391 (1979): pp. 371–375.

GOULD, R. G., and LUM, L. F., eds. *Communications Satellite Systems: An Overview of the Technology*. New York: Institute of Electrical and Electronics Engineers Press, 1976.

GRIBBIN, JOHN. 'What Future for Futures?' *New Scientist* 84, no. 1187, pp. 21–23.

HALLET, JEAN-PIERRE. *Congo Kitabu*. New York: Random House, 1964.

HARRIS, MARVIN. *Cannibals and Kings: The Origins of Cultures*. New York: Random House, 1977.

HAWTHORNE, J. B. 'Model of a Kimberlite Pipe.' *Physics and Chemistry of the Earth* 9 (1975): pp. 1–15.

HOARE, COLONEL MIKE. *Congo Mercenary*. London: Hale, 1967.

HOFF, CHRISTINA. 'Immoral and Moral Uses of Animals.' *New England Journal of Medicine* 302, no. 2, pp. 115–118.

HOGG, GARRY. *Cannibalism and Human Sacrifice*. New York: Citadel Press, 1966.

JENSEN, HOMER; GRAHAM, L. C.; PORCELLO, L. J.; and LEITH, E. N. 'Side-Looking Airborne Radar.' *Scientific American* 237, no. 4 (1977): pp. 84–96.

JONES, ROGER. *The Rescue of Emin Pasha*. New York: St. Martin's Press, 1972.

KAHN, HERMAN; BROWN, WILLIAM; and MARTEL, LEON. *The Next Two Hundred Years*. New York: Morrow, 1976.

LILLESAND, THOMAS M., and KIEFER, RALPH W. *Remote Sensing and Image Interpretation*. New York: Wiley, 1979.

LINDEN, EUGENE. *Apes, Men and Language*. New York: E. P. Dutton, 1975.

MARTIN, JAMES. *Telecommunications and the Computer*. Englewood Cliffs, N.J.: Prentice-Hall, 1969.

MARWICK, M. G. 'The Sociology of Sorcery in a Central African Tribe.' In *Magic, Witchcraft and Curing*, edited by John Middleton. Garden City, N.Y.: Natural History Press, 1967.

MIDGLEY, MARY. *Beast and Man: The Roots of Human Nature*. Ithaca, N.Y.: Cornell University Press, 1978.

MOORE, C. B., ed. *Chemical and Biochemical Applications of Lasers*. Vol. 3. New York: Academic Press, 1977.

MOOREHEAD, ALAN. *The White Nile*. New York: Harper & Brothers, 1960.

MOSS, CYNTHIA. *Portraits in the Wild: Animal Behavior in East Africa*. London: Hamilton, 1976.

NOYCE, ROBERT N. 'Microelectronics.' *Scientific American* 237, no. 3 (1977): pp. 62–70.

NUGENT, JOHN PEER. *Call Africa 999*. New York: Coward-McCann, 1965.

ORLOV, YU L. *The Mineralogy of the Diamond*. New York: Wiley, 1977.

PATTERSON, FRANCINE. 'Conversations with a Gorilla.' *National Geographic* 154, no. 4 (1978): pp. 438–467.

——. 'Linguistic Capabilities of a Lowland Gorilla.' In *Sign Language and Language Acquisition in Man and Ape: New Dimensions in Comparative Pedolinguistics*, edited by Fred C. C. Peng, pp. 161–202. AAAS Selected Symposium 16. Boulder, Colo.: Westview Press, 1978.

PETERS, WILLIAM C. *Exploration and Mining Geology.* New York: Wiley, 1978.

PREMACK, ANN JAMES and DAVID. 'Teaching Language to an Ape.' *Scientific American* 227, no. 4 (1972): pp. 92–100.

PREMACK, DAVID. 'Language in a Chimpanzee?' *Science* 172, no. 3985 (1971): pp. 808–822.

RICHARDS, PAUL W. 'The Tropical Rain Forest.' *Scientific American* 229, no. 6 (1973): pp. 58–69.

ROTH, H. M., and others. *Zaire: A Country Study.* Area Handbook Series. Washington, D.C.: U.S. Government Printing Office, 1977.

RUMBAUGH, DUANE M., ed. *Language Learning by a Chimpanzee: The Lana Project.* New York: Academic Press, 1977.

SABINS, FLOYD F. *Remote Sensing Principles and Interpretation.* San Francisco: W. H. Freeman, 1978.

SANDVED, KJELL B., and EMSLEY, MICHAEL. *Rain Forests and Cloud Forests.* New York: Abrams, 1979.

SAPOLSKY, HARVEY M. *The Polaris System Development.* Cambridge, Mass.: Harvard, 1972.

SCHALLER, GEORGE B. *The Mountain Gorilla, Ecology and Behavior.* Chicago: University of Chicago Press, 1963.

——. *The Year of the Gorilla.* Chicago: University of Chicago Press, 1964.

SPUHLER, J. N. 'Somatic Paths to Culture.' In *The Evolution of Man's Capacity for Culture,* edited by J. N. Spuhler, pp. 1–13. Detroit: Wayne State University Press, 1959.

STANLEY, HENRY M. *In Darkest Africa,* 2 vols. New York: 1890.

TERRACE, H. S. *Nim.* New York: Alfred A. Knopf, 1979.

——. 'How Nim Chimpsky Changed My Mind.' *Psychology Today,* November, 1979, pp. 65–76.

TURNBULL, COLIN M. *The Forest People.* London: Jonathan Cape, 1961.

——. *Man in Africa.* Garden City, N.Y.: Doubleday, 1976.

——. *The Mountain People.* London: Jonathan Cape, 1973.

VAUGHAN, JAMES H. 'Environment, Population, and Traditional Society.' In *Africa,* edited by Phyllis M. Martin and Patrick O'Meara, pp. 9–23. Bloomington: Indiana University Press, 1977.

WILSON, EDWARD O. *On Human Nature.* Cambridge, Mass: Harvard, 1978.

YERKES, ROBERT M. and ADA W. *The Great Apes: A Study of Anthropoid Life.* New Haven: Yale University Press, 1929.

ZUCKERMAN, ED. 'You Talkin' to Me?' *Rolling Stone,* June 16, 1977, pp. 45–48.